9 Historical Women Win More than a Blue Ribbon at the Fair

THE
Blue Ribbon
BRIDES
COLLECTION

Cynthia Hickey, Gina Welborn
Jennifer AlLee, Angela Breidenbach, Darlene Franklin,
Carrie Fancett Pagels, Amber Stockton,
Niki Turner, Becca Whitham

BARBOUR BOOKS
An Imprint of Barbour Publishing, Inc.

THE
Blue Ribbon
BRIDES
COLLECTION

Contents

Requilted with Love

by Carrie Fancett Pagels

Dedication

To my sister, Linda Joy Fancett White,
for making fairs and special events so much fun when we were growing up!
This one's for you, Sis!

Acknowledgments

I want to thank my husband, Jeffrey, and son, Clark, for bearing with me and assisting in the balloonist research. They've always been great brainstormers and helpful in discussing research with me, and I'm really grateful for that.

Thank you to Vicki McCollum, my critique partner and freelance editor for this project—I couldn't have done it without you! And thank you to Becky Fish, my insightful editor from Barbour for all her help. I'm grateful to Gina Welborn, who brought this project together with Cindy Hickey, and to my fellow authors for this project, who are all great ladies to work with!

I appreciate my Pagels' Pals Readers Group so much. Whether it is for prayer support, or a beta reader (special thanks to beta readers Tina St.Clair Rice, Regina Fujitani, and Elizabeth Lopez), or to promote my work, these ladies have been there for me. Hugs to all! Thank you to the *Overcoming with God* blog "Angels": Diana L. Flowers, Teresa S. Mathews, Noela Nancarrow, and Bonnie Roof, for being there for me through everything!

I often borrow names in my writing. My childhood friend and a fellow writer, Denise Drefs McLean, was one of the early encouragers in my writing. I'm so glad to have her on the page with my heroine, Sarah, who is named for a lovely young reader from North Carolina. One of the faithful Christian fiction readers I'd really wanted to include in this work was Judy Strunk Burgi, who was struggling with the same cancer that had claimed my mother. So I named my heroine's state fair supervisor after this lovely lady. Sadly, Judy left us for heaven before I got to tell her. But she lives on in my memory, and in a fictional version in this story.

Chapter 1

Across the narrow train aisle from Sarah, a matron examined her Friday newspaper, the bold print headline proclaiming ANOTHER BALLOONIST SUCCUMBS IN KALAMAZOO.

The woman's companion, a silver-haired man with a drooping mustache, tapped the paper. "Why do those foolish young men engage in such folly?"

Indeed, why did they? Neither Sarah Richmond nor the lady had an answer.

"Mama, won't there be a balloon show at the fair?" asked a boy in the row diagonal and forward from Sarah.

"Not after last year's. . .mishap." She patted the boy's hand.

Mishap? The death of a balloonist before thousands of state fair attendees in Detroit? Sarah wouldn't call that a mere mishap. She chewed her lower lip. Her fiancé's death, now *that* could be referred to as such. A niggling began in her conscience. She had to stop blaming Arnold for his death. But new determination rose up against the hospital staff who might have been able to save him had they been more diligent. If her quilt won the blue ribbon, she'd tell any journalist who'd listen that Battle Creek wasn't the only place in the state that needed to provide excellent health care to its citizens. And if a wealthy fairgoer wished to purchase her quilt, she'd contribute the money to the small hospital in her community.

Beside her, a schoolteacher from Ohio patted Sarah's arm. "You might not want to keep tugging on that beautiful quilt, dear. Not if you hope to win a prize at the fair."

She hadn't realized she'd been pulling at the fabric's scalloped edges. "Oh. . .yes." Her fingers traced the red-and-yellow tulips she'd worked to cover her first wedding quilt's design. Patting the folded quilt, Sarah smiled at the lady, who'd been visiting family up north near the Straits of Mackinac, where Sarah resided. "Thanks."

Her seatmate resumed her knitting, aided by the light streaming through the window. Fatigue washed over Sarah. Before long, her head nodded.

When she awakened, the little family had departed, as well as the older couple.

The conductor angled through the narrow passenger aisle. "This is your stop, miss."

"Thank you." Sarah rose and stretched. She smiled at the schoolteacher. "I pray your trip will be pleasant and you get home safely."

"Thanks. I hope all goes well at the fair."

They exchanged good-byes, and Sarah departed the train, the sounds of happy greetings carrying back from the platform. There'd be no one there to meet her here at the fairgrounds. Her aunt would be picking her up later, after Sarah had registered.

The railway man took her satchel. "I imagine we'll get pretty busy at this stop once the fair begins." He held out a hand for her, and she accepted it.

"Thank you." Sarah stepped down onto the landing. "Do you think someone could direct me to Home Arts Pavilion?"

"Certainly." The conductor waved at a dark-haired man attired in a jumpsuit. "I need some help for this young lady."

"Me?" The man's deep voice expressed confusion.

"Yeah, you. Ain't ya wearin' one of them state fair getups for a reason, young man?"

Michigan State Fair was emblazoned on his upper left pocket. The man looked to be in his late twenties or early thirties. He stood a head taller than the conductor and shot him a look that would've quailed even her rowdiest brother. Deep-set, dark blue eyes dominated his face. High cheekbones turned the faintest shade of rose, as did the full lips beneath his Roman nose. Sarah suddenly felt dizzy and closed her eyes.

"Are you all right, ma'am?" The worker's baritone voice made her knees weaker.

The railway man jerked a thumb toward her. "That quilt she's got bundled round her is goin' in the contest. And she's got that satchel."

The stranger bent his head closer to hers, and she caught a whiff of sandalwood and something else she couldn't quite identify. "Any other luggage?"

She carried her most cherished possession, her quilt, which had become an albatross since Arnold had died. Sarah shook her head.

"That's it?" His handsome features crumpled in confusion. "No trunk?"

"No."

"All right." A faint smile tugged at his lips, sending a quiver through her.

"I can manage if you'll point me to the Home Arts Pavilion. I need to register."

"No, ma'am. I'll carry this for you."

"It's miss." Not that he needed to know her marital status. "Miss Sarah Richmond."

"Grant Bentley. Pleased to meet you, Miss Richmond." His eyelids lowered halfway. But instead of the usual slow, salacious appraisal of her buxom figure as he scanned her appearance, his features tugged in sadness. Then a faint smile flew past before he once again settled into a mask of. . .what? She was unaccustomed to such a reaction. Now his features fixed, as though he'd schooled himself in indifference.

"Thank you for your help, but I don't want to trouble you." The discomfort this man stirred in her wasn't something she could name. Suddenly she didn't feel safe around him. Not that he'd harm her. More that he could crack something in her heart that had hardened to stone.

"No trouble at all." He set off, and Sarah struggled to keep up with the handsome man's long strides.

"Can you slow a bit?"

"Sorry." He grinned down at her, the corners of his eyes crinkling.

They continued on, but Grant stopped for no one, instead giving a brief greeting in reply to the women or a half grunt to the men, one of whom called him "Professor." A strange greeting, but perhaps young gents in the city used different nicknames than they did up north, where often one was called by his nationality.

As they passed by each section of the front of the fairground, Mr. Bentley pointed out the attractions. "The bicycle race is held over there." He pointed to a long, elliptical track.

As they passed rows of small buildings, all labeled for different fair submissions and events, someone belted out the tune "Slide, Kelly, Slide." Sarah hummed in time with the lyrics.

"Do you know this ditty?"

"I do."

He stopped, and they found the source of the music. A piano had been set up on a platform near a beer wagon, surrounded by fair workers. "Let's sing it."

Sarah laughed but then joined her mezzo soprano with his mellifluous baritone. She hoped he didn't want to partake of the beer offered there, not that it was any of her business.

When done, he crossed his massive arms, his armbands dark against the crisp white of the jumpsuit sleeves. "You possess a beautiful voice."

"As do you."

They exchanged a long glance, and her heart skipped a beat.

"I used to sing in our church choir."

"Me, too."

A dapper gentleman in a gray-checked suit strode toward them, pulling a gold watch from his vest pocket. His eyes skimmed Sarah's figure before focusing on Mr. Bentley. "You just need to hook that balloon up to the city's gas valve on Main Street to fill it."

A muscle in the handsome worker's jaw jumped.

With a curt nod, the suited gent snapped his watch shut and rushed off toward the beer wagon.

"Who's that?" Sarah watched the man push through the crowd to the front of the line.

"He's one of the fair managers."

"And what did he mean about the balloon? I heard they'd canceled that dangerous ridiculousness because of the death last year in Detroit."

Mr. Bentley's mouth opened, but no words came out.

Of course, he had no control over such things and merely had to do as directed. Sarah frowned. "Another of those aeronauts died just yesterday in Kalamazoo."

He ran his hand over his lips and chin.

Sometimes she spoke out of turn. How many times had she had to do as directed by her father at their farm, without questioning him?

They walked on in silence. She deliberately avoided his sapphire gaze. Soon he stopped at the pavilion and set her bag down by the registrar's desk.

"Here you go, Miss Richmond."

She grabbed his arm, sensing the firm muscles beneath his gabardine uniform. "Thank you for your help. I appreciate it."

Grant tipped his head and sighed. "I'll come back to check on you when my work is through."

Absolutely nothing in the man's tone indicated he harbored anything more than altruistic motives. And for some reason, that annoyed her. Wasn't she pretty enough, dainty enough that he'd like to see her again? And why was she thinking such things? After losing two fiancés, she would never risk her heart on a man again.

——◦●●•——

Grant surveyed the newly built dining hall. Everything here, at what would be the permanent home for the Michigan State Fair, was newly built. Although he and his business partner weren't technically state fair employees, anyone displaying or engaged in commerce at the event could eat in the cavernous building. Rows of windows punctuated every wall, save for that where the kitchen workers served up hearty food.

His friend and partner, Lee Hudgins, joined him in line. "This is some mess hall, isn't it?"

"Top notch." As was the young woman he'd directed to the pavilion earlier.

Long tables, set up picnic-table style, were flanked by benches. The few ladies in the room sat primarily at the end of the benches. Several tried futilely to manage their bustles, sitting cockeyed to do so. Silly contraptions.

"Humph," Grant snorted. "We've been tethered."

"What?"

"The fair manager told me just now." Grant ground his back teeth together.

"Like hucksters?" Lee grimaced. "Showmen?"

"But we're not circus performers. We're engineers." One day soon, massive balloons, unlike anything ever seen, would carry crowds of people into the air. With an engine there would be more control, too.

"Tethered. How will we make any money?" The son of a prominent Virginia congressman, Hudgins, like Grant, was bullheaded enough to think he had to prove himself on his own. Hence their need of capital.

When they reached the counter, Grant inhaled the scent of poultry, potatoes, and a sharp odor that prickled his nose. He pointed to a huge bowl of yellowish vegetables. The server, a woman with wisps of silver curls framing a pleasant round face, beamed up at him. "Turnips?"

Turnips? The Bentley household had never deigned to serve turnips before Grant had been turned out, after college, for refusing to follow his father into the banking business his ancestors had built up in New York. If he'd been willing to tuck tail and crawl home, though, he'd likely be welcomed.

"Yes, madam, I'd like to try them."

Hudgins cast a sideways glance at him.

The woman's eyes widened. "Try them? Have ye not et 'em before?" Her thick Irish accent recalled that of Cook's at home, and for a moment, Grant could picture her scolding him for not at least trying the oyster soufflé she'd prepared.

"He has, ma'am." An elbow jutted into Grant's side as Hudgins laid on his Southern drawl, thicker than the gravy being poured over his potatoes. "I believe he's meanin' he's nevah had them with fried chicken before."

She glanced between the two of them then finished filling Grant's plate.

Hudgins leaned in. "Any okra, ma'am?"

"Don't be askin' fer none of that up here. Too many former Union men ain't too happy to even hear a Rebel drawl, much less et their food."

With that caution, Grant headed toward the closest table holding space for two men. Working men attired in either the uniform of a state fair worker or in laborer's clothing occupied most tables. The newly constructed buildings still required work before attendees arrived several days hence.

When a lady hastily removed her half-eaten tray of food from a table and departed, they slid into the vacancy. Across from them, two men with dirty blond hair stared hard, one wiping his greasy fingers across the front of his streaked tan coveralls. They looked to be brothers, with matching squashed noses. One had a bandanna around his neck that might have once been red. The other's neck sported a nasty faded pink scar, perhaps from a failed garrote attempt. The back of Grant's neck tightened.

Hudgins bit into the chicken and sighed. "Almost like Mama made."

"You South—" the stranger across from Hudgins began but then suddenly his chin jutted upward, his eyes fixed on someone in the front.

The other brother whistled. "That's some kind of woman."

"Just my type."

"Yup." After setting his chicken on his plate, the scarred man motioned his hands into a pronounced hourglass shape and winked at Grant.

Heat crept up his neck. A gentleman didn't make such lewd gestures nor respond to them. He dipped his spoon into the diced turnips and raised them to his mouth. Foul smelling. He took a bite. Nasty. Like the brothers across from him. Grabbing his tin cup of ginger ale, Grant took a swig.

"You two, take a hike." The one with the neckerchief jerked his thumb to the end of the table. "We need room."

"Not a chance," Lee mumbled around a mouthful of potatoes.

The click of a knife opening got Grant's attention. Even in this room full of people conversing and the scraping of chairs and tables as they came and went, he'd discerned that warning sound he knew all too well. A man on his own in the world better recognize danger, immediately, if he wished to maintain his life and his wallet.

"My friend can take you." Hudgins grinned at the brothers, a dimple deep in his right cheek making him look far younger than he was—and deceptively innocent.

The two strangers laughed. "Kin he now, ya heah?" Mocking Lee wasn't a good idea. The "friend" Lee spoke of meant a combination of fists and his pistol, always strapped somewhere on his person.

Both men ceased guffawing and stared just behind Grant, dual jaws dropping open and then clamping tight.

Someone's skirt brushed against Grant's arm. He looked up into the dark eyes of the young lady he'd rescued earlier.

Lee shot to his feet. "Ma'am?"

Exhaling, Grant stood, too. "Miss Richmond."

Lee poked Grant's side. "You two met?"

Her face flushed pink. "Earlier."

When the pretty brunette glanced down at them, the brother with the open knife closed it shut. His leer revealed several blackened teeth. "They's just leavin'."

"Weren't ya, fellas?" The brother narrowed his eyes.

"Indeed we were." Grant focused his attention on Sarah. "Might you wish to take your meal outside with us, miss?"

She glanced first at the laborers and then back at Lee. "Lovely notion."

Over the brothers' protests, Grant and Lee rose.

Outside, Lee located a bench beneath a large maple tree, whose leaves were beginning to change. "Let's sit yonder."

"The cafeteria crowd seems a rough sort. They may cause you extreme discomfiture." *Or worse.* Grant wouldn't allow himself to contemplate what devilry these men were capable of.

<hr />

Sarah *was* discomfited. "Those men. . ." She shivered. The way they looked at her, like she was a whole plateful of fried chicken they'd like to consume, had made her skin crawl.

"Not fit company for a flea-infested hound, much less a lovely young lady."

Mr. Bentley cleared his throat. "Miss Sarah Richmond, this is my friend Lee Hudgins."

"Nice to meet you. What do you do at the fair?"

"We help." The way Mr. Bentley's lips tightened, he appeared embarrassed of their job. No shame in being a groundskeeper.

Dressed in button-up jumpsuits, the two men made a handsome matched set. And far more gentlemanly than she'd have imagined the fair employees would be. Sarah nibbled her lower lip. God was good. She'd been through the loss of two men she'd expected to marry. She'd never fall in love again, not even if the man's wavy dark hair begged to be pushed off his forehead, not even if his full lips invited her to. . .

"Miss Richmond?"

"Oh!" She blinked, trying to re-collect herself. She balanced her tray on her lap. "I should say grace."

Right before she closed her eyes, Mr. Hudgins grinned like her brothers did when they had a secret. Was it he or Grant who had something to hide?

Dear Father, please bless this food, and keep me safe. Thank You for helping me earlier.

"Yoo-hoo!" Striding up sawdust-strewn walkway, Aunt Bonnie waved.

Mr. Bentley leapt to his feet. He turned to Sarah. "Do you know this woman?"

Mr. Hudgins languidly rose and waved.

"There stands the bane of my existence." Mr. Bentley muttered so low, Sarah almost didn't hear him.

Chapter 2

Grant forced his teeth to unclench. The whirlwind heading toward them held in her wake the sweetest little girl he'd ever met. Lila Swanson's temperament resembled a gentle lake breeze, while her mother's conjured hurricane images.

Keeping his voice low, Grant bent toward the beautiful young woman. "Do you know her?"

"That's my aunt Bonnie." A furrow formed between her lovely dark eyes. "She couldn't possibly be the bane of anyone's existence."

Had those words actually slipped from his mouth? He rubbed his thumb over his lower lip.

Serenely, Miss Richmond set her tray aside, stood, and wiped crumbs from her wrinkled dress. If Grant's sister had ever presented in such disorder, her lady's maid would have fainted dead away.

"Cousin Sarah!" Lila clapped her hands. "I told you it was her, Mama!"

"Yes!" Sarah laughed.

When the girl prepared to run, Mrs. Swanson grabbed ahold of her daughter's arm and held fast, preventing her from sprinting toward them. Perhaps Lila was more like her mother than Grant had thought, for she broke free and raced toward them.

"Mr. Grant!" Lila flew past him and launched herself into Miss Richmond's embrace.

When Mrs. Swanson came within twelve paces of them, she gazed with disapproval at the two men.

"Ma'am." Hudgins flinched, something he only did when downright aggravated.

"What're you two doing here?" Widowed several years, Mrs. Swanson touched the side of her head, absent today of her ever-present black mourning hat.

Miss Richmond released Lila. "They're working here."

"Are they?"

Sarah swept her aunt into her arms.

What would it feel like to have Sarah Richmond in his arms? Hugging him so close? *Focus, Grant.*

"So glad to see you out of mourning. Papa will be glad." Sarah stepped back and took her aunt's hands.

Sunlight filtered through the oak tree whose red leaves gently drifted down. Nearby a group of acrobats tumbled, threw one another in backward flips, and jumped on top of one another's shoulders.

A vendor pushed a cart past with hot apple cider, and Lila ran off to it, calling over her pinafore-covered shoulder, "Mama, can I have some?"

Widow Swanson wouldn't have brought in a crop last summer if Grant's uncle Franklin hadn't helped. Grant strode toward the ebony-haired youth who commandeered the cart. "Cider all around, please."

Charcoal-black eyes met his, and the boy nodded. With a jug of cider left near the day's end, the vendor might've been left with waste and not enough profit to take home. He named the price, in a heavy accent. Grant fished out the money and added a little extra.

Lila grabbed hers and took three long sips before walking slowly toward her mother. The immigrant boy counted the coins. *"Grazie."*

"Prego." That tour of Europe and all those years of university hadn't totally gone to waste.

A grin split the Italian boy's face.

Lee and Grant carried the tin mugs to the ladies.

"Thank you, Mr. Bentley." Sarah's flashing eyes met his with more appreciation than what hot cider should bring.

"At your service, ma'am." He bowed.

Mrs. Swanson accepted hers from Lee, staring at Miss Richmond, then frowned.

"What is it, Auntie?"

"Sarah Richmond! Where's your mourning attire?"

Grant frowned. Her aunt could hardly expect this vivacious young lady to still mourn an uncle who'd died three years past.

"Papa didn't think it was right for me to wear it."

"But Arnold was your intended."

How long ago had her fiancé died? A pang of sympathy shot through him.

Miss Richmond squared her shoulders. "Mama said we weren't yet wed. . . ."

"Pshaw. I'll lend you some of my black gowns. You've a right to mourn properly."

Had he mourned sufficiently for Jonetta? He'd set off on a cross-country balloon exhibition almost as soon as she'd been laid to rest. So he and Miss Richmond had this awful loss in common. A chill coursed through, recollecting the image of Jonetta dying.

"Love again. . . ," she'd urged him. But he couldn't. Had Miss Richmond's beloved uttered similar encouragement to her? Moisture gathered in his eyes.

Hudgins elbowed Grant. "Best gather up these cups and be moseying along."

Aunt Bonnie tended to hurry the horses through ruts and then slow the pair on the flat road. But they arrived in one piece.

They approached the white wood-framed farmhouse sitting on over fifty acres, dominated in season by hay, now mown and sold.

An odd, rhythmical series of thumps sounded across the fields. "What's that noise?" Sarah jumped down from the carriage, straining to listen over the horses' whinnies.

"One of the Bentleys' lunatic inventions, I imagine." Aunt Bonnie sighed.

Franklin Bentley always seemed like a kindhearted and helpful man, when they'd visited. Maybe the loss of his wife brought about this change.

Seth, the hired hand, exited the stable and jogged toward them. At the buggy, he assisted her aunt down.

"Thanks, Seth. Please bring in my niece's baggage."

"Sure thing." He grinned up at her. "Good to see you, Miss Sarah."

"You, too, Seth." The man never seemed to grow any older. From the time they first met, he'd worn the same style plaid shirt covered by denim overalls, and farm boots, a perennial red bandanna wrapped around his neck. In the summer, he donned a straw hat.

As Lila ran off, calling, "Mr. Box!" for her dog, the two women strode toward the house.

The square, two-story building was sturdy but plain, with no bric-a-brac nor decoration on the exterior. Inside was another matter. When they entered the kitchen at the back of the house, Aunt Bonnie's fondness for emulating *Good Housekeeping*'s décor recommendations apparently didn't extend to carrying out the recent suggestion that collections should be periodically "culled" to make room for the new. Another layer of lace dripped from her furniture. Fancy teacups filled her glass-fronted case to overflowing. And not one item had been stored since Sarah's last visit.

The scent of cinnamon and baked apple enveloped the chamber, making Sarah's mouth water. Her aunt removed her sweater and apron and hung them on the oak pegs by the door. Sarah followed suit.

The door slammed, and Lila carried her beagle inside as Mr. Box licked her cheeks. As a puppy, he'd been housed in a slat box with blankets. Little Lila would point and say "Box" when she wanted the puppy brought out, and the name stuck.

"We're so glad you can stay with us." Lila handed her pet over to Sarah.

"Thank you." Mr. Box squirmed in her arms.

"Lila, don't pester your cousin with that dog." Aunt Bonnie pumped water at the sink.

Lila took her dog.

"Have a seat." Aunt Bonnie retrieved a wall lantern and a match from the engraved metal match dispenser. After removing the glass globe, she adjusted the wick and lit it.

Sarah pulled back a chair from the oval walnut table and sat. Aunt Bonnie placed the lamp in the center on a crocheted doily.

Lila put her pup down and wrapped her arms around Sarah's neck.

"You gonna be seeing Mr. Grant a lot at the fair?"

"Why?"

"He's handsome." Lila sighed.

Sarah's heartbeat picked up. "Mr. Bentley is attractive. But I'm not here to make men friends."

"Why not? Ya ain't got old Arnold anymore."

Aunt Bonnie's face blanched. "Lila! Watch your manners. One doesn't discuss the dead so casually."

Sarah bent her head over the ginger tea and sipped.

"Sorry." Her cousin uttered her placating word without the least bit of sincerity, which made Sarah smile.

"Everyone has been tiptoeing around me for so long, maybe it's best if Lila speaks her mind." Mama and Papa acted as though saying his name would cause Sarah to burst out crying. And she had, for the first few weeks. But then an icy coldness, like the Straits of Mackinac freezing over in winter, seemed to envelop her heart.

"*The Ladies' Home Journal* says one must mourn the dead with great decorum." Aunt Bonnie bobbed her head in agreement. "Did you have a lock of his hair put into a keepsake, dear?"

Sarah frowned. Perhaps folks who lived nearer the city did have some strange notions, like Pa had said. "No. I didn't."

"But a picture of him in his casket?"

Sarah felt her eyebrows rise higher than they ever had before. "Certainly not, Aunt Bonnie." She slowly took a long sip of tea.

Her aunt's lips formed a pout. "Well, you know it's done in the city. They even place the deceased in a chair and take a picture of them."

Nearly spitting the sweet tea out, Sarah stared at her aunt, but Aunt Bonnie gazed across the kitchen at a framed portrait of Uncle Elwood, who'd passed away years earlier.

"I wish I had more photographs of Elwood."

Lila rolled her eyes. "I sure wouldn't be lookin' at any old picture of Dad after he was kicked by that mule. No, ma'am."

Aunt Bonnie blinked rapidly at her daughter. "Yes, sweetheart, you're right. Now, let's finish our tea and get Sarah upstairs into her room."

"It's our best guest room." The child beamed. "The one your folks always stay in."

"With the boys off on the lakes, we've got it all cleaned up nice."

Her four cousins, all grown. . . Thank God, Aunt Bonnie had this little girl to keep her company after her husband died. Bittersweet memories of how her uncle doted on the child rose up, and tears pricked Sarah's eyes.

"In the morning, don't expect the rooster to wake you." Aunt Bonnie's face crinkled in disgust. "Mr. Hudgins will likely be out there running one of his engines at daybreak."

How sad that the man possessed knowledge of mechanical inventions yet worked a menial maintenance job at the fair.

"I'm hoping it might be quieter out here with those two working at the fair."

Lila linked her arm with Sarah's.

She grinned down at her cousin. "Yes, that sounds very good." With Grant working at the fair every day, perhaps they'd keep running into each other.

Aunt Bonnie clutched her hands at her waist. "You can use my bicycle to get to the fairgrounds on good days, like tomorrow. But on the rainy days, either I or Seth will drive you to the train station or the fairgrounds."

"Could I share a ride with Mr. Bentley's guests?"

"Oh heavens, no!" Aunt Bonnie's eyes widened. "Far too dangerous!"

Lila tugged at Sarah's arm. "Don't ask."

Chapter 3

What was that infernal noise? Grant struggled to open his eyes. He inhaled the musty odor in his uncle's second spare bedroom, rolled onto his side, and rose. He opened the window.

Cock-a-doodle-do carried from across the way. The Swansons' rooster often had competition from the engines in his uncle's barn. *Not today.*

They'd overslept. He and Lee needed to get into the fairgrounds. Quickly, he moved to the washstand and poured water from the blue-and-white porcelain pitcher into the bowl. He washed his face, patted it dry with a linen towel, and then combed his hair. Would the image in the rosewood oval mirror appeal to Miss Richmond? And why concern himself with such things? He grabbed his coveralls, dressed, and hastened down the hall to knock on Hudgins's door. "Get up!"

From within, his friend groaned.

"We're late." Grant emphasized the latter word by clapping his hands.

"It's Saturday. We're not on a schedule. Not yet." Bedsprings creaked, something thumped against the wood floor, then Hudgins threw open the door. "Make coffee. We'll eat the cake Bonnie sent over for your uncle—he won't mind."

"I don't know about that." Lately Mrs. Swanson had brought food over with each entreaty that they keep the engine noise down. *As if we could do that.*

If Uncle Franklin continued to consume the widow's cakes, he'd soon need several new pairs of dungarees to accommodate his expanding girth.

Presently, Lee and Grant were shoving buttered coffee cake into their mouths, chased down by coffee.

"We should offer her a ride."

Hudgins didn't have to specify which female *her* was. Grant knew. He'd thought of nothing but Sarah all night long, which was why, when he'd finally fallen asleep in the wee hours of the morning, he'd not been able to rouse himself at his usual time. Now they were late. And carrying a young lady with them would only slow them further.

"She's likely already gone."

Ten minutes later, submitting to Hudgins's repeated requests they stop at the Swanson's farm, Grant pulled into their lane and drove up alongside the handyman. "Is Miss Richmond here?"

"Gone."

"Told you so," Grant grumbled under his breath to Lee.

Seth waved toward the road. "Took the bicycle to the train station and caught the early bird. Maybe you fellas oughta try it sometime."

The Swansons' beagle came bounding out the farmhouse door and leapt at Grant. He bent and lifted Mr. Box into his arms. "We should take you up on a balloon ride with us, old fellow."

Mrs. Swanson stood in the doorway, eyeing their vehicle, which she called his "idiotic death trap." She handed Lee a basket. "Sarah left without this. I guess it's too big to balance on the bike."

"Right kind of you, ma'am." Lee accepted the large wicker contraption and seemed to stagger under the weight. "What's in here, Miss Bonnie?"

"First"—she counted down on her fingers—"there's my prize-winning canned peaches; then pound cake, which won at our county festival; then my fried chicken, best of Central Michigan Fair in '85; my corn bread muffins; and more."

"You're sending all that with one gal?" Hudgins flexed his arm slowly, like a weight lifter, before gently setting the basket on the floor of the backseat of the carriage.

Her cheeks reddened. "I added more for you fellows since you're going to keep watch over her. All kinds of strange folk come into those fairs, don'tcha know?"

"Yes, ma'am. I reckon so."

"Thank you, Mrs. Swanson. We'll do our best." Grant offered her what he hoped was a winning smile. Watching over the pretty Miss Richmond should be no chore at all.

The early train arrived as the sun rose over the gorgeous new fairgrounds, casting a coral glow on the whitewashed buildings. Sarah made her way directly to the almost-empty Home Arts Pavilion. Her carpetbag, holding quilt and sundries, weighed her down more than she'd imagined. By the time she set it down by the linen-covered registration table, her arms ached worse than after milking an overfull cow.

"Good to see you, again." The registrar, about Mama's age with soft brown waves framing a pretty face, smiled up at her.

"Thank you, Mrs. Burgi."

"I have your table information." Judith Burgi flipped through a box of what looked like recipe cards and pulled one out. "Number twelve, shared with Miss Denise Drefs."

"From Newberry?"

"Yes." Mrs. Burgi beamed, as though she'd just handed Sarah a blue ribbon. "Do you know her?"

"I do. If only I'd known." They'd met at the county fair. "We could have traveled together."

"She brought her mother's quilt to display." A muscle in Mrs. Burgi's jaw twitched. "It's rather unusual."

"Oh." Sarah wasn't sure how to respond. "I'm sure it's lovely."

The registrar's lips compressed into a thin ribbon.

When no further comment was forthcoming, Sarah picked up her bag. "Thank you, Mrs. Burgi."

Within the hour, the pretty young blond joined Sarah and caught her up on the latest town news. "With the new asylum opening, we'll have many nurses coming to the area. It'll be even harder to meet young men."

"I've no desire to meet any men." Sarah blurted out the words without thinking.

Arching a golden eyebrow, Miss Drefs gently inclined her head toward the building's door. "With that gal here, I doubt we'll have to worry about meeting any fellas."

Sarah swiveled around. Even a hayseed like herself recognized Mamie DuBeau, whose wealthy father owned DuBeau's Department Stores. On the weekends, Papa picked up the *Detroit Free Press*, reading it from front to back. Sarah enjoyed scanning the social columns, which frequently mentioned Mamie DuBeau. Her fiancé was reported to be an industrial engineer-inventor. How exciting, to spend time creating new machines.

From front and center of the pavilion, Mamie DuBeau sauntered right toward Sarah and Denise. The lovely brunette patted the side of her upswept hair. Attired in a midnight-blue wool walking suit, a glittering hat pin secured her matching feathered hat. She could have stepped out of a *Godey's* ad. Or more aptly, from one of the DuBeau Department Store advertisements in the *Detroit Free Press*.

To Sarah's surprise, the woman paused at their rectangular table, her catlike green eyes scanning her from hatless head to the scuffed tips of her work boots. "Good day. I'm Mamie DuBeau."

Resisting the urge to shove her hand at the woman, having read it was considered unladylike, Sarah nodded. "Sarah Richmond. Nice to meet you."

Her friend offered her hand, and the Detroit society miss lifted her nose in the air, ignoring her.

With one long, manicured finger, Mamie pointed to the ceiling. "That's mine." The feline expression on her face reminded Sarah of when the cats had gotten into the creamery at home.

Suspended from a golden bar, with two gilded eagles on each end, an exquisite American star quilt dominated all others.

Sarah's mouth went dry. What chance did she have?

Denise straightened to her full height, taller than both women, nearly the height of Sarah's eldest brother. "I'm showing my mother's quilt."

"Where is it?"

Miss Drefs unfolded what should have been a log cabin quilt but appeared more like a child's paint box had exploded on a quilt backing.

The Detroiter's nostrils curled.

"I haven't found a workman to hang it yet." Denise ran her hand over the quilt, protectively.

"We brought in our own help." Mamie's face became a regal mask. "My father owns DuBeau's. He sent a work crew over after hours to hang mine in the best spot."

When Sarah and Denise blinked at her, the beauty added, "He has friends among the State Fair Commission who wanted to help out."

Feeling like the air had been sucked from her lungs, an image of Arnold flashed before Sarah's eyes. The hospital staff had made every effort to save him. If she won, she'd wanted to donate the prize money to the medical staff. And she wanted to use the publicity to promote fundraisers for the clinic. The hospital's understaffing and lack of care for her sweetheart were what she believed led to his death.

The annoying woman fixed her green gaze on Sarah. "What brings you to the fair?"

Sarah had had enough of the woman's condescending tone, which reminded her of the nurses who made up every excuse under the sun as to why they'd not changed Arnold's bandages nor gotten him up like the doctor had told them to do. She frowned. "Same as you, I expect."

"Oh?" Her perfect lips puckered. "Have you something to display?"

Sarah narrowed her eyes at the woman, wondering what she'd look like if her maid hadn't spent hours dressing her up like a doll. Denise, if she swapped out her pretty but serviceable clothes, would outshine this upstart. Sarah slapped her hand down on her quilt, which had been unfolded into quarter width. "Here it is."

"Oh, I thought that might be your cloak. It looks wide enough."

A frisson of anger shot through Sarah. As Denise had, she stood her tallest and looked down at the shorter and much thinner woman. Wealthy, privileged, dressed in the latest fashion or not, this girl needed a set down. Sarah had entreated Arnold's nurses to improve their methods, but they'd only briefly complied before reverting back to their poor care. "Forgetting your manners are you?"

Jaw dropping open, eyes wide, Miss DuBeau swiveled away, leaving behind the overpowering scent of her tuberose perfume.

Sarah patted her folded quilt. Once again she'd lost her temper, like she had over and over again as Arnold fought to recover without receiving consistent help. Mama called Sarah her even-keeled girl, but those nurses at the hospital had gotten under her skin like chiggers, as did Miss DuBeau. As much as she'd like to ignore insults and incompetence, she simply couldn't.

Glancing down at her clothes, her hot cheeks flaming, she'd like to shrink into a tiny bit of cotton and stuff herself into her quilt and hide. Her best dress had been decorated with new buttons, lace on the hem, and ribbons edging the seams. But standing near Mamie DuBeau made her mother's and her efforts at fashion laughable. Even Denise's pretty blue cotton day dress made Sarah's look worn out. Which it was.

Denise wrapped her arm around Sarah's apron-covered waist. "Don't let her get to you."

She took two steps back and appraised Sarah. "Perhaps she's jealous."

"Of me?"

Why had the society miss headed straight to Sarah? It was strange.

Grasping the ties to Sarah's apron, her new friend pulled them tighter then wrapped them around her waist, pulling them in once again, emphasizing Sarah's small waist and her generous curves.

Denise pointed toward the door. "There's a couple of fellas over there with their eyes bugging out of their heads, instead of helping put the quilts up."

Sure enough, a trio of swarthy men ogled Sarah from across the room. She turned away and drew in a deep breath. Maybe Mama was right about men in the cities. They weren't civilized.

Grant's heartbeat ratcheted up as Lee and he strode out from their barn. He'd not felt this light of heart when they'd been setting up their balloon shed, but today longing filled him. "Let's see who's already here setting up their booths."

The beautiful, brand-new grounds covered acres. Lovely trees and flowers—all separating him from Sarah Richmond.

Hudgins winked at him. "How about the Home Arts Pavilion first?"

Feigning a groan, Grant put his gray cotton workman's cap on, pulling the bill low over his forehead. "Good a place as any, I suppose."

"Ya'll come on then, ya heah?" Hudgins liked to lay his accent on thick sometimes, which could land them in some trouble.

"Behave yourself today."

"Spoilsport."

Grant stiffened. Jonetta had often called him that. But as she lay dying, she'd apologized, saying he'd been the most stalwart friend she'd had.

Hudgins pulled an apple from his pocket and tossed it in the air as they walked, catching it with ease each time. Once in a while he'd pause, wink at a lady, and then grin if she blushed.

"Don't even think of trying that number on Miss Richmond." Grant nodded at a trio of gents setting up a canopy. The scent of rich coffee carried on the breeze. "Wonder how she takes her brew."

"Probably full-bodied, sweet, and creamy." Lee's eyebrows waggled in self-amusement.

Grant stifled the desire to throttle his friend. "I'll inquire."

"Why?"

Grant's index finger involuntarily twitched, which it did when he was aggravated, working like a telegram operator sending a message. "That's my business."

"Speakin' of business, ya ever think about givin' up on using our engines to navigate?" Lee scratched his chin.

Grant's need to create an engine that would help maneuver much larger and navigable balloons to far places had become a sore topic. "We've already had the military sniffing around our shop in Detroit."

"Meanwhile, everyone else tryin' this seems to be meetin' an untimely end."

"Let me pray on this some more." And get into the Word more than he had been.

"Maybe it's good we're tethered," Lee muttered.

They walked on to the massive hall, which reeked of sawdust and paint. Men, and some women who never should have been up on the ladders in their bulky skirts, hung quilts.

As they moved through the thin crowd, a curvy woman standing high atop a rickety ladder half turned toward them. His breath caught in his throat. Both at the image of her feminine form so prominently displayed and because of the danger of using that weathered old ladder that looked like it should be heaved onto a trash pile.

"Mr. Bentley! I'm so glad you and your friend are working today." Sarah Richmond, her dowdy gray skirt flaring out near the top rung, called down to him. When she swiveled around, one hand grasping the side, it began to sway.

"No!" He thrust out his hand.

The ladder tumbled, heading straight at several ladies who shrieked.

Grant rushed forward as Sarah hurtled down.

Chapter 4

O h!" Strong arms caught her, and Sarah grabbed Mr. Bentley's neck and shoulder. Instead of the scent of paint and fresh lumber, ever present on the new site, she inhaled something spicy mixed with the faint odor of engine oil. She felt his knees bend and then struggle momentarily to straighten as she dipped in his arms. She marveled that he could manage her and her ample curves so easily. She'd feared he'd fall. "Thank you, but I think you'd best set me down."

This close, his pupils appeared large and black, with only a thin line of rich chocolate brown around the rim. He didn't release her, nor did he seem to breathe. Perhaps she'd knocked the stuffing out of him. Finally, he sucked in a breath and blinked. "Miss Richmond."

Gently, he lowered her. When he let go, a chill seemed to take the place of his warm hold. She crossed her arms and clutched them to her body. "I'm awfully glad you're working today."

Nearby, Mr. Hudgins pulled the ladder away, as a bevy of quilters watched, tittering. Goodness, Sarah could have landed on one of them. Denise joined her and Mr. Bentley. "Are you all right, Sarah?"

"Nearly broke your neck," Mr. Bentley muttered. He bent to pick up his hat from the floor then dusted it off against his leg.

Sarah bit her lower lip.

Denise clutched her hands to her chest. "What your friend did was so brave!"

"I could've been knocked unconscious." Mr. Bentley patted his thick hair.

Mortified, Sarah was at a loss for words. She glared at the irritating workman who'd possibly saved her life. "You might be too thickheaded for that to have happened."

His handsome features contorted, and his face reddened. "Do you not think before you act?"

Mr. Hudgins strode back toward them.

"You got up on that ancient contraption." Grant's voice rose.

"Now, Grant. . ." Mr. Hudgins laid a hand on his friend's arm, but Mr. Bentley shook it off like a snake.

"You could have died right in front of all these ladies. Can you imagine the horror that would've caused?"

Around them, heads turned and women gaped. The hall suddenly became eerily quiet.

A whisper-soft voice within her urged, "*Forgive Arnold.*"

Tears pricked her eyes at the conviction she knew was from God speaking to her heart. She'd thought she'd forgiven her fiancé for volunteering at the Wild West show, only to inflict horror upon the spectators, his family, and her when he was seriously injured. Worse yet, his lingering death without proper medical attention.

Mr. Hudgins ran his finger around his collar, bringing to mind Arnold's priest, who didn't seem to know quite what to say to Sarah. She wasn't, after all, his wife. Would be no one's wife.

Her eyes flitted back to Lee Hudgins's collar. A decidedly white, starched, and possibly celluloid dress collar gleamed beneath his jumpsuit. Incongruous for a workman. She directed her gaze to Mr. Bentley whose Adam's apple bobbed above a similarly pristine white collar. His eyes glazed over, as though he, too, was lost in thought.

"Why didn't you wait for someone to help you?"

Once again, Mr. Hudgins tried to lay a hand on his coworker, but Mr. Bentley threw back an arm, almost striking the other man on the nose.

"Why would you put yourself in danger's path and not consider all those who care. . ." His voice trailed off.

Sarah didn't need a scene. Yet every word he hurled at her she'd spit out at Arnold after the accident. Almost verbatim. A chill swept over her. She could've sworn God stood right there with her. And of course He was with her. There was nowhere she would be without Him. Even in a pavilion full of ladies who'd just seen her make a fool of herself.

"I fear your conduct is becomin' most ungentlemanly." Mr. Hudgins's accent thickened. "Miss Richmond is *not* your mother."

Not his mother? Why would he say that?

Mr. Bentley spun on his heel and stormed from the hall.

Her heart beat wildly. Good thing she'd sworn off men. The last two she'd cared for had died. No more heartbreak, nor pining over what could have been. No putting up with male tantrums in a public setting. No more quilting long hours on a wedding quilt that would never be hers. No additional embellishments to this quilt. She spun around to see where her quilt had fallen.

Denise offered it to her.

"Thank you." She pressed it to her bosom. The hours of wishes, dreams, and love that had gone into every stitch would soon belong to someone else. At least she prayed that would happen. If she attracted enough attention with it, she could sell it for a good price. And if somehow she beat out Miss DuBeau and the others for the blue ribbon and was interviewed by the papers, she'd be sure to point out that more state dollars needed to go for hospital care in the Upper Peninsula.

Lee Hudgins swept his hat off. "Forgive my friend, ladies. He lost his mother in an accident that he witnessed."

"Oh." *How horrible.*

"I fear you, Miss Richmond, received the wrath a twelve-year-old boy could not vent on his mother."

Sarah drew in a long shallow breath. "I see. I'm sorry."

Taking two steps toward him, Denise extended a slim hand. "I'm afraid we haven't been introduced. I'm Denise Drefs, Sarah's table partner."

Mr. Hudgins stared for a moment too long at Denise's proffered hand. Then he bowed, took her hand in his, and pressed a lingering kiss atop it. "Charmed, Miss Drefs. My name is Lee Hudgins, but I insist you call me Lee."

Denise seemed to have swallowed her tongue. Lee was a very handsome man and eloquent for a groundskeeper. Perhaps he'd received a good education and had fallen on hard times. Why did neither man ever seem to have equipment with which to conduct their work? Odd.

Still rattled by her fall, Sarah set the quilt on the table and leaned in. "Are you all right?"

"I believe so."

"Well, then." Mr. Hudgins cocked his head at her. "I'll be on my way."

"Wait. You're working right now, aren't you?" Why were they there?

Mr. Hudgins cast a sly glance. "I believe we are, although I've been abandoned."

"Would you hang my quilt?"

Stroking his golden mustache, Mr. Hudgins scanned the room.

When he didn't move, Sarah's ire rose. "If you're going to wear the state fair uniform, they may expect labor from you."

"At your service, Miss Richmond." Grant's friend bowed low. "I reckon you're right, ma'am. If I were a worker here, I sure would be workin' to get paid."

If he were a worker? When he straightened, Sarah narrowed her eyes at him.

Lee strode to the wall and grabbed a sturdier-looking ladder.

Denise giggled. "He's adorable, don't you think?"

"Right now Tweedle Dee and Tweedle Dum aren't exactly on my good list." She crossed her arms. Something was strange about those two, a kind of *Alice in Wonderland* conundrum she'd unravel.

Lee returned, unfolded the ladder, and took the quilt from Sarah's arms. "Ladies, do ya mind holdin' the ladder?"

With wide doe eyes, Denise gazed up at him. "I don't mind."

Sarah stifled a groan. While Denise might be there to find a husband, she definitely was not. And she wasn't about to join the coterie of ladies who gawked at the two men wherever they went. She had better things to do. But at the moment, she couldn't remember what they were.

She rubbed her arms. Grant Bentley had just saved her life. She'd have joined Arnold in heaven or been severely injured if he hadn't caught her.

Her heart had hardened after Arnold's death. Now, despite his harsh words, Grant Bentley stirred emotions she'd crammed, like bits of stuffing, into each flower she'd appliquéd on the quilt. Flowers that couldn't completely cover the pattern underneath. The hopes and dreams and colors beloved by a young woman hoping to marry and begin her life.

<hr />

Grant paced in front of the Home Arts Pavilion. Why had he lost his temper with Miss Richmond? She could've been killed. Like Mother. He closed his eyes, recalling his mother taking the steeplechase jumps in their fields, unaccompanied. She'd been training to impress Father's New York society friends. Following her on his pony, Grant got to her too late. He found her crumpled on the ground, arms and legs askew like one of his sister's rag dolls. Then he'd screamed for his father.

A trickle of sweat ran down the back of his neck. Grant swiped it off. From somewhere nearby the faint music of a Southern spiritual rose up. He strolled in the direction of the a cappella singers. He recognized some of the Detroit African Methodist Evangelical church members. The choir stood, singing on risers that would be used for performances once visitors were allowed on the fairgrounds.

As they practiced "Give Me Jesus," a thousand chills swept over Grant. Mother had loved the hymn. He blinked back moisture in his eyes. The chorus repeated and rose, drawing more people closer. When they finished, the onlookers clapped.

The director turned. "We give all the glory to Jesus, friends."

The choir members stepped down from the stands and streamed out toward the main fairgrounds, some clapping each other on the back. A few of the quilting-bee ladies waved shyly at Grant, and he waved back, winking at Mary, who baked the best pies on God's green earth.

Nearby, a trio of men unleashed a barrage of profanity. Luckily, the church members had moved out of earshot. A rant of cussing like that in the state of Michigan could land you in jail, and surely these men knew it. When the men removed their slouch hats and quarter-turned toward the home arts building, Grant recognized the two miscreant brothers from the cafeteria. The taller one elbowed the other.

Grant stepped back and pulled his cap low, wanting to see where they went. A bad feeling grew in his gut.

When the three passed, Grant overheard the older brother cajoling the other two. "You two chicken? She's the fair's greatest prize."

What young lady did they speak of?

"She's got this"—the scarred brother made exaggerated curving motions—"going on and more."

Grant picked up some trash from the ground, tossed it in a nearby basket, and followed the men.

"Fresh as country cream. Unspoiled, if you know what I mean."

"So you want me to keep an eye on her?" The other man, whom Grant hadn't met, pulled a jackknife from his pocket and began cleaning his filthy fingernails.

"Me and little brother want to find a place where we can spend some time alone with that pretty quilting-bee lady."

They had to be speaking of Sarah. Who else matched her description?

Confronting the men would do no good. He had no proof. But he could make sure someone followed Sarah. And warn her to never be alone on the grounds.

Thank You, Lord, for letting me overhear this. My temper got the better of me, but You used it for good, just as You promise in Your Word to use all things for our benefit.

From here on out, he'd be spending much more time with Miss Richmond. And he'd have to trust God with that, too.

———— • ◆ • ————

Ten minutes into the process, Lee still awkwardly tried to even out the quilt.

Sarah cupped her hands around her mouth. "A little more to the left."

Shouldn't the Southern gentleman be more adroit with such a chore? And why weren't Lee and Grant out doing whatever chores the fair workmen did?

Movement near the front of the pavilion caught Sarah's eye. Mamie DuBeau whispered to another well-dressed woman, behind her lace-gloved hand. Even if Sarah lost to this privileged woman, perhaps she'd garner a purchaser. Miss DuBeau claimed if hers won, her father would have it displayed at his flagship store in Detroit along with the second- and third-place quilts. If she was a runner-up, perhaps someone at DuBeau's would buy the quilt.

Thankfully, Miss DuBeau remained at the front of the building. Mr. Hudgins finally descended the ladder.

"Why did you and Mr. Bentley come here this morning?"

His mouth flapped open like brook trout, and he stared past her.

Grant Bentley, his face red, strode toward them. He leaned in and whispered something to his friend.

Lee's eyes widened. "Are you sure?"

"Absolutely, but I don't think she saw me."

"Who are you talking about?" Denise, like Sarah, was unaccustomed to people whispering to one another. It wasn't polite.

Lee shoved his hands in his pockets. "Mamie DuBeau is here."

Sarah frowned. Why should they care?

Moving slowly toward them, chattering with a plain woman dressed in a dun-colored walking suit, Miss DuBeau held center court. Not everyone could afford to bring in their own help, which the wealthy young woman had. But after all, wasn't this what Mr. Bentley and Lee were being paid for?

Grant glanced up and scowled. He clambered up the ladder.

With a toss and a few tugs, he positioned her quilt overhead. Beside her, several women moved closer and gasped.

"It's beautiful."

"Gorgeous."

Even though she could detect Miss DuBeau's heavy scent nearby, a thrill of pleasure shot through Sarah. But when she turned and caught the malicious look the well-to-do young lady shot her way, her enthusiasm deflated.

"How did you appliqué those tulips over the rings without them puffing out too much?" Mamie's friend inquired.

"And how long did it take?" an older woman with a heavy Polish accent asked.

Miss DuBeau narrowed her eyes. "That had to have been hundreds of hours. There's no way you could've done that by yourself."

"Five years. . ." and two wishes for marriage dashed and an extra pair of spectacles because her eyes had worsened from all the close work.

"Well then, I think that disqualifies you." Mamie smirked, her green eyes glittering.

"What do you mean?" Sarah clasped her collar, suddenly feeling a choking sensation.

"I believe the guidelines state the quilt must have been completed within a year."

"And you would know that how, Mamie?" Grant's voice rang out behind her.

She turned to see his eyes shooting daggers at the beauty.

"Why, Grant Bentley, I know a great many things that might surprise you. Such as why you're at this fair."

Chapter 5

When Mamie finally slunk off to her own table, Grant exhaled the breath he'd been holding. Sarah watched him, chewing her lower lip. It was an adorable sight and a sharp contrast to Miss DuBeau's prissy behavior.

"I can't believe Mamie is here." Grant's gut clenched.

"You ain't just whistlin' 'Dixie,' brother." Lee feigned to wipe sweat from his brow.

"At least Heinrich isn't." *Thank You, God.*

"Yet." A rare scowl altered Lee's fine features. "But where she is, trouble is close behind."

A growl emerged from Grant's throat before he realized what he was doing. Trouble was named Heinrich Stollen, who seemed to lurk at every turn. No matter what engineering society meeting they attended, he always found a seat near them. Stollen would question them on their progress on engines that he, too, was developing.

"How do you know Miss DuBeau?" Miss Drefs brushed at some imaginary wrinkles in her gown.

Miss Richmond wore an expression Grant hadn't seen in a while. Could it be? Once, at a party, Jonetta's face had gone into a pucker of jealousy when she'd been introduced to his sister's close friend, a sweet girl he'd known since childhood.

"She's engaged to our competitor." There, Grant offered the truth.

Miss Richmond's face relaxed. "Competitor?"

"We're engineers. Inventors working on refining small engines."

"Inventors? Engineers?" Miss Richmond looked like she'd swallowed a peach pit. "No wonder."

Denise laughed. "We'd been chatting earlier about how we just couldn't believe you two fellows looked like groundskeepers."

Grant unfastened the top six buttons of his coverall. Beneath, a tailored, superfine navy suit hugged the white linen shirt. "Since we've no pressing business today, how about you ladies come to lunch with us?"

"I spied a splendid spot in the central park area, ya'll." Lee directed his comment to Denise.

When Miss Richmond simply stared at him, Grant placed his hand over his heart. "I understand your reticence. I apologize for my earlier behavior. It won't happen again."

Her pretty face pinked up as she fought a smile. "All is forgiven. But in future, please be more direct with me."

"With us," Denise added.

Lee ran his thumb over his lower lip. "I suppose we should confess we've got a basket loaded with food from your aunt."

Sarah gave an exaggerated sigh. "All blue ribbon quality, too; she told me several times last night as she prepared it. I wondered what she was up to."

"A challenge to keep up with her accomplishments, Miss Richmond."

"Did ya wonder if she was sendin' that to Franklin and us for our dinner tonight?"

With a melodic laugh, Sarah shook her head. "All I knew was I surely couldn't bring that on my bicycle. So Denise and I were going together to the cafeteria."

Grant raised his hand. "Please, spare me worry and don't enter that establishment again, Miss Richmond. With those woods surrounding the cafeteria, and some criminally minded men finding it a favorite, please avoid that eatery."

Sarah blinked up at him. "Mr. Bentley, thank you for your concern. I give you leave to call me Sarah. After all, you've saved my life."

"And please, call me Grant." He grinned. "Sounds much better than other names I've been called."

Lee stifled a chuckle. "*Crazy Yankee* being my favorite."

Two hours later, still reclined on a blanket in the park, they sipped lemonade, nibbled on banana bread, and continued to share all kinds of information, as if they were long-lost friends. When a breeze stirred the gently falling maple leaves and chilled the air, the young women shivered.

"Sorry all the tables were taken, ladies, or I'd have wrapped that blanket around you."

"Makes a right good barrier between us and the ground though." Lee gazed at Miss Drefs like a lovesick puppy.

She giggled like a teenager instead of a young woman in her twenties.

Sarah lifted her napkin to her lips and gently wiped biscuit crumbs away. "Do you think Miss DuBeau is correct about the one-year policy?"

He laughed. "Mamie would make up any new rule and get her father's cronies to add it if she could get away with it."

Lee tapped two fingers against his forehead. "Best get yourself a copy of the original guidelines."

"What's she doing at the Home Arts Pavilion, anyway?" He feared Mamie and her fiancé were there spying on him and Lee. "Is she a judge?"

Sarah and Denise exchanged a long glance.

Don't tell me. It couldn't be. But Grant couldn't help asking, "She's entered a quilt?"

"Yes," Sarah and Denise agreed.

Lee choked on his lemonade, and Grant gave him a moment before he whacked him a few times on the back. Lee waved him off.

"Which quilt did she claim was hers?"

Sarah dipped her chin. "Claim? Do you mean you don't think—"

"I'd be certain Mamie could no sooner fashion a quilt as she could build a bridge."

Other than the chattering of chipmunks and sounds of leaves rustling, silence settled over the group. A train horn in the distance announced its arrival at the fairgrounds.

"You have to enter your own quilt or represent the quilter." Denise pulled her straw boater lower and adjusted the red ribbons on it.

Sarah gently touched Grant's sleeve, sending a frisson of electricity through him.

"Did you see that American album quilt, the one highest overhead?"

"I believe it's one the ladies quilting bee at the Detroit African American Evangelical church sewed."

"What?" Sarah's gasp caused several passersby to gawk at them.

Lee scratched his head. "I reckon that's the one where each lady was stitchin' a different kind of big block."

"All heavily embroidered. I even sent to New York for some of the silk thread. We use that in our—" He caught himself before saying *balloons*.

Lee stacked his dishes. "Our shed along the Detroit waterfront is near the church."

"It's our office—not a shed," Grant grumbled. "Our laboratory." Truthfully, it was little more than a small warehouse. Why did he suddenly care what Sarah thought of his workplace? Why did he want her to approve? He was beginning to care too much about her.

His friend rolled his eyes, and Denise laughed.

"Lee and I often stop by the AME church."

"On Thursdays they do quilt tops." Lee winked. "And bring sweet potato pie. Or pecan."

"And we're not hesitant to bring in supplies for certain pies, if the ladies are willing." Grant patted his girth for emphasis. He'd missed the ladies' pies, but Mrs. Swanson had given the churchwomen a run for their money with her baking.

"With Grant's engineering eye for detail, I'm reckonin' he would know if that's our church ladies' quilt."

"It is."

Both Denise and Sarah gaped at him. After running the tip of her tongue over her lower lip, which did something strange to Grant's insides, Sarah exhaled a sigh of satisfaction. "Which means Mamie's submission is disqualified."

"Yes'm." Lee grabbed another chicken leg and gnawed.

"He's an endless pit." But Grant, too, grabbed another piece of chicken, savoring Mrs. Swanson's fine cooking.

"Whoever marries these two fellas better know how to cook." Denise flipped open the top of the nearly empty hamper.

Grant grinned. The notion of one day finding a wife didn't hurt so much anymore. His brittle heart was softening.

"Sarah, if you and Denise are available this afternoon, can we take you on a tour of the grounds?"

"Oh no." Denise pulled a watch fob up on the chatelaine attached to her sweater. "We best get moving. We're late."

Sarah shot up. "Can you clean up and take the basket for us?"

"Yes'm." Lee saluted.

"Thanks. We have to return to our duties." Sarah linked her arm through Denise's, and they strode off.

Grant bent and picked up the plates, scraping all the remnants onto one plate he emptied into a nearby trash container. He'd grown up on a fashionable Hudson River estate, yet an Upper Peninsula farm girl had just ordered him to do chores for her. Again.

The funny thing was, he'd be happy to do just about anything she asked him to do.

31

Especially if, someday, God allowed him to be rewarded by her warm hugs and kisses. And more. He better rein in those thoughts.

"What are you grinnin' about?" Lee arched one brow.

Mimicking his friend's and his own mother's heavy accent, Grant said, "I 'spect ya'll reckon ya know already."

"Yes, sir, I 'spect I do." Lee gave a little salute.

The two worked together, thoroughly cleaning up the area. They were accustomed to forming an efficient team, putting everything back in order each night wherever they were. Despite his easygoing veneer, Lee was compulsive about ensuring all was in its place. He surprised Grant by tossing the last biscuit at him.

When Grant dodged the projectile, a beagle with huge eyes trotted up.

"Mr. Box, what are you doing here?" Grant patted the dog's head.

Lila held the dog's leash tight. Mrs. Swanson scurried up behind her daughter and glared at them. "Are you wasting my good food?"

"No, ma'am." Lee wiped crumbs from his mouth.

"Mama, it wasn't wasted. See?" Lila pointed to Mr. Box, who contentedly ate the biscuit.

"Well, at least give us back the hamper to bring home."

Would she be disappointed it was practically empty? Were the Swanson's having hard times? He, Lee, and Uncle Franklin had helped bring in a good harvest with Seth.

Lee easily hoisted the cloth-lined wicker hamper and passed it to the dour woman. She set it on the ground and opened it.

After counting through the plates and cups and utensils, she removed lids from the food containers. Bonnie Swanson looked up at them. "You ate all that food?"

Grant cringed.

"Yes, ma'am. It was right good, too."

"Delicious," Grant agreed.

"And you ate it all?"

"Yes'm." Lee patted the midsection of his coveralls. "Exceptin' for that half biscuit Mr. Box is enjoyin'."

A huge smile covered the woman's face. "How nice to know my efforts were appreciated."

"First rate—blue ribbon quality through and through." Grant meant it, too.

Bouncing on her toes, Mrs. Swanson gave a little sound of triumph. Appearing regal as any queen, she held Lila's hand and took the basket in the other. "We'll take this to the carriage and then come back to check on Sarah."

For once, Grant was completely grateful for the irascible woman's actions. But he couldn't effusively praise her for checking on her niece. With Mrs. Swanson providing oversight, those hooligans wouldn't dare get near. Relief coursed through him.

"Mrs. Swanson, let me carry that back for you. Lee, you take Lila to the pavilion, and I'll bring her mother shortly."

The tiny woman gasped and looked up at him as though Grant had suddenly grown horns. But then she smiled, offered him the basket, and extended her arm.

They promenaded onto the walkway as though they were aunt and favorite nephew.

The notion made him grin. How long had it been since one of his elders, other than Uncle Franklin, expressed any approval of his actions? He'd left home after a parting of the ways with Father and had never looked back. Nor had he received a dime of support from him after Jonetta's death. But wasn't that his own fault for not communicating with him?

———•◦•———

Monday morning, rested, renewed, and refreshed from their Sunday off, Sarah and Denise practically ran up the groomed walkways to the pavilion.

"I think I might meet my goal." Denise's white teeth gleamed in the sunlight.

"Oh?"

"I'm here to meet a husband, and maybe I have."

"A husband?" Sarah felt her eyes widen. "The fair only lasts a week." Did Denise think Mr. Hudgins could ask her to marry him in so short a time?

"I know, but there are few eligible bachelors where I live." Her lower lip protruded in a pout. "Besides, I'll have been here for almost three weeks before it's over."

Sarah didn't want her friend to be hurt by the flirtatious Southerner. At least both Lee and Grant were churchgoers and had attended yesterday's service.

Denise huffed out a sigh. "I know Lee might just be practicing his charms."

They slowed as they neared the building, inhaling the faint scent of new paint. "He seems to get along with you."

"And Grant with you."

Sarah raised her hand. "I've no interest in a beau, much less a husband." Although seated in the pew with him the previous day, she couldn't deny such thoughts had flitted through her mind.

"That's where we differ. And maybe Lee won't work out, but here there are all those workmen who built these gorgeous fairgrounds, and most of them young."

"If that's your only criterion, come visit my brothers; they're all under twenty."

Denise laughed. "I'm too old for them."

"They're ornery, sullen, unkempt, and irreverent on occasion." Sarah arched a brow at her friend. "As are most men."

"But are they handsome?" Denise's gaze led to where Mamie DuBeau stood framed in the doorway, a tall and distinguished-looking young man gazing down at her in adoration.

"I don't think he's a workman."

———•◦•———

The sun set earlier every evening. After making sure Sarah's aunt and cousin had driven her home, Grant loaded their bicycle into the back of the horseless carriage. He shoved his goggles into place, wishing his pal would stop aggravating him about Miss Richmond.

"I loved your latest oh-so-clear explanation of what we're doin' at the state fair," Hudgins called over the noise of the engine.

"Do you really think I'd tell her we're giving balloon rides?"

"Our engines will eventually put massive dirigibles floatin' overhead. If we keep on your course."

In Grant's Bible study, as well as at church, the Holy Spirit had nudged him to reconsider his plan to create engines that could power massive balloons. "One day. But we really don't need to discuss our business with her. She's just here for the quilting exhibition. Leave it at that."

His partner laughed into his gloved hand. "As if you believe she didn't spark your interest."

"Probably too much like her aunt Bonnie." Although his uncle's neighbor was turning out to be quite a peach, after all. By Mrs. Swanson's report, she'd stuck with Sarah like glue all day.

"Do ya think Sarah is the same one Mrs. Swanson said buried two or three of her beaus?"

"We know about the one for sure." Two or three? How did anyone get over that? He'd wondered how such a comely young woman could still be single at her age. She had to be nearing her late twenties.

"Denise told me it was some kind of bad accident and reported it in all the papers up north. But she didn't say anything about another beau or two dyin'."

Grant gripped the steering wheel, guiding the vehicle around a deep rut in Holt Road. "Mrs. Swanson, obsessed by death as she is, likely exaggerated. And yes, if I was a betting man I'd wager this prototype that this is the very niece she was discussing."

"Want to take a chance on being number three or four, old man?"

Hudgins acted as though Jonetta had never existed. He had no intention of discussing this with his friend. It was off-limits. Wouldn't serve any purpose to dredge up. He frowned as a heavy weight of sadness settled on his chest.

The two rode on in silence, save for the engine noise and the gentle wind. They'd had to light the battery-powered headlamps, and it helped but didn't fully illuminate the road. They were operating on prayer and faith God would get them home, especially in some parts of the country road, rutted from wagon wheels.

"There's the Swansons' farm. Swerve to the left and miss that pothole."

Grant maneuvered the vehicle around it then turned into the Swansons' drive. Light glowed in the kitchen window. Sudden warmth burned in his heart. How soothing it must be to come home to a light in the window and loved ones waiting for you. With Jonetta, their home would have been an estate near his father's, and their life a whirlwind of social engagements. Yet now, somehow, his heart longed to arrive and find Sarah opening a jar of her aunt's famous peaches and adding a dollop of fresh-churned ice cream she and the children had made.

What a dolt I am. He had no children. What was he thinking? He had no wife. And he certainly didn't farm, nor would he ever.

Lord, if You're moving me in that direction, give me some kind of sign. I'm afraid. You know it. I can't hide anything from You.

He parked the car and left the engine running, not wanting to restart it given they were simply dropping off the bicycle.

The screen door swung open. Lila waved to them, a lamp in her hand. She hung the kerosene lantern on the side of the house. "Come on in and see what we made!"

"Sure thing, sunshine!" Lee hopped out, removed the bike, and rolled it over beside the house.

Grant removed his driving gloves, lagging behind.

The door reopened. Sarah stood, lamplight illuminating her lovely face and feminine figure. Looking at her felt like coming home. Although he tried to shake off the feeling, Grant couldn't. Chills coursed down his arms.

"Grant. Come in."

"I'm coming."

"Lila and some of her friends churned ice cream for the last hour, hoping you'd stop in."

Mrs. Swanson popped her head out behind Sarah and waved. "Hurry up, if you want any of my blue ribbon peaches! Lee is about to pour himself the whole mason jar."

Grant's jaw dropped open. He'd asked. God had answered. Never had he thought the message would come via the state fair. But it just had.

Chapter 6

They exited Uncle Franklin's house to a morning crisp and clear. Sunshine illuminated the maples like a summer's bonfire with oranges, reds, and yellows. Each color vied for prominence. Grant couldn't linger. He hopped into the driver's seat as Lee, already hunkered down beside him, pulled his slouch cap over his eyes.

Grant planned to spend as much time as he could with Sarah. Her aunt and cousin were busy today canning spiced apples, an all-day affair. His stomach growled.

As though reading his mind, Lee groaned. "Wish I had me some of Miss Bonnie's cinnamon apples topped by whipped cream right now, instead of waitin' for dinnertime."

"At least we've been promised that as our dessert this evening, so don't complain."

"You know you're thinkin' the same thing."

"I am," Grant growled. "Uncle Franklin's oatmeal mush may be filling, but it lacks taste."

"Filling?" Lee straightened in his seat. "I can hear your stomach growl over the motor." He grinned. "I'll buy you some cookies and hot cocoa from the Italian boy."

"I'll accept that offer." He settled back into the seat and didn't look up again until they'd arrived.

After they'd garaged their horseless carriage in a barn at the edge of the field, Lee stretched and yawned. "Inspection time."

The balloon was secured where today it would be filled.

Grant and Hudgins set to work. They examined each seam of the balloon, the ropes, the basket, and all the apparatus to ensure everything was in working order, as they had done every day since they'd transported it to the fairground.

"If only we could get our engines workin' well enough to fly this balloon up north, over the Straits of Mackinac. I reckon we could drop down on Sarah's family."

Spine stiffening, Grant straightened. "Why?" He'd just read of an accident in Germany, where a respected engineer's motor caught on fire and caused his death while aloft in the countryside. Surely his friend didn't wish to prematurely try their motor on such a long trip, although Grant, too, had been tempted. "Would you wish to spy on her people?"

"To help you out." Laughing, his friend pulled on a brass fastener, which held tight. "I wouldn't call it spyin'."

"My father sailed in a balloon up over the James River in your beloved Virginia. What would you call his endeavor?"

"That was war, my friend, or Northern Aggression, but your pa may call it *reconnoitering*."

"He'd been discharged by his superiors to do his patriotic duty." Grant rubbed the back of his neck, which, despite the cool day, was damp with sweat from his work in the enclosed building reeking of dust, engine oil, and decaying wood. "What you propose is simply snooping."

"Snoopin'?" Hudgins wiped his brow with a red handkerchief. "Why, that's what your uncle called Miss Bonnie's visitation, but that ain't it at all."

"Anyway, how would learning more about Sarah's family behoove me?"

"You really are dense in the head sometimes, Bentley."

Grant feigned a swat, and his friend ducked. "Come on, let's go set up our booth."

The two men carried the bulky wood structure out onto the pasture at the end of the fairground. In the short time it took them to secure it, several young women had clustered together on the edge of the field, gawking at them. Grant swiveled away. Women seemed to be getting bolder, even the well-dressed ones, as these were.

"I think Miss Bonnie comes to the fairground to see what is transpirin' between you and her niece."

"As long as she keeps an eye on Sarah, that's fine."

Nothing needed to happen to that pure-hearted young woman. Recalling the feel of her form in his arms brought about desires to find a wife he'd thought long passed. He'd lost Jonetta and never wanted to suffer that way again. But lately in studying the Word with his uncle at night on the farm, something stirred in his heart. Maybe it was just the love of God. The answer from the Lord he'd received last night at the Swansons' farm had him ready to seek out Sarah and keep watch over her.

"Grant? Grant Bentley?"

"That filly's headin' straight for us. What do you want me to do?" Hudgins moved between Grant and the oncoming woman.

Grant swiveled to face Mamie DuBeau. Despite her beauty, she failed to draw him as Miss Richmond did. She continued toward them, accompanied by the other young women he'd spotted earlier. He didn't need this schemer to spread the word he'd one day inherit a large estate in New York, the son of one of the wealthiest families in the Hudson Valley—if Father didn't disinherit him.

"There's trouble," Hudgins drawled.

"You're not kidding." Grant exhaled loudly.

Soon the women were upon them. He nodded briefly to each, eliciting giggles from two.

"Miss DuBeau." He inclined his head in her direction. She'd never forgiven him for rejecting her interest in him, and he'd always feared she'd extract retribution.

"It *is* you!" The schemer pulled her skirt aside, revealing elaborately decorated shoes unfit for a field.

"What brings you out into the field?" *Lord, please don't let Stollen be here.*

She peered around him. "Is that a balloonist booth? I'm sure Heinrich will be delighted."

<hr>

"Are you ready, dear?" The matron in charge of the tea and coffee service wheeled the cart toward Sarah.

Part of her work at the fair was offering tea, cookies, and sandwiches from a rolling cart.

"I think so." This should be easy compared to farmwork.

"Here's your apron." Mrs. Burgi passed a frilly white apron to Sarah.

Sarah eyed the top piece's narrow, lace-edged rectangle. "I don't think that will fit." It wouldn't begin to cover Sarah's ample bosom.

"It fits anyone. The ties all adjust." Mrs. Burgi untied the top and, eyeing Sarah, resecured a knot that allowed the apron to lie lower. She slipped it over Sarah's head.

Patting the midsection, Sarah examined where the fabric stretched across parts not needing accentuation. Across from her, she caught Denise's startled gaze. Subtly, her friend shook her head no.

The registrar tied the apron's waist so tightly Sarah gasped.

Sarah's cheeks heated. At least Miss DuBeau wasn't there.

"Now, first go up to the officials' table and offer them tea or coffee. Then pastries or sandwiches."

"Yes, ma'am."

"Don't worry, Miss Richmond, you'll do fine."

But as Sarah wheeled the cart toward the judges' station, she grew aware of most of them, male and female, blinking at her torso. This is how God made her—wasn't that what Mama always said? She was meant to be a curvy woman and had no reason to be ashamed. Drawing herself up tall, she kept her features serious and, whenever possible, met people's direct gaze. No apologies for God's handiwork.

No apologies from Arnold when taken home by God to live with Him forever.

She blinked back tears. Sarah sensed in her soul she'd expected Arnold to apologize for something he had no control over. He'd been in an accident, injured, and couldn't fight the infection that set in. It wasn't his fault, even though he'd chosen to go along with the Wild West Careeners' invitation to ride with them. He'd grown up riding horses almost every day. His parents owned a Percheron farm. But when something spooked his borrowed horse at the performance, he'd been thrown. His life was soon gone and hers altered forever.

"Miss?"

"Hmm?" Sarah looked into the warm brown eyes of a portly gentleman attired in a tweed suit. His name tag indicated this was Hershel Thomas, the chairman.

"Might I have what you're offering?" His face was kindly, like Papa's, and there didn't seem to be any insinuation in his voice.

She blinked at him.

Mr. Thomas pointed to the tray.

"Oh! Yes, sir. Let me pour."

From somewhere behind her, she heard men's low voices as someone neared. She bent to retrieve a cup and saucer from the bottom of the cart.

Someone snickered behind her. "Got us the best view in the whole house, fellas."

Choosing to ignore the comments, her hands shook as she poured coffee.

The judge's dark eyes widened as he looked past her and then slightly beyond.

"Hey!"

She heard a scuffling sound. The other officials gasped. Sarah turned to see Grant and Lee hauling several large men out of the pavilion, the rude men's arms twisted behind their backs. Sarah sucked in a deep breath, her heart pounding. But she had to perform her duties, so she turned back to face the next official.

A middle-aged woman in a snug pink day suit pushed her spectacles up her narrow nose. "At least we have good security."

Mr. Thomas nodded then addressed Sarah: "I'm sorry I didn't speak up for you, young lady." The judge patted the unusual arms of his chair. *A wheelchair.* "War injury has prevented me from keeping up my gentlemanly responsibilities."

After having served the officials, Sarah scanned the pavilion. Quilts dotted the entire building, giving the place a beautiful, homey feeling, despite its cavernous size. Personality and artistic style reflected in each creation. Clearly the quilt Miss DuBeau entered was the most beautiful.

There'd be no blue ribbon for Sarah. No money for the clinic. Reconsidering her unacknowledged anger toward Arnold, she wondered, did her motivation stem from anger toward Arnold and not from the godly desire to improve the small hospital? Part of her hoped to embarrass the staff. But they'd operated on a limited budget in a rickety old building and were doing the best they could.

God help me. Make my heart right.

------◆◆◆◆------

Grant and Lee held the two miscreants hostage while Mrs. Burgi summoned the state fair security guards.

"We ain't done nothin' wrong, 'cept admire a pretty gal!" The foulmouthed men continued to deny their words as Lee whistled the "Angelina Baker" song.

Several younger quilters came forward but stopped about six feet away. When one of the men leered at the prettiest one, Lee elbowed him hard.

Two burly men from the fair police entered the building and joined them. When they stopped and saw who was clutched tight at the registrar's booth, the men exchanged a knowing glance.

The quilter wearing the most prominent bustle spoke out, pointing at the disrupters. "They stopped at our booths and made. . .lewd comments to us."

"We'll take care of this. These two are leaving and never coming back." The guards accompanied them away.

Thank You for Your help, Lord, and please keep them far away from Sarah.

Now for his next chore. Followed by Lee, Grant quickly wove through the gathering crowd of mostly ladies in the building. He located the chairman of the committee. But when he looked into the deep brown eyes of "Uncle" Hershel Thomas, he almost swallowed his tongue. "Sir?" was all he managed to rasp. *Father's friend, now confined to a wheelchair.* Did Father likewise suffer with his war injuries?

Dark eyebrows knit together. "I'd stand and shake your hand, Grant, my boy, but no miracle yet."

Grant bent and grasped the man's warm hand. "How are you?"

"Missing New York some, but Lansing has been good to me. Research is coming along well." Father's closest friend from the military had spent a great deal of time with the family during Grant's youth.

"That's wonderful. Last I'd heard you were promoted to associate professor of biology at Yale."

He waved his hand. "Michigan offered me full professorship and my own lab."

Grant scratched his head. "Which made you qualified to judge quilts?"

Hershel laughed. "Filling in for a professor in the art department."

"Ah, well, I've a question for the officials about the rules."

The women who flanked him raised their eyebrows.

Grant leaned in. "Miss DuBeau entered a quilt created by a church quilting bee in Detroit, near my shop."

The trio exchanged glances. The woman in pink removed her spectacles. "That's a grievous charge. Have you proof?"

"Ma'am?" Lee stepped forward.

Grant sighed, sensing Lee would attempt his Southern charm on a group that included a veteran with legs damaged by the Rebels. "Not now, Lee."

For once, his friend hushed.

Hershel cocked his head. "If the real quilters come forward, we could disqualify Miss DuBeau and see if the churchwomen wish to enter under the group category."

"Let me get Miss Mary right quick."

When Lee trotted off, Grant jerked a thumb toward the door. "Earlier, we heard them practicing their choral performance."

Several judges from the end rose and joined the huddle. Soon Hershel explained the situation.

"I hate to embarrass Mr. DuBeau; he's been good to the fair," said a tall, angular man.

Sarah pushed her cart away.

Hershel waved for Grant to follow her. "A lovely young woman, Grant. Reminds me of your dear mother, rest her soul."

Sarah—like his mother? Mother had been quite femininely endowed like Sarah and offered better, softer hugs than his stick-thin nanny had. In Sarah's eyes, as well as Mother's, often glowed the soft light of loss. Mother had lost both a husband and her life in the South. His mother possessed a bedrock faith, which he suspected Sarah did, as well.

"What are you waiting for, son?" The voice, undeniably his father's, caused Grant to freeze.

Facing his father, he took in the silver-streaked hair and slight stoop.

When Father opened his arms, Grant didn't hesitate. The faint scent of lime brought back a rush of memories. Of riding through the fields as a family. Of dinners spent gathered around the long mahogany table, the chandeliers alight with candles. Of the day of Jonetta's death, inconsolable, when Grant had left New York State.

"Frank's kept me apprised, but I wanted to see you," Father whispered as he patted Grant's back.

"I've missed you, sir." This might be the closest he would get to apologizing.

Grant drew in a deep breath as the two men separated. Swallowing, Grant glanced past to where Sarah poured for Mamie's table. What would that vixen do if she became disqualified because of Grant's report to the judges? "You'll forgive me, but I need to—"

"Chase down a beautiful woman?" Waving him away, Father moved toward the judge's table. "Lieutenant Thomas! More civilian duties for you?"

Chapter 7

Five days had passed since Sarah first enjoyed a fairground tour with Grant. The previous day they'd strolled among the oaks and maples, arm in arm, and he'd shared that his father had arrived all the way from New York. Her stomach growled. She'd hastened out of the house that morning without so much as a muffin, and at lunchtime she'd gotten busy with a quilting demonstration, where she'd daydreamed about Grant instead of paying attention. Only two days remained for the fair. Sarah drew in a deep breath.

She needed to focus on finishing her afternoon hostess duties. Sarah pushed her cart toward the alcove where workers would wash the dishes. Her heartbeat's acceleration announced an impending reprieve—and time with the man she was falling in love with.

Struggling to untie the apron's neck, she sensed heat from someone behind her.

"May I?" Grant's husky voice sent a shiver through her.

"I have it." With her back to him, Sarah fumbled with her apron's bow. With him so near she couldn't concentrate.

"Allow me." He moved closer, right behind her. She'd never been so aware of a man's presence as at that moment.

He tugged at the bow, his knuckles brushing against her lower back. She jumped. "Sorry, Sarah, but someone got a knot in here."

"Denise tried to help me earlier—the ties kept coming undone."

She froze as he worked the knot, her heartbeat loud in her ears. When he paused, she turned to face him. "Can you help me turn it to the front and I'll work at it?"

He said nothing. Behind him, a stream of visitors flowed into the building, ladies adjusting their hats, the men accompanying them looking bored.

Looking up into his blue-as-Lake-Michigan eyes, her mouth went dry. All thoughts fled. The pupils of his eyes grew wide and dark. He leaned in. Was he going to kiss her? Right there in the home arts building?

Grant jerked away and rubbed his forehead. Averting her gaze, Sarah tugged at the apron to turn it. With a couple of strong pulls, she'd almost had it around her hip, when Grant grasped it.

"Here, you need to lift it higher to your waist." Deftly, he pulled and brought the knotted tie front and center.

"I can't believe I couldn't manage this maneuver myself." She looked up at Grant's gleaming smile. It was worth the struggle to be so close to him that she could. . . What? Step into his arms?

Forcing her eyes to the knot, she loosened the tightest part and then pulled the ties free. "Voilà!"

Grant took the apron from her and hung it on a peg.

"May I accompany you on the Grand Promenade?" Grant offered his arm.

"We're comin', too." Lee trotted up, followed by a sheepish-looking Denise.

Soon, the other couple came alongside. Sarah breathed more normally than she had moments before.

After they exited the building, Denise pointed to the multiple rows of low buildings populating the grounds, all gleaming white in the sun. "Seems strange that everything is brand-new."

"Almost everything." Lee gestured to a gypsy's faded wood caravan parked by the music stands. "That wagon has seen better days."

Frowning, Sarah remembered how the previous day a gypsy woman had asked to tell her fortune and she'd refused. Sarah knew what lay behind her—two men she cared deeply for, dead. And only God knew what was ahead. She'd have to start trusting Him to heal her heart.

Grant pulled Sarah's arm through his as they fell into an even cadence, unlike the irregular patter of her heart.

"Our buildin' is an old barn." Lee gestured toward the fairground's north edge.

"Really?" Denise brushed a stray lock from her forehead.

They strode on. Grant pointed to a juggler on the green. He picked up his pace. "Always wished I could try that."

Wooden benches, six deep, surrounded a chalk circle on the lawn. Just beyond, a man practiced a trick with a little mutt—the pup up on his back legs balancing a ball on his nose.

<hr/>

Grant needed to tell Sarah about the ballooning. Every time he was about to explain, he felt like his lips clamped shut.

The juggler, the Italian youth who'd offered them refreshment earlier in the week, changed out his india rubber balls for narrow wooden bowling pins, which would surely hurt if they landed on his head. Grant clapped in appreciation as the young man performed. *Young and working both a cart and performing a juggling act to make ends meet.* At least Grant had a small inheritance from his mother he and Lee used to pay their expenses. If only they could get one of their motors to work reliably to steer a balloon and power it farther. Maybe Lee was right. Maybe they needed to get out of the balloon business and focus on their engines.

Father and Mr. Thomas had requested a meeting with him. Were they going to suggest he move back to New York? Give up his dreams? He pushed the concerns aside and focused on the performance.

With Sarah snug beside him, Grant's thoughts wandered where they shouldn't stray. What would it be like to have Sarah in his arms? To kiss her, like he'd almost done earlier? To make her his own? He pressed his eyelids closed as sweat broke out on his brow.

As the acts transitioned out, a young boy came through, hawking raffle tickets. "A penny for a chance to ride the balloon!"

The boy glanced between Lee and Grant, but when he opened his mouth, Grant silenced him by placing his index finger to his lips. Didn't need the little fellow blurting out they were the balloonists.

Sarah rolled her eyes. "Can you imagine anyone wanting to do something so dangerous?"

Denise laughed. "I would."

"People get killed in those contraptions." Sarah scowled.

"You could just as soon be struck by lightnin'."

"But in a balloon, you deliberately put yourself in peril." Sarah's plaintive tone pulled at his heartstrings.

"We should go take a look tonight." Denise cocked her head.

"Shall we keep walking?" Grant abruptly stood. "I just wished to see the juggler."

<hr />

What in the world was the matter with Grant? Why the reaction to the balloon discussion?

Denise looked like she might cry. "I want to see the trick dog, please."

"Sit!" Lee commanded Grant.

He lowered himself back to the bench, glaring at his friend. His fierce countenance could curdle milk.

The boy with the raffle tickets had circled around again. He stopped by Grant. "Buy a chance for a balloon ride, sir?"

Grant made a shooing motion with his hand. Although he was being rude, relief coursed through Sarah that he didn't wish to buy a ticket.

"Pooh." Denise fished around in her coin purse. "Wait!"

The red-haired boy turned around. "Yes, miss?"

"One raffle ticket." She handed the penny to Grant.

He sighed and passed it to the child, who handed him a small cardboard raffle ticket. Grant gave it to Denise, but his eyes were fixed on Lee.

The Southerner winked. "I hear the men who operate the balloon exhibition are old pros at this."

"Old?" Grant's offended tone made no sense.

Lee chuckled. "I doubt those *young and handsome* balloonists would let you be killed."

A muscle in Grant's jaw twitched. Then the performance began, and all were silent.

After the show, they passed by the arena for the horse races. Grant steered them away from the track while Lee shot him a sympathetic glance. Seemed Grant, too, wasn't fond of horse shows. Poor Arnold. He'd been so excited. He'd reminded Sarah of when he was a ten-year-old boy, and she eight, and he'd jumped his pony over a hay bale to make her smile. They'd been friends all their lives. She chewed her lower lip, aware of the powerfully built man beside her. Although she'd loved Arnold, he'd never inspired the feelings she had for Grant, and in such a short time.

"Can we see your barn?" Denise pulled on Lee's arm.

"Why in the world would you want to see that?"

"Come on!" Denise motioned for Sarah to follow.

Sarah pulled free and ran after her friend, her skirts hiked up above her boots.

Heading north past the balloonist exhibition, she spotted Mamie and her beau exiting a large old barn. What were those two doing there?

Grant and Lee caught up with the ladies just in time to catch Stollen leaving their workspace. "What are you doing here?"

Fisting and unfisting his hands, Grant fought the urge to strike the intruder.

Stollen tugged at the lapel of his snugly tailored striped suit. "That's no way to treat your supporters."

"Supporters?" What game were they up to?

Mamie twirled her lacy parasol. "Just wanted to make sure you'll be taking us up for our ride tomorrow night."

"We ain't fixin' to take you nowhere." Lee's eyes narrowed into slits.

Mamie ignored him. "Father purchased all the tickets for the first ride after dinner."

"What?"

"Can't wait to see you use one of your motors." The socialite lowered her umbrella and tapped it into the dirt.

Lord, thank You that I listened to You and kept our most valuable prototypes at Uncle Frank's barn.

"That won't be happening." They'd been tethered. And if he admitted it to himself, it had been a far too dangerous idea.

"Maybe you can take us all the way to Detroit? Don't you even want to try?" Stollen's lightly accented voice and insinuating tone irritated Grant. "Isn't that your goal—to show how superior your product is?"

"Heinrich, would you like to replicate your German friend's outcome?" Grant forced steel into his voice. Lee had asked Grant the same question that very morning.

"Ach! Nein."

Mamie tapped Stollen's arm. "What's he talking about, Heinrich?"

"Franz died." Stollen's eyebrows furrowed together.

"Died?" Her eyes widened.

"Ja. Crashed badly. In France."

Sarah slumped, and Grant caught her in his arms.

━━━●◆●━━━

Dizziness overwhelmed Sarah. Someone held a cup of juice to her lips. Sarah took a few sips. She was seated on a bench, with a warm arm wrapped around her.

Her fuzzy vision cleared. Straight ahead was a large, multicolored balloon. A fair attraction that belonged to Grant and Lee. She pressed her eyes closed.

"Drink some more, Sarah."

"She didn't eat anything all day." Denise paced between Sarah and the offensive sight of the brilliant balloon. "Sarah was too occupied with something. . . ."

Or rather someone. All those daydreams ceased *now.* Here was a man who risked his life and others for the thrills. *How silly I've been. No more.* She forced herself to breathe slowly and evenly then finished the juice.

Grant leaned in. "I'm sorry. I didn't want you to learn about our business like this."

Sarah waved him off dismissively. "It's of no consequence to me. What you do is your own affair."

"But. . .I. . ." Disappointment washed his handsome features. "Let's talk about this later."

"We're busy tonight. Canning." That was true enough, but Aunt Bonnie had said Sarah could invite Grant.

"What about tomorrow?"

"Tomorrow?" There was absolutely no tomorrow for her and this man. "I don't think so."

"I told my father we'd take dinner with him on Friday."

The fair would be over then. Sarah would be going home. Alone. What harm could one meal do? "Fine."

She felt anything but fine as she rose and they resumed their walk, this time with her arms crossed and walking stiffly beside Grant.

Their good-byes at the pavilion portended their relationship's permanent severing. When Grant left, Sarah sat at her table and cried.

Chapter 8

Thursday. It was almost halfway through the day, and tomorrow brought the end of the fair. Grant was running out of time. He rubbed the side of his head, where an ache had begun earlier, right after Sarah had said she was "too busy" to walk with him.

"If only my attempts at placating Sarah would go as smoothly as our balloon trips," Grant groused to Lee, walking back to their stand. They'd stayed aloft, tethered by dual winches, long enough to satisfy all the customers, the skies blue and the wind even. Their hired assistants had experienced no problems with the extra ropes.

"Seems you've stepped in it real good, partner!" Lee's laughter aggravated Grant.

Gritting his teeth, Grant ground out, "At least you get the joy of taking the DuBeaus up tonight. It's your turn."

"Ain't that fine?" Lee whistled.

Grant sighed. "When we get back to the balloon, let's make sure everything is perfect."

"Any problems earlier?"

"No, but who knows what Stollen might try?"

"Ya think Heinrich really expected us to display our new engine and how it works on balloons?"

Men had died trying to accomplish exactly what he and Lee were aiming for. Today, for the first time, it had hit him what that meant for those who cared for him. He'd kept everyone at arm's length since losing Jonetta.

"You know the ideas you had for better motors for our horseless carriage?" A breeze ruffled the autumn leaves, swirling them around the two men. "Perhaps we should focus more on those notions."

Lee kicked his boot into the soil on the pathway, sending up a clump of dirt. "Yeah?"

Swallowing back guilt, Grant considered how every time Lee had an idea he'd wanted to pursue, he'd steered him back to the notion of a huge balloon powered by engine that could carry many people far distances. Was this an imitation of his father's dream? Of an elaboration on Father's foray into Virginia during the war? Was it to show him he could go farther, do it better than he had? That Grant would have stopped his mother from. . .

Something deep and dark welled up in him. He swiftly fled, weaving in and out of the crowds of people. His heavy burden lightened then lifted heavenward, like a balloon finally untethered.

* * *

The tension in the Home Arts Pavilion felt palpable to Sarah. Although the judges had listened to the Detroit quilters in private, rumors had quickly circulated as to what the consequences would be. The lead quilter, "Miss Mary" as Lee had called her, kept her head high as she and the other quilting-bee members strode from the building and their formal grievance meeting in silence.

Mrs. Burgi gave Sarah a gentle push. "Serve them now before they speak with that pretender." The disgust in the sweet-natured registrar's voice surprised Sarah.

After the AME Quilting Bee had been heard, another private meeting was to be held—this one with Miss DuBeau.

Sarah pushed her cart toward the pavilion's center and the judges' table. Earlier she'd decorated it with fall leaves, apples, and tiny pumpkins. Prior to the churchwomen's arrival she set out cucumber sandwiches, pecan tarts, and miniature apple turnovers. Now she brought both tea and coffee service for the judges. Her hands shook as she set up afternoon tea for them.

Mr. Thomas, seated in the middle, presided over the group. He smiled at her when she poured his coffee. She continued serving each judge.

Mamie DuBeau, attired in a coral linen walking suit with a prominent bustle and French lace–edged blouse, moved alongside Sarah's cart. Mr. DuBeau, looking more dapper than in newspaper photos, followed his daughter. He carried his top hat under his left arm and a black, silver-headed walking stick in the other.

Mamie tipped her nose in the air and avoided Sarah, but her father offered a gentle smile. The beautiful socialite nibbled her lower lip.

"Good day, esteemed judges." Mr. DuBeau bowed toward the table. "I'm Cyrus DuBeau, here from Detroit."

"We all know who you are, sir." Mr. Thomas's voice was gruff, despite the humble delivery by Mr. DuBeau. "State your business."

Red crept across the man's high cheekbones. Mamie's face contorted, but then a mask of serenity replaced her livid expression. She stepped forward, clasping her hands. "I'm afraid there has been a misunderstanding."

"Such as?"

"I was supposed to display the quilt I brought as a group submission from a local church. However. . ." She glanced down at her ivory kid, button-up boots. "I incorrectly completed the paperwork."

"And submitted it as your own?"

She lifted her chin. "Nowhere on the form did it have a section for all the church members' information."

Mr. DuBeau touched his daughter's shoulder. "I fear I haven't trained my daughter how to complete paperwork. I've always done it for her. I take responsibility for that error in judgment."

"So this quilt was to have been submitted on behalf of the church group?" Mr. Thomas rubbed the bridge of his nose.

"Yes."

Several of the judges simply stared at the DuBeaus.

"But it's too late to be reentered for judging."

Mamie's shoulders edged up toward her ears, like a chastened child.

Mr. DuBeau tapped his cane. "I'd hoped to display the quilt at my flagship store in

Detroit, as the winner of the blue ribbon."

"A pity the churchwomen will suffer from your daughter's mistakes." Mr. Thomas fixed his eyes on Mamie, who wouldn't meet his gaze.

"Mamie shall make amends to them, I assure you."

"We're afraid we've also voted Miss DuBeau may not submit in any state fair category for two years."

Mr. DuBeau stiffened. "She'll be a married lady by then and too busy keeping household."

Mamie raised her chin and glared past her father at Sarah, who only then realized she'd simply stood there like a ninny, listening in.

The socialite's eyes narrowed. "I'm no longer engaged, Father. I fear Mr. Stollen's fascination with those silly, boring balloons has come between us. I'll not sit by for years while he works on an engine for them to become more than they were meant to be—a simple diversion. And I have no plans to begin quilting, either."

Mr. DuBeau's mustache twitched. "There you have it, esteemed judges. You shan't be troubled by my blunders or my daughter's in the future."

A smirk settled on Mamie's face.

Sarah hastily placed the last creamer at the end of the table and pushed the cart toward the alcove. Mamie and her father passed nearby, her father's scolding words too low for her to hear at first, but then his voice raised a touch. "If all you want is excitement and a handsome face, you'll only find sorrow. A marriage is based on sacrifice by both parties and mutual love and respect. You'll never find that if you keep putting yourself first."

After steering the cart into the quiet alcove, Sarah removed her apron. Had it only been yesterday that Grant had almost kissed her? Even though it was she who sent him away that day, his absence today rippled through her like physical pain. Would the sadness of losing him outweigh the anguish she'd experience if he died in a balloon crash?

"Trust Me," a still, quiet voice nudged her.

I want to trust You, Jesus. I want to rely on You, but right now I can't seem to get past myself. Like Mamie. Tears filled her eyes.

"Lean into Me."

<hr />

The sun began to dip in the autumn sky. Father and Mr. Thomas drew in closer as Grant commandeered the first winch, and his strongest assistant managed the second. Hired helpers clutched the additional safety ropes. They'd worked hard all week long. Might as well give the assistants a bonus, because Lee and Grant would, by no means, raise enough money to keep their engineering shop in Detroit going. Tethered.

Lee assisted Mamie into the basket. Her father drew in beside her. And Stollen, a sulky look on his face, stepped in, too. Soon, ballast was emptied, and Grant and his helper loosened the winch, as the balloon ascended into the air.

From the periphery of his vision, Grant sensed someone watching him. He continued to focus on the DuBeau contingent, not wanting to be distracted. A gentle breeze stirred the fragrance of autumn leaves and apples—and a distinctly feminine scent he associated with Sarah: lilacs and roses. He daren't look around, though. They allowed the balloon to move higher into the cerulean skies. He looked up to see Mamie clutching not Stollen's arm, but her father's. Even from this distance, she appeared pale. Grant made a slashing motion at his throat and the other wincher also stopped.

He cupped his hands around his mouth and called up, "Are you all right?"

Mr. DuBeau gazed down with obvious affection at his only child. He patted her arm. Mamie nodded and DuBeau jerked his thumb upward.

Breathing slowly in relief, Grant and his helper continued to unwind the tether rope. Once they reached about a thousand feet, a cheer went up from the crowd. He resisted the urge to turn and count how many observed. But from the sounds of chatter in the background, the numbers were growing.

Footfalls hurried toward him. "Sir?"

Grant didn't stir as the ticket boy came alongside him. "Yes?"

"We sold out all the tickets."

"All?"

"Yes, sir."

Grant could feel the boy's smile, even though he didn't look. Instead, he kept his gaze fixed on the DuBeaus.

"Folks said if Mamie DuBeau and her pa could go up, so was they!"

He almost cringed at the child's grammar but didn't correct him. "I'll honor our agreement."

"Whoopee!"

All the ticket sellers were promised unlimited drinks and food from the Italian boy's cart if they sold out.

If they sold out. That meant they'd made enough to hold on to their lease. If they did a real aeronautical show, with a parachute drop, maybe they could finance their new prototype.

A stiff wind blew leaves up from the ground. Between the excitement of their sales, the strong breeze, and the sensation that Sarah was nearby, Grant struggled to keep his focus on the tethers. Tomorrow promised to be a long day. How could he make things up to Sarah?

Chapter 9

It's the last day of the fair and your only chance! You can do this." Denise patted Sarah's arm.

"I know. I have to do this." Having seen the night before that the balloon was tethered and appeared quite safe, Sarah almost looked forward to going up.

"Lee is such a sweetheart. I was so surprised when he brought those tickets by."

"Yes, but without Grant."

"Grant tried to speak with you yesterday, but you said you were too busy." Denise's gentle chide brought tears to Sarah's eyes.

She'd prayed for an answer, and God had provided. Lee had explained how the winches worked, one on each side, and the balloon ride was secured. Sarah had to try. Only God knew the time and place in which someone's time on earth would end. She had to trust that He knew best.

The autumn sun rose higher in the early morning sky.

"What a long line!" Sarah pointed.

As they approached, Lee jogged toward them and practically dragged Sarah and Denise to the front of the line, over the protests of the people ahead of them. "Guests of honor!" he called out.

Grant's eyes sparkled as Sarah shyly moved forward. "You're really going up?"

"I am." She raised her chin. *I can do this.*

"All right." He pointed at Lee and then the winch. "We're going up alone. You two can go next."

"Ya might start a riot, old man."

"I may be over thirty, but I'm not old."

This virile man was anything but old. Strength radiated through Grant's arms as he led Sarah to the balloon basket and assisted her in.

She was doing this. Really going up. Grant's hand brushed against hers as he secured the basket door, sending a thrill through her. "Hold on."

He gestured for them to begin and tossed a sandbag out.

As the balloon propelled upward, Grant wrapped his arm around her waist. The warmth of his palm penetrated her cotton dress, sending tingles up her spine. "I'm not a youth. I know my own mind. And if I have figured correctly, you might be of the same persuasion."

Sarah swallowed. They ascended higher, the crowd beneath them growing larger even as the people appeared smaller. "I'm not sure what you mean."

Confusion flashed over his handsome features. His lips, which she longed to have pressed against her own, twitched.

Grant turned her toward him, and she clutched at the rail, despite feeling quite stable in their perch. "I'm trying to say that I care very deeply for you, and even though we've known each other a short time, I feel close to you."

Though she was aware the balloon continued to rise, ever so slowly, the only thing she could contemplate was Grant Bentley. He edged forward, his shoes nestled between her low boots, and pulled her into his arms. As she released the rail, his head inclined toward her. Then his mouth covered hers, and nothing else existed. Nothing but the two of them, high above the earth.

She was safe. Perfectly safe. In his arms.

———◆●◆———

Were they engaged now? Grant wasn't sure he'd actually asked the question. But judging by the crowd's excitement, they thought so.

Reporters crushed in. "When is the big date, Professor Bentley?"

Grant cringed at being addressed by the aeronautic honorary title of *professor*.

A Lansing photographer snapped a picture of Denise hugging Sarah, who gazed wide-eyed at Grant. "Let me get one of the happy twosome."

"We've heard of couples getting married in a balloon, but this is the first engagement we've gotten wind of." Danny Williams, from the *Detroit Free Press*, scribbled on his notepad. "When's the wedding date?"

A fracas began in the background. People shouted as the crowd parted for someone.

"What's happening?" Williams called out.

"Dunno!" Another man answered as he jumped up on an overturned box. "Someone's rushing the balloon!"

"Hey!" Lee called out as two men jumped into the basket.

A policeman's shrill whistle pierced the air.

Grant pushed past the journalists to Sarah and wrapped an arm around her. Beyond her, the two brothers who'd threatened her stood in the basket, whacking at the winch ropes with long knives.

"Stop them!" Two policemen ran across the field.

The balloon lifted off. Ballast rained down, and the men and balloon shot upward.

Lee moved alongside him. "Suppose they know. . ."

Danny elbowed Grant, pencil raised. "Will those two be able to land safely?"

"Short of a miracle, no."

———◆●◆———

"I'm so sorry about your balloon, Grant." Sarah's heart still pounded from their fast walk to the pavilion for the presentation of home arts awards.

They arrived just in time to hear Mrs. Burgi announce, "And the blue ribbon for individual quilts goes to. . ."

Sarah gripped Grant's hand tighter than a vise. All the way there, he'd urged her to do as he did: to pray and give the matter over to God—both the fiasco that had just occurred and the possibility of winning the blue ribbon.

"Sarah." Grant grinned down at her, affection in his eyes.

Her heart leapt. "Yes?"

"You need to go up." Grant bent down and kissed her cheek. "Congratulations."

Lee nudged her. "Ya need to hasten up there before someone else grabs that silk ribbon."

Denise giggled, and Sarah's feet finally managed to move as Mr. Thomas called out, "Ahem! Again, I give you Sarah Richmond, this year's winner of the blue ribbon."

That afternoon, Denise came out to the farm to style Sarah's hair. "Looks just like the new style in the latest *Godey's* magazine."

Sarah patted the side of her upswept hair. "Thanks for helping."

Applying pomade to some of the curls, Denise sighed. "I wish I was going."

"But Lee will be coming here with Grant's uncle."

Denise laughed. "Lee confided that I shouldn't miss tonight's 'big doin's.'"

"Oh?"

"I'm hoping. . ." Her friend blushed.

With some of Aunt Bonnie's jewelry, a borrowed cloak from Denise, and her boots freshly polished till they shone, Sarah went downstairs to await Grant's arrival. She'd be in his horseless buggy that evening. Dangerous or not, she'd trust God to get them to the restaurant near the Grand River, which edged the fairgrounds.

When he arrived, Grant escorted her out to what he referred to as his latest "prototype." She enjoyed the ride, and they reached the restaurant much sooner than they would have in a horse-drawn buggy. They didn't have to worry about finding a stable, either. Sarah and Grant entered the hotel's restaurant through the large varnished oak doors ten minutes early.

Sarah marveled as the hostess led her and Grant past cherrywood tables, covered with pristine white linen tablecloths and fresh flowers in crystal vases at each table. Silver place settings were laid out, with starched napkins at several empty tables. They were directed to a corner table with plenty of space around it for privacy, obviously one of their best in the restaurant. The candelabras were higher at this table, and lit, to add more illumination than the gas-lit sconces on the wall provided. Mr. Thomas was waiting for them, along with another man.

"My father, Herbert Bentley. And this is Sarah Richmond."

Mr. Bentley's deep blue eyes met hers. "Good to officially meet you, Miss Richmond."

When his father made to rise, Grant gestured for him to sit. He pulled out a chair for Sarah and sat beside her.

The gravity of meeting Grant's father suddenly weighed on her. On their drive, Grant shared that with their balloon destroyed, he and Lee would be unable to continue to use the device to raise funds for their research.

Sarah wondered at what effort it must have taken to get Mr. Thomas up the stairs and into the restaurant with his wheelchair. He steepled his fingers. "The two culprits are in City Hospital. Busted up by their crash into the trees."

"But they'll probably survive." Mr. Bentley's eyes took on a sheen.

Sarah's eyes, too, welled up, realizing Grant's father likely felt as she did—that Grant could easily have perished in one of his flights, if not now then later, had he continued.

Grant held up his hands. "Well, all of that's over for me and Lee, now."

Clutched in her lap, Sarah's hands shook. Grant placed his warm hand atop them, bringing her comfort. She looked into his dark blue eyes and saw something there that made her draw in a deep breath.

"They make a handsome couple, don't they?" Mr. Thomas grinned at them.

Sarah's cheeks heated.

"Sure do." Mr. Bentley accepted a menu from the waitress.

The petite red-haired woman gave them each a copy. "I recommend the Kansas City steak tonight. It's real tender and comes with roast potatoes and asparagus."

The two older men passed her back the menus. "You're speaking our language, ma'am," Mr. Thomas quipped.

"Same here." Grant returned his.

Sarah knew she couldn't eat a whole steak. She'd be lucky if she could manage to eat at all.

"How about our house salad, miss?"

"Perfect." What was in it? It didn't matter. A rock had settled in her gut.

"We need to talk about a few things tonight." Mr. Thomas tapped the table. "One thing is I want in on the partnership. Twenty-five percent."

"Twenty-five percent of a defunct company is nothing, sir." Grant leaned his head toward Sarah. "I believe I'll be helping on Sarah's dairy farm for the foreseeable future."

"Not if I have anything to say about it." Mr. Bentley's determined face brooked no arguments. "Twenty-five percent for me, too."

Grant puffed out a sigh. "If you mean as investors—"

His father raised a hand. "We have a deal that will sweeten the pot."

"Oh? I'm listening." Grant raised his water glass to his lips and sipped.

"We'll donate to the funding of a new clinic in Northwoods, in honor of the winner of the quilting contest."

A thrill shot through Sarah. "Really?"

"We have it on good authority that she wishes to improve the health care for residents of her community."

"Sounds like bribery to me," Grant drawled.

Sarah elbowed him. "Sounds like a winning proposition."

<hr />

Grant drove Sarah back to her aunt's farm in a daze. Father and Mr. Thomas were now his and Lee's partners. Lee had already agreed to assume lead, and they'd pursue his motorized vehicle engine designs. Sarah had visibly relaxed when he'd shared that news.

From the kitchen window, lights shone bright. Laughter echoed outside the small farmhouse. After parking the conveyance, they hurried inside.

Seth had a mug of punch raised. "I toast the happy couple!"

Bonnie and Frank hugged.

Lee extended his arm toward the two. "I'm proud and privileged to give you Mr. and Mrs. Frank Bentley."

Lila bent and hugged her pet. "I got a new daddy, and you do, too, Mr. Box!"

"What on earth?" Sarah clutched Grant's hand.

Joining them, with her dog trotting behind, Lila took Grant's free hand. "I'm your cousin now, Mama says!"

"If those two got married, then that's true."

"They're hitched, and we saw it!" Lee wrapped his arm around Denise, and she blushed.

Mr. Box trotted off toward the farmhand. He licked Seth's leg, where a piece of cake had clung.

"Have some cake." Bonnie wiped tears from her eyes and pointed to a white cake heavily frosted with her famous stove-top, prize-winning concoction. It would definitely not be served at the Kelloggs' Health Reform Institute in Battle Creek.

"Married?" Sarah blinked.

Lee leaned in to whisper: "If the story the *Detroit Free Press* is fixin' to run is right, they ain't gonna be the only Mr. and Mrs. Bentley in the family."

"Nor the only blue ribbon bride." Grant pulled Sarah into his arms and bestowed a lingering kiss.

Author's Notes

The 1889 Michigan State Fair in Lansing was supposed to begin the use of a permanent site for the fair (which had rotated through other cities such as Grand Rapids and Detroit). A huge investment was put into making the grounds fabulous. Unfortunately, maintenance costs and other fiscal difficulties arose, and the fairgrounds were later sold to Oldsmobile.

In this time period, balloonists really were referred to as *professors*, an honorary title, and as *aeronauts*. Many balloonists died as they engaged in more spectacular demonstrations, such as parachute descending. Ground assistants could be injured, especially the inexperienced. Those involved in ballooning were widely varied. Many were inventors—like my hero—or military—like my hero's father (balloons were used during the Civil War). Additionally, aerial photographers, cartographers, and artists, as well as showmen and thrill seekers made use of balloons. Some weddings were really performed in balloons.

Three main types of balloons are coal gas (less common and more stable for Michigan's climate), hydrogen (highly flammable), and heated air. Helium came after this time period. The wind commonly shifted during landing, and this brought about the most mishaps. Sand was often used as ballast. To ascend, ballast had to be tossed off, and to descend, the upper flap of the balloon was opened, releasing the air. Upon descent, without a means to ascend again nor ballast to hold the balloon down, one way to control the balloon was by a drag rope. Imagine being a farmer in the field, as a struggling balloonist wildly gestures for you to grab some lines, which he throws down. You might be the only thing between the "professor" and yonder trees, preventing possible injury or death. Balloons were expensive and had to be recovered, if possible. Dirigibles were the next big thing after this era, and what my hero is working toward—a larger balloon with the capacity to be steered over long distances. Given the dangers of these huge dirigibles (remember the Hindenburg), I think my hero made the right choice, don't you?

Carrie Fancett Pagels, PhD, "Hearts Overcoming Through Time," is an award-winning, multi-published, Christian historical romance author. Twenty-five years as a psychologist didn't "cure" her overactive imagination. Although a "Yooper" by birth, and a Michigander, she currently resides with her family in Virginia. She's a self-professed "history geek." Carrie loves to read, bake, bead, and travel – but not all at the same time! You can find her on her website www.carriefancettpagels.com or on her two group blogs: OvercomingwithGod.com and ColonialQuills.org.

Seven Medals and a Bride

by Angela Breidenbach

There be three things which are too wonderful for me, yea, four which I know not: the way of an eagle in the air; the way of a serpent upon a rock; the way of a ship in the midst of the sea; and the way of a man with a maid.
PROVERBS 30:18–19

Chapter 1

May 1, 1893

Bettina Gilbert gawked at the White City from a bench on the hurricane deck of the steamship as she balanced a sketchbook on one knee, a white lace glove in her lap to avoid blackening it with graphite smudges. The clouds clearing from their early morning drapery drew away as if a cord were pulled on a stage, revealing the glow of bright white classical structures gleaming in the spring sun. Heaven might as well be laid out before her. The Peristyle's forty-eight Roman columns, one for each state, and its gateway arches spread the massive colonnade across the park's waterway entrance butted by the mammoth casino on one side and the matching music hall on the other. From the distance, the shape made by the harbor buildings seemed more like Bettina pictured the Lord's giant throne room, regal and triumphant, calling believers into His presence.

Could she capture that sense of incredible royalty in a sketch before the boat docked? The cacophony of the crowd on board rumbled with unencumbered excitement to discover the Columbian Exposition of 1893. The noise of the crowd on the pier walkway rolled across the short distance to collide with the clamor on the boat as if one hand met the other in wild ovation. Did the angelic chorus sound as loud? God must have rather the regular headache. Bettina pressed lace-clad fingertips to her temple.

"Beautiful from this vantage." The expressive awe in the man's words tickled her ears, a calm center in the explosion of buzzing energy. His voice soothed her spirit like the sun on her shoulders eased the shivers after the morning's rainy start. "We're blessed with unusual opportunity."

Against the rising roar from inland, where hundreds of thousands listened to President Cleveland's opening address and those on the dock scurried to see the great man press the golden key to open the fair, this man's quiet words subdued Bettina's frayed nerves. "Yes, astonishingly so." She slipped the sketch pencil into her hair and turned into the sun, barely escaped from its cloudy curtains, to find her fellow passenger.

Lifting her gloved hand to block the glare, she caught a glimpse of a mustache and dark hair under a bowler as she waited out the signal bell clanging orders to the steamship's crew. Then a woman with several well-dressed children, girls in matching gray frocks and boys in matching gray knickers and vests, jostled into an open space, hindering a good view of her congenial companion.

He must have given way—as a gentleman should according to her father. Refreshing, since manners seemed sorely lacking as more and more travelers bore down on Chicago the last few weeks. Well, it'd been a pleasant interlude among the din. She returned to her sketching.

"Antoine, qu'est-ce que je dis? Ton frère. . ."

French. Bettina tried to ignore the poor mite's scolding for shoving a sibling, but her love of language and sense of unrequited adventure meant a tiny bit of intentional eaves-dropping. Poor bored Antoine was picking on his brother. She knew exactly what that felt like. Her pencil flew. The boy's face, eyes full of longing, took over the upper corner of her page, watching the city from afar.

Who were all these people? What were their home countries like? Why were they here, specifically? The magnitude of the crowds everywhere she looked already drained her people patience. She'd much prefer peeping into a microscope or testing soil samples. But then, she still had to find a way to meet the man she hoped would have a place for her to continue her research. Dr. Kelsey would be here, at the exposition, taking part in the congresses before massive audiences. She couldn't arrive on that day and expect to be prepared. No, coming early to investigate was a wise choice.

She cast a quick consolation glance at the boy who wanted to be done with the wait-ing. It had to be harder still for a small boy to wait when the World's Fair seemed only inches away and as yet so inaccessible. Would anything be as thrilling for him again in his lifetime? Or hers? The boy turned to face away from his family, nose in the air as if watching a seagull. An elbow popped out and jabbed his little brother, setting off another squabble. Then he pretended a wide-eyed innocence as his sibling overreacted to the injury, sending his mama into another fit of French scolds.

Oh no. Bettina rolled her lips inward and tightened them to keep from laughing. Anyone could tell what a finger-shaking at a nose meant. How many strangers had caught her brothers, or her, acting just this way during childhood? She focused on shad-ing dimension into the numerous arches of the Peristyle rather than be an encouraging party to the French lad's mischievous antics. French boys and Irish American boys. Not so different. Although she seemed to get away with a few pranks as the middle child to keep her four brothers in line, it was survival of the fittest as far as she was concerned. Adding an eight-year-old sister into the family meant jostling for a new pecking order.

Bettina peeked back at the boy. "I see you," she mouthed at him and signaled between their eyes in case he didn't speak English.

He rewarded her with a knowing grin.

She tipped her pencil to her hat—ending the silent, secret language of mischievous middles.

His grin grew.

She'd take one-on-one communication any day over parties and crowds. Then she caught sight of another gaze. A little breath wedged in her throat at the handsome strang-er's nod of detection. He'd noticed the exchange and joined in the humorous moment. Bettina lowered her lashes and turned toward the dock, a warm blush creeping across her cheeks. She whispered to herself, "No distractions." My, but she liked the confident look of him.

Approaching the already teeming dock doubled the volume and drowned out her ability to think. Today national and international experts began to gather and share scien-tific discoveries and potential medicines derived from the study of plants. The upcoming congresses promised to educate and entertain on every topic imaginable. Winning a slot to present her own paper on strategic crop planting for maximum harvest both excited and terrified her. Only the possibility of gaining a position close to home at Oberlin College convinced her parents the summer in Chicago would be worth the sacrifice of letting their daughter go for a short time. But would anyone even want to hear an unknown, let alone a woman botanist, speak on farming techniques? Hopefully one Reverend Doctor F. D. Kelsey and his colleagues. She pushed the anxiety away and concentrated on her plan.

Bettina knew where each one of the featured displays would be housed as well as the illustrious names in botanical science she wanted to meet. She'd gleaned several from research papers at college, and thanks to the detailed articles in the *Chicago Tribune* for the last year or so, she knew which would be speaking or participating with an exhibit. Sharing her work was less about the audience and more about attracting an expert mentor, preferably the good Reverend Doctor Kelsey, to help her navigate her budding botany career.

The daily speakers in the congresses, where the learned of the world convened to educate and enlighten, held both the key to her future and an example of how she should conduct herself when it came her turn to present. While others took in the sights and exotic experiences like camel rides, Egyptian mummies, and Mr. Ferris's wheel on the specially dubbed Street of Cairo, Bettina intended to expand her horizons professionally by studying the scholars she wished to intern under for an advanced degree. She didn't have time for thrill seeking if the few remaining positions that fit her need for a situation near Cleveland, and her parents, were at stake.

The signal bell clanged its arrival announcement. Closing the sketch pad, she eyed the jam of families, including the French lad still pestering his little brother. The mishmash line flowed out from the stairwell and disappeared down two decks toward departure. That could take awhile. A few minutes more to remember the awestruck moment the White City boardwalk spread like a welcome mat to every nation would be worth the delay disembarking after the mass exodus off the steamboat. But then she'd visit each botanical and agricultural exhibit first. Of all the places possible, admiring and studying the leading experts' work at the World's Fair had to be the best opportunity to find a master mentor for a degreed botanist.

Bettina's heart drummed in her ears, matching the thrum of the antsy throng. Brilliant minds would walk here this summer. She wanted the chance to meet them, discover unknown species, uses for plant materials, and better ways to manage crops to feed the masses—and one day be considered accomplished among those brilliant minds.

She flipped open the page on her sketchbook again, tucking the loose referral letter from her professor safely in the back pages with her carefully planned list of activities, and tugged the pencil from its mooring under the small purple hat. Flaxen strands floated free of her loose chignon and danced in the breeze over her shoulders as she bent to draft a smart line drawing of her first view from Lake Michigan. She studied the entrancing architecture, ducked again to feather in a little shading for the lagoon, and then shifted on the bench for a better angle to finish the brilliant white, elegant casino left of the pier. The beaux art domes on many of the structures seemed similar. She started counting, dipping the end of the pencil as she ticked off each one in sight.

"That's an astounding representation," the same man's voice said as he leaned over her shoulder, blocking the morning sun.

Bettina gasped and dropped her sketchbook. It slid down her navy skirt and lodged near her boot—until she moved to pick it up at the same time the ship's paddle wheel chugged, jerking into reversed direction as it moored alongside the dock. Skittering across the planked decking, still wet from the earlier drizzle, the book careened toward the edge. She stood to give chase.

He shot to the rescue, dropping to a knee and snagging the book by the corner before it slid under the boat's rail and over the side. As he rose, the pages blew open and fluttered in the breeze, loosing one to float free, lolling on a current.

Her reference letter! "Catch that!" She lurched, arm outstretched, and bumped the handsome stranger into the railing as they both reached for the paper. Her pencil sailed from her fingers and plunged into the waves. She scrambled for a handhold and clutched for the page, losing her balance. Her gloved hand slid at the same time as her boot, pitching her forward, off her feet, in the direction of water lapping against the hull.

The man grasped Bettina around the waist a moment before she tumbled into Lake Michigan three decks below.

She squeaked like a strangled seagull as his saving strength cut off all airflow.

One arm tight around Bettina, he snagged the errant page from the teasing grasp of the breeze as it blew inward and tipped toward the water, missing its pencil mate. Setting her back on her feet, he let her loose. "Are you all right?"

Dragging in a deep breath, Bettina clasped the white lace at her throat. "Yes. I don't know what would have happened if you hadn't stopped me." She swallowed as she glanced down at the deep, dark water. "Thank you."

"I'm sorry I caused you such distress during a delightfully peaceful moment in all this hullabaloo." He offered her the page. "Miss—" He waited.

Goose bumps erupted as he spoke. "Bettina Gilbert." Was there a nip in the wind?

"Miss Gilbert. I feel I owe you some sort of compensation for damaging your art and for the appalling scare."

The way he said her name with that hint of pleasure in his tone sent little tingles down her spine. "No, please, this is the way I take notes." She meant to make quick eye contact, just to be polite, but that one glimpse led to a smile sparkling in his blue eyes. "I–I'm not an artist." She might not have drowned in the lake, but his eyes drew her like a bottomless well. Dark brown, wavy hair refused to maintain the combed-back style of the day in the humidity.

"Notes?" Bettina's admirer brought her attention back to the pad as he thumbed to the pencil drawing of the Grecian columns, domes, and spires on the neoclassical architecture. "That's about as creatively detailed a note as I've ever had the pleasure to view. Wait until you see the art on display at the exposition. I've previewed a few in the Manufacturers and Liberal Arts building. Your 'notes' could rival many of the exhibits."

Coloring, she shook her head. "I appreciate the kind compliment. I've developed the ability to sketch in order to log my studies as a botanist." She shook her head, but a bemused smile touched her lips. "Not an artist." Holding out her hand, Bettina asked, "May I have my sketch pad back, please?"

Rather than returning it, the man had the gall to take a step away from her. "Might

I glance through at a few more?"

"I really wish you wouldn't. Some of my notes are"—she paused, searching for the right word—"personal. I know it looks like random sketches to you, but those pictures are more like a diary of my thoughts."

His smile disappeared. "My apologies. I meant no intrusion." He gave the scuffed-up book back. "Luke Edwards, from Montana. Pleased to make your acquaintance, though under less than favorable circumstances."

"Pleased to meet you, Mr. Edwards." She gave him a polite nod and shook his outstretched hand with her ungloved one. "I'm sure the circumstances were unavoidable." Sparks tingled in her palm at his touch. She glanced up, back at their clasped hands, and up again. Did he feel the energy, too? Retrieving her hand, she blurted out the first thing that popped into her head. "You don't look like a frontier cowboy." Brilliant observation. Could she take that comment back? "What brings you to the fair?"

"Not everyone in Montana is a cowboy, Miss Gilbert." He pointed to the bench, offering to sit with her. "Perhaps you'd let me—" The wind curled its fingers and snatched through his dark hair, triumphing in glee as the gust grabbed the bowler off his head and tossed it a goodly distance into ship center. He pivoted to see where it'd blown off to and then back to Bettina. "Pardon me a moment." For a man in a formal suit and starched collar, he dodged nimbly through the shuffling travelers as the boat anchored.

Bettina tried to hold back a grin. But watching the good-looking Montanan dive and resurface among the throng reminded her of a duck bobbing for fish, albeit unsuccessfully. She shouldn't laugh at his misfortune. But there he was again, bopping up with a hand signal for one more moment. She couldn't help herself. She giggled and pressed her fingers against her mouth. Their eyes connected. For a brief moment, she saw into his heart. Bettina knew something shifted in hers. She lowered her hand to wrap her waist where he'd held her from disaster, and realized she'd lost a glove. Peering around and under the bench, she couldn't find it. She stood to search for her hero. Possibly he'd found it along with his hat? But Mr. Edwards had disappeared in the press of oncoming fairgoers, and she was pushed along the ship's railing toward the gangway by the last rush of passengers.

Chapter 2

Hat in hand, thanks to a quick-acting fellow, Luke searched for a dark purple velvet hat with matching ostrich plumes and a white blouse in the shoulder-to-shoulder sea of humanity moving off the ship. If he didn't find her now, the possibility of getting to know Miss Bettina Gilbert over one of those novel carbonated sodas shrank exponentially on the six-hundred-plus acre grounds. She'd had a navy-blue jacket over her arm to match her skirt. Possibly she'd donned it?

Straining to see ahead, he slid on a small object along the wooden deck. Picking it up, he saw the pitifully dirt-laden lace resembled a rag more than an expensive ladies' accessory. At the very least, should he find Miss Gilbert, he could gallantly return her missing glove. Ladies spent a lot of money on custom gloves. Perhaps she could salvage the pair by dyeing them in tea? Reason enough for pocketing it.

The fact she fascinated him, and wasn't one of the many chosen by his overly helpful self-appointed matchmakers, propelled him to weave in and out of the queue until they closed ranks at the narrow departure point. "Excuse me." He zigged into an opening. "Pardon, if you don't mind." He zagged into another break between bodies until he'd made it down both sets of outer stairs.

At the top of the gangway platform, he caught sight of a purple blur bouncing a few feathers at the entrance to the moving walkway. As it had yet to operate, she skirted the construction with the sway of the crowd—and then, shorter than most, she was gone as if swallowed by a wave. Luke inched forward toward escape from the suffocation of shoulders, umbrellas poking at him, and the heat of so many bodies squashed in too small a space.

On the pier, still navigating the narrow boardwalk, the crowd parted, thinning at the harbor Peristyle as they accessed the fair's sidewalk system. Surely a proper miss would avoid the casino. But her sketches of the architecture? Maybe she wanted a closer look.

Luke threaded through the massive columns acting as the entrance gate, searching up and down the rowed arches. Not a hair. He hightailed it to the highest point of the nearby footbridge spanning the first man-made lagoon, centerpiece for the Court of Honor. With dozens of people passing over, he stopped and scanned as far through the fair walkways as he could for the enchanting Miss Gilbert and her distinctive purple plumes. No luck. She'd vanished into the vast opening-day masses. Evidently God had other plans in mind for his potential wife, if He planned one at all. *Would You mind, Lord, if I—*

"Mr. Edwards, did you manage to acquire the chairs and bring them back?" Mrs. Lydia Fitch asked. The lady's sister lived near downtown Chicago and had sold the

Montana women antique replacements for two broken pieces of exhibit furniture. With the state's contingent working together, though spread throughout several buildings and varying exhibits, he'd agreed to oversee the shipment after the disastrous arrival of a smashed crate. Though why he couldn't meet the ship at the dock escaped him.

In the mass arrivals, he couldn't find a trace of Miss Gilbert, while the woman who'd made a top project out of his matrimonial status could find him in a wink. Though only receding thunder from the morning's rainstorm, Luke distinctly felt the heavens laughing. *You do have a sense of irony, don't You, Lord?*

Luke plastered on a patient smile. "Yes, ma'am, I did. I'll have the chairs off-loaded and brought over once the harbor master clears them." Truth be told, he enjoyed all the fuss the ladies made over him. They'd adopted him as if he were a favored nephew when they learned he wanted to come to Chicago and find a wife. The male to female ratio back home leaned heavily against him, regardless of his business success and ownership of both a silver and a copper mine. But a little less zeal wouldn't be amiss. Somehow he hadn't been able to impress on the Montana ladies that he was perfectly capable of finding his own wife.

"We do need a respite for weary attendees and a comfortable sitting area for those watching after our work in the pavilion salon."

He chanced another scan of the grounds over Mrs. Fitch's head. Well, not if pretty prospects kept disappearing.

She followed his gaze. "Are you looking for someone in particular or admiring the view?"

He stuck his hands in his pockets and gave his attention to Mrs. Fitch.

Without a hitch, she turned back and continued. "Were you taken with my niece? She's had quite the successful debut. The young men are lining up. I'm sure I could put in a good word for you with her parents."

"Uh, I didn't realize—" The very tender girl in question seemed more interested in needlework than discussion. She might be a bit youthful for his twenty-nine years. But then he'd thought the reason for the trip into the city had to do with replacing chairs for the botanical exhibit. He surely should have known better where Mrs. Fitch was concerned. He could be convinced to meet the pretty girl again. Wait. Botanical…botanist… if Miss Gilbert's interests drew her to the Montana flora, then he might find her there. Though he had no idea if she came for the day or if she'd return frequently through the summer. Was she even a Chicagoan? Luke's mouth went dry. What if she came from another country? His search could be enormously more difficult.

Mrs. Fitch tapped his elbow. "Would you like me to formally introduce you?"

"Yes." An international bride might take more logistics but not unreasonable ones. Wait. Introduce him to whom? He gulped. "What?" In the few weeks since they'd arrived to set up their agricultural and mining displays, his several supporters were championing his marital opportunities with such fervor that they'd begun a daily habit of scouting every available lady working anywhere nearby. Some aware and some curiously clueless to the machinations of his determined "aunts." Evidently the mission was to first determine his interests. They might be more successful if they'd simply listen to him. He liked a woman with a strong personality who knew her mind. Any other might not be prepared for his home farther out on the range than in the city. Helena was very modern, but he wouldn't have the miracle of electricity for a while yet, regardless of owning a copper mine. His self-appointed matchmakers had their own ideas of what a perfect counterpart looked like, and so far it hadn't yet agreed with his. Was he searching for the impossible?

"I'll invite Janey to see one of your talks."

The Mining and Mineral building should have been far enough away from the Woman's building to deter such regular romps through his day, but they had him outnumbered. It almost seemed as if they had assigned shifts. "But—"

"You can tell her all about our silver Lady Justice statue. Just leave out the part that she's modeled after that hussy actress from New York, will you? Why they couldn't use one of our lovely Montana ladies as the model. . ." She shook her head then brightened at her decision. "Yes, that'll be a good start."

"Mrs. Fitch—" If it hadn't been frenzied enough, opening day seemed to set off a race to be the lady who found Luke Edwards a wife that was almost as important as whether they'd out-win the men in medals.

"No, no need to thank me. We promised to bring home a bride for you, and that's quite what we'll do."

He stopped searching the distance and turned to look at his doting friend. *Was* there a competition going on? If he didn't find a wife first, he might be trampled by the sweetest, most well-intentioned cupids, with Mrs. Fitch, Mrs. Moore, and Mrs. McAdow in a three-way tie for the lead. Who said women weren't competitive?

"You know, it'd be so lovely to have family around. You might be quite taken with Janey once you get to know the little angel. She's quite talented and would make quite the perfect wife for a success-oriented young man like yourself, if you're looking for a smart match. You are truly looking for an accomplished homemaker, aren't you?" She didn't seem to breathe between sentences. The opposite of her shy niece.

Quiet. Contemplative. That personality might do well with his, but he still needed to feel an attraction. The moment or two he'd waited in the sunroom with Janey could hardly tell the full story. Neither had been aware the meeting was contrived for their benefit. At least he wasn't.

"I've heard of young men sowing their wild oats. I'm sure that's not you. Though you haven't really shown much interest in the few you've met thus far. Janey, now, she's quite a girl, don't you think?"

He couldn't help it, the word seemed to have been planted in his skull. "Quite." He nodded. "Mrs. Fitch, you haven't set up a contest between you all?"

"A contest? Why, what foolishness. No, the only contest I know of is to see who gets more medals, the men or the women." She tapped his arm with her folded fan. "That wouldn't be happening, either, if those lummoxes hadn't crowed they'd bring home the most and only given us ten percent of the budget. And how is that going for the men, Mr. Edwards?"

A tiny purple speck caught his attention in the distance against the backdrop of a white wall like an iris rising from a late winter snow. Luke squinted against the bright sunshine. How had she managed to get that far ahead?

At this point, he had a choice to make. Let go of the first girl who'd captured his interest or indulge his curiosity about the adorably humble botanist-not-artist with olive-green eyes, a shapely figure, and the prettiest smile he'd ever seen. "Mrs. Fitch, would you excuse me?"

"Certainly." Her words trailed behind him. "Shall I see you with the chairs—"

"Yes, this afternoon sometime." He dashed north, in the direction of the state buildings. "Miss Gilbert! Bettina Gilbert!"

Chapter 3

Bettina toured several state manors filled to the brim with displays of every kind touting their local prides and products before entering the exhibits in the Woman's building. The incredible size of this one building could easily take her the day if she gave each pavilion its due. Talented women around the country shared their art, inventions, and business endeavors. Basics like clothing design, gardening, and canning had a spot as well. With daily awards in progress, a jar of peaches already had its pretty blue ribbon proudly placed center front in Georgia's booth. Corn and wheat throughout the cavernous structure held the most ground from states like Illinois, Iowa, and Nebraska.

A few new growth records intrigued her, as did the artistically displayed farming achievements hanging on walls and in specially built presentations kiosks. The grains and grasses, whether woven or glued, portrayed everything from mosaics to decorative rope to corn husks twisted into rose bouquets. An ear of corn from Iowa could feed two people! Every so often, she sketched ideas to reference in her talk during the congresses next month. When had the world birthed innovation any more than now? She hadn't even been inside the largest building Mr. Edwards mentioned. His fine-looking face sprang to mind, and she scanned the area. Silly. She'd met him all of twice in the space of an hour. It would take a week to explore those exhibits she'd planned to see, let alone all those not on her list. A man was not on her list. Even one as extraordinarily heroic and handsome as Mr. Luke Edwards.

Bettina straightened her shoulders and continued through the building's magnificent offerings. She rounded another corner and took in the beautifully designed scientific botanical display the *Chicago Tribune* publicized as being created with precise classifications by the Montana women and a "not-to-miss" exhibit. Did he work this huge stall? A building inside a building, more accurately. Bettina slowed her pace and searched the faces around the area as well as inside the display salon.

Montana's new botanical discoveries proved fascinating. Ten frames hung on an immense carved and polished wood pillar; books filled with seeds and pressed flora lounged on stands, and some on a highly polished table. Braided grain stalks and weavings covered the pavilion walls. The assortment of pinecones and the decorative arrangement showed the skill of florists as well as interior designers. Another ten frames of beautifully preserved wildflower bouquets, with a card noting Emil Starz as the preparer, fashioned an impressive visual of the variety and scope found in the mountainous region. She wanted to see this wild country in person. Blue eyes and dark hair flashed into her thoughts yet again. If only he knew how often in the last few hours she'd been disappointed not to find him in the crowd. Statistically speaking, an irrational hope. Though didn't the statistics rise around his home state exhibits? How had a chance meeting taken over her mental processes? She blinked rapidly. Her parents would never approve.

Bettina touched the edge of a book to admire the seed-to-flowering phases, pressed and pinned in order of each stage as recorded by a Mrs. Jennie Moore. Every entry in perfect systematic order from kingdom to species, just as the article foretold. An occasional watercolor recorded a shrub or a leaf on a page representing a plant too large to put in the book. Unlike much of the vegetation in Illinois and the surrounding states, she'd not encountered several of the Rocky Mountain species before. The small *Lewisia rediviva*, known informally as the bitterroot flower, was not only beautiful but edible? She filed that tidbit into her journal with a quick line drawing and notation. How wonderful to walk among the fresh discoveries of the frontier. Probably the closest she'd get, knowing Mama's feelings on how far Chicago was from Cleveland already.

"You would think he was smitten!" one well-dressed woman said to a small nearby group. They all wore matching black skirts and ornately embroidered white blouses with ruffled high-neck collars. A banner, in the colors of the new state flag, draped shoulder to hip embroidered in yellow-gold thread with the state name. The Montana women aimed to impress and were doing a good job of it, too, in their opening-day costumes.

Bettina perused the woven wall hangings, inhaling the earthy scent of grain and the various grasses. The decorative presentation kept her mind wrestling with the longing to see it all in its natural habitat—until snippets of the nearby chat showered her with accidental gossip.

"Lydia, he hasn't shown a bit of interest in any particular girl yet. None of us has uncovered the most likely candidate. Your Janey still has as much chance of landing him as any other girl at this point."

"I do believe I heard him calling out to a Miss Gert or Bert. . .possibly Stuart." The woman, Lydia, apparently, tapped a gloved finger against her cheek. "I'm sure I heard the name Serena. What do you suppose running after someone like that could mean otherwise? He's smitten, I tell you." She waggled that gloved finger at her friends. "Ladies, your duty to our poor, single Mr. Edwards is to find this Serena Stuart. His happiness may depend on it."

Oh dear, that poor Mr. Edwards would find himself married, whether he liked it or not, soon enough if these ladies had their way. He was both charming and heroic. Bettina touched her hand to her waist where he'd held her from falling. Whoever he chose would be a fortunate girl.

Lydia nodded. "Yes, that's the name. I'm sure of it. Though it makes me heartbroken that Janey may get passed over by such an eligible bachelor. She's quite a catch, you know, for any of our Helena millionaires. He'd be a lucky man to have her."

"They'd make a lovely couple," another woman agreed.

Bettina sneaked a quick glance at Lydia. She seemed genuinely disappointed her niece hadn't yet impressed this revered saint of a man. Mr. Edwards appeared to have earned admiration from those who knew him well—and one who didn't, if she admitted the truth.

Several other ladies, evidently friends, bobbed their heads in agreement while tsk-tsking Mr. Edwards's lack of taste. One said, "We'll simply have to help him see her virtues so he doesn't dismiss her lightly. But our promise is to help Mr. Edwards come home with a bride by the end of summer. I would truly hate to fail such a wonderful man after we all agreed to help. If I were only twenty years younger."

They all giggled with her.

"Jennie, you're right," Lydia responded with a sorrowful sigh. "We must help him be sure of his choice. Don't you think I should still invite my niece to come down? He couldn't have had much time to meet her. I sent ahead and made sure my sister knew of the prospect. I do so want family near, if there's a chance."

The smile slipped out. The ladies seemed so invested in their matchmaking project even if one or two had ulterior motives. She'd heard men outnumbered women in that fledgling state. If her parents wanted her safely married to a bright, successful man, she could always use that suggestion. Though she'd have a hard time keeping a straight face if she declared she was moving to Montana to have her pick of husbands. They knew she'd never dare move so far away, not after all they'd given her. Loyalty was such a small thing to give back to those who loved her wholeheartedly without expectation of repayment.

Bettina put her hands behind her then remembered the missing glove. Her mother was a stickler for observing social custom. Tucking her bare hand into the pocket of her walking skirt, she focused full attention to the lines of the grain weaving. She shouldn't be listening to what didn't concern her. But her thoughts squiggled back like doodles on her sketch pad. So the man from Montana was already sweet on a gal. A little pang of disappointment hit her. She'd have liked to—oh, what did it matter? If not that girl, his cherubic matchmakers had another in mind already. Did he have days or weeks until ignorance changed to wedded bliss? She had no doubt these Montana ladies meant to take home as many winning medals as possible *and* a bride for Mr. Luke Edwards.

How romantic to find a sweetheart at the Columbian Exhibition. Wouldn't that make a grand story for future generations? The world to choose from, and two lovers find the one in all the earth meant for—well, it wouldn't be her story. Not yet, anyway. Although, at the rate these ladies wanted to interfere, it may not be his choice, either, though he might think it was. She choked back a giggle, pretending a light cough, as several other visitors filled in around her.

"Lydia, we've been remiss." One of the ladies pointed to the gathering fair attendees perusing their pavilion. "We have visitors."

"Hello." One of the women approached Bettina. "My name is Jennie Moore." She offered a handshake. "This is Mrs. Lydia Fitch and Mrs. J. E. Light. This exhibit has been completely created and designed by the women of Montana." The loving pride of both their handiwork and home state glowed all over them.

"Goodness." Bettina indicated the page she'd read about the bitterroot flower. "You're the one who cataloged all these specimens so well."

Mrs. Moore nodded, a little flushed with pleasure at the compliment. "That one, the bitterroot, is a favorite of my friend Mrs. Mary Long Alderson of Bozeman. She's nominating it for our state floral emblem, though it may take a while to happen."

"It would be a worthy choice. I believe I've noticed each of your names on the cards here and there." *And I may have overheard your conversation.* "What an honor to meet all of you ladies." She shook hands around the small circle. "I'm Bettina Gilbert."

"What questions do you have about our great state of Montana or the vegetation there?"

"As a botanist, I'm impressed with the care given to the science, including the sequence. But the beauty of your display is something to behold." She waved toward the enormous rows of braided grain stalks climbing the pillars holding up the gazebo-style cross-slat roofing.

Mrs. Moore beamed. "We've been working on this since they announced the White City would be built. Dozens of us collected specimens from all over the state. One of our ladies even rode around the range toting her children in a wagon searching for seeds and specimens not yet discovered. She went farm to farm and town to town where the trains couldn't go."

"That's very much what I want to do—discover!" Bettina's passion for the topic flared. "I'm hoping to work for the new head of Oberlin's botany department. I'd like to integrate what I've learned in college to applied use—determine how to really help people with my abilities." Images from her childhood, of dirty street water tainted by sewage and very little food, clamored in her head with the memory of not being allowed to kiss the cheek of the woman who birthed her. To say good-bye as her birth mother died in filthy rags, on a dirty mattress, in a room that stank of piled-up waste. Then she was gone from the pneumonia that chased typhoid all too commonly, the good doctor said. In all that grief and pain, Bettina remembered the intense hunger that cramped her belly. A feeling she hadn't ever forgotten—along with the odors of garbage, sour breath, and death.

"Clara should take her under her wing." Mrs. Fitch suggested.

"Lydia has worked tirelessly to produce seven hundred specimens here while our friend Clara McAdow—oh, there she is now." Jennie Moore waved at her friend across the wide aisle. "Yoo-hoo, Clara, come meet this lovely gal." She continued extolling Mrs. McAdow's contributions. "Clara has worked on another display in the Horticulture building, but she rubs elbows with the likes of Reverend F. D. Kelsey. I believe he's the one at Oberlin?" She waited for Bettina's agreement.

They knew him? Maybe Montana wasn't the far frontier. "Yes." Bettina nodded. "I've read his work but not yet had the pleasure to meet such an esteemed scientist. It's his department I've applied to. But the referral letter from my professor didn't arrive until just this week. I brought it with me hoping for the chance to pass it to him in person."

"We'll get you introduced properly, then, shall we?"

Mrs. Fitch enthusiastically added, "Who knows where that association may lead? I imagine assistants for his department are chosen from those he knows, don't you?"

Besides scientific interests, it seemed the Montana ladies had a talent for being well connected in society regardless of their distant homes. The world seemed a little smaller all of a sudden. *Thank You, Lord!* But what could she offer these mavens in return?

Clara joined the growing circle as the passersby ebbed. The women buzzed at her like bees dancing with the hive queen and filling in what she'd missed.

Clara shook hands with Bettina. "You'll enjoy Reverend Kelsey. He has such a quick mind for Latin, being well versed in the language through his theological education. His mind snaps through the genus and species as if he's conversing with friends at a dinner party. But then, everyone is his friend." She turned to the group as a whole. "We're in the running for another medal for our scientific botanical display! I heard the judges debating over at the Iowa booth."

"That would make seven!" Mrs. Fitch clapped her hands. "Now what will those men say when we mount those awards for all to see!"

"I don't know that we can beat the Iowa display though." Jennie leaned against the table, hands bracing beside her hips for balance. "Did you see how many ways they managed to decorate with corn? Really, right down to rosettes out of husks. Colorado isn't going to do well, not with those heavy frames sagging off their pillar."

"Of all the displays that shouldn't win, I think it's that man from Ireland claiming no good oatmeal can be made in America. Can you imagine the gall?" Mrs. Fitch plunked her fists at her ample waist and shook her head.

"Our prairie farmers will just have to grow heavier oats." Jennie Moore's eyes twinkled as she tossed her head with a little snap, punctuating her words. "But first we women need to take home more awards than our men. They're edging up on us with the mining and minerals."

"You don't think they're serious, do you?" Bettina tilted her head a tad and scrunched her nose. "A mining display is so different from a scientific botanical display."

"If those coffee-slurping, backslapping men think they can breeze in here and insult our efforts, then why not beat them and show those cowboys what we can do?" Mrs. McAdow pointed her finger all around the group, but her grin betrayed her. "You all heard the challenge when they laughed at us back home. Then giving us ten percent of the budget and keeping the rest. Do we put up with that, or do we stand up for all womankind?"

In the next thirty minutes, well over a dozen Montana women hobnobbed about their plant studies, specimens, and chances for exposition medals. Bettina had a sense of belonging in the camaraderie, though the women had varying levels of involvement. For most it was about advancing Montana's natural resources and establishing the state's emergence into the national marketplace. Their common goals, scientific language, understanding of the world, and undeniably passionate interest in the botanical life God created burst from Bettina like the sun cresting the horizon. Even the merriment of a good-natured race against the men excited her.

Bettina mentally counted around the circle, wanting to pinch herself. A dozen women talking her language, and not about whose blooms were the prettiest, as in her mother's gardening club. The beauty of flowers notwithstanding, her fascination lay in the elegance of God's infinite design and how to best steward it to help her fellow man. "I want to believe it's possible to find a solution to the poverty and hunger in our nation. What if we could cultivate at higher yields or find new varieties of plant nourishment like your *Lewisia rediviva*?"

For a girl who didn't socialize much outside of her studies the last few years, Bettina couldn't stop from asking more questions if she tried. "Mrs. Moore, I noticed the bitterroot is designated as edible, and the Indians believe it has some sort of medicinal value. Can we develop that into sustainable crops? Are there other Montana plants that grow naturally that might be helpful this way or grow in other locales? Are there great expanses of land rich enough for farming?"

"You do have an inquisitive mind and a good heart. Bettina, is it?"

"Yes, Mrs. Moore," she nodded. "I hope to find answers to those questions. Answers that will make a difference in the lives around us. What if these new discoveries eradicated typhoid?" Still too common and rampant in Chicago even fourteen years after— she shivered away the image of a woman dying and brushed away the memory of tears on a cheek. "May I reference your work in my upcoming talk?"

"You may." Mrs. Moore leaned in and grasped Bettina's hand. "And call me Jennie, please. Together"—she motioned to the group—"we'll see what we can do to help you. But you simply must consider coming to Montana."

Was that a wink at the other ladies?

"It'll be a great pleasure to get to know you while we're here." Jennie looked around the circle of women. "Wouldn't that be something you'd all like to do as well?" At their wholehearted agreement, she added, "It's much better to have many different perspectives than to rely on only one acquaintance."

Mrs. Fitch nodded. "Call me Lydia. It's settled, then. Come spend time with us here at our exhibit. We could use a knowledgeable volunteer."

Bettina couldn't afford not to accept. These maven matchmakers had a penchant for connecting people. And she needed connections in her field to get one of the few positions at Oberlin or another university that would gain her access to grants and permissions for studies. *That's all they meant, right?*

"Miss Gilbert?" Luke Edwards rolled in a cart with several carved wooden chairs on it—and one no longer truant black bowler on his head.

Jennie's rounded eyes couldn't look more surprised than Bettina's—or Lydia's. The rest of the gathered group tossed meaningful glances like popcorn.

"Gilbert," Lydia burst out. "Yes, I suppose that's what I heard earlier."

Definitely not the kind of connection Bettina wanted the Montana women to focus on for her. O-h-h. Is that what Jennie's invitation to Montana was about? Bettina wanted a career, not romantic associations. What if these ladies all thought her purpose was husband hunting? No, no, no. Better to extricate herself as quickly as possible and keep her prospects professional. "Mr. Edwards, good to see you found your errant hat. Nice to see you again."

"O-o-h," said the three cupids collectively, looking one to another.

"I did. A gentleman caught it for me near the stairwell. I also found your, er. . ." He noticed the odd looks from his doting supporters. He cleared his throat and pulled something from his vest pocket nearest his heart. ". . .glove." Without taking his eyes off the trio, as if keeping them in check, he handed over the heavily stained accessory. "Although, I think my hat fared better."

"O-o-h," they sang in whispered unison while gaping at the heavily stomped, no longer white, lace glove. The ladies who hadn't been present for the earlier conversation in the pavilion expressed confusion.

"I'm sorry for the condition," he added, "further aggravated by my own shoe, I'm sure."

Bettina took the soiled glove and smiled through her discomfort at being the center of attention. She darted a glance at the ladies she'd been so at home with moments before.

"I do hope it can be salvaged."

A sage nod accompanied by a long look between Lydia and Jennie drew Mrs. Light's attention to the situation as she returned to the group. Lydia made a tiny head tip toward Luke Edwards and then Bettina. Mrs. Light responded with a slow nod in silent understanding, as did the rest of the circle.

Was everyone in on the matrimonial prospects of Mr. Luke Edwards? And they thought she might be one? The vaulted ceiling that seemed a mile above earlier suddenly closed in on Bettina. "I'm sure it'll be fine. Though I've felt quite awkward with only one since." She held up both hands and shrugged. "What can a girl do when she's away from home? I best find another pair. Well, again, thank you." She stepped backward.

Luke stepped forward, waltzing into her retreat as he cupped her elbow. "I tried to catch you after the steamboat, but you'd gotten too far ahead of me."

If Luke Edwards was sweet on someone he chased from the steamboat, that meant— No! A hot flush stole up her throat.

Then he offered another, more tangible surprise. An elongated, elegant, but very thin box tied with a purple satin ribbon. "I picked these up at the Spanish fashion counter to ease your distress. I used yours to match the size. I hope they'll fit."

He replaced her gloves? Such a costly gesture, and an unnecessary one. "I couldn't, Mr. Edwards, but thank you."

"Oh, what a shame. I suppose that means you don't accept my apology." He looked crestfallen.

The circle of women gaped, first at the pretty box and then at Luke Edwards and then halting on Bettina, all in sync as if a string passed before a row of kittens. Their eyes fastened on her, watching, waiting. Would they pounce to protect their favored son?

"Of course." She rushed to soothe the group as well as the man. "Of course I accept your, uh, apology. I simply meant your gift is too—"

"Small?"

Their personal audience gasped, audibly and again in unison.

Panic fluttered in Bettina's stomach. She'd never experienced a gift so thoughtful— and romantic—at the same time a fear so palpable that she'd make a misstep.

He untied the ribbon and opened the box, revealing delicate Spanish lace fit for a much more elegant lady than she could ever hope to be. "I'll search for a different pair until you are satisfied if these aren't to your liking."

"No, please." She touched the beautiful paper, almost afraid to lift the precious gift. "They're truly lovely."

"Not as lovely as the woman whose art I ruined and glove I stained under my shoe. Will you accept?" He gave her a questioning smile. "I do hope to be in your good graces here forward."

"I, uh, yes." Her lips parted as she gazed into his shining eyes and took the box. "Thank you." She backed away. "Ladies, it's been a delight. I hope to see you again."

"Wait!"

"Yes, Mr. Edwards?"

He tugged at his collar. He raised his eyebrows expectantly at his champions. "Ladies, could you excuse us, please?" If there was a little heavier emphasis on *please*, Bettina couldn't fault him.

"Of course, dear." Lydia patted his arm. "We'll just, uh. . ." She looked around. "We've other business to discuss." They scattered around the pavilion salon, talking in twos and threes.

"Miss Gilbert, would you do me the honor of allowing me to buy you one of those refreshing sodas?"

"A soda?"

She caught an interested peep or two darting over a shoulder here and there. Then a not-so-quiet whisper: "Could she be the one?"

"Do you think?"

"He hasn't shown such passionate interest. . ."

"Shush, they'll hear us."

Bettina's face burned. If she turned his invitation down, would she insult him and ruin her budding opportunity with the Montana women?

"No expectation except that I'd like to enjoy your company for a few minutes." He closed the distance between them, keeping his smiling eyes on hers. "I'd be honored if you'd accept." He thumbed back over his shoulder. "And I think they're rooting for me."

What could she say? "I—" If he worked with these women, he'd know soon enough they'd invited her to volunteer this summer and that she'd accepted. Might as well be on good terms with Luke Edwards, too. Good terms with Luke Edwards could easily become a problem if the uneven patter of her heart was a sign. Or the weakness in her knees that grew as he came closer. Or the fact that she loved the timbre of his voice.

"Unless, of course, another day would be more convenient. I wouldn't want to impose on any plans you might have already."

No one pretended to be talking anymore. Tiny nods of encouragement and a flutter of fingers from Lydia Fitch told her to go with him.

She inclined her head. "I am a bit thirsty"—she saw Jennie's nod telling her to accept—"for a soda."

A small sigh from a dozen women, let out at the same time, resembled the sound of rustling leaves through the rafters.

Chapter 4

Have you heard of candied popcorn?" Luke pointed at the busy booth on the thoroughfare. An ornate sign advertised A CRACKER JACK, SWEET CONFECTION OF POPCORN WITH PEANUTS AND MOLASSES INVENTED BY FREDERICK WILLIAM RUECKHEIM AND BROTHER. The aroma of buttery popcorn and rich molasses wafted over to them, floating in the warm late-spring air. His mouth watered at the scent.

Miss Gilbert indulged his sudden curiosity. "Cracker Jack. Yes, it's delicious. Would you like to taste it?" Slipping her hand through his elbow, she tugged him along as she shared what she knew. "There's a little shop that started selling earlier this year near where I live. It's fun to get some and share it during readings, picnics, and parties."

They parked themselves at the back of the long line. "That good?"

"Sweet chewy popcorn and peanuts in a candy sauce? Delectable." She craned to see the front of the line. "I wish it wasn't so sticky, but I can't resist."

"Then I'm sure I won't be able to, either." He didn't just mean the Cracker Jack stand as he looked at her.

When Miss Gilbert glanced up, her green eyes caught the light. All he could do was stare.

Then she asked him to put words together coherently. "Why don't you tell me a little about yourself? Until today, the only thing I knew about Montana is that it became a state four years ago. That's not very long to become civilized. I'm so curious." She gave him a half smile. "Well, and I now know much more about the flora from visiting your exhibit."

"You realize there's more than one Montana exhibit? We're a diverse population for as few of us as there are."

"I haven't been as far around the fair as I'd have liked today." She turned her head and lifted a shoulder slightly. "The sheer size of it is daunting. I've been able to take in several agricultural and botanical displays. But I didn't look for any particular state presentations, other than a quick walk through a few buildings."

"Why did you come, if not to experience the world at your fingertips?"

"I came to connect with botanists more than anything." She looked to see how the line was moving. "What other exhibits should I see when I come back?"

She planned to come back! What would she enjoy? "There's the Montana building, full of crafts and skilled workmanship. You'll learn our state has talents and resources that rival any in the known world. We're much more civilized than you think." He gestured at his attire. "Why, we even wear up-to-date fashions."

She giggled. "That sounds like an interesting exhibit. What else?"

The mining exhibits would likely fascinate the scientist in Miss Gilbert, but Luke was after the opportunity to properly court her, if she wasn't already spoken for. If she believed Montana offered civility and culture, there'd be one less hurdle to leap should she consider him husband material. "Then this evening one of our ladies will sing at the opening of the music hall." He decided to take a chance. "Do you like music?"

"Yes." She moved forward with him in the line. "But we're supposed to be talking about you."

"I like music."

She laughed and his heart pounded a little harder. A wife with a gentle but quick laugh. Yes, that would be a good quality. Humor could help weather hard times.

"What kind of music do you like?"

"All kinds."

"Ah, too general, I'm afraid. Please be more specific."

More specific? That answer would satisfy most women. Could that mean true interest? He thought for a moment. "I suppose I enjoy marches that inspire and invigorate, like John Philip Sousa, and songs with words."

She looked a little surprised. "Songs with words?"

"Songs I can sing when I'm working or want to take my mind off something difficult."

"Oh, that's interesting." She considered his answer. "Then you like to sing as well. See? I learned something about you. Music is cultivated, so therefore"—she paused and gave him a mischievous look down her nose—"I declare thou must be civilized."

Her playful expression made him smile. "We Montanans are relatively sophisticated, Miss Gilbert. We're even a cultured people. I'd be happy to prove it if I may escort you to the concert tonight?"

She grinned but shook her head. "I do appreciate your thoughtful invitation. But I've promised to return home before dark. My parents are worried enough that I'm off alone."

She's from Chicago. "How did you manage to pull off such a feat, then?"

"I explained the need to make connections with people I admire in my field. It's not appropriate to take parents along for potential business contacts."

"Wise on both counts." They finally reached the stand, and she waited while he ordered. Hands full of a box of fresh caramel corn with peanuts sprinkled through it, Luke guided Bettina to the soda shop and managed to order sandwiches and sparkling refreshments in half the time it took to obtain the sweets. They found a shady spot next to a tree surrounded by droves of fairgoers picnicking or resting on the lawn and a duck quacking on the pond.

"All right, your turn. What interested you in botany?" He separated a chunk of sticky stuff from the rest. He leaned back against the tree and chewed a bite as he listened, amused at the delicate way she handled the candied corn. Neither had chosen the sandwiches first.

"When my oldest brother began studying medicine, my father bought a microscope. I thought it was the most fascinating toy ever. I put everything I could find under it. Plant life fast became my favorite." She picked a blade of grass. "Did you know you can see leaves breathe under a microscope? Actually, they're undergoing photosynthesis and creating oxygen so we can breathe. But the way light becomes food in, say, a blade of grass, is amazing." She spun it between her thumb and forefinger. "Don't you think?"

He thought he understood. "Where I see a blade of grass, you see a whole different world. Is that it?"

"Yes." Miss Gilbert tilted her head. "But it's more. I see ideas, solutions to many of the problems our world faces, like starvation and disease. Can you imagine what it would be like to discover a way to optimize crops for higher production? How many more people could we feed if crops produced even ten percent more? Lack of nutrition is the highest cause of illness and mortality. What if a new plant enzyme cured a childhood disease? Who's going to cure tuberculosis?"

"You see all that in a plant?" He frowned. "What do you see when you look at an animal, then? Or a human being?"

She peeked up from under the short brim of her pretty purple hat. "Complex. Human nature is part of that package."

He chuckled. The woman before him could be described as that and then some. "How does one study the complexities of human nature?"

She dipped her chin and brushed her fingers across the grass.

He couldn't see her face except for the gentle slope of her cheek and the length of her graceful neck. His fingers itched to brush her soft skin the way she touched the lawn.

"I don't know. That's why I chose plants." She raised her face to him. "I've never been very comfortable with people. At school"—she gestured back toward the Woman's building—"and with people who enjoy the science of botany, I know how to communicate. But I'm less of a social person than most. I don't understand how to—"

What was it about this woman that made him want to encourage her? "You're doing fine with me." *Very fine, as a matter of fact.* He doubted the conversation would be as stimulating with her if all she wanted to discuss were dresses, shopping, and gossip. "I've never thought of a blade of grass or a leaf breathing or making oxygen so I could breathe. You look at creation differently than anyone I've ever met before."

Miss Gilbert grimaced. "I know. Again, I don't know how to make small talk, no matter how hard I try. Hence, my mother fears I'll never marry." She shrugged.

"No beau, then?"

"No."

Not spoken for. If he could leap for joy at the news, he would. He checked his excitement so as not to push her away. He might be on a time schedule with only these few months, but she didn't need to know it. "I take it that's not on your favorite topics list, either?"

"Marriage isn't a bad topic. I just don't know of many men who want a woman who wants to work after the wedding." She repositioned her legs, curling them on the other side. "My father says most men aren't enthused about a woman driving the cart at full speed. But I'm not ready to hand over the reins and darn socks. I like the challenge of accomplishment."

The curve of her hip drew his fascination as she moved into a more comfortable position. He needed a wife and quick! But he didn't want only that. The miners who'd met and married their mail-order brides in one day didn't always have the happiest homes. He'd watched too many disastrous examples, even abandonment, because they couldn't work things out. He knew a few miners with beautiful wives at home who worked and lived at their stakes, avoiding married life after spending so much money to bring a wife to Montana. He didn't fear marriage. But he sure feared being in the wrong marriage. Slow it down and get the right wife, his father had said. Get to know her first. Wasn't that what he was trying to do?

He swallowed and put his mind back on her words. "So you're not ruling out marriage, if the right fellow came along?"

"No. I look forward to finding the right fellow, as you say. I don't think he's going to be all that easy to find. They all seem to want wives who dress pretty and pop out lots of pretty babies." She clasped a hand over her mouth. Her eyes widened and her face flared a peachy pink.

Luke reached out and tugged her fingers away, brushing her lips with his thumb. "Please, don't be embarrassed with me. Not all men want that kind of wife. Makes for dull evenings if there's nothing to talk about, don't you agree?" He held her fingers loosely entwined between them in the grass. "People need to find common ground and know they have interests to share before picking a mate." Would she pull away?

She didn't immediately. She offered a smile and slow nod, though she lowered her eyes again as her face cooled. "Ah, but I think you have your own matchmaking dynasty back there." Dusty brown lashes hid her thoughts.

"I'm sorry if they embarrassed you. They mean well. I've told them this is something a man has to do himself. I don't think they believe me though." He gave her a wry grin. "Some of us are looking for a smart wife who makes a man think and can hold her own. Montana is a place that needs men and women who want to develop her resources. There's opportunity to create the future there for goal-minded people." Releasing her hand, he leaned in and touched her chin, willing her to lift her gaze to his. When she did, he added, "Some of us are intrigued by women who have goals and dreams."

Her green eyes illuminated. "Oh."

"But hopefully she won't rule out children," Luke half teased.

Her face relaxed into a bright smile. "A woman like that might be convinced." She rose to her knees. "I really need to be going. We're staying in a town house in the city this summer. The omnibus schedule should get me home before dark, if I hurry."

"I'll see you to the stop." He stood, offering a hand to help her rise. As she brushed grass from her skirt, he picked up the residue of their late lunch. He deposited the empty box and cups in the receptacle as an exotically dressed runner with a wicker seat on wheels attached to long handles approached. "It's a long walk. Would you mind a rickshaw to the gate?"

"Delighted."

He signaled the driver. "Front gate, nearest the downtown omnibus stop, please."

She placed her hand in his and stepped into the wicker seat basket. "I've traveled by steamship in and rickshaw out. Today's been an adventure the whole way through."

He climbed in beside Miss Gilbert.

The runner raised the long wooden bars to his hips and headed toward the main gate, city side. A short ride later he collected a few coins from Luke and set off after another fare.

"When will you return?" Luke walked with her to the omnibus stand.

"I haven't a set schedule, but I did agree to volunteer at the Montana pavilion with your friends. I suppose I should stop in tomorrow morning to set a schedule?"

"I'll let the ladies know to expect you." He'd find a reason to visit, often. Deep down, he knew the wife he searched for, prayed for, hoped for—Miss Bettina Gilbert—needed time to come to the same conclusion.

The approaching horses clopped to a stop, drawing the long carriage to a halt. Ten to twelve passengers filed down the three wooden steps. Very few looked to be leaving on this omnibus. With concerts at several points and hours left for the midway to run yet, the transportation system would be heavily taxed a few hours from now.

"What do you actually do at the exhibit, besides buy candied corn and entertain tourists?" she asked with a light tone.

"I don't work at that exhibit, Miss Gilbert." He took her hand to assist with boarding the rear steps into the long carriage. "My purpose here is to promote the mineral, ore, and mining industry of Montana to the world."

She stared at him. "You're a miner?"

"Yes and no. I'm a mine owner looking for opportunities to grow and attract business from the resources in my state. And I admit that I hope to find a wife who would enjoy doing those things with me." He squeezed her fingers. "I'll be looking forward to seeing you again."

She snatched back her hand. "It was nice meeting you, Mr. Edwards. Thank you for a lovely afternoon. I don't think we have those commonalities you're looking for."

Had he offended her by being honest? "Miss Gilbert?"

She disappeared into the omnibus.

What just happened? He stared after the departing vehicle taking away the one woman he wanted.

Chapter 5

The month of May had passed into a lovely June. The flowers and trees burst colorful beauty all over the carefully planned grounds. Bettina volunteered two to three days a week, though she remained cautious around Luke Edwards. Getting involved with someone so far from her ideology would be a disaster. Her personal feelings about mining notwithstanding, how could she compromise? After all, his goals cost lives while hers saved them. But, oh my. My, my, my how she liked his magnanimous personality. His low laugh that sent ripples through her belly. Liked the confidence in his walk and the breadth of his shoulders.

With the Mining and Mineral building at a distance, it hadn't been too hard to keep space between her and Luke as well. But she couldn't seem to take her eyes off him when he arrived with supplies or to assist one of the other ladies. Unfortunately, Lydia or Jennie managed to notice, or were they intentionally watching her reactions?

Scholars and the audience could readily rip apart her farming theory during her slot at the scientific congress tomorrow if she didn't have the new research incorporated. Research that hadn't been released during her last year at college. Afterward, Clara McAdow promised the introduction to Reverend Doctor Kelsey. Would he feel she'd earn her place at Oberlin? Without the repeated practices her friends encouraged, it wouldn't be possible at all.

"But can you imagine what this new knowledge means, Lydia?" Bettina leaned across the table in the center salon of the Montana pavilion, grateful for this opportunity. What a blessing to rehearse and debate the ideas in her demonstration with Lydia and Jennie acting as devil's advocates. "Since the agriculturists here in Illinois discovered crop maturity advances from south to north as much as twelve miles per day, farming strategy could revolutionize how we produce food on a grander scale. Look at the hundreds of miles from south to north in Montana alone."

Nodding, Jennie measured the distances. "What you're saying is we could gain approximately twenty-six more growing days across the country with this strategic crop planning and at least add a good portion of those growing days in Montana."

"Yes!" Bettina clapped.

Lydia waved a hand in the air. "Bettina, we have to take climate into account. Much of that south to north line is along mountainous terrain. If the chemistry isn't right. . ." She let the comment hang in the air like a hawk on a current. Sooner or later that hawk would dive for a mouse.

Bettina gave her a curious look. "The chemistry?"

Jennie and Lydia exchanged glances.

"It's like good relationships. If you sow on fertile ground and pull the weeds of misunderstanding regularly, then your tender crop has a chance," Jennie said.

Bettina's brow crinkled. Were they talking about farming and harvests? "I'm sure you're right." She swept a hand from bottom to top over the map in the almanac. "By teaching farmers to plant crops with longer growth cycles farther south and plants with shorter growth cycles to the north. . ."

Out of the corner of her eye, she noticed Lydia and Jennie were sending silent hand signals. But as soon as she looked up, the ladies suddenly seemed to be smoothing a hairdo or skirt.

"Hmm? What were you saying, dear?" Lydia smiled. "Do go on."

Bettina finished her tactical theory, though another was forming having nothing to do with wheat or corn or feeding the masses. ". . .those extra days, amount to be determined by the clime and. . .chemistry, can mean excess to send to cities, raising farmer income while filling higher populace needs." She stood up fast as the two ladies snapped their eyes on the map with guilty looks.

"I see. But you realize the last day of frost in Montana is not until quite late in May. Quite different than Illinois." Lydia pointed at the northern area of the state.

Were they beleaguering the climate point for a reason? Studying their uncharacteristically bland expressions, Bettina was sure the two had a secretive conversation going on they didn't want her to know about. But about what?

"And this area might be up to a week earlier some years but not others depending on weather cycles. I think you're better suited to choosing crops for your comparison study by climes. Crops would mature prior to the early known frost we can often experience. The length of growing days can be fickle, as can the heart."

Lydia nodded. "There's a natural harmony that has much to do with matching seed to soil type, water, humidity, sun, wind, pollination, and so many other factors. Some of the chemistry you might be able to control. And then there's the synergy, the spark of creativity you cannot control, like love. That part of life is God's design."

"I have the distinct feeling that either you two are wanting this conversation to go in another direction or I've gone over the possible objections so many times I'm boring you."

"I certainly wouldn't have intruded," Lydia said with a tongue-in-cheek tone. "Would you, Jennie?"

"No, I'd never." Jennie's eyes twinkled.

"But now that you've asked." The older woman's expression turned motherly, and compassion enveloped her every word.

"Yes, now that you've asked." Jennie nodded to Lydia. "Go ahead, you're the one he came to for advice."

"We're concerned there's been a misunderstanding." Lydia watched Bettina closely as she asked, "What is it that keeps you avoiding our dear Luke?"

Mr. Edwards had talked to Lydia? Heat flushed up from Bettina's high collar.

"Did he insult you?" Lydia locked a hand onto a hip like a mother ready to set straight a son. "If an apology is in order, then, by all means, give him the opportunity. After all, he's respected for his integrity."

"It's not about an apology. He hasn't done anything untoward." Bettina leaned against the pavilion pillar, leaving the large book open on the table. The sturdy support at her back helped with the two-against-one situation. "Mr. Edwards is, well, he is. . ." She wove her fingers together and focused on her palms. "Our beliefs in progress and the future are too different. We're too different." She let out her breath slowly at their disbelieving expressions. For ladies who loved to talk, their silence spoke in thunderous volumes. Her mother wouldn't let her get away with such a vague statement, either. "You both know what I came here for, and it wasn't to find a man."

Jennie crossed her arms. "There's nothing saying you can't find both."

"It's not that he isn't a very attractive man, Jennie, he is. He's going to make some woman a very good husband. He's wildly handsome, confident, caring, kind—"

"Just not for you, even though you find him so appealing?"

Appealing. Apt description. "No, not for me. I don't want to be sidetracked from the dreams in my heart." She reached out a hand to her new friend. "You understand, don't you?" she asked as Jennie clasped both hands over Bettina's. "A mine owner. No, I can't fathom the destruction. And how he could send other men into danger." The comforting grasp encouraged her. "If there isn't a common goal, then it's too dangerous to step into the fire."

"Some pine trees need fire to propagate." Lydia smiled at Bettina's consternation. "Oh my dear, when you grow older you begin to realize that each person can have their own goal. You don't have to chase the same dream to help the other reach theirs. Marriage is about helping your mate, not doing it for them."

"I hadn't thought of it that way." Bettina rubbed her teeth across her bottom lip. "But if those goals are complete opposites, aren't the two destined to clash constantly?"

"You might think a little more on it." Jennie squeezed Bettina's hand. "I don't believe you've given him a fair chance. Do you?" She slid an arm around Bettina's shoulder in a gentle hug. "He's asked to speak with you, and yet you turn him away. Learning more about what our Mr. Edwards does might help you see him in a different light. A hasty decision is the cause for many a mistake."

"We do believe you've been a tad hasty. But then again, if it's not possible in your mind, I'm sure my niece wouldn't mind getting to know our Luke." Lydia looked at Jennie. "Isn't that right?"

"Yes, yes. I'm sure there's potential with Janey." Jennie wagged her head as if imparting solemn news. "You mustn't feel we're pushing the most eligible bachelor in Helena on you."

Lydia wobbled her head, too. "No, no, you mustn't. Although it occurs to me you've assumed the outcome without proper research. One must be sure of their facts."

Even with the older women's wisdom rolling through her mind, Bettina couldn't come up with any option that would offer compromise to a man who owned a mine and lived off the sweat and blood of others. But feelings she didn't expect reared up at the thought of this Janey capturing his attention. Feelings she didn't like one bit. What did she want with a rich mine owner when her own father died in a coal mine, poor as could be? But was it fair to Luke Edwards, the way she'd locked him out with no explanation? A good scientist at least observes the facts. And a lady offered courtesy to those she disagreed with. But would mending that fence leave her heart open to—

"You sent for me, Mrs. Fitch?" Luke strode to the table, nearly out of breath. "What's the emergency?" He gave a curt dip of his head to Bettina.

Bettina's eyes widened as she stepped back. "Emergency?" She looked up into his blue eyes. "Oh, I feel terrible. I've been going on and on about the Illinois discovery. Forgive me, Lydia and Jennie. Please take care of whatever it is you must do. I'm happy to watch the display for you."

Lydia deepened into a pink one shade deeper than the bitterroot's petals. "Dear boy, there's no emergency." She glanced at Bettina. "I simply sent one of the ladies to ask that you stop in when you had a chance."

"When I—"

Now she understood how he must feel with all his matrimony prospects being managed by such helpful friends. They'd kept her talking long enough for someone to fetch him. Was the mention of Janey's interest another ruse then, too?

"Would you be a dear and explain to Miss Gilbert here what your plans are for your mines? A little on how you've changed practices to protect nature will do. Of course, we all know the strides you've made in mining safety protocol."

Bettina would have turned tail and skedaddled out of there. But Lydia put an arm around her waist and wasn't letting go.

He looked between the two women. His eyes narrowed. "I think I'm on to you, Mrs. Fitch."

"Me? I have no idea what you could mean, dear boy." She feigned an innocent, wide-eyed expression. "Go ahead, I'm sure this is going to fascinate us."

"If Miss Gilbert is at all interested, she's welcome to attend one of my talks at the Mines and Mining building. I'll be sure to go into detail for her." He gave them all a nod. "Enjoy your afternoon, ladies."

"Oh, my dear." Lydia's face looked worried as she watched him walk out. "You must at least go to one of his talks. It appears that though he may not have offended you, you certainly did offend him. You were on at least a first-name basis the last few weeks."

* * *

Luke had been by the Woman's building several times in the last few weeks. He'd managed to find reasons to check in with the ladies but only garnered a good snubbing from Bettina Gilbert for his trouble. For a man who ran several mining crews of rough characters, that woman could make his knees quake with a single glance. Something no other had been able to do. The ladies made sure to continue their quest to find his perfect mate while Mrs. Fitch made a few attempts to smooth the way for him with Bettina. But nothing swayed her. He'd met more women in those few weeks and he couldn't remember half of them. Why couldn't he forget her?

He knew when he spotted Mrs. Fitch listening politely to his presentation about silver, gold, copper, and other Montana mining successes she had news of some sort—or she'd given up on patching his rift with Bettina. "Though mining can be competitive, the Kimberley Diamond Mining Company has underwritten this entire exhibit with contributions from more than twelve counties sharing over fifty tons of specimens. The gold nuggets you see are dwarfed by the forty-eight-ounce giant here." He placed a hand on the mother of gold nuggets, enjoying the amazement of his guests. "In addition, please note the sapphires, rubies, and garnets native to our mountainous state." He moved to steps near the middle of the room. "Now I'd like to share a little about our Lady Justice, who was commissioned by the state fair board. Mining companies across the state worked together to promote the health of the industry in her creation. The solid gold plinth she stands on is on loan from the Spotted Horse Mine of Maiden, Montana, and measures two feet on each side. The lady herself is solid silver belonging to two men loaning equal measures for the mold pouring. She holds a level balance of silver and gold, and her sword denotes the battle of justice for all."

The mingling nations were often represented in the fairgoers through exotic dress, language, and customs. He knew some followed his gestures but couldn't follow all of his words. "You'll note our twelve-foot-tall Lady Justice has her eyes uncovered." He pointed up. Then for the sake of the foreign children, Luke bent his knees and flashed his fingers open in front of his eyes, garnering a round of giggles. "In researching the concept of justice portrayed this way through the centuries, we discovered she's only been blindfolded the last two hundred years. In Montana, we don't want Lady Justice to turn a blind eye. Contrary to the idea that she be blind to individuals, we believe in individual freedom in Montana. Though often portrayed in marble and stone, this is the first time she's been immortalized in a precious material like silver. Are there any questions?"

Mrs. Fitch raised her hand.

He took a breath, drawing deep. "Yes, ma'am."

"My niece would like to know, who modeled for the lovely statue?"

She wouldn't have asked that particular question normally. He knew exactly how she felt about the choice of model. Now he knew Mrs. Fitch's purpose in attending another one of his talks—she'd resumed her matchmaking. So even she'd made no progress with Bettina, whose avoidance communicated volumes. She wasn't interested. His heart squeezed. It was hopeless. Was it time to give up and turn himself over to the three women who had his well-being at heart? If he wanted a wife, he had to get that pretty botanist out of his head.

Her niece stepped into view. Jeanne. No. Joanne. No. *J*, it starts with a *J*. With any luck one of the ladies would drop the lovely girl's name before he had to admit not remembering it. He smiled at the young lady and warmed to her returned smile.

"That's a wonderful question, Mrs. Fitch." He waggled a finger with a dramatic flair, bringing grins from the little ones dressed in colorful satins. "And a controversial one as well. Montanans had their own idea of a feminine model, chosen from young ladies who lived in our state. But our executive director over the Montana World's Fair Board, Mr. Bickford, and the artist had other ideas. Ada Rehan, the famous New York actress, stands before you, immortalized in precious metal."

The crowd oohed at the mention of the well-known actress with a bit of a questionable reputation, and the story-behind-the-scenes that Luke shared.

"Our citizenry didn't appreciate a nonresident actress chosen over the epitome of Montana womanhood. However, Miss Rehan fit sixty-two of the sixty-eight artistic points of beauty. Who can argue with an artist and win?" He chuckled with the attendees who understood English. "Our newspapers still tried to mount a campaign up to the very last moment. We are a stubborn people." He lifted his arms then let his hands fall against his legs. Another short burst of appreciation for his light wit rippled around the central space inside the Grecian columns surrounding the booth.

"Miss Rehan posed for the statue mold. Then the mold was poured from Montana silver provided through the First National Bank of Helena due to the work of Mr. Samuel T. Hauser and Mr. William A. Clark of Butte on March 18th."

Janey—the name suddenly came to him—sidled closer to her aunt and sent him a flirty smile. Perhaps he should open his mind if Mrs. Fitch believed Janey could be a good wife. She was of age and very attractive. Could she relax and converse as they grew to know each other? He could at least try. How could one form an opinion in such a short first visit? Then again, he'd only had an afternoon visit with—

"Mr. Edwards?"

He knew that voice, and his blood raced at the sound of it. "Yes, another question." He searched the growing crowd for the presence of the woman he'd hoped might give him a chance. People filled in the standing-room-only aisles inside and around the mining exhibit. Touted as a not-to-be-missed feature, the Montana Mining and Minerals hadn't let up in its popularity in the first month.

"Mr. Edwards, do tell us if you think you might run out of this precious silver any time soon?"

"Excellent question, Miss Gilbert." Was that it? Had she worried about his livelihood since the silver pricing downturn began? She didn't seem like the type to be that concerned about security, but what did he know of a woman's mind? He could quell that concern. "As a matter of fact, no. The silver deposits in Montana are nowhere near running out, regardless of the Silver Act redirecting purchases to the gold standard. Last year alone our state produced enough silver to cast a thousand of these statues, if they'd been needed, and still have plenty left over to mint a thousand silver dollars in addition."

"You mean that ripping the land apart for financial gain is worth the scars left behind? What about future generations? What about rehabilitating the natural resources? What about the danger to the men?" She had a fierce expression. "What a waste of God's green earth." She turned to leave.

"Kindly let me offer a response, Miss Gilbert."

"I can't imagine that you'd have one, Mr. Edwards."

"But I do." The crowd parted as he stepped down off the dais at Lady Justice's feet and walked into the great hall beyond the pavilion. Many followed him while others that hadn't fit inside the booth merely needed to turn a bit. "Tell me about how cities are built without wood or quarries. How should dentists fill cavities without gold? And without coal, how can the iron horse ship food to distant places or bring more coal to warm tenements?"

"I'm sure those things—"

"Are important to civilization?"

"Of course. However, we must act with conservation and safety in mind. When the land is changed and it can't regenerate, then what direction have we set but one for destruction?"

How could he get across to her the need for mining with her mind set in stone? "And copper? Copper conducts electricity." There must be copper in his veins, because she'd managed to get his blood surging. "How do you suppose we provide electricity to cities, hospitals, or homes in the future if we have no mining for this resource?"

"Resources that may not be replenished if done irresponsibly."

"You are assuming all mining is done irresponsibly, Miss Gilbert. Civilization demands support. Through our mining and mineral opportunities we better the lives of everyone on this planet." Isn't that what she'd told him she wanted? To uplift the lives of the less fortunate?

"What about the lives of those men in the mines? Tell me your answer to that, Mr. Edwards." She crossed her arms and tapped a foot.

"I'll tell you about the jobs responsible mining provides, and then I'll tell you about all the families those working men feed. Without mining, our entire nation would lose a major industry for our populace. Children would go hungry with fathers out of work. Do you propose we let that happen?"

Mrs. Fitch moved into his line of sight. She gave three small, sharp shakes of her head at him.

If he didn't end this impromptu debate, there might be no coming back with Bettina Gilbert—and they needed to talk. She had to give him the chance to clear up the misunderstanding that he couldn't comprehend. "Ladies and gentlemen, thank you for attending. Be sure to see my two favorites, the Statue of Liberty made of salt and the Silver Lady next door in the Colorado pavilion, on your tour through the rest of the building. Thank you."

The crowd applauded. A few voiced their appreciation while a family from somewhere in Asia ducked their heads to him in a small bow as Bettina whirled and stomped away.

Was it mining, safety, or something else that bothered her? Luke glanced around for Mrs. Fitch and Janey.

Mrs. Fitch threaded through a few people. Was she disappointed or delighted Bettina offered less competition to her niece? "Oh, Luke. How could you?"

Disappointed. He turned his palms up and sighed. "What was I supposed to do? She wants to help people but doesn't understand there's more to it than feeding them bread." He pushed his hands into his pockets and stared at his shoes.

"She's a smart girl. She will understand if you take the time to help her."

"She doesn't want to have anything to do with me now." He looked down the cavernous aisle she'd exited. A city girl who despised his way of life would be the worst choice for a miner's wife, wouldn't she? So why couldn't he get her out of his head?

"I think you're misreading the situation, dear." She patted his arm. "If she didn't want to know you, she wouldn't have come. She's been miserable, though trying not to let anyone notice. Time to stop avoiding the conflict and get started on securing yourself a wife."

"Aunt Lydia? Mr. Edwards?" Janey managed to squeeze through the crowd and join the two of them. She looked fetching in a light pink day dress and straw sun hat covered in an array of pink and white flowers. The pink bow at the right of her chin brought a youthful color to her complexion. "Is everything all right?"

"Yes, dear."

Why couldn't he have fallen for a sweet, simple girl like Janey? "It's just 'Luke.'" He took her fingers in a genteel greeting. "Janey, thank you for coming. Did you enjoy the presentation?" he asked as he released her hand.

"It was a bit technical for me, but I enjoyed your beautiful speaking voice."

"Ah. Technical. That could dampen my tour for some." He looked at Mrs. Fitch to add her opinion.

She merely glanced away at the stack of copper bricks behind Lady Justice.

"I'll take that under advisement."

Janey fluttered her lashes, seeming to preen that he'd considered her thoughts a valuable commentary.

Mrs. Fitch glanced between Janey and Luke, gave an almost imperceptible tilt of her head the direction Bettina had gone, and pressed her lips together. Then she raised her brows, signaling with her eyes down the aisle, as if to say, *"I think you have somewhere to be, young man."*

If she offered, albeit silently, he'd take her advice and go. "Pleased to see you again, Janey. Will you ladies excuse me?"

He waved to one of the other men in the far corner to take over and heard Mrs. Fitch behind him.

"He is a bit too slow for you, Janey dear. I have another fellow much more charming in mind."

Luke choked back a laugh as he headed out the south entrance, through grand doors that led to the lagoon in the center of the Court of Honor.

"Bettina!" He couldn't believe it. She stood in front of the colossal fountain depicting Columbus's arrival in America. She turned at his call with red-rimmed eyes and tears streaking down her cheeks that could create a fountain of their own.

Shame for the way he'd spoken to her doused any fire he'd felt at her words. Somehow they had to clear up the mess they'd made—and it started with humbling himself. He stood beside her, waiting for her to accept his presence.

She turned back to the water trickling off the fountain's oars and splashing below Columbus's feet as he stood on the bow searching for the shore. Could they find dry ground?

"Bettina, will you forgive me?" He said it softly without demand or expectation that she should.

She looked up into his eyes, searched his soul for what seemed an eternity, and then offered her own apology. "I've made assumptions about you and judged you harshly without merit. The apology is mine to give, not yours. By meeting you, I came face-to-face for the first time with the kind of monster I blamed for my father's death in a mine collapse." She dropped her eyes to his chest. "I'm an orphan."

"But you speak of your parents as if they're alive."

"I'm adopted. Adopted by the doctor. . .the doctor who couldn't save my mother. But he could save me, as sick as I was with typhoid, too."

"I don't know what to say."

"Just listen. When I heard you were rich, that made me angrier, because I assumed that you made money from the suffering of others. The monster in my mind I'd built up all these years finally had a face."

"But—"

"I know." She turned to face Columbus again as if she drew strength from the cascade of water, helping her pour out her story. "You weren't a monster. The more I've watched you, the more I've discovered a man of kindness and integrity. A man who cares about others and serves without resentment. You brought water, food, and ran the smallest of errands for all of us"—she let out an ironic chuckle—"you made sure everyone else was taken care of first, before yourself. I couldn't understand it or release that monstrous picture I'd built in my head even though my eyes could see."

He lifted a hand, palm up, and held his breath. Would she touch him?

She placed her hand in his and a jolt rocketed through his body. They watched the light reflect on the splashing surface. The mist cooled the hot, still summer air around them. He released his breath slowly, evenly, so as not to disturb the moment, and listened to her heart.

"After my father's death, my mother had no choice but to move us into the city." She jutted her chin toward town. "Chicago. She did everything she could to survive. Things she wouldn't have had to if my father hadn't died. Then typhoid struck and people started dying in the epidemic. First my little brother, he was four." She swiped away a tear dangling from her chin. "Then my mother fell ill for weeks and still tried to take in laundry. Eventually she caught pneumonia. That finally took her. She hadn't worked in so long, we had no food. I begged on the streets while she slept, tried to help wash clothes, and began to get ill as well. But a neighbor took pity and called for a doctor to look in on our family."

He tightened his hold on her hand, wishing he could carry this pain for her. Pain he'd had no idea he churned up like tailings from a mine poisoning the very ground it'd come from. That she could bear up under the weight of it made him admire her that much more for her strength. For the desire to change the circumstances of others like herself.

"On my mother's deathbed, she told me not to be afraid, that the doctor was here to help me. He wouldn't leave me alone." She smiled at the ground and then gave him a sidelong glance that said she understood as an adult now what her mother had tried to do for her. "I don't know whether he felt pressured or some form of guilt, but that doctor agreed to take care of me. He promised my mother he wouldn't leave me behind when she breathed her last." Her mouth worked a moment, though no words came out. She took a deep breath. "Right there, in that hovel, she gave me into the safekeeping of the doctor. And then she was gone. I was eight. He kept that promise, even refusing the neighbor's payment for his visit. He knew our neighbor was a very poor man." She smiled, her tears drying. "He still says he got the better part of the deal in a daughter. My parents adopted me, educated me, and have never treated me with anything but the deepest of love. I'm so blessed. But there are so many others who have no one to rescue them from starvation, disease, and poverty. That's why I'm so driven. Someone has to help the others."

She inspired him to want to do more, to help her live out the calling on her that seemed God ordained. If only he'd known sooner. "I'm so sorry my ignorance caused you further pain."

She shook her head, the tiny ribbons down her back fluttering as the breeze off the water picked them up and dropped them back down. "You've done nothing wrong. What I want to say is thank you. Thank you for helping me face my childhood demons and forgive people caught in circumstances beyond their control." She blinked in the sunshine as she gazed up at him. "If you consider me unworthy of your—"

Luke took her in his arms and held her close. "I consider you most precious." Then he realized the liberty he had taken and released her. But he whispered into her ear as he pressed her hand to his heart, "The most precious of women."

Chapter 6

Bettina's knees trembled faster than a lady's fan flickered on a blistering day. She knew her talk was well received. She'd answered every discussion question from the audience with aplomb, according to her father. He'd said it with his chest puffed out while Mama beamed on his arm. Yet her heart rat-a-tatted like the drummer in the John Philip Sousa concert Luke had taken her to last week. Had she impressed Reverend Doctor Kelsey enough to win the position at Oberlin?

First he shook hands with her father, congratulating him on raising a fine young scientist. Then he turned to her mother and praised her skills of turning out such a gracious child. Then, finally, he addressed Bettina.

"Young lady, you have a quick mind and very thorough research methods. You've worked hard to create a possible plan to help the masses."

She brightened. He saw her vision, her—

"But I see a flaw in your theory."

Her stomach hit her boots, and the blood in her body followed it. "A flaw?"

"You focus too much on the overview to bring about results because of the intensity of your passion to save the poor right now. Would you consider coming at your research from a more practical angle?"

Practical? Wasn't that the entire basis of her theory? That it could be put to use for practical solutions? "Please, sir, where might I improve?"

His face relaxed into an inviting smile. "That's exactly the question I wanted to hear. It shows me you're open to criticism that will help you grow as a scientist and as you undertake this project long term."

"But the flaw?"

"Your vision will give you the passion to keep working toward your goal. However..."

Flaw. However. She hung on his words, leaning in to understand.

"...I'd advise you to focus not en masse but on the exponential. Study the cause at its root, or we cannot repeat the result intentionally. Do you look over a field of wheat and say it grows because of the sun?" He pulled the boutonniere from his lapel. "If I dissect this flower and glean all I can from it, but I haven't grown it and observed it in various situations, how can I say what I observed will be repeatable?" He replaced the button mum. "By starting with one, I can determine how and why it thrives best. Then, once I understand how it flourishes, I can expand to help it and others like it prosper. Understand the organism at its most elemental level and you'll be able to build outward from there. Then, would you consider it wise to include observations from others? Consider those who work with the crops. What have they observed year after year? You have much work to do yet."

His wisdom opened her eyes to the flaw. She didn't have enough information to guarantee success yet. "Yes, I understand. Thank you, sir."

"I came because your application stood out. Rarely do I see such high marks in overall laboratory work. I invite you to be part of my team because I see in you a person who desires to make the world a better place through your science, if you'll temper your enthusiasm for immediacy and focus on causal research. Can you cap that passion and channel it into tedious work for the greater good?"

"Yes, yes, sir!"

"Good. Then we'll see you this fall at Oberlin."

She hadn't even remembered to give him the reference letter!

<hr />

"My darling girl, we couldn't be more proud. But it's for men to be so driven. Shouldn't your education be enough?" Mama wanted grandchildren, specifically granddaughters. One surprise daughter hadn't been enough with four boisterous sons. She hadn't been part of Bettina's early childhood to dress her and show her off. Two of those sons, Robert Jr. and Daniel, produced a passel of boys but not yet one girl. Of course, neither Bruce nor George would marry for another few years. "With what you know, your children will be well educated. Goodness, you'll rule any garden club in the city. Change is made in the parlor, influencing people, not out in the fields. Imagine the lives you could influence." Marion Gilbert swept her hands out as if gathering the grand downtown Chicago coffee house into her fold. Mama had a gift for gathering people to her and, once there, never letting them go. Her loyalty was renowned among those who knew her.

"Mama, botanists might belong to garden clubs, but they don't plant pretty flowers for the hobby of it." She covered her mother's hand on the table. "Don't you understand, I want to feed thousands of children through my science, not a few from my stove?"

Her mother slid back in her seat as if she'd been slapped. Tears glistened, though she blinked rapidly. "I suppose being a mother isn't enough to contribute to society. I understand."

How had her passions insulted her mother so deeply? "Mama, that's not what I meant. Motherhood is truly God inspired. But I'm not ready for that yet."

"You're twenty-two. How long do you think you have to pass on those brilliant genetics, when you haven't even married yet?"

"I think what your mother means is—"

"Robert, I know what I mean." The tears gone, red spots on her cheeks flashed the signal a storm would let loose any second. Bettina's adventure gene seemed a wild card to Mama.

"What if I could influence farmers with my discoveries? What if each person I educate could affect the lives of hundreds or thousands? Can't you see how that would make daily life better for all mothers?" Bettina bowed her head. "What if what I achieve could have helped a mother"—her voice thickened—"who died like mine? Couldn't that be enough?"

Ever the peacemaker, Papa stepped in. "Bettina, we understand how important it is to you to be involved in bettering society. We've never besmirched your beginnings, nor would we now. Your birth parents were hardworking, honorable people. It's only natural you want to help those who weren't as fortunate as yourself. Accept the position, if you wish—" He held up a hand to stay Mama's objection. Then he looked at her as he finished. "At least it brings you home to Cleveland. We'll talk more then about other future prospects."

"There are plenty of important volunteer opportunities for married women right in Cleveland."

Papa closed his eyes for a moment.

"Mama—"

"Bettina." Her father's raised eyebrows and stern tone stopped any further discussion. He snapped for the waiter. "The end of the summer, then we'll talk in the privacy of our home."

The six-block walk wouldn't have been too difficult, but the July temperatures already rose steadily into the nineties by midmorning on clear days. With not much of a breeze off the lake, Bettina would be a puddle of perspiration before starting her shift to relieve the ladies for luncheon. With the heat and Mama's worry for her safety in the city, ensconced in safe transportation rather than alone on the streets might appease her overly protective sensibilities. Right now Bettina did not need to challenge her mother further. She would keep using public transportation as she'd agreed when they rented the city town house for the summer.

Bettina boarded the World's Fair omnibus, leaving her parents to a little Friday shopping. She chose the first empty seat toward the back door, hoping for a little draft of fresh air, and drew out her hand fan. Flicking her wrist, fanning away the scent of horse and human, the morning celebratory brunch with her parents had taken longer than she expected. They seemed bent on convincing her against going anywhere away from home. How could she help the children of Chicago or any other city if she never experienced the farms or understood the challenges of farmers outside the sprawl of buildings? Traveling the nearby countryside couldn't be that outrageous as part of her position at Oberlin. Why couldn't she have waited to share the details of the position until the summer ended?

Bettina waved out the side window to her parents as the carriage moved away from the curb. "I'll be home before dark or I'll send word and be sure I have an escort." She called the reassurance to Mama, who waved back until she was out of sight. Knowing Mama, the discussion with Papa had just begun. Bettina leaned her head against the wooden wall. Only nine and she was exhausted.

The horses clipped along at a brisk pace toward the city-side entrance. A few blocks shy of their goal, one of the horses whinnied. The carriage lurched, sliding Bettina a few inches on her bench into the woman next to her. Another loud neighing at the sound of a crack and the carriage whipped forward as the nose crashed into the street. Bettina let out a screech, with the yells and screams of other passengers adding to the chaos, and then smacked headlong into the bench in front of her. As the horses' high-pitched whinnies continued, the omnibus carriage wrenched forward, ripping. The back door flew wide as Bettina's body slammed into it, then she tumbled over the steps, just missing the edges as they burst up toward her with the runaway draft team's frantic thrust forward. She thudded to the street and rolled in a tangle of skirts, arms and legs flailing, as the brightly painted vehicle careened onto a corner, flopped onto its side, dragging for another twenty feet until someone caught the horses.

As Bettina pushed herself up to see, a crowd ran to help her.

———————•◆•———————

"Where has she gone?" Luke wanted to congratulate her on a speech well done. To tell her Montana needed scientists like her. To tell her he needed her.

"I believe her parents took her to a restaurant just outside the grounds to celebrate. I don't think she could eat a bite beforehand. For an early morning event, that was a large audience. Can you imagine a young thing like that speaking to fifteen hundred people? Brilliant girl, just brilliant!" Mrs. Fitch gave Luke a sympathetic look. "They'd never have found seating inside at breakfast, you know. Those lines don't seem to go down no matter what time of day or night."

Luke paced the pavilion floor in the Woman's building. One thing Bettina was not— late. She had some sort of internal clockwork in her head he couldn't explain. Worry gnawed in his gut the way mice worked a rope. He'd slipped away from the auditorium this morning so as not to disturb her discussion with Reverend Doctor Kelsey. Though he prayed for her as he left the building, he also prayed for God's will. Luke hoped God's will aligned more with his desire to marry Bettina than Bettina's desire to work for the scientist. But he knew better than to superimpose his will over God's. It didn't hurt to let the Almighty know what he wanted though. And she'd planned to meet him at the booth.

"I'm sure she was simply detained discussing her talk's success with her parents," Mrs. Fitch soothed. "She was quite dazzling."

"Yes, she was." *Quite*, he brooded. "But I need to see her before I go. She doesn't know."

"You haven't told her yet?"

"No, I didn't want to cause her any stress before her presentation at the congress. She was as nervous as a puppy around fireworks this last week."

"Mm." Mrs. Fitch hummed an agreement as she rearranged the seating, putting chairs back into the inviting arc she preferred. "When do you leave?"

He picked up a chair and walked it over as she pointed out the spot to leave it. "In the morning. There just isn't any choice left to me."

"No, I suppose there isn't." She put a hand on his arm. Mrs. Fitch's eyes told the story of years. Years of watching men build the frontier by scratching in the ground to create civilization. "I've learned in my time that things have a way of coming around for the better."

"I hope you're right, Mrs. Fitch. I hope you're right."

"Luke, don't leave things hanging if you want one special bride." She patted his arm. "Go find her and spend the day together before you get on the train." She dug in her satchel. "I have Bettina's schedule. You know she loves her schedule. No surprises for that girl. She's written which restaurant she'd be at with her parents if her talk went well. Yes, here it is." Handing it over, she suggested, "Pray about it. Let her know how you feel. Then let God direct her path." She tipped her head and shrugged. "Maybe she'll even go with you. But you won't know unless you take the chance. And you, my boy, have nothing to lose."

"Thank you, Mrs. Fitch."

"Off with you now. Go get your girl."

Luke grabbed for the thick leather harness. He bellowed a deep baritone, "Whoa, whoa there." As the draft horse drew to a dancing stop, he gentled his voice to calm the team, fighting the adrenaline it'd taken to capture them and their runaway omnibus.

Passersby raced to help him rescue and then comfort the injured passengers. He lifted several women out of the sideways vehicle through the broken windows. He checked inside for any more unable to get out on their own and found it empty, jumbled with belongings. Then he spotted Bettina's favorite purple ostrich plumed hat lying in the street!

"Bettina Gilbert!" He yelled through cupped hands down the city street the direction the horses had come. A splintered wheel, spokes poking up, lay in the center of the road. He sidestepped it, racing toward another circle of people as a man redirected other carriages to turn and go around the block before reaching 61st Street.

As he jogged closer, he glimpsed a dove-gray skirt between people's legs. "Please, let me through. Let me through. I'm her friend."

She lay on the ground, dirtied by the road but surprisingly in better condition than he'd expected. Hunkering down, he asked, "How badly hurt are you?"

She touched her elbow where a little tear showed a scrape. "A few bumps, but if you'll help me up—"

Shuffling his arms under her knees and shoulders, Luke clasped her to his chest. "I was terrified."

She gave a breathy laugh. "Me, too."

Luke stood, and the gathered crowd let him through with a few pats on his shoulders as he carried Bettina to the sidewalk. He set her down on the curb and held her at arm's length as he looked her up and down. "Are you sure you're not badly injured?"

She looked up into his eyes, making him want to melt with relief. "I have a few bumps and a nice tidy headache. But the worst was I had the wind knocked out of me. Is anyone else hurt?"

"A few more than others. But they're being taken care of now."

"That's good." She leaned against his shoulder. "I think I should change clothes before going back to the booth."

"Mrs. Fitch gave you the rest of the day off. I was coming to ask you to spend it with me. But it might be best to take you home to rest and have your father examine you."

She sat up straight. "No! I'd prefer we keep this incident between us. If Mama caught wind that I'd been. . .oh, no, no, no." She pushed against him. "I'll go home, but only to freshen up and change."

"All right." He looked her over one more time. "Then I'd like to take you somewhere peaceful where we can have a quiet conversation."

A starry smile spread across her lips. Lips he wanted to taste more than candied caramel corn or sparkling sodas or the world's most enticing delicacy. Tonight, he would.

"Bettina, what I'm trying to say is I have to go home to Montana. Tomorrow morning. My train leaves at seven." The same time she'd presented today. Could he see seven in the morning the same again?

"Why now? There's still months left of the exposition."

He sat with her on the island park bench. The craze of the carriage crash, crowds, and commotion of the fair across the canal. Surrounded by the peace of the Japanese lanterns glowing along the shaded path and the respite of Wooded Island, Luke took her hand in his. "Would you come with me?"

"Why can't you stay?"

"It's the silver. Since the government has replaced it with the gold standard, silver has been falling. Falling hard enough that I have to close one of my mines. Now the Reading Railroad has entered bankruptcy, steel has fallen. It's a deluge of one thing after another. I have no choice but to close one of my mines and let men go." His eyes blinked hard several times.

"Will you come back?"

"I don't know." His voice faltered. "I don't know when or if I'll be able to come back."

She watched the way his thumb moved over her knuckles in soft brushes, and her heart broke for him. "What happens now?"

"I'll try to relocate as many men as I can from the silver mine to the copper. With electricity coming on strong across the country, it's possible the demand will remain. But there aren't enough jobs in one mine to absorb all the men from another." Luke ran a hand across the back of his neck. "I'm putting dozens and dozens of men out of work. Men who have families."

His pain flooded her body. She finally understood the other side of the mining equation. The sense of responsibility he felt for people who relied on his jobs to survive. "I'm so sorry."

"To look a man in the eye, while you know his fate yet he does not?" His face reddened while he rasped out, "That burden should belong to God only."

She wanted to hold him. To tell him she loved him and would stand by him through this terrible time. And yet, as she ached for Luke and the painful decisions he must make that would affect so many lives, so many families, Bettina knew the heaviness of that burden well. Knew the burden of looking a man in the eye and telling him what would change his fate. She knew she had to tell Luke no.

She lifted her gaze to his, tears burning, and swayed into his arms like the cobra who'd danced to the flute. A cobra whose grace belied the bite to come. He lowered his mouth to hers. A kiss she wanted to lock in her heart forever. Her first kiss—and her last. There'd be no other for her. She knew that as much as she knew he'd come for a wife. Salty tears mingled at their lips. She dropped her arms from his warm, strong neck.

He lifted his head and searched her wet face. "You're not coming then, are you?"

Bettina scrubbed a hand across her cheeks and looked away at the same green grass that she'd told Luke breathed life into the world. The same green grass she'd study to find out why it grew so fast almost anywhere while other plants didn't. Green grass that tickled her nostrils with the scent of heaven after a rain. She kept her eyes glued on the green grass and gave an almost imperceptible shake of her head. "How can I?"

"You can because you love me."

"And I love my family." She raised her face to his. "You don't understand." She stood and took a step backward.

"No." Luke stood and reached out for her, but Bettina backed away again. "I don't."

"My parents never considered turning me out or giving me over to the state. Instead, they made me part of the family. My education, it's all because they poured love into me. I need to use it, Luke."

"If they love you, they want you to be happy."

"But don't you see? I can't be happy if I bring them even a second of pain. All I am I owe to people who owed me nothing and yet gave me everything." She leaned toward Luke, toward the life she wanted but couldn't have. "I cannot now, or ever, hand them betrayal like that."

He gathered her against him, tangled his fingers into her hair, and held her tight. "I love you."

"Luke, I do love you. But since I can't go with you, I—" Bettina swallowed back the lump in her throat that seemed to grow thorns, jabbing them into her. "I think you should take Janey with you." Tears coursed down her face, wetting his shirtfront. "I need to know you'll be happy. Then I'll be happy, too, every time I think of you. Every day." She disentangled herself and walked into the life she'd chosen.

"Bettina, please."

She stopped, turned her head, and said with finality, "No."

Chapter 7

November 1, 1893
Helena, Montana

Luke met Frankie Shanahan on the porch as he tied his horse off. "Haven't seen you in a while. Did you bring me some mail?" The teenager who once led a group of newsies now held a more trusted messenger position when not in school.

"Got a letter from someone named Miss Gilbert."

Luke bounded down the steps into his yard. "Let's see it."

Frankie flipped open his saddle pack and pulled out a newspaper and a tan envelope.

Luke opened the envelope, scanned the message, and looked at Frankie in awe. "She's coming." He hooted, tossing his hat in the air and grabbing the sixteen-year-old in a bear hug. "She's coming now!"

Both men, one nearly to adulthood and one on the cusp of matrimony, dusted off their hats, grinning like fools. "She'll be on the same train as our contingent returning from the exposition!"

"I'm right pleased for you, Mr. Edwards."

"The train's due in a couple hours."

"I wouldn't be too far behind it, then. Some other fella might be snatchin' yer girl."

Luke laughed, but they both knew the truth of his words. He sobered and took off toward the barn. "Frankie, there'll be an extra tip in your pay this month. You've made me a happy man!"

Two hours later, Luke checked each window as the train pulled into the station. He ran along the length of it, searching as passengers stepped off, thrilled to be home. Then time froze as Bettina stopped in the doorway, searching the platform until she found him. Her smile bloomed, beckoning him to her as if a golden lasso dropped around his heart and tugged.

Bettina held out a hand, clad in the fine Spanish lace gloves he'd given her that first day, and took his, walking straight into his arms. Arms that had ached to hold her against a heart that had shredded in Chicago. He breathed in her scent as he pressed his mouth against her neck. "You came."

He brushed off a tap on his shoulder.

"Excuse me, son, but that's my daughter, and you haven't asked my permission to be so free with her."

Luke jumped back and stuttered. "Your—your—" He shot a look from the taller, well-dressed man in a vested suit to Bettina and back again. He turned to Bettina, one thought on his mind. "You did come to marry me, right?"

"Yes." Bettina's musical laugh soothed his sore soul. "Mr. Luke Edwards, I'd like to introduce my father, Mr. Robert Gilbert, and my mother, Mrs. Marion Gilbert."

He greeted them but noticed several men hanging around the train watching with curious interest. He wasn't taking any chances with the most precious woman in the world. "Sir, if you'd give me permission to marry your daughter, I promise to love and protect her every day of my life."

"Wait a moment. I haven't finished." A mischievous smile played around her lips. "I'm sure you'd like to meet my brothers, their wives, and my nephews. . . ."

As she named them all, he took in the large family gathering around them under the awning of the small Helena train depot. He swallowed. She told him she'd never leave her family behind. How many were there? Shock must have registered on his face as he kept nodding at each person. "Uh, pleased to meet you. And you. And you. . ."

Mr. Gilbert held out his hand. "We're glad to meet you, too, son."

Luke shook the older man's hand.

"Our little Bettina about pined away missing you. If I were to deny you, I don't think she'd ever forgive me."

It took a moment to sink in, but then Luke grinned at his future father-in-law. "I'll do my best to see she's happy."

"Now, let's see about making this official once we find our lodgings."

Nodding, Luke stared around the uneven circle. The sheer volume of them and the luggage being unloaded. What would he do with them all?

Bettina leaned in and whispered. "Papa has taken a position at St. John's Hospital, as has my oldest brother. They're sending carriages around." She pointed to another man corralling a toddler. "You remember, that's Daniel."

No, but he nodded.

"Daniel will be working as a pharmacist. He has yet to determine whether the local pharmacy has room or if he'll need to open another."

"Ah, I see." He gazed at her as she spoke. "And what about you and your dreams? You're giving them up for me?"

Her brows drew together. "Absolutely not." She folded her arms and announced, "I've been given a grant to study farming techniques in the West as part of a greater program being run through Oberlin."

He moved to wrap his arms around her and then stopped, remembering Mr. Gilbert's warning. "May I?"

"You may."

He kissed his bride soundly as he heard Mrs. Fitch say, "There, you see, we've brought home seven medals and a bride. Well done, ladies."

Angela Breidenbach is a bestselling author, host of *Grace Under Pressure Radio*, and the Christian Author Network's president. And yes, she's half of the fun fe-lion comedy duo, Muse and Writer, on social media.

Note from Angela: "I love hearing from readers and enjoy book club chats. To drop me a note or set up a book club chat, contact me at angie.breidenbach@gmail.com. Let me know if you'd like me to post a quote from your review of this story. If you send me the link and your social media handle, I'll post it to my social media with a word of gratitude including your name and/or social media handle, too!"

For more about Angela's books (especially more Montana-inspired romances) and podcast, or to set up a book club chat, please visit her website: http://www.AngelaBreidenbach.com

Twitter/Pinterest/Instagram: @AngBreidenbach

Facebook Author Page: http://www.facebook.com/AngelaBreidenbachInspirational SpeakerAuthor

A Taste of
Honey

by Darlene Franklin

Dedication

Life inside a nursing home can be very lonely without contact from the outside. Someone I had never met before took me on as a ministry. Whenever I need to make purchases, she stops by. Whenever I need a ride to church or to the store, she takes me. Whenever I need help finishing a project, she finds the time to help. Sue Blackmon, you exemplify everything a servant of Christ should be. Thank you for your friendship.

It is not good to eat much honey: so for men to search their own glory is not glory.
PROVERBS 25:27

Chapter 1

Spruce Hill, Vermont
July 1896

Edith Grace checked her outfit, making sure she was prepared to garner as much honey as possible in one trip. Harvesting honey for free from her neighbor was a deal made in heaven, as far as she was concerned. At the fiftieth annual Rutland State Fair, she intended to make her mark as the best baker in all of Vermont, thanks to Mr. Oscar's honey.

He had taught Edith how to harvest the honey from the supers over the hollow logs, called log gums for some reason. Today was the third time she had donned her veil and thick gloves to gather the liquid gold by herself. She approached the log gums with caution. Experience had taught her that bees didn't want to sting her. It cost them their lives, after all. But experience had also taught her some stings were inevitable. Although she wasn't allergic, they still hurt and itched. Another reason she harvested as much as possible at one time—so she could wait before returning.

She loved this meadow. The honey only made it sweeter. Every wildflower native to Vermont swayed in the gentle breeze. No two varieties looked alike, from the green boneset that blended with the grass, to the brilliant magenta of an Indian cucumber root, to the yellow marigolds and violets that bloomed in every shade of the rainbow. Standing at the edge of the meadow, watching the flowers, the mild buzzing of bees flying to and from flower to colony made her smile every time she saw it.

It was time. She put cotton balls in her ears to lessen the sound of bees buzzing and approached the third log gum. She blew smoke into the log to encourage the bees to fly away and lifted the bowl-like super.

The honey poured into the pail, and the bees were attracted to the scent. Gloves protected her hands, the net protected her face and neck, and honey slowly filled the pail.

The sound of a thousand angry bees assaulted her ears, but Edith ignored them by singing softly to herself. However, the noise grew louder, different.

Someone yanked the super from her hands, her pail toppled over, and the precious honey oozed down the side. She lunged for the pail. Something—someone?—stood in her way, and she fell to the ground. The crash unsettled one glove, and bees dived on her skin. One sting. She struggled to stand. Another bee stung her hand, then a third.

She made it to her feet, her hand on fire, and her wagon on its side, losing what honey she had gathered. She stepped toward it but stumbled.

Strong arms caught her and picked her up. "I'm sorry." He ran to the shelter of the trees and beyond before he sat her on the ground.

If her hand didn't hurt so much, she would yank the veil off and give the stranger a piece of her mind. He had caused the loss of several pints of honey and the attack on her hand. Then he had whisked her away to safety. In his strong arms she seemed to weigh no more than—a bee. The silly analogy took her mind away from the pain for a moment.

He was talking again. Something about her bonnet? She flinched at the fear of another sting. Thick fingers touched her neck, unbuttoning the clasps that kept the bee veil in place. A fly landed on her nose, and a mosquito's sting pierced the film of sweat on her forehead.

She raised her hand to wipe it off, the hand that had been stung, and she yelped. That—paw—so swollen that she could hardly see her fingers. The salty sweat burned her skin.

"Let me see that." Her rescuer knelt down next to her, and something about him looked familiar. But she couldn't place the face.

"I take it you're not highly allergic to bees." He held her throbbing hand in his, strong and calloused from hard work.

Her laugh came out as a groan. "This is bad enough." She wanted to scream.

"If you were allergic, you'd be dead." The man spoke in clipped tones.

"That doesn't help when you feel like your hand is a pincushion. Ow!" Her voice raised to a howl.

"That's one out." He held the short stinger where she could see it. "You are hurting, but this represents the life of a bee. They were living happy lives until you threatened their home, and they gave their lives defending it."

A second dig in her hand, another yelp, and he held up the second stinger.

"Haven't you ever heard of tweezers?" She squeezed the words out of her throat as he slid a thin blade under her skin for the third stinger.

"That would only release more venom into your system. If you're going to play with bees, you should know that."

Who was this stranger who happened to know so much about bees? Apiarists weren't all that common.

He lifted her hand close to her face. "I believe that's all. Now I'm going to unbutton your sleeve. Your wrist is swelling as well." He put his threat to work.

How dare he? Edith jerked her arm, but he didn't let go. Instead, he held it over her head like a child wanting to answer a question in school.

<hr />

Grant Oscar's quick trip to the field his father left fallow hadn't turned out as expected. First he had discovered a woman harvesting honey from log gums on his family's land and then the nasty exchange she'd had with the bees. He hardly recognized the tomboy he'd left behind in this amazing beauty.

She didn't seem to recognize him at all. She struggled to free her arm as if from a stranger. He loosened his grip. "Do you think you can stand up?"

She jumped to her feet. "I'd appreciate it if you would see if there is any honey left in my jug and bring it to my house when you have time." She held her injured hand gingerly. "I'll have to return to get more once I've healed." She took a couple of steps and stopped. "I should tell you who I am and where I live." She cradled her hand. "And thank you for getting me away from those bees. I'm—"

"You're Edie Grace, and your parents' farm is about two miles west of here." So she hadn't recognized him. "My home is closer, so you're coming with me. You need to get ice on that hand." He watched as his words sank in.

"Grant Oscar?"

"That's me."

She took a step and wobbled, and he wrapped his arm around her. "Let's get going. I'd go for my horse, but that would just jostle your hand further."

She nodded in agreement, her lips compressed in a straight line from pain, her hand looking angrier than a crying baby. He almost wished he had been around to watch her grow up.

When he had left Spruce Hill nine years ago to enlist in the navy, he had enjoyed visiting new ports and distant lands. Over the years it had grown tiring. His desire to see something besides the ocean on a daily basis combined with his father's failing health brought him back to the farm that had belonged to his family for more than a century. He hadn't known the herculean task ahead of him—bringing it back from the brink of bankruptcy.

He kept them under the trees, following the fringes of the meadow. Edie winced every time she brushed a branch, but she didn't complain. When at last they reached the cultivated fields, corn and bean stalks marked the pathway to the barn. The sun beat on their heads; her forehead glistened and her body trembled. "Do you want to rest?"

She shook her head. "No."

"At least drink some water." He handed her his canteen.

As she shook her head, she stumbled, and he grabbed her arms to keep her from falling. Unfortunately, his hand clamped on her right wrist. Tears squeezed from her closed eyes.

He uncapped the canteen and handed it to her. "Please, drink. I don't want you to faint before we reach the house."

She took a sip and then a deep swallow. "Thank you, Mr. Oscar."

"Grant, please."

The water helped, and a few minutes later they arrived at the house.

She stared at the porch stairs and then at her hand. She drew in a deep breath and stepped up without holding on. The three steps to the front door took an eternity, but at last they crossed the threshold.

Edie walked gingerly to the closest seat, the sofa. She made it, too, with only a single wince. She attempted to straighten her skirts with her left hand. "Why, hello, Mr. Oscar."

His chair faced the front window, looking over the farm. The stroke he'd suffered four months ago had robbed him of clear speech and he didn't move well, but he loved to watch what was going on.

"Gr." That's about as much of his son's name as he could manage. "Miss Grace."

Edie sprang from her chair as if her hand didn't hurt a bit. "Mr. Oscar." She kept her hand at her side, where he couldn't see it. "You must be glad to have your son home at last."

Chapter 2

L et me get some ice for that hand," Grant said. He disappeared from the room.

He'd better run away. Edith had been the one to find his father on the floor, as still as death, on Easter Sunday. Mr. Oscar was so proud of his son in the navy—just look at the photograph of him in uniform.

The problem was that after Mrs. Oscar had died, Mr. Oscar had gone into a steady decline, and his son wasn't there to do anything about it. Even after the stroke, Grant hadn't made it home for almost four months.

"Miss Grace." Mr. Oscar struggled with the words, but his smile was all that mattered.

"Sit down so I can take care of you properly." Grant stood behind her, water dripping from the towel wrapped around an ice chip he had broken from the block of ice in their kitchen.

Mr. Oscar was getting agitated, probably wanting to know what had happened. "The bees got to me today." She held out her hand, swollen and red. How much worse it would have been if Grant hadn't taken care of her.

Of course, if Grant hadn't surprised her, she probably wouldn't have been stung in the first place.

Mr. Oscar indicated that he wanted to be turned around, and Grant complied. His eager eyes watched every movement his son made, as if ready to take over if he didn't do a good job.

The ice provided instant relief to the heat, and he gently laid her affected hand on the arm of the sofa. "Keeping it elevated a little will help." Grant grabbed one of the pillows his mother had embroidered. "Try this." He slipped it under her arm.

It felt awkward, and uncomfortable, but Edith agreed with the course of treatment. She had studied the appropriate treatment for bee stings when she had decided to harvest honey by herself. She should thank him for helping her.

He frowned. Once he was satisfied she was as comfortable as possible, he plopped down in a well-worn chair by the fireplace. "Pa, did you know Edie is taking the honey from the meadow?"

All the good feelings Edith had fostered for Grant soured. "Taking your honey? Do you think I'm stealing it?"

Grant looked at her as if she were the one who didn't know what was happening. "My grandfather put up those log gums, on our land. You're the one who told me that."

Mr. Oscar was trying so hard to say something that she feared he would have another stroke, so she rushed to explain. "Of course I know the log gums are on your land. I talked with your father about it, last winter." She didn't want to explain her reasons—her dreams—to this man who seemed determined to think poorly of her. She would approach it as she had with his father.

"I had researched the market price for honey. I asked if I could possibly have a discount if I harvested it myself. He insisted I take what he had already brought in for free. I refused." She smiled at the memory. Maybe the father and son had something in common—stubbornness. "We compromised. I agreed to take it for free, and he agreed to let me harvest it."

"And look how well that turned out. Your hand stung so badly you can't use it."

"You ran into me, as I remember, and knocked over the pail I was using to collect the honey, so all that work—and pain—was for nothing."

Grant's eyes narrowed. "I suppose you thought you could use all the honey this year since he's in no shape to harvest it himself."

What had happened to the young lad who always had a kind word for her, to make him so suspicious? "As a matter of fact, I intended to ask if he wanted me to bottle all of it and sell it at the farmers' market. Bringing him the money earned, of course."

Mr. Oscar nodded and banged his hand on the chair. Even Grant couldn't ignore his father's approval.

Grant tipped his head to the side, doing some kind of mental calculations. "What happened this morning is unfortunate. Give me a few minutes." He disappeared in the direction of the kitchen and returned with a picnic basket filled with jars of honey. "Hopefully this will replace the honey you hoped to gather today."

"It's too much—"

"Don't thank me yet. Use it wisely, because there won't be any more honey coming from that meadow."

"I'd be happy to pay, if that's the problem." The particular assortment of plants and flowers gave that honey—and therefore her baked goods—the best taste in the county. She intended to prove they were the best in the entire state at the Rutland Fair in September.

"Money isn't the issue." Grant shook his head. "We're going to plow it under and farm it."

"But what about the bees? The honey?" The answer to her question dangled there, but she didn't want to grasp it.

"There won't be any more honey after we harvest the last of it. It's time that field starting earning money."

"But you sell the honey. . . ." The more Edith sputtered, the redder Grant's face grew. He didn't care about the honey. He didn't care about the beautiful meadow, alive with sights and sounds and aromas.

"Who owns that meadow, Miss Grace?" Her name sounded like an expletive.

"God." The word came out of her mouth before she could call it back. "His name isn't on the deed, but He made it, perfect just the way it is."

Grant's mouth flapped open then he closed it and swallowed. "And I suppose you've left your property the way it was before the first settler came to Spruce Hill? Do you know there were no bees in America until Europeans brought them here?"

She hadn't known that. "I apologize. I had no right to say what I did." Now that she had humiliated herself, she wanted to get out of there as quickly as possible. "My hand is much better now. I'll go home." She looked at the basket brimming with honey. Oh, how she wanted to take it with her, but she didn't trust her arms to handle the weight. "I appreciate the gift, but I'll have to come back for it."

Mr. Oscar struggled to say something. Edith hugged him. "It's all right. Everything will work out."

She wanted to walk out of there without another word, but her upbringing demanded better of her. "Welcome home, Mr. Oscar. Your father is very glad to have you here." She unwrapped the towel and ice from her hand and laid them in the sink. "Thank you for taking care of me." She headed for the door. Was the man going to let her go without saying another word?

"Don't worry about it. I'll bring it to you." Grant wasn't ready to say good-bye. "I'd like to hear why this honey is so important to you."

She flicked a glance at his father and shrugged. "Will it make a difference?" Those soulful, gray-green eyes said more than her words. It mattered to her, a great deal. She crossed the porch and descended three steps. Once her feet landed on the ground, her back straightened and she turned around. Her eyes now more green than gray, she said, "If you bring the honey in the morning, you can stay for breakfast."

The way she moved, musical perfection in a female form, made him want to watch. He was as bad as a man on shore leave, ready to marry the first woman who looked at him kindly. He had withstood that temptation, but his years at sea had worn away his comfort in the presence of the opposite sex.

Something about Edie—Edith—Miss Grace—confounded him, at a time he could least afford any distractions. "Bother." He went inside and shut the door.

"No." When Pa shook his head, his whole body wobbled with it. He didn't like Grant's ideas for the farm, but they had to do something to save the only home his father had ever known.

"We're talking again tomorrow." Grant headed for the kitchen to fix lunch. If he gave every penny he had saved, they could postpone the inevitable. But they needed a long-term solution. And what about his own dreams? He didn't want to spend money on a farm that had been on the brink of financial ruin for most of his life. His father had the heart of an angel—that is, if an angel lived in a poorhouse because he gave everything away.

Including the honey. Grant would have to call on all the discipline he had developed in the navy to cope with neighbors who were taking advantage of a sick old man.

Even Miss Grace? Especially Miss Grace, if she was using the honey for her own gain.

Pa's head had fallen forward as he was sleeping. Grant brought a bowl of vegetable soup to his father's side, and his eyes fluttered open.

Grant pulled up a chair and guided his hand to his mouth. "I know you want Miss Grace to have the honey, as long as she wants it. You don't want to change a single thing." Grant looked out the window at the front lawn. The lilac bushes were a little more straggly than when Mama was alive, and the rosebushes should be dug up and thrown into a mulch pile. Things had already changed, and his father didn't see it.

"Work out." His father steepled his fingers together in prayer. "God."

Where was God in all of this? The question Dad raised all day and into the morning when Grant headed for the Grace farmhouse. The neighbors had pulled together to plant the crops after Dad's stroke, but the fields looked neglected. Weeds choked the edges, and everything needed irrigation. The farm would earn a smaller return than usual, and their medical expenses had risen. Was there an end in sight?

If he hadn't gone to the navy, would things have gotten this bad? Grant shook this head to clear those thoughts away. "What if" questions didn't matter. What if his younger brother hadn't drowned when he was ten years old? That's when he'd first become friends with young Edie. She missed Grant's brother as much as he did.

Ma, the perfect farmer's wife, died of grief a few years later, which helped push Grant out the door to the sea. Somehow Pa had lived past all that loss with a smile in his heart, even now with the stroke. That was Grant's one reason in trying to save the farm. Losing it might be the one loss his father couldn't survive.

He rounded the corner and found himself a few feet away from the front door to the Graces' home. He checked his appearance, making sure his shirt was properly tucked at the waist, ran a hand over his hair, and rubbed his smooth chin—why he would take all that trouble for a woman who had given him nothing but trouble yesterday, he didn't know.

Delightful smells wafted through the air, the scent of baked bread and spices and something else that was tantalizingly familiar. He was drawn to the house as certainly as Hansel and Gretel found the witch's gingerbread house.

Only his witch was a young woman with hair the color of red cedar and emeralds sparkling in her granite-colored eyes. She appeared on the doorstep. No wonder the children had succumbed to temptation.

Chapter 3

The look in Grant's eyes changed from contemplation to that of a befuddled lad, and Edith released a long breath. When she'd arrived home the previous evening, she had discussed the confrontation with her mother. She couldn't help it when Mother dressed the wounded hand.

"You catch more flies with honey than with vinegar." Mother said the words in perfect seriousness, although they both smiled. But neither mother nor daughter could contain their laughter. "In all seriousness, you are more likely to gain the young Mr. Oscar's favor if you are as sweet as the honey you crave than if you demand he honor the verbal agreement you had with his father."

A long string of "buts" had led to Edith's capitulation and to the care she had taken with her appearance this morning. She had exchanged yesterday's dress for a green calico with so many flowers that she might have plucked her skirt straight from the meadow. The green flattered her coloring. She might not have the beauty of a Gibson Girl, but she could turn a man's head when she tried.

And then Grant appeared. His years at sea had given him an extra swagger, something that would draw a woman's eyes.

She shook her head in an attempt to rid her mind of such foolishness and went outside. He waved a hand in greeting.

"Good morning, Mr. Oscar. I didn't expect to see you so early." She waved back with her bandaged hand then pulled it back. "You added more honey. That wasn't necessary."

"You planned to fill your pail. I want to be certain you have at least that much." He pulled a wagon full of mason jars, carefully packaged to prevent breakage. The number held far more honey than her single pail could have carried. The generosity of the gift brought tears to her eyes. She tucked a stray strand of hair behind her ear. "Once we get the jars inside, I have something for you as well."

He nodded. Before she blinked twice, he lifted the wagon and set it on the porch as if it weighed no more than a sack of potatoes. "I'll leave the wagon on the porch so it won't dirty up your floor, but now we don't have to climb up and down the stairs." Even with a jar in each hand and a third hugged to his chest, he still managed to open the door by himself.

Edith called after him. "The pantry is to the right of the kitchen."

"I remember." His voice floated back in her direction.

Edith picked up two jars. Grant had already returned. He hustled back and forth, finishing two trips to every one of hers. Of course, he probably had a thousand things planned for the day and wanted to take care of this business as quickly as possible.

Every time he walked through the kitchen, he passed by the dried-apple cake she had made as part of her honey-not-vinegar approach, but he paid no attention to it. She began to despair.

Soon they emptied the wagon, reaching the kitchen at the same time. Edith stopped in front of the door, blocking the exit. "I was hoping you would sit a spell and eat some of my dried-apple cake. I, um. . ." The words she meant to say flew out of her head while she stared at him, all muscled and manly, his stance commanding, probably a result of walking on a boat plowing through choppy waves.

He sat down and ended her quandary. "I smelled this as soon as I came into the yard. It's been teasing me every time I walked by."

Her cheeks warmed. She kept her back to him as she poured cups of coffee, grabbed two plates with cutlery and a sharp knife to cut the cake.

Since this was a new recipe, she had several questions about his reaction. The original recipe called for rum in the brown sugar icing, but they didn't keep spirits of any kind in the house. The adjustments she'd tried on the first batch left it grainy and thick, so she used her standard honey glaze on this batch.

She cut him a standard-sized slice. "Enjoy. You're welcome to eat as much as you want." She cut a similar-sized slice for herself and added a small pitcher of cream and another of honey on the table. "If you want regular sugar, let me know."

"I drink my coffee black." He glanced at the pitcher of honey, as if questioning its presence on the table.

"So do I." She nibbled on the cake. This latest batch turned out better than she'd expected, raising her hopes for the fair.

But what did Grant think? He took one bite, then a second, and a third. He ate it all without speaking or drinking his coffee. He crushed the last crumbs under his fork.

"Have another slice." Edith cut a larger slice and handed it to him. He could eat the entire cake, as far as she was concerned.

<hr>

Grant stared at his empty plate sheepishly. He hadn't devoured a sweet like that since he was a child and he almost choked on a cookie. "That was good." He rubbed his stomach to emphasize his point while his mind traced a rabbit trail. "I can't place the spice, but it seems familiar."

A satisfied look crossed Edie's face. "It should smell familiar. I made it with your honey. You're eating the meadow." She paused. "The crops you plant will taste good, but you can't get honey that tastes like this anywhere else in the world. Unique. Like all of God's creation."

The fork stopped midway to Grant's mouth. "The glaze."

"And in the cake as well. I only use a little cane sugar."

Grant took a larger bite. It settled on his tongue. He didn't know much about cooking. He and Pa managed okay, especially since the church ladies brought them meals at least once a week. "If I thought I could bake it myself, I'd ask you for the recipe."

Edie sat up straight in her chair. "Would you go so far as to say it's the best cake you've ever had?"

The question mattered to her, but he'd play along. "Well, I don't know, Edie." He loved the way his use of her old nickname made her cheeks turn pink. "I've tasted cakes all over the world."

Her shoulders slumped for a second then she straightened back up. "Perhaps I should ask if it's the best cake you've ever had in Vermont. Even in all of New England."

"America?"

Her backbone stiffened again. "Perhaps."

"Very well." He brought up a generous chunk of cake on his fork and took it in his mouth. He let it linger. It was definitely American, familiar flavors like cinnamon and apple, a distinctively American variety that made similar fruits the world over seem like imitations.

The cake was sweet and slightly sticky. "It does taste like the meadow."

Edie clapped her hands together. "So tell me. Is it good?"

"I'll take another bite to be sure." He had fun teasing her, drawing out this interaction. "The best in Spruce Hill, definitely, unless a new baker has moved to town since I left." He ate a third bite. "The best in Vermont? I've eaten at the best restaurants in Montpelier and across New England. I've never tasted an apple cake to match this one."

She jumped up and covered her face with her hands, laughing gleefully.

"But I had an apple cake in Washington State that might give it a run for its money." He gobbled down the rest of the slice and reached for the knife. "I need another slice to make up my mind."

Edie laughed. "You can eat the whole cake if you want to. I may have to meet the lady in Washington State at some point in the future. If they ever hold a national fair." She picked up a jar of honey from the pantry. "I intend to sweep the baking competition at the Rutland State Fair so I can raise the money to start my own business. And honey from the Oscar farm is going to get me there."

Her posture, her voice, could have come from a boat's captain rousing the ship's crew to battle. Perhaps she should be a politician and not a baker. Then again, with her spirit, she'd run a successful bakery.

He wished he could let her have all the honey she wanted. She had spunk, and he admired spunk. But his family's needs came first. "Look. I don't know how much honey you need. I hope you have enough for the fair and beyond." With all the pint jars in her pantry, she shouldn't run out any time soon. "And of course, once we harvest the rest of the honey, before we plow the field under, you are welcome to purchase the rest."

"That is your right, of course." She took the cake plate from the table and wrapped it loosely in a towel. "Make sure your father gets a slice. He's said it takes him to the meadow in his dreams." After standing uncertainly for a moment, she sat back down. Her fingers trembled where she held the coffee cup. After a bite of cake, a smile had replaced her tears. "I'd love to hear tales of your days at sea."

Her smile might be a mask, but he applauded her courage. "I joined the navy to see the world. The world turned out to be weeks on the open sea, with nothing in sight but water, water, everywhere. I did see many interesting sights." His stops at ports around the world had mostly reminded him of the need for the Gospel, both in places that had never heard and places with churches over a thousand years old. He hungered to share the Gospel with them.

Only now he was back in Spruce Hill, farming. Edie wasn't the only person whose dreams were in danger.

Chapter 4

A week had passed since Grant had tasted Edith's apple cake with a honey glaze and declared it the best he'd eaten. That fact made Edith ridiculously pleased and afraid at the same time. Because just as surely as he liked her cake, he intended to destroy the source of her honey. Something was driving him to destroy the meadow, God's masterpiece of color and sound and taste.

Edith wanted the meadow to stay the way it was. Too much was changing in 1896. Every day something new was invented that every American wanted. Why, just in her lifetime, look at the telephone, electric lightbulbs, cars that ran without horses, and even pictures that flickered on a screen like real life. The next century, less than four years away, was bound to have more changes to come.

Maybe they would have better ovens to cook with. They might even come up with a way to bake that didn't involve measuring ingredients and all the little touches that made her cakes unique. That would be unfortunate.

Taking the meadow away would be another change for the worse. How could she change Grant's mind when she hadn't seen him once in the past week, not even at church? Maybe he had stopped attending while he was away.

Instead of worrying, she busied herself in the kitchen, testing recipe after recipe, adjusting for honey instead of sugar. Today marked her third attempt to use honey in sugar cookies.

"I should just give up." Edith sat by the table, resting her elbows on the flour-covered surface, her face on her hands.

"I heard that." Mama pulled up a chair next to Edith and put an arm over her shoulders. "You might have better luck making a molasses cookie."

"I already did that," Edith mumbled between her fingers. "What's the point? Sooner or later I'm going to run out of honey. Sooner or later everything's going to change. And I'll be an old lady stuck in the past, who couldn't succeed at the one thing she wanted." *And who couldn't find love*, but she wouldn't say that out loud.

Her mother stood. "Get out of that chair and take off that apron. Dust yourself off. It's time you get out of this kitchen."

Edith didn't want to move, but she didn't want to mix any more ingredients either. She dusted herself off as much as she could. Hopeless. She'd better not run into anyone after they left the house. "You're not taking me to town, are you?"

"No. We're just going for a stroll." After they filled a couple of canteens, they headed for the family cemetery, where their ancestors were buried. The land had belonged to Mama's family, and she had inherited it as the only child of her parents' old age, just as

Edith was her parents' only child. She'd like three or four children herself. Sniffling, she drew her still-floured hand across her nose. There she went with her foolish dreams again.

They stopped along the way, picking flowers that might have been there when her ancestor received the land from the Crown for service in the French and Indian War. The latch squealed a little as they went. "We've been coming here all my life." The fence was a recent addition, when Papa put it in a few years ago. Edith headed for the same grave she went to every time, a pair of twins who had died at birth, and placed the tiny Queen Anne's lace at their tombstone. Her family had replaced the original crosses with small headstones. There weren't that many graves for one hundred twenty-five years of family history. She pulled away the encroaching grass, showing that someone remembered.

Mama placed her flowers by the earliest grave, the first wife of the first settler. "You know, Edith, this place that is so special to us was once a forest, thick as those bees who make all your honey. And there were no paths to mark the way. Even a trip to get water meant danger."

Edith knew the story. That first wife had fallen in the river on a cold winter's night and died from fever.

"Close your eyes and imagine this place like it was back then."

Edith stretched the tendrils of her mind to the past, to stories she had heard.

"My grandmother spoke to me of days spent clearing trees and burning the stumps and how hard it was to plant even a small garden. But they did it, because that was their dream." Edith felt her mother's eyes on her. "I expect the Abenaki who used to live in these forests were upset with the change."

Edith opened her eyes, taking in the acres growing gleefully by the grace of the sunshine and water God provided. "And someone brought the bees."

"Ah, yes, and helped spread flower seeds. Especially after our two families decided to leave that meadow untouched, to separate our farms and to enjoy the land together."

Was her mother saying the meadow belonged to both families?

"It's time you get to know the property that will be yours one day. Years ago, fathers used to take the boys along the boundaries, pounding on rocks along the way, memorizing the land that belonged to them. Nowadays we look at a piece of paper and numbers, but nothing beats walking it." Mama opened the gate.

"Let's start today. Head to that meadow you prize so much. And remind yourself what the changes meant to this family."

———— ⚫ ————

Smoke had driven bees out of the first log gum, giving Grant access to their private treasure. The protective veil made clear vision impossible, and the super dripping with honey was heavy. He couldn't imagine how the petite Edie had managed on her own. But she had, until he knocked her over, and the pail with her.

He had spent the past week checking the status of the crops already growing. Work he'd expected to take two days took four instead. After that, he checked if any crops planted in early August could grow before frost set in. In some parts of the country, they could grow two crops a year. Not here, and certainly not in August.

On Sunday he'd taken time to slip into church during the hymn singing and left during the pastor's final prayer, not wanting to get caught up in conversation. Or to run into Edie again and struggle with guilt over making her dream so much harder to accomplish.

The task of harvesting the honey, which he had expected to take a day, was moving as slowly as everything else this past week. So far he had filled a gallon and a half from this single super, and he might finish another one before lunch. He replaced the super on top of the log and headed for a stump by the side of the field to rest for a minute.

"Yoo-hoo! Mr. Oscar." An unrecognizable lady's voice penetrated his headgear, but he didn't dare take it off this close to the bees.

It wasn't Edie. He would recognize her voice anywhere, unlike the hundreds of men and women he had met around the world. "Mrs. Grace?" He hazarded.

"Yes."

"Where are you?"

"Five yards north. Maybe ten west."

He thought that's what she said. He walked north, stopped. "Do I turn here?"

"Yes."

Did he dare take the bonnet off yet? No bees buzzed around his head. The memory of the bees who fed on Edie's hand sprang to mind.

"You're here."

Grant removed his headgear. Edie had come, with her mother. "Good day, Mrs. Grace. Ed—Miss Grace." Her nickname kept wanting to escape his tongue, but she deserved better. "How lovely to see you again." Even as he welcomed them, he wondered what they wanted. One more thing to slow down his progress on the day that was already stretched too thin.

"You look parched," Edie said. The name suited her, suited her voice. Full, strong, yet sweet and comfortable. She handed him a canteen. "We brought two."

"Thanks." He poured a generous portion into his mouth, let it swish around, and swallowed. "Will you need any more honey? I expect to finish harvesting this by—" When? "—tomorrow, I hope. Should I set aside any of it for you?"

Edie and her mother looked at each other. "Before we talk about the honey, we have another issue to discuss with you. We were going to come by later, but since you're already here. . ." Edie took a deep breath. "I just learned part of this meadow belongs to my mother."

What? "This meadow has always been Oscar land. Everyone knows that."

Mrs. Grace shook her head. "We'll have to get a surveyor to determine the exact boundary line—"

A surveyor?

"—but my parents said the two families kept the meadow as a buffer between them, where they could meet or enjoy the peace of nature. It's only a few square feet of the total acreage after all. When the bees came, that was an additional blessing. We were happy to let your family have the honey, since they set up the equipment." Her facial expression turned serious. "But, yes, part of the land belongs to me."

Grant's temples pounded, and he felt light-headed. This meadow might not belong to his family? His one last slender hope shredded. He closed his eyes and fought for control.

"Are you all right, Grant?"

Grant locked on to the granite in Edie's eyes like solid rocks to support him. "If that's true, why have I never heard about it?"

Her eyes remained a steady gray, only a few flecks of green. "I never heard about it until today either. I can't say I'm sorry about having a say about what happens to the meadow." A small smile played around her lips, but she suppressed it. The green flecks flashing in her eyes suggested her feelings were stronger than her words. "But I do regret that it came out now. I know you are seeking to do the best for your father and your family's future."

What future? He almost blurted the words out but caught himself in time. They walked such a thin line of losing the land. In the depths of Grant's heart, he knew his father needed to remain on his land in order to recover.

But Grant had learned one thing from his years in the navy. Never show weakness, whether to an enemy or to those in your command. "I will have to verify what you are saying."

Edie nodded, but her mother spoke up. "The county clerk's office has the record of the property lines. But as far as the meadow goes, the decision to leave it fallow was no more than a verbal agreement."

Edie cocked her head at Grant, her eyes shading toward a pine green. "Whatever is done with the meadow must rise not only out of what is legal but what is right." Her injured hand was clenched at her side, as if prepared to do battle.

Chapter 5

A week later, the Graces prepared to meet with Grant and the land surveyor to determine exactly where the boundary line stood. If the Lord saw fit, the log gums would stand on Edie's side of the boundary line. She glanced at her bee bonnet, wondering if she should bring it with her in case walking the property involved getting close to the bees.

If only Mr. Oscar could come to the meeting. If he knew about the common property, it explained his willingness to give her the honey. Grant was a different matter altogether. When they spoke last week, he stood as if at attention, a man used to getting his way. Even though he was of average height, his demeanor commanded respect. But underneath that solid exterior, she sensed fear. His father's health? Something more?

"Are you ready, dear?" Her mother called up the stairs.

"Coming." Edie brought the bee bonnet, in case one of her parents wanted it. She trotted downstairs. "Thank you again for letting me accompany you."

Her mother looked her up and down and smiled, as if aware of the extra pains Edith had taken with her appearance. "Of course, you must. It's your inheritance. In the same way Grant Junior must take part. We don't want a shadow of uncertainty hanging over the next generation."

Her expression indicated she wanted to say more.

"What is it? I will listen, even if I disagree." Edith might still live at home, but she was no longer a child and would decide for herself.

Her mother looked away. "Wait until your father gets here."

Papa came upon them and looked from mother to daughter. "Tell me what's going on."

Mama sent a pleading look at Papa. "We've often talked about the serendipity of our farm sharing a boundary with the Oscar farm, and the closeness you and Grant shared when you were younger. Look at the way he calls you Edie. You hate it when anyone else uses that nickname, but your face goes all pink when he says it."

Edith squirmed. She remembered those days of near hero worship, which only deepened when Grant joined the navy. But now she had put away childish things. Were her parents hinting at something more?

"Grant Junior is a fine young man, a lot like his father. What a blessing of the Lord. We have often wondered, hoped even, that the two of you might find happiness with each other." Her father beamed at her, as if he had just given her pure gold.

Edith nearly collapsed. How dare her parents try to play matchmaker for her? Did they think she needed the dowry of her land to be an acceptable bride for Grant or anyone else? She drew on her training in discipline. "I wish to be known as the best baker in

New England. I hope to start a business that will provide an income independent of the farm. Marriage would interfere with the dream I believe God gave me."

Her parents exchanged looks, and her mother spoke for both of them. "But, my dear, you see, marriage to the right man will only make your success sweeter. And turning your back on love will make you sour and bitter, no matter how sweet your baked goods taste."

Edith chose not to answer. The truth behind their words stung her heart. She did want more. Success, a business—yes, even love. Once she had dreamed of Grant, when she was but a girl and he was so handsome in his uniform. But she had grown up and couldn't see a future with the man who saw only dollar signs in the meadow.

But wasn't she just as bad? She loved the meadow and wanted it to stay unchanged. But she also wanted its honey, for her business to succeed. How was that different from Grant's objective?

It would take the wisdom God gave Solomon to figure it all out. While people said God worked in His own time, she had a deadline. For her to succeed in the baking business, she needed the recognition of winning a blue ribbon at the state fair. But what good would winning do if she couldn't replicate the flavors because she no longer had the honey?

Did Grant have some need, some urgency, to plow under the meadow, something that drove him the way the fair, and all the opportunities it represented, drove her? If so, he should speak up. Maybe he would today.

Edith tuned back in to her parents' conversation. "It is unfortunate that Mr. Oscar can't come today. The land belongs to him, and he is still of sound mind, from what I've heard."

He was, which made Grant's decisions all the more perplexing. Maybe they had discussed it, and only her wishful thinking implied Mr. Oscar Sr. would never agree to farm the meadow.

"The surveyor is here already." Mama pointed to Mr. Nelson waiting at the boundary stone.

"And there comes Grant," Papa said. The wagon he drove trundled over the ground.

<hr />

Grant looked over his shoulder. "Are you doing okay back there, Pa?"

"Yes."

He could imagine a wide smile on his father's face. This was the first time Pa had left the house since Grant had returned home. "I'm glad you could come today."

"Thanks." Pa's speech was still unclear, but he could usually make his intent understood. Lately it had improved, and Grant hoped he could make himself understood today.

When Grant had told him about the boundary line running through the meadow, he'd nodded his head in violent agreement. Perhaps that fact lay behind his father's reluctance to plow under the meadow to begin with, but he couldn't communicate it clearly.

The Graces approached from the opposite direction, although Edie had separated from her parents. Her carriage, her confidence, her beauty, took his breath away.

When he'd joined the navy nine years ago, she'd shown signs of the beauty now in full bloom. On his last visit home, Pa had hinted at romance between the two. Grant had scoffed at the idea of marriage to anyone. Now that he was destined to settle down, the idea no longer seemed ridiculous.

Was there any chance Edie felt the same way? Had she remained unmarried because she was pining for him? He shook his head. Foolishness.

Mr. Nelson, the surveyor who would decide the fate of the land, waited for them at the boundary rock. Grant got his father settled in his chair on the ground. Their roles had reversed. The child who once looked up to the father could now pick up the shrunken man as easily as a schoolchild.

Edie dashed forward. She flicked a smile in Grant's direction but bent down on one knee in front of his father. "Mr. Oscar, how delightful to see you here today! I wasn't expecting such a pleasure." She lifted a hand to touch his cheek, and Grant's father slowly lifted his hand to place over hers, leathery fingers over delicate white skin. "Edie—"

"Yes, Mr. Oscar. It's Edie."

She didn't mind her nickname when his father used it.

"I wish we had talked about this"—she flung her free hand in an arc, indicating the field surrounding them—"before now. But I've been praying that we find a solution to the questions plaguing us today."

Grant's father nodded.

"Is everyone here?" Mr. Nelson's high-pitched, nasally voice made it hard to take him seriously.

When everyone agreed, he said, "Let's get started."

All chatter ceased as five faces turned in his direction.

He pulled a piece of paper from a leather packet and put on a pair of wire-rimmed glasses. "I was able to find the original land grants from the Crown to Mr. Oscar and Mr. Putnam—that's Mrs. Grace's grandfather—for their service in what we now call the French and Indian War." He cackled to himself. "Did you know that our first president was once a surveyor? Just think if he had surveyed this land. However, I believe he performed that service on the Ohio."

If the original document had been done by George Washington, that would solve all their financial problems in a heartbeat. It would fetch a pretty penny at auction.

"The good news is that the description of the boundaries—the western boundary of the Oscar land and the eastern boundary of the Putnam claim—match. There is no question about where the boundary lies. So let me start with the first point of reference."

Grant held his breath. If the boundary followed a straight line, the starting point would reflect how the meadow was divided.

Nelson took out a compass and paced until he found the right spot. "We are standing at the northern end of the boundary line." He smiled. "Or we would be, if that big rock wasn't in the way."

"Boundary rock," Edie said.

Her words echoed Grant's thoughts. He looked right and left. The rock lay slightly past the halfway point. If the boundary followed a straight line, his family owned close to two-thirds of the meadow. He relaxed a smidgen. The log gums almost straddled the line.

"If you, sir—Mr. Oscar Junior—will walk twenty paces south, measuring with this chain."

Grant walked forward the required distance. He passed two hives to the north—on

Grace's side of the boundary land. Mr. Nelson checked his notes. "You've reached the second coordinate given on the description."

That suggested the boundary was going to change direction.

"Now turn to the north—your right. Walk fifteen paces with the chain."

Grant planted a rock on the chain to keep it from moving and turned north. After a couple of steps, he hesitated. Fifteen paces would place him uncomfortably close to the third log gum.

Edie joined him where he stood. "Would you like some company?"

He glanced at her hand, which had returned to normal, and praised her silently for her courage. "I would appreciate it." They continued pacing to fifteen, which took them less than a yard past the hive. Standing still at this spot was uncomfortable, with bees buzzing around and behind them. One of them landed on Edie's head. He reached for her hand, and she allowed it. The slight tremor in her hand didn't relax until Mr. Nelson verified the spot.

From the third hive they moved twenty paces to the south, passing two more log gums before Mr. Nelson called for them to turn west again. So far that made two log gums on Grace land and three on Oscar land.

The boundary returned to the original line and passed the sixth and final bee log gum.

The beehives were split evenly, three for each family. Had whoever set up the contraptions originally done that on purpose?

Edie looked at Grant and smiled. "Oh dear. It seems the Lord intends for us to find a compromise, since He split the honey between us."

"And since you will keep your log gums, how can I use that parcel of land for farming? The bees don't respect boundaries." He tried to frown, but his mouth refused to cooperate. "God must have a sense of humor."

Chapter 6

Three log gums stood on Grace land. Edith couldn't stop smiling. That should supply all the honey she needed for as long as she needed it. Would the Oscars object if she moved the remaining log gums to her side of the boundary? They shouldn't mind, since Grant had planned on destroying them all when he plowed the land under. Would the smaller parcel produce as much honey?

When Edith glanced at Grant, she knew he wasn't pleased. He didn't own all the land he thought was his all along, but the Oscars still had the larger portion of the parcel, and the thorny issue about the honey could be easily resolved.

"What's troubling you, Grant?" She spoke quietly so only he could hear her.

He ground his teeth together, which informed her more certainly than anything else that the result hadn't pleased him. "I should be laughing. God's played a pretty trick on me."

A puzzled frown replaced her smile. "What more could you want? I have plenty of honey, and you have most of the land to farm." A thought struck her. "Or did you hope that the shared meadow was a tall tale and you did own all the land after all? Perhaps we ought to put up a fence so that our grandchildren don't make the same mistake a hundred years from now."

His face went red at the same time she realized what she had said. If they had grandchildren together—she wouldn't allow her mind to go in that direction. She would rather be a spinster than marry a man so they could join their farms together.

"You don't know anything."

She barely understood his words, the way his mouth hardly moved, his jaw shut tighter than a sealed can of peaches. "Then explain it to me. We're friends. At least we used to be, and I am very fond of your father. I would never do anything to harm either one of you. But I don't understand what difference a few square feet of farmland can make."

She needed to calm down. The meadow had been her sanctuary for years, a place she could come and commune with the God who created it all. She breathed in and out. Bees flew around their heads and hands. How beautiful the creatures were, the furry black and yellow stripes dancing around the black center and yellow petals of the sunflower.

"You wouldn't understand." Grant repeated his answer and walked in the direction of their parents. He wouldn't let things rest until they resolved the situation.

Picking a sunflower, she pressed it to her face and breathed in the sweet smell before twirling the flower between her fingers. She started pulling off the petals. *He loves me. He loves me not. He loves me.* The final petal said "He loves me." Edith looked toward heaven.

"You love me. I already knew that. But is there someone else?" She looked at Grant and shook her head.

Her mother was smiling, apparently as happy with the outcome as Edith was herself. Papa was paying Mr. Nelson for his services. Edith looked behind them and saw the posts wavering in the wind. They would need to get them firmly planted so no one—that is, Grant—could question the boundary markings.

Grant was on his knees, talking with his father face-to-face. That showed a good side to him. Mr. Oscar was shaking his head, as if he disagreed with something his son had said.

Grant moved closer, his knees almost touching his father's. Did Mr. Oscar feel intimidated? Not that Grant was doing it on purpose. She decided to join them. What harm could it do? She walked to the wagon and gave Mr. Oscar a quick hug.

"Honey yours." He smiled at her.

"Half of it is, at least. And that's probably as much as I need." She stood to face Grant. "Do you want to secure the boundary posts, or shall I? Or perhaps you want something more permanent—like a fence?"

Mr. Oscar shook his head, and even Grant had the grace to blush. "We could do it together." Grant's mouth quirked into a crooked grin. She blinked, taken aback at the humor. "And no, I don't want a fence. We'll find another solution."

"Leave alone." Mr. Oscar pounded the ground with his cane. "God's way."

Her parents interrupted. "Now we know how the property is divided, we all need time to think about what we've learned. Then we can iron out any problems together. Shall we come to your house in a week?"

"Two days," Grant said.

Edith's eyebrows raised. *Why so fast?*

"We'll be there on Friday, then." Mama made arrangements for a picnic lunch. "Are you ready to head home?" she asked Edith.

Edith wanted a few minutes alone with Grant, to see if he would open up to her, but Mr. Oscar needed to get back home. "If you have time this afternoon, why don't we both work on fixing the poles? We can make quick work of it."

Grant opened his mouth, and she feared his refusal. "That sounds wise. Two o'clock?"

"I'll see you then." Edith followed her parents, dropping the stripped flower.

⁃⁃⁃⁃⁃●◦●⁃⁃⁃⁃

Grant picked up the sunflower and stared at its brown center. Pulling the petals seemed so unlike her. It reminded him of the child's game to determine a boy's interest. For a second, he hoped that's what she had done and what the answer was.

"Edie like you." Pa pointed to the flower.

Grant shook his head. "She thinks I'm crazy to plow the meadow." He picked up his father and settled him in the back of the wagon.

"You are." Grant felt the cackle against his chest. He secured the chair so it wouldn't roll off the wagon and wiped a weary hand over his forehead. "I'm not going to argue with you about it today. Let's ask God for an answer neither one of us has come up with yet."

Maybe he should ask Edie. That one was full of ideas and wasn't afraid to speak her mind.

When they reached the house, Grant again lifted his father. Pa was so worn out, he couldn't lace his arms around his son's neck, making it harder to carry him. Grant himself was tired by the time they settled inside the house. "I could use a cup of tea with honey right about now." He might as well enjoy it as long as he had it.

The answering smile on Pa's face decided the matter. While the tea was brewing, Grant threw together ham sandwiches and drew a couple of pickles from a jar.

The honey tempted him to run his finger around the rim of the bottle after he sweetened his tea. The first cup went down so quickly that it almost burned his throat, but the smooth honey eased the pain.

After lunch, Grant settled Pa in his favorite chair by the front window for his afternoon nap. Grant went over the account books again, checking for a loophole he had missed the first three times he had looked. Pa hadn't kept business and household expenses separate, so Grant couldn't tell for certain what had created the debt. Back in 1893, during the bank crisis, Grant found a few entries that suggested his father had helped his neighbors out. The numbers were listed without names. That was Pa, generous without protecting his future. He'd probably say that was God's job.

Grant glanced at his father. If he asked, Pa might refuse to answer. And would Grant understand the names, with his garbled speech?

The day's mail contained mixed news. One request for payment had been returned, the client having moved without a forwarding address. Grant's temples pounded while he checked the balance in the account book. Fifteen dollars. The amount wasn't ruinous, but every extra penny mattered.

On the other hand, another envelope revealed payment in full for one of the larger accounts.

Unfortunately, unpaid accounts outnumbered the paid accounts. For businesses affected by the bank crisis, Pa had either written off the debt or continued to carry it. Not only so, he continued to sell to them, long past the point of financial sense. He didn't seem to understand that he couldn't feed anyone if he didn't keep the farm.

If Grant had been home, he might have seen the danger signs earlier. If he had been home, he could have eased the workload his father carried and perhaps prevented his stroke. If only. He couldn't change the past, and he had asked God's forgiveness. He still felt the daily panic, and he lashed out at the closest person. Even Pa, which made Grant even angrier at himself.

And also at Miss Edie Grace, who with her winning attitude and determination represented all the things the Oscar farm needed. Pa was right. She'd make someone a fine wife, a fine farm wife, and she was pretty, smart, a believer—everything a man could want. But while she might love Grant Oscar Sr., she had made it clear how she felt about the junior version.

Maybe today when they pounded in the poles, he could help rectify that.

The final piece of mail was a circular that Grant dangled over the trash can until the headline caught his eye. FIFTY-DOLLAR CASH PRIZE FOR BEST VERMONT-MADE PRODUCT in celebration of the 50th annual Rutland State Fair. Other cash prizes promised for the best in produce, animal husbandry, and housewifely arts.

Grant rapped his fingers on the desk. Most of this year's crop was average at best, given the intermittent care. But if the honey was as good as Edie claimed it was, maybe, just maybe, they had a product to enter into the fair. If it won, he could sell the honey at a heightened price.

Suddenly he wished he had all six hives instead of the three that he had once vowed to plow under.

The flyer gave details about the various competitions and what products belonged in which category. He'd have to give that some thought. And he'd have to learn quickly how to transform honey from the comb to the honey found in a jar.

On the opposite side of the flyer he found a list of amusements, as well as the always popular pulling contests. He ran his finger down the list. Yes, there was a strength contest for men. Not lifting weights, but pulling loaded wagons, the yoke across his neck instead of his faithful oxen's. Did the contest offer prize money? Yes. Not as much as the unique Vermont product, but every penny would help.

He shook his head. Not if he injured himself.

Before he left to join Edie in the meadow, he gathered supplies and checked on his father. A part of him wanted a fence, craved that precise definition, like the markings on a uniform indicated rank. The same way he wished his father kept better accounts.

At least this path, leading from his house to the meadow, followed a well-defined pattern. They had crossed from house to house often enough to wear the grass down.

"We shall come rejoicing, bringing in the sheaves." Edie was singing at the top of her voice, as she sometimes did when working outdoors. He chuckled. Did the irony of the words strike her the same way it did him? She wouldn't be pleased if he grew sheaves in her fair meadow.

At the edge of the meadow, he admired her from a distance. The ribbons on her hat fluttered in the breeze. As she raised her arm to hammer the wooden post, her form was alluring. If the fair gave a prize for feminine beauty, she would win.

The fair's strongest man and loveliest lady—some would say they were made for each other. If only Edie could agree.

Chapter 7

"Edie!"

At the sound of Grant's voice, Edie smiled. She hoped he couldn't see how widely her mouth stretched or the heat that entered her face as soon as she heard his voice. Instead, she pounded the hammer once more to give herself a chance to cool down.

When she straightened, he stood less than a yard away from her, and she knew he had seen every expression on her face, just as she could see a simmering excitement in him. Did she dare hope she was the reason?

He took another two steps forward, and she smelled the mixture of masculine cologne and sunshine that she had come to expect from him. "My name is Edith." She said it more to put some emotional distance between them than because she disliked the nickname.

He shook his head. "Edith is the name of a schoolteacher or a heroine in a play or maybe a ticket taker at a theater." He pointed a finger at her before continuing. "You are Edie, all sunshine and summer and happiness, no matter what the time of year is."

That statement doubled the heat in her cheeks. "While Grant is the name of a United States president who won the Civil War, saved the Union, and freed the slaves. Very appropriate for a man who chose to join the service."

"He led the army, not the navy." Smiling, Grant shrugged. "But today I am the Grant whose ancestor received a land grant from King George."

She giggled.

He opened his toolbox and checked the post she had hammered into the ground, ringed with stones wedged to keep it in place. He nodded as if to say "well done" before walking two feet farther down the property line.

Their silly exchange about their names reminded her of more carefree times when they were friends and he would laugh at her jokes, even though the girlish thoughts of a fifteen-year-old must have struck him as foolish. But he had never made her feel foolish. He took her seriously. Which is why she had expected him to understand her desire to succeed at the state fair.

His hammer pounded the wood, the muscles in his arm outlined under his skin as he drove it into the ground. He could finish the job in half the time without her and do it better. Did he want her company? Another short burst of heat tickled her neck.

While he worked, he began whistling a song she didn't recognize. The melody and rhythm reminded her of the sea. She had only seen the Atlantic once, when they had taken a week's trip to Old Orchard Beach in Maine. The rhythm of the waves pounding the sand, the white sails skimming across the water were imprinted on her mind.

She made a notch in her post and slid the thick twine into it before tying it in place and walking in a straight line to Grant. It wouldn't hurt to treat Grant like a friend and not like an opponent. "I like that song. Is it one you learned in the navy?"

He flashed white teeth in a smile. "Life aboard a ship can get tedious, and music helps keep us focused. Although I'd rather not repeat the words in the presence of a lady."

"Grant." She laughed, slightly scandalized.

He shrugged. "I once heard that the melody to 'A Mighty Fortress Is Our God'—you know, Martin Luther's song?—was bar music." He banged the post one last time. "This one's ready for your rope."

He watched as she cut a notch in the post and secured the rope. "I got a notice about the Rutland State Fair today."

She tightened the rope. "I didn't think you were interested in the fair. Do you plan on going?"

"I believe I will. I may even enter one of the contests." He took the paper from his back pocket and handed it over. "Because it's the fiftieth anniversary of the fair, they are offering fifty dollars for the best Vermont-based product. If my honey is as good as you say it is, maybe it could win."

Talk about a surprise. "That's a good idea." But fifty dollars for the best Vermont-based product? The thought buzzed around Edith's head as loudly as a bee. If she could win the baking contests and convince them of the seriousness of her business plan—if she won, she could open her business right away.

Grant had already moved to the next post. And now he intended to enter his honey. She pulled the rope tightly as she walked to him. "If we both entered honey from our side of the boundary line, I wonder if they would taste the same."

The hammer came down on his thumb, and he bit back what might have been a curse word. "You wouldn't."

"Of course not. Even though they might taste different, depending on how the raw honey is processed." She lifted her chin. "But I will enter baked goods from Edith Grace's bakery, and they might win."

He was holding his hand, and she felt bad for worrying about the fair. "Let me see that."

When he held it out, she could see a large bruise forming on his thumb. "That's nasty. You might lose your fingernail."

"It's happened before." He pulled a canteen from his toolbox and took a swig. "Why do you want to open a bakery? Do you plan on leaving the farm?"

Because she didn't plan to wait for some man to rescue her from spinsterhood, and she wanted to do something besides help her mother around the farm. "Because I'm a good baker, and I believe people will want to buy what I make. I'd like to start small, with a shop in town, perhaps, but I would like to see the day when my pastries are served in restaurants all throughout New England." She sighed. "Fifty dollars would go a long way toward getting me started."

Of course Edie wanted to win the money, to start a business. Sitting at home had never satisfied her. She needed a passel of little ones to keep her busy. Why hadn't she married?

Were the bachelors of Spruce Hill blind to her beauty and sweet nature? She didn't just want a career like teaching; she wanted a business. And he couldn't deny she made the best baked goods he had ever tasted.

Why did he ever think he could win? He couldn't even pound in a post without ruining his thumb. He pressed on it. It didn't hurt, much. He could finish the job.

Edie had already tied the rope and headed for the first spot where the boundary turned north. Kneeling down, she dug in the earth with a spade. He couldn't blame her for wanting to win. He admired her for it. Of course, it was possible neither one of them would win.

She finished with the hole and stood. "It should be ready for you." She looked at the ground, a light pink dusting her cheeks. "I decided it was foolish for me to pound in the posts when you do it so much better than I do." She glanced at his hand, where his thumb had begun to swell. "Unless you're injured."

"I'm okay." With that, he stuck the pointed end of the post in the ground and aimed the first blow on the top. Edie watched until he finished the job, then took over with tying the rope. "I've decided it's okay if you call me Edie. What you said was so sweet."

"It's true." His voice sounded gruff, and he cleared his throat. "You're also graceful, so your name suits you marvelously."

"If you keep saying things like that, people may think you are courting me." She flickered eyelashes at him, the green in her eyes dancing like fireflies.

Would that be so terrible? The words trembled on his tongue, but he caught them in time. Sooner or later, she would learn about the perilous state of the farm and might think his primary interest was financial so they could join their farms. "As long as we remain friends, who cares what people say?"

The green light in her eyes died. "Your father was afraid you might come home with some foreigner for a bride." Although she said it as a sentence, he could hear the implied question.

"I never met that one. Never had time to get to know anyone. I'm hoping I might find someone, now that I'm home." Let her puzzle that out. Was he talking about her, or not?

Instead, she appeared to ignore that statement. She finished tying the knot and walked halfway to the next corner, which left her only a few feet away from the beehives. "Are you still planning on plowing your side of the meadow under?"

"I haven't decided." Which was the truth. "There's a lot of things to fix around the farm. I'm starting to think I should get everything in working order before I decide what to do with the meadow." No matter which way he put his mind around the problem, he couldn't find a way to make quick money. He pounded his frustration about the situation into the post, and his thumb throbbed in protest.

"What does the doctor say about your father?" Edie tightened the strings of her hat and stepped a few feet farther away from the bees. "I'm the one who found him after his stroke. I was scared you would be coming home to a funeral."

Grant shook his head. "It's day to day. I should spend more time with him, working with him each day."

"You're doing so much. Don't blame yourself."

"I should be able to do more. I have to do more." He didn't want her pity. Platitudes designed to make him feel better boomeranged, heaping an extra helping of guilt on his back.

As soon as he finished the post, she claimed it with her busy hands. "You can't do it all yourself—run the farm, make improvements, help your father. We haven't been over there since you came home, in case you'd think we were interfering, and we heard you let Mrs. Phillips go. You know if you ever need help—"

"I only need to ask. I know." The problem was, what they needed most was cold, hard cash. And Grant Oscar wasn't a beggar. Neither one of them was.

They turned their backs on the hive and headed for the corner, the bees leaving them alone. "Are you scared that the bees will want a second helping after what happened the last time?" One of the critters chose that moment to leave his stinger in Grant's sore thumb.

He dropped the hammer, which landed between them, the wooden handle tapping the toe of his boot. The post tilted sideways, and he grabbed for it. It pushed against his thumb before it reached the ground. He wrapped his knuckles over the throbbing joint and stopped the pretense of working.

Edie had already moved away from the log gums, in the direction of his house. "Get away, before they bother you again."

He picked up the hammer with his left hand and placed it in the toolbox without further mishaps. "I can't even pound a few posts in the ground without making a mess of things."

"When you were in the navy, you didn't have to pound posts into the water." Edie kept a straight face as she said the words.

His aching thumb cut his laughter short. "You're right. Anchors drop through the sea, eager to reach the end of the rope." He cast about for another topic to occupy his mind. "Would you mind showing me how to get the raw honey ready for human consumption?"

Green glowed like question marks in her eyes. "It's the least I can do after everything you've done out there." They reached the lawn in front of the house. "But when we go to the fair, I intend to use every means at my disposal. I want that grand prize."

"I wouldn't have it any other way." Grant grinned. "May the best man—"

"—or woman—" Edie said.

"—win." Grant offered his right hand, his thumb still throbbing, for a handshake. Edie pressed back, strongly. She would be a formidable opponent.

Chapter 8

Whether or not Grant wanted help, Edith wouldn't leave them to manage the house on their own. Before he returned home, she had spent time daily with Mr. Oscar, fixing him meals, helping him eat when needed, encouraging him to talk. At first she had to beg him to get out of bed.

Grant's homecoming had perked up his father's spirits tremendously, but he still enjoyed her company. How could she stay home, knowing Mr. Oscar was sitting in his chair, waiting for her visit? She hoped she helped him—his speech had improved slightly—but the blessing she received far outweighed the price. She didn't think she would be so content in his situation.

Especially since his son stayed too busy to take care of his father. She wanted to confront Grant, but how could she, when he had his hands on something every minute? The daily farm chores overwhelmed him, but he was doing them all by himself. No wonder he acted crazy.

She opened the door to his bedroom, as she did each Monday, and grabbed the sheets for the laundry. The furnishings were sparse and never seemed to move. The bookmark in his Bible changed places, suggesting he read it.

Maybe that came from living in close quarters on a ship. Without brothers and sisters to share the space, she had filled the emptiness with knickknacks and moved her favorite things about.

She carried the sheets downstairs. Mama washed the Oscars' laundry with their things. Her family didn't mind, but people were beginning to link her name with Grant's.

"If he doesn't hire that housekeeper back pretty soon, Edith girl, I'll have to ask him what his intentions are." Papa had said that two weeks ago. He wouldn't leave it much longer.

Edith would like to know the answer as well. His long johns hung on her clothesline. Things didn't get much more personal than that. But he kept her at a distance, hardly friends.

She carried the bundles to the wagon and came inside to visit with Mr. Oscar for a few minutes. Grant should be here in—she glanced at the grandfather clock in the parlor—seven minutes exactly. They were in the process of canning the honey, every morning at nine thirty.

"Good morning." Mr. Oscar enunciated his words more clearly all the time. "Pretty."

He said things like that all the time, but they still brought heat to Edith's cheeks. "You're looking dapper yourself, Mr. Oscar." She took the seat beside him. "It's too bad you can't see the fields from here. Your son has done a good job taking care of them."

Mr. Oscar waved that concern away. "He worries."

"I've noticed. I've reminded him a time or two that God sends the sunshine and the rain. You can work hard, but God makes the plants grow. And He delights in giving us good gifts."

Sorrow crossed Mr. Oscar's face. "Hard."

Edie sat back. Mr. Oscar had lost his wife, his older son, his remaining son had left home, and then the stroke. Even her own parents had struggled with not having children. She knew of three tiny graves, and there had been others, before she was born.

Grant had no wife or children, so what troubled him so? Men. Who could understand them? And magazines suggested men found women difficult to understand.

Mr. Oscar held up a penny and gestured at her, a question in his eyes. *A penny for your thoughts?*

She gestured to the sky. "I was just thinking that God is the only one who can truly understand men and women. Because we don't understand each other very well."

Mr. Oscar garbled in what was his version of a chuckle, and Grant came up the porch steps, right on time. A smile swept across his face when he spotted her in the window, and she wiggled her fingers in response. History and proximity tied them together, as well as friendship and a common faith in God. It didn't hurt that he was handsome as well. She held back a sigh.

She disappeared into the kitchen and returned with her latest recipe, honey blueberry muffins, with a special honey butter. She couldn't serve the butter at the fair, but it made the hot bread so much tastier.

She tried out a different recipe every day on her greatest competition.

If only the fair allowed two winners.

⸻ ⬥⬥ ⸻

Grant sniffed the air appreciatively as soon as he opened the door, trying to place the aroma. Edie liked playing a game with him. *Strawberry? Definitely not. Raspberry—no.* "Blueberry."

"I can't fool you." Edie clasped her hands under her chin, her cheeks a rosy red, excited as always when she offered a new treat. He hoped she got the bakery she wanted, because it brought her so much happiness—and her food would spread it around.

"Oh, and more honey butter, please." He split a muffin in half and spread butter on it. The honey butter might sell even better than honey by itself, but that put their two products in the same bin.

A single bite indicated a new ingredient. "Cinnamon." The word came out of his mouth as garbled as his father's speech. He should know better than to talk with his mouth full. He swallowed and tried again. "The cinnamon is good."

"Just a dash." She smiled as she spoke. "I'm glad you like it."

He ate another muffin and set aside two to share with his father later. He could probably eat more if he didn't know she liked to take them home for her parents to taste.

She did have a home of her own. As much as he enjoyed having her here every day, eating her food, helping with his honey—pretending they were a couple—she belonged somewhere else. He had to stop the pretense, but he couldn't bring himself to let go of her companionship.

They took a few minutes to clean up from the snacks before they started on today's batch of honey, the last he had unless he harvested some more. The raw honey was already on the stove when he came in, ready for them. It wasn't as difficult as he expected, but it was time consuming. Nobody wanted honey with globs of wax or pollen in it. If he heated it too long, it became too thick to pour.

Edie went down the row of jars, checking the seal on them and nodding her approval. She knew, as he did, that they had finished the honey. That he didn't need her to return tomorrow, or until the laundry was finished. And that left a hole in his heart.

She clasped her hands behind her back. "These should do well at the fair."

"I was thinking that your honey butter would also attract buyers." He held his breath.

"It's so easy. Anyone could do it."

He counted to five. For such a talented woman, she was overly humble. "But not everyone does, and not everyone can. I would love to sell it with my honey, but it belongs with your baked goods."

"Oh." A confused expression crossed over Edie's face.

Pa brought his hands together in a quiet version of his former vigorous clap. "Work together."

The idea struck Grant with the force of hurricane winds. *Of course!* "I think that's a great idea."

When Edie didn't respond, he noticed her hand trembling where it touched the jar of honey. "My bakery." The words came out in a whisper.

"You'll still enter the baked goods contest. We can put them together as a business proposition at the fair. Nothing more Vermont than this. Vermont ingredients and Vermont recipes."

"But if we win? Are you suggesting we go into business together?" The green in Edie's eyes had died out, leaving them dead granite gray.

"Would that be so terrible? We've been a good team these past few weeks, you and I."

"Is that all this has been for you? A business partnership?" The last glimmer of green winked out, and she removed her apron. "I'll come back later to pick up my things. One of my parents will bring back your laundry."

She moved so quickly, he hardly had time to react. When he reached the door, she was already down the porch steps. "Edie. That's not what I meant." She had reached the meadow path by the time he came outside. He stood at the steps, yelling, "I love you, Edith Grace!"

He had embarrassed himself in front of God and all creation, and she ignored him, scurrying away as if he were a dangerous varmint. His shoulders slumped, and he sat on the top step of the porch.

Something rattled behind him—the window. Grant twisted around and saw his father standing up from his chair. What was Pa thinking, doing something dangerous like that? Even as Grant sprang to his feet, his father collapsed.

His father had fallen back into the chair at an odd angle. When Grant tried to help, Pa pushed him away. "Go. Edie."

"Not until I know you're okay."

Pa stopped fighting. It only took a few minutes to help him into his seat after that.

"Go." His father pounded his cane on the floor, rattling the window again.

"I will." Grant took one step back toward the door. "As long as you promise not to move until I get back." He took a second step.

Pa lifted his right hand, finger twisted saying okay. Grant kept him in sight until he reached the door. He jumped from the porch and sprinted in Edie's direction, hoping to catch up with her before she got to her house.

He glimpsed her across the meadow and called for her. She didn't stop. "Edie! Please!"

She turned around. His heart flew high in his chest and propelled him across the distance separating them. He couldn't read what was on her face—anger? Hope?

Up close, his heart slowed down when he saw the green gleaming in her eyes. She was as uncertain as he was.

She handed him her canteen. "Here. Take a drink and catch your breath." The tiny smile accompanying her words gave him hope, but he didn't know what to say. She waited, not filling the silence with chatter.

Before she gave up and left, before he felt too discouraged to ask, he blurted out the first thing that came to mind. "I feel like Moses, slow of speech. Slow to see what was right in front of me. I have nothing to offer you, Edie Grace, but I hope you're willing to wait while I prove myself to you." There. He had said it. He could only pray she would agree.

Chapter 9

Edith's mind scattered everywhere, not ready to respond. Grant was so disheveled, clothing tangled with branches and trampled through mud, sweat matting his hair to his head.

And his thumb—the nail had turned black and the skin had swollen around the bee sting. "Your poor thumb." Tears threatened her eyes. For the life of her, she couldn't think what else to say.

He froze in place. "I may not be much, but I deserve an answer."

Drops fell on her face. Several fell before she realized rain was adding itself to her tears. She giggled. "Even God Himself is crying over two such foolish people."

Grant didn't laugh.

She knew her answer. Yes—but she didn't want him to think she'd marry him out of pity. "I will answer your question on one condition."

He looked at his hat, now in his hands, as if it held the answers. "What's the condition?"

"That we enter the fair together, like you suggested. Give our best and see what God and the state of Vermont make of it."

Puzzlement filled his eyes. Good. That was better than the desperation she had seen before.

"Are you saying you will only allow me to court you if we win the state fair?" Grant asked.

"Not exactly." She crossed her arms over her chest, where the rain had begun to soak the cloth. "You can court me while we prepare for the fair. Afterward, you can decide whether you want to marry me." Now she had nearly proposed to him. This wasn't how things were supposed to happen.

Her suggestion brought a smile to his face. "Then you can expect a proposal on the last day of the fair. And we will win." In one swift move, he pulled her into his arms and kissed her, briefly, on the lips.

She remained in his arms. A ridiculous smile covered his face, matching hers. The rain came down harder. "I need to get home." She looked at the laundry sitting in the wagon, getting wetter every minute. Dragging the heavy load through the mud underfoot would be difficult.

"I'll take the laundry back. We'll take care of it, somehow. It's not your worry anymore."

"But I—we don't mind—"

He put a finger to her mouth. "We have a business to get off the ground. Let's start the day after tomorrow. After I get things settled at home." With a grin and a wave, he left her behind, her knees wobbling as she wondered about everything that had happened that morning. She felt shiveringly happy, as warm as a day in July.

She shivered more on the way home, and Mama wrapped her in a blanket and sat her in front of the stove as soon as she walked through the door. "A cup of tea and a bowl of soup for you, and then you get yourself dry and clean and go to bed." Mama hummed as she went around the kitchen, all happiness and sunshine at odds with the rainstorm.

Halfway through the soup, Edith almost fell asleep. She followed her mother's advice and went to bed, dreaming of seeing Grant again the day after tomorrow.

When she woke again, her mother sat on her bed, gently shaking her. "Edith, please. Take some food."

Sunshine streamed through the window to the east. She had slept through the night. Something tickled her throat and she coughed, a chest-rattling cough. Mama handed her a glass of water, which Edith gulped down with gratitude.

"I'll bring you tea and honey later. But I want you to eat a bit of chicken soup first." Mama dipped a spoon into the steaming bowl.

"I can feed myself." Edith pressed her hands into her damp pillow to reach a sitting position. Her gown stuck to her back and made her movements cumbersome. She shivered, and her hands trembled. "What's wrong with me?"

"You've been sick, dear. The soaking you got during the rainstorm stirred up a bad cold." Mama directed the soup spoon at Edith's mouth, and this time she took it without complaint. By the time the bowl was half empty, her eyes drifted closed. She slipped down to a prone position and slept.

The next day, she woke up, fully alert. Her illness felt like a long dream, one that couldn't possibly be true. In addition to her parents, Grant had been there, too. Mama said he chattered about the honey and how they were going to beat the competition at the fair.

How many days had passed while she had been sick? What would happen to the new beginning she and Grant had planned? Or was that part of her impossible dream?

She wasn't going to spend another day in bed. She pulled herself into a sitting position and slipped her legs over the side of the bed.

"Edie." Grant's voice snapped through the air.

Edith glanced over her shoulder and yelped, pulling the sheet around her.

He covered his eyes with his hands. "Stay right there. I'll go tell your mother that you're awake." He turned his back to her and scuttled out of the room like a mouse escaping a cat.

Edith wiggled her toes, feeling the smooth texture of the boards beneath them, the warmth of the sunshine on her face. Someone had changed her gown and her sheets, so she felt clean and new—and whole. Ready to eat bacon and eggs and maybe a couple of pancakes. She stood for a moment, in case she wobbled. Although the bedding and her gown were clean, the air smelled stale. The window revealed a brilliantly blue sky and leafy trees, inviting her to open it and let fresh air in. She took a couple of steps and tugged on the window.

It didn't move, even when she leaned on the windowsill. Just a little extra oomph and it flew up a couple of inches, sending her arms through the opening and pressing her face against the glass.

Her mother rushed across the room and pulled her back as if she might break the glass and fall out the window. "Edith, what are you doing?"

"It smells like a sickroom in here." She wiggled out of her mother's arms. "I'm fine, truly."

"It is good to see you feeling better." Mama hugged her then held her at arm's length. "Are you ready to eat?"

"Everything you have." Edith closed her eyes, imagining the feast she wanted to consume, but that left her a little dizzy. "I want to go to the kitchen." She walked to her wardrobe and reached for a dressing gown.

"Let me help you with that." Mama eased the gown over her arms. "Grant is eager to speak with you."

<hr />

"Mama says you wish to speak with me." Edie's cheeks burned red, and not from the fever that had raged through her body for several days. They contrasted sharply with her pale forehead and the dressing gown that hung loosely from her frame. Her hair fell in a tangled braid down her back.

Grant didn't care. She was still the most beautiful woman in the world to him.

"She wants to eat. I told her I'll fix her whatever she wants," Mrs. Grace called over her shoulder.

"Then let's get you to the kitchen." He rushed ahead to the kitchen and pulled out the chair for her. The project he had undertaken with Mrs. Grace filled the kitchen. What would Edie think?

"Bacon and eggs coming up," Mrs. Grace said. "But you might wish to sample the dishes from Edith's Good Eating."

Edie didn't take the chair Grant offered her. Instead, she walked along the counter, staring at every loaf of bread, cupcake and muffin, cookie and pie. She reached the door that led into the pantry and poked her head around the corner. Cards featuring her recipes hung from string nailed along the shelves. Bottles of honey with bright red and blue ribbons and labels saying "Grace Meadow Honey" filled the shelves. So far he couldn't tell her reaction.

Edie walked down the pantry, adjusting a bottle here and there. When she studied the cards, he wondered if she could tell he had copied them himself, from her recipe box. He'd even baked a batch or two.

"Your mother and I tried the revisions you had indicated. You may want to adjust them again, of course. But I thought people might like to buy some of your favorite recipes, if you don't mind giving away some of your secrets." He had given her the gift he thought she wanted, a chance to win at the fair.

"When did you do all this?" Her hand gestured down the length of the pantry.

"Your food is ready. I fixed you some honey corncakes with your blueberry honey butter." Mrs. Grace's voice carried across the room.

Edie's mouth worked as she repeated the words. "I don't have a blueberry honey butter."

"You do now." Mother smiled.

Grant held the chair and helped her scoot close to the table. She bit into the crisp bacon and swallowed. He let her finish a batch of eggs before he spoke. "Do you know what day it is?"

She laid her fork on her plate. "How long was I sick?"

"You've been in bed for ten days." He saw the wheels turning in her brain.

"Then the fair starts. . ."

"In three days."

The beautiful green dancing lights in her eyes dimmed, replaced by a rocky gray. "Then I haven't got a moment to lose." She laid down her silverware and attempted to push back from the table.

Grant held to the chair, not allowing her to leave. "You cannot go to the fair if you aren't well."

"You're not the one to decide whether or not I will go to the fair." She thrust against the chair with such strength that it drove his belt buckle into his stomach, and he cried out. When he let go and clutched his stomach, she sank back into the chair. "And now I've hurt you again. I'm surprised you want to see me, with the hammers and bee stings I bring your way."

Tears stained her eyes, tears that saw all of her dreams disappearing.

"Aw, Edie, don't worry so. I've done everything I can to get your things ready for the fair."

Before she could respond, Mrs. Grace interrupted. "Edith Mae, listen to me. He's been here day and night. When he hasn't been at your side, he's been in the kitchen finishing with the honey or helping me with the recipes. He spent hours copying all those recipes."

"It's nothing—" Grant said.

Mrs. Grace wouldn't let him finish. "He even brought his father over here, moving in so he could take care of both of you. If you make a fool of yourself and get sick all over again, well, I'll—" Mrs. Grace ran out of words.

Edie's eyes changed colors as quickly as a kaleidoscope, suggesting her emotions were going in a circle like a carousel, up and down, and circling around until they stopped where she started. "Forgive me for being so thoughtless." She blotted the tears from her face and eyes and finished her glass of milk. "Now, I believe I'd like to try one of those honey oatmeal cookies and maybe a bit of gingerbread."

Mrs. Grace hurried away to the pantry. "I noticed those recipes had been changed," Edie said. "I want to taste and see if they deserve the Edith Grace seal of approval."

Grant's facial muscles stiffened, until her cheeks dimpled. "They could taste like clay and I would still think they were the best desserts I've ever tasted. Anything done with such selflessness deserves a golden crown in heaven." She placed her hand on his arm. "Thank you."

Mrs. Grace returned with the cookie and gingerbread. Edie bit a piece of the cookie first. "This cookie is definitely a winning recipe. It tastes like there's an extra ingredient in it, something not listed on the card."

Grant couldn't stop the smile from forming on his face. "That's because you can't put love in a jar."

Chapter 10

The first day of the fair dawned with a hint of fall in the air. Edith counted on the strength the Lord promised to get through the next few days. The doctor had pronounced her well enough to travel but cautioned her to be careful. The fair demanded a lot of stamina.

They had traveled to Rutland by wagon, but Edith looked forward to seeing motor-cars at the fair. One dealer had already set up an exhibit with two shining machines. Half-a-dozen men crowded around it, studying the engine the way ladies might examine a particularly well-made dress.

"You'll have to find time to visit the cars, Grant." Edith stapled a green-checkered bunting to the front of their booth.

He hovered over her on a stepladder, placing a custom-made sign overhead. Edith had insisted that they call the business "Oscar Farms" since they had named both products after her family.

Once he finished, he came down and put his arm around her shoulders. "Oscar Farms, Grant Oscar and Edith Grace, Proprietors." Pride rang through his voice.

"That sign alone makes me feel good. In spite of everything." She waved her hands. "God let us get here. Adding a Bible verse to the labels was smart."

"After all, 'How sweet are thy words unto my taste! Yea, sweeter than honey to my mouth!'" Grant wiggled his eyebrows. "I could mention some other verses about honey, but I don't think anyone wants to hear that they'll vomit if they eat too much of it."

Edith pretended to gag. "That's only common sense." She stepped back to study the effect. If heart, hard work, and quality alone could win, they'd jump to first place in a minute.

Grant joggled her arm. "Ladies are gathering for the baked goods competition."

Edith's stomach flip-flopped. Winning at least a couple of the baking competitions would make their bid for business that much stronger. No one cared about also-rans. "You'll have to stay here. We can't leave the booth unattended."

Mama appeared like an answer to an unspoken prayer. "I'm sorry I didn't get here earlier. I was caught up in admiring the quilts. But I'll take care of the booth so both of you can hear the judges' decisions."

Edith managed a "thank you" as her feet headed for the corner of the pavilion. With Grant and her mother's help, she had met her goal of entering all six categories of baked goods. She had her eye on the grand prize that stood four feet from the ground, for the best baker out of the hundreds spread before the judges. The ten-dollar monetary award would be nice as well.

Several women greeted Edith. In her first competition last year, she had shocked the competition by winning the quick-bread division for her apple walnut loaf. That had started her dream, in fact. If she could win one category, the only one she'd entered, why not try for all?

Mrs. Rowe, a lady with a commanding presence both in height and girth, approached. "She's won the grand prize for the past three years," Edith whispered to Grant.

"So glad to see you again. May we expect to see your apple walnut quick bread again this year?" Mrs. Rowe smiled like a cat waiting to pounce on a mouse who dared to come too near.

Edith held her head high. "Why, no, Mrs. Rowe. I've made something different."

Mrs. Rowe studied the tables, as if trying to guess which plate held Edith's entry. "Perhaps it's that rich plum cake."

Edith held back a giggle. "Why, that lovely cake must be your entry. I'm sure it's delicious." But not as good as hers was, God willing.

A hush settled across the crowd as the judges marched behind the tables. Edith wouldn't want to be in their shoes, differentiating among dozens of entries from a single bite. The verse about too much honey and vomit came to her mind, and she hoped they didn't get ill from partaking of so many delicacies.

Cookies came first. One judge had to break one in pieces because she couldn't bite into it. It remained in her mouth a long time before she could chew it. The unfortunate baker's face turned as red as her hair, and she buried her head against her husband's chest.

Grant would care if she lost the contest, but he wouldn't hold her in his arms. Those strong arms that could make a woman swoon.

The judges tried her honey ginger cookie without visible reaction. That was true of most of the tastes, so she told herself not to worry.

After every taste they made notes. When they finished, they retired to a corner and compared notes. A few quick minutes later, they had reached their decision. The lead judge headed down the table, placing the third-place yellow ribbon by a plate of sugar cookies, the red second-place ribbon by snickerdoodles. Edith held her breath. If she hadn't placed at all, she would be heartbroken.

With a broad smile, the judges placed the blue ribbon by her honey ginger cookies. She spun around, wanting to cheer. Instead, she offered congratulations to the other ribbon winners.

Ladies offered her congratulations as well, including Mrs. Rowe. That spoke well of her, because her snickerdoodles came in second.

Grant didn't say a word, but the joy gleaming in his eyes said it all.

One blue ribbon made Edith hunger for more. When she won a second blue ribbon, for her blueberry honey quick bread, and then a third, the congratulations turned into astonishment, and Edith could hardly hear what anyone had to say.

By the end, she had won four blue ribbons and two second-place ribbons. Her knees felt rubbery. Grant placed his arm around her, and she held on like an anchor, anxious to know whether the last big prize was hers.

One of the male judges picked up the trophy, and the room held its collective breath. Grant wasn't sure who was more excited, him or Edith. She should win. No one else had come close.

The judge cleared his throat, and Edith's fingernails dug into Grant's arms. "We have a clear winner for the best baker in this fiftieth anniversary competition, since she placed in every category. Congratulations go to Edith Grace, of Edith's Good Eating."

The trophy dwarfed Edith. She placed it on the table while she spoke. "Thank you so much. I appreciate winning in the presence of so many wonderful cooks in the state of Vermont. And most of all I want to thank God, who answered my prayers."

With that, Grant took the trophy before it dropped on Edith's foot. "May I take a photograph for the paper?"

Edith agreed—why not? A photo would draw attention to the trophy, and their business. After the powder flashed, the reporter asked, "Miss Grace, do you have another trophy you wish to announce?" He pointed to Grant, who was holding the trophy.

Grant couldn't help smiling, but he didn't take the bait. "You'll hear from us again. We expect this to be the first of several wins for Oscar Farms." With that, he settled the trophy against his shoulder and slipped his other arm around Edie's elbow to lead her away.

The trophy brought a lot of attention to their booth. Both women and men sampled her baked goods, and she introduced them to the "winning ingredient"—the honey. If they wished, she let them sample the honey butter, which sold as quickly as the bread. Win or lose, the Oscar Farm products were off to a good start.

Edith's confidence in the honey proved true when it won its category. With five blue ribbons, two red ribbons, and one grand trophy, they should fare well in the business competition.

Grant couldn't measure how much he hungered for a win. He craved, needed, to settle their debts and make certain the farm was on a secure financial footing before he would officially ask for Edith's hand. He decided against the pulling contest after he saw the contestants hardened by years of scrabbling out a living in spite of Vermont's harsh climate.

A different set of judges made the rounds throughout the day. "I wish we could see the other booths as well." Edith rearranged the display to catch the eye as their supplies dwindled.

"Your mother will bring us news," Grant said.

She didn't answer, and he understood. He wanted to see for himself as well.

The judges didn't make it to the Oscar Farms stall until the afternoon was well advanced. Over half of the baked goods had sold, leaving empty spaces on the shelves. Both the stickiness of honey and the creamy smear of butter had left their marks. Edie was wiping it down as best she could, one eye on the judges, one on the shelves. She scrubbed at one particularly stubborn spot and then dried it off.

The judges—three men, all of them successful entrepreneurs—approached. "Miss Grace. Mr. Oscar." The youngest of the men, handsome and charming enough to win the ladies, spoke first. "Congratulations on your performance in the baking competition,

Miss Grace. We have been looking forward to trying some of these amazing recipes."

The second judge, round and friendly, pointed to the fifth blue ribbon. "I see you won first place for your honey as well. Well done."

Both Grant and Edie smiled at that.

Edie looked worried. He could almost read her thoughts. *What if they're disappointed?* "I have been sampling her cooking ever since I returned from the navy, and I haven't tasted anything like it in all the world."

The silent judge raised an eyebrow at that statement, but when he bit into a cookie, pleasure chased away any doubts about his opinion. "Your baking speaks for itself. But what makes the honey special?"

Edie spread honey butter over a muffin before handing it to them. She also offered each judge a honey dipper to sample the honey by itself, leaving the explanation to Grant.

"As you know, honey takes its flavor from the sources of the pollen. All the flowers God saw fit to put in Vermont fill the meadow where our log gums stand. When I was in the navy, I brought a jar of honey with me. Whenever I was homesick, I'd taste the honey and be reminded of all that was good and right at home."

The final judge let the honey drip into his mouth. "You may be on to something."

The trio didn't ask any additional questions before they proceeded to the next booth. Edie's green-glazed eyes mirrored the worry in his heart. His mouth felt too dry to speak, so he sipped from a glass of water. "Let's shut down our booth and enjoy ourselves for the rest of the day."

"Good idea." She grabbed a box and started filling it. Their laughter released some of their tension as they packed their goods in boxes and baskets and covered the stack with a blanket. "Let's go see the motorcars, shall we?"

Amazing that oil from the ground could make a car move without horses. If anything made him envious, these beauties would. "They say these things can go as much as twenty miles an hour."

"Oh, Grant." Edie put her hand to her mouth. "If we win, we must get one of these things. I could sell my baked goods to so many more places if we could ship them faster."

The salesman noted their interest. "They say engineers in Europe are making engines with wagon beds behind the cab. They call them trucks. But for now—you're right, this car could revolutionize your business."

Grant's jaw clenched while Edie chatted as if buying a car were possible. When they paused their discussion, Grant said, "Let's find your mother and head to the hotel."

Edie glanced over her shoulder one last time before they got too far. "Buying a car would be a good investment, Grant. Of course, we need to come up with a business plan first."

Grant shook his head, not trusting himself to speak. Once they picked up Mrs. Grace, the two women talked so much that he just listened—and hoped they wouldn't notice.

He was wrong. Once they reached the hotel room, Mrs. Grace went to the dressing room. Edie turned on Grant. "After the day we had, I expected to celebrate. Instead, you look like you've gone to a funeral."

"No. Yes." He blew out a deep breath. "I can't afford a car, not now, not in five years—I don't know if I can ever get one. There's something you don't know, the reason why I need to win that prize."

Her forehead wrinkled. "So, you—we—can get our business started more easily."

He shook his head. "I—Pa and me—need the money for the farm. Pa's missed several payments. If we don't pay, in full, we'll lose the farm." He turned his back to her. "I should have left the navy a long time ago, but I didn't know how bad things were."

"I didn't know." Edie circled around so she was facing him. "Why didn't you tell me? We can work things out."

He stepped away from her. "There is no 'we' until I know I can support a wife." He knew he sounded angry. In truth, he was desperate.

"Pardon me." Mrs. Grace stepped into the room. She had heard the entire humiliating confession. "Sit down. There's something I probably should have told you a long time ago."

The women sat on the hotel chairs and Grant took the bed. Mrs. Grace spoke again. "Grant, your father never told us that he was having problems. And Edie, there's something you don't know. Mr. Oscar loaned us money that helped us save our farm back in '93. And he said we could pay him whenever we had the money. We were waiting until we'd harvested the last of our crops this year, but—we have the money. He should have asked."

Edie gaped at her mother, and Grant was sure a similar expression appeared on his face.

When Mrs. Grace mentioned the amount, Grant couldn't believe it. If his father loaned that much money to other farmers. . . "The bank may work with us if we can give them that much."

"As soon as we get back to Spruce Hill, I'll make sure the money is transferred to your bank. We should have done it months ago. If you win, we want you to use the prize money to start your business."

"So what do you say, sailor man?" Edie had her hands on his lapel.

"That tomorrow won't come soon enough." Grant leaned forward and kissed her briefly. She ran for the dressing room, her cheeks a bright red. His joyous laughter followed her.

Epilogue

The three judges stood on center stage, where music had played and magicians had performed tricks. But tonight's announcement of the winning business was the final act, the highlight of the fair.

The handsome younger man stood behind the podium, one of the other judges on each side. "We had a difficult time choosing the winning business. Every entry shows the ingenuity and diversity of life in our beautiful state. But we can only award one company fifty dollars."

He paused while an aide brought in a gigantic check, with the amount of fifty dollars written on it. "Before we announce the final winner, we want to recognize several businesses that came close to winning. You will each receive a blue ribbon and our very best wishes for a successful future."

"Maple Notch Dairy." A pair of men who could have been twins came forward to receive the ribbon.

"Beecher Motorcars." The salesman who had sought to sell them the car yesterday took the blue ribbon.

"And, finally, a company that needs no introduction for everyone who was here for the baking competition, Oscar Farms, which includes both Edith's Good Eating and Grace Meadow Honey."

Grant and Edie stepped forward, managing to smile in spite of deep disappointment. And a worry that Grant might never marry her now.

Grant whispered to the judge, who said, "Mr. Oscar would like to say a few words."

"Yesterday a reporter asked Miss Grace if she expected to take home any other trophies. We are blessed to be recognized with this blue ribbon. But the sweetest, best trophy I could hope for can't be found in a bank or in a jar of honey. It's the heart of the most wonderful woman I know, Edith Mae Grace. Edie, will you do me the honor of marrying me?"

She looked up at him, her right hand crumpling the ribbon. "All you had to do was ask."

He lifted the hand holding on to the ribbon up high in the air, and the audience broke into applause.

Bestselling author **Darlene Franklin**'s greatest claim to fame is that she writes full-time from a nursing home. She lives in Oklahoma, near her son and his family, and continues her interests in playing the piano and singing, books, good fellowship, and reality TV, in addition to writing. She is an active member of Oklahoma City Christian Fiction Writers, American Christian Fiction Writers, and the Christian Authors Network. She has written over fifty books and more than 250 devotionals. Her historical fiction ranges from the Revolutionary War to World War II, from Texas to Vermont. You can find Darlene online at www.darlenefranklinwrites.com.

Altered Hearts

by Gina Welborn

Dedication

To my mom's sister, Marsha Carl.
When I was younger, I used to think you were the coolest aunt in the world. I loved all the crazy clearance sales at Michael's in Watertown, and appreciate that you let two teenage girls do the gift wrapping—three pieces of tape only! I hope this story does your home city proud. (P.S. You're still pretty cool.)

A Special Thanks
To Fish at Joe's in Monroe, Louisiana, for sharing their experiences (good and bad) in starting a new business.

To Angela Breidenbach, Jennifer AlLee, and Susanne Dietze for joining me in the Daily Word Count Challenge. Best fun I ever had finishing a manuscript. The chatting during the breaks: priceless.

To my gluten-free boxer-Lab, Kansas, for protecting me from all the UPS, FedEx, and USPS delivery guys and gals who come to our front door. I feel safe.

—◆•◆—

"Land speculation was the mania of nineteenth-century America. The way to make money was to buy land cheap (or to get it for nothing) and sell it at a higher price. It was the falls of the Big Sioux River that made this location a prime townsite. . . . [Railroads] not only distributed goods to the smaller cities and towns of the region, they brought agricultural produce and people to Sioux Falls. By 1920 its population was two and one-half times larger than in 1900."
—GARY D. OLSON AND ERIK L. OLSON, *Sioux Falls, South Dakota: A Pictorial History*

"I am more than ever pleased with Sioux Falls after seeing it. I confidently believe from what experience teaches me that Sioux Falls is certainly destined to be the Minneapolis and St. Paul of this country, if not its Chicago."
—A VISITOR FROM MAINE, *The Argus Leader*, June 15, 1889

"We ford the Sioux, climb a big hill beyond and there lies at a little distance the prettiest of towns, Sioux Falls. We see it through the fading day—too late to visit the 'Niagara of the Northwest,' so we stop at a good hotel for the night."
—MISS CARRIE PEABODY OF DUBUQUE, IOWA, November 7, 1877, upon visiting Sioux Falls

For they that are after the flesh do mind the things of the flesh;
but they that are after the Spirit the things of the Spirit.
ROMANS 8:5

Prologue

Germania Hall, 220 West 9th Street, Sioux Falls, South Dakota
Saturday afternoon, September 1901

Fifteen-year-old Reba Diehl gripped the back of her father's sleeve, her heart pounding against her chest as he maneuvered her through the crowded aisle. With her other hand, she gripped the program. She twisted and turned and stood on her tiptoes to get a better view. The brocade silk curtains, wrought-iron decorations, stained glass, plaster carvings (so much to see!), and what she missed because everyone in the noisy theater topped her by a foot or more. . .well, Father had promised to take her to the balcony once the show was over.

The crowd thinned as they neared their seats. A tall girl, who couldn't be much older than she was, strolled onto the stage wearing a sparkly turquoise dress and carrying a fiddle. Reba gasped. The girl's heart-shaped face looked so much like that of famed Gibson Girl Evelyn Nesbit. The piano player and the fiddler started a song that sounded similar to the folk music their Norwegian neighbor Mr. Bergdorf played. People began clearing the aisle to find their seats. Crowd noise lessened. Calls went out for candy and popcorn.

"For my birthday girl." Father motioned to the last two unoccupied chairs on the front row. He then slid the tickets inside his suit coat.

Reba sat in the second chair, leaving the aisle seat for her father. She laid the program in the lap of her blue Sunday dress then glanced around, awed at what she saw. To think the four hundred chairs could be removed for dances, dance classes, wrestling, and banquets. Like the other theaters in town, Germania Hall was, as Reba had read in the *Argus Leader*, a "window to the world."

She drew in a deep breath then released it slowly and a bit raggedly. "I can't believe I'm here."

The lady to her right leaned close. She smelled like a bouquet of flowers and wore a straw hat covered with ribbons and feathers. "Dearie, is this your first show?"

Reba nodded.

"Miss Maud Harrison is the newest addition to the program," the woman whispered, and her eyes sparkled with the same anticipation Reba felt. "I saw her one-act comedy sketch, 'The Lady Across the Hall,' in Chicago last winter. Tonight is her last performance in Sioux Falls."

"Is that her?" Reba pointed to the fiddler.

"Goodness, no. That girl is the dumb act."

Reba frowned at the fiddler, whose eyes were closed as her bow floated against the strings. "Why is she the dumb act? She's so pretty."

The woman smiled sweetly. "The opening act is the weakest and usually has no dialogue, thus is considered *dumb*. The first performer exists simply to notify the audience the show has begun."

As the woman turned her attention to the man on her other side, Reba opened the program. The first two pages contained advertisements, including a full-page ad for the Bee Hive Department Store her father had taken her to yesterday. She flipped the page.

GERMANIA HALL
Daily Mats. 1:30   Evenings 7:30
12   ALL STAR ACTS   12
TIMETABLE
FOR THE WEEK OF SEPTEMBER 21ST

Under the timetable was a list of the twelve acts, of which eleven—including Miss Maud Harrison—were named. As lovely as the fiddler played, she was nothing more than "Musical Selection."

How was that any different than being known as the youngest Diehl? Or the surprise Diehl? The unexpected one? Born after a dozen pregnancies, three of which ended in miscarriages and one in stillbirth. Embarrassed to admit at the age of forty-four, and with three grandchildren already, that she was carrying again, Mother had kept her pregnancy secret as long as she could. "*In case it didn't take*," she had explained ever since Reba could remember.

She hadn't wanted it to take. While Mother had never said those words to Reba, Reba knew that's what her mother had hoped. Maybe even prayed.

The unwanted one—that's what she was. To her mother.

Reba's vision blurred, but she blinked away the tears. She wasn't going to cry about what she couldn't change. Her father loved her. He liked spending time with her. He liked her as his daughter, as his youngest child. As a person. He never made her feel unwanted.

She rested against Father's arm. "Thank you for bringing me to the city."

He placed a kiss on top of her head.

A candy butcher stopped next to Father. "Sir, would you like a treat?" The mustached man withdrew two paper sacks from the basket that was supported by a strap around his neck. "I have lemon drops, cream candy, stick candy, rock candy, butterscotch, licorice, popcorn, and Cracker Jack."

Father looked to Reba. "Your choice."

"No, thank you."

Father's ashy blond brows rose, yet he didn't question if she really wanted some. No matter how many times he insisted money was no object, she knew it was. Mother had made sure they both knew her disfavor with the weekend trip. The money Reba had made selling her show ewes and ram at the county fair needed to go to purchase a new divan and side chairs. Reba didn't need to see Sioux Falls, any more than Father did. Waste of money, the trip was.

In the forty-two years her parents had been married, not once had they visited the big city together. Mother abhorred riding on the train. Mother saw no reason to leave home. Mother had grandchildren and work to attend to.

Reba smiled in hopes of convincing her father she was content without candy. They had one more day in Sioux Falls. She refused to waste their fun money on sweets.

Father waved the candy butcher on.

While the man made his way down the front row, Reba flipped through the program filled with advertisements for everything—anything—a person could want. Mother didn't know what she was missing. If she did, she would never want to return to the farm.

Just like Reba didn't.

And one day she wouldn't return. Somehow she'd find a way to escape to a better world.

She closed the booklet then and gripped her father's hand. "Father, I think I'd like to live in Sioux Falls," she announced as the fiddler played a somber second tune.

Father's blue-eyed gaze shifted from the stage to her. "You would give up everything you know to live here? You would leave the farm and your family? You would leave me?"

Reba's heart tightened. She nodded.

His eyes almost looked watery, and he seemed troubled. No, not troubled or worried or even anxious. More like. . .well, like sad. And older than his sixty years.

She opened her mouth to tell him she wouldn't leave. But nothing came out. Besides her father, there was nothing for her back home. No bright future. No life-to-the-fullest like Reverend Frieke had preached about last week. She refused to grow up to be miserable like her mother. She wanted pretty hats, caramel popcorn, and afternoons spent at the theater.

Reba started to let go of Father's hand.

His fingers tightened around hers. "Reba Diehl, you are braver than I have ever been."

Chapter 1

"A becoming hat or bonnet may be equal to a letter of recommendation, for it is the practice of many people to judge the character of an individual by the clothes which he or she wears."
—JESSICA ORTNER, *Practical Millinery*, 1897

Turner County Fair, Parker, South Dakota
Late August 1908

With a record fifth win at this year's fair," yelled the announcer through the megaphone, "Miss Reba Diehl!"

Reba released the breath she was holding. Her hat was the best in show.

As applause broke out, she was engulfed in hugs and congratulations. The best part about entering her creations in the Turner County Fair was how friendly and encouraging everyone was, even when their fair entry didn't win.

"Miss Diehl," the announcer said, "please come to the stage for your ribbon. Coming up next, the Division of Culinary..."

After the last hug, Reba smoothed the front of her good luck white pongee silk dress and nervously checked the pin securing her favorite black hat onto her hair. Of all the ribbons she'd won today, this one—Class 142, MILLINERY, Ladies' Hats—meant the most. She glanced around for Levi, but the crowd was too thick and she was too short to see over anyone's head. Surely he was around somewhere. Certainly. He knew how important this win was to her. He, more than anyone, would understand what this meant.

Reba smiled as she climbed the gazebo bandstand to accept the blue ribbon for the straw hat bedecked with handcrafted silk flowers and leaves. Hours cutting petals and curving the fabric. Hours stitching. Hours taking what she saw in her mind and turning it into a masterpiece. Her cheeks ached already from smiling so hard.

Because that's what her hat was—a masterpiece.

She vigorously shook hands with the four members of the fair's Department of Women's Work. With a thank-you, she accepted the ribbon from the superintendent, Mrs. Gertrude Wright.

"This was your best hat yet. Congratulations!" Mrs. Wright touched Reba's arm, stilling her from walking away. "Miss Diehl, please reconsider my offer. It's far too generous a scholarship for you to pass up. You would be a valued addition to the teaching staff."

Reba nodded, even though she had no intention of attending college, regardless of where it was located. No matter how many blue ribbons she won for darning stockings, patching old garments, or repairing buttonholes, her future did not include earning a degree in home economics. Having a degree meant becoming a teacher, and Mrs. Wright, also the dean of Home Economics at Sioux Falls College, had already offered her a job upon graduation. Reba certainly didn't want to teach college girls how to darn, patch, and repair, which was only a fraction of the household management curriculum. If she wanted to manage a household and teach, she would stay on the farm and have a quiver full of children.

She offered a polite thank-you then headed to the stairs.

Mrs. Wright called out, "You will receive an enrollment packet in the mail next week!"

"Oh, all right. Thank you!" Reba accepted hug after hug as she made her way through the crowd surrounding the bandstand. She wasn't a seamstress. She wasn't a teacher. She certainly wasn't a country girl content to stay on the farm.

She was a milliner.

She made hats. Blue ribbon–winning hats.

And she had plans—grand plans.

Levi Webber hooked his thumbs around his suspenders as he watched the Ferris wheel turn. A soft breeze blew across his forearms, bare from his rolled-up sleeves. This year he'd convince Reba to ride the wheel with him. Tonight. At sunset. Twilight never ceased to amaze him with its ability to transform a fair into something a little bit mysterious, a little bit exciting, and even a little bit dangerous. . .and yet all the while sending out sweet echoes of laughter and romance. What girl could resist that? Sitting high above the fairgrounds at twilight would be the perfect time to choose the date for their wedding.

Of course, he'd have to not look at her when they talked, because when he did look at her, after a minute his ears would stop listening. Reba was the prettiest girl he knew. When he walked through the cornfield, he couldn't help but brush the tips of the cornstalks. Her hair was as golden, as silky, as touchable. Lately, not touching it was becoming more and more of a struggle.

He loved her too much to bring her any dishonor.

That they were marrying soon was a blessing. Next month was a good time to marry.

Levi resumed his stroll along the midway, determined to find the perfect gift for his girl. For as long as he could remember, she had loved the fair as much as he did. Carnival workers cajoled youngsters and old-timers into their lairs. In the distance was the sound of BB shot hitting tin cans. He passed signs hawking food—FRESH ROASTED CORN!—and games. He paused at SHOOT A BASKET, WIN A BEAR and watched two boys throw a dozen brown balls at six apple baskets nailed to a wall. None sank.

The game operator patted one boy's back, leaving a chalky handprint. "Lemme let you in on a secret. That balloon dart game over there is the easiest one to win."

After an exuberant "thank you, sir," the boys dashed in the direction the game operator had pointed.

The man slapped his hands together, wiping off the chalk, then looked to Levi. "I bet you could win a stuffed bear for your girl."

"I doubt I'd be that lucky."

"Don't be a pessimist. Have more faith."

"What I need is more skill, not more faith." Levi adjusted his flat cap. "Thanks for the offer. My fiancée would prefer a sweeter gift." He continued on, passing a row of tents, buffeted by the smell of sausage competing with the smell of fish. The wind direction favored the fish, perhaps explaining why the line was longer at that stand.

The bandstand within eyesight, Levi stopped at a display of canned fruit. Mrs. Diehl's pantry was as full as his mother's was, but what it lacked was—

He picked up a jar, its lid covered in blue gingham. "Did you grow these peaches?"

"Sure did." The seller stepped to the table while his pregnant wife stayed in her chair, knitting.

Levi studied the perfectly ripe fruit. He'd never heard of anyone successfully raising peaches in South Dakota. "How did you get them to endure the climate? I've been trying to grow peaches up in Brookings for the last six years. I've tried Bokhara No. 3 and some of the Iowa peach seedlings, and even planted a few pits of the Bailey, the Leigh, the Alberta, and the Early Canada. What few trees have survived have only produced fruit buds."

"We're from Minnesota," the wife said. "This is my cousin's booth. His wife has several entries in the culinary division. They're announcing winners now."

The seller tipped his straw hat. "You own an orchard?"

"No, sir. I worked at the South Dakota State University Extension to pay for my degree." Levi couldn't contain his smile. "Horticulture is a hobby of mine. I'm determined to grow peaches someday. My fiancée loves them."

"What's your degree in?"

"Agricultural business. And accounting," he answered with less passion. He'd have earned a degree in horticulture if he'd had the time and finances. . .and the support from his parents. "My family owns the largest dairy farm in Turner County. We're expanding, and they need me to do the accounting and paperwork." Levi didn't flinch as the man seemed to see into his soul and recognize the discontent he had tried to hide.

The man raised a brow. "Well, now, have you tried grafting the peach on native plum stock and on sand cherry?"

"Yes, sir. I grafted right on the ground or a little below it into a young sand cherry stock, using a wedge-shaped scion. Did it very early in the spring before the buds start."

The seller nodded approvingly. "You're doing that right. Try bending the trees at the roots in the fall and keeping them covered with straw or mulch in the winter. Don't cover them, because the moist earth is apt to rot the buds."

Levi shook the seller's hand. "Thank you. I'll take two jars."

After paying the couple, he headed in the direction of the Women's Work building. Reba loved peaches. His feet ached to run to her, to show her what he'd bought. Ever since returning home from college, he couldn't stop thinking about her and their future together. Come spring, he'd plant her an orchard. The land she'd inherited from her grandmother had the perfect spot for one. God had certainly blessed him with the perfect wife and the perfect house on the perfect piece of land.

Levi clenched the jars of peaches to his chest as he wove through the crowd. The only thing standing between him and his perfect future was—

He grinned.

Nothing.

Chapter 2

*". . .while certain rules will always apply more or less to the details of construction, yet there
are few rules which can ever be applied to the manipulation of trimmings."*
—Practical Millinery

Miss, I'll give you two dollars for your blue-ribbon hat."
Reba didn't have a chance to respond before a second man said, "I'll pay three!"

"Three and a quarter," offered another man in a three-piece suit that looked to be tailored specifically for him, as did the fancy silk dress worn by the redhead holding on to his arm. The pair looked out of place—more suited for an urban environment like Chicago or New York.

Reba glanced back and forth between the three men. The bidding continued, and a crowd grew around display table number eight in the Women's Work building.

"I saw a hat similar to it in Macy's," the stately redhead said to the woman next to her. "It was imported from Paris and was priced at thirty dollars."

Several people gasped.

The bidding ended at half the Macy's price tag. . .only to start up again on the very hat Reba wore. Within minutes, she had a handful of bills and a list of names and addresses of people interested in buying her hats. She'd never sold one for more than a dollar before, but today she'd sold two for over twenty times that. She gave her blue-ribbon hat to the redhead and accepted payment from the husband.

She then placed the money and the list on the empty display table and removed her favorite black hat with white silk flowers and ostrich feathers. She handed it to the other winning bidder. "Thank you, sir. I'll send word when my shop opens." As Reba continued to utter her thanks, the crowd wandered off.

The man nodded. "If you're interested, there's street-front space in the Edmison-Jamison building in Sioux Falls. It's the best place to attract traffic from the Bee Hive next door. My wife will be thrilled for Sioux Falls to finally have a milliner of your caliber." He withdrew a business card from inside his suit coat. "I am a loan officer at the Metropolitan Bank. Come see me next week."

"Thank you," she said, not taking the card, "but I don't need a loan." She tucked a loosened blond strand behind her ear. "I sold the land I inherited from my. . ." Her words trailed off when the banker's gaze shifted to something—someone—behind her. It couldn't be her father because he was at the cattle arena with her nephews, Hans and Peter.

"I'll inform my wife about your boutique." He pressed his business card in her hand then tipped his hat. "Good day."

Reba turned around and winced. There stood Levi with a most unflattering scowl on his bearded face, which was enough of a confirmation that he'd overheard the discussion.

This wasn't how she'd planned on sharing the news. However, in light of recent events, as Father had warned her earlier this morning, this discussion was one she and Levi needed to have.

She laid her hat pin on the table.

"I won five blue ribbons," she said to break the silence, "and sold two hats for twenty-four dollars. It's unbelievable! People want my hats. If I'd have brought more, I could have sold them."

Levi's eyes narrowed. "I don't care about the hats," he said, walking to her. "You sold our land."

Reba choked on her breath. "Our land? No, I sold *my* land inherited from *my* grandmother."

He slammed the two jars of peaches he'd been carrying onto the display table. "You had no right to sell it without talking to me first."

She blinked rapidly, trying to make sense of his response. She'd never seen Levi angry. Or possessive. Or rude. If he truly cared nothing for her hats, then he'd been lying to her when he'd expressed interest. If he had been lying, what else had he been dishonest about?

"I'm twenty-two years old," she said in a quieter voice than his had been. No need to draw attention to their discussion. "Who are you to tell me what I can or can't do with what is legally mine and mine alone?"

"I'm your fiancé." He crossed his arms and glowered down at her. While he was the shortest Webber, he towered over her by a good eight inches. "We're getting married next month."

"What? Who told you that?" She felt her mouth gape as she stared at him, waiting for some sign that he was jesting

He didn't blink. He didn't smile.

He continued to glare.

"Do you think we're engaged?" she asked, because—well, she was too shocked to think of something to say otherwise.

"Yes." His tone couldn't have been more confident. "Ask anyone."

Reba nearly stamped her foot. "I don't care what anyone else says. You never proposed to me. Never, Levi. Not once in any of the letters you sent during the six years you were at college did you mention marriage. . .or courtship, for that matter. Not once this past summer did you speak of getting engaged. Not once have you said, 'I love you, Reba. Will you marry me?'"

Then there was the fact he'd never kissed her. Or held her hand. Not that she was about to say that aloud. He might think she wanted him to kiss her, and she didn't.

"We aren't engaged," she said firmly.

He yanked his cap off his head. "What did you think"—he flapped his hat in the space between them—"this was?"

"Friendship."

"Fr–friendship?"

At the befuddled look on his face, she started to feel sorry for him, but then he said, "*Everyone* knows we are a couple."

"I didn't know," she argued, "and you are presuming that other people think it."

He raked his hand through his dark hair. "You've heard our mothers talking marriage."

Reba rolled her eyes. "They've been talking marriage since we were children. Two Webber-Diehl marriages aren't enough for them. As the youngest in each of our families, and the only two not married, *and* with farms next to the other, we seem like a logical match." She knelt and lifted the black table covering to expose the basket she'd stored under the table. Standing, she rested the basket on the table. "I value our friendship. You are more a brother to me than any of mine have ever been."

His mouth opened then closed. Redness crept up his neck and into his cheeks.

"I'm sorry, Levi, I truly am," she said. "I did not mean to embarrass you. Had I known you viewed our relationship more intimately—" Her own cheeks warmed as she said the last word.

With those green eyes, his strong jaw, and a well-fitted white shirt, Levi Webber attracted female attention. She'd seen ladies back home and here at the fair admire him. Circumstances would be easier if she had developed wifely feelings for him. No—actually that would have made things worse. Levi Webber grew up a dairyman, went to college to be a better dairyman, and would die a dairyman. Farm life was what he lived and breathed. If she had fallen in love with him, leaving him and the life he'd planned for them would be exponentially more difficult.

She'd hope they could part ways as friends. But now that she knew he saw them as a couple—well, how could this end amicably? Someone was going to be hurt.

He was going to be hurt.

But it was his own fault. Not only had he presumed they were courting, he'd also presumed she would say yes to his marriage proposal without him actually having to propose.

She withdrew a blue handkerchief from inside the basket. "I sold my land because I'm opening a millinery in Sioux Falls." She folded the fabric into a triangle then tied it over her hair, the flap covering the loosely braided bun. "My father knows and is supportive. He helped negotiate a premium price for the land. A sweet Hutterite couple bought it."

He tapped his hat against his thigh. "What will your monthly expenses be? How many hats will you have to sell to stay in business? How will you have time to make hats, sell product, and advertise? Do you know simple baseline accounting? What is your timeline for turning a profit?"

"Why do you want to know?"

"I don't think you realize that there's more to running a millinery than making hats," he said, his irritation clear.

"I know there's more," she bit off.

He snorted and jerked his head. "Your problem is you have always been a success. Every time you've entered the fair, in every category, you've won a ribbon. Winning ribbons doesn't mean you have the skill to run a business. You have greatly overestimated the number of South Dakotans who want to wear silly feathers and flowers on their heads."

Reba snatched up the money and the notepad. She held out the money. "*This* is proof that people will pay for silly feathers and flowers." She held up the notepad. "*This* is a list of people who want to buy silly feathers and flowers to wear on their heads."

"Sometimes things work out. Sometimes they don't." He sighed wearily, his brow furrowing. "Too often they don't. Do you have a plan for what happens when your shop fails?"

"Ha! There's your problem, Levi. You always assume the worst will happen." Reba tossed the money and notepad inside the basket, adding also the hat pin. "Life hasn't been easy for me. My mother—" Her voice cracked. "You of all people know what I've endured at home. I haven't succeeded at everything I've tried. The difference between us"—her eyes burned with tears, and she sniffed—"the difference is that when I try something, I believe I'm going to succeed. It may not happen the first time, but given enough tries, it will happen. Hope never disappoints."

People, though, did.

People also liked to remind her what a disappointment she was.

She rested her hand on his forearm. "I've been praying that God would reveal His will for my life. He's closed doors while also giving me signs that this is the path I am to follow."

"That's not always the best way to go," he grumbled. "When you use circumstances—good and bad—as a determination of God's will for your life, you start thinking that because the Bible says God is good, God must always be behind the good things. Then when bad things happen, you question your faith in God and in His goodness."

She patted his arm. " 'O ye of little faith.' "

"It's not faith I need more of." He claimed the jars of peaches from the table and placed them in her basket. "Take these."

"You should keep them."

"No, I bought them for you."

"Why?"

He didn't answer. Nothing in his expression indicated his actions were because he was deeply and passionately in love with her. If he loved her, he would have been there for the award ceremony. If he loved her, he would support her decision to open a millinery.

That he didn't love her was good. She wasn't in love with him, and unreciprocated love was terrible.

She knew that from experience, from the worst sixteen months of her life five years ago. If Levi hadn't taken her to Mrs. Shaw's estate sale and bought her the vintage millinery set, she may have wasted more months fruitlessly loving Gustov Browning. For as long as she could remember, Levi had been her closest friend. Some days it felt like he was her only friend.

Reba gave Levi a tender smile to cover the strange ache in her chest.

She looped the basket's handle around her arm. She had taken four steps away when she stopped and looked over her shoulder. "Did you say something?"

He shook his head.

How odd. She could have sworn he said, *"Because you're my girl."*

He slapped his cap back on his head. "I'll see you at the wagons." And then he turned around and headed to the exit.

Reba sighed. This wasn't how she wanted their friendship to end. She'd always enjoyed talking to Levi and enjoyed not feeling obligated to fill the silence when he had nothing to say. She liked his ability to make people feel at ease. He was a good listener. She just wished he would be a little more hopeful, a little more optimistic that everything would work out how God willed it.

And it *would* work out, because God had made a way.

Chapter 3

*"An experienced milliner is capable of designing entirely new
and original patterns of shapes; and without even measurements
as her guide, she produces the idea which her brain has conceived."*
—*Practical Millinery*

*Edmison-Jamison building, 9th and Phillips Avenue, Sioux Falls
Monday, October 5, 1908*

Reba clasped her hands together on the lap of her black skirt to hide their shaking. She refused to look like a female wilting under pressure. She could do this. She had to stay calm, to not look like she was panicking or that her pulse was racing. Was she sweating? She was. She could feel the moisture on the back of her neck.

"Mr. Smyth," she said with a smile, "Brookings is sixty miles north of Sioux Falls and one-third the population. Three women there own millinaries, a fourth manages a music store, a fifth the general store, the sixth is the superintendent of the hospital, a seventh a school principal, and everyone in this part of the state knows Mrs. Gerlach, the proprietor of the ever popular Wayside Inn. If Sioux Falls is to overcome her past of being the divorce capital of the country, then, in honor of Helen McKennan, creator of the city's first public park, let us work together to make Sioux Falls a city of opportunity...a city of prosperity for both sexes."

Mr. Smyth leaned back, his chair squeaking. He smoothed his bushy gray mustache as he looked from Reba to her father and back to her. "Impressive speech for one so young."

Father nodded. "Reba has spent the last year interviewing women business owners. She is not venturing into this lightly."

Mr. Smyth crossed his arms. "Are you sure you want to do this? Do you realize how risky opening a new business is, especially for a female as inexperienced as you are?"

Reba kept her gaze on the building manager yet swallowed to ease the tightening in her throat. His questions echoed the ones Father had begun asking after she'd told him she wanted to open a millinery, and had continued to ask even as they'd ridden the train to Sioux Falls this morning. Was she sure? Yes. Did she realize the risk? Yes. Now, though, was not the time to let caution restrain her dreams. With great risk came great reward.

She motioned to the proposal she'd prepared. She'd spent more time on it than any essay in high school. "On page three is a list of the benefits to me of leasing a street-level shop in the Edmison-Jamison building. Phillips Avenue is the principal retail thoroughfare in Sioux Falls. Having my millinery there is the key to its success."

"In good conscience," Mr. Smyth said, "I must recommend you lease a less expensive location, build up your clientele, and in time move to Phillips Avenue, if you deem it worthwhile."

Father shifted in his chair and looked her way, silently expressing his agreement with the building manager.

"I considered that," Reba admitted. Her straw hat seemed to have doubled its weight, and the stuffy room needed a window opened.

"Mr. Diehl, please talk sense into your daughter."

"I have tried." Father turned to Mr. Smyth. "We discussed the benefits and costs. Reba is an adult, and this is her money—thus her decision. You could lease the space to her and have a guaranteed six months' rent. Or you could reject her offer and gamble that another interested person will come along. You lose nothing by leasing the space to her. Any loss is Reba's to bear."

Mr. Smyth tapped his desktop. "Mr. Diehl, I'm a father myself. Both of my girls are about your daughter's age. One has a child already; the other is carrying. I'd be remiss not to point out that what your daughter would spend on six months' rent would buy one of those mail-order houses from the Sears catalog. She needs a husband, not a business."

"She—"

Reba touched her father's arm to signal that he should let her respond. "Sir, I want to be a milliner, not a wife. What I decide three—four—years from now could be different."

Mr. Smyth continued to tap his desk.

Reba added quickly, "I am not naïve enough to believe the moment my millinery opens I'll have customers. Please give me a chance." She motioned to her proposal again, which he finally opened. "You'll see my plan includes realistic one-month, three-month, and six-month goals." Thanks to her father's insight. She would've asked Levi for advice about her proposal and for accounting tips, but he'd been avoiding her since the fair. "All I'm asking for is a six-month lease. If in that time I've not met the agreed-upon goals, then your prime lease space returns to you."

Mr. Smyth turned his attention to her proposal. He lifted a page then flipped to the next and then the next. With a shake of his head, he closed the cover. "Come back tomorrow and I'll have the contract ready for you to sign. And bring a bank check."

"Oh thank you, thank you, thank you." Reba stood and shook his hand. She claimed her tapestry bag.

As they walked to the door, Mr. Smyth said, "I recommend you rent a room at the Cataract Hotel just next door. Or at Fogerty's Boardinghouse. It's about an eight-minute trolley ride from here."

Father shook Mr. Smyth's hand. "We will be back in the morning."

Reba hurried to the stairs. She paused until her father caught up. "I told you God's will was for me to open a millinery. I won at the fair. People were willing to pay me many times what my hats cost to make. And now I have a prime boutique space on Phillips Avenue. God has piled on the blessings. Every time I've thrown out a fleece, He has answered in confirmation."

Father gave her an odd look. "I hope you have that same confidence when circumstances don't go in your favor."

Reba released a loud sigh. "You sound like Levi. Have faith!"

"It is not faith I am lacking," Father muttered. "I know how much you dislike math."

"Accounting is not like doing algebra. I'll be fine."

They turned the corner and descended from the second floor.

"Mr. Smyth will eventually see the merit in leasing to me," Reba said, her excitement speeding up her words, echoing them off the walls. "He will."

Father pointed his hat at her. "You will have to work hard to bring in customers. You will need to spend extra money on advertising. You must pay the bills promptly and keep a detailed budget. No rounding up. You must add and subtract to the penny."

"Oh, I will." She stopped at the ground floor and pirouetted. "I'm so happy I could dance."

Father plopped his hat on his head. "Before you dance, we need to examine your shop. You need to make a list of what needs to be done to prepare your boutique for customers. Come along." He nudged her to the arched front doors and outside onto the ten-foot-wide paved sidewalk.

Two shop spaces were next to the entrance to the Edmison-Jamison building. One was taken by Huss Bakery.

Reba breathed deeply. "I am going to love working here for the smell alone."

Father's gaze shifted to the building to their right. He frowned. "We should check the boardinghouse first. The hotel looks expensive."

Reba eyed the five-story brick building. Its first-floor café had street access. She'd heard the restaurant inside was one of the finest in the city. But as lovely as the Cataract was, a boardinghouse was a better use of her funds. She motioned to the left, to the west side of Ninth Street. "The Metropolitan Bank is right down there. Should we get the bank check now or wait until morning?"

Father checked his watch. "Let's wait. We'll take the streetcar to the boardinghouse then walk back this way. It's a good day to check walking time. Remember, time is money, so you must always calculate how much you could accomplish if you didn't have to spend time traveling to work. Also, when running a business, it may be worthwhile to pay someone to do a trivial job so you have time to do the one demanding greater skill. Consider costs and dividends."

"I don't want to spend money on an employee until business is more than I can handle."

"It's your millinery." She could tell by his tone he disagreed with her decision.

They waited until the electric streetcar came to a stop.

Reba hitched her tapestry bag in the crook of her arm then lifted the front of her skirt to keep it from brushing against the dirt-hardened street. When she had the time, she would alter her work dresses to ankle length. No sense letting the streets ruin a hem. Come to think of it, in light of the number of times she'd have to walk to the trolley if she lived at the boardinghouse, the added cost of living at the Cataract may outweigh the inconvenience of crossing muddy streets. Thankfully, it hadn't rained in over a week.

Father helped her into the streetcar.

Reba slid onto a wooden bench, the car bumping as passengers climbed on and off. She rested her bag in her lap.

Father sat next to her and crossed his legs, "What about Levi?"

That took her aback. "What about him?"

"You broke his heart."

"I did not." She shifted to face him. "Why do you bring this up now?"

Father did nothing but raise his brows, which she suddenly realized (like his beard) were more white than ash blond. Sixty-seven wasn't old. Or at least it hadn't seemed old until today.

The streetcar started into motion.

"You can look at me like that all you want," Reba said, smiling, "but I don't know what you're trying to say."

"Levi's a good man"—he patted her arm—"and good for *you*."

Reba sighed. That he was good for her was irrelevant. She liked Levi. She really did. She missed talking to him, missed confiding her fears and insecurities. He was smart. Far smarter than she was. So how could he have presumed they were engaged? How could he have allowed Mother and Mrs. Webber to plan his—their—future? And why? One thing she'd learned with her mother was that if you gave her an inch she'd take a mile. Levi knew that, too. Not everything parents wanted for their children was the best thing. Someday he'd have to realize that, or else he would lose out on doing something God wanted him to do because he was too committed to what his parents wanted him to do. He was going to miss so many wonders because he was stuck on the farm.

"Levi has been my closest friend my whole life." She growled under her breath. "But he allowed Mother's and Mrs. Webber's plotting and planning to ruin our friendship. There's no telling how many other people believed we were engaged because he told them we were. An engagement always begins with a proposal. There was no proposal. I want a proposal. I want a man to say he can't bear the thought of life without me. How could Levi just assume we were engaged?"

Her father's lips tightened at the corners, his eyes almost amused. "Could you consider marrying him?"

For a moment Reba was speechless.

Something began to tug at her. It twisted and turned in her chest. She had long learned to live with being a disappointment to her mother, but she simply could not bear to disappoint her father—her dear *Vati*. She swallowed to ease the tightening in her throat.

"Do you want me to?" she said quietly.

Please, say no. Please, don't make me feel selfish like Mother did.

Father's brow furrowed. His gaze focused on something outside the trolley window. "I want you to marry the man *you* want to marry, not the man your parents or anyone else has chosen for you to marry. Marriage is hard, Reba. But it can be wonderful, too. Love makes the hard seem less hard and the wonderful more wonderful, especially when you know your mate was your choice because, as you say, you couldn't bear the thought of life without that person. So choose wisely."

Had Mother been his choice or his parents'? Had the marriage been arranged, as Levi said his parents' had been? She wanted to know, wanted to ask. She'd never heard Father criticize Mother to anyone. Her parents had eight children, thirty-two grandchildren, and eight great-grandchildren. They'd been married for almost fifty years. She wanted to believe they had married by choice and for love. When Father said things like this, though, she wondered.

The truth was, Mother was a hard person for anyone to love.

The trolley came to a stop.

Passengers climbed off and on.

Reba leaned forward and placed an affectionate kiss on her father's bearded cheek. "If God desires for me to marry Levi, then God will have to show me."

In a gentle tone, he asked, "Would you be open to his courtship?"

She thought for a long moment. She'd never looked at Levi as a suitor. While he had his good traits, his future had been laid out by his parents. A dairyman he would always be. She was never going back to the farm. If she had to live in that smothering environment, she'd become as bitter and spiteful as her mother. It wasn't that farm life was torturous. She knew many people who loved it.

Life on the farm merely wasn't for her.

As the trolley started in motion, Reba settled back against her seat. "Any possible feelings for him are inconsequential. I don't believe Levi actually wanted to marry me. I'm not his choice. I was convenient for him. He's never had to make an effort to court a girl, because I was always there."

Father nodded with apparent understanding. . .and maybe even agreement. "What if he makes an effort?"

"He won't." That strange ache was back again in her chest. She turned to the window. The dust from the road, even if blown occasionally in her face as the trolley whizzed along, was a minor inconvenience compared to travel on a wagon or inside a suffocating carriage. "I know Levi. There's nothing he loves more than raising corn and cows."

"Have you listened to him talk about his work at the Extension Office? That boy loves horticulture more than cows."

Reba released a soft *humph*. That was news to her. "Clearly he and I aren't as good friends as I'd thought."

Father patted her hand. "Sweetheart, know one thing: men don't like to change. Ever."

"Then that's proof he won't make an effort."

Diehl Farm, north of Parker, South Dakota
Sunday, October 11

"May I speak to Reba?" Levi asked as politely as he could with Mrs. Diehl glaring through the screened door at him, her usual expression. He tapped his cap against his thigh. "She wasn't in church this morning. Nor Mr. Diehl. I figured they were sick."

Her lips were tighter than the pinned gray curls around her head. She dried her hands on the apron around her waist. "The pair left over a week ago for Sioux Falls."

Left? Levi ignored the burst of panic in his chest. He needed to talk to Reba. He had to make things right.

He clenched his cap. "When will they return?"

"If they had any sense," she said haughtily, "they would have never left, but everyone in Turner County knows Mr. Diehl can't say no to his youngest daughter. Don't matter that the girl is as senseless as they come."

Reba had her flaws, as did everyone, but senseless? She was smart and good-hearted, and could cheer anyone up, because she knew how to make the best of any situation.

Levi looked at the setting sun. Red-gold streaks painted the horizon. He'd spent many an evening on the Diehls' covered porch in the swing, watching the sun set. Every time he returned home from college, he could find Reba on the porch waiting for him.

He faced Mrs. Diehl again, her scowl unabated. "How long will they be gone?"

She shook her head. "Go home, Levi. She's not coming back. Ever. She filled a wagon with those crates of hat goods she ordered from the East Coast. She might as well just burn her money. You should be thankful she jilted you. Mr. Diehl's youngest daughter has a wanderlust that can't be tamed. She rebels against all that's good for her. Better for her to leave you now than leave you after you marry."

He felt his spine stiffen. The need to defend Reba prodded at him. Mrs. Diehl, though, was the type of woman who never admitted when she was wrong. Trying to convince her of that was futile. Could he fault Reba for wanting to leave home? Her mother had none of Abraham and Sarah's joy at having a child in old age.

Why Sioux Falls?

The air was fresher out here in the country. They could have married and lived on the land Reba had inherited from her grandmother. Sixteen miles down the road on one hundred and sixty perfect acres.

"All right then." He started to leave then stopped before backing onto the step. "When will Mr. Diehl return?"

"Maybe tomorrow, maybe next week." She muttered something under her breath. "He's helping his youngest build hat stands. If he calls, I'll let him know you stopped by. It'll be dark soon. Grab one of Peder's lanterns from the barn."

"Thank you, but I rode over instead of walking." Levi tried to smile. Every time he spoke to Mrs. Diehl he felt worse for wear. Too often he'd sat by in silence, listening to her rebuke of Reba. What kind of man did that make him? A coward who wouldn't defend the woman he loved. But not anymore. He straightened his shoulders. "Mrs. Diehl, her name is Reba, and she's your daughter, too. She has as much sense as anyone."

After a *pffft*, she closed the door. The bolt latched.

Levi slapped his hat on his head. He slid his hands in his coat pockets then trudged down the steps. As he walked to where he'd tied his gelding, he spared a glance over his shoulder. Light glowed in the front window of the two-story white-framed farmhouse. The Diehls had never had to worry about money, not any more than any other farmer in Turner County did, but neither were they wealthy. Save for Reba, their daughters had married well and their sons had found good women. If Reba wanted something different, who was he to criticize?

Mrs. Diehl was right. Better for Reba to jilt him now.

There were girls back at SDSU whom he could court. Nice girls. Girls who loved life on the farm. Girls who were content being a wife and mother.

Levi stopped at the hitching post and untied the reins. He rested his forehead against his saddle. Why did Reba do this? What was she thinking?

Reba didn't know anyone in Sioux Falls. She had never lived away from family. She had never been gone from home for more than a few days. During the six years he attended SDSU, he'd missed his family. He'd come home at every opportunity. What Reba needed wasn't life in Sioux Falls. What she needed was a place she felt loved and valued. Where she felt like she was a valued contributor. Where she wasn't criticized and belittled.

What she needed was to marry him and move into his parents' home. They loved Reba. They'd welcome her. The four of them could have the perfect life, just as he'd imagined. Everything Reba needed to be happy was here in Turner County. It was just at a different house—his house.

Tomorrow, he'd go to Sioux Falls and convince Reba to come home. And if she still wanted to make hats, she could make them here. His mother crocheted. Every woman needed a hobby. A good husband supported his wife's leisurely interests.

Chapter 4

"[A] foundation of wire will prove stronger and better fitting. Those wires which we place around the divisional lines of a shape we may call the ROUND wires; while those which keep the shape erect. . .are called the SUPPORTS."
—Practical Millinery

The next day

Levi admired the awning over the door to Reba's shop. Unlike the weathered, dingy white one over the next-door bakery, hers was crisp, bright white, and clean. There in the glass, centered and etched near the top of the window, were the words:

R. DIEHL
FINE MILLINERY

Underneath the wording was a display of fancy hats and a sign saying OPENING NOVEMBER 2. A wall of white fabric, about half as tall as the window, blocked any view into her boutique yet left space above it for natural light to come into the shop.

He knocked on the door.

A trio of young ladies exited the bakery, all wearing fancy hats like the ones Reba favored. One said, "Oh," and the other two gave him friendly smiles.

The "oh" girl said, "Hello. The millinery won't open for another two weeks."

"I know the owner."

The brunette regarded him intently. "Is she, umm, your sister?"

"She's my fiancée."

Her smile fell.

One of the ladies with her tugged on her arm. "Come on. Mother said we have to have our shopping done by noon."

Levi watched as the trio continued on until they reached the entrance to the Bee Hive Department Store. With the trolley, automobiles, and horse-drawn vehicles on the road, there were a lot of people passing by. He had to give Reba credit. She'd chosen an excellent location for her millinery.

He knocked on the door again, this time with more emphasis.

Within moments, a clicking sounded. The door opened.

Mr. Diehl's frown turned into an immediate grin. "Levi, it is good to see you." He propped the door open by wedging a triangular piece of wood under it. He brushed his hands on his paint-stained overalls then shook Levi's hand. "Come in, come in. I need to have Reba put a bell for the door on her shopping list."

Levi climbed two steps then entered the well-lit shop smelling like it had been painted and wallpapered recently. Along each side were white shelves and cabinets with red-and-gold geometric-stripe wallpaper. Two mirrors were diagonally across from each other. He could see how that made sense—who wanted to see the reflection of a mirror inside a mirror inside a mirror and so on?

"Tomorrow the men are coming to install the tin ceiling tiles," Mr. Diehl said, drawing up next to Levi. "Reba bought a crystal chandelier to go in the center of the ceiling, and she'll have wall sconces around the room."

"Seems a bit fancy for South Dakota."

"Women like pretty things."

"You've done a lot of work in a week."

"Nah, we just had to clean the place then paint and hang wallpaper. All the cabinets are from the previous tenant." He slapped Levi's shoulder. "What brings you to Sioux Falls?"

"Reba." Levi turned to the back entrance, which must lead to a workroom. "Is she here? I need to talk to her."

"I imagine you would." Her father's voice lowered. "Look, son, you've not ever had to worry about chasing my daughter or compete with another man for her attention. If you truly love Reba, you're going to have to convince her."

"I love her enough to come here."

Mr. Diehl patted Levi's shoulder. "Let me let you in on a little secret. Women take a lot of convincing. Even when you do convince them of your feelings, you still have to remind them daily or they start doubting again." He turned and cupped his hands around his mouth. "Reba!"

"Be there in a jiffy!" was her response.

"Seeing what time it is. . ." Mr. Diehl motioned to a stool. "Why don't you have a seat? I'll run down the street and pick us up something to eat from the café." He grabbed a well-worn straw hat from the counter.

Levi settled on the stool.

Mr. Diehl hadn't been gone a minute when Reba strolled into the room, wearing a loose calico work dress that did nothing for her petite figure. Even so, she was beautiful enough to make his eyes ache from staring.

<hr>

Reba stared at the clipboard in her hand. "Father, I have some extra dollars in the decorating budget. What do you think about buying a few—" She looked up. "—plants? Levi, what are you doing here?"

He jumped to his feet, snatching his cap off his head, his hair falling forward. "I came to bring you home." He said it in his usual confident-of-my-decision-because-I-know-what-is-best tone.

"N-no," Reba stuttered. "I've invested hundreds of dollars into starting my millinery. I'm not leaving now, no matter what you say."

As his green eyes—one obscured by a lock of walnut-colored hair—studied her, Reba regarded him carefully. How odd. She'd always thought of Levi as a fairly nice-looking man with no exaggerated or distracting features. Now, as he stood there in his three-piece Sunday suit, and even with a bit of sadness in his eyes, she decided he was an eminently handsome man. Certainly a plus in his favor. He should have no problems finding a young woman attracted enough to him to forsake indoor plumbing.

"I've thought about what you said at the fair before you ended. . .us." He cleared his throat. "You were right."

Reba stayed silent.

He raked his fingers through his hair. "I never proposed, so I had no right to presume we were engaged. The way I see it, there isn't only one person in life who can make us happy in marriage. My parents agreed and suggested that, since you insisted we would only be friends, I make a list of other girls I could court. I know that's not romantic of me to admit, but you'll only get the truth from me." He cleared his throat. "I made a list of eight girls. When I couldn't decide which girl to contact first—well, that's when I knew."

"Knew what?" she said and didn't feel bad at the wariness in her tone.

"There could be another girl who could make me happy in marriage, but I don't want to look for her. I want you, Reba Diehl. You."

"Y–you want me?"

He nodded and gripped his cap with both hands. "Love is a choice, and I choose to love you. Will you marry me?"

He sounded serious. He looked serious. But her heart didn't flutter, her breath flee, or her body feel wistful and warm. Even if he truly did love her—and she had her doubts— she wasn't in love with him. And he couldn't carry the love load for the both of them. Granted, not all marriages began with love. Levi's parents' marriage hadn't, but Reba didn't know a couple more doting, more attentive, more in love. And they'd been married for forty-eight years.

"You don't love me. You only want to marry me because I'm comfortable and convenient." Reba held up a hand. "Wait. Hear me out. Let's say I married you—and please, do not presume I have agreed—how often would we come to town? Not Parker Township. I mean Sioux Falls."

"We could visit a few times a year." He must have seen something in her expression, because he added, "One weekend a month. During the summer we'd stay for a week."

That was his concession. *That* was what he figured it took for her to toss away the hundreds of dollars she'd spent so far on starting her business.

One measly weekend a month and one measly week in summer.

With a *humph*, Reba set her clipboard on the nearest butcher-paper-covered counter. "Do you like horticulture more than cows?"

He gave her a strange look. "What does that have to do with us getting married?"

"Nothing—everything. We've never talked about what you like." She released a frustrated breath. "Do you enjoy doing accounting for the family farm?"

"It's why I went to college," he grumbled. "Don't you want to be a wife and mother?"

"Yes! Someday when I'm ready."

He waved his hand at nothing in particular. "So you're going to waste hundreds of dollars on a hobby until you decide you're 'ready' to be a wife?"

Reba froze. She wanted to argue that this wasn't a hobby, that if Levi moved to Sioux Falls, she'd be open to courting him. If their feelings for each other changed—deepened into real love—then she could see herself marrying him. If he moved. If he changed. If he realized life back home wasn't as wonderful as life here.

Reba moistened her lips. In a soft voice, she said, "Levi, do you really like living at home with your parents?"

"Yes." And there was that implied "*Why shouldn't I?*"

Father was right. Men don't like to change.

"Don't you want your own home?" she asked.

He didn't have to speak for her to know his thoughts. He'd had his soon-to-be-own-home. . .until she sold it and the land it was on.

"My parents agreed to give us their bedroom," he said, "and they would take one of the rooms on the second floor. They adore you. They want to do whatever they need to make you feel welcome."

At the sound of a *rumble rumble rumble pop pop*, Reba looked out the open door to the street. A blue automobile drove past, and two horse-drawn wagons followed. The trolley should pass by soon, too. On the other side of Phillips Avenue, people were walking along the sidewalk. A group of men passed by her shop door.

She met Levi's gaze. "I don't want to live with your parents. I don't want to leave this life I've started here in Sioux Falls. This is where my customers are."

A little muscle under his eye twitched. She'd never known him to lose his temper. In fact, Levi was the mellowest, most patient, take-it-all-in-stride person she knew. But when that muscle twitched, she knew he was irritated.

"Why are you doing this?" he snapped.

"Making hats brings me joy."

"You can make them at home."

"For whom?" she said, losing her patience. "I've sold a hat to every lady I know in Turner County. Farmers' wives have no need to own lots of hats, so I must find more customers. I need women who will buy multiple hats."

"Why?"

She scowled at him. "Because I love making hats! No matter what I do, my mind goes back to a new idea I have. I have to make it. I have to. Drawing a picture of it isn't enough. I have to see it come to life. Don't you have anything you *can't* not do? Or is accounting and managing a farm what brings you joy? It's all right if it is. God made us all different. We're not obligated to love doing the same things."

He didn't answer.

She didn't mind. He was considering her words. She liked his willingness to hear a different perspective and even to change his mind when he realized he was wrong. Were it not for his predilection to farming, he would make a good husband for her.

She gave him a few moments to think before she said, "Just because you planned for us to marry doesn't mean that's how it's supposed to be. And don't you dare tell me us marrying is God's will for our lives, because if it were what God wanted, don't you think He would tell both of us and not just you?"

A glimmer of something—anger, sadness, or maybe disappointment—flashed in his eyes. She didn't think he was going to respond until he said, "So your answer is no."

Reba nodded. "I want a man who is willing to move mountains for me. We both know you aren't him, and that's all right. Maybe we could make each other happy in marriage, but maybe there's someone better for you and for me. Maybe you should go look for her."

"Understood." He slapped his cap on his head. "Good-bye, Reba. I wish you well."

Before she could say, "And I wish you well," he was out the door.

Her heart didn't tighten, nor did she feel any need to chase after him. Instead, she looked to her clipboard. She stared at the numbers she'd written down.

For a long, long time she stared.

She hadn't wanted to hurt him. Grandmother used to say, "The blunt truth sometimes can be the kindest words." She wanted Levi to be happy and to be loved.

He'd made a list of eight girls?

She was still standing there, staring at the clipboard, when Father returned.

"I have food." He strolled up to her, carrying a paper sack. "Where's Levi?"

"He returned home."

"I see." Father rested his straw hat and the paper sack on the counter. "Do you want to talk?"

She shook her head. "I need to focus on the future, not the past."

Chapter 5

"When a hat is larger in the head than the wearer finds comfortable, the size can
be quickly reduced by stitching a round bandeau into the crown of it."
—*Practical Millinery*

Great Northern Railway Depot

Levi found a seat at the back of the passenger train, several rows away from the nearest person. He tossed the bagged lunch he'd bought inside the depot onto the bench.

How could Reba say he didn't love her? He wouldn't have come all the way to Sioux Falls to ask her to marry him if he didn't love her. He wanted to marry her because of who she was, not because he'd gotten used to the idea of marrying her.

"You only want to marry me because I'm comfortable and convenient."

Levi winced. That wasn't a fair statement for her to make. She didn't know his heart. When a man loved a woman, he knew. He just knew. When he imagined his future, he could see her there. He could see her reading to their children. He could see her serving them dinner and sitting by the fire darning his shirt. His mother did those things and never complained. Why didn't Reba want that?

He rested his head against the window.

"I'm comfortable and convenient."

She believed that's how he saw her.

Levi released a frustrated breath. His relationship with Reba *was* comfortable. *She* was comfortable. She was easy to be around. That comfortableness about her wasn't a flaw. Knowing he had a great girl back home while he was at school had kept him from wasting his time, finances, and emotions on courting, like many of his friends had. He'd been able to focus on studies and have extra time to conduct horticulture experiments at the Extension Office.

Convenient wasn't a flaw, either. When the fruit you'd picked tasted good, why go sampling other fruit? Reba was a kindhearted, good-natured, God-fearing woman. He knew it. He knew her. How many girls would he have to court before he found one he liked being around as much as he liked being around Reba?

"I want a man who is willing to move mountains for me. We both know you aren't him. . . ."

He struggled to find an argument in response. If there was a mountain needing moved, Reba would do it herself. No obstacle intimidated her.

The whistle blew and the train started into motion to take him home and away from Reba. Amazing how the tracks took a person *to* and *from* something at the same time.

Levi straightened in his seat, an epiphany dawning.

He was a train on tracks. He could, move on from Reba, continue his life as planned, and find another girl to marry, or, move to Sioux Falls, let her get the millinery out of her system, and do whatever necessary to convince her she was ready to be a wife. His wife.

Reba had such a knack for succeeding at anything she tried, the odds were she would succeed. But if she didn't succeed, if her business failed—he wouldn't rub salt in the wound. No, he'd comfort her. He'd help her find a better outlet for her creativity.

The key was convincing her to marry him and move home before she spent all the money she'd made from selling her grandmother's land. Tomorrow he would talk to his father and brothers. Surely there was an acre of Webber land along Baseline Road, just outside of town, that he and Reba could buy. Granted, Parker wasn't Sioux Falls. It was town.

Three months should be all the time he'd need to win Reba back. This was mid-October. That meant they could have a St. Valentine's Day wedding.

Perfect.

With a satisfied grin and a restored appetite, Levi grabbed the paper sack with his food.

Webber Farm, north of Parker, South Dakota
Five days later

Levi stood at the head of the table that Ma continued to cover with her favorite white crocheted tablecloth even though his brother Daniel could be counted on to spill whatever he was drinking. His parents and four older brothers sat in silence, clearly mulling over the seven-point plan he'd revealed about how to convince his girl she loved him more than her business. A nice Saturday morning breeze blew through the double windows, fluttering the lace curtains and cooling the room.

Levi hooked his thumbs around his suspenders. "Please keep in mind this will only be for three months, and I won't leave the farm until I've finished up what I need to do here."

Pa nodded. "We can manage without you for three months." He looked to Solomon, Ruben, Daniel, and Israel. "Are you four good with this? Solomon, this means you'll have to go back to doing the accounting."

One by one, his brothers nodded.

"Where are you going to get a job?" Ruben asked, being the firstborn he was.

Levi shrugged. "I don't know yet."

Solomon and Israel exchanged glances.

Daniel sipped his coffee.

"He'll find something," Pa said, grinning. "He graduated from South Dakota State University. Everyone will want him to work for them."

Levi's cheeks warmed. "I thought I'd apply first at the John Deere Plow Company. It would give me opportunity to study that new cornstalk chopper they have."

"Ask them to pay you in tractor parts," Ruben suggested.

Solomon and Israel grunted their agreement.

Daniel pulled the plate of pastries to him. He dunked one in his coffee then took a bite.

"While you're in Sioux Falls, your mother can make wedding preparations." Pa looked to Ma. "Do you think you can handle that, or were you going to go stay with

Martha after the baby arrives like you did with the last one?"

Ma ran a finger around the rim of her coffee cup, her gaze absent.

Levi sat next to his mother. "You look troubled. What are you thinking?"

She focused on him. "What are you going to do when Reba doesn't agree to marry you and return home?"

Levi drew a blank.

She would agree. His plan was solid. Logical.

Reasonable.

Ma rested her palms on each side of his face. "I love you dearly, you know that?"

Levi nodded as best he could with her grip still on him.

"There is a time in every mother's life when she looks at her son"—she gave a pointed look to Solomon, to Daniel, to Ruben, and to Israel, and then smiled at Levi—"and thinks, 'I have raised an idiot.' Fortunately, your older brothers developed sense. I am sure you will, too."

Keeping his face even to hide his annoyance, Levi removed her hands from his face. "Reba *will* come home."

"So you expect her business to fail." Ma scowled at him. "Or are you just hoping it will? Because for your plan to work out, that's what will have to happen. Levi, that girl isn't going to fall in love with someone who thinks her dreams aren't important. She will fall in love with a man who supports and encourages her."

Levi flinched. He wasn't hoping Reba would fail. He merely recognized her business failing as a possibility, because he was a realist.

Ma continued to stare at him, knowingly, as if she could see what he wasn't admitting to himself. What kind of man hoped his girl's dreams failed?

That's *not* what he was doing.

He jolted to his feet. "I'm going to Sioux Falls to win back my girl. We'll be back in three months. Ma, any help you can provide with wedding plans is appreciated."

"Excellent," Pa said with a slap to the table. "Now that we have that settled. . . While you're in Sioux Falls, I want you to talk to the bank about a loan so we can look at expanding. I'd like to start building in the spring."

As his brothers argued about where best to build the larger milk barn, Levi watched his mother. She circled her finger along the rim of her coffee cup, lost again in her own thoughts. He could tell her his plan would work. He could list all the sound, sensible reasons. He could say he was doing this because of his love for Reba. Or—

He could prove it.

Chapter 6

*"In tying a flower, extreme lightness must be exercised in the handling,
and, if necessary, the cotton should be left rather loose in
order to avoid pulling the flower in at all."*
—Practical Millinery

Sioux Falls
Monday morning, October 26

Reba stopped counting electric trolley poles as she reached the intersection of Ninth and Phillips. She inhaled slowly to steady her breathing then checked her wristwatch. While she'd probably walked quicker than she would on a regular basis, she'd cut four minutes off her best time while walking from the boardinghouse to the millinery. That she didn't have Father with her lessened her time, too.

She sighed. Him being here to help her set up the boutique had been the best two weeks of her life. And all they'd done was work in her millinery during the day and return to the boardinghouse for supper and sleep. No theater visits. No trips to the park. The only shopping they'd done was to buy things for the store.

But he couldn't stay forever.

He needed to go home to the farm and to Mother.

"You won't be alone," Father had said before boarding the train yesterday. "God is with you. He will never leave you or forsake you."

She knew it. She believed it. But that hadn't stopped her from crying her way from the train depot to the boardinghouse.

A trio of young women strolled past, dressed in the style Reba had quickly adopted— white shirt and matching ankle-length skirt, thin black tie, black stockings and shoes. Instead of a simple straw hat, she wore a more elaborate one with feathers and silk flowers. Until she opened the boutique, there was no need to wear her nicer dresses.

With a firm grip on her tapestry bag, Reba hurried across Ninth Street. She reached the front of Huss Bakery when she noticed someone was standing in front of her millinery. She took a hesitant step forward. Then another. And another. A man in a black suit leaned against the door, legs crossed at the ankles, arms folded across his chest, a flat tweed cap over his face to shield his eyes from the morning sun.

Reba placed her foot on the bottom step. "Levi, what are you doing here?"

He slid his cap off his face. "I'm here for you."

A loud groan escaped before Reba could stop it. "I told you—I'm not leaving."

"Then I'll have to convince you."

Reba hurried up the steps. "No! I'm not convincible."

"We'll see." He cocked an eyebrow, his lips easing up in a mischievous grin. He was flirting with her, and the worst part was—some little part of her wanted to flirt back.

"Levi, don't look at me like that."

174

"I can't help it," he said, his tone serious. "I love you, Reba Diehl, and I'm not leaving. You were right about me never courting you like a suitor should. I'm going to now. I'm going to prove to you that my love for you is real."

A little pain grew in her chest. She must have taxed herself too much in walking so quickly to the millinery. "Don't do this. Don't make this hard on either of us. Your family needs you at home."

"They can manage a little while without me."

He moved closer. . .much closer. So close that her breath caught in panic over his nearness. Her heart began to beat a little faster. He wouldn't draw her to him and kiss her. He just wouldn't. He was Levi Webber. He wasn't some rogue in a dime novel. His father was a deacon. His grandfather had been a deacon. His great-grandfather. . .well, she had no idea, but she did know Levi was a decade from becoming a deacon himself. If the man had believed they were engaged and not kissed her, then he certainly wouldn't now when he knew full well they weren't engaged. Or even courting.

Yet—

He took her hand, the one not clenching her tapestry bag, and raised it to his lips. "I'm not leaving without you." His kiss brushed against her skin with aching tenderness.

She nodded, unable to think of another argument, unable to look away from his lovely green eyes. Dozens of people could be on the street watching them, and she didn't care. She wanted to relish this moment—this feeling she was about to float away—as long as possible. She liked this confident, romantic man standing in front of her. Since he was willing to leave the farm to woo her, then maybe he would be willing to leave the farm forever to win her love.

Levi cleared his throat. He took a step back. "I took a room at the Cataract, and I have a job interview later this week at the John Deere Plow Company."

"How. . .uhh. . ." Reba gave her head a little shake to clear the muddle he'd made of it. "How could you have arranged all that this morning? It's only eight o'clock."

He shrugged. "I arrived on Friday."

"What? Why didn't you come by?"

"I had plans to make."

"What plans?"

He winked. "Courting-you plans."

Reba nipped at her bottom lip, accepting that nothing she could say could convince him to move on with his life. "All right."

"All right?"

"You may court me." Ignoring the pleasure she felt in saying those words, Reba reached inside her tapestry bag for the key to the boutique. She tapped the key on his chest. "You'd better believe me when I say I'm not going to fall in love with you. I promise, I'm not going to live on a farm ever again. Sioux Falls is my home."

Grinning, he took the key from her. "What can I do to help?"

<hr />

The next morning Reba arrived at her boutique to see Levi sitting on the front step, using a folded newspaper to shield his eyes from the sun. "There's my girl looking pretty as a penny."

Her heart increased its beat, yet she responded, "I'm not your girl."

A smile curled one side of his mouth. His handsome face said it all—*"You'll always be my girl."*

"Levi, please go. You have other things you can do," she said as she climbed the steps.

He followed. "Not really."

"I'm just making hats today."

Levi took the keys from her. "What can I do to help?"

She eyed him. "Don't you have a job interview?"

"Tomorrow."

"Shouldn't you be preparing for it?"

He gave her a bemused look.

"Oh, good gracious." Reba slid between him and the door, blocking the lock. "Is this going to be a habit for you?"

He looked heavenward and frowned, as if he was giving her words some serious thought. "Takes three weeks of repeat behavior to make something habitual."

"Good," she said. "You can't keep this up for three weeks. You need a job. Better yet, go home."

"Three weeks is no time at all when you're with the woman you love." He winked. "Besides, the way to win a girl's heart is through her hat."

"I'm fairly certain that's not how the saying goes," she said with some enjoyment.

"It's not?" He gave her a bland look. "Then I shall have to find some other way to court you." He gripped her arms then lifted her out of the way so he could unlock the door. "I know you aren't in love with me. I know I've done a poor job conveying my feelings. I love you, and I will do whatever necessary to convince you my love is true. Now let's get to work. Your boutique needs to be ready for its grand opening."

Reba watched as he unlocked then opened the door. He smiled, motioning her inside. She smiled. Whatever had come over Levi—well, she liked it. Clearly Father had been wrong. Men could change.

<hr />

Late afternoon
Saturday, November 6

Levi crossed his arms and leaned against the workroom's threshold as Reba spoke with the last customer in the boutique. She seemed like someone of importance, with her mannerisms and air. The two women stood at the full-length mirror. The statuesque brunette tipped her head left then right, evaluating the gold silk ribbon covering the black straw hat. Reba stood on the footstool she needed when attending to a tall customer. In her hand she held an assortment of hat pins from the Sterling Company in Rhode Island. Not that the name had meant anything to him. "Refined ladies," Reba had explained, "would know."

Apparently so, because she'd sold all but the four in her hand.

She'd even sold the enameled sets that came in velvet-lined presentation boxes with DIEHL'S FINE MILLINERY imprinted on the satin. He'd never thought of giving her hat pins. Nor would he have guessed that most of those presentation boxed sets would be purchased by men to give to their sweethearts. In all the times he'd been in Reba's boutique, he'd never seen a male customer. Mr. Diehl had been right: women liked pretty things. And if anything could be said about Reba's boutique, pretty was an apt description.

He glanced about the millinery, impressed at the sight. He'd visited the two other millineries in Sioux Falls, but neither of them were on the main thoroughfare through town, nor were they decorated as elegantly as Reba's. Neither smelled of flowers. Reba's did because she'd placed potted orchids around the room. What woman wouldn't want to shop at a boutique like Diehl's Fine Millinery? Clearly, enough of them in Sioux Falls did. After six day of sales, all but four hats had sold. If Reba kept selling at this pace, she'd be out of stock by noon on Monday. Deservedly so.

She wasn't only good at making hats. She thrived at selling them.

Reba knew how to sell beauty because, ever since he could remember, Reba had sought beauty, had drawn beauty to her. It was no wonder she wanted more than life on a farm. It was no wonder she wanted more than to be the wife of a dairyman.

Ma had been right—Reba would never fall in love with him as long as he thought her dreams were unimportant and her hard work was nothing more than a hobby. He had to support and encourage her. But if he did that, and her millinery continued to succeed, then she would never come home with him. He was a dairyman, not a city slicker.

How could he compete with all of this?

Laughter came from the front of the shop.

His stomach turning sour, Levi ducked into the workroom. He sank onto the chair beside Reba's workbench and leaned forward, his head in his hands. It wasn't supposed to happen like this. He'd compared the prices of her hats, pins, and sundry items against the prices at the Bee Hive Department Store next door. Everything she sold was more expensive. A few items were even twice the price!

With sales like this, there'd be no reason for her to close the millinery in three months. No reason for her to come home with him.

The bell tied on the front doorknob jingled. After a pause, it jingled again.

The customer must have left.

Levi checked his watch. Sixteen minutes after five. He released a wry chuckle. This was the earliest she'd closed all week.

Reba dashed into the workroom.

Levi stood, opened his mouth to speak, then—

BAM!

She hugged him tight. "She bought my hat! Oh, Levi! I couldn't believe it was her—did you see her? Did you? She's as beautiful as a Gibson Girl, and she bought *my* hat." Reba released him. She lifted her hands over her head and twirled like she was six instead of twenty-three. "This is the best day ever!"

Levi nodded. "I can see that."

Reba clasped his arm then bent over, her face red and splotchy as she gasped for air. "Oh, my goodness, oh, my goodness. My heart feels like it's going to explode."

"Who was she?"

"Musical Selection."

"Huh?"

She burst out laughing.

Levi stared in awe. He'd never seen her so elated. He swerved her over to the chair and nudged her into sitting. "Catch your breath and explain."

Reba's lips formed an O, and she released her breath slowly. Her face returned to its normal color. "For my fifteenth birthday, Father took me to Germania Hall. That woman was the first performer. She was listed as 'Musical Selection.' Today, Miss Claire Van Dyke is the headline performer at the New Theater. She bought my hat. Do you realize what this means?"

"Women will want your hats because Miss Van Dyke wears one?"

"Exactly!" Standing, she gripped his arms. "I hoped to sell through my inventory after three months. Father said six months was more realistic, which was why he advised I sign a six-month lease, but I've almost sold out in six days. Can you believe it? Miss Van Dyke ordered two more. Several singers she knows in St. Paul will be here next month. She suggested I stock up because her friends love to shop."

"That's great. You're really good at making hats."

"You sound surprised."

Levi shrugged. He was surprised at her skill, at how quickly her business was succeeding, and at how unsettled that made him feel. "My news isn't as exciting, but I got the job at the John Deere Plow Company. I start Monday. It's only inventorying right now, but—"

Reba squealed and hugged him tight. "I've been praying that God would open the door if it was His will for you to stay in Sioux Falls. This is exactly what we need."

Levi grinned. Not *I* need. *We* need.

She tilted her head to the side in a bashful manner. Then she smiled, which was all the encouragement he needed. Hoping she couldn't see his hands shake, he cupped her face and brushed his lips against hers. She didn't respond by kissing him back, but neither did she pull away. Instead, she sighed. And so he kissed her again. This time she responded.

If he'd only kissed her months—years—ago, they'd be married already and could—

Levi drew back a little too abruptly. "Uh, we should eat. Supper. Go now—the, uh, restaurant down the street. . .they. . .I made reservations."

She frowned at him. "I can't."

"Can't?" he echoed.

"I have orders I need to fill. I can't eat. I need to make more hats." She glanced around the room, nipping at her bottom lip. "There's so much to do."

Levi nodded. "I'll bring something back here for us to share."

"Thank you."

As they walked to the front door, something pricked at his mind. Something she'd said about—

"Did you say you signed a six-month lease?"

She stopped at the door. "October 6 to April 6."

"Six months? I can't stay here that long."

She looked like she was about to say something but then thought better of it. "How long did you plan on staying?"

"Three months."

She nodded slowly, her expression losing its joy. "Go home, Levi. I won't change my mind. I'm not giving up my millinery because I enjoyed kissing you."

He stepped outside yet blocked her from closing the door. "Reba Diehl, I'm not giving up on you. I'll escort you to church in the morning."

Chapter 7

"No matter whether a city be under siege, a country perplexed with overwhelming
questions of national well-being, or a nation plunged in the awful intricacies of war,
Fashion still holds her sway, changing with surprising rapidity,
in spite of obstacles of never such appalling magnitude!"
—Practical Millinery

Diehl Fine Millinery
Wednesday, December 30, 1908

Yes, Levi, I'm writing it down." Reba shifted the telephone to her left ear, raising her shoulder to hold it in place. She yawned. Blinked her eyes to chase the blurriness away in order to finish another batch of silk leaves. As she wrote on the notepad, she read aloud her handwriting. "Dinner. Six p.m. I promise I won't forget this time."

"I also have tickets for—"

The bell on the door jingled twice.

"Oh," she gasped, cutting him off. "I have a customer." *Finally.* "Good-bye." She dropped the headset into the base and the pen onto the notepad. After a quick check to ensure her dress was free of loose threads and clingy silk scraps, she hurried into the boutique. "Good morning and welcome to Diehl's Fine—" Reba stopped abruptly. "Oh, Mrs. Wright, what a lovely surprise."

"I don't mind snow, but wind. . .*brrr.* It's near freezing out there." Mrs. Wright tucked a manila envelope under her arm then removed her gloves. Her cheeks and nose were red. The snowflakes on her woolen coat and fur hat quickly disappeared.

Reba met the older woman at the center display table. "At least it's not a blizzard. What kind of hat can I interest you in today? I have a new assortment of hat pins from London."

Mrs. Wright's gaze shifted about the millinery. She had to notice how thin the displays were. Did she realize the number of potted plants having taken over spaces formerly occupied by hats? While Diehl's Fine Millinery wasn't devoid of stock, inventory was a fraction of what she should have available. To have product to sell, Reba needed to hire someone to work the boutique while she focused on hat construction, but she couldn't afford to hire someone without dipping into the next six months' budget. She may have to make a compromise. Ladies couldn't buy a hat if there weren't any hats available. And with Easter only months away—

"Is something wrong?" asked Mrs. Wright.

"No, no, no. I was—it's nothing. How are you?"

Mrs. Wright's face lit up. "I'm doing wonderfully. For Christmas, Mr. Wright took me to see our youngest son in Cedar Rapids. Our daughter-in-law is expecting their first."

"Congratulations."

"And congratulations to you. Word is, Diehl's Fine Millinery makes the most superb hats in all of Sioux Falls. I had to come by and see your boutique."

"Thank you." Reba turned to face the shelves filled now with folded yards of fabric instead of hats. "I do have a few hats in stock, but most ladies elect to place orders. The first step is to decide on colors. If you'd like to peruse the silks, I'll go—"

"I'm not here to buy anything."

Reba's smile fell. Why would the dean of Home Economics at Sioux Falls College come to her millinery if she didn't want a hat? A sinking feeling spread throughout her belly.

The scholarship.

"I meant to respond to your letter," Reba blurted. "Truly I did, but after the fair, I had to start packing for the move. It slipped from my mind."

Mrs. Wright motioned to the Queen Anne chairs in the sitting area. "Could we?"

"Oh, of course." Reba followed Mrs. Wright to the red velvet chairs. "It was wrong of me not to notify you I was turning down the scholarship," she said as they were seated. "I'm deeply sorry."

Mrs. Wright laid the envelope on her lap and placed her gloves on top. "I had a feeling you wouldn't accept it."

"I appreciate the offer, but"—she shrugged—"college isn't for me. This millinery is my heart's desire."

"I can tell." Mrs. Wright looked impressed as she again glanced about the room. "It's exquisite. There's nothing like it in Sioux Falls. I like how you used the 60-30-10 principle."

"60-30-10?"

"Sixty percent red, thirty percent white, and ten percent gold." She laid the manila envelope on the marble-topped coffee table. "You brought in texture with the walnut center table and smell with the orchids and potted plants. You have a natural decorating sense." She slid the envelope across the table. "I want you to reconsider your decision."

Reba looked at the envelope but didn't take it. "I don't want to go to college."

"Why not?" Mrs. Wright said, her tone gentle.

"I don't enjoy cooking or canning or cleaning house. I don't want to take classes in household management." She leaned forward to nudge the envelope back to Mrs. Wright. "Making hats brings me joy. This is what I want to do."

"Is it?"

"Yes, it is."

Mrs. Wright nodded her head slowly, like Father did when he was thinking of a response.

Reba shifted in her chair.

"I was here opening day," said Mrs. Wright.

"I didn't see you."

"You were too busy taking money."

Reba glanced at her watch. Eleven fifteen. She needed to get back to work.

Mrs. Wright continued with: "You aren't as busy taking money anymore, are you?"

Reba managed not to choke. How did she know? She couldn't know. But the question was too pointed for her not to reply, "Customers prefer customizing."

"Do they prefer it"—Mrs. Wright paused—"or is it a matter of they have no choice?"

A heavy sigh was all Reba had in response.

Mrs. Wright eyed her measuringly. "There's not enough time to make the hats needed to keep up with demand without skimping on quality, and that's something you can't do. You had to decrease your business hours from six days a week, nine to five, to Wednesday through Saturday, noon to five, to have time to work on orders. Yet even with more time to focus on hat making, you keep having to lengthen the amount of time to fill an order. Inventory is low. Customers are becoming more dissatisfied. Word is spreading. Consequently, fewer customers stop in, and custom orders continue to decrease. By the look on your face, I can tell you are wondering how I know this."

Of course she wanted to know! But admitting it was another thing.

Mrs. Wright leaned forward and slid the envelope back to Reba. "After my mother's death, I helped my father manage his bakery. Once he passed away, I sold it, because I knew I didn't have the skills, talents, or abilities a successful business owner needs. I hated the long work hours and little sleep. It's not joyful living, is it?"

Reba swallowed an indignant *humph*.

"Bring the enrollment papers to my office next week. Classes start February 1."

"I have a business to manage."

"Take two credit hours a week, and open your shop only on Fridays and Saturdays."

"This is a business, not a hobby."

"How long can you keep it afloat?"

"All new businesses struggle the first year," Reba said in her defense. "Come spring, I'll be able to hire help. Winter is always a slow period for sales."

Mrs. Wright stared at Reba for a long moment. "Well, then. . ." She stood, pulling on her gloves, and walked to the door. "You have time to change your mind."

Reba followed her. "I'm flattered by the offer."

Mrs. Wright reached out and tucked a stray lock of hair behind Reba's ear. "I know making hats brings you joy. Take a look in the mirror and ask yourself if running a business does. Does paying bills and ordering supplies fit your talents and abilities?"

Reba said nothing at all.

As Mrs. Wright left the shop, a burst of wintery air bit at Reba's face. She quickly closed the door. Crossing her arms and rubbing them, she hurried to the potbellied stove at the back of the boutique. She added a scoop of coal then sat on a nearby footstool to enjoy the warmth. She didn't have to look in a mirror to know she looked ragged. She felt it. Her parents had never seemed the worse for wear on only six hours of sleep a night. Right now she would give anything for six hours of slumber.

What a fool she'd been to think she understood what it took to manage a business! She should have listened to Father and to Mr. Smyth. Maybe they were right. Maybe she should have opened a smaller shop in a less expensive part of town. Maybe she should have asked Levi for business advice. Or hired him to manage the accounting.

Reba's eyes burned with unshed tears. Her chin trembled, yet she fought the urge to break down. "I don't understand, God. You promised whatever I asked for in Your name would be given to me. I took the time to figure out Your will. I know You opened this door. It's not supposed to be like this. It's supposed to be abundant." Her voice choked. "You promised abundance."

That doesn't mean immediately, she reminded herself.

Right. Hard work and patience. And if push came to shove, she could dip into her savings and hire a shopgirl. Maybe an accountant.

Reba took a deep breath. "It'll work out," she said in a firm voice. "I'll find a way to make it work." She pushed off the footstool and headed straight to the workroom.

The time for crying and moping had passed. She had hats to make.

Chapter 8

"Never put more stitches than are absolutely necessary to keep the material in place."
—*Practical Millinery*

John Deere Plow Company
Monday, midafternoon, February 8, 1909

W e'll bring it to Parker by train next week." As another gust of wind rattled the windows, Levi stepped around his desk to shake Mr. Olander's hand. Selling to their neighbor to the east of the Webber farm was the easiest sale thus far. "It's a great tractor. I'm sure my father will be over to try it out. He'd like a new tractor but needs a cornstalk chopper more."

"He has the money to buy both."

"That he does."

Mr. Thayer peeked around the corner. "Levi, after you finish here, lock up, will you? I need to get on home. The power's been flickering on and off, and Bertina is nervous."

"Of course." Levi caught the keys the store's manager tossed him.

"That's the signal I need to be going." Mr. Olander pulled on his greatcoat. He grabbed his gloves and hat from off Levi's desk. As they walked across the empty-but-for-them showroom, he slid his hands in his gloves and said, "Looks like the snow has picked up."

Levi frowned. The wind howled, blowing thick clouds of snow across the street and limiting visibility to less than a block. The trolley trudged slowly down the snow-laden street.

"Think it'll taper off soon?" he asked.

They stopped at the large window to the left of the door. Mr. Olander touched the glass and looked at the sky.

With a *humph*, he tugged his hat down over his ears. "Levi, I suggest you go check on Reba," he said in a grim tone, still staring out the window. "I've seen enough snowstorms to know this one is going to blow through the night."

Levi nodded.

Mr. Olander looked back at him. "You mind me asking a personal question?"

Levi braced himself for a question about why he and Reba hadn't married yet.

"During the summer when you were home from SDSU, you remember how you'd come over every Tuesday morning for coffee and Berliners?"

"Yes," he said hesitantly. "Uh, I was really there for the company. Mrs. Olander's jelly doughnuts were a fortunate bonus."

"A bonus they always are."

Another gust of wind rattled the window.

Mr. Olander's gray brows drew together. "You would always tell us about what you were growing at the Extension Office. When you showed me all the equipment in the showroom, whether you were talking about buggies, plows, or tractors, you had that

184

same gleam in your eyes. You never had that gleam when you talked about your business classes. Did you get those degrees in accounting and agricultural business because you wanted them or because you felt obligated because that's what the family wanted you to do?" He patted Levi's shoulder. "Mull on it for a spell."

Levi dipped his chin enough to convey he would.

Mr. Olander looked as if he wanted to say more. His blue eyes grew watery, his voice tightened. "I'm a farmer because my father was a farmer. I never thought I had a choice. My son joined the navy because he wanted to be a sailor. It wasn't until he died in the sinking of the USS *Maine* that I realized I would rather he die doing what he loved than live doing what he hated."

Throat too tight to speak, Levi nodded.

"The, uhh. . ."Mr. Olander cleared his throat. "The missus is buying fabric over at Fantle Brothers. Good thing we've already booked a hotel room. This is not a night to be traveling." He hurried outside to his automobile.

Levi watched as the wind continued to howl and the snow fall. He enjoyed plowing the cornfields. He enjoyed bringing in the harvest. He didn't so much enjoy milking or breeding or castrating. For all that he could tolerate about cows and sheep, hogs were a blight on his senses. But farming was a job, a good job. Like his father and grandfather, he was supposed to be a farmer.

Out of obligation?

His degrees were to help the family. He couldn't walk away from his duty. While his brothers and parents agreed he should move to Sioux Falls to court Reba, they expected him to return. Family stayed together.

Like her mother and grandmother before her, Reba was supposed to become a farmer's wife, yet she'd chosen to walk away from what was expected of her. Her mother considered her a rebel. Her father considered her brave. If he was being honest with himself, last summer he would have agreed more with her mother. Now he wasn't sure. If his father wasn't a farmer and he could choose any job he wanted to do, what would he do? What would he do because *he* wanted to do it and not because it was what anyone else wanted or expected? What brought him joy?

Spending time with Reba did.

He couldn't make a living doing that.

Move her, Lord, or move me. Change her or change me.

Of all the words his mother had advised him to pray, these were his most fervent of late. Something had to change. But what? As long as Reba felt fulfilled by making hats and managing her millinery, things wouldn't change.

Snow and wind battered the windows. The lights flickered.

Levi rushed to the telephone on his desk. He grabbed the receiver. No sound. He clicked the base. "Hello?" Nothing. The lines were down. He snatched his greatcoat, hat, scarf, and gloves. Knowing Reba as he did, he knew she wouldn't have left the millinery. . .not when she had work to do.

Reba jolted awake at the pounding on the boutique's front door. As her eyes adjusted, she looked down at what she'd been sleeping on. Mrs. Lister's hat! Well, what remained of it. Wonderful. She shivered. How strange. She'd never had a problem with the potbellied stove not warming both rooms. With a gentle slap to her cheeks, she stood, yawned, and gave her head a shake. How long had she been asleep? She checked her watch and gasped. Ten minutes after six. She'd started working on that hat right after lunch.

The pounding on the door continued.

She grabbed the key from her desk and hurried into the boutique. "I'm coming," she called the moment she noticed the white sky and almost horizontal sheets of snow beating the window. No wonder the millinery was cold; no telling how close to zero degrees it was outside. She stopped at the door. "Levi?"

He unbundled his snow-covered scarf from around his face. "Hurry up and unlock the door," he said, his words muffled by the wind and the glass.

She turned the key.

Levi burst inside and slammed the door closed. Snow fell from him, pooling at his feet. "G–g–gather w–w–what you n–n–need," he said, shivering.

"Warm up first." She pulled him over to the stove then added more coal. Shouldn't take long to warm the room. "What's going on?"

His eyes widened. "Do you n–n–not see the b–blizzard outside?"

"Please don't patronize me."

"The trolley stopped running," Levi snapped. He knelt closer to the stove, removing his gloves. He laid them and his scarf on the top of the stove to dry as he warmed his hands. "You won't make it back to the boardinghouse on foot without freezing first."

Reba looked to the window even though the snow was too thick for her to see anything outside. She'd been in a blizzard before. The best course of action was to stay put and bundle up. "I have enough coal to keep the boutique warm for the rest of the week. I can scoop snow into my lunch pail. It'll melt, and I'll have water. I keep a stash of emergency rations as well. There's a couple old blankets in one of my trunks in the workroom. Father may have packed a cot, too. Let me go—"

Before she could take a step away, Levi stood and grabbed her arm. "You're not staying here."

"Where am I supposed to go?"

"The Cataract."

"The Cataract?" Reba shook her head. "No. If I'm going to be snowed in anywhere, I'll stay here. Here I can get work done."

"Would you stop being so stubborn and let me help you?"

"It's more likely all the rooms are already filled with people stranded by the storm."

"I stopped there first to book rooms for you and me. There's no way I'll make it to my boardinghouse, either."

Reba felt her mouth gape. The price of a room at the Cataract, plus meals— One night or two wouldn't break the bank, but she'd heard of blizzards lasting days. There were too many better things for her to spend her savings on.

"I'll be fine here," she insisted. "I grew up on a farm. I know how to survive a blizzard. Sometime in the night the snow will stop falling. There's a snow shovel in the back room. I have an oil lantern and candles in case the power goes out." She shrugged. "I don't need to stay at the Cataract."

Levi studied her. "I love you too much to allow you to stay here alone."

What? He couldn't stay here through the night. It wasn't appropriate. "Be reasonable," she cautioned. "People would find out, and we will have to marry."

He shrugged.

Reba gritted her teeth. She refused to allow a storm, a man's stubbornness, and propriety to force her into a marriage she didn't want. At least not now. "Fine. I'll go, but only after I've packed up some supplies."

* * *

The Cataract Hotel
The next afternoon

SIOUX FALLS' WORST IN MANY YEARS—or so it was, according to the *Daily Argus Leader*. Twenty-one inches in fifteen hours. Yet for all the storm's wrathful glory, it only made page eight. Of all the days to put an advertisement in the paper, today would have been it. Right below a photograph of the snow at Ninth Street and Dakota.

With a weary sigh, Reba laid the paper on the counter then sipped her coffee. She didn't need the paper to tell her snow had piled six to eight feet high in the street overnight. She'd discovered that herself when she tried to leave the hotel after lunch. The thermometer outside the front door read zero degrees. While the snow had stopped raging an hour ago, she expected the temperature to be about the same.

But at least the hotel had heat and electricity.

"Would you care for a slice? Freshly baked." The waitress offered Reba a slice of pumpkin pie.

Reba lifted her coffee cup. "I'm fine with this, thank you." Unlike the food in the Cataract's café, the coffee was unlimited. . .and free. Since she was stuck here until the sidewalks were clear, she might as well enjoy the stay. Frugally, of course.

* * *

Noon, Wednesday, February 10

Reba sipped her coffee and looked from her third-floor window at the snow piled in the street, covering the trolley tracks. Mayor Doolittle had been up since five o'clock organizing snow removal, or so she'd heard someone say this morning in the café. Somewhere along Phillips Avenue was Levi with hundreds of other volunteers, helping the fire department shovel snow into wagons that would then be emptied into the Big Sioux.

Her stomach growled.

Coffee and toast for breakfast. Coffee and toast for lunch.

Fortunately, this evening Levi would buy her dinner. Tomorrow the sidewalks would be all clear and she could return to the boardinghouse. Until the streets were clear for traffic, there was no reason to open the millinery. Since the boutique was normally closed Sunday through Wednesday, that meant she had a full seven days to focus solely on making hats.

"The storm is God's blessing in disguise," she said before finishing the last of her coffee. It had to be. She'd had more rest in the last two days than she'd had since the millinery opened. Instead of waiting on customers today, she had all the time in the world to work on hat orders.

After one final glance at the street below, Reba walked back to the bed strewn with silk flowers in a rainbow of colors. She smiled. "I can make this boutique a success."

She took her seat at the desk and continued making silk bows. Occasionally she glanced at the black telephone within arm's reach. Levi had promised to call when he finished shoveling snow. More than occasionally her stomach growled, which led her to think about dinner, which led her to think about Levi, which led her to wonder if he would kiss her again. The last time was when they'd gone home for Christmas. After the hayride, he'd chased her into the barn. She'd been laughing, blissful and breathless, and he'd kissed her. While the cows mooed and their bells jingled.

She'd never liked a cow barn until that moment. She'd never believed he was in love with her until that moment, either.

Reba smiled.

She'd never imagined their lives together until then. It could happen.

Move him, Lord, or move me. Change him or change me.

The words Mrs. Webber had encouraged her at Christmas to begin praying lingered in her mind. For her and Levi to have a future together, something—someone—had to change. They could find a compromise. She would find a compromise.

With a whispered "amen," she returned her attention to her needle, thread, and pink silk bow.

As she worked, the sun lowered in the sky, casting shadows about the room. It wasn't until twilight had descended that the *knock knock knock* sounded.

Reba dropped the needle and bow and ran to the door. She opened it, and her breath caught.

Levi stood there, grinning. His hair looked damp, but he smelled of bergamot cologne and wore his Sunday suit. "Been missing me?"

Reba smiled. "I had other things to occupy my thoughts."

He glanced inside her room but didn't step over the threshold. He whistled. "Looks like you've been busy."

"Thankfully, I had the leaves and flowers already cut." She eyed him. "You seem pretty happy for having spent the last ten hours shoveling snow."

"I've never had such fun freezing my fingers and toes off. We started out on. . ." As he spoke about his day, he motioned with his hands.

She'd never seen a man's eyes sparkle, but his did. Like emeralds glistening in sunlight. She was growing fanciful. And she didn't care. She almost giggled. He was happy. Joyful. Exuberant. The truth was obvious—Levi Webber loved living in Sioux Falls. She could see it on his face, hear it in his words. Before his self-determined six-month stay here ended, she would help him see he loved city life more than country living.

It was the perfect plan. It would work, too.

The two of them could actually have a future together. . .because he loved her and she loved him.

She could have stood there all day, staring up at him, listening to him talk about the people he worked with and new friends he'd made, but her stomach growled.

Levi laughed. "I suppose you're hungry."

Reba gave him a mischievous grin. "A little."

He offered her his arm. "Let's find some food, and then I'll tell you about the invitation I received to the fire department's St. Valentine's Day ball. Be prewarned: I shall be asking to escort you."

"Be prewarned: I shall say yes."

Chapter 9

"The sharp edges must be bound neatly and thinly with the mull muslin or sarsnet,
so that they do not mark the velvet, and, for the same reason,
any flaw or blemish upon the shape must be removed."
—*Practical Millinery*

Noon, Saturday, March 27

This is the *third* time you haven't had my order ready. I like you, Miss Diehl, I do, but this is not how I expect a business to be run. Cancel my remaining orders and keep the deposit."

"Please, Miss Van Dyke, I'm—"

At the click, Reba knew Miss Van Dyke was no longer on the line to hear her apology.

She rested the handset in the receiver and looked to the bulletin board above her desk. For every order she'd filled in the last month, another one called to cancel. This time she didn't feel the usual despair over a cancellation (over four to be precise). Instead, she felt angry.

Reba jumped to her feet. She ripped Miss Van Dyke's orders off the board. "I don't need your orders!" she spat, not caring how vicious she sounded. No one was in the boutique to hear. No one had been in all week. She crumpled the papers and tossed them onto the open accounting book on her desk. She grabbed the bell that had fallen off the front door and threw it against the curtains blocking the workroom from the boutique. Stupid bell.

Her gaze shifted to the manila envelope on her desk. Another six-month contract. Another looming deadline. Mr. Smyth wanted to know by Monday if she was going to renew the lease. He had another interested party.

She needed to order more pins and more supplies. That cost money.

She needed to put advertisements in the paper. More money.

Hire a shopgirl. Hire an accountant. More and more money.

Her chest tightened as if a giant were squeezing the air from her lungs. "I don't know what to do, God." Blinking away the sudden tears in her eyes, she picked up the phone. She cleared her throat. "Operator, put me through to. . ." She steadied her breathing while the operator made the connection. *Please, let Father answer. Please, let Father answer.*

"Hello?"

Reba released the breath she was holding. "Oh, Vati," she said, falling back to her childhood name for him, "I—" Her voice caught. Tears flowed. She struggled to get out her words and to keep the cries in. "I don't know what to do." *Gasp.* "I have no customers." *Gasp.* "They keep canceling orders. It's not supposed to happen this way."

"Oh, sweetheart."

"Mr. Smyth brought the new lease by last week."

"You don't have to sign it."

"But I do!" she exclaimed. "Don't you see? I've invested so much in the millinery. I can't quit now. I can't give up because things are tough. I will never go back to the farm. But I don't understand why God would guide me into starting my own business, only to let this happen. He promised an abundant life. He promised all things would work together for my good. I did what God told me, but there's no abundance here. I'm miserable. Why won't God fix this? I keep praying, but He's not answering."

It sounded like he placed the receiver down on the kitchen table. The legs of a chair scraped against the floor. He must have sat down.

After a long silence, he said, "Reba, what makes you think God told you to open a millinery?"

She dried her cheeks with the back of her hands. "I laid my fleece out like Gideon did, and sign after sign confirmed this was God's will."

"I see." His *I see* was less *I hear you and am impressed you heard from God* and more *I've heard this before, and I'm mulling what to say in response.*

Before he could start in with a lecture, she blurted, "I prayed that if God wanted me to do this, you'd be supportive. When I told you what I wanted to do, you said everyone needed a dream and that you'd do all you could to help me."

"Sweetheart," came his gentle voice, "God had already told Gideon what He wanted him to do—to lead His army. Gideon put that fleece out to confirm it was God's call and not his own selfish ambition."

"You think I made a selfish decision?"

"Would you have given up the idea of moving to Sioux Falls and opening a millinery if I hadn't been supportive?"

"Of course not! This was what I wanted—"

"You wanted."

Tears blurred her eyes. "If you believed I was making a selfish decision, why didn't you stop me? A loving parent would have."

Silence lingered.

Finally he said, "There is nothing wrong with pursuing a dream. What's wrong is when you use circumstances to determine God's will. If I constantly stopped you from making a poor decision, you would never learn to take care of yourself and never learn to deal with the frustration of making a mistake. The way I looked at it, the millinery could succeed as easily as it could fail. I wanted you to succeed. I believed you could." His voice tightened. "Either way, Reba, *you* would be fine, because you always have a place to come home to."

The truth of his words hurt. Deep down in her heart it hurt. It wasn't just because of the money she had wasted in learning how to fail. For weeks she'd convinced herself she could have a successful business and a life here in Sioux Falls with Levi.

She drew in a deep breath. "So you want me to come home and marry Levi?"

"I want—" He released a frustrated sigh. "Reba, you are the type of person who doesn't stay down when she falls. You're braver than most people I know. You are smart, too. But being smart and being able to make beautiful hats doesn't mean you have the skills needed to run a business, and that is all right. You have to give yourself permission to fail."

Reba didn't say anything. She examined the few orders remaining on her board. She'd invested a little over a fourth of her land money in the millinery. If she hired a woman to take care of customers, she could focus on making hats. If she ordered some inexpensive, premade hats, she could appeal to a less affluent clientele. She could also sell flowers for individual purchase so ladies could add them to hats they already owned. Or. . .she could fail and be all right with it.

Move him or move me. Change him or change me.

The prayer echoed in her mind.

"Reba, are you still there?"

"Yes. I was thinking."

"About?"

"What to do after I stand up. I may have another option."

He cleared his throat. "You should talk to Levi about your plight. He'd give you good advice, maybe help with the accounting."

"There's no point. He's already informed his manager at John Deere that he is quitting on April 3." She switched the telephone to her other ear. "I think he's going to propose tonight."

"This is good."

She didn't know whether to laugh or cry, so she took another deep breath and straightened her shoulders. "I love him, Vati. I do." She paused. "I feel terrible saying this. I can live with a broken heart. But I can't live with spending the rest of my life on a farm, even if it's with Levi."

He sighed.

She sighed, too. "Would you give up indoor plumbing for an outhouse? I can't. I like electricity and fans that blow cool air. I love riding the trolley and going to the theater, ice-cream parlors, balls, baseball games, and the park. I like attending a church where there are dozens of people my age. I like meeting people who've experienced life outside of South Dakota. Hearing that, do you still want me to come home and marry Levi?"

"No. If you did, you would wither and die inside."

Tears brimmed again in her eyes. "How do I know what God wants me to do about the lease?"

"This may be hard to hear," he said slowly, "but sometimes God doesn't care what job we take or which city we live in. Those aren't moral decisions, and He can bless us no matter what we do. God is more interested in building your character than building your hat shop."

Reba closed her eyes. "I've been too busy making hats to talk to God."

"Take time to talk to Him. . .and to Levi. That boy loves you."

"I know. I love you."

"I love you, too. Call me after you've made a decision about the lease."

"I will." After a quick good-bye, she hung up.

"You're right."

Reba jumped, her heart nearly stopping in shock upon hearing Levi's voice.

He held up the bell. "This wasn't on the door."

"It broke an hour ago. I…uh, how—how much did you hear?" She took a deep breath and stood very still, waiting.

"I thought—" His voice caught. "If this bell hadn't been broken, I wouldn't have been able to walk in without you knowing. Sometimes the doors we step through aren't ones God opened." He stepped forward and placed the bell on her desk then looked at her with tear-bright eyes. "I think we can take this as a sign. I appreciate knowing where I stand with you. Good-bye, Reba. I wish you the best with your boutique."

He left, slipping through the curtains and out of the millinery as silently as he'd arrived.

Reba stared blankly ahead.

Could his hearing what she said be a sign? She didn't know, not anymore.

"I can't go backward," she whispered. "Oh, God, what am I supposed to do?"

Chapter 10

"When it has been satisfactorily fixed, so that it is quite even, and the first row not unduly hidden in any part, the two can be sewn together."
—*Practical Millinery*

Webber Farm
Sunday afternoon, April 4

L evi, would you get that?" Ma yelled from the kitchen.

"All right," he yelled back, descending the staircase two steps at a time. Probably some of his parents' friends out visiting. He opened the door.

Mr. Diehl pushed his hat back on his head. "I was wondering if we could talk."

"Who is it, dear?"

Levi looked over his shoulder. "It's Mr. Diehl. We'll be on the porch." He stepped outside, taking care to close the door in case Ma decided to eavesdrop.

Mr. Diehl sat in a rocker.

Levi leaned back against the porch railing, legs crossed at the ankle, elbows on the railing. "I suppose you heard the news?"

"That you and Reba aren't courting anymore?"

"Yes, sir."

"Seems I did." His brows rose. "You look to be handling it well."

Levi tried to digest this. He'd never had a broken heart before. Considering he hadn't taken to the bottle, spent the day wailing in grief, or done anything to be regretful of in the morning, he supposed he was handling it well. As best a man could. He supposed in a few days the numbness from the shock would wear off. Ma said it would. But if he saw Reba talking to another man, he doubted his response would be as levelheaded.

He shrugged. "Not much I can do to change the situation."

A glimmer of something flashed in Mr. Diehl's eyes. "Do you love her?"

Levi nodded. "I want her to be happy." He looked to the left—the milking barn. He looked to the right—a cornfield. "I thought it was a matter of her not liking cows and looking out of her bedroom window and seeing corn all the way to the horizon. It's more than that. She likes culture. There's no one around here who understands that creative, artistic drive in her. I'm not sure I even understand it."

Mr. Diehl nodded. "She likes pretty things. Always has. Her mother—" He slapped his thigh. "Well, that's that." He stood and walked to Levi. He clasped Levi's hand. His other hand settled on Levi's shoulder. "Let me give you a piece of advice my father gave me, twenty-four years ago. 'When you are no longer able to change the situation, you are challenged to change yourself.'"

His parents had said as much last night, after apologizing for causing him to feel like he had no future except for that on the farm. His brothers could manage without him. His parents could manage without him.

194

But could he manage without Reba?

He could. He knew he could. The crux was, he didn't want to now, any more than he had six months ago. His love for Reba had only grown and deepened, matured.

That, though, could change.

Levi swallowed, drowning under the sudden surge of emotions. "I can be—" His throat tightened. He shook his head and took a deep breath. "Given time, I can be happy without her."

Mr. Diehl patted his shoulder. "*Given time* can be an awfully long time."

"Yes, sir, it can."

It didn't have to be.

Change her or change me. Move her or move me.

Levi looked to Reba's father. . .and smiled. "There is another possibility."

<hr />

Sioux Falls College
Tuesday, April 6

Reba laid the manila envelope on the desk and sat in one of the chairs across from the dean of Home Economics. Her hands didn't shake, yet she could feel a nervous flutter in her stomach. "I wanted to drop this off," she said. "The papers are all filled out, except for the one accepting the scholarship. I'd rather you consider giving it to a girl in my church. Her contact information is in the envelope. I've already spoken to the bursar about tuition and fees and visited the ladies' residence hall to make arrangements for this fall."

Mrs. Wright's eyebrows rose in shock, but she recovered quickly with a smile. "Excellent. I'm delighted you decided to enroll." She shifted through a stack of papers on her desk and pulled out a booklet. "Fall classes begin in August. Here is a schedule of course options."

Reba took the proffered booklet. "Thank you." Standing, she slid it into her tapestry bag. "I would love to stay and visit, but I need to return to the boutique. There's a little more packing to be done before I hand over the key."

"I am sorry about the millinery. You make beautiful hats."

Reba chuckled. "If you could see my accounting book, you'd realize that hats are about the only beautiful things I make."

"My husband balances our checkbook because he says I can be too creative with math. I take no offense to that." Smiling, Mrs. Wright walked around the desk to shake Reba's hand. "May I inquire what prompted your decision to close the millinery?"

"Something you said planted the seed, actually."

"Oh?"

They started toward the office door.

"I realize now God has gifted me with certain talents, gifts, and abilities." Reba released a wry chuckle. "Managing a business isn't one of them. The only thing I liked about running a millinery was decorating the shop and making hats. That doesn't mean I can't still make hats. It means I shouldn't be making hats as a business. I spoke to my father, and he agreed that college would be a good place for me to figure out what I want in life. Maybe I will become a home economics teacher. Maybe I will learn interior design. Maybe I will decide I want to do nothing more than be a wife and a mother. I don't know what my future holds, and I am all right with that."

"Congratulations, Miss Diehl, on learning what too many of my students have yet to figure out."

"And what's that?"

"That it is all right not to have all the answers."

They stopped at the threshold.

"Until August. . ."

Reba smiled. "I'll be looking forward to it."

***

Reba climbed off the trolley and enjoyed a leisurely stroll toward the intersection of Ninth and Phillips, the sun bright and cheerful. Gone was the anxiety she'd felt in the last month as she approached the millinery. She had about four hours before the omnibus would arrive to haul her trunks of fabric, millinery tools, and office supplies to the boardinghouse. The inventory worth selling she'd sold. During the last week, she'd finished the last of her orders, including the four Miss Van Dyke had canceled, as well as every other canceled order. While not all received the exact hat she'd ordered, they'd each received a hat. Doing it was the right thing, even though it had been a cost to her. No matter how many times she heard "*Oh, you didn't have to do that*," she knew she had to. For her own conscience.

When she wasn't doing alterations for the Bee Hive Department Store, she'd make hats for the church summer auction.

As she strolled, automobiles honked. Dust occasionally swirled in the air as buggies, wagons, and automobiles drove past. Busy street. Lots of pedestrian traffic, too. Sioux Falls fairly bustled with life. This weekend she'd buy a ticket to the vaudeville Levi said—

Reba smiled to cover the ache in her chest each time she thought about Levi. She should call him. Or write a letter.

She stopped at the corner and inhaled. Manure. Engine oil. Freshly baked bread. Not the best combination, but the sweet smell was familiar. Was home.

Grip tight on her bag, she hurried across the street. No more time to dawdle. She had to pack. She had to—

Reba stopped in front of the bakery. Someone was standing in front of her millinery. She took a hesitant step forward. Then another. And another. A man in a black suit leaned against the door, legs crossed at the ankles, arms folded across his chest, flat tweed cap over his face to shield his eyes from the morning sun.

Her heart beat frantically.

She nervously placed her foot on the bottom step. "Levi?"

He slid his cap off his face and grinned. "Took you long enough. I considered looking for you but had no idea where to start. Mr. Huss didn't know where you were. He did, however, have a hot-cross bun to sell me, along with a free cup of coffee."

"Why—uh, why. . ." She gripped her bag with both hands. "What brings you to Sioux Falls?"

"I thought about what you said."

"And?" she prodded.

He tapped his cap against his thigh. "I figured out something after talking to my parents and to your father." He moved down a step. "I can live anywhere and be happy." He moved another step. "I can live without you and learn to be happy about it." He stood on the ground next to her. "But I don't want to learn that."

Reba tried to speak, but her throat was tight, and her eyes were blurry.

He flipped his cap on his head, his gaze locked on her. "You said you wanted a man who would move a mountain for you. I'm the mountain."

"You're the mountain?" she echoed, trying desperately to catch her mind up with her heart. He'd come back *for* her—was that what he was saying?

He nodded. "I'm the mountain you need moved."

Not just *for* her.

He came back to *be with* her. To marry her. To create a life with her in Sioux Falls.

Reba glanced around. They had an audience. Oh, it wasn't but a dozen or so people, but still. . .

"Is this a proposal?" she managed to say.

"Eventually." He grinned. "Next week I start working for the SDSU Extension Office here in Sioux Falls. I don't want to be a farmer, but I do want to help other farmers be better farmers." He withdrew a red satin-covered jewelry box. "Reba Diehl, I have this ring, and I would like to ask you to marry me, but"—he rubbed the back of his neck—"if you say yes, then I'm going to kiss you. Seeing we're out here on the street and all—"

Several people chuckled.

Feeling her cheeks warm, Reba opened her bag and withdrew the key. She held it up.

Levi took the key from her. "Race you to the door."

ECPA-bestselling author **Gina Welborn** worked for a news radio station until she fell in love with writing romances. She serves on the American Christian Fiction Writers Foundation Board. Sharing her husband's love for the premier American sports car, she is a founding member of the Southwest Oklahoma Corvette Club and a lifetime member of the National Corvette Museum. Gina lives with her husband, three of their five Okie-Hokie children, two rabbits, two guinea pigs, and a dog that doesn't realize rabbits and pigs are edible. Find her online at www.ginawelborn.com!

Better with Butter

by Jennifer AlLee

Chapter 1

Fallon, Nevada
June 1916

I f she didn't take a break soon, she was sure her fingers would snap clean off.

Ella Daniels sighed. Despite the fact that it was a warm summer's day, she was cold to the bone. Butter was a tricky medium. Not only did she have to work in the icehouse so the sculpture would hold its form, she had to continually dip her hands in ice water to keep her body heat from melting her creation. Her hands had had all the abuse they could take for at least a few hours.

She covered the half-formed cow with a wooden box and placed a slab of ice on top of that, just to be safe. As soon as she left the icehouse and shut the door behind her, she began to peel off layers: woolen scarf, long coat, and a long-sleeved flannel shirt that had once been her father's. She hung each piece on hooks so they'd be easily retrieved later, after the feeling came back into her hands.

If only she worked in a normal medium like clay or marble, she could spend hours sculpting. Not only that, but her creations would last more than the length of a state fair. Still, there was plenty to do. The sculpture she'd just left was a small-scale version of the nearly life-size one she'd be making in a few months. She still needed to make some sketches, decide on the final design, and build the frame to support several hundred pounds of butter. Rubbing her hands together to warm them, she set off for the barn. Time to visit her favorite model.

Geraldine let out a low, soulful moo as soon as Ella entered the barn. The Jersey cow put her pretty head over the half door of her stall and looked at Ella with expressive, doe-like eyes.

"Hello, my pretty girl." Ella pulled a stub of carrot from her skirt pocket and held it out on a flat palm. The cow slurped it up, her velvety muzzle skimming Ella's skin.

Unlike the other cows at the Daniels Dairy Farm, Geraldine was a pet. Ella had raised her from a calf, bottle-feeding her after she was rejected by her mother. That had been five years ago, about the time Ella decided to try butter sculpting as a way to grab public interest in the dairy. Naturally, Geraldine had been her first model. Over the years, Ella's sculptures became a record of Geraldine's life, getting bigger and more impressive.

"What shall we do this year?" Ella leaned against the door and stroked the cow's neck. "A garland of flowers around your neck? A sassy hat?"

"Why stop there? How about an evening gown?"

Even before Ella turned at the sound of the deep voice, she knew who was walking toward her. Maxwell Sinclair was just as handsome as the last time she saw him, over a year ago.

"Hello, Max. I didn't know you were in town."

"Visiting the family."

"I see." Ella crossed her arms. "And what brings you to our lowly little farm? Have you finally decided it's time to leave the fake butter business?"

Max chuckled. "It's not fake butter; it's margarine. A completely different and far superior product."

"You make it in a factory, not a farm." Ella wrinkled her nose in disgust. "It can't possibly be better than butter."

"Ah, yes. Making something from milk drawn from a cow in a barn full of heaven knows what kind of contamination is bound to be *much* healthier."

Ella bristled at Max's sarcasm. How dare he malign the dairy? He'd worked there himself until he left a year ago. He'd started when he was just sixteen, and over the next ten years he'd cleaned the barn, tended to the cows, maintained the milking machine, and done just about everything a dairyman could do. He'd become her father's most trusted employee. Not only that, but he'd become part of the family. The betrayal of his decision to join the Joy Margarine Company had cut deep.

"Why are you here?" Ella asked, her voice flat.

Max frowned. "I wish we could put the past aside and move forward. Are you going to stay mad at me forever?"

Yes, I am, because I loved you with my whole heart and you broke it the day you left.

But Ella would never say that to him. Instead, she just repeated herself. "Why are you here?"

"I see how it is." Max puffed out an exasperated breath. "I came because I wanted to talk to your father. We didn't part on the best of terms, so I was hoping to mend fences."

Of course. She hadn't for a moment thought he might have come to see her. Still, the confirmation of that fact left her feeling hollow.

"Dad's in the milking barn. You're free to talk to him. Unless, of course, you're afraid of all the contamination in there."

His eyes narrowed, and he looked like he was about to toss out a snappy comeback. Instead, he put his hands in his trouser pockets and nodded.

"Thank you. Take care of yourself, Ella." He walked away but threw one more comment back over his shoulder. "See you around."

———◆●◆———

That had been a spectacular failure.

Max left the small barn and stalked toward the bigger one, shoulders hunched and hands still in his pockets. What had possessed him to look for Ella? He should have known she still had a chip on her shoulder. Why couldn't she understand that he left the dairy for something better, but he didn't leave her? He'd hoped that time would have softened her, dulled the sharpness of his departure. Obviously that wasn't the case. Hopefully, Walter Daniels would be more sensible than his daughter.

Upon reaching the milking barn, he took one more deep breath of semifresh air. Then he opened the door. Just as he remembered, the smell of cow hit him in the face like a warm, moist wall. That was one of the many reasons he preferred margarine. No cows were involved.

As dairies went, the Daniels Dairy was one of the best. Walter made sure the place was clean, the equipment well maintained, and the cows taken care of. At the moment, about a dozen cows were lined up in a row, their halters attached by rope to a feeding trough in front of them. They happily munched and swished their tails while being milked. Four men were doing the milking, so the other eight cows waited their turns.

The clank of an empty milk pail hitting the ground got Max's attention. Walter Daniels was walking toward him, looking serious.

"Well now, if I didn't know better, I'd say Max Sinclair stopped by for a visit. But that can't be, since Max works for the enemy now and knows better than to darken my door."

Obviously Walter's sensibilities were aligned with his daughter's.

"Come now, Walter." Max grinned and used his best let-bygones-be-bygones voice. "It's been over a year. You can't still be upset."

"Can't I?" He quietly gazed at Max, as if taking inventory. "You broke her heart, you know."

He looked Walter straight in the eye. "I know. But it was never my intention. I'll always regret hurting her. And you."

It was unusually quiet in the barn. The only sounds were the cows chewing and the occasional clink of a harness when one shook its head. Even the *ping, ping, ping* of milk shooting into the tin pails had ceased as the men stopped to watch the exchange.

Walter looked in their direction and swatted his hand through the air. "Get on with you, then. Nothing going on over here that's any of your concern."

That was all it took for the milking to resume.

Walter turned back to Max and sighed. "My father used to say life is too short to hold grudges, and I suppose he was right." He held his hand out.

With a solemn nod, Max took his hand and shook it. "Thank you."

"Just don't make me regret it."

"Of course." Max smiled and looked around the barn. "The place looks as good as ever. How many head do you have now?"

"About fifty Jerseys." He pointed in the direction of the men on their stools. "I've got four hands that do nothing but milk."

Max knew that. Each cow was milked twice a day, and each man was probably responsible for about a dozen cows. Walter most likely took up the slack. He wouldn't be surprised if Ella pitched in, too, when she wasn't sculpting.

"Quite a few dairies are using the new milking machines," Max said. "Have you considered switching over?"

Walter pulled a face. "Not a chance. I don't trust those things. Hard to keep all the tubes clean, so it's easier to contaminate the milk. Besides, they're not good for the cows. Nope, we get a cleaner, healthier product doing it the right way."

Max held back a laugh. To Walter, there was his way, and there was the wrong way. Anything new and innovative couldn't be trusted. He'd undoubtedly fought pasteurization tooth and nail.

They spent awhile talking about the business, the milk yield, how much butter was produced. Talk of butter naturally brought the conversation back around to Ella.

"I assume she'll be going to the state fair this year," Max said in a way he hoped sounded casual.

"Oh yes, she's coming with me. And Geraldine, of course." Walter chuckled. "You know, people who go every year have watched that cow grow up, in real life and in butter."

Max nodded. "People do love the butter sculptures. That really was a stroke of genius, using them to advertise the dairy."

The pride was so apparent in Walter, his chest seemed to puff up on the spot. "Wish I could take the credit, but it was all Ella's idea. That girl is something else."

"Yes, she is."

And she should be something else. She shouldn't be tied to a dairy farm with her hands in a greasy, smelly cow byproduct. She should be someplace where she could use her creativity in something permanent and beautiful. But that would never happen as long as she felt responsible for the dairy's success.

Max steeled himself. The real reason he'd come to see Walter could very well get him unceremoniously booted out of the barn. But it could also pave the way for something better for everyone concerned, especially Ella. There was no turning back now.

"Walter, there was something I wanted to talk to you about. . . ."

Chapter 2

The grounds of the Nevada State Fair were a swarm of activity, even though it wasn't open to the public for another two days. Ella had been coming to the fair with her father since she was a little girl, and every year it was the same. Vendors set up their stands, unfurling banners for amazing items that every home had to have or treats that would make your mouth water at the sight of them. Workmen unloaded trucks by the various exhibition buildings. In the livestock area, pens and stalls were filled with horses, pigs, cows, chickens, and every kind of animal one could imagine finding on a farm.

Ella walked up to the whitewashed fence on one of the swine enclosures and waved at the man on the other side. "Good morning, Mr. Evans. Those are some fine-looking pigs."

Felix Evans was probably only in his fifties, but he'd looked about seventy for as long as she'd known him. Still, he was wiry, energetic, and always convivial. When he smiled, Ella suspected he'd lost at least one more tooth since the last time they'd met.

"Thank you, Miss Daniels. Yep, you can't go wrong with Berkshires. Now others, they prefer the pale-skinned Yorkies, but not me. Dark skin, darker meat. That's a good pig! I expect we'll be taking home a ribbon or two."

He said almost the same thing every year. Ella chuckled. "Good luck to you. And to Mrs. Evans. I assume she's entered in the canning competition again?"

"Absolutely." Mr. Evans nodded enthusiastically. "It was a good year for peaches. She canned some beauts. And she's got a great pie to make for the recipe contest. That is, if I don't eat it before the judges get to it."

Laughing along with him, Ella backed away from the fence. With a cheery, "See you later," she was on her way.

Looking around her, Ella couldn't help but be in high spirits. There were times when she wished her world was bigger than just the dairy. She yearned to live in a big city, where everyone didn't know everything about her and she could stretch her artistic muscles. But then there were days like today, when she was surrounded by other people living the same kind of life she did. She felt the camaraderie, the community. At times like that, she couldn't imagine her life any other way.

A chorus of moos greeted her as she approached the bovine enclosures. Since she was the only butter sculptress at the fair, the Daniels Dairy had been given their customary space in the center, complete with its own icehouse. Next to it, Geraldine was happily ensconced in a special stall all for her. In a large corral beside that were the ten Jerseys her father had brought to sell.

Digging in her skirt pocket, Ella found the treat she'd brought. "Here you go, gorgeous."

As Geraldine munched the carrot, Ella scratched her behind the ear. This would be a good time to start working on the sculpture. The wooden frame, which she'd created already, was in the icehouse and waiting for her to apply the base layer of butter. It was much more a laborious task than an artistic one, so she always did it ahead of time. There was so much she needed to do in private with the doors shut before the crowds arrived day after tomorrow. Ella rubbed her hands together, anticipating the coming chill. Might as well get to work.

Before she could open the door to the icehouse, she heard the sound of someone clearing his throat.

"Excuse me."

She turned around to see a man in a light brown suit. He tipped his flat-topped straw hat and bowed slightly. Ella smiled at him. "May I help you?"

"I believe you can. More to the point, I believe we can help each other." His voice broke and a red flush crept up his neck from beneath his celluloid collar. "What I mean to say is. . .oh dear. My name is Orville Henderson. I'm with Igloo Ice Works, manufacturers of dependable iceboxes for over fifty years."

She shook his hand after he extended it. "Nice to meet you, Mr. Henderson, but I think you want to speak to my father. He owns the dairy and makes all the purchasing decisions."

"No, I'm not trying to sell you anything. Are you the butter sculptress?"

"I am. Ella Daniels."

He looked so relieved, she might as well have told him she'd discovered the Fountain of Youth. "Wonderful. Wonderful."

She waited for him to explain, but he just kept nodding and smiling. Finally, she had to prompt him.

"Why do you want to talk to me?"

"Oh! Oh, yes, of course. Sorry. Your sculptures have done so well advertising the dairy, I was hoping you could do the same for me. For us. For Igloo Ice Works, that is."

The poor fellow was having quite a time expressing himself. Rather than tell him flat out she had no interest in promoting anything other than the family business, she clasped her hands together, gave him her full attention, and waited for him to continue.

"You see," he said, "we'd like to sponsor your sculpture this year."

Now she had to say something. "Sponsor? As in, pay?"

"Yes. We agree on a fee, and then I can put our advertising on the side of your icehouse."

A poster or two on the wall didn't sound so bad. "Is that all?"

"Well, actually, no. You see, Igloo has an exhibit in the Homemaker's Hall. We'd like to demonstrate how well our icebox works by keeping one of your butter sculptures in it."

"Oh dear—"

"Not a full-sized sculpture," he rushed to assure her. "Something small and easy."

Small and easy. There was nothing easy about sculpting with a medium that melted almost as soon as you touched it. He had no idea what he was asking.

"Mr. Henderson, I'm sorry. If I'd known ahead of time, we might have been able to work something out. But there's no way I can make an additional sculpture on such short notice."

The man was crestfallen. "Are you sure? Perhaps—"

"I'm sure."

"I see. Well, of course, I understand." He sighed. "Would you mind if I took a look in your icehouse? Just a professional courtesy. I like to see how they're configured and if I can do anything to improve the efficiency."

"Be my guest." Ella motioned to the building.

Giving a brief nod, Mr. Henderson hurried over, pulled open one of the big doors and disappeared inside, closing the doors behind him. Ella supposed he was more comfortable by himself, surrounded by ice. Why else would he willingly go into the frigid space? Which reminded her, she had been about to get working on her project before Mr. Henderson showed up. Now, where had she put the valise with her overcoat and scarf?

She was double-checking the area next to Geraldine's stall when another voice called out, but this one was so familiar, she didn't need to look to know who was coming.

"Miss Daniels," Max boomed. "Is that you?"

What was he doing there? Was she never to be allowed to get to work?

"You know perfectly well it's me," she sputtered at him while tromping around the stall. "What in the world do you— Oh."

Max wasn't alone. The man beside him sported an imposing mustache and was dressed a bit too well for the fair. When he smiled, she caught the faint sparkle of a gold molar just beyond the corner of his mouth.

Motioning to the man, Max made introductions. "Miss Daniels, this is Mr. Philip Stanley."

He held out a gloved hand. Ella hesitated, knowing that, after a day of setting up her work area and petting Geraldine, she would likely mar the pristine white cotton, but when he showed no signs of retreat, she acquiesced.

"Pleasure meeting you, Mr. Stanley," she said as he pumped her arm.

"And you." His eyes swept the paddock and stopped when he got to the icehouse. "I understand you're the one who sculpts cows from butter."

Before she could answer, Max jumped in. "She's the very one. For years, she's been proving that butter is hard as a rock."

"What?" Ella couldn't hold back her shocked reaction.

"The detail she gets is amazing," Max continued. "It's definitely not something you can do with margarine."

Mr. Stanley nodded. "Yes, you want something that holds its shape if you're sculpting a statue. But not if you're spreading it on a fluffy homemade biscuit."

Ella glared at Max. How dare he bring this stranger to meet her if all they were going to do was insult her? "I don't see how this is any business of yours."

"I'm so sorry, miss." Mr. Stanley put his palm against his chest, giving her such a fake look of contrition it was insulting. "I should have explained that it actually is my business. I'm with Majestic Electric, maker of fine electric appliances, such as the Sure-Frost Refrigerator."

"How nice for you." Ella looked at Max. "What is the meaning of your visit?"

Max glanced at the other man, who nodded. "I wanted you to meet Mr. Stanley to make a point. The electric refrigerator is the wave of the future, the same way that margarine is. Iceboxes and butter are things of the past. It won't be long before both of them disappear in favor of what's newer and better."

"Which is why," Mr. Stanley added, "Majestic Electric has decided to partner at this fair with the Joy Margarine Company."

Rather than scream at them, which is what she really wanted to do, Ella remained calm. "What do you mean by 'partner'?"

Max hooked his thumbs under his suspenders and rocked forward on the balls of his feet. "Majestic Electric is sharing advertising with Joy."

"Together, we'll show how the same refrigerator that keeps your ice frozen will also keep your margarine at a perfect, spreadable temperature." Mr. Stanley slapped Max on the back. "The housewives are all going to beg their husbands for one."

Ella's mind was whirling. She'd never really believed that margarine was a threat to their business. To her, it was a fad, like mismatched socks or collecting lost hairpins. No one in their right mind would ever choose a tub full of chemicals over a stick of wholesome, rich butter. But what if she was wrong? The icebox manufacturers certainly had reason to worry. Maybe she did, too.

The door to the icehouse opened, and Mr. Henderson walked out, looking a bit red in the nose and cheeks.

"Everything in there looks good. You obviously know what you're doing."

There was no time to think. Ella simply acted. She rushed to the man's side and linked her arm through his then pulled him up to the other two gentlemen.

"Congratulations, Mr. Sinclair, but you're not the only one with news."

Confusion clouded Mr. Henderson's face. Meanwhile, Max frowned. "Oh, really?"

"This is Mr. Orville Henderson, of Igloo Ice Works, maker of fine iceboxes." Ella smiled broadly. "Igloo is partnering with the Daniels Dairy."

Max wagged his finger from one to the other. "You mean. . ."

"Yes." Ella looked Mr. Henderson in the eye and nodded, hoping he'd understand. When he began to smile, she looked back at Max. "Igloo is sponsoring my sculpture this year."

Chapter 3

The first day Max walked into the milking barn of the Daniels Dairy he'd met fourteen-year-old Ella. Her hair hung down her back in a lopsided, messy braid and her worn, brown work dress was soiled around the hem from heaven-knew-what. But when she looked over her shoulder and smiled at him, her fingers still wrapped around the cow's teats, he felt like the earth shifted beneath his feet. The warmth of her smile and the sparkle in her eyes had him absolutely smitten. Ten years later, he still thought she was the most beautiful woman he'd ever known.

She was also the most stubborn, irritating, opinionated woman on the planet.

Walking to the Hall of Innovations, he nodded and made appropriate noises as Philip prattled on about the workings of the Sure-Frost Refrigerator, but hardly a word the man said registered. Max couldn't stop thinking about Ella.

He had hoped the news of his company's partnership with the appliance manufacturer would prove that margarine was a serious product. Dairy farmers were understandably uneasy about anything that would cut into their profits, but they couldn't ignore the inevitable. Ella was smart. Surely she would understand. Not for a second could he have guessed that she'd obtain a sponsor for the dairy, too.

"What do you think, Max?"

"What?" Max shook his head. "I'm sorry. What did you say?"

"You're thinking about the milkmaid, aren't you? I don't blame you. She's a pretty thing."

Yes, he had been thinking that. He *always* thought that, but Philip had no business thinking it. "I was thinking she and her sculpture will get a lot of attention. It will be hard to compete, especially since Joy wasn't given a spot in the Homemaker's Hall."

"That's because it's so much better than the old-fashioned option. Margarine is new, it's modern. It belongs in the Hall of Innovations, right alongside Majestic Electric." He slapped Max's shoulder. "That's why we're a great team."

"Of course, you're right."

"I almost always am." He laughed. "Back to what I was saying before, when you were daydreaming. We should talk to Walter Daniels, appeal to his good sense. Help him see it's just a waste of his time and money to fight progress. He's the owner, after all."

Max shook his head. "Remember, I used to work for them. I know how they do things. Walter is one hundred percent in charge of the livestock, but anything specific to the business end of things is left to Ella."

"Ella, huh?" Philip's smile turned slightly lecherous. "How well do you know her?"

Well enough that I want to punch your smug face. "We worked together for several years."

He chuckled. "That could help, too. You might know something we can take advantage of. Give us some leverage, so to speak."

Max stopped dead in his tracks. Philip was a few steps ahead when he realized what had happened. He stopped, too, and turned back to look at Max.

"Something wrong?"

"I need to make something clear. I have no intention of taking advantage of anyone. I want to be successful and do a good job for my company, but I will not sink to dishonest tactics."

"Whoa! Hold your horses there, son." Philip put his hands up in surrender. "You've got me all wrong. I didn't say you had to be dishonest."

A warm flush crept up the back of Max's neck. "Good. My apologies for overreacting."

"I understand. You've got principles. That's a good thing." The genial attitude disappeared, replaced by a face so serious, he might have just told his mother died. "But you need to remember something. This is business. It's not a game, not a family matter. There's a lot more at stake here than you and your feelings. You may have to get pretty close to that line of yours and do things you don't feel good about. Are we clear?"

Max looked back in the direction of the Daniels Dairy enclosure. They were far enough away that he couldn't see Ella anymore, but he knew she was there. And he knew what needed to be done.

"We're clear," Max said.

They started walking again, this time in silence.

———————•◦●◦•———————

"You agreed to what?"

Walter Daniels was usually a very calm man. Ella could count on the fingers of one hand the number of times she'd seen her father flustered. This was one of those times.

Following him through the pasture, she nearly had to run to keep up with him. "It's not really a big thing. He's going to pay us to put advertising on our icehouse, and we get to advertise the dairy over at his display for free."

"Not a thing in this world is free." He walked faster, swinging the empty pail in his hand like a pendulum. "What do we have to do for them?"

"You don't have to do anything. I agreed to create a butter sculpture for them to keep in their display." Ella hoped this would placate her father. Instead, it just increased his agitation.

"Another sculpture. Which means more butter, which is less that we have to sell. Those silly sculptures may be made of butter, but I'm not!"

Ella stopped and watched her father walk away. She couldn't have been more shocked if he'd doused her with a pail of milk. He'd never said anything negative about her sculptures before. Not when she originally told him about her crazy idea to promote the dairy. Not when she did her first sculpture at the fair and most of the other farmers had laughed at the foolishness of using so much of their butter on such a frivolous endeavor. No, he'd supported her for her ingenuity, encouraged her not to be swayed by the opinions of others, and when her sculptures began to draw crowds of fairgoers, he'd bragged to anyone who would listen about his talented daughter. Now he called them silly and seemed to think they were a waste of money.

Up ahead, her father left the paddock and went into the outbuilding where they kept their supplies. With a sigh, Ella trudged in that direction, keeping her eyes on the ground to make sure she didn't step in something she shouldn't. By the time she reached the gate and looked back up, her father had come out of the building and was leaning on the fence.

He opened the gate for her, his expression somber. "I'm so sorry, darlin'. I didn't mean what I said. You know how proud I am of you."

Ella nodded. She was sure her father hadn't meant to say what he did, but he still said it. So there had to be a grain of truth in the sentiment.

"You're right, Papa. I shouldn't have made the deal with Mr. Henderson. At first, I said no, but then Max came, and he just made me so mad—"

He frowned as he cut her off. "Wait, Max was here? What does he have to do with it?"

She didn't want to admit how her mood could be swayed by a conversation with Max, but there was no avoiding it now. "The Joy Margarine Company has an exhibit in the fair this year. Max came by to gloat about it and to introduce me to his sponsor, a Mr. Stanley from the Majestic Electric Company."

"Let me guess. They're touting the new electric refrigerator?"

"Yes. Both of them were going on and on about the superiority of margarine, and Mr. Stanley was so. . .so. . .arrogant about the whole thing. Well, I just decided right then that the dairy should have a sponsor, too." She hung her head, realizing what a rash decision she'd made. "I'm so sorry."

Strong arms encircled her as her father drew her into a hug. "You have nothing to be sorry for. You did the right thing."

She hugged him back then pulled away to look him in the eye. "I did? Really?"

"Don't sound so surprised," he said with a laugh. "You have a much better head for business than I do. That's why I let you handle so much. Honestly, I don't know why I snapped at you. I suppose I'm just feeling a bit of stress lately."

"About what?" Stress wasn't something her father usually gave in to.

"Oh, life in general. Things are changing so fast. I haven't felt quite right ever since last year. . . ."

The sentence trailed off, hanging between them in midair, not needing to be verbalized for both of them to hear the rest of it: *when your mother died.*

"There's a war going on in Europe that we'll likely be joining," he continued. "Wars almost always mean rationing, and that's an opportunity for the margarine companies."

She'd heard rumblings of that already from women at church and in town. "You can't be saying you think they're right."

"Not entirely. No one will ever convince me that margarine is superior to butter. But it may be necessary for a time. Before long, people will get used to it. And once someone is used to something, they're not likely to go back to what they did before." He shrugged. "It's the nature of people."

Ella chewed on her lip. There had to be a way to sway the public before margarine became an even bigger problem. "Max and Mr. Stanley kept talking about how much better margarine is, but we know they're wrong. And we're going to prove to every single person at this fair how wrong they are." A plan began to form, and like a lightning bolt streaking from the heavens, inspiration struck. She knew exactly what she would sculpt for Igloo Ice Works.

Grabbing her father's hands, Ella laughed out loud. "Margarine may be the wave of the future, but we're going to show them what every wife and mother out there already knows. Everything is better with butter!"

And while they were at it, she'd show Max that she was better off without him, too.

Chapter 4

Ella was up to her elbows in butter. Literally.

For the last two days, she'd immersed herself in what she now called the "Better with Butter" campaign. Planning just the right subject for the Igloo minisculpture had been more challenging than anticipated. Because she didn't have any materials, not to mention time, to construct a frame, the sculpture had to be something solidly built. So, the peacock that she originally thought of creating couldn't be standing. Those skinny little bird legs wouldn't hold up the rest of the butter body, and fanned out tail feathers would most certainly bend under their own weight. After an hour of sketching, she finally hit on the perfect way to pose the bird. Then, she immediately set to creating it, working until the wee hours.

The finished peacock sat on a block of ice, waiting for her to take it to Mr. Henderson. Meanwhile, Ella fought exhaustion as she worked on the first layers of her sculpture of Geraldine. This part of the process didn't require precision, so she was able to wear gloves, which allowed her to spend more time in the icehouse. She hadn't even bothered to bundle up, hoping the cold air would be invigorating.

Scooping up handfuls of partially softened butter from a nearby bucket, she couldn't help but wonder what Max was doing right then. No doubt he'd had a good night's sleep. If he was even awake this early, he was probably enjoying a hearty breakfast and a cup of strong coffee before heading to the fairgrounds. Meanwhile, she'd never left, catching a few hours' sleep on a cot in the supply room and munching on an apple for breakfast.

Max had no idea what it meant to be a dairyman. Oh, he'd worked at the dairy for years, but as soon as a more comfortable opportunity presented itself, he'd run after it. A real dairyman didn't do that. The dairy was in your blood. It was part of who you were. Her mother knew that. Even after she was diagnosed with cancer and everyone, including her father, had begged her to stay in the hospital, she'd refused.

"The time will come when it's my time to go," she'd told Ella. "And when that time comes, I don't want to be surrounded by strangers, looking at white walls and hospital equipment. I want to be right here in the home I built with your father. I want to be able to look out my window and see the cows grazing in the pasture. This is where I belong."

Ella blinked against the tears that stung her eyes. Even more than a year after her mother had died, thoughts of her were still bittersweet. Max had been with them during it all. He'd done extra work around the dairy in order to free up Ella so she could care for her mother. He'd supported Ella, encouraged her, held her when she cried. They'd grown so close. She came to depend on him, she even thought she loved him. And then, four short months after the funeral, he'd left.

With a bit too much vigor, she slapped more butter on what would become the cow's left hind leg. She had to stop thinking about Max, her mother, and everything that could go wrong. It was time to focus on the good things in her life. Ella firmly believed that a person's mood translated into their work. It wouldn't do to create an angry, hurt version of Geraldine.

The door to the icehouse cracked open, and her father stuck his head inside. "You doing all right?"

"Wonderful," Ella chirped, using the happiest voice she could muster.

"Good. You've been in here so long, I was afraid you might have frozen in place."

Oh dear. How long had she been in there? "What time is it?"

"Almost eight."

Ella rose from the stool she was sitting on and stretched, pointing her fingers to the ceiling. "This is a good time for a break."

"Good. You need some rest."

"No time for that." Ella stripped off her gloves and work smock and draped them over the front part of the wooden frame, which still was butter-free. "I need to visit the Igloo exhibit and deliver their sculpture."

He protested, as she knew he would, but Ella stood firm. With his help, they loaded the crate on a hand wagon. A few minutes later, she pecked a good-bye kiss on his cheek and set off up the dirt path to the exhibition buildings. It was rough going at first, trying to avoid rocks and other impediments. She said a little prayer of thanks when the dirt of the livestock area gave way to the paved footpaths of the exhibition area.

The inside of Homemaker's Hall was a flurry of activity. One half was reserved for home goods that had been entered into various competitions. Rows and rows of canned preserves and fruits, intricately stitched quilts of every color imaginable, and needlework samplers that must have taken months to complete vied for space with one another. Each piece was more delicious, more beautiful, more breathtaking than the next. As she did every year, Ella marveled at how much talent was on display.

The other half of the great hall was full of exhibits of products to make home life better. It wasn't hard to find Mr. Henderson. He stood in front of a giant painted canvas with a scene that came straight from the arctic: a white landscape, a polar bear prowling in the distance, up front a domed igloo, and beside that, two penguins cavorting in the snow. Off to one side was the newest model of the Igloo icebox. Mr. Henderson was hunkered down beside it, checking something underneath.

Ella pushed the wagon up to the display. "Good morning, Mr. Henderson."

He jumped up and rushed over to meet her. "Good morning, Miss Daniels. You're looking lovely today."

She appreciated his kind words, even though she suspected he was merely being polite. "Thank you. Are you ready for the crowds?"

"Yes, absolutely. I was just double-checking the drip pan, and all is well." He eyed the crate expectantly. "Might you have brought me something?"

"As agreed, here is your butter sculpture. Would you mind helping me lift it?"

They put the crate on the table, and Ella carefully lifted out the sculpture. Mr. Henderson moved the crate out of the way so Ella could set it down.

"Oh my." His voice was hushed as he bent slightly, putting his face close to the statue so he could get a better look.

The peacock was sitting in a nest, delicately designed so you could see each strand of grass or hay, or whatever they made their nests out of. The peacock's tail made up half of the sculpture, stretching out behind it, fanned out and laying on the ground.

"What do you think?" Ella asked.

Mr. Henderson shook his head as he straightened up. "I've never seen anything like it before. It's beautiful."

Ella smiled. She was quite pleased with how it had turned out, and even more pleased that Mr. Henderson liked it.

"It's not just decorative, you know." Ella pointed to the tail feathers. "I designed it so that each one of these can be removed." She took a dull knife from her skirt pocket and demonstrated, cutting off the last feather on the back row.

Mr. Henderson gasped as if she had mutilated a priceless painting. "Why would I want to do that?"

Ella grinned. This was the best part. "Because now, you have a pat of butter. Which you can put on a delicious slice of freshly baked bread."

Eyes wide, Mr. Henderson seemed to understand where she was going. "I didn't realize your sculptures were edible."

"Usually, they're not. But I made sure this one is. I used fresh, clean butter, sterilized my carving tools, and kept my hands clean. I thought, what better way to convince people how good butter is, when it's kept in an Igloo, of course, than to let them taste it? Every day, I'll make more feathers to replace the ones you've used." She grinned at him. "Just make sure you don't take any slices from the body."

"That's a wonderful idea. But there's one problem," he said with a frown. "I don't have any bread."

Ella laughed and swept her hand in the direction of the other half of the building. "But you have access to so much of it! All you have to do is talk to one of the bakers. I'm sure you can find one or two who would like to partner with you, as well."

Mr. Henderson was visibly impressed. "Young lady, I think you may have missed your calling. You should work in advertising."

They both laughed together at the idea.

"I'm perfectly happy at the dairy, but thank you."

After a few more niceties, Mr. Henderson gave Ella the advertising for her to put on their icehouse, and Ella was on her way. When she left the hall, she glanced to her right. The Hall of Innovation was just two buildings down. Maybe she should take a look at the Majestic Electric display. Just to keep an eye on the competition.

<hr>

Max took a step back, admiring the sight before him. Majestic Electric had outdone themselves. As one would expect, their display utilized the newest in electric lighting and showcased their greatest innovation, at least as far as the modern housewife was concerned: the electric refrigerator. Right beside them was the display for the Joy Margarine Company and the next greatest innovation, although the modern housewife might not know it yet: margarine.

Philip came up beside him and slapped him on the back. "It's a thing of beauty, isn't it?"

"Sure is."

"Look, I've got to go take care of something, but I'll be back in a jiff."

Max looked at him askance. "Now? The gates open in ten minutes."

"Not a problem." He jerked his head toward the display and the dapper young men who were putting out the final touches. "John and Eric can handle things till I get back. Nothing's going to go wrong, kid."

He certainly hoped not. As Philip left, Max went back behind his table to finish prepping. One thing the margarine companies had learned early on was that housewives were more likely to try their product if it looked familiar. But margarine was a dull white color when it was produced, so they'd added food coloring to give it that butter-yellow color. Then, the dairy industry had made a stink about the health of the consumer and the safety of the food, and a law was passed that margarine companies couldn't add any dyes to their product. But there was no law saying they couldn't add food coloring after the fact.

Max took a small bottle of yellow food coloring from his jacket pocket and opened the margarine container that was already on his table. He squirted in a few drops and mixed it together until he achieved the right hue. *I'm not doing anything wrong*, he told himself, as he did every time he went through the process. Margarine was now sold with bottles of food dye, so customers did the same thing he was doing at home. Still, it felt somehow dishonest, as if saying his product wasn't good enough to start with.

As if confirming this concern, a shadow fell over his table and a sweet female voice said, "Still doctoring the chemicals, I see."

Ella. What was she doing here?

Smiling with what he hoped appeared to be confidence, he looked up at her. "Miss Daniels. How unusual of you to leave the. . .*intensity*. . .of the bovine enclosures and venture to this side of the fair."

"True," she said with a nod. "As a rule, I don't have business in this area. But I just delivered a delicious and lovely butter sculpture to Mr. Henderson at the Igloo Ice Works exhibit, and I thought I'd stop in and see how you were getting along."

"You shouldn't have. Really." Max slipped the bottle of food dye back in his pocket and replaced the lid on the margarine container. "I'm sure you have a lot to do back in your own space."

For a moment, her lips pursed and her eyes narrowed. Then, the corners of her mouth rose in a smile reminiscent of the *Mona Lisa*. "Yes, I have a cow to sculpt. And advertisements to place on our reliable icehouse."

She took a step backward and her heel caught on a stray electrical cord. One moment, she looked like the *Mona Lisa*. The next, she looked like Edvard Munch's *The Scream*. Her arms flailed, and though she tried to right herself in midair, it only made things worse. A cry of pain escaped her as she landed hard.

Max was around the table and down on one knee by her side before the Majestic Electric fellows had time to look up from their pamphlets.

"Are you all right?"

She looked up at him as if not sure what he'd said. Then she squeezed her eyes shut, took a deep breath, and looked at him again.

"I'm fine. I think." She put her palm on the floor and tried to push herself up then thought better of it and stopped. "Would you please help me stand?"

Max put one arm around her shoulder, put his other hand beneath her arm, and pulled her to her feet. Then she took a step forward and nearly collapsed again.

"I think I sprained my ankle."

Without asking for permission, Max scooped her up in his arms. She gave a little yelp then put her arms around his neck to hold on.

"What do you think you're doing?"

Max shifted her a bit, getting a better grip so as not to drop her. "I think I'm going to carry you back to your father."

"You can't do that."

"Far as I can tell, I either carry you back, or I leave you in a heap on the floor, which would just be plain bad for business."

She let out a little huff of air that tickled his throat. "Fine."

Max got the attention of John. Or Eric. He didn't know which was which. "Would you mind manning my display until I get back? Thanks."

As he carried Ella outside, Max tried not to think about how she was pressed so close against him, he could feel the heat from her body through his shirt. Or how her hair rubbed softly against his chin. Or how her fingertips grazed the skin of his neck. None of that mattered. He was helping a woman in need. That was all.

When he pushed through the doors to the outside, he headed for the steps but stopped when Ella gestured wildly with one hand toward the side of the building.

"Are you trying to tell me something?"

"I left my pushcart over there. I need to take it back with me."

Max shook his head. "I can't carry you and push that thing at the same time."

"You don't have to carry me. Let me sit on the cart."

There were already quite a few people milling about the fairgrounds. What would they think if they saw him pushing her on a cart like a bushel of potatoes? Still, it would be easier than carrying her. And it was her idea.

"All right."

There was a box on the cart, which he assumed held the advertising she'd mentioned. He had an irrational desire to "accidentally" knock it off but restrained himself. Instead, he set her down gently.

"Make sure you tuck in your skirt." He moved behind the handle. "Don't want it getting tangled in the wheels."

She did as he asked then looked over her shoulder at him. "Thank you."

He nodded then gave the cart a good push. "Hang on."

As expected, they received their fair share of looks. Some appeared horrified, others bemused, still others laughed. Several children clamored for their turn to ride the ride, only to be told by their parents not to stare. Rather than sit in quiet embarrassment, Ella began to wave at the people they passed.

"What are you doing?" Max hissed.

"I'm pretending this is a parade and I'm on a float." She sat up a little straighter, waving to the folks on one side then on the other. "Who's to say this isn't the first parade of the fair?"

The last thing he wanted to do was encourage her, but he couldn't hold back his laughter. Why did he expect anything less from her? After all, this was the woman who decided she could help the dairy by creating cow statues out of butter. Being the queen of her own little parade made perfect sense.

Her cheerful mood was contagious. By the time they arrived at the Daniels paddock, Max had joined in, sending up the occasional salute to particularly enthusiastic watchers. He was starting to feel quite jolly, until Walter Daniels caught sight of them and ran out of the corral.

"What in the world happened? Ella, why are you riding on that cart?"

She looked up at her father and threw her arms wide. "Oh, I thought it would be fun to ride down the street with everyone staring at me."

Frowning, Walter turned his eyes to Max. "What did you do to her?"

Of course, that was the thanks he got for trying to help. "Nothing. She tripped on a cord and twisted her ankle. This seemed like the best way to get her back here."

"Is that true?" Walter asked Ella.

"Yes, Papa. Max was a perfect gentleman. Well"—she looked up at Max with a sly grin—"maybe not perfect, but a gentleman nonetheless."

Max snorted. "I need to get back to the hall. I leave you in the capable hands of your father. Take care, Walter."

"Just a minute. Stay right here." Walter stalked around the side of the supply building. He came back a moment later with a stack of papers, which he thrust at Max. "Maybe you'd like to explain this?"

As Max shuffled through the papers, Ella craned her neck, trying to get a look.

"What's wrong?" she asked. "What are those?"

Walter crossed his arms in front of him. "While you were gone and I was tending the cows, someone decided to plaster our icehouse with that, that, garbage."

Max frowned. He'd never seen Walter upset enough to sputter, but the man had every right. They were posters made by the Dairy Council, but someone had painted them to alter the meaning. One featured cows that looked diseased. Another poster asked "What's in your butter?" and showed a fat rat sitting on a butter stick. He stopped looking, not wanting to see the rest.

"This is awful," Max said, passing the papers to Ella so she could take a look. "But why do you think I'd know anything about it?"

"Because I think you put them up."

"What?" Max and Ella uttered the shocked word at the same time.

"When could I have done it?" Max huffed. "I've been with Ella for the last half hour."

Walter shook his head. "It happened right after Ella left."

Max looked down at Ella. "Would you please talk some sense into your father?"

But Ella was biting her lower lip, her brow creased with concern. "You would have time to put up the posters and still get back to the hall before I arrived."

"Before you arrived for a visit I wasn't expecting?" Max barked out a harsh laugh.

"That would make me not only a vandal but a fortune-teller. I assure you, I am neither."

Walter took a step closer as if to challenge him, but Ella reached out and put a hand on her father's wrist, bringing him to a halt. Then, with a motion of her head, she indicated the fence where several visitors had stopped to watch the unrehearsed show before them.

"Max," she said, "I think you should go now."

He absolutely did not want to leave without convincing them that he'd had nothing to do with the slanderous posters. If he did, it was almost like admitting guilt. But there was no way to have a calm, reasonable talk with Walter at the moment, even if they didn't have an audience.

"Yes, I should be getting back to the hall and take care of my own exhibit."

Turning in a quick about-face, he strode down the path and away from Ella, her father, and their smelly cows.

Chapter 5

September 12, 1916

Homemaker's Hall was always crowded but never quite so much as this. The closer Max got to his destination, the thicker the crowd became, until finally he reached the concentrated mass of women gathered in front of the Igloo exhibit. The closely packed bodies raised the temperature at least ten degrees, making him glad he'd left his jacket back at the Joy display.

A handsome young man wearing a smart Igloo Ice Works uniform was speaking to the crowd. "For years, Igloo has been the brand you know and trust, keeping your food fresh and at the perfect temperature, and that hasn't changed. Our newest model has even more features you'll love. Remember, with Igloo, there's no need to worry about electric wiring or power availability. Our trusty icemen make sure you have everything you need."

Orville Henderson was off to the side, a place Max was sure he felt more comfortable. He stood behind a table, handing something to the ladies in front of him. It wasn't until Max made it all the way through the crowd that he saw what it was.

Even if it hadn't been made out of butter, there was no mistaking Ella's work. The peacock was lovely, although its tail was thinning by the second as Orville cut off butter feathers, put them on slices of bread, then handed them out.

"Excuse me." Max slid between two matrons who were discussing which flour produced the best bread, and got as close as he could to Orville without attracting the man's attention. Then, he watched.

The butter sculpture rested on a slab of ice, keeping it cool enough to hold its shape. The bread, however, was on a platter that was on top of three bricks, which no doubt had been heated to keep the bread warm. A small sign next to it announced that the bread was provided by blue ribbon winner Mavis Beechum. It was a smart move, involving another exhibitor. Max frowned to himself as he scanned the excited crowd. Ella was definitely getting more out of her partnership than Max was from his.

"Ladies, now, there's no need to worry." Orville spoke up as some of the waiting women began to jostle one another to move closer. "There are more feathers in the freezer of the Igloo. And we have more coming every day."

More feathers? Max considered this new information. Ella must be making replacements. How was she finding time to do this and create her usual sculpture?

The canvas at the back of the display rustled, and Max noticed there was a slit in the middle that extended to the floor and went right through the center of the igloo. A moment later, as if his thoughts had made her appear, Ella came through carrying a full buttery tail of peacock plumage on a wooden tray covered in wax paper. The man in the Igloo uniform also saw Ella and made a big deal of her to the crowd.

"Here she is, ladies, the closest thing we have to an Eskimo and the queen of butter sculpting, Miss Ella Daniels of the Daniels Dairy."

Blushing slightly, Ella smiled and nodded at the announcer then looked out over the crowd, smiling and nodding as she went.

And then her eyes landed on Max.

Her smile melted into a frown, and Max wondered if the butter in her hands would melt if she didn't set it down. She turned, gave the tray to Orville, then walked up to the announcer and whispered something to him. He glanced at Max, nodded at Ella, then addressed the crowd.

"Ladies, let me introduce another exhibitor here at the Nevada State Fair." He motioned to Max. "Mr. Sinclair represents the Joy Margarine Company. It seems they're as interested in butter as all of you are."

Orville's eyes grew wide when he finally recognized him. Then, without appearing to think it through, he buttered a slice of bread and held it out to Max. He refused it, but it didn't matter. The women around him laughed, and the announcer jumped on the opportunity.

"You see, even the people who sell margarine know that everything is better with butter!"

Coming to check up on the Igloo exhibit had been a bad idea, but there was no undoing it now. Pasting on a smile, he stepped up onto the stage and addressed the crowd.

"I agree that everything is better with butter." A whisper of surprise rippled through the ladies in front of him. He moved toward Ella, enjoying the shock on her face. "But," he said, raising his voice, "I absolutely believe that everything is marvelous with margarine!" To emphasize the point, he bowed low, and when he straightened back up, he grinned and winked.

The crowd loved it. Laughter and applause came at him like a wave, encouraging him to say more.

"I hope you ladies visit me in the Hall of Innovations for a sample of something truly delectable."

One woman waved at him. Several giggled behind gloved hands. Beside him, Ella grabbed his wrist and pulled him closer.

"Come with me," she said.

She glared at Max, but he looked her straight in the eye. "Yes, I believe you and I should talk."

He followed her to the back of the stage and through the opening in the painted igloo. As soon as they were safely behind the display and away from the eyes of the onlookers, Ella stiffened, arms rigid at her sides, fingers curled into tight fists. "How dare you come over here and cause a scene."

Max let out a huff of frustration. "Me? I caused a scene? What about you?" He gestured back with a slash of his hand. "I was just standing there, watching, not saying a word. There was no reason to point me out to that man so he could throw verbal barbs at me."

"Quit acting put-upon. You took full advantage of the situation. Everything is marvelous with margarine? Please. As if that vile product could possibly compare to butter."

She shook her head. "No matter how much you dislike me, I never thought you would stoop so low. First the posters, now this."

Two things struck Max. She still thought he was responsible for the posters, which irked him. And she thought he disliked her, which irked him even more.

"Ella," he said in a low, calm voice, "no matter what you think, I have never, ever disliked you."

She blinked. Her fingers relaxed, and she pressed her palms against the sides of her skirt. She blinked again. Max allowed himself an instant of satisfaction at the fact that he had managed to render her speechless. Then he decided to speak up before she returned to her old self.

"We are in competing businesses, yes, and I plan to do what I can to promote my product. But I won't do it by hurting you or the dairy."

For a moment, she dropped the protective shield she kept up and looked at him, really looked at him, the way she used to. Thoughts of their time together filled his mind: talking for hours, laughing as they chased down a rogue cow, sharing their first kiss behind the milking barn. . . How he had loved her.

He reached out, and his fingertips grazed the curve of her cheek. "Ella, I—"

She jerked back as if he'd cut her. "No. I'm sorry. But after everything. . .I just can't." She hurried away, sliding between booths, where she disappeared into the flow of people.

What had she meant? Can't what? Can't trust him? Can't think about their time together? Can't admit she still loved him?

Max slammed the door on those thoughts. They were part of another time, one they couldn't get back. He needed to focus on the present. He had a job to do, and he'd best get back to it.

But first, he needed to stop by the bakery displays and find something on which to sample his margarine.

<hr />

By the time Max had made his way back to his own exhibit, he'd managed to banish thoughts of Ella Daniels from his mind. For the most part. It had been over a year since he left the dairy, and he still thought about her nearly every day. He'd come to accept the fact there was no way to completely remove her from his memory. Instead, he threw himself into his work.

Stepping up on the raised platform, he thanked Eric for taking over during his break and sent him back to the Majestic Electric booth. Max set down the box he was carrying and took out a sack filled with fluffy biscuits. He'd failed at several tries to find a homemaker who didn't sneer at his proposal. Then he met Susan Reynolds, a progressive young baker who was thrilled to be associated with margarine. She was so happy to be involved, the single Miss Reynolds also gave him a plate, a knife, and an invitation to join her family for Sunday dinner. He politely declined the dinner but took everything else with a smile and effusive thanks.

Max took a container of margarine from the Majestic Electric refrigerator next door and put it on the table. Then he worked on the biscuits. As he cut them into thirds—so there'd be enough to go around—and arranged them on the plate, people began to stop in front of his table. Unlike Homemaker's Hall, the Hall of Innovation was populated by a majority of men. Regardless, the lure of free food was apparently enough to grab their attention. Thankfully, several were accompanied by their wives. Max knew that, while the men held the purse strings, the women really made most of the buying decisions, especially when it came to food.

This was going to work out better than he'd hoped.

Max smiled and addressed the people as he worked. "I'm so glad you came to see what the Joy Margarine Company has for you. How many of you use margarine already?"

Only two hands were raised, and those only to shoulder level. He was used to people who were embarrassed to admit they used margarine. Chances were good at least half the crowd had but wouldn't admit it.

"In that case, let me show you the best thing to happen to biscuits since God created honey."

Wanting to show them the entire process, Max took the lid off the container and used a spatula to scoop the contents out into a glass bowl.

"As you can see, fresh margarine is white. It's perfectly fine to use it as is, but many homemakers like to give it a little color first. That's why, with every purchase of Joy Margarine, we include a bottle of food dye."

Max hadn't realized until the moment he reached for the bottle that he wasn't wearing his suit jacket. "Excuse me one moment." He retrieved it from the back of the chair he'd left it on, dug in the pocket, and found the bottle. Returning to the table, he held it up for the crowd to see.

"I'll tell you a secret." He continued talking as he removed the lid and poured a few drops into the container. "Dairy farmers like to say that margarine is inferior because we have to add coloring. What they don't tell you is that color is added to butter, too."

A few surprised gasps came from the crowd as he mixed.

"The coloring doesn't change the taste or the quality of the margarine in any way." He held the bowl up, showing how he'd managed to achieve an even, pleasing yellow tint. "See how lovely that is? And it was easy, wasn't it?"

Affirmatives rose from the crowd. Several of the women were smiling, and one clutched her husband's arm and whispered in his ear. He had them on the hook. Now it was time to reel them in.

He picked up a piece of biscuit. "Here's something you can't do with butter." He slathered on a generous amount, spreading it easily with the knife. "Soft and smooth. Spreads like a dream. Now, who wants to be the first to try it?"

Almost everyone responded, except for a burly man in the front. Max could tell by looking, he was the kind of fellow who was skeptical about everything. If he could win this man over, he'd tell everyone he knew about how fabulous margarine was.

"Here you go, sir." Max held the biscuit out to him. "Why don't you give that a try?"

The man hesitated, but eventually he took it, raised it to the woman beside him as though offering a toast, then popped the whole thing in his mouth. Max watched closely, wanting to experience that split second when skepticism turned to delight.

What he saw was skepticism turning to shock then to disgust.

The man coughed hard, his eyes bulging and watering. The woman pulled a handkerchief from the pocket of her dress and handed it to him. He promptly spit out the partially chewed biscuit and wadded up the cotton square, all the while coughing and retching. Max jumped down from the stage and pounded the man on the back.

"Are you all right, sir?"

"Stop hitting me!" It came out as a strangled cry.

"I'm sorry," Max said. "I thought you were choking. I—"

The man put up his hand in a signal for quiet. He leaned over, hands to his knees, and took several deep breaths until the coughing subsided. When he stood up straight, he looked at Max.

"That was, beyond a doubt, the worst thing I've ever tasted in my life."

Max wasn't sure what to do. He'd never seen anyone react that way. "I am sorry, sir. Perhaps it was the biscuits? I should have tasted them first."

Another man who was right in front of the table reached up and grabbed one. All watched expectantly as he smelled it first then pinched a piece from the side and popped it in his mouth. "Nope. That's a good-tasting biscuit, right there."

Unhappy rumblings spread through the crowd as the people began to walk away. Desperate to save the situation, Max jumped back on the stage and called to them. "It was probably just a bad batch. Let me get another container."

The unfortunate taster, whose face was still blotched with red from the exertion of coughing, shook his head. "What, and let you kill me this time? No thanks. You couldn't pay me to eat that vile stuff."

As they walked away, Max made out bits and pieces of what they said.

"Batch probably went bad in the refrigerator when the electricity went out."

"Told you it was bad."

"See, butter is better."

Max tossed the biscuits back in the sack then he stared down at the bowl of margarine. What had gone wrong? He picked it up, looking closer, and then it hit him.

The smell.

Margarine had no discernable smell. But he was definitely getting a whiff of something pungent as he brought the bowl closer to his face. It almost smelled like. . .onion?

That was crazy. He put the bowl down then used his index finger to swipe up a bit of margarine. One taste was all it took to convince him. It was definitely onion.

How had that happened? He was relatively confident there wasn't an onion anywhere in the building, so how had the margarine become tainted? Someone must have altered it on purpose. But why? He'd taken the container from the refrigerator in the Majestic Electric exhibit. They were his partners. Not only that, but someone was watching what went on at all times. No one could have gotten to it. Which left only one answer.

The food dye.

He unscrewed the cap and held it beneath his nose. After muttering a few impolite words under his breath, he put the cap back on. It smelled as though someone had pressed the juice from an onion and added it to the bottle. Somehow, someone had managed to sabotage his food dye, therefore ruining the margarine. Now at least one man, and probably many of the others, would forever have a negative impression of the product.

Whoever did it would have to know that he mixed the coloring into the margarine as people watched, and know that he kept the bottle of dye in his jacket pocket. A thought popped into his head, just the seed of an idea. He tried to ignore it, to push it away, but the more he tried, the more it grew.

He stepped to the edge of his display and motioned to the one next door. "Eric!"

The young man hurried over. "Already time for another break?"

"No. A question. When I was gone before, did anyone come behind the table? Maybe go over to the chair?"

Eric cocked his head to one side as he thought. "No. Not that I saw."

If he was there the whole time, there was no way he would have missed it. "Did you stay here the whole time?"

"Almost. At one point, quite a few people were asking questions, so I had to go help John. But it was just for a few minutes." Eric frowned. "Why? Did something happen?"

"Maybe. Don't worry about it. Thanks."

Max moved slowly back to the table. He picked up the bowl and dropped it into a trash basket. It hit the bottom with a thud at the same time Ella's words rang in his ears.

"As if that vile product could possibly compare to butter."

He didn't want to believe it, but it made sense. When she'd come by the other day, he'd been mixing color into the margarine. She'd seen him drop the bottle in his pocket. Today, she would have had plenty of time to sneak into the exhibit. It was a terrible thought, but who else would do such a thing? She already believed he'd tried to undermine her, so why not respond in kind?

Ella had sabotaged him.

Chapter 6

Maybe partnering with Igloo hadn't been such a good idea.

Ella got up from the stool, her stiff joints protesting with every move. She stretched her muscles, reaching for the ceiling then pressing her fingers into the small of her back and leaning backward.

She'd spent far too long in the icehouse, but she didn't have much of a choice. The time it took to fashion new peacock feathers for Mr. Henderson had cut into her cow sculpting time, putting her behind schedule. She was heading into the third day of the fair, and she had only gotten the basic form of the cow done. By now, she should have been finishing off the fine touches on the head. The people who'd been coming by to watch her do that had been disappointed to find the icehouse doors closed. She had to open up to the public tomorrow. But first, she needed to warm up.

Stepping outside, she was shocked to find she'd worked so long, the sun had gone down and now the moon was out, grinning like Lewis Carroll's Cheshire cat. Papa had brought her food at some point, though Ella didn't know exactly when. He'd admonished her not to work too hard then had gone off to meet some farmer friends whom he only saw once a year.

Ella sighed. It would probably be another night of sleeping on the cot. A low moo got her attention, and she walked over to Geraldine's stall.

"You want my attention, too, do you?" She rubbed the cow's nose. "Don't worry. Tomorrow, you'll get all the attention you want."

"Miss Daniels!" A voice boomed behind her. "A word."

She whirled to see Max. He looked decidedly unhappy, which unnerved her almost as much as the fact that he'd called her Miss Daniels.

"Being rather formal tonight, aren't you?"

Max's frown deepened. "It seems we've gotten to that point. After today, you made it clear that there's nothing between us anymore but animosity."

"Oh, that." Ella sighed. "Max, I'm sorry. I've been thinking about it, and I realize I may have gone a bit too far."

"A bit? You altered a food product."

"What are you talking about?"

Either he didn't hear the question or he chose to ignore it. "Thanks to you, at least a dozen people are now convinced that margarine is abhorrent. But even worse, that man almost choked to death on the sample I gave him. Is that what you wanted? To kill somebody?"

Now Ella was getting upset. "I was apologizing for the words we exchanged earlier. I have no idea what you're talking about. You should know there's no power on earth that could make me touch margarine."

Even in the moonlight, Ella could see the red on his neck rising from beneath his collar. "But you have no issue with touching the dye bottle, do you?"

"You are making no sense whatsoever. Now, if you'll excuse me, I have more work to do. Good night, Mr. Sinclair."

She marched right back into the icehouse, only to have Max follow her inside.

"Oh no," he said, pulling the door shut behind him. "We're not finished."

Ella pressed the heel of her palm against her forehead, trying to hold back the dull throb that was becoming an incessant pounding. "Please, listen to me. I didn't do anything to your margarine, or your dye, or anything you own. You have to believe me."

"Really? The same way you believed me when I told you I didn't paper the walls of this building with libelous posters?"

What did he mean by that? "Are you finally admitting that you did it?"

"No!" Max ran his fingers roughly through his hair. "I'm saying that I did not do it, and you had no right to do what you did today."

Ella jammed her fists on her hips. "I didn't do anything!"

They stood that way for a moment, fuming and glaring at each other.

"This is ridiculous," Ella said. "I will not engage in a screaming match with you. Stay here all night if you wish. I'm going to the storage room, and if you follow me in there, you'll find yourself at the pointy end of a pitchfork."

She stormed past him to the door and gave it a good push. Except it didn't budge, and Ella bounced backward, stumbling over her feet.

"What in the world?" This time, she approached the door with caution and pushed. Still nothing. Then, as panic began to rise, she grabbed the handle and shook the door.

"Step aside," Max said. "Sometimes, you just need a man to handle things."

The glimmer of satisfaction she felt when his try was as useless as hers quickly faded as the reality of their situation sunk in.

"We're locked in here."

<hr />

"How does something like this happen?" Max paced from one end of the building to the other. "Why would the door to an icehouse lock on its own?"

"It doesn't." Ella stood in the corner, hugging herself against the cold. "Someone must have come by and put the lock on."

"With us inside? No one is that stupid."

"Whoever it was must have thought the building was empty."

"Then that person was deaf, because there's no way he could have missed us yelling."

Ella shrugged. "I have no idea. But it looks like we're stuck in here until my father comes back in the morning. No amount of pacing is going to change that."

Max stopped short and looked around, assessing the situation. Thankfully, the building wasn't completely full of ice. Because of the need to leave space for Ella to work on the butter cow, a good-sized section was empty, the floor covered in straw.

"You're right." He walked up to her. "We won't freeze to death in here, but it's going to be rather uncomfortable. I suggest we stay close to each other to keep warm."

Her eyes flicked away from him. "As long as we're in here, I could keep working on the cow. That would be the reasonable thing to do."

"Or, we could sit on the floor together and try to get a little shut-eye," Max said. "You look exhausted."

That was all it took to convince her. "I am tired. All right."

As Ella settled herself on the floor against the wall, Max looked around for anything he could use as a covering. There was a coat, a smock, and a pair of gloves in her work area.

"Here you are." He draped the coat over her knees and handed her the gloves.

Her nose wrinkled. "Those gloves are stained with butter. No matter how much I wash them, it never all comes out."

"Put them on. You're trying to stay warm, not going to a ball." He sat down next to her and covered himself with the smock.

Now that they were sitting together, their sides pressed against each other, he had no idea what to say. So he made inane conversation.

"It's too bad you don't keep wood and matches in here. We could build a fire."

"Then all the ice would melt. And the cow."

"But it would be cozy."

She chuckled. "I suppose. And if the butter melted off the cow, then we could burn the wooden frame underneath."

"If we had some bread, we could make toast and soak up all the butter."

Ella looked up at him, and for the first time in longer than he could remember, she laughed. Not a fake, polite laugh, but a real chortle that came from deep down. It warmed him more than any fire could and gave him the courage to take a chance.

"Would it be all right if I put my arm around you? To conserve warmth, of course."

Her laughter dying down, Ella nodded. "Seems that would be the sensible thing to do."

He draped his arm over her shoulder, tucking her in under his arm. It only took a moment for Ella's tense body to relax, and she leaned against him, resting her head on his chest. They stayed that way for a while, quiet, with nothing but the sound of their breathing in the space. Max shut his eyes and let himself remember another time, when the only thing he'd wanted was to be with her and he couldn't imagine a future without her. How had everything gone so wrong?

"Max?"

He opened his eyes. "Hmm?"

"You really didn't put those posters on the icehouse, did you?" She didn't move as she asked the question.

"No. I really didn't."

"I believe you."

It was as though someone had lifted a great weight from his shoulders he hadn't even known he was carrying. All the energy he'd put into defending himself and being upset with Ella had pressed down on him, making him unhappy and unreasonable. With her belief in him came a sense of calm and clarity.

"And you didn't do anything to ruin the margarine sample, did you?"

She gave her head a slight shake. "No. I would never."

"I believe you." Without even thinking, he lowered his lips and kissed the top of her head.

"Max?"

"Hmm?"

"Did you just kiss my head?"

He heard the humor in her voice. "As a matter of fact, I did."

"That's what I thought." She pressed a little closer to him.

Perhaps getting locked in an icehouse together wasn't such a bad thing. Max didn't know if it was the frigid temperature or the fact that they had no choice but to talk to each other, but they were finally talking about things that mattered.

"Can I tell you a secret?" Ella asked.

He squeezed her shoulder. "Of course."

It took her so long to speak, he thought she'd changed her mind. But then she took a deep breath. "I really don't like butter."

Max was at a loss. Saying she didn't like butter was like a singer saying she didn't like music. It didn't make sense. But he had to say something. "You don't? Well. That's. . .surprising."

She pushed away from him just enough so she could look up into his eyes. "It's awful, I know. The butter sculptures were my idea, but I thought I'd only do it once or twice, and then the novelty would wear off and I could move on to something else."

Now he understood. "Instead, they just became more popular, and you felt you couldn't stop."

Shaking her head, her eyelashes fluttered as if she was trying not to cry. "I love my father, and I love the dairy. I do. But I don't know how much longer I can stand this."

"Have you said any of this to Walter?"

"No. It would break his heart."

Max didn't agree. "He might be disappointed, but he'd understand. I think what's most important to your father is your happiness."

"I suppose." Her eyes shifted and she looked past him, as if seeing something in the distance. "But I can't help but think of my mother. She wouldn't quit on Papa. How can I?"

Ah, now they were at the crux of it. "Your mother was a remarkable woman. The dairy was her life. That was her choice. But it doesn't have to be yours."

She looked back at him. "What do you mean?"

"Ella, you have a great talent. You should be exploring that, creating art in clay, marble, stone, anything else. Just because your family dedicated their lives to the dairy doesn't mean you have to. You need to decide what will make you happy. That's the life you should have."

"Like you did."

There was accusation in the statement but also something else. An unspoken question.

"I did what I had to."

"Why?" She blinked, and a tear escaped and ran down her cheek. "We made plans together. You told me you loved me. What was so wonderful about working for a margarine company that you had to leave?"

"It wasn't a farm. I grew up on a farm, and I knew I didn't want that life. Then I tried the dairy, but it didn't fit me any better. I had to find a way out."

"Without me."

Max huffed out a breath. "When your mother got sick, I watched you. How you took care of her. How the less she could do, the more you did, trying to take her place at the dairy. You were as determined as she was not to leave there. If I'd asked you to come with me, that would have put you in a terrible position."

"You should have let me decide for myself."

"Maybe, but I didn't want to hurt you more by making you choose between me and your family."

Every fiber of Max's body wanted to touch her, even as his mind screamed it was a bad idea. He ignored the screaming. Caressing her cheek, his fingertips wove into the hair at the base of her neck. Her eyes widened in surprise.

"Ella?"

"Hmm?"

"Can I tell you a secret?"

Her lips parted slightly, and she nodded.

"I've made a lot of mistakes in my life, but the biggest one was leaving you."

His head dipped, slowly, giving her time to stop him if she wanted. Instead, she leaned toward him. Their lips were so close, he could feel her breath. Just another fraction of an inch—

A heavy pounding on the outside of the door made them jerk apart from each other. Then a voice called out.

"Ella! Are you still in there?"

It was Walter.

Ella scrambled to her feet. "Papa! Yes, I'm in here. So is Max."

"What? Wait a second. Hold tight."

As Walter did something on the outside, Ella stripped off the gloves and the coat, returning them to where they'd come from. Slowly, Max stood up. He was glad they wouldn't have to spend the entire night in there, but the timing was abysmal.

When Ella turned to look at him, her face was flush, and there was a hint of a smile on her lips. "I'm glad we were able to talk."

He nodded. "Me, too. Think we can pick this back up later?"

Her smile widened. "Absolutely."

There was the sound of a key scraping in the lock. A moment later, Walter was standing in the open door, looking like he'd found an elephant in the icehouse.

"How did you two end up locked in here?"

"It's a long story." Max moved to the door, clapping Walter on the shoulder as he walked by. "I'll let Ella tell you. For now, I need to get some sleep."

As he walked down the path, he could hear them talking, although he couldn't make out what they were saying. Max smiled. He should have been thinking about who'd put the lock on the icehouse door, but it was the last thing on his mind.

For now, all he could think about was the kiss that almost was, and the promise of the kiss to come.

Chapter 7

September 13, 1916

Ella chose to sleep on the cot, but it wouldn't have mattered if she'd slept on a slab of stone. Exhaustion sent her to sleep as soon as her head touched the pillow.

The sound of urgent mooing woke her at 6:00 a.m., and she sat up quickly, filling her vision with sparkling pinpricks. She'd slept later than usual, and now her father was trying to milk the cows by himself. After a quick check in the mirror to fix her hair and an attempt at smoothing the wrinkles from her skirt, she grabbed a pail and hurried outside.

"You should have woken me, Papa."

Five cows were still tethered to the fence, waiting to be milked. Walter looked up from the one he was working on. "I figured you needed some extra sleep. You've been burning the candle down to the wick."

Her milking stool was waiting for her, right by the feed trough. She grabbed it as she walked by and settled at the cow beside her father. Wordlessly, she got down to the business of milking. The steady rhythm of the milk shooting from the cow's teats and pinging against the pail had a soothing effect. As she worked, her mind wandered back to the previous night. The conversation with Max had been a long time coming. She was glad they'd had it, but still, in the light of a new day when she wasn't locked into an ice-cold room for heaven knew how long, she couldn't help but wonder about the sincerity of it all. Had Max meant what he said? Did he really regret leaving her? And why had she admitted how much she'd grown to dislike butter?

"I had a real good talk last night with Hank Jepson, one of the other dairymen." Walter interrupted her thoughts as he finished milking one cow and unsnapped the rope from her halter.

"What about?"

"Oh, how the industry is changing. What we need to do to compete." He poured the milk from his pail into a tall, metal milk can then moved his stool to the next cow. "Hank's looking to expand his business. He's ready to pay top dollar for a good herd. I don't guess anyone has a better herd than we do."

Ella stopped milking and looked in her father's direction, even though her view was blocked by the Jersey. "You're not thinking of selling them, are you?"

"Of course not. No." He kept on working. "Although, it did get me thinking."

Resuming her milking, Ella tried not to do too much thinking of her own and simply listen.

"The times are changing, and it will take a considerable amount of work and investment to keep up. I'm not sure I'm up for it."

"We're doing just fine, Papa." Just fine might be an exaggeration. Ella kept the books, and she knew there were months when they barely squeaked by. Still, they had enough to keep the dairy running, pay the bills, pay the workers, and keep food on the table.

"We wouldn't be well at all if it weren't for you."

"Papa—"

"No, now listen. I never told you this, but five years ago, we were on the verge of going broke. If you hadn't come up with the idea of doing butter sculpture and getting everyone talking about us, we would have lost the dairy."

It was a shocking revelation. Back then, she hadn't kept the books. In fact, she'd been looking into the idea of attending college and trying to figure out how to convince her parents it was a good idea. She'd known they were having financial problems but not the extent of it.

Max's words came back to her. *"You need to decide what will make you happy."* She should talk to her father, tell him what she'd told Max. But how could she after what he'd just disclosed? He was obviously worried about keeping the dairy running. What would it do to him if he found out she wanted to walk away and do something else?

For now, she would keep her feelings to herself.

They continued working, saying nothing, listening to the *ping, ping, ping* of milk in the pails.

———— • ◆ • ————

"Mark my words: good Americans love margarine!"

Max spoke to the crowd that had gathered in front of the table to try the samples. After opening a brand-new bottle of food dye, carefully mixing it with the margarine, then spreading it on pieces of fresh biscuits, Max had tasted it himself. It was perfect. And he only had to eat two more pieces in front of the crowd to convince them that trying his product wouldn't kill them. Today should go a long way to correcting the previous day's debacle.

Just as expected, a man piped up with a question. "How does eating this make me a good American?"

He had the crowd's complete attention as he explained that rationing was imminent, and how margarine was a more readily available product. The inevitability of entering the Great War was on everyone's mind, even if they tried to ignore it. Finding another way they could support the fight for freedom, small though it may be, was encouraging. It would have been quite a mercenary way to sell something, except that Max firmly believed what he was saying. Not everyone could go overseas to fight, but this was something everyone could do.

For the next two hours, he interacted with the sea of people that flowed past the Joy exhibit. He answered questions, offered samples, complimented housewives on their smart attire and husbands on their excellent taste in women. It wasn't until his stomach began to rumble that he realized it was dinnertime.

Right on cue, Eric bounded over from the Majestic Electric exhibit. "Time for dinner."

Max looked at his watch. "Thank you. What about you? Don't you ever take breaks?"

Eric shrugged. "When I need to."

With another thanks and a promise to be back in half an hour, Max hopped off the stage and hurried toward the exit door.

Being at the state fair, there was no shortage of cut flowers available. After a quick detour to purchase a bouquet, he hurried to the livestock area. He passed coops of chickens, pens of pigs, and corrals of horses. Sheep, goats, ducks, turkeys. . .it was a menagerie of farm animals and smells that usually would have curled his nose hairs. But nothing could dampen his mood or wipe the smile off his face. He was going to see Ella.

When he entered the Daniels Dairy area, there was already a group of mostly women and children standing in front of the open doors of the icehouse. They watched as Ella, wearing her smock but not the gloves, stood beside the replica of Geraldine, carefully sculpting details into the hindquarters. Muscles were emerging, the tendons visible in the lower legs, hip bones pushing up from beneath the skin. It really was amazing how much she could do with such an odd substance.

After waiting ten minutes, Max made his way carefully through the crowd and went into the icehouse. She was so engrossed in her work, she didn't even notice.

"Excuse me," he said, holding the flowers in front of his face.

Ella looked up. "Oh, I'm sorry, you can't—" Max moved the flowers, and Ella laughed. "Never mind. You can."

As he handed her the bouquet, a chorus of *ooh*s and *ahh*s came up from the crowd.

"Say," one woman called out, "isn't that the Joy Margarine man?"

Ella and Max exchanged a look. "I think that's my signal," she said. Then she turned to her audience. "I'll be taking a break now, but if you want to come back later, you can see how much progress I've made. Feel free to visit Geraldine. She loves the attention."

They weren't happy about missing whatever was about to transpire between the margarine man and the butter lady, but they moved on. Max shut the doors but not all the way.

"Good idea," Ella said. "We don't want a repeat of last night."

Max grinned. "I wouldn't remind repeating part of it."

She lowered her eyes, but her smile widened, bringing to life a dimple in one cheek. "True. It wasn't all bad. Thank you for the flowers. They're lovely."

"I was thinking it's a shame for us to spend all this time here and never get to enjoy the fair like a regular visitor. Would you do me the honor of strolling the grounds with me?"

Her smile fell and her brows lowered in a frown. "I'd love to, but I can't. I have to do more work."

Max nodded. "All right. How about tomorrow?"

"Yes." The smile returned and her eyes sparkled. "Same time?"

"Perfect." He leaned down and brushed a kiss on her cheek. "Until then."

He left the icehouse and went in the direction of the exhibition halls. But before he was out of her sight, he looked over his shoulder and saw Ella, her nose buried in the flowers. Then her eyes met his, and she waved. He waved back and forced himself to keep walking. Tomorrow couldn't come fast enough.

Chapter 8

September 14, 1916

In all the years she'd been coming to the fair, Ella had never really taken the time to experience it. The newly installed electric lights shone down on the brightly colored stalls and displays. There was so much to see and do, it was almost overwhelming. That and the fact that she was on the arm of Maxwell Sinclair, the man she'd loved, and lost, and seemed she might be able to love again, was quite an assault on her senses.

They bought their dinner—hot dogs and pink lemonade—from one of the many vendors calling out to everyone who passed. They strolled through horticultural displays, listened to a band playing in the pavilion, and visited the midway, where Max attempted, and failed, to win a prize for her. It was a wonderful evening, and it was over entirely too fast.

"I suppose it's time to take you back now," Max said as the clock tower chimed for the eighth time.

Ella sighed. "We both have to be up early, so, yes."

As they walked the dirt roads through the livestock area, Max took her hand. Happily, Ella intertwined her fingers with his.

They hadn't talked about their respective businesses at all, but now that their date was almost over, Ella wanted to bring something up.

"I talked to my father yesterday about the dairy."

"Really?" Max sounded surprised. "You brought it up?"

"No, he did. He said he talked to someone, and it got him thinking about the future, about competition, whether or not he wanted to keep the dairy at all."

Max didn't respond right away. "Did he say who he talked to?"

"One of the other farmers. Mr. Jepson, I think."

"Oh. All right." He sounded relieved.

Ella looked sideways at him. "Is something wrong?"

"No. Not at all."

They came around a bend in the road, and Ella gasped. She could see the Daniels buildings and corrals. The icehouse was glowing, and smoke billowed out under the doors.

It was on fire.

Ella dropped his hand and ran. Max began calling out to anyone who might be around to hear him.

"Fire at the Daniels Dairy! Get the fire crew! Hurry!"

Ella had almost gotten to the icehouse when Max grabbed her arm and jerked her to a stop.

"Let go! I have to do something."

Max's face was grim. "What do you think you can do? The two of us can't stop it. We need the fire crew."

Panic rose, almost strangling her. She looked around wildly. "My father. Where is he?" She ran to the supply building, but he wasn't there. Whirling, she ran back toward the burning building. "He might be in there."

Max stopped her again. "He's not. Didn't you tell me he spends evenings visiting with the other farmers? I'm sure that's where he is."

His words sounded positive, but the look on Max's face said something else. It said what Ella was thinking but didn't dare say: *If he is in there, it's too late.*

The pounding of running feet sounded behind them as a group of men filled the yard. Relief flooded Ella as she saw the man leading them was her father.

"Papa!" She threw her arms around him, hugging so hard he had to pry her hands loose.

"I'm fine, darlin'. Now let me get to work." Max moved to join him, but Walter shook his head and pointed at Ella. "You stay with her." Max didn't attempt to argue.

Within moments, the men had formed a bucket brigade and were scooping water from the trough and throwing it on one side of the building. A moment later, the clang of the fire wagon bell sounded. The yard was a flurry of activity, but Ella wasn't watching it. Now that she knew her father wasn't in danger, she could think of what was really happening.

Even before the men and fire crew started dousing the building, water had been seeping out under the doors and around the foundation. Mixed into the water was a pale yellow substance. She stared at it, unable to tear her eyes away, even when Max tried to hug her to him.

Melted ice. Melted butter.

Her sculpture was gone.

———— ••• ————

The fire was out. The remnants of the icehouse were a soggy black mess. The doors had fallen off when the wood around the hinges became unstable. Like a great gaping mouth, the doorway left the inside on display for anyone who wanted to take a look. But no one did.

When Ella finally allowed herself to cry, she couldn't stop. Max held her, whispering soothing words in her ear as she sobbed into his shirt.

"I'll take her now." Walter put his arm around Ella and maneuvered her away from Max and into his own arms. He squeezed Max on the shoulder. "Thank you."

The attention of her father seemed to help. The crying subsided, becoming sniffles and the occasional gasping breath.

Walter looked at the icehouse. "I don't understand how this happened. There was nothing in there that would start a fire."

Max considered it. "Could it have been a short in the electric light?"

"No." Ella shook her head. "I turned the light off when I left. And I locked the door."

"She's right," Walter agreed. "I double-checked it before I went to meet my friends."

The answer was obvious, although Max had no intention of being the one to say it. The only way the fire could have started was if someone set it.

"Maybe this is a sign," Walter said. "Maybe I should take you up on your offer."

Ella pulled back from her father. "What? What offer?"

No, Max thought. *Not now. Don't bring it up now.*

"Max brought me an offer from the Joy Company to buy the dairy."

"When did he do that?"

"A few months ago. That day he came by. They think it would make a nice place for a processing plant. After tonight, I'm thinking they might be right."

With snail-like slowness, Ella turned her head toward Max. Her mouth was set in a grim line, her eyes narrow. "You."

The one syllable hit him like an arrow finding its target. "No. I didn't do this." She just stared at him, until he had to say something else. "You know it couldn't have been me. We were together when it happened."

"That doesn't mean you didn't get someone else to do it." A groan escaped her lips, and she put her face in her hands.

"What's wrong?" Walter looked back and forth between them. "What are you trying to say?"

Ella put her hands down. "It was all a lie. Everything you said to me, the encouragement, that you still loved me. You made me trust you, and then you took me out tonight so we wouldn't think you did this."

Walter glared at him. "Is this true?"

"Of course not." Max felt helpless.

"You want my father to sell the dairy. Then you told me I should leave the dairy." Ella looked away. "You'd do anything to get what you want."

"I would never hurt you," Max said. "Either of you."

"You hurt me once before. Why should now be any different?" Ella looked up at her father. "Can we go, please?"

"Of course."

As they started to leave, Walter stopped and addressed Max. "Don't come around us anymore."

Father and daughter walked away, leaving Max alone in the smoldering remnants of what might have been.

Chapter 9

September 15, 1916

Stories about the fire spread through the fair, hopping from one exhibitor to the other like hungry fleas on a pack of dogs. Rumors abounded. Some said the fire had been set by Max Sinclair in an angry attempt to undermine the competition. Others said Walter Daniels had set the fire to gain sympathy and to point the finger at Max. Very few believed it had been an accident. The wildest theory was that Ella Daniels had set the fire in order to destroy her statue and hide the fact that she just wasn't as talented as she used to be.

Manning his exhibit, Max fought the urge to speak up every time someone came up with another ridiculous idea. He wasn't even interacting with the crowd like he used to. Instead, he put out the margarine samples and sat back in a chair, watching them pick up pieces of biscuit as they walked by. He just had to get through that day and the next, and then the fair would be over. He could go home and put this all behind him.

Except he doubted he could ever forget. Holding Ella while she sobbed, the look of anguish on her face, which then changed to anger. The cold steel of Walter's voice as he told him to stay away. The hollow ache in his gut whenever he thought about what had happened. There was no way to escape feelings like those.

"Why the long face?" Philip Stanley sauntered over to him, one hand in his trouser pocket.

Max grunted. "Haven't you been listening to the gossip?"

"What, that?" Philip laughed. "Don't let that get you down, son. People are talking, and that's always good. You've just got to use it to your advantage. Turn a negative into a positive."

Had he heard him right? "How can any of it be positive?"

"Easy. If Daniels hadn't been such a champion of iceboxes, there would have been no icehouse, so there wouldn't have been anything to burn. It's just another reason why the electric refrigerator is safer and better."

"All right," Max said slowly. "That's a positive for you. But how does it help me?"

Philip smiled, but it was forced and somehow brittle. "We're partners, remember? What's good for me is good for you, and vice versa. Now that the butter cow is gone, so is the milkmaid, and that's good for both of us. What's not good for me is the way you're moping around here, scaring off potential customers."

An uneasy feeling crawled up Max's spine and prickled the base of his neck. Philip sounded like he was happy about the fire. Max stood up, taking advantage of his height, and looked down at the man.

"What did you do?"

Philip tried to look shocked. "How can you ask me that?"

Right then, he knew. He had no way to prove it, but there was something he could do. He stepped close to Philip and looked him straight in the eye. "Our partnership ends now."

Any congeniality he'd tried to imitate disappeared. "You don't want to do that."

"Yes, I really do. Furthermore, I'm leaving today. I refuse to be associated with a man like you."

"You're making a big mistake." Philip took a step back and shook his head. "Joy will not be pleased that you left a day early. And you can be sure I'll let them know what a disappointment you turned out to be. Don't expect to have a job to go back to."

"Not a problem. I was thinking of changing careers, anyway." Max plucked his jacket off the back of the chair. "Just tell me one thing. If you're so dedicated to being my partner, why did you sabotage the food dye?"

Philip cocked his head. "You really don't understand this business at all. There's no reason for me to sabotage you. But who does have a reason?"

With that, Philip returned to the Majestic Electric exhibit, immediately calling out to the people nearby with his carnival barker voice.

Philip was right about one thing: Max's work for the Joy Margarine Company was over. He left all the promotional pamphlets on the table, as well as the rest of the margarine and biscuits. Then he walked out of the building. He needed to talk to Ella, but first, he had one more stop to make.

Inside Homemaker's Hall, even more talk circulated about the fire and what had caused it. Max was sure he saw several exhibitors point and whisper as he passed by. He kept his head down and kept walking until he reached the Igloo exhibit.

Orville Henderson was slicing feathers off the extremely bare tail of the butter peacock. When he caught sight of Max, his eyes grew wide with fear. "What are you doing here?"

"I just want to ask you a question."

"All right."

"Why did you put the onion juice in my bottle of food dye?"

Orville blanched, confirming what he knew to be true.

"It was because of the posters," Orville stammered. "I. . .I didn't want to hurt anybody. I just wanted to teach you a lesson. I never thought you'd burn the icehouse down."

"I didn't," Max said with controlled intensity. "Stanley did that."

Mouth dropped open like a cod fish, Orville stared at him. "Somebody could have been hurt. Even killed. You have to report him."

"I would, but I have no proof."

Orville hung his head. "I'm so sorry."

Hopefully, his guilt would move him to assist Max. "Right now, I need to convince Ella that I had nothing to do with any of it. Will you come with me and talk to her?"

"I can't."

Max took a step closer. "Listen here—"

"Wait. You don't understand." Orville held his hands up to ward him off. "I would if I could, but they're gone."

"Gone? Are you sure?"

"Absolutely. Miss Daniels came by early this morning to tell me. She apologized that she couldn't give me any more butter for the peacock. Such a shame."

Orville kept talking about what nice people they were, but Max had stopped listening. He turned and walked away. His last hope of making amends with Ella had just vanished.

Chapter 10

September 30, 1916

The clay was a red lump of nothing, just waiting for her to shape the beauty within it. Ella smiled, excited about the challenge. It was good to have something to smile about again.

After the fire, neither she nor her father had the heart to stay at the fair. Hank Jepson had been happy to purchase the ten Jerseys Walter had brought for sale. After she'd talked to Mr. Henderson, being careful not to run into Max when walking through the exhibit halls, they'd loaded up Geraldine and headed home.

Ella had spent the next two days in bed. Finally, Walter had coaxed her out with the promise of making her french toast, just like when she was a girl. It was the one thing she knew he could make without burning, so she'd come downstairs. Sitting at the family table, sharing breakfast, they finally talked about everything that had happened. Then they talked about what could happen. It had been enlightening.

As much as her fingers itched to dig into the clay, Ella knew she had to wait. They were expecting company, and she couldn't give a proper greeting with red-stained hands. She draped a wet cloth over the clay to keep it moist then went outside.

It was a beautiful day. Geraldine wandered in the pasture, along with the two other cows they'd decided to keep. Once her father had made up his mind to sell the dairy, things had moved quickly. Mr. Jepson had been so pleased with the cows he'd already purchased, he jumped at the chance to acquire the rest of the herd. Walter also made a good deal on most of the equipment. Now, the milk barn was mostly empty, as was the icehouse where Ella had done her sculpting.

There would be no more butter, no more butter sculpting, and no more butter-stained clothes. That part of her life was over, and she was ready to move on to the next part.

Gravel crunched beneath tires as a car came down the drive. Ella smiled to herself. The representative from Joy was right on time.

She walked up to the car just as the driver opened his door and got out.

"Hello, Max."

He looked utterly confused. "I assume this is the reason I got my job back."

Ella nodded. "Papa refused to deal with anyone but you. If Joy wanted to buy the dairy, then you had to represent them. They must really want this property."

"I guess they must." Max swallowed hard, as if afraid to go on. "Ella, I don't. . . What does this mean?"

She reached into the pocket of her skirt and pulled out a folded piece of paper. "This should explain it."

He took the paper and unfolded it. It was a letter. "Dear Miss Daniels," it began, "I must inform you of an egregious error I made, as well as grievous misdeeds done by Mr. Philip Stanley." His eyes jumped down to the bottom of the page. "My most sincere apologies, Mr. Orville Henderson."

"I don't believe it," Max muttered.

"I was quite surprised when it came. He explains everything."

"And you believe him?"

Ella nodded.

She could see the relief as it surged through Max. "Thank God. Now you know the truth."

"Thank God, indeed. I've been thinking about that. About how God can use something terrible and turn it into something good." She smiled at Max. "I thought I'd lost everything that night, but since then, God has done some big things in my life."

He reached out as though he wanted to touch her, but then drew back. "What kind of things?"

She tapped her lips with her finger as if thinking. "I told my father how I feel about butter and what I really want to do. And he told me that he was tired of trying to keep the dairy going. As it turned out, we both wanted something else."

"That's great. Is that all?"

"No, there's one more thing." Now it was Ella who held out her hand. "A very important thing."

Max took her hand. "You have my complete attention."

"Good. Because God showed me how important love is, and how once you find it, you can't let it go."

Squeezing her fingers in response, Max nodded his agreement.

"I love you, Max. I don't know if you still feel the same about me, but I had to tell you. I had to make sure you know."

A laugh burst out of him. "I've loved you for so long, I don't remember a time when I didn't."

He pulled her close, wrapped his arms around her, and kissed her. He pulled back and held her face gently between his palms, looking down into her eyes.

"Marry me," he said.

"Yes. Oh yes."

They laughed together and shared another kiss. Then Max stepped back, straightened his tie, and cleared his throat. "I suppose we should get the business out of the way."

"Of course. Let's get that out of the way."

He leaned into the car and took some papers out of a briefcase. "This is the contract." Before she could respond, he held it up and ripped it in half.

Eyes wide, Ella placed a palm flat against her chest. "What are you doing?"

"This property really isn't right for processing margarine." He looked around shaking his head. "I have a much better idea. Something that involves having a place for you to work on your art and filling up the house with many children. Why don't we go talk to your father about it?"

He offered her his arm, and Ella took it. There was no wiping the smile off her face now. God was obviously still working in mysterious ways. And that was just fine with her. She may not have won a blue ribbon at the fair, but she'd come away with something much better: a future.

Jennifer AlLee believes the most important thing a woman can do is discover her identity in God—a theme that carries throughout her stories. She's a member of American Christian Fiction Writers and RWA's Faith, Hope and Love Chapter. When she's not spinning tales, she enjoys board games with friends, movies, and breaking into song for no particular reason. Jennifer lives with her family in the grace-filled city of Las Vegas, Nevada. Please visit her at www.jenniferallee.com.

Driven to Distraction

by Becca Whitham

Dedication

For my in-laws, Bob and Marilyn Whitham
~and~
For Jody Turner and Denise Keenan:
Childhood friends who, for different reasons, color my memories of the fair.
Do the Puyallup!

Prologue

Comisky Park
Chicago, Illinois
April 1917

Robert Montgomery wrapped his cold fingers around the steering wheel of the stripped-down Model T. The machine-gun staccato of an unmuffled engine hammered his eardrums and gasoline fumes stung his nostrils.

"Time for a little razzle-dazzle, eh, big brother?" Mitch shouted their good-luck phrase from the passenger seat. He lifted his long-handled polo mallet like a jousting lance and stared at the opposite end of the field, where two cars were lined up rim to rim between goal posts. "Theo Caplan looks like he's ready to blow a gasket."

No surprise there. Theo Caplan was always threatening retribution for one thing or another. The rivalry between Caplan's Crusaders and the Montgomery Marauders was the bitterest on the auto polo circuit. Spectators flocked to their matches, which was exactly what the Auto Polo Association wanted when, eight months ago, they'd teamed up the Crusaders and Marauders for a yearlong tour that stretched from coast to coast.

Except this time, Theo's retribution was personal.

Glancing to his left, Robert checked on his teammates. Bruce held his mallet above his head, eyes forward, while Eddy gripped the wheel, thumbs up. They were ready.

Robert returned his attention to the field's center and inhaled as the referee lifted his flag. Robert revved up the engine; the crowd roared. At the opposite end of the field, blue flames leapt from the Caplan's Crusaders cars.

The flag dropped.

Four cars raced toward a dingy white ball. Eddy let up at the prearranged spot, and Robert steered left to give his brother first shot at the ball.

Hanging on to the roll bar, Mitch stood on the running board and swung, pounding the ball fifty feet toward the Caplan's goal posts. Theo Caplan drove straight at Mitch. Slamming the car into REVERSE, Robert whirled the steering wheel, catching the brunt of the impact on the front tire. Mitch leapt clear as the two cars tangled.

A cheer lifted from the crowd.

The referee held up the flag to indicate a stop in play until the damage could be assessed.

Shifting gears again, Robert turned his wheels to see if they would disengage. With a grind and pop, they were free. Mitch jumped back into the car and they were off, racing toward the ball. Now that the first collision was over, Robert's nerves settled. "Razzle-dazzle!"

Mitch gave his signature response: "Tally-ho!"

But Theo didn't seem interested in playing polo. Every chance he got, he rammed Robert and Mitch. Even the newest Crusader, a Frenchman who spent more time recruiting Americans for the Allied Powers fighting in Europe than playing auto polo, was eyeing Theo askance.

After fifteen minutes of the abuse, Robert's temper had reached a boiling point. The shrill whistle calling for the first break in play saved him from retaliating in a way he'd only regret later. He climbed out of the car and looked into the stands.

The sight of Jolene, palms pressed against her white cheeks, curled his hands into fists. How dare Theo cause her undue distress! Auto polo was dangerous enough without a madman behind the wheel.

The Montgomery Marauders huddled behind their goal posts gulping down cups of water. While Robert's father discussed strategy going into the second period, his mind wandered.

She'd said yes!

As soon as the polo match ended, Jolene Caplan would run away with him and become Mrs. Robert Montgomery. Neither of them was happy about eloping, but given the bitterness between their families, it was the only way they could be together.

He cut another glance into the stands. Her large white hat with a blue bow shaded her face, but he'd memorized the curve of her cheek, sky-blue eyes, and sweetly bowed lips. Two months ago, when they were in Los Angeles, a movie producer had begged her to join his cast of starlets. Jolene laughed while retelling the story, as though the producer needed new glasses or a psychiatrist.

A rare beauty, his Jolene, and totally unaware she turned heads wherever she went.

Fingers snapped under his nose. "You with us, big brother?"

With a start, Robert returned his attention to the strategy session. "Of course."

Mitch snorted. "Sure you are."

A shrill whistle ended the break.

Robert, Mitch, Bruce, and Eddy made a beeline for their respective cars.

Jimmy, the team mechanic, met them halfway. "Eddy, watch your left front tire. The wood is a bit splintered but not bad enough to be replaced yet. Robert, try to avoid at least *one* collision, all right?"

The criticism burned Robert's eardrums as he slid behind the wheel and waited for the second period to begin.

"You know what you're doing, right?"

Robert ground his teeth at his brother's question.

"Right?"

"Of course I know what I'm doing!" Keeping his left foot on the brake, Robert stepped on the gas pedal with his right foot to rev the engine and drown out further annoyances.

The flag dropped, and he snatched his foot off the brake. Speeding toward the ball, he noticed that Eddy was keeping even with him instead of hanging back by half a car length. As the cars drew closer together, Robert saw Theo and the other Crusader driver shifting their eyes, trying to determine which Montgomery car was taking lead.

At the designated spot, Robert veered left, expecting Eddy to slam on his brakes as they had practiced earlier that week.

Eddy didn't brake.

What? Was I supposed to—?

A quick swerve right avoided a collision with his teammates, but the cars bumped wheels, lifting the left side of Robert and Mitch's car into the air. Mitch jumped off the side. Theo's reactionary swerve was too late, and Mitch slammed into the front of the Caplan car with a sickening *thunk*.

Robert crashed into the elevated edge of Theo's car sending it into a full roll. Robert's car slammed back to earth with a bone-jarring bounce.

He leapt from the Model T and raced to where his brother lay, facedown and unmoving, in the mud.

Chapter 1

Western Washington Fair
Puyallup Valley, Washington
September 1918

Jolene Caplan swiped a strand of blond hair from her mouth with a greasy knuckle, no doubt leaving another smudge of oil on her face. Oh, for a hot bath and clean clothes, but her chances of either before the afternoon auto polo match were slim to nil. Dad was treating the rematch between Caplan's Crusaders and the Montgomery Marauders like it was on par with the Great War raging in Europe. He'd been in the repair tent four times to check and recheck her work, something he never did unless he was nervous.

Jolene sighed. Seventeen months had passed since that terrible day—with Robert gone to war as penance—and she still hadn't found a way to tell her parents why the accident was her fault.

"Are you in here?"

Jolene turned at the sound of her mother's voice. "I'm here."

The tent flap opened. Mom pushed Cousin Theo through, his wheelchair slow to move on the uneven ground. Mom wore a cloth mask over her nose and mouth—protection against the deadly influenza outbreak—but Theo's had slipped around his neck.

Jolene set down her wrench and walked to her cousin. "Good morning, Theo. How are you today?"

Theo lolled his head in a rhythm of his own. "Aaa. Aaa."

Mom patted his shoulder. "Doesn't he look nice?"

"Yes, indeed." Jolene wiped a dribble of spit from the corner of his mouth with a clean edge of her rag and replaced his cotton mask. "Very spiffy."

"Today is a very special day, isn't it, Theo?"

At the significant look her mom gave her, Jolene frowned. Special day? It wasn't Theo's birthday or any occasion she could think of. Was Mom referring to this rematch with the Montgomery Marauders? Her stomach flipped. Oh no. . .had there been a team meeting to discuss how to best exact revenge for Theo's broken neck?

Mom grinned and leaned close to Theo's ear. "Should we tell her what the occasion is?"

"Aaa. Aaa."

"Yes, I think you're right. We'd better not spoil the surprise." Mom scrutinized Jolene from head to toe. "However, I don't think we would be remiss in suggesting she get cleaned up and change into something *very* pretty."

Jolene fixed a smile on her face, but her heart dropped. No, it wasn't the match. There was only one reason to get fancy in the middle of the day: Pierre was going to propose.

"Go on, child. Your father says everything looks fine for the match later." Mom smoothed Theo's blond hair to one side. "I've laid out an outfit for you, and your father is heating water for a bath."

"Must I"—at her mother's frown, Jolene trapped the word *accept* inside her throat—"go this moment? I need two more minutes to finish up."

Mom's face relaxed. "Two minutes." She wheeled Theo out of the tent, leaving behind the weighted air of expectation.

Jolene bowed her head. Pierre's proposal had been coming for months. He was a good man and would make a fine husband, but it would be like marrying her brother. With his curly dark hair and chocolate-brown eyes, he was certainly handsome enough. . .only Jolene preferred straight sandy-colored hair and caramel eyes.

But the dream of marrying Robert Montgomery—the only man who'd ever made her heart sing—died when he told her not to wait for him, to find someone more worthy of her, and not to grieve should he fail to come home from the war.

Men were so stupid! If he'd asked, she would have waited a lifetime for him.

Maybe Mom was right. Maybe it was time to be realistic. A girl who spent nine months out of the year traveling from one side of the country to the other didn't have many marital options. And even if Robert had asked her to wait, the obstacles between them were stacked as high as the grandstand's roof.

Ever since she'd attended her cousin's wedding and watched Mary Ellen walk down the aisle on her beaming father's arm, Jolene dreamed of the day it would be her turn. She wanted the mother of the bride and of the groom to weep happy tears, the fathers to slap each other on the backs, and for her and her new husband to leave the church showered with good wishes that would last long after the rice blew away.

Even more, over the last few months she'd fought an ever increasing longing to leave the life of a traveling show, to settle in one place with a little house where she could grow vegetables, flowers, and children.

All things that would happen only if she married someone her parents found acceptable. Someone like Pierre.

She'd been willing to throw their approval away to marry Robert. A foolish decision she'd not make again. Her parents loved her. Marrying against their wishes wasn't romantic; it was a sure way to start a marriage on rocky ground.

And yet. . .was marrying a man she didn't love because her parents *did* approve of him any better?

Jolene rubbed her aching temple. "If there be another way, Lord, please show it to me."

"Miss Caplan?"

Her head snapped upright. "Yes?"

A middle-aged man peeked through the tent flap opening. He wore a tan three-piece suit and brown-and-white wing-tip shoes. His straw hat was decorated with a brown ribbon and a small cluster of black and brown feathers tucked in one side. "Do you have a moment to speak with me?"

"The cars will be on display before the match this afternoon."

His face creased with a broad smile. "I'm not here about the cars, miss. I'm here to offer you a position with my company."

She squinted at him. "A position?"

"If you wouldn't mind. . ." He opened the tent flap wider but didn't step inside.

Apparently he was a stickler for propriety. A good sign. "Of course." She wiped her hands on the blue rag, tossed it on the table with her repair tools, and walked into the sunshine. "May I ask your name, sir?"

"Horace Walpole, at your service." He pinched the brim of his straw hat and dipped his head. "And you are Miss Jolene Caplan, correct?"

"Yes." Jolene stuffed her hands in her pockets. When she was dressed in greasy coveralls, she never knew if she should extend her hand to shake like a man or dip a polite curtsy like a lady. She settled for looking him in the eye. "How can I help you?"

He withdrew a small piece of paper from his inside coat pocket and held it out. "I represent the Dayton-Wright Aeroplane Company."

She took the card. His name was printed in small letters above the larger ones of his company and their location in Ohio. "Wright? As in Orville and Wilbur Wright?"

"The very ones." He grinned like she'd passed some kind of test. "We believe aeroplanes will revolutionize travel in the next twenty years the way automobiles have the past twenty. We are looking for an adventurous female who will travel the country as an aerial stunt pilot to show off the safety and maneuverability of our aeroplanes."

Her heartbeat quivered like a sputtering engine. "Stunt pilot? But I don't know how to fly a plane."

"Hardly anyone does, Miss Caplan, and most who do are fighting the war. We want to make aeroplanes. . .friendlier, so we're recruiting women. Don't worry, we'll teach you how to fly."

As Mr. Walpole described the job, she listened, scarcely able to believe what he was saying.

He must have noticed her shock, because he offered her a kind smile. "I realize this is a great deal to think about, but I do need an answer by the end of today."

Jolene's jaw slid down. "Today is awful fast, sir."

"I'm aware, but I'm heading back to Ohio tomorrow morning. You are our first choice for this position, Miss Caplan. We can train anyone to fly, but we want you. Your face is one that can launch a thousand ships, as the saying goes. Your family name is known, you're clearly able to handle the nomadic lifestyle of traveling cross-country, and your skill as a mechanic means we can also train you to fix your own plane." His smile seemed a little too bright. "There are plenty of others who would be willing to fill the role given the generous salary."

Had he already told her the amount, or was he fishing for her to ask? "Which is?"

"Two thousand dollars a year."

She pressed a hand over her open mouth. In the last few months, she'd sneaked out to visit a few banks within walking distance of the various fairs and exhibitions on the circuit to ask if she could purchase a house on her own. All of the loan managers had said the same thing: "A single woman is too great a risk. Of course, if you were married. . ."

But two thousand dollars a year! In one year, she would be able to buy a house without a bank loan! With a home of her own, she could get work, find a church, and seek out some nice woman to teach her gardening and canning. She might even find a man both she and her parents loved. In two years? Why, she'd have enough money to live comfortably for three or four years in case finding work or a husband proved difficult. Or that might even give enough time for the Montgomery and Caplan families to reconcile so she and Robert—if he made it home from the war and still wanted her—could marry.

Mr. Walpole's brown eyes twinkled. "I thought that might sweeten the offer."

Jolene nodded.

"Does that mean you'll take it?"

Behind him, Jolene's mother beckoned with broad sweeps of her arms. Jolene waved to acknowledge she saw. "I'll have to discuss it with my parents, Mr. Walpole, but I will get back to you before day's end."

"Excellent." He clapped his hands together. "I'll be in the grandstand to enjoy the auto polo match this afternoon. I'll look forward to hearing from you by then if not sooner." He pinched his hat brim again and walked away.

Jolene stared after him, her legs unwilling to obey her mother's summons.

Two thousand dollars. A place of her own away from constant bitterness, regret, and expectations. The offer was too good to be true.

Especially since it came with the opportunity to fly!

When the team had been in Cincinnati ten months ago, her birthday present was a ride in a hot-air balloon. It had been the most magical experience in her twenty years. As the balloon lifted, so did her spirit, until she felt so close to God she was certain she could touch His face. Since then, every bird overhead made her long for the freedom of flight.

She tucked Mr. Walpole's business card deep in her coverall pocket and walked toward her mother, each step as labored as if molasses coated the soles of her shoes.

"Who was that?" Mom put a hand on the small of Jolene's back and pushed her up the three steps into the house-car.

"Just a man I thought wanted to see the cars." It wasn't a complete fib. Jolene picked up the bar of soap, towel, and change of clothes sitting on the kitchen table. "Is my bath ready?"

"Yes." Mom grabbed one of Jolene's hands. "Please try to get all this grease off before you put on the gloves. They're brand-new."

Jolene trudged back outside. Her bath was a half barrel filled with water. Three folding screens formed a triangle of privacy. What she wouldn't give for a house with indoor plumbing and a bathtub she could actually sit in.

After secreting Mr. Walpole's business card in her skirt pocket—she couldn't risk Mother finding it when she washed the coveralls later in the day—Jolene stripped off her clothes and stepped inside the barrel. The water was already tepid. As she scrubbed black grease from her skin with the harsh lye soap, one thought plagued her:

Robert, my darling, if only you had left me with hope. . . .

Chapter 2

Robert swung his crutches forward and leaned into another step. The fairgoers parted around him, some offering salutes as he passed.

A broken ankle was a small price to pay to leave the battlefield. The way things were going, the war would be over before he was healed and could be sent back.

At least he hoped so.

He'd joined the army to cure himself of loving Jolene Caplan. It didn't work. But the horrific view of what family feuds cost when the warring parties were a German kaiser against his cousins, the king of England and the tsar of Russia, cured Robert of whatever nonsense stood between his parents and Jolene's. It also cured him of wanderlust. He'd seen enough of the world. He wanted a home and family.

With Jolene.

Robert shuffled through the crowd until he found the Fisher Scone booth. Jolene's sweet tooth would eventually draw her to the gooey goodness of a fresh-baked pastry filled with melted butter and sweet raspberry jam.

Unable to resist the delicious treat himself, he purchased a scone and ate it while surveying the area for the best place to wait. An entrance to the grandstand provided concealment. He wanted to surprise her, but he didn't want anyone from his family or hers to find him before he was ready. When he reached the spot, he rested his back against the portico wall and eased the crutches from under his armpits.

Fear trickled down his throat.

What if she'd forgotten all about him? He'd told her to find someone new, someone more worthy. What if she had?

His hand fisted around the now empty scone wrapper.

A large white hat with a blue bow bobbed closer. Robert's heart pumped like he was waiting for the command to advance. He tossed the wrapper in a nearby garbage can and pushed away from the wall, balancing his weight by angling both crutches in front of him.

The crowd parted enough for him to glimpse her face.

Jolene.

How he'd missed her!

She got in line to purchase a scone. He fitted the crutches under his arms and took a step toward her.

Look at me. C'mon, sweetheart. Look over here.

As though she heard his silent plea, Jolene turned and looked right at him. Her blue eyes widened and her pretty mouth dropped open. Her glowing beauty stole his breath.

"Robert?" She made her way through the crowd, picking up speed as it thinned.

"Hi, JoJo."

She threw her arms around his neck, knocking him against the wall and bumping his ankle cast, but he retained enough balance to toss away one crutch and press her close.

Burying his face in her neck to hide unmanly tears, Robert inhaled her unique perfume of sunshine and gasoline.

"Robert. Oh, *Robert*."

"I'm here, sweetheart. All in one piece."

Her shoulders started to shake, and cool wetness soaked through his uniform.

Every doubt about whether or not she still loved him dissolved. "Marry me, JoJo. I was an idiot to think time and distance would change my love for you. Say you'll marry me. I can't be away from you again."

She sobbed harder and tightened her hold around his neck.

He'd survived barbed wire, mustard gas, and mines on the battlefield, but he was going to die of strangulation if she didn't ease up.

It was a good way to die.

He bent lower. "Say yes. Don't think about what your parents will say or what mine will say, just say yes. I'd get down on one knee, but. . ."

A little hiccup of laughter rewarded him.

"At least let me go so I can kiss you."

Her hold loosened.

He angled his head and captured her lips in a kiss. She tasted sweeter than a Fisher Scone and felt like heaven in his arms. He pressed her closer, deepening the kiss to fill his starving soul with her goodness. Dreaming of her—of this kiss—kept him sane and fighting through the inhumanity of war. He was never letting her go, not until death parted them.

The sound of rushing water roared in his ears.

Jolene pulled away and lowered her head. Was she hiding?

Robert looked around to see why. A grinning mob formed a semicircle around the grandstand portico, clapping and whooping like they were watching an auto polo match. A few people near the back turned to frown at something.

Robert swallowed.

Jolene's dad and the French mallet man who'd ridden beside Theo Caplan the day Mitch died pushed their way through the crowd.

Hampered by his inability to stand on both feet, Robert did his best to shield Jolene while turning to face the enemy. "Look, sir, let me explai—"

Mr. Caplan swung a right hook. Robert's head snapped sideways. Pain exploded along his jaw.

<hr>

Jolene screamed. Robert staggered back, nearly taking her down with him. Hands gripped her upper arms. Dragged her away. Twisting and turning, she couldn't break the hold. "Let me go!"

"Hey!" A group of men pushed through the gawking crowd. The Montgomery

Marauders Auto Polo Team. All four of them, in matching blue shirts.

Jolene was tossed sideways. Pierre rushed to meet the men's upraised fists. She stumbled into the crowd. "Help me stop them. Please."

Her voice was drowned by shouting—calls for the police clashed with hollers of encouragement to the combatants.

She pushed against bodies to get to Robert, but a group of men stood, backs to the fray, arms spread wide. An impenetrable line.

Jolene jumped, ducked, and kept pressing forward to catch glimpses. Robert lay on the ground, hands and body curled to protect his white cast. His crutches too far away for him to grab. Two Montgomery team members had pulled her father away, holding his arms while a third punched him in the stomach. The fourth Montgomery and Pierre traded blows. Was Robert bleeding? "Oh, *please*! I need to see!"

This was all her fault—kissing Robert in public!

They'd been so careful before, always finding somewhere public enough that their love for each other didn't lead to impropriety yet private enough to keep from being discovered by either of their families. Until the day Theo discovered them holding hands. . .a discovery that led to such heartbreak for them all.

Jolene shook the thought away. She'd spent the last seventeen months wondering and worrying without a single letter from Robert. And now he was here, she needed to touch him. To reassure her arms and hands that he wasn't a ghost. To hold him close and smell his skin and feel his sandy-colored hair prickle against her palm.

Shrill whistles cut the air. The crowd parted for a couple of uniformed officers rushing forward. The two men holding her father let go. He slumped for an instant then stood tall, his jaw clenched.

Jolene rushed through in the police officers' wake. Robert sat up. Other than the beginnings of a swollen lower lip, he looked remarkably undamaged. She knelt down and held his hand close to her cheek. "Are you okay?"

He nodded, but his lips were rimmed in white.

"Miss, please, move away." One of the two police officers held out a hand and helped Jolene stand. "We need to take some statements, so you'll have to wait until we're done, if you please."

She *didn't* please, but she nodded and stepped to the side. Her father grabbed her arm, keeping her from retrieving Robert's crutches.

The taller officer turned to the crowd. "Can anyone tell me what happened here?"

A chorus of voices answered, their shouted words mingling together into unintelligible babble.

"You there"—the officer pointed to a distinguished-looking gentleman in a derby hat—"what say you?"

"As best as I could tell, the soldier was kissing his girl when that one"—he pointed to her father—"came roaring up and decked him. Then those four in the blue shirts jumped in and were pummeling that one and that one."

A few voices called out affirmations of the version.

The officer turned to Jolene. "Are you the girl?"

She nodded.

"Then you'll have to come down to the station with us, too."

At that, all four of the Montgomery Marauders started defending their actions and pleading with the officers that they couldn't leave the fairgrounds because they had an auto polo match in a few hours.

"Then you shouldn't have started a brawl." The tall officer tapped a finger against the black billy club hanging from his belt.

"If I may. . ." Her father tipped his head sideways with a touch of deference. "The fight was a publicity stunt that got slightly out of hand. No one in the crowd was hurt, as you can see."

"Except this soldier here." The shorter officer, his girth and height nearly proportionate, hoisted Robert to his feet. "What say you, Corporal? You want to press charges over this. . .publicity stunt?"

"Of course he doesn't."

Mr. Montgomery pushed through the crowd and stood next to her father. A casual observer might not detect the hatred between the two men, but Jolene saw it in the raised tendons running down her father's neck and Mr. Montgomery's tight smile.

The tall officer took off his hat, his bald spot shocking on a man so young. "And who might you be?"

Mr. Montgomery extended his right hand. "Charles Montgomery. And this is Mr. Oliver Caplan. We own the two auto clubs that are competing at three this afternoon."

Her father stepped forward and shook the officer's hand as well. "Yes, folks, if you want to see a real fight, you just come for the match and we'll show you a good one."

By the looks of disgust on several faces in the crowd, Jolene guessed many of them were planning to turn in their tickets rather than watch the match.

That would not be good, not when finances were already stretched thin.

Mr. Montgomery stepped close to Robert. "And my son here will be competing just to show you that there's no real harm done."

<hr />

Robert snapped his jaw shut. Apparently it was too much for Dad to say, *"Good to see you, son. How are you doing, son? How come the army sent you home early, son?"*

The police officers huddled together for a moment before the taller, almost bald one said they wouldn't make any arrests. "However, you pull another publicity stunt like this one, and we'll clap you in jail faster than you can blink."

Mr. Caplan whispered something to the Frenchman. He nodded, and the two men wrapped arms around Jolene's waist, forcing her to walk away.

Since he had no desire to end up in a jail cell, Robert let her go.

For now.

His father smiled for the crowd, but his nostrils flared wide as if venting exhaust from an engine. He leaned his head close to Robert's ear. "What your mother will say when she finds out you went to see a *Caplan* before coming to see her, I dare—"

"Don't." Robert twisted away from the staring strangers, gingerly balancing his weight by touching his boot cast on the ground. He didn't care about preserving the facade of geniality, but this was private business. "I'm not some gullible spectator who will fall for a trumped-up dog-and-pony show to increase sales for your precious rivalry."

"Trumped up?" Dad stooped to pick up the crutches and scanned the thinning crowd like he was trying to find their owner. "Your brother's death may be old news to you, but it's still as fresh as the day it happened for me. I'll never forgive the Caplans for taking him from me. Never."

Seventeen months and the hatred was still vitriolic. Robert gritted his teeth against the pain in his ankle, jaw, and heart. No amount of time or distance would ever make his father forgive him.

Robert held out his hand and waited until comprehension dawned on his father's face. "You might have considered why the army sent me home before volunteering me to drive today."

His father handed over the crutches. "Nonsense. You're a better driver with a broken—what? Leg—?"

"Ankle."

"—and one hand tied behind your back than the idiots I've got now."

Jimmy, the mechanic and the only blue-shirted Montgomery Marauder Robert recognized, glanced their way and pressed his lips into a thin line.

Way to inspire the team, Dad!

Robert tucked the crutches under his arms and swung his good leg forward. "Can we discuss this someplace more private?"

His face hard, Dad pointed to his left. "This way. Your mother will be anxious to see you."

What was left of the crowd parted as Robert, his father, and the four team members headed toward the team camp. Soon, the uniformed Marauders were lost in the shifting sea of fairgoers.

Jaw and ankle throbbing, Robert's palms slickened with the effort to remain upright.

Pop!

Robert ducked and threw his hands over his ears. Steel bands wrapped around his chest. He gasped in shallow bursts and clawed at the bands, the instinct to run shooting adrenaline through him. *Need to run. Need to get away. Need to breathe.* The steel bands held strong. A small voice struggled to be heard over the shouting inside his head. *Safe. Safe. No guns. No artillery fire. Nothing to fear. Just a sunny day at a fair far away from the front lines.*

"You're making a spectacle of yourself."

The criticism jerked Robert upright. He filled his lungs with sweet air and blew it out with a shudder. Both crutches were lying on the ground, the padded armrests flung farther than the bottom tips so they formed a V with his feet at the center point. Pitying glances showed in faces all around him. He straightened. "My apologies."

"I wasn't sure if I should slap you or just keep hanging on, so I settled for something in between." The steel bands released Robert's chest as his father leaned down to pick up the crutches.

"Of course." Robert touched his cast to the dirt for balance and lifted his chin to stare at the mighty Mount Rainier, grounding himself in the Puyallup Valley instead of the trenches of France. At Walter Reed, he'd been told that sudden noises could set off a reaction, but he'd ridiculed the warning—much to the doctor's amusement. Now he understood those knowing smirks.

The padded end of a crutch bumped against his chest.

Robert grabbed hold and fit it under his armpit, repeating the process with the second one a moment later. He started forward without looking at his father.

"I'd like to see my mother now."

Chapter 3

Once they were far enough away from the grandstand, Jolene opened her mouth to apologize, but Pierre gripped her elbow and sent her a *"Don't talk"* look.

"Might I have a moment to speak with your daughter, Mr. Caplan?" Pierre's voice was as tight as his fingers.

Dad crossed his arms over his chest. "Certainly. Only let's have no repeat of the kind of behavior that got us into this mess, shall we?"

As though the kiss, rather than the man she'd been caught with, was the problem.

"But of course, Mr. Caplan. I have too much of the respect for your daughter." Pierre's tone was smooth as oil, but a vein pulsed at his temple. Jolene let him pull her past the game booths and lunch counters. As they passed the fruit and vegetable displays, she craned her neck to see the winning entries, but Pierre's grip forced her to keep a brisk pace.

"Pierre, please. Can't we slow down?" She pried at his fingers on her elbow.

He let go and lifted his left hand, palm up. "This way, if you please."

They continued until they found a quiet spot. Pierre laid a handkerchief on one of the hay bales marking the boundary between the fairgrounds and parking lot. Jolene sat and rested her hands in her lap.

Pierre looked at a place over her head. "I am of a surety that you know your parents wish us to marry."

A hard lump of dread weighed down her heart. "I'm aware."

He smoothed his thin mustache with his thumb and index finger. "But you are of the desire to marry Robert Montgomery. This I have known for many months."

Jolene gasped. "How?"

He stared at her, eyebrows slightly elevated. "You were not all the time discreet before he left for *La Grande Guerre*."

"Did you say anything to my parents? Or. . .anyone else?" She checked to make sure no one could overhear them.

"Jolene, *ma chère*, do you think your love for this man is secret now?"

Heat crept up her neck. "No. I suppose not." Though she wanted to think that, except for Theo knowing, it had been until today.

"And do you think your parents will allow you to marry this man?" Pierre slid his hands into the pockets of his tweed pants. "Is this why you make a display of yourself in public, to make them agree?"

"No." At least, she didn't think so. "I was simply overcome at the sight of him after so long." She hung her head. "It was foolish beyond permission, I know. But I do want to marry him."

"Are you. . .of a surety?"

His hesitation made her face hot and her hands cold. "What do you mean?"

He sat beside her and gripped his hands until the knuckles whitened. "I do not ask to make you angry, chère. I ask because I am all the time wanting what is best for you, and I am not sure that it is a man who would make you the source of scandal."

"He wants to marry me. He said so."

"But of course he does. This is not in question." Pierre tapped his thumbs together. "*Will* you marry him? Against your parents' wishes, against *his* parents' wishes, and even against what might be your best interests?"

Face burning, Jolene wriggled and tugged at her skirt until she no longer sat on the coin purse tucked in her pocket. "A girl doesn't publicly kiss one man and expect to get an offer of marriage from someone else."

Pierre inhaled sharply. "What you mean, of course, is that you do not wish to receive an offer of marriage from me now that Robert Montgomery has made his feelings known." He fingered the button over his heart. "Do you know what kind of man he is? Now?"

Jolene's heart hiccuped. "What are you saying?"

"War changes men, ma chère. There may be injuries to your Robert that are much harder to mend than broken bones, *non?*"

If he'd said it with malice, it could be dismissed. That he said it with such tenderness demanded consideration.

He studied her. "I know you do not love me as you think a woman should love a man, but you know me, my Jolene. You know my character, and you know a woman can learn to love a man."

What was she to do with this Pierre? No brother's voice vibrated with such ardor. She'd always assumed they shared a mutual, though filial, affection rather than a romantic one. She'd also assumed Pierre shared her reticence in considering marriage, but now. . .

Had he been in love with her all this time?

Even if he had, she needed time—time to know her own heart—now that Robert had returned. But how was a girl to explain such a thing to a man?

As though he sensed her inner struggle, he took her hand and held it between both of his. "*Cherie, l'amour*—love—is a thousand choices over a thousand days that lead to a thousand more. There should be passion, this is sure." He stroked his thumb across the back of her hand. "The friendship we share will bind us, as will the way of a man with a woman, and the children of our union."

She disengaged from his grasp and walked away from the arguments that, much as she hated to admit it, were terribly similar to the ones she'd been considering an hour ago. Before Mr. Walpole. Before Robert. Before the kiss.

"You have a most difficult choice to make, ma chère. After this day, you must marry someone."

Because a girl didn't kiss a man in public and not shelter her reputation with an engagement and marriage.

Jolene stopped walking and bit down on her bottom lip.

"I am sorry to be so blunt, but. . ." Pierre came alongside her. "As I have said, you know me. We are friends, and if you will allow it, we will grow to love each other with a passion you cannot begin to imagine now. But I am going home to *La Belle France* next month. I must make the plans to travel for one person or two. I do not ask you to answer me this moment, but I will ask it by the end of today." He picked up her left hand and pressed a warm kiss onto her cold fingers. "Choose wisely, ma chère."

As he walked away, Jolene pressed both hands to her heart. Such a good man. One any girl would be lucky to marry. And he was right, she could choose to love him.

But did she want to?

———— •◦•◦• ————

Robert heard his mother singing before he knocked on the door to the house on wheels. "Mrs. Montgomery? I have a telegram for you all the way from—"

The door swung open, nearly hitting him in the face. His mother raced down the steps. "Robbie!" She pulled his neck down into a hug so tight, he couldn't dislodge the crutches digging into his armpits. "Thank You, Lord. Thank You for bringing my Robbie home."

As he absorbed her tears, Robert adjusted to the shock of grief-etched lines beside her mouth and across her brow. Her hair was almost white now, not lightly salted auburn, and she'd lost so much weight her skin sagged.

His father coughed. "I'll leave the two of you." The subsequent swish of air and the crunch of boots on straw announced his departure.

More relieved than he should be to have his father gone, Robert basked in the embrace of the parent he knew loved him more than her own life. "Hi, Ma."

"Let me look at you." She pushed against his shoulders and scanned his face. "You look like you haven't eaten a decent meal since you left."

"I haven't, and whatever you're making smells delicious. Might a weary soldier get a bite?"

"Of course. Come on in." She proceeded into the house and turned to watch, anxiety in her green eyes. "Do you need help?"

"Can you take this?" He handed her one crutch then half pulled, half hopped to get up the three steps. Once inside, he curled and twisted his body until he could sit at the little table. "Whew!"

His mother smiled at him, but it was tinged with concern. "How long ago did this happen?" She took both crutches and propped them against the wall behind him.

"A few weeks ago. The doctors said it wasn't too bad, but I might walk with a limp the rest of my life."

She rubbed a palm over her heart. "Oh, son. I'm so sorry."

He lifted one shoulder. "It's nothing compared to—" Images of mangled bodies stopped his words. "I got off lucky."

Her mouth trembled and tears leaked from the corners of her eyes, as though her sympathetic heart understood every word he hadn't said. She leaned down to kiss his forehead. "Of course. And I'm lucky to have you home."

Robert closed his eyes against the piercing joy of her nearness. The thought of two women had kept him going during the worst moments of war: Jolene and the dream of her kisses, and his mother and her home-baked bread. He breathed in the yeasty smell of her apron and felt something inside his spirit relax. Being here, more than landing in

America or even seeing Jolene, said he was home.

Safe.

Ma squeezed his collarbone and stepped to the stove. "Why didn't your father stay?"

And the moment was over. "You know how it is between us."

She bowed her head, took a deep breath, and released it in a rush. "I had hoped. . ." Ma squared her shoulders and reached above her head for a bowl. "Never mind that now."

Robert felt small for ruining her happiness, but some things couldn't be repaired, and he was tired of fighting.

She ladled thick stew into the bowl and set it on the table. "Go on. You need a little fattening up."

He took a spoon from the wooden rack built into the windowsill beside the table. "Thanks, Ma. It smells wonderful." He bowed his head and gave thanks for the food, promising God a longer prayer later to account for all the blessings of the day. At the first bite of beef, carrots, onions, and potatoes swimming in savory tomato sauce, Robert moaned with pleasure.

Nothing beat home cooking.

Ma smiled. "In a few more minutes I'll have some fresh bread for you, too."

Heaven!

"Your father will be coming back for his lunch soon, so you'd best tell me what I need to know before he gets here." She ladled stew into a bowl for herself then sat at the table opposite him.

Between bites, Robert told her what happened under the grandstand. She ate in silence, interrupting him only when it was time to take the bread from the oven. "And how did Jolene's father feel about you kissing her in public?"

Robert swallowed the last bite of stew. "He smashed his fist into my jaw and then whisked her away. I didn't exactly have time to ask for her hand in marriage."

Ma tucked a strand of hair behind her ear before opening the oven door. "I see. And you've told your father you intend to marry her?" The trepidation in her voice spoke volumes. Her hands shook a little as she placed the golden loaves on top of the stove.

"Not yet." He was proud to love such a wonderful girl. He wasn't giving her up, not for anyone. "But nothing will keep me from marrying her, not him or even you."

Ma turned one bread pan upside down. A golden loaf slipped into her towel-covered hand. "If you want to marry Jolene, I'm all for your happiness. But do you know that Jolene wants to marry you?"

Remembering their kiss put a grin on his lips. "I'm fairly sure she does."

Ma sliced the heel from the loaf, buttered it, and set it on the table. "Fairly sure?"

He'd said the words in jest. That she took them seriously stung. He opened his mouth to tell her so then frowned. Come to think of it. . .Jolene hadn't said yes.

Robert took a bite of bread. It tasted like clay.

"Were you able to keep up a correspondence with her while you were away?"

Away. Not "at war." The distinction shouldn't bother him, but it did. "I was trying to get over losing her. I didn't think exchanging letters was a good idea."

"And it's unlikely Mr. and Mrs. Caplan would have allowed Jolene to accept them if you did." Ma pinched off a piece of bread and held it in front of her lips. "You know she's been seeing quite a lot of another man."

Robert sat back. "Are you trying to tell me she doesn't love me? Because she kissed me readily enough."

"She kissed *you*, or did you kiss *her*?" Ma slipped the piece of bread into her mouth.

"What difference does it make?"

Ma raised her chin. "Are you telling me you would be so ungallant as to force a woman to marry you because she kissed a soldier come home from war?"

Amazing he could still feel ten years old. "No."

"Son, I'm not trying to rain on your parade, but you have to consider that, even if you didn't get over Jolene these past seventeen months, perhaps she got over you."

Robert pushed his empty bowl away. "Then how do I win her back?"

Ma's shrug wasn't encouraging. "I remember her from before Mitch. . ." She pressed a fist against her lips. "Seventeen months, and I still can't say it."

"It's okay. I know what you mean." He'd lived ten lifetimes in those months.

She swiped a finger under each eye. "Before the accident, Martha Caplan, Jolene, and I used to chat sometimes. This silliness between the teams wasn't a good enough reason to avoid the only women who understand what it's like to live as we do. I know Jolene. At least I knew her once, and I don't think her personality has changed. She's a sensitive girl. She'll not marry without her parents' blessing. If she hasn't already lost her heart to the other young man, you'll need to make peace between our families before she'll agree to marry you."

"She agreed to—" Robert clamped his lips shut. Ma didn't need to know that Jolene once agreed to elope with him. That Mitch was dead because Theo caught them planning where to meet. Robert went to war to pay for that mistake. No need to bring it up on his first day home.

"Agreed to what?"

Ma's question sent his brain scrambling for a suitable answer. Nothing came. He shoved another piece of bread in his mouth and mumbled, "Never mind."

Chapter 4

Jolene wandered around the fairgrounds, eventually finding her way back to the scone booth. As she stood in line, she listened to the speech about Fisher Flour Mill and its exceptional milling process, which was the reason the scones were so light and fluffy. She passed the display of Paulhamus Farms jams and jellies, proudly claiming responsibility for bringing Fisher Scones to the Western Washington State Fair and for providing their delicious filling.

She paid ten cents for the scone, but its warm sweetness couldn't distract her from her troubled thoughts. Had Robert changed from the man she fell in love with? Was Pierre right?

Pierre. . .

What was she going to do about him? Her parents approved of him, but did they know marriage meant she would move to France? It would serve Dad right if she married without letting him know that.

Not that she should make such a choice because she was angry with her father right now. How could he have punched Robert—he was crippled and in uniform! Surely, if Robert had turned violent from the horrors of war, he would have retaliated. Instead, he did nothing but try to protect himself. Still, was one incident enough to judge his character after seventeen months apart?

Which brought her tumultuous thoughts full circle, with no resolution in sight.

She licked crumbs from her fingers and searched for a garbage can through the thick crowd.

"Miss Caplan, were you looking for me?" The man who'd proposed she join the aeroplane company waved at her.

What was his name again?

She waved back, put a smile on, and waited for him to zigzag through the crowd. "Hello, again."

He tipped his straw hat. "Miss Caplan. I'm hoping you have good news for me."

"Actually, I—"

"Excuse me."

Jolene turned at Robert's voice. Her heart leapt at his approach, but her eyes scanned the crowd to see if any of the Caplan's Crusaders were nearby. "What are you doing here?"

He gave her an odd sort of frown, turned to the older gentleman, and stuck out his hand. "Hello, sir. Robert Montgomery."

"Horace Walpole." He shook Robert's hand and winced before tugging his hand away. He squinted up at Robert. "Have we met before?"

"Yes, sir. When you came to France to train mechanics in repairing your company's DH-4 planes."

Mr. Walpole's smile seemed to freeze. "I see. Well, Miss Caplan and I were discussing a job offer."

Robert stiffened. "She's not interested."

Jolene gasped. How dare he speak for her! They weren't engaged, and not likely to be if he'd turned into an overbearing brute.

Mr. Walpole's eyes shifted between Jolene and Robert. "Shall we finish our business later, Miss Caplan?"

After shooting Robert a speak-for-me-again-and-I'll-hit-you-myself glare, Jolene nodded. "Certainly, Mr. Walpole. I look forward to speaking with you later today."

He tipped his hat and melted into the crowd.

Jolene turned her attention to Robert. His jaw was starting to tinge purple. What a wretched day he'd had! Jolene's indignation faded a degree. A reprieve was needed, not another battle. "How long have you been waiting?"

He planted his crutches in the ground. "A minute or two. I figured you'd be back, since you didn't get your scone earlier."

How well he knew her.

"Do you know what kind of man he is? Now?" Pierre's questions reared their ugly heads.

Jolene didn't want to think about potential problems. She wanted to enjoy Robert's safe return and the fact that she no longer had to hide her love for him. "I guess we let the cat out of the bag earlier."

He bent closer. "Yeah. I think we'd better talk about that."

Jolene longed to touch his cheek, but they were in enough trouble. "Where would you like to go?"

Rising to his full height, he looked over top of the crowd. "There's a bench over there"—he jutted his chin toward the flower displays—"that's empty for now."

"How about I go ahead, and you follow at your own pace?"

His gaze sent a thrill through her. "I'd follow you anywhere, Jolene Caplan."

Blushing, she walked where he'd indicated. She could feel Robert's eyes on her all the way to the empty bench. She sat and waited for him to join her.

He eased himself down and set the crutches on the ground beside him. "What job did Walpole offer you?"

Reprieve over. "Aerial stunt pilot."

"For Dayton-Wright? Absolutely not!"

A few fairgoers gawked at them.

Robert glared right back. "Do you know what we called the Dayton-Wright DH-4 planes over in France? Flaming coffins, that's what. And they want to put a *woman* in one? Over my dead body."

Jolene smiled at his protectiveness. "Since Mr. Walpole said they want me to demonstrate the safety and maneuverability of their planes, I doubt they'd put me in one that was dangerous. But if I turn him down, I prefer to tell Mr. Walpole my own way."

"My Jolene. Always the peacemaker."

Was he insulting her? Just because she chose to use soft words and to speak when tempers weren't inflamed didn't mean she couldn't stand up for herself. Her way was better than throwing punches first and shouting later.

To prove it—to herself if no one else—she changed the subject to something less inflammatory. "Did you work on planes, then?" She traced a circle on her kneecap.

"I worked on whatever kind of engine they put in front of me for as long as they'd let me." He scratched his neck. "But eventually they needed me more in the trenches."

Jolene sensed his reluctance to say more, but Pierre's questions needed to be answered. "Are you. . .okay?"

He went still. "You mean other than a broken ankle?"

The familiar crook in his nose, those tawny eyes, and the angles of his jaw lured Jolene to believe she still knew him, but seventeen months and a war stood between them. And maybe even more. "The papers have started talking about something called *shell shock*."

"And you want to know if I'm suffering from it?" No mockery laced his question.

Thank heaven he was taking her seriously. Jolene nodded.

A wry grin twisted his lips. "An hour ago, I would have laughed at you, but not now." Goose bumps pebbled her skin. "Why?"

He looked out over the fair crowd and told her how he'd made a fool of himself over the pop of a balloon. "The doctors say my reaction is normal and to expect loud noises, especially if they're sudden, to startle me for as much as six months. But I've seen shell-shocked soldiers. You can tell them by the hollowness in their eyes." Robert opened his eyes wider and grinned. "See. All here."

Sweet relief filled her lungs. "I'm glad you're home."

Robert shifted on the bench, his grin fading. "Are you? I mean, are you really?"

Had he missed the whole part about kissing him like a wanton woman?

"I mean"—he scrubbed at his scalp like he was trying to remove a layer of skin—"I know you kissed me and all, but. . ."

But? She didn't know this faltering Robert. He'd always been so sure of himself. Of her. Of their love. Her heart began to race. "I don't know what you're saying."

He rolled his shoulders. "Look, before I left, I told you not to write. To forget all about me."

The words stabbed afresh. He'd wanted a clean break—a chance to get over her and for her to get over him. She'd been miserable for days. Her mother thought she'd caught a cold. "I remember."

Robert gripped his hands together in front of him. "Well? Did you?"

She squinted like it would bring his confusing words into focus. "Did I what?"

He lowered his head and closed his eyes. "Did you. . .forget about me?"

"Forget about you? Do you think I would—?" She lowered her voice. No point in causing another public spectacle. "Do you think I would have kissed you like that if I'd *forgotten* about you?"

Robert heaved a sigh that seemed to come from his toes. "Thank goodness." He grabbed her hand and started to babble. "I was afraid maybe I had kissed you and you didn't kiss me back, and I didn't know if that was true, so I wasn't sure what to think."

Jolene squeezed his hand. "Silly boy."

Robert swiped a hand against his cheek.

If she acknowledged his tears, it would embarrass him, so Jolene looked around for a new topic of conversation. "Did you see the displays of fruits and vegetables?"

"No, but I'm guessing you have."

"Not yet. I got a little sidetracked by a certain soldier." She stood and tugged on his hand. "Would you come with me?"

With an exaggerated huff, he let go of her hand and bent to retrieve his crutches. "If you insist."

Grinning because his show of reluctance was exactly what she expected—and therefore proof he was still her Robert—Jolene waited for him to stand before sauntering toward the displays of canned goods stacked in layers of color.

They started with the vegetables. Asparagus, beans, and pickles in shades of green with an occasional red, white, or blue ribbon hanging from jars to indicate winners. Many of the fairgoers around them offered Robert a nod or salute. A few of the women gripped his hand to thank him for his service and ask if he knew their son or nephew, brother or cousin.

He didn't, but he answered each with a solemn assurance that no news was good news and that the war was winding down.

Pride swelling her heart, Jolene stood beside him soaking in these stolen moments where everyone around them assumed they were a joyful, reunited soldier and his girl enjoying a sunny day at the fair.

They moved to the fruit where pale applesauce and canned pears gave way to the orangey yellows of apricots and peaches.

Jolene picked up the winning jar of peaches, feeling the weight of it and turning it in her hand to observe the perfect golden slices touched with red slivers at their core. Unbidden, tears sprang to her eyes. "Do you know why I spend every free moment at every fair wandering through the canned fruit and vegetable entries?"

Robert bent his head closer to her lips.

"Because this"—she fingered the blue ribbon hanging from the jar—"is the embodiment of my dream: to live in one place long enough to grow my own fruit tree, pick and preserve its goodness, and win a blue ribbon at the local fair."

A hand touched the small of her back. "I know. And I want to give it to you more than you can possibly imagine."

All the obstacles to such a rosy future filled her lungs to bursting. She saw one way, but if she spoke it aloud, would her dream dissipate like vapor?

Robert leaned close to her ear. "Last time we. . .I mean. . .you were willing to run away and marry me. I still want that. Do you?"

She set the can of peaches back on the display before her shaking fingers dropped it. This conversation—this heartbreak—had been looming since the moment she saw him under the grandstand. To drag it out was unfair to him and her. "What I want is peace between our families. I want to welcome your parents into our home the same way I want you to welcome mine. I want our children to love both sets of grandparents."

And she didn't know how that would happen other than for Robert to ask for and receive permission to marry her.

He swung his crutches and shuffled away from the beautiful display of canned fruits.

Following, her steps weighted, Jolene absorbed the sight of Robert—his broad shoulders tapered into his waist, the tan uniform crisp except for the horizontal creases from sitting with his back pressed against a seat, and the long legs. She engraved the sight into her mind so that, in the years to come, she might remember every part of this man who held her heart—

But might never again hold her hand.

⁂

Robert leaned into another step, his eyes watching the uneven ground, taking in the shoes in various shapes and sizes parting like the Red Sea before him.

If Jolene followed him, she was silent. Just as well. She'd said enough already.

What a fool he'd been, running off to war hoping it would solve the problems he'd left behind. Hoping, somehow, that distance would bandage the wounds, and silence salve the rift.

It didn't work.

Nothing he'd done after losing Mitch had worked.

He'd give his right arm—no, his very life—to take back what happened that day. It was all his fault, from getting caught holding Jolene's hand to losing his focus in the middle of a match.

All.

His.

Fault.

A bale of hay came into view. He'd come to the edge of the fairgrounds with nothing but a parking lot for cars, buggies, and a few horse-drawn carts beyond the hay boundary.

End of the line. Nowhere to go but back the way he'd come or in an endless loop around the perimeter. He sensed rather than saw Jolene's presence. Part of him wanted to yell at her to go away, but the greater part longed to draw her near and never let go. To kiss her until she admitted she was as crazy in love with him as he was with her, and that she'd defy her parents to become his wife.

Because defiance has worked so well for you, hasn't it?

His sarcastic conscience hit with the force of a hammer.

The first rule of any conflict, whether on the field of play or the field of war, was to change tactics when the one you were using didn't work. And the first rule of love was to put your beloved's needs above your own. What Jolene wanted was right and good.

If only the chance of success wasn't so slim.

Robert closed his eyes to gather his courage. "If I ask, and your father says no, what will you do?"

A swish of fabric. The faint scent of gasoline. "I don't know."

"That's not good enough, JoJo. Promise me you won't run off to be an aerial stunt pilot." He gripped the handles of his crutches until his palms ached. "Promise."

"Then you prefer that I marry Pierre and live in France?"

Pain lanced through his chest with the force of a bullet. He bit back a groan.

"Do you?"

He couldn't get the word past his tight lips, so he nodded. Jolene deserved to marry, to have children, to grow her fruit trees even if they were planted in foreign soil.

"Then you must promise me something in return, Robbie."

The sound of his nickname in her voice turned his legs to rubber. Only the brace of his crutches saved him from falling to the ground. "What?"

She touched his elbow, a gesture of love and caring that rippled in agonizing waves through his body. "You must promise to find some sweet girl to marry."

Open himself again to the pain of love and loss? "Never."

Chapter 5

Jolene dropped her hand and stepped back. What was she supposed to do now? Was saying he wanted her to marry Pierre, then refusing to marry himself, Robert's way of making her give in and run away with him?

The temptation was fiercer than when Mr. Walpole offered her the chance to fly.

When Pierre asked if she knew who Robert was now, a small part of her hoped she didn't. Because Robert, despite all his good qualities, had a streak of arrogance. He thought he could bend people to his will with the force of his convictions. Of course, that wasn't all bad. Men with solid, unshakable beliefs were good for someone like her. . .someone who bent too easily for the sake of keeping the peace.

She had hoped—even prayed—that war would knock some brashness out of Robert. Apparently it hadn't.

Jolene hung her head and took another step back. Her parents' approval of the man she married meant too much to her, and she'd not be swayed from it. Not even by Robert.

Changing him wasn't her job. Neither was changing her parents. The only person she could change was herself, so the question remained. . .

What was she supposed to do now?

Robert twisted his torso then used the crutches to make his legs follow. His ashen skin and dull eyes were those of a soldier facing a suicide mission. "I'll ask, JoJo. I don't think it will do anything but pound the final nail in the coffin of our dream. But for you, I'll ask."

She inhaled. The acidic scent of hay tickled her nose and lined her lungs. Perhaps he wasn't as stubborn as he used to be. So perhaps she needed to be a little more forceful about what she wanted instead of always choosing the path of least resistance. "Then I'll go to my parents and tell them that I want to marry you."

A pathetic attempt at a smile lifted the corners of his tight lips. "Good. I'm. . .I'm sure that will help."

Tears burned her eyes. She put a trembling hand over her mouth to hold in a useless contradiction. How sweet of him to try and bolster her spirits. Before her tenuous control over her emotions fractured, Jolene whirled around and stumbled toward the staging area for the auto polo teams.

Within four steps, she knew something else. She turned back in time to see him rub his chin against his shoulder, leaving a patch of darker tan cloth. "I won't marry Pierre, Robbie. I can't. Not when my heart belongs to you. So, if my parents say no, I'll be saying yes to Mr. Walpole."

His eyes blazed. "Over my—"

"Dead body?" She tilted her head to one side. "No, Robbie. Not yours, and probably not mine."

His chin snapped up an inch. "*Probably* isn't good enough."

Aching with love for this man who wanted to protect her, she put a hand up to keep him from coming closer. "Nothing in this life is guaranteed, darling. You and I know that better than anyone. If it's my time to die, then it's my time. I'll fly to my heavenly mansion, plant fruit trees in the backyard, and learn how to can peaches from my sainted grandmother. What I will no longer do is order my life around what others think is best for me."

Spinning around, she gulped down strangling sobs and walked toward the fight she'd been avoiding since the day she fell in love with Robert Montgomery.

Five minutes later, she approached the repair tent. Her father would be making one last check before they drove the cars to the grandstand area for viewing. Sure enough, his blond head was bent over the engine of the second car from the left.

"Daddy, do you have a moment to talk?"

He looked up, his grease-smudged face sobering the moment his eyes met hers. "Sure, baby girl. What do you need?"

Eyes stinging, she dropped the tent flap and stepped inside. She'd never wanted to be a mechanic, but Theo's injury had forced the entire team to adapt. A part of her loved the challenge of puzzling out how to restore life to mangled cars. Sometimes, if she tried hard enough, she could make the tent's canvas walls a sanctuary.

Not today.

"I. . .I want to. . ." Jolene dropped her eyes. Her fingernails were still rimmed in black. She picked at the grease and struggled to form the words inside her head so that, when they came out, her father would understand. "I've had a job offer."

Metal clanged against metal. "What kind of job?"

The frayed skin around her thumb began to bleed. She held it to her lips and swallowed down the coppery tang of blood mixed with oil.

"I asked what kind of job." His tone of voice made it sound like she was asking to become a fallen woman.

"A mechanic. Sort of."

"Define *sort of.*"

Jolene raised her chin. She could at least look like she felt brave. "A Mr. Walpole from Dayton-Wright Aeroplane Company wants me to become an aerial stunt pilot to show off the safety and maneuverability of their planes. He says that they will teach me to fly, and since I'm already a mechanic, they can train me to fix my own plane, too."

Her father ran his tongue along his top teeth, ending with a little slurp. "And you're asking for my permission to leave us?"

Heart hammering so hard she could feel it to her toes, Jolene squeezed her hands into fists. "No, Daddy. I'm almost twenty-one years old. If I want to take this job, I will."

His blue eyes widened. "I see. So, why are you here?"

He knew why she was here. He had to! Didn't he? "Because. . .because I love Robert Montgomery."

"Ah." He bent over the engine once again.

His dismissal heated her skin. Jolene stomped forward. "Define *Ah!*"

He didn't look up. "It means I've been waiting a long time to have this conversation."

Jolene's legs wobbled. There was no place to sit, so she settled for leaning against the worktable and hoped no grease would stain her navy skirt. "How long have you known?"

"Since the moment Theo stormed into the repair tent at Comisky Park breathing fire because he caught you and Robert holding hands and whispering in each other's ears."

Jolene's lungs seized. "So you've known all this time?"

The question wasn't about her and Robert, it was about her guilt, but to say that outright was more than even her new resolve to be more forthright could muster.

His blue eyes were the saddest eyes she'd ever seen—sadder even than Robert's a few minutes ago. "It wasn't your fault, Jolene. It was mine. I should have stopped Theo from driving like a madman that first quarter, but to my everlasting regret, I said nothing."

How many others thought the accident that left Theo Caplan an invalid and Mitch Montgomery dead was their fault? Heart swollen with pity, Jolene lurched into her father's waiting arms. "Why didn't you stop Theo?"

He hugged her a little tighter. "I knew my little girl was in love, and I needed to see if it was with a boy or a man. If Robert had behaved in the second quarter the way he did in the first, I would have given my permission."

At least he didn't know she'd planned to elope and deny him the opportunity to walk her down the aisle.

"But now?" The bitter question came from behind her.

Robert.

Jolene rotated enough to see him, while keeping her arms around her father's waist. "Robbie. Not now."

He swung his crutches forward and stepped inside the tent. "I think now is as good a time as any. After all, I need to know what I'm up against."

* * *

Robert watched Mr. Caplan's face as he dropped his arms from around Jolene's shoulders. He seemed older than even a few hours ago, but the firm set of his jaw meant he was still a force to be reckoned with. "Go on, baby girl. This is between me and Robert."

Jolene's beautiful blue eyes flitted between him and her father.

"It's okay." Mr. Caplan kissed her forehead and gave her a little push. "I promise not to deck him again."

After eyeballing her father then Robert, Jolene gave a little sigh. "I'll be in the house-car with Mom." As she passed Robert on her way out of the tent, she whispered, "Praying."

Robert longed to sit down but dared not. This was a battle, no mistake, and he intended to use every advantage—including his two inches of height superiority. "I love her, sir."

Mr. Caplan waited until the flap of the tent closed, dimming the light inside to a muted gold. "I know. That's not the problem."

Robert sucked in a breath. "Then what is?"

With narrowed eyes, Mr. Caplan took a step closer. "I think you know."

His heart thudded against his rib cage. Jolene's dad was laying down a challenge. If Robert identified the problem, he'd be one step closer to winning the girl of his dreams.

Sickening dread settled over him—the same dread that surrounded him when he'd stood in a foxhole, rifle ready, the stench of his own sweat tempting him to surrender.

Robert slouched against the crutches and closed his eyes. He needed to think and couldn't do it while staring Mr. Caplan down.

If he were a father and someone was asking for permission to marry his daughter, what would be the most important thing to know about the man? "I'm a hard worker, Mr. Caplan. I don't have a job yet, but I'll find one."

"I know."

"I'll treat her right, sir. I'd never hurt her or intentionally cause her harm. I'd lay down my life for her. And I'm sorry for kissing her in public like that when I didn't have the right to do it. But aside from that lapse, I've always put her reputation above my"— Robert swallowed past the humiliation of the next word—"desires."

"I know."

"Well, then, why'd you hit me so hard?" Robert opened his eyes and rubbed his jaw.

Mr. Caplan smirked. "Not bad for an old man, huh? Truth is, I didn't recognize you at first, and then. . ." He picked a blue rag off the worktable and wiped at the grease on his hands. "Well, then I thought you might be kissing her to force my hand. It wasn't until later I realized my mistake."

Good to know. But it wasn't helping Robert figure out what Mr. Caplan considered the greatest obstacle to granting his permission for Jolene to marry Robert.

He gulped down air. His lungs were on fire and his brain frozen.

Jolene's sweet voice filled his head. *I want to welcome your parents into our home the same way I want you to welcome mine. I want our children to love both sets of grandparents.*

Oh no.

Hanging his head, Robert stared at the ground. "I can't. . .I can't make my father love her, sir."

"And I can't let her marry into a family that won't welcome her." Mr. Caplan's scuffed white-and-brown wing tips appeared. "What you're too young to realize is that marriage isn't just between two people, it's between two families. Any couple that starts a life together without the support of their families does so at their peril, because someday your wife is going to want to wring your neck like a chicken, and if your mother-in-law isn't supportive of your marriage, she'll tell her daughter *exactly* how to do it."

In spite of himself, Robert laughed at the image, but the humorous moment accentuated the gap between him and Jolene's father. Time to face the awful truth. "My father hasn't forgiven me, sir. I don't know how to get him to forgive you."

Mr. Caplan's eyes went shiny. "Neither do I, and I've tried."

The statement hung between them like a referee's flag stopping play until the damage could be assessed. "When?"

"As soon as I found out we'd be competing against each other again. I wrote your father a letter asking if we could put the past behind us. He wrote back telling me where I and my desire to reconcile could go to rot." Mr. Caplan swiped a hand through his hair. "We used to be friends, your dad and I. Did you know that?"

"No, sir." No longer worried about appearing superior, Robert hauled himself to the closest car and maneuvered his sore body into the passenger seat.

Mr. Caplan remained silent until Robert got settled. "Thirty years ago, when we were fresh from the schoolhouse with no future but taking over the family farms, an automobile race came through town. Your dad and I begged to be allowed to quit our chores long enough to stand on the side of the road and watch it. There were only two cars, and they were slow as molasses in January, but they were the most exciting thing two farm boys had ever seen in our sixteen years. For weeks afterward, your dad and I met after our chores were done and dreamt of the day we'd run away and become automobile racers. We made a pact that nothing would ever ruin our friendship and had every right to believe we'd be able to keep that promise. After all, if the fight over Mary Alice Kuhlman—the most beautiful girl in School House Seven—couldn't come between us, nothing ever would."

Robert had heard the story of the race that came through Oshkosh, Wisconsin, but never with Oliver Caplan as a part of it. "How much of the seven hundred dollars required to purchase that first car was yours?"

"Half." Mr. Caplan shook his head. "We were a team back then. Automobile companies were trying to sell the longevity and dependability of their cars, so the races were long-distance and required at least two drivers so one could sleep while the other drove."

"What went wrong?"

Mr. Caplan lifted his right shoulder. "A little jealousy here, some hurtful teasing there, and then—when racing became an individual sport—I got offered a sponsorship as a solo driver and took it. Your father never forgave me."

The skin on the back of Robert's neck tingled.

"And that's my biggest problem." Mr. Caplan held up a hand to forestall any comment. "Because here's another thing you don't understand yet: one day you are going to have to forgive Jolene. It might be a big thing; it might be small. It might be a year from now or ten years from now. It doesn't really matter. Marriage requires hefty doses of forgiveness on a regular basis. You're too in love for me to judge your character on this issue. Whether you like it or not, most men grow up to be the spitting image of their fathers. So, Robert, if you were in my shoes, would you entrust your daughter to a man you feared had never learned to forgive?"

Chapter 6

As Robert left the repair tent, he looked around for Jolene. She said she was going to be inside the Caplan house-car, but he expected she never made it past the tent door and had been listening to him and her father the entire time.

Because it's what he had done so he could interrupt at the opportune moment.

Robert slumped into the crutches and rubbed his jaw. He wanted to find Jolene—to kiss her one last time—before going to see his father. Before asking the impossible: if he'd let go of his anger so his only surviving son could marry the daughter of his bitterest enemy.

Not hard to guess his father's response.

The panic that had overtaken him earlier began to creep up his spine. He cut a sweeping glance over his surroundings to tether himself in the here and now instead of the foreign soil of war. Evergreen trees covered the hills like a thick carpet. White clouds floated in a blue sky and occasionally blocked the sun as they traveled east. Birds, not bombs, flew overhead. The dirt beneath his feet was covered with straw, not blood.

He was as far away from the front lines as a man could get, but his heart still pounded like a misfiring engine.

A group of men wearing red shirts approached. The Caplan team. Robert beat a hasty retreat—well, hasty for a man on crutches. He headed for the Montgomery camp, reminding himself to breathe.

His father was standing outside the Montgomery repair tent, a hand shading his eyes. "There you are."

"Dad, we need to talk."

"Not now. We need to get you ready for the match."

Robert shook his head. "I can't drive."

Dad reached inside the tent flap and pulled out a blue shirt. "Like I told you before, you can drive better than—"

"It's not that." Robert stared into his father's face. Was Mr. Caplan right that sons inevitably turned out like their fathers? If so, the bitter lines around Dad's mouth would etch into his own face one day. "I have something important to ask you."

"You put this on and drive, and I promise the answer will be yes." Dad held out the shirt.

Robert's head spun for a moment, then his heart sank. "You must not know what I want to talk to you about."

"Leaving the auto polo circuit? Your mother already told me."

"She did?" It wasn't what he and Ma discussed, but perhaps she was trying to ease her husband into letting go.

"Now put this on, and let's get you in that car." Dad shoved the shirt into Robert's hand.

Jolene often said he should choose when to confront an issue rather than attacking it head-on the moment it came up. Perhaps she was right. "Okay, Dad. I'll drive, but we *will* have a conversation after the match, and I'll remind you of your promise. Do we have a deal?"

"Fine. Fine." Dad turned and disappeared into the repair tent.

Trying to change shirts while balancing on one leg and keeping crutches from falling proved too difficult. Robert sat on the steps to the house-car, breathing in the lingering scent of his mother's bread as he changed into the Montgomery team shirt.

"I can't believe you're doing this."

Robert looked up to find Jimmy standing a few feet away. "No choice, buddy."

Jimmy's face hardened. "I'm not your buddy, Robert Montgomery. We weren't even buddies back when I was the mechanic." He took a step closer and jabbed a finger under Robert's nose. "I'm driving now, and if you drive in Frank's place, you might find that the Caplans aren't your only enemy out there."

<hr />

Jolene gasped when she saw Robert behind the wheel of one of the Montgomery's cars. What was he *thinking*? If he survived the match, she was going to kill him with her bare hands.

"Good afternoon, Miss Caplan."

Heart sinking, Jolene smiled at Mr. Walpole. "Good afternoon, sir. I hope you're ready for a great match."

"I always enjoy a show of skill, whether on the ground or in the air." Though there were plenty of available seats in the grandstand, Mr. Walpole sat beside her. His tenacity had just crossed into browbeating.

Jolene needed time and another conversation with Robert before she gave Mr. Walpole her answer. Robert hadn't talked to her after the conversation with her father, and when she tried to follow up, Dad shooed her away because it was time to get ready for the polo match.

Did Robert have permission to marry her or not?

On the heels of that question were twenty more. Listening to Robert stammer over asking if she still cared for him, and then his willingness to speak to her father when, seventeen months ago, he'd been dead set against it. . .well, clearly he'd changed. So had she. Were they still a good match for each other? Could they go back to how it was before, or was she remembering the past with too fond an eye? Why was he playing in the match? He knew how much she wanted to leave the circuit. He'd been willing to give it up to elope. Had he changed his mind?

"Is that Robert Montgomery driving?" Mr. Walpole's question sent Jolene into protective mode. She might abhor the idea, but she'd not let an outsider criticize Robert or either auto polo team.

Jolene angled her head toward the Montgomery side of the field to pretend she needed to see for herself. "I believe it is."

"Well, now. Isn't that an interesting twist?"

Jolene stiffened and exerted all her willpower to remain seated. "What a lovely day we're having."

"It is." Whether Mr. Walpole sensed it was safer to turn the topic of conversation or just enjoyed discussing trivial matters, he kept up a light banter for a few minutes before the roar of engines prevented further discussion.

Checking the stands, she was grateful to see almost every seat taken.

Until the match started.

When the flag dropped, Robert drove straight for the center of the field, but the other Montgomery driver didn't move. The Caplan drivers headed for the ball, one pulling up in time for the other to take lead and let Pierre swing. Robert's car arrived at the exact same time, except his mallet man didn't swing.

Robert spun his car around and drove at the ball again. When his mallet man still didn't swing, the crowd hushed. Pierre pounded the ball through the Montgomery goal posts with no opposition from the car still parked there.

Booing split the air.

Jolene pressed a hand against her pounding heart. What was going on?

Two more Caplan goals were scored in an identical manner, and booing drowned out the four unmuffled engines.

The referee held up his flag while retrieving the ball from behind the Montgomery goal posts for the third time. Before returning to the field of play, he stopped to say a word to Robert's father. Mr. Montgomery, face deep red, marched to where both team cars waited. Whatever he said worked because, when play resumed, both cars entered the fray—although, to Jolene's trained eye, the Montgomery mallet men weren't making much of an effort.

By the end of the first period, the score was five to zero in the Caplan's favor and the booing was back.

Oddly, Robert drove his car almost off the field rather than parking behind the goal post and walking to where the team gathered to discuss second-period strategy.

"I guess they're trying to hide the boy's broken leg." Mr. Walpole's observation was as unwelcome as his presence.

A few minutes later, the car reappeared with a different driver. Robert, crutches in place, walked out far enough to catch Jolene's eye. He shook his head, his mouth flat and tight.

Jolene bit down on her bottom lip to stifle a sob. He'd failed. The bitterness between the Montgomery and Caplan families would rob her of her greatest dream. Therefore, she'd settle for a different one.

"Mr. Walpole, I accept your job offer. Where should I meet you and when?"

———◆●◆———

Jolene didn't stay to watch the rest of the match. Instead, she hurried to the house-car and began packing. Mr. Walpole was meeting her at the main gate in an hour. She couldn't afford distractions. At least that was the story she told herself while the truth—that her parents, Robert, and everyone else who'd try to talk her out of leaving were too caught up in the auto polo match to miss her—nibbled the edges of her fraying composure.

When her small suitcase was stuffed to bursting, she set it aside long enough to pen a note.

> *Dearest Mom and Dad,*
>   *I have accepted Mr. Walpole's offer to become a stunt pilot. My decision has nothing to do with being angry or upset. As you know, Daddy, I was hoping Robert would be granted permission to marry me. I understand why you said no, but my disappointment is acute. I have agreed to work for Dayton-Wright for one year. I hope that when I'm done, the bitterness between you and the Montgomery family will be laid to rest.*
>   *I'll write again when I'm settled.*
>   *I love you with all my heart,*
>
>   *Jolene*

A tear fell and smudged her signature, but she didn't have time to fix it. The match would be over soon, and she'd lose her opportunity to slip away. Besides, she was crying so hard a new note would end up as nothing but ink blobs.

After a final look around the traveling home she loved and hated in equal parts, Jolene stepped outside and closed the door behind her.

Robert watched the rest of the match from the sideline. Although he hated to admit his father was right, the level of play had declined significantly in the past year and a half. Many of the fans left after the first break, and several more trickled out until the grandstand was half-empty by the time the Crusaders beat the Marauders ten to four.

Dad had screamed himself hoarse during the match, so the team meeting afterward was short. Once it was over, the guys disappeared fast. Either they were still mad about Robert driving or they wanted to skedaddle before Dad took them to the woodshed for their first-period stunt.

Robert and his dad were loading mallets into one of the cars when Mr. Trotter, the head of the Auto Polo Association, marched to their side of the field, his face shiny red and eyes blazing. He was hauling Mr. Caplan along by the elbow and, when he got close enough, grabbed Dad's arm. "You two, I swear I'm going to have your guts for garters. What were you *thinking*? I give you one simple instruction—make it a good match—and you turn what was supposed to be the triumphant return of the greatest rivalry on the circuit into a laughingstock. Do you not understand what's at stake?"

Silence.

Robert scooted his crutches back. He didn't belong here.

"Stop right there, young man." Mr. Trotter pointed a finger at Robert's nose. "Don't think you're getting off without your fair share of a lecture. I don't care if you have *two* broken legs." He returned his attention to Dad and Mr. Caplan. "Unless I hear a good reason for what happened out there, I'll ban both your teams from ever playing auto polo again. I'll not have the bitterness between you ruining the sport."

After a few tense seconds, Dad glanced at Robert. "My boy's the best driver the circuit's ever seen, and I challenge anyone to dispute that." He shot a belligerent glare at Mr.

Caplan before returning his attention to Mr. Trotter. "You said make it a good match, so I put my best players on the field."

"Three of whom then didn't play!" Mr. Trotter ripped the brown felt hat from his head. Wisps of white hair stood straight before flopping sideways on his pink scalp. "The entire association is losing momentum. We're trying to *attract* people, not scare them away by looking like complete lunkheads. You"—he glared at Robert—"did you know what your teammates were planning?"

"I knew they weren't happy, but I had no idea they meant to boycott. I removed myself as soon as"—Robert leveled his gaze on Dad—"I fulfilled my promise."

Mr. Trotter's mouth opened and closed twice. He turned to Mr. Caplan as though suddenly recalling his presence. "And where were *you* while all this was going on?"

Mr. Caplan lifted his eyebrows a fraction. "Do you have an issue with how my boys played?"

"Their conduct on the field was fine, but what about that nonsense under the grandstand this morning?" Mr. Trotter jammed his hat back on. "Did you think I wouldn't hear about that?"

Mr. Caplan's eyes narrowed to slits. "Let's just call it another—how did you describe the last Caplan-Montgomery match?—unfortunate event."

Dad's breath hissed on the way in. "You, too?"

"Made me so livid I couldn't see straight for a full minute."

"What are you talking about?" Mr. Trotter's face echoed Robert's confusion.

Mr. Caplan yanked a piece of paper from his hip pocket, unfolded it with jerking impatience, and thrust it at Mr. Trotter. "This."

Instead of reading the letter, Mr. Trotter patted his front jacket pockets—first on the right side then the left. Not finding what he was searching for, he started patting his pant pockets.

"Never mind your glasses"—Dad grabbed the letter—"I'll tell you what it says. I've read it so many times I have the stupid thing memorized."

Dear Mr. Oliver Caplan and Mr. Charles Montgomery,

I am writing to inform you that the Auto Polo Association will no longer adjust the tour schedule with the expressed intention of avoiding a rematch between your teams. We hope you can resume your rivalry without undue antagonism over the unfortunate events of your last meeting. Your first meeting will be September 16, 1918, at the Western Washington Fair in Puyallup, Washington. If you have any questions or concerns, please direct them to me at the above address.

Sincerely,

Albert J. Lindsay for William B. Trotter

Dad finished reading and poked a finger in the middle of the page. " 'Unfortunate events?' " His voice rose. "Is that how you describe what happened when my boy was killed and his maimed?"

Mr. Caplan gripped Dad's shoulder. "I couldn't have said it better myself."

Robert squeezed his crutches until his fingers begged for mercy. He didn't move, hardly even breathed for fear the small gesture of friendship would blow up and obliterate them all.

Eyes flitting between the two rivals, Mr. Trotter stepped back.

"I. . .I got his letter and yours on the same day." Dad rubbed his jaw. "Afraid it may have colored my reply just a bit."

Remembering what Mr. Caplan said was in that reply, Robert held his breath. Was it possible that some of what had been said and done in the past was distorted by the heat of the moment or ravaging grief?

"I should have stopped Theo." Mr. Caplan's words were so soft, Robert wasn't sure he heard them correctly.

Dad scratched his earlobe. "Plenty of blame to go around."

There it was! Would Dad *ever* forgive him? Robert tightened every muscle in his face to keep from shouting the question at his fath—

"I never should have let my boys try a maneuver they hadn't mastered in practice."

Robert lost his balance and nearly fell. "What?"

Dad turned around. His suntanned skin was tinged with gray. "Robert? What's wrong?"

The dirt beneath his feet quaked, but no one else seemed to notice. Robert sucked down air. "What maneuver are you talking about?"

Cocking his head to the left, Dad narrowed his eyes like he was trying to understand the question. "The one where you and Eddy were to keep even, then he was supposed to do a hard left at the last moment. Between Eddy waiting a hairsbreadth too long and the damage to his tire. . ."

Whatever else Dad said got lost. A floating sensation overtook every limb. Robert held on to his crutches like they were the only thing keeping him on solid ground. "So. . .I didn't. . ." Mitch's death wasn't his fault? Could it be true?

Mr. Caplan reached out and touched Dad's sleeve. "I think your boy blames himself for his brother's death."

Dad's eyes pinched at the corners. "Is that true, son?"

Robert nodded, his lips still unable to form words.

Dad stumbled back a step and grabbed his suspenders. "Is that why you went tearing off to war without so much as a word to me? Because you thought I blamed *you*?"

Robert cast his mind back, forcing himself to relive the terrible grief following Mitch's death. Whom *did* he blame? The truth was like a slap across his face. "No, Dad. *I* blamed me and couldn't handle the guilt. I decided you couldn't forgive me because I couldn't forgive myself."

Both Dad and Mr. Caplan stiffened then slowly turned their heads until they were staring each other in the eye.

"I. . .do you think—?" Dad tipped his head toward Robert.

"That your boy is on to something? That we blamed each other out of our guilt?" Mr. Caplan rubbed his bristled cheek. "Maybe."

Dad stuffed his hands in his pockets. "Yeah. Maybe."

Was that an apology? Robert didn't want to ask for fear the answer was no.

Mr. Trotter bobbed his head once. "Well, I'm glad you two are finally over this nonsense."

"Nonsense?" Dad and Mr. Caplan spoke in unison and turned to stand, shoulder to shoulder, facing Mr. Trotter.

Instead of withdrawing, Mr. Trotter grinned. "Nonsense I said, and nonsense I meant. Oh, not the loss of your boys—that's a tragedy and no mistake—but this rivalry between you when God made you brothers. If I've accomplished nothing during my tenure as president of the APA other than get Charles Montgomery and Oliver Caplan to be friends again, I'll retire happy."

The sun reappeared from behind a cloud, as though God echoed the sentiment from His seat in heaven. Robert added his own plea for good measure. *Please, God. . .let this small foundation hold up. Let forgiveness be built on it in the days and months ahead.*

Dad's shoulders inched down. "Hating you hasn't done me much good."

Mr. Caplan's shoulders began to shake, and laughter rent the air. "Charlie, has anyone ever told you you're miserable at kissing and making up?"

Dad shrugged. "My wife. All the time."

Grins still in place, the two men faced each other.

"Friends?" Mr. Caplan stuck out his right hand.

Dad shook it. "Friends."

Unable to hold back any longer, Robert leaned forward and tapped Mr. Caplan on the shoulder. "Does this mean I can speak to Jolene?"

The small flick of Mr. Caplan's head toward Dad reminded Robert of the second half of the man's objection.

"Right." Robert swiveled on his crutches to face his father. "Dad, do you have a moment?"

Eyes narrowing, Dad bounced his gaze around the three faces staring at him. He focused in on Mr. Trotter. "We done here?"

Trotter put his hat back on. "I'm done."

"Let me walk you back." Mr. Caplan swept his left arm toward the exit, indicating Mr. Trotter should precede him.

As the two men walked away, Robert heaved a deep breath. "I'm not sure if you know that Jolene Caplan and I were seeing each other before I left for the war."

Dad's jaw loosened. "You were?"

"We felt we needed to hide our. . .well, our love because of the rivalry between the Caplan and Montgomery teams." Robert grunted and shook his head. "We thought we'd done pretty well, but then Theo. . .that day. . ."

"I wondered what had gotten into that boy." He scratched his neck. "Did Ollie know?"

Ollie? Oh, Mr. Caplan. Robert clamped his teeth together and tightened the corners of his lips to keep from grinning. "Yes, sir."

"The whole time?" Dad lifted his derby hat and finger-combed his markedly gray hair.

Sobered by the reminder that he'd caused his parents undue distress, Robert ducked his head and cleared his throat. "I don't think Mr. Caplan knew until Theo told him."

"And your mother?" Dad shook his head. "Never mind. I'm sure she knew you were in love with the girl before you did."

"Probably." His heartbeat sped up, like an engine revving before the main event. "I. . .I want to marry her. If that's okay with you."

Dad squinted then glanced to where Mr. Caplan was still chatting with Mr. Trotter. "Let me guess, you won't get permission from Ollie to marry the gal if I'm not going to let her be on the team, so to speak."

Robert nodded.

"Nice girl. Got nothing against her." He replaced his hat, tugging the brim until it shaded his eyes. "Don't know her very well, but you're man enough to make your own decision, I guess."

"So. . .?"

A smile split his father's face. "Got a hankering to be a grandpa."

Robert's racing heart skidded to a stop. "Is that a yes?"

Dad slapped him on the shoulder. "That's a yes."

Tossing his head back to give a whoop, Robert miscalculated and lost his balance. The crutches slipped forward while he fell back and landed on his rear in the mud. Pain shot through his leg when his broken ankle bounced on the ground, but he didn't care. His only thought was finding Jolene to tell her the good news.

Mr. Caplan raced over. He and Dad pulled Robert upright. "You okay, son?"

Not sure which father asked, Robert reached for the crutch his father held out. "Better than—"

Mrs. Caplan appeared at the opposite end of the grandstand field. Alarm creased her forehead, and she pushed Theo's wheelchair at a reckless pace.

Mr. Caplan ran toward her. "What?"

She waved a piece of paper then grabbed the wheelchair before it toppled. "Jolene's gone!"

Chapter 7

Jolene stopped to purchase another scone as she headed to meet Mr. Walpole. The bitter taste in her mouth needed something sweet to counteract it.

Pierre appeared just as she took her first bite. His red shirt was stained with dirt and sweat, but his face was clean and dark hair damp.

Oops. She was supposed to answer whether or not she planned to marry him and move to France.

"I see you have the bags packed, but you have not given me your reply." He stopped a foot away and crossed his arms over his chest.

Swallowing hard, Jolene coughed to dislodge a crumb that got stuck on the way down. "I'm sorry, Pierre. There was so much going on today, I totally forgot about..." The affront on his face stopped her from saying the rest. "I'm sorry."

Her repeated apology deepened his scowl. "A man does not wish to hear that the woman he has offered to share his life with has forgotten such a thing."

Jolene held out a hand. "I know. I shouldn't have said that."

After a moment of staring into her face, Pierre turned his palms up and shrugged in a decidedly French manner. "It is the way of the heart, non? Your Robert returns and all thoughts of poor Pierre flee your pretty head."

Yes, but she still shouldn't have phrased it that way. Jolene set the scone on her brown suitcase. "I do love you, but as a brother. You deserve someone who will fall victim to your charm and yearn to spend a lifetime staring into your handsome face."

A quivering grin fought through the stern lines of his mouth. "With logic like that, how can I stay angry with you for rejecting me so heartlessly?" He dropped a glance to her suitcase. "May I ask where you are going? Because, if you plan to elope, I will act the brother you claim me to be and toss you over my shoulder to carry you back to your parents."

"No need for dramatics." She told him about her new job, and his scowl reappeared. "I've already agreed to a yearlong contract, so banish all thoughts of tossing me over your shoulder."

He stared at a point some distance behind her. "I do not think I will need to."

Jolene swiveled so fast, her skirt flared. "Robert."

His speedy crutches left a trail of alarmed fairgoers in his wake.

Bending to retrieve her suitcase, she knocked the scone into the dirt. Sparing an instant to regret the wasted money and loss of her favorite treat, Jolene straightened her spine and held the battered leather in front of her chest.

"Do you wish me to remain, *ma soeur?*"

Jolene shook her head but didn't turn to see if Pierre left. Her entire focus was on Robert and the firm set of his squared jaw.

Lord, give me strength to stand strong.

Robert was out of breath by the time he reached her. "What do you. . .think. . .you're doing?"

"Keeping my word." Jolene curled her toes inside her shoes.

He went white. "To whom? Walpole or the Frenchman?"

Sick with dread, Jolene pulled the suitcase tighter. She hated fighting. If only she hadn't stopped for the scone.

"Answer me, JoJo." Robert's tone lashed her shredded nerves.

"Which would you prefer?" The audacious question flew from her lips as though someone else put the words in her mouth.

The stunned look on Robert's face echoed her surprise. "What do you mean?"

Heart pounding against the brown leather, she inhaled a tremulous breath. "Which would you find easier to accept, me marrying Pierre or becoming a stunt pilot for a time?"

He leaned forward to put his face nearer to hers. "Neither."

Intimidated but unwilling to show it, Jolene put a finger on his shoulder to push him back. "No fair, Robbie. You don't get to win by changing the rules of the game."

Robert didn't budge. For a long moment, they stared at each other while Jolene did the only thing she could think of to do. . .

She prayed with all her might for wisdom and resolve.

———◦●◦———

"A soft answer turneth away wrath."

Had the Bible verse come from the Frenchman as he passed, or was it an echo inside Robert's own head? He swallowed down the angry words forbidding Jolene from going anywhere. What was it Captain Moller always said? Be careful you aren't so focused on winning the battle that you lose the war.

"Sorry, JoJo." Robert straightened his spine and focused on a distant point to break his intimidating stance and stare. He didn't feel sorry. He wanted to tear someone's arms off. But he'd just witnessed what harboring bitterness and resentment had done to two lifelong friends. To not learn from their mistakes was foolish. "Let me start again. May I ask where you're going?"

Jolene placed a soft hand on his arm. "Thank you for asking so nicely."

The urge to grab her hand and never let go sent heat up his arm and neck.

"Would you like to sit down so we can discuss this?"

No! He wanted to stand right where he was, blocking her path. Wanted to ask why she was leaving when he'd gotten permission to marry her. But she didn't know that. He'd silently told her the opposite less than an hour ago. Upbraiding her for avoiding him, when he'd been doing the same thing with her, was stupid. He looked over the crowd. "I don't see a bench available nearby, but I think we can have a little privacy in that"—he pointed with his chin—"grandstand entrance."

"Okay."

As they made their way through the crowd to the empty portico, Robert slowed his breathing. Another Bible verse came to mind. He couldn't remember the exact words, but it was something about the importance of listening over speaking.

Jolene rested her suitcase on the cement then gripped her hands together. Tears leaked down her cheeks, but she didn't speak.

What had she done?

"I. . ." She looked up at him with those blue eyes, and his heart splintered. "I've accepted the job with Dayton-Wright."

Relief stabbed his ribs. She wasn't marrying the Frenchman. But images of flaming planes, the screams of pilots, and the smell of burning flesh sent terror racing through his veins. Robert closed his eyes to block out the vision. His stomach rolled and bumped like he was back in the car the day Mitch died.

He couldn't lose Jolene. Not like he'd lost his brother. Or like he'd lost too many friends on the battlefield. If she died, he'd never forgive himself.

Oh, God! Was that the lesson he was supposed to learn? That he couldn't prevent bad things from happening? Couldn't force God to protect his loved ones? Couldn't keep blaming himself for not bullying the future and forging it by sheer force of will?

"It's only for a year."

Jolene's voice beat against his eardrums. So much could happen in a year. So much could happen in an *instant*.

"Please say you don't hate me."

Robert's eyes flew open. "Hate you?" He reached out with one hand, bending an inch to trap the crutch under his arm. "I love you so much my heart can't hold it all."

She stepped closer. Her hat brim was too large for contact, so Robert removed the hatpin and hat. Jolene tilted her head and stepped forward.

He wrapped his free arm around her waist and drew her close, fingers still clutching her hat. Bending his head, he memorized the fragrance of her hair and the way the fine strands tickled his nose. "Only for a year," he repeated for his own benefit.

Her cheek rubbed up and down against his chest. "Maybe by then, our parents won't hate each other and we can—"

"But they don't hate each other anymore." Robert bent his head closer to her lips. "Your father has given me permission to court you."

Instead of melting into his kiss, Jolene pushed him. Hard. "*What?*"

Staying upright took all his concentration for a moment.

"But you. . .you. . .didn't you?"

"Huh?"

Jolene lowered her brows. "You said—or at least I thought you were telling me—that you didn't get his permission." She flattened her lips and shook her head, imitating how he'd spoken to her across the length of the grandstand.

"Yeah, but that was before the match was over." Briefly, he told her about the meeting with President Trotter and how it had healed the rift between their fathers. But instead of coming back to his arms, she peppered him with more questions: Who said what? What did he think about what was said? What did her father think? What had her father said when Robert talked to him earlier? How did Robert feel about that? And so on until he leaned down and kissed her just to shut her up.

"No fair, Robert," she murmured against his lips when he pulled back. She wrapped her arms around his waist, though, and sighed. "We can last another year, can't we?"

"Of course we can." He'd wait forever if it meant being together.

She lifted her head. "Besides, this will be good for us."

Her words brushed across his neck and set his skin on fire. Robert forced his brain to concentrate on what she'd said instead of how much he wanted to kiss her again. "Good, how?"

She started to pull away, but he tightened his hold on her waist. "Because we've been apart from each other too long."

He cocked his head to look down at her face. "What kind of convoluted logic is that?"

He was too slow to react when Jolene pressed her hands against his chest and stepped back. "We need to get to know each other again—who we are *now* instead of who we were seventeen months ago."

"Still not following your logic, JoJo."

Her lips curved, sending his heart into triple time. "I'm not the same girl you left behind, and you've endured"—she shook her head, the light in her eyes dimming—"unimaginable things. Don't you see? We've both changed."

"My love for you hasn't."

She placed a gloved hand against his cheek. "Nor mine for you, but how we feel about each other must be tempered by common sense. I want a house and permanence, but you—"

"Want the same thing."

Jolene frowned. "Do you? How would you know? You've not been home long enough to know what you want. Perhaps a staid life won't suit you. In six months, you may long to return to the auto polo circuit."

Was that what was keeping them apart? "Jolene, sweetheart, listen to me. I've had enough wandering around for a hundred lifetimes. I'm staying put from now on."

"Then prove it to me." Jolene patted his cheek. "Get a job and figure out who you are and what you want. Write me long letters full of all those emotional details you men hate so much. Tell me how much you miss me, what you're doing, and how much better it would be if I were here with you."

"Mushy-gushy stuff, you mean." He pretended to find the idea exasperating. The impatient part of him did, but what she wanted was right and good. Her insistence on getting her father's permission had turned out well, and chances were this would, too. "How long before you leave?"

She checked her necklace watch. "I'm already late."

As she bent to pick up her suitcase, Robert grabbed her hand. "You have to promise me something before you go."

The suitcase remained on the ground. "What?"

Heart thumping hard, Robert mulled over the best way to express his emotions. "I. . . I need you to be careful, JoJo. You check and double-check and then triple-check every piece of equipment. You don't take any unnecessary risks. You don't let them put you up in a plane you don't know backward and forward. Promise me."

Her smile was tinged with sadness. "I'll be careful, Robbie. I promise. But you have to promise that should something happen to me, you won't shut yourself off. You're too good a man and will make someone a fine husband. Don't rob the world of your children, Robert Montgomery. Promise me."

The very thought twisted his stomach. "I can only promise to *try*, JoJo, because I won't lie. I can't see my life with anyone but you."

Jolene searched Robert's face. His amber eyes met hers, and she saw his heart. Far from trying to manipulate her, he was fighting to let her go. To put her needs ahead of his. To love her sacrificially. Her knees went soft. If he asked her one more time to stay, she'd throw her arms around his neck and never let go.

Why, oh *why* had she agreed to take the stunt-pilot job? And why did her own logic about the year apart being good for them hollow out her chest?

"I need to go." Jolene wriggled free and grabbed the suitcase. He took it from her and transferred it to his left hand. How he held it and his crutch, she didn't know. Or care. She was fighting tears and legs that had suddenly grown roots.

Robert stuck out his right elbow, and she looped her white gloves through his tan uniform sleeve. "Ready?"

If she opened her mouth, she'd beg to stay. So she nodded and strained to pull her right leg free to take a step. Then the left leg. And right. Left. One foot in front of the other, each step a little easier than the last.

Mr. Walpole waited beside the gate. When he saw Robert, his smile drooped. "Miss Caplan. I hope you still plan to come with me."

"I do."

The muscles in Robert's arm rippled.

Jolene let go and immediately felt cold. Alone. Unsure. She held out her hand and waited for Robert to give her the suitcase.

Instead, he held it toward Mr. Walpole, who grabbed the handle. "Sir, I'm going to be real honest here." Robert didn't let go of the suitcase. "I'm not happy about this—not one bit—but Miss Caplan has made her decision, and I'll honor it. However, if I find out you or anyone at Dayton-Wright has risked her life by knowingly putting her in a faulty aeroplane, there won't be a place far enough to run from my wrath. Understand?"

Mr. Walpole's Adam's apple bobbed twice. "I understand."

Robert relinquished the suitcase. "Now, if you don't mind, I need a minute to kiss my gal good-bye."

Jolene didn't see if Mr. Walpole left them alone or not. Her eyes locked on to Robert.

"I love you, JoJo Caplan, and I'll be waiting right here one year from today. . .plus a week for travel, but no more, hear?" He removed her hat. When had it gone back on her head?

Throat aching from all the words crammed together begging to be said, Jolene found the most important ones. "I love you, too."

Robert's fingers dug into her hair and tilted her head toward him. "You ready?"

She started to nod, but the look in his eyes stopped her. She quit breathing for a moment then dragged air into her stinging lungs.

"Because"—he leaned down, his lips so close to hers she felt their heat—"I'm going to kiss you so's you know exactly what's waiting for you when you come home to me."

Epilogue

One year later. . .plus a week for travel

Robert kept his cold fingers wrapped around the steering wheel of the Model T.

"Darling?" Jolene twisted on the passenger seat to face him. "What's wrong? You haven't said a word since we left the church."

He dared a look. Dressed in her bridal clothes, she was so beautiful his eyes hurt.

"This is supposed to be the happiest day of our lives, but you look like you've swallowed a persimmon." Her lips smiled, but her eyes were pinched at the corners.

The celluloid collar around his neck tightened. "I. . .well, I have another surprise for you."

Her expression eased. "You mean other than this new car? Which is lovely, by the way."

"I'm glad you like it." He'd spent a year refurbishing what had started out as a shell. Last September, Jolene's dad had offered him a car too beat up to drive to the next fair. His dad, not to be outdone by the generous offer, donated a new set of tires. Over the following twelve months, Robert spent every night after work piecing the car together. Some of his coworkers at the Boeing Airplane Company caught the spirit and started picking up bits and pieces—a hood ornament, running boards, and even some leather seats—as they found them.

It had been a good way to pass a year while waiting to marry his sweetheart. And saved him enough money that he'd put a sizable down payment on a little house near the Duwamish River, where he'd already planted blueberry bushes, a plum tree, and some berry vines. That was his third surprise for Jolene, and a good thing, too, if the second one turned out to be a huge mistake.

Robert let go of the steering wheel and set the brake. "Remember how your dad lectured me about one day us needing to forgive each other. That it might be for a small thing or. . .or maybe a big thing."

Wariness crept back into Jolene's blue eyes. "Yes."

"Well, I did something I thought would be funny, but it just occurred to me that a woman might not want her wedding reception plans messed with, not even by a husband who thinks she's the bee's knees."

Jolene's skin turned pink. "What did you do?"

"Maybe I'd better just show you." He popped out of the car and headed around the hood to open the door for his wife.

His wife!

He was never going to get tired of calling her that. As long as she forgave him for this.

They walked toward the small Elks Club they'd reached ahead of their wedding guests. He opened the door and let Jolene walk inside first. His surprise was front and center.

Jolene broke into peals of laughter. "That's. . .perfect."

Relief filled his lungs. "Thank goodness."

She set her bouquet down on the table. "And the best part is that I can do this." Jolene picked one golden triangle from the tower that substituted for a wedding cake and sank her teeth into a freshly baked Fisher Scone.

Becca Whitham (WIT-um) is a multipublished author who has always loved reading and writing stories. After raising two children, she and her husband faced the empty nest years by following their dreams: he joined the army as a chaplain, and she began her journey toward publication. Becca loves to tell stories marrying real historical events with modern-day applications to inspire readers to live Christ-reflecting lives. She's traveled to almost every state in the United States for speaking and singing engagements and has lived in Washington, Oregon, Colorado, Oklahoma, and Alaska. She can be reached through her website at www.beccawhitham.com.

First Comes Pie

by Niki Turner

Chapter 1

Western Colorado, 1920

I t was a perfect apple: round, smooth, undamaged by birds or insects. But it was just beyond her reach. Lorelei wedged one bare foot into the fork between two branches and stepped off the ladder. Leaning into the trunk, she reached into the fruit-studded limbs. The apple snapped loose with a twist of her wrist.

She rubbed the fruit against her sleeve, gratified by the shine that appeared. A smile curved her mouth. She tucked the apple into the voluminous front pocket on her black-and-white checked overalls. Then grabbing the trunk with both hands, she inched her free foot toward the top rung of the battered ladder. When her toes found purchase, she shifted her weight back.

The sharp sting on the base of her big toe took her by surprise. She jerked her foot away. The hornet escaped unscathed. The ladder crashed to the ground behind her with a clatter. Lorelei scrabbled to find a secure grip. Rough bark bit into her fingers as the force of gravity overrode her attempt to save herself.

Emmett Dewey had himself an apple rustler. The idea spurred a crooked smile. Surely an apple rustler wasn't too dangerous. He crept forward, spotting an ancient ladder and a small, bare foot poised on the top rung.

When the ladder crashed to the ground, Emmett leaped forward, arms out. He caught the falling figure. The impact took them both to the ground.

The creature stealing his apples came up punching and kicking like an Irish street brawler. Emmett scrambled to his feet. Fists raised for battle, he faced the thief. His red haze of fury cleared. He dropped his hands, along with his jaw.

Her strawberry-blond hair, cropped in a chin-length bob, was mussed, random tendrils tickling the sides of a heart-shaped face. Her baggy overalls failed to disguise her feminine attributes.

"You're a girl. I'm sorry," he blurted, appalled that he'd apprehended her.

"You're sorry because I'm female?"

Emmett shook his head. "No, I'm not sorry about that. . . ." He flushed. "I'm sorry for. . .for catching you the way I did."

It was her turn to redden. "You broke my fall. Thank you."

He cleared his throat. "You're welcome. Are you aware this is private property? You're trespassing."

She blinked cool gray eyes. "This property belongs to Otto Starkey."

"I beg to differ. Mr. Starkey is the former owner. It was sold at auction. To me."

Lorelei examined her rescuer. He was tall—at least six feet—and strong, judging from the way he'd caught her free fall. He was also well versed in self-defense. Even when she'd used most of the tricks her Welsh father had taught her, the man hadn't flinched.

Then what he'd said registered. Her clenched fists dropped to her sides, horror and grief marching over her soul. She'd attended Otto's funeral, offered her condolences to his relations. They'd said nothing about selling the property. Grief gripped her. The orchard had been Otto's life, but his family wouldn't have cared. They'd abandoned the old man years ago. With their ambivalence they'd stolen her last hope for the future.

"What about his will?"

The stranger shook his head. "Wasn't one, as far as I know. The deed passed to his next of kin."

Lorelei suppressed a groan. She'd urged Otto to draw up a will. He'd promised to do so, promised to leave word that she would always have access to the orchard. But his death had been sudden, and he hadn't followed through.

"Why did you buy it?" She fisted her hands on her hips.

"It seemed like a good idea."

"What do you know about apples?"

"I like to eat them," he replied with a lazy drawl that made her think of warm summer afternoons and tall glasses of fresh-squeezed lemonade.

She stomped her foot to shake off the image. "What are your plans for the property?"

He grinned. Lorelei rocked back on her heels, struck dumb. No man should be graced with a cleft chin *and* dimples, in addition to sparkling blue eyes and a headful of wavy golden hair. It wasn't fair.

"I'm leaning toward selling the place."

Lorelei's heart lurched. It was bad enough that Otto had shrugged off this mortal coil before the trees he'd planted with such care produced their best crop. It was worse that this stranger had no comprehension of the treasure he now owned.

"You can't do that!"

He cocked his head. "Why not?"

Her eyes stung. "Otto was my friend." She'd spent the last year and a half making sure he was getting enough to eat. She sought a distraction to stop the tears before they started. Her shoes. Where had she put her shoes?

He cleared his throat. Her serviceable black lace-ups—courtesy of the 1918 Sears catalog—dangled from his outstretched hand. She lunged toward them, but he held them out of reach.

"Why shouldn't I have you arrested for trespassing?"

She crossed her arms over her chest. "You don't even know what you've bought."

"I'm fairly sure it's an orchard, with a very ramshackle cabin in one corner. That's what the deed said, at least."

She gasped again. "You bought the cabin, too?"

"I did, and for much more than it was worth, but that's one of the risks of buying sight unseen."

"He built that cabin with his own hands when he homesteaded this place," Lorelei said.

"That explains the lack of amenities. Adding indoor plumbing and electricity is at the top of my list of things to do."

The man was confusing. "So you intend to stay? I thought you were going to sell."

"I can't sell the place as it is and make a profit. I'll be here for a time."

"How long?"

"Isn't that a rather personal question when we haven't even officially met? Why don't you tell me what's so important to you about this orchard?"

The apple in her pocket banged against her breastbone. Without Otto, if she were to have any hope of winning the Apple Pie Days contest she would need this man's cooperation. She shifted from side to side. Her toe was beginning to itch. She withdrew the apple from her pocket and balanced the golden fruit, kissed with a rosy hue on one side, on her palm.

"This is a Colorado Orange."

The stranger narrowed his eyes. "That's an apple."

"The *variety* of the apple is called Colorado Orange. Otto grafted these trees years ago from cuttings he brought from Fremont County. They're quite rare."

"What does that mean, in layman's terms?"

Lorelei cupped the apple in her palms, warming to her topic. "It means this variety of apple is unique and, I believe, particularly well suited for pies."

"So that gives you a license to steal them?"

She stared him down. She was not a thief. "Mr. Starkey was my silent partner."

A brisk breeze swirled through the orchard, sending dust and debris flying and making speech impossible. When the air settled around them, Lorelei tucked the apple back in her pocket.

"Partner in what?" Emmett asked.

"Mr. Starkey was helping me create a contest-winning pie."

"What contest?"

She blinked. "It's nothing."

"Seems like it's something to you."

Good grief, were all her thoughts revealed on her face? All her hopes for the future were pinned on winning the contest, but he didn't have to know that.

"Apple Pie Days is Rifle's annual festival. Every lady in town bakes six pies. People come from all around to enjoy free pie and coffee. An Apple Pie Days queen will be crowned, based on who has the best pie. I think I can win if I use Otto's apples."

His scrutiny burned like a brand. She resisted the urge to squirm.

"What do you get if you win?"

Lorelei dug her fingernails into the fleshy pads of her palms. Did the man ever stop asking questions?

"A lovely blue ribbon and the Apple Pie Days Queen title." She peered at him from beneath her lashes, unable to meet his straightforward blue gaze. How did you explain desperation to a stranger? He would think her real idea foolish, at best. An idea struck her. "It would increase the value of the orchard for you when you're ready to sell."

He lifted one eyebrow. "So you want to use my apples, and if you win this contest, it will benefit me when I sell the property?"

Could he not simply give her the apples and move along?

"Yes, I believe it would." She raised her chin. If he refused to cooperate, she'd come up with another plan. Silence stretched between them until her nerves zinged with tension.

"I'll think about letting you use my apples, if you'll allow me to give you a ride home."

Chapter 2

She had the most amazing face. Emmett watched the play of thoughts and emotions cross her features. It was like reading a living book.

"You do live around here, don't you?" he asked.

Her eyes narrowed in suspicion. "It's not far. I can walk."

Another gust of wind scoured the orchard, silencing them both.

"It's getting dark." He gestured toward the western horizon in full sunset. "You shouldn't be walking alone on the road this late."

"I don't even know your name."

"Nor I yours."

She examined him in the deepening twilight. He offered what he hoped was a trustworthy smile.

"Lorelei Boyd."

"A pleasure to meet you, Miss Boyd. My name is Emmett Dewey."

"Mr. Dewey." She pointed at her shoes. "May I have those, please?"

He extended his hand. She plucked her shoes from his grasp, plopped onto the dirt, yanked her balled-up stockings out of the toes, and put them on. Emmett averted his eyes to avoid staring at her slender ankles and shapely calves.

"My car is parked by the cabin."

"If I let you drive me home, I can use the apples?" she asked.

He held out his hand to help her up. She hesitated. To his surprise, she slipped her small, cool fingers into his palm. He pulled her to her feet then released her. He shoved his hand in his pocket, trying to ignore the tingle where their skin had met.

"It's a start," he replied. "I'm still thinking about it."

He thought he heard something like a growl from her throat.

"Fine," she muttered, stomping toward the cabin.

Emmett followed. He had to hurry to keep up on the half-mile jaunt. Had he not decided to walk through the orchard after a cursory examination of his latest acquisition, he wouldn't have heard or seen her. *She could have fallen and been injured*, he thought.

When she spotted his 1919 yellow Paige roadster, her sudden intake of breath swelled his pride. The car was his sole luxury, his splurge. Beyond basic expenses and the costs to renovate properties he bought, his profits were sent home to his mother.

"She's beautiful," Lorelei murmured, hands hovering over the sleek curve of the front fender.

"I think so." He opened the passenger door for her.

Miss Boyd trailed her slender fingers over every available surface in the interior, appreciation evident in her soft sigh and gentle touch. Emmett swallowed, unnerved by his response to this woman. He climbed into the driver's seat and shut the door with more force than he intended. "So, where's home?"

She pointed. "Two miles west, then take a left at the big stand of cottonwoods."

He started the engine. Reaching over, he popped open the glove box and withdrew two pairs of goggles. He handed Lorelei a pair. "You don't want a bug in your eye."

She put them on. "Thank you. I've already got a hornet sting on my toe. I'd rather avoid any more contact with insects this evening."

"A hornet sting?" he asked as he pulled on his goggles.

"Did you think I just fell from the tree?" Her tone was incredulous, as though the concept was inconceivable. "I was stung by a hornet."

Emmett shifted the car into gear and gave it some gas. "I've fallen from trees for lesser reasons," he replied, steering the automobile into a U-turn.

"I haven't."

They both fell silent. He had to drive slowly. The Paige wasn't designed for rural Colorado roads.

"Do you often go to the orchard alone?" he asked.

"Yes." She stared straight ahead, body tense, fingers curved around the door handle.

Questions raced through his mind. Was she married? Single? Didn't anyone care that she was out alone so late?

"Thank you for the ride. I appreciate it," she said. "It would have been a long walk in the dark."

"You're welcome. I'm sorry about your friend Otto." He thought she might be fighting tears, but when she spoke, her voice was strong.

"Me, too. I wish I'd had a chance to say good-bye." Otto had gone into town to see the dentist and collapsed. He'd died just a few hours later.

Emmett slowed at the stand of cottonwoods.

"You can let me out at the turn, if you'd like."

"What kind of gentleman only takes a lady partway home?"

Emmett steered the roadster onto a narrow dirt lane, slowing even more to navigate around the deeper potholes. He should have rented a truck or something else more suitable for the rural roads. He braked outside a modest single-story farmhouse with a wraparound porch. She slithered out of the passenger seat.

"Thank you for the ride," she called, already halfway up the porch steps. The door flung open, and light flooded out. Emmett blinked at the glare.

"Where have you been, young lady?" boomed a baritone voice in an accent Emmett couldn't place. "You know I don't like you out after dark alone."

"Sorry, Da. I was at the orchard." Miss Boyd attempted to slip past the bulky figure, but instead of letting her pass, the man stepped forward. Emmett's eyes adjusted to the light. He identified a bearlike man, thick in the middle, with arms that seemed too long for his body. While Miss Boyd had called him Da, Emmett couldn't see a single similarity.

"Lorelei, where are your manners? You could at least introduce the gentleman who brought you home in his automobile." The word *automobile* was spoken syllable by syllable.

Emmett shut off the engine. He steeled himself and got out of the car. Back straight, head up, he ascended the steps and extended his hand. "Emmett Dewey, sir."

The man engulfed Emmett's hand in his own. "Brian Boyd."

Emmett kept his expression mild, even though the bones in his hand were grinding together in the man's grip.

"Is that Lorelei?" Another voice rang from within the cozy confines of the farmhouse.

Emmett shoved his bruised hand into his pocket. A soft, round woman came into view, drying her hands on her apron. She had the same strawberry-blond curls as her daughter, hers sprinkled with white; the same smattering of freckles over nose and cheeks; and the same steady gray eyes.

"Child, you'll be the death of me." The woman wagged a reproving finger at her daughter.

Miss Boyd frowned. "Please don't say that, Momma." In a rush, she flung herself into her mother's arms. "Otto's family auctioned off his land."

Mr. Boyd peered at Emmett through small, dark eyes. "Is that true? The wee German fellow's family sold his orchard?"

Emmett nodded. "I bought the property at auction."

"Otto was a good man." Mr. Boyd shook his head. "I suppose I should thank you twice, once for bringing my daughter home and once for not having her arrested for trespassing."

"It's not a problem—"

"You'll join us for pie and coffee." It wasn't a request. "Maggie, dear, would you put on a fresh pot of coffee and take out Lorelei's pie for our new neighbor?"

"Of course, Brian." Mrs. Boyd patted her daughter's shoulder then leaned toward Emmett. "It's nice to meet you, young man. Thank you for bringing my girl home."

"You're welcome, ma'am."

Mr. Boyd clapped him on the back hard enough to make him suck air and propelled him inside after the ladies.

They took a sharp left into a warm kitchen. The men sat opposite each other at the scarred kitchen table while the women prepared cups of steaming coffee and plates of warm apple pie.

"So you've bought an orchard and a rattrap of a cabin." Mr. Boyd appraised Emmett. "Judging from that automobile, I wouldn't have pegged you for the orchard-owning type. Is this a new venture for you?"

"I intend to fix the place up and sell it for a profit," Emmett replied.

Mr. Boyd chuckled. "You might be better off to dismantle the cabin and start over from scratch."

Emmett rubbed his forehead. He'd thought the same when he first saw the place, but that would take far more time and expense than he was accustomed to investing on a single property. "What is it that you do, sir?"

Mr. Boyd flexed massive arms. "I came here from Wales to work the New Castle coal mines. After the second mine explosion in 1913, I bought land. I'm a sugar beet farmer now." He grinned. "My Welsh ancestors, all coal miners, are turning in their graves."

Emmett's own father had died in a Kentucky mine cave-in, leaving his mother to raise five small boys on her own. His three older brothers had followed their father's example: one died in an accident, one was ill with black lung disease at thirty, and one continued to pry coal out of the earth day after day, biding his time until the next disaster struck. Unwilling to perpetuate the tradition, Emmett had left home at sixteen to find his fortune. He'd done well for himself as an entrepreneur, and as a result, his youngest brother was currently at Princeton studying architecture.

"I'd say that was a wise choice, with a family to provide for," Emmett said.

"We do what we must for our womenfolk," Mr. Boyd agreed.

"And your womenfolk, in return, take care of you." Mrs. Boyd placed mugs of dark, rich coffee before them.

Miss Boyd followed, distributing plates laden with thick slices of apple pie. "This is number twenty-three," she said to her mother.

Emmett examined the pie. The crust was flaky and golden brown. Chunks of apple tumbled onto the plate, speckled with spices. He stabbed a piece of apple with his fork, added a bit of crust, and raised it to his mouth.

Delectable. He closed his eyes as flavors burst across his senses like fireworks: golden apple coupled with rich red cinnamon and clove and allspice and a surprising hint of citrus. It was reminiscent of the clove-studded oranges his mother had made every Christmas and surpassed all the apple pies he'd ever tasted. Delicious. Decadent. Delightful.

"So?"

His eyes sprang open. All three Boyds stared at him.

"It's excellent." He dabbed his mouth with a napkin Mrs. Boyd had passed him.

"Do you taste the citrus?" Miss Boyd asked.

"I do, yes. It's definitely different." Emmett swallowed his second bite, which was at least as good as the first.

A wide smile graced Miss Boyd's face. "That's the Colorado Orange from Otto's orchard."

"I think this one is a winner," her father said between bites.

Miss Boyd shook her head. "You say that about all of them."

Emmett swallowed his third bite. "What do you mean by 'number twenty-three'?"

"She's been working on the best recipe for Apple Pie Days next week. This is her twenty-third version." Mrs. Boyd said.

She speared Emmett with a steely gaze. "But without Otto's apples, it would be an ordinary apple pie."

Emmett's mind danced with possibilities, not the least of which was finding a way to see more of Miss Lorelei Boyd. He'd trained himself to see potential, to analyze opportunities, and to choose the course most likely to guarantee success. He took another bite. Lorelei Boyd's pies oozed with juicy potential. He wiped his mouth again and placed the napkin on the table.

"I tell you what, Miss Boyd. Now that I've tried your delicious pie, I'd like to consider affording you the use of my apples as your new silent partner."

Relief washed over her face. Then a frown creased her lovely forehead. "On what terms?"

She was sharp—something he appreciated.

He pushed back from the table. "I never make a business deal without sleeping on it."

"A wise practice." Mr. Boyd nodded his approval.

Mrs. Boyd sipped her coffee, her gaze shifting between Emmett and her daughter.

Emmett focused on Miss Boyd. "I'll come by to present my terms tomorrow."

Her frown remained. She hesitated so long he thought she might turn him down flat. When she finally murmured her agreement through pursed lips, he let out a breath he didn't know he'd been holding. So did her parents.

"Excellent," he said. "When is a good time for you?"

Mrs. Boyd stood and collected the empty plates and forks. "Why don't you come for lunch, around one o'clock?"

"Mother!" Lorelei hissed.

"I'd like that very much, ma'am. Thank you."

"Lunch it is," Mr. Boyd said, hefting his bulk out of the chair. "I'll see you out."

"Good night, Miss Boyd," Emmett said.

"Mr. Dewey." She was still frowning.

He followed Mr. Boyd to the porch, said a polite good evening, and got back in the Paige. On the drive back to his tiny room at the Clark Hotel, his mind whirred with possibilities.

Lorelei Boyd's pie was nothing short of amazing, worth far more than a blue ribbon and a title in a local contest. The excitement he sensed when he came upon a lucrative prospect stirred his senses. Usually that meant property of some sort in an excellent location, but he'd invested in other things over the years on a hunch, and those hunches had almost always benefited his bank account.

* * *

Lorelei rose before dawn, nerves abuzz over the terms—*ransom*—Emmett Dewey would demand for the use of "his" apples. She dragged on clean overalls, this pair blue-and-white-striped, over a plain white blouse. Her mother would urge her to put on a dress, but since Mr. Dewey—whose sparkling smile and beguiling dimples had invaded her dreams—had already seen her in her overalls, what was the point?

By the time the sun cast its light through the kitchen window, Lorelei was sifting flour into the speckled enamelware bowl she used for mixing piecrust.

Momma shuffled in, yawning. "My goodness, you're up bright and early."

"I want to have a fresh pie for lunch in case Mr. Dewey needs added encouragement to let me use Otto's apples." She squeezed the sifter handle faster, until flour flurried into the bowl like a miniature blizzard.

"Do you think he'll change his mind?"

Lorelei measured salt, dumped it into the bowl, and stirred the dry ingredients together. Then she pried the lid off the tin of lard. "How would I know? He's a perfect stranger, and now I have to partner with him on the most important thing I've ever done." She counted spoonfuls in her head as she scraped lard into the bowl.

Momma filled a cup with coffee from the pot on the stove and took the seat opposite her daughter. "Now, Lorelei, it's just a pie contest. It isn't life or death."

Lorelei pressed her lips together. She hadn't told her parents her real reason for wanting to win the contest. She used the tines of the fork to cut the lard into the salt and flour mixture. "Well, it's something I care about very much, and he doesn't care about the apples or the orchard."

Momma sipped from her cup. "It would seem he does. Have you prayed about it, Lorelei? Perhaps you're putting too much stock into this contest, allowing the idea of winning to become an idol in your mind."

Lorelei grimaced. She knew it probably looked like that from her mother's perspective. "I'm sorry, Momma. I should pray about it. Who knows?" She shoved a fist into the bowl of dough with unnecessary force. "Maybe Emmett Dewey is a godsend."

Momma smiled. "Perhaps he is, dear girl." She rose and put her cup beside the sink. "I need to get the eggs. One of the hens has turned into an egg eater. If I figure out which one it is, we'll be having chicken and dumplings for supper."

The back door banged shut after Momma. Lorelei kneaded the crust a few more times before turning the lump of dough onto the oilcloth. When she picked up her favorite rolling pin, she knocked loose a stack of envelopes that hadn't made it to her father's desk. She bent to pick them up. Cold dread prickled her flesh when she saw the return addresses. All six letters were from the bank.

They'd been getting letters for months. After the first few, her father stopped opening them. Curious, Lorelei had read one and discovered the bank was threatening to foreclose on the family's modest, forty-acre homestead if they didn't pay additional funds, citing incorrect paperwork and errors in establishing property value. For weeks after opening the letter, she'd mulled solutions. An article in *Ladies' Home Journal* about a woman who sold a cookie recipe to a high-end restaurant inspired a plan to sell a winning pie recipe for enough money to save the farm.

Lorelei shoved the letters back into place. Whatever Emmett Dewey's terms were, she would agree to them because Otto's apples were the secret to winning the contest.

"Is something wrong?"

Lorelei jumped at the sound of her mother's voice. "No. Just tired."

Momma transferred the morning's eggs from her apron to a wooden bowl on the Hoosier cabinet. "None of the eggs had holes pecked in them today, so maybe that hen was being temperamental."

Lorelei offered her mother a benign smile. "We can hope so. Da gets cranky when he doesn't have his fresh eggs in the morning."

Chapter 3

Emmett paced the post office corridor, hat in hand, waiting for Jimmy's reply. He'd met Jimmy Clarke in Chicago five years earlier. The two had become long-distance friends. Now he hoped that friendship would come in handy for Jimmy, and for Miss Lorelei Boyd, who had haunted Emmett's dreams the night before.

"Telegram for Mr. Emmett Dewey." The postmaster's voice echoed through the empty halls. Emmett shook his head. The man was less than ten feet away, and Emmett was the only other person in the building. As he took the telegram, he thanked the elderly gentleman. He moved to the front window to read Jimmy's reply:

SOUNDS LIKE A WINNER *Stop* GLAD YOU REMEMBERED I WAS LOOKING FOR NEW RECIPES *Stop* MEET YOU THERE NEXT WEEK *Stop* JIMMY *Stop*

Emmett grinned. Now he had to convince Lorelei Boyd to sell her prized apple pie recipe to the largest lunch-counter chain in America. But he would wait until after the contest.

━━━━◆●◆━━━━

Lorelei stirred crispy bits of crumbled bacon into fresh steamed green beans.

"Trying to impress the young man?" Momma asked from her seat at the kitchen table, which was already set for lunch. "You know your father and I are content with salt and a dab of butter."

Lorelei made a face. "We had some bacon left over from breakfast, that's all." Was she trying to impress him? Maybe she was because she needed those apples, but she thought her mother suspected she had different motives. She wiped her hands on her apron. Maybe she should change into a dress.

Da boomed into the kitchen.

"Look who's here already!"

Lorelei's head turned toward her father and their visitor.

Mr. Dewey tapped his hat against his thigh and smiled. *Oh, those dimples.* Lorelei blinked and looked away. She blanched cold then flushed hot. Tiny beads of sweat peppered her forehead. She swiped at them with the back of her hand, appalled that she would react so strongly to Emmett Dewey's presence.

"Welcome, Mr. Dewey. It's good to see you again," Momma said, rising. "Can I get you something to drink?" In her gracious way, she didn't mention his early arrival.

"No thank you, ma'am. Mr. Boyd has offered to give me a local tour before lunch."

His voice was deep and smooth like the sweetest custard, with its slow Southern drawl.

"I suppose you're taking your car, Mr. Dewey?" she asked.

"Why, yes," Mr. Dewey replied, brows drawing together in confusion.

Lorelei stared at her father. Da's chin dropped to his chest. He turned a dark red—she knew from whom she'd inherited her tendency to blush. Lorelei smothered a grin. Da loved all things mechanical. She wasn't surprised he'd finagled a ride in Emmett Dewey's fancy automobile.

"Why don't you come along?" Mr. Dewey asked. "If it's all right with your father, of course."

Startled, Lorelei caught Emmett's bold, blue gaze. A shiver rippled down her spine.

"Me? No, I can't." She searched her mind for a reason to refuse while her heart clamored for another ride in that beautiful car. "I have a pie to bake."

He took a step forward. "We can wait."

"That's an excellent idea," Da said. "Come along, Mr. Dewey, I'll show you everything there is to know about sugar beets. By the time we're done, Lorelei will have that pie in the oven." Da patted his daughter's arm, kissed Momma's cheek, and herded Mr. Dewey out the front door before Lorelei could ask what he'd decided about Otto's apples.

------ ◦●◦ ------

With surgical precision, Lorelei made three identical slits in the top crust before sliding the pie into the oven and latching the door. This particular recipe, number twenty-four, might be the winning combination. She'd blended her grandmother's no-fail, award-winning crust with a filling compiled from Otto's suggestions, her mother's recipes, and a hundred-year-old cookbook she'd unearthed in an abandoned barn.

Lorelei pulled her journal from a shelf, opened it to the next blank page, and scribbled the unique combination of ingredients she'd used under a heading of "Twenty-Four." When she was done, she flipped back through the pages, scanning what she'd written.

She'd rated every version with stars from one to five, along with detailed notes about taste and texture. Thus far, none of her efforts had earned five stars, despite her parents' ebullient praise of every pie she produced. She turned to the beginning of the book and reread the words she'd scribbled on the flyleaf.

Nothing is impossible with God.

Winning the Apple Pie Days contest and having an award-winning recipe to sell was the only way Lorelei could see to save her family.

Footsteps interrupted her thoughts.

Lorelei looked up. Mr. Dewey stood in the kitchen doorway. Her pulse quickened.

"Your father wanted to know how long until you were ready to leave."

Lorelei slapped the journal shut with a snap. "I'm ready. I'll ask my mother to take the pie out when it's done."

He smiled. "We'll be out front."

She tucked the journal into its place on the shelf.

"Momma?" she called.

"Yes?" Momma replied from one of the back rooms.

"Will you take the pie out for me? I'll set the timer. I'm going with Da and Mr. Dewey."

"Of course, dear."

Lorelei set the dial on the wall-mounted timer, tossed her apron over the peg behind the kitchen door, and hurried outside. She squeezed into the middle of the roadster's front seat between her father and Mr. Dewey, who offered them goggles. Da refused, saying he liked the wind in his face. Lorelei put them on. She chuckled at her bug-eyed reflection in the tiny rearview mirror, causing Mr. Dewey to smile and her to flush with pleasure.

———◦●◦———

Emmett's hands trembled when he wrapped them around the steering wheel. Lorelei Boyd's effect on him hadn't diminished overnight. If anything, he was now painfully aware of her, pressed against his right side from shoulder to hip in the front seat of the roadster.

As they drove, following Mr. Boyd's erratic directions, Miss Boyd talked about the local residents. Opal Roberts's baby was due any day. The Raley family was having a barn raising the following weekend. Ancient Mr. Green was moving in with his son and daughter-in-law. Emmett envied her connection to her neighbors, to community.

When they braked outside the Boyds' home after their tour, the acrid odor of scorched apple pie tainted the air. Lorelei flung herself out of the car with a shriek and raced into the house.

"That doesn't bode well for lunch," murmured Mr. Boyd.

"As long as lunch involves more than pie, we should be all right." Emmett opened his door and stepped out of the car.

"You don't understand," Mr. Boyd explained as they fell into step. "Winning the pie contest has become everything to her. You'd think her life depended on it."

Inside they found Miss Boyd and her mother on opposite sides of the table, a blackened apple pie between them like a coffin awaiting its pallbearers.

"It's my fault," Mrs. Boyd said to her husband. "She asked me to take it out of the oven. I didn't hear the timer."

"It's all right, Momma. I'll make another."

"You're out of apples."

Miss Boyd groaned.

"Perhaps Mr. Dewey could run you down to his new orchard and collect some more?" Mrs. Boyd suggested.

Three pairs of eyes focused on Emmett. "I'd be happy to do that, if it would help you out."

Miss Boyd shot him a wary glance. "Momma, could you mix up another crust?"

"Of course." Mrs. Boyd dusted her hands on her apron. "Mr. Dewey, I'm afraid you'll have to stay for supper."

Miss Boyd's gaze snapped to her mother then back to Emmett, who blinked and swallowed. Miss Boyd did not look like she welcomed the invitation.

"I don't want to make a nuisance of myself, ma'am."

"Nonsense." Mrs. Boyd waved a dismissive hand. "We're glad for the company."

"I'll need to get those apples started soon if we're to have pie in time for supper." Miss

Boyd gave him a wide berth on her way out of the kitchen.

"I made up some sandwiches for you to take along." Mrs. Boyd reached for a small basket on the table and passed it to Emmett.

"Thank you very much, ma'am." Emmett hurried after Miss Boyd.

Chapter 4

Miss Boyd was silent on the ride to the orchard. At the cabin, Emmett switched off the engine. He leaped out and hurried around to open her door.

"Thank you," she said.

He helped her out of the car. "You're welcome."

"Have you made a decision? About the apples?"

"I have. But I would prefer to share the terms of my offer after dinner."

Her lips compressed into a flat, thin line.

"I'm going to eat what your mother sent along." He plucked the basket out of the car and flipped back the calico napkin. Inside he found two sandwiches wrapped in waxed paper, a mason jar full of lemonade, and two cookies. He handed one of the sandwiches to Miss Boyd.

"I don't understand how my mother could forget about the pie and still remember to make sandwiches she didn't know we'd need," Miss Boyd muttered, unwrapping the sandwich. "Eat fast. I need to get back soon if we're to have a pie today."

"How many pies have you made to prepare for this contest, Miss Boyd?" Emmett unwrapped his own sandwich and took a bite. His brain went blank. Toasted slices of homemade bread wrapped around tangy egg salad. Maybe the best egg salad he'd ever had. He might be able to get Jimmy to buy Mrs. Boyd's egg salad recipe, too.

Miss Boyd chewed and swallowed. "I've made a lot. I'll make as many as it takes." She took another bite then rewrapped the remainder and dropped it into the basket. "Let's get to it. The best trees are on the other side of the orchard."

He followed her through a pathetic excuse for a gate dangling on a single broken hinge. A brisk breeze cooled the air, warning of autumn's impending arrival, reminding Emmett he intended to be gone before winter, off to California or Mexico or somewhere else warm and sunny.

The orchard was a less peaceful setting than he'd envisioned when he signed the paperwork. Hornets and yellow jackets gorged on fallen fruit. Flocks of starlings squawked their disapproval at being interrupted from their feasting. The sickly sweet smell of decaying fruit filled the air.

When she reached for the rickety ladder she'd been using the day before, he laid a hand on her arm.

"You can't use this. It's not safe."

"I've been using this for months."

"Isn't there a better one around here?"

She laughed. "Have you looked at this place? Everything is at least thirty years old. I think the ladder is one of Otto's newer purchases."

"Then I'll climb. You can direct me to the apples you want."

She eyed him with unabashed skepticism. "You're going to climb trees in your suit?"

He shrugged out of his jacket and draped it over a branch. "There. I'm at least as ready to climb trees as I was when I was a boy."

She laughed again. He liked the sound.

"I can't picture you as a boy."

"I was a terror."

"I bet you were," she murmured.

She stopped beneath a squat tree and craned her neck to inspect the fruit overhead. "These look good." She stretched on tiptoe for one particular apple, but it was out of reach.

Emmett gripped her around the waist and boosted her into the air like a ballerina. The apple popped off its tether. He lowered her to the spongy ground.

She held out the fruit. "Perfect."

Yes, she was. He inhaled sharply. She was also an unexpected complication.

* * *

Lorelei tried to keep her head from spinning off her shoulders and into the clouds. Her flesh tingled where he'd touched her, and her legs were weak. Was she coming down with something?

He plucked the apple from her palm and rubbed it against his shirt until the rosy-gold skin glistened. "Can I eat it?" he asked. "Or do they all have to be saved for pies?"

"Go ahead." She gestured at the fruit-laden branches. "This is the best crop Otto ever had. He would have been proud." Her eyes prickled with unshed tears.

Emmett bit into the apple with a satisfying crunch. A smile spread across his handsome face as he chewed. "Excellent," he mumbled.

"I've forgotten a bag for the fruit. I'll run back to the cabin. Otto kept a stash of old flour sacks on hand," she said.

"I'll do it." He swiped a drop of juice off his chin with the back of his hand. "While I'm gone, you decide which apples you want." He took another bite and strode toward the cabin on long legs that ate up the distance.

Envisioning the dapper gentleman as a wild little boy brought a smile to her mouth.

Don't get used to having help, Lorelei. He's a short-timer. Focus. There's more at stake here than a handsome man who plans on leaving as soon as he can make a profit.

She sat on the ground, careful to avoid squishy apples and hornets—her toe still throbbed—to remove her shoes and stockings. With muscles honed by years of experience, she hauled herself into the arboreal realm where she'd spent much of her childhood. She was, in some ways, more comfortable in the branches of a tree than she was on terra firma.

She scooted from one branch to the next until she found one that gave her perfect access to a swath of fruit untouched by birds, insects, mule deer, or the voracious ground squirrels that inhabited the region. She straddled the branch, thankful for her overalls, and began plucking apples and tucking them into her pockets.

She'd expected to hear him return, so when he cleared his throat just below her, she shrieked, clutching the branch to keep from falling. Apples tumbled out of her pockets, pelting his head and shoulders.

"Ouch!" He jumped back, rubbing his scalp.

Lorelei sucked in air. "Stop sneaking up on me!"

He scowled at her. "I wasn't trying to sneak up on you. Maybe you need your hearing checked."

She returned his glare. "My hearing is fine." She glanced at the apples that had fallen. "Did you find a bag?"

He raised one arm, dangling not one but two grubby canvas sacks from his hand. "I told you I could do the climbing."

"I saw no reason to wait for you, and"—she ignored his disapproving look—"I found a perfect branch to pick from. Can you hold one of those bags open?"

"As long as you promise not to bean me with any more apples." He rubbed his head again.

She chuckled. "No guarantees. I climb trees well, but my aim is terrible."

"I guess if I want more pie I'll have to take the risk."

He dropped one sack on the ground by her shoes and used both hands to hold the other one open. Lorelei pulled the remaining apples from her pockets and began loading the bag. When her pockets were empty, she reached for more fruit from the surrounding branches, using her legs for balance.

"This spot is cleared. I need to switch." She scooted back to the trunk and shimmied to the ground. The full sack sat beside her boots, but Mr. Dewey was gone. She rotated. The man moved like a ghost.

"Up here," called a deep voice.

A shiver rippled down her spine. She jerked her head up. He was perched on a branch in the next tree, exactly where she would have gone. She'd never met a grown man who could—or would—climb trees.

And he did it for her.

When they returned to the car, Mr. Dewey scooted the bags of apples to one side to make room for her feet. It was a sweet gesture.

He opened her door, waited for her to get in, then rounded the front of the car and slid behind the steering wheel.

"Have you considered what you're going to do with the rest of the harvest this year? It's a shame to let it go to waste," she said.

The engine roared to life. "I hadn't thought about it. Do you have any suggestions?"

Lorelei inhaled, surprised he would ask for her opinion. "A few families around here are really struggling right now. If they could come in as gleaners, it would help them."

"That's not a bad idea," Mr. Dewey replied. The car lurched forward, and the wind hit her face.

Chapter 5

Emmett carried both bags of apples through the back door into the kitchen, muscles protesting after his unaccustomed activity in the orchard. He looked at Miss Boyd. "Where do you want these?"

"Over there." She pointed to an empty spot on the floor near the sink. "I appreciate the help."

Standing up, he brushed his hands on his trousers. "I enjoyed it. It's been years since I had a reason to climb a tree."

Mrs. Boyd came into the kitchen. "Would you care for some iced tea, Mr. Dewey?" She squeezed her daughter's shoulders with one arm and Miss Boyd leaned into her. Emmett swallowed, missing his mother. He was long overdue for a visit home.

"If it's no trouble, ma'am."

"Momma, I need the table. I've got to prepare these apples if we're to have pie before midnight," Miss Boyd said.

"We'll take our tea to the porch, dear. We won't be in your way." Mrs. Boyd faced Emmett. "Mr. Boyd's out there now, if you'd like to join him."

Emmett found Mr. Boyd on the porch swing, feet propped on the railing, eyes closed, and head back. Emmett took a seat in a nearby chair. "Long day, sir?"

Mr. Boyd's eyes flickered open. "I've the gout. Had to come in before I was finished."

Emmett made a sympathetic sound. "Do you have help?"

"I've got a couple local boys. And we usually hire a crew for harvest."

Emmett frowned. He'd seen the fields of sugar beets today, frothy green tops marching along in tidy rows. Twenty-five of the forty-acre parcel was in sugar beets. It was a lot of work for one man and some part-time helpers.

Mrs. Boyd shouldered the door open, carrying a tray with tall glasses of iced tea garnished with sprigs of mint. Emmett took one. She handed one to her husband and took a seat next to him.

Mr. Boyd kissed his wife's cheek. "You're a good woman, Mary Margaret Boyd."

Her blush took ten years off her face. She turned eagle eyes on Emmett. "So, Mr. Dewey, tell us what brought you to the wilds of western Colorado."

He opened his mouth to reply, and the door opened.

"Momma, where's the crust you made?"

"I put it in the icebox. Here. . ." Mrs. Boyd pushed up and bustled through the door after her daughter.

The men sat in silence for a time, sipping tea and listening to the magpies and redwing blackbirds chattering in the cottonwoods behind the house. When Mrs. Boyd reappeared with her daughter in tow, Emmett smiled at them both.

"Now, where were we?" Mrs. Boyd retook her place on the swing. "You were about to tell us where you were from."

"I'm from Kentucky, ma'am. My family settled there before Daniel Boone came through. Coal miners." He nodded toward Mr. Boyd.

"So how did you find your way here?" Miss Boyd hopped up to sit on the porch rail, feet dangling.

"I left home at sixteen, ended up in Florida, and made a connection with a real estate broker who helped me get started. I made some money and headed west, state by state. In short, I buy property—mostly at auction—improve it, and sell it for a profit. I follow the property auctions."

Miss Boyd's eyes narrowed. "You're an opportunist."

He dipped his head. "You could say that."

Mrs. Boyd frowned. "Mr. Otto's property, you bought it to sell it again?"

He nodded. "Yes, ma'am. Once I fix it up a bit."

Mr. Boyd snorted. "More than a 'bit,' I think."

Emmett chuckled. "It is pretty rough. I'll start working on it this week. I ordered some things from the hardware store this morning."

"You do your own construction?" Mr. Boyd asked, brows lifted.

"I do, for the most part."

"And once you sell the property?" Mrs. Boyd asked. "Then what will you do?"

"Move on. Head to California or Arizona for the winter, look for more opportunities there." He glanced at Miss Boyd. She looked away.

"Don't you want to settle down? Have a place to call home?"

Emmett flinched. He did want that. Someday. His mother regularly asked him if he'd found a place to "land" and a girl to "settle" him. Again and again he told her no. But now he felt the first stirrings of change.

Chapter 6

The meal was excellent, but the pie was exquisite.

The Boyds deluged their daughter with praise. Her pie was amazing, the filling incomparable, the best they'd ever had. They wiped their mouths and gushed.

Emmett worked his way through his piece silently. Miss Boyd's focus on him was like sunbeams through a magnifying glass while he scooped up a new bite, chewed, and swallowed. He repeated this process until his plate was empty. When he finished the final morsel, he laid his fork down and dabbed his mouth with the cotton calico napkin Mrs. Boyd had provided.

"It's good," he said. The Boyds sighed with relief.

Miss Boyd leaned toward him. "It's good, but what? What's missing? I know something is missing. More cinnamon? More nutmeg? Clove?"

Emmett pushed his chair back. "I said it's good."

"But it's not good enough," Miss Boyd insisted. "What would make it perfect?"

Emmett closed his eyes and considered. "Is there such a thing as a perfect pie?"

Chairs scraped across the floor, and he heard footsteps leaving the room. When he opened his eyes, her parents were gone. Miss Boyd's eyes glittered, chips of volatile shale.

"What would make this one"—she waved a hand over the remaining pieces in the dish—"better?" Leaning toward him, she whispered in a conspiratorial tone, "You saw how my parents responded."

He nodded.

"That's how they react to every pie. Every. Single. Pie. It doesn't matter what it looks like, what it tastes like, or what I put in it. I could probably switch the sugar with salt and they'd still gush."

"They love you."

She rolled her eyes, which were fringed with dark lashes. A testament to her father's Welsh origins, Emmett surmised.

"And I love them, too, but for this I don't need a pat on the head. I need an honest opinion."

Emmett looked at her. *Honesty, eh? All right.* "The pie is delicious. Yesterday's pie was delicious. I'd be willing to bet all your pies are delicious."

"So will you let me use Otto's—your—apples to win the contest? Are you willing to take Otto's place as my silent partner?" she asked.

"Will you agree to my terms?"

She crossed her arms over her chest. "What terms?"

Emmett took a deep breath. "I want a sample slice of every pie you make between now and the festival."

"All right."

Emmett held up one hand, palm out. "And one more thing."

She grimaced. "I knew that was too easy."

"I get to decide which pie recipe you enter in the contest."

Gray eyes widened then narrowed to slits. "Why?"

He considered his answer. He didn't want to tell her about Jimmy or his notion that her pie recipe was saleable, lest she get her hopes up and then be disappointed.

"Because they're your apples?" A rosy flush mottled her fair neck and cheeks.

He stretched a conciliatory hand across the table. "Listen, you're right. If your pie wins the contest, the property value of Otto's orchard will increase. I want to be involved in the process. You can understand that, right?"

— ⬥●●⬥ —

Oh, she understood. It was all about the money. But for him it was adding some extra zeros to his plump bank account. For her, it was survival.

Should she tell him her parents' property was in danger of foreclosure? Would he change the terms of their silent partnership? Her mind raced, recalling his words. He was an opportunist. He'd admitted it. If he knew their farm—which bordered Otto's on one side—was in trouble, he was liable to run straight to the bank and snatch it up for himself. She looked around the familiar kitchen and pushed down her panic.

"I'll bring you a sample of each pie and allow you to choose which recipe I enter in the contest," she said. And then, mimicking him, she held up one hand, palm out. "But that's all I'll agree to. Your name will not be on my contest entry. My entry will be mine alone."

He smiled.

Lorelei blinked. "What are you grinning about?"

"You're a formidable negotiator, Miss Boyd. That's a skill I appreciate."

A smile flickered around her mouth, but she stifled it. "So we're in agreement, then?"

"We are."

She gestured toward the remaining pie in the dish. "So what about number twenty-four? What's wrong with it? Is it something with the crust, or with the filling? I know it's not the apples."

That made him laugh. She had such incredible faith in the Colorado Orange and so little in her own ability.

"I've only tried two of your pies. That's not a good basis for comparison."

"But what do *you* think?" She gripped his forearm. "Am I on the right track?"

Her desperation was tangible. He understood competition and wanting to win, but her intensity bordered on obsession. He chose his words with care.

"I believe if you continue to produce such excellent samples, your chances of winning any apple pie contest are excellent."

She averted her gaze and released his arm. "I hope you're right," she murmured, more to herself than to him.

"Have faith, Miss Boyd. Your pies are excellent."

She blinked. "Thank you." For a beat their eyes met and held. "I usually bake in the morning, so I'll bring your sample tomorrow afternoon after lunch."

"I'll look forward to seeing you." He stood. "And now I should get going. Thank you for your hospitality."

He bid good evening to her parents, who were snuggled together on the porch swing like newlyweds.

He thought about the Boyds on his drive back to his empty hotel room. Mrs. Boyd had asked him if he wanted to settle down. He did, someday. That was how he answered his mother when she asked him about it, every time he spoke to her.

He genuinely liked Lorelei Boyd. But his lifestyle, his livelihood, would force him to leave her behind in a matter of weeks. And that was what he wanted, wasn't it?

Lorelei pulled pie number twenty-five out of the oven. She placed it on the table to cool and took off her apron.

"I feel terrible that you are only taking Mr. Dewey a piece of pie. Why don't I make him a lunch?" Momma said, coming into the kitchen.

"No, Momma. This is a business deal, that's all."

"But he seems like such a nice young man. And handsome, too."

"That's neither here nor there."

"So you don't deny it?"

"Are you testing my vision? Of course, he's handsome, but—"

"Who's handsome?" Da interrupted.

Lorelei's face flamed. "Nothing, Da. Momma is being silly. I'm going to walk down to the orchard and deliver Mr. Dewey's pie after lunch. And then I'll probably stop to visit Opal."

"All right, dear."

"You be cautious, Lorelei. There's been talk of vagrants in the area again. Be back before dark."

Lorelei shuddered, thinking how easily Mr. Dewey had come upon her in the orchard. "I'll be careful, Da."

Chapter 7

With less than a week until the festival, Lorelei's days fell into a pattern. She rose early, did her chores, tweaked her latest recipe, and baked the day's pie. After lunch, she packed a piece of pie for Mr. Dewey and walked to the cabin.

Today she spotted him on the roof, unrolling tar paper over the places where he'd removed rotted shingles. His sleeves, rolled up past his elbows, exposed strong forearms as he wielded a shiny new hammer. She shaded her eyes with one hand and watched him. She hadn't expected an opportunist to be such a hard worker. But then, many of the things she'd learned about Emmett Dewey were unexpected.

Their daily visits afforded opportunities to chat, either before or after he critiqued the day's pie, and every day he had surprised her with his wit, his intellect, and his faith.

"Hello!" she called out. "Do you want to take a break?"

He stopped, hammer in midswing, and turned. When he saw her, he smiled and waved. "Perfect timing! I'll be right down."

Good grief, she could see those dimples from a distance.

He unrolled the last bit of tar paper and tacked it down before swinging over the side of the roof onto a shiny new ladder. She met him beside a small folding table and chairs, which had been delivered with the ladder. She placed the container with his slice of pie on the table while he washed his hands at the cistern spigot.

"So, what's special about number thirty-six?" he asked, smoothing his hair off his forehead with damp fingers. He always asked, which surprised her. And he remembered what she said, which surprised her more. It was as if he took a genuine interest in the process. Or maybe he was interested in her? She set that notion aside as unbelievable.

"I adjusted the cinnamon, as you suggested, and added a tiny bit of molasses as an experiment," she said, taking a seat opposite him.

He picked up his fork and took his first bite. He chewed, closed his eyes, chewed some more, and swallowed.

"Nope. The molasses takes away from the distinct flavor of the apples," he said. "It's good, don't get me wrong, but this isn't your winner."

She sighed. "I thought so, too."

He finished the piece of pie and stretched. "Listen, I'm done for the day. Can I give you a ride home?"

"Driving me home wasn't part of our contract," Lorelei said.

"Doesn't have to be part of a contract," Emmett drawled. "I'd like to take you home." The dimples appeared, and she couldn't help but acquiesce.

Lorelei's heart pounded when she approached the cabin the next day. She had a sample of pie number thirty-seven in one hand and two fishing poles in the other.

She'd protested her da's suggestion. Emmett Dewey was an opportunist, she'd insisted, and he was headed out of town as soon as he could sell Otto's place for a profit. Her father had frowned, his thick black brows forming a V. The young man was alone in a strange place and deserved kindness and friendship, he said. When Momma chimed in with the scripture about being kind to strangers who might be angelic visitors, Lorelei yielded, mostly to silence her parents.

Emmett came out of the shed, brushing cobwebs and dust off his clothes in a choking cloud.

"Are you all right?" she asked.

He looked up, startled. "I'm fine. I upended what I thought was an empty box." He swiped a hand over his face. His eyes brightened at the sight of the fishing poles. "You going fishing?"

She swallowed the nervous lump in her throat. "My da thought you might want to go along. He said you told him you missed fishing."

A broad smile spread across Emmett's face. "I haven't been fishing in years. I'd love to join you."

She propped the fishing poles against a tree and handed him his slice of pie. "No molasses today, and a little more lemon zest, as you suggested."

Emmett was impressed by Miss Boyd's ability to unearth worms and drop the wriggling creatures into an empty can.

"Where to?" he asked once they were in the car, fishing poles poking above the seats. She gave him directions to the river.

The waters of the Colorado River were far different from the Mississippi and Ohio Rivers he was accustomed to. White-capped rapids alternated with smooth, still places where, Miss Boyd informed him, the undercurrent was dangerous.

He followed her through a marshy stretch of willows. She stopped at a small clearing on the bank where wide, flat rocks offered perches.

"This is a good spot," he said, watching her settle onto a rock near the edge and begin to prepare her pole.

"It's my favorite," she said. "Sometimes I just come down here to sit and watch the river. It's hard to believe this water will end up in the ocean."

She had that dreamy look again. The one that made Emmett wonder what she was thinking. "Have you ever been to the ocean, Miss Boyd?"

"No. But I'd like to see it someday," she said.

They both fell silent. Emmett found himself thinking he'd like to be the one to show Miss Boyd the ocean for the first time. She yawned and stretched.

"Tired?" he asked.

"Thinking about the contest has been keeping me awake at night."

Thinking about *her* had been keeping him awake at night. He was watching her when his fishing line went taut. The pole, which he'd been holding in one relaxed hand, flew into the water. He lunged and caught it just before it bobbed downstream but lost his balance in the process. He hit the water face-first, arms outstretched, with a splash.

The water was deeper than he'd expected, and shockingly cold. He floundered, keeping hold of the pole, and struggled to find his footing. When he got his feet under him on the slippery rocks, he turned and headed back toward the bank.

Lorelei had propped her pole in the sandy soil and hurried to where he had toppled into the river. Her hands were pressed against her mouth, as if in horror, but her gray eyes danced with mirth. It took him a moment to realize she was laughing at him.

He strode through the water with some difficulty, tossed the pole, with its empty line, to the bank—the trout had made a break for it during Emmett's gyrations—and reached for Miss Lorelei Boyd.

She squealed when he tugged her against his cold, soggy frame, river water soaking them both. She put both hands against his chest and pushed back, but he bent his head and pressed his mouth to hers.

After a moment her hands slipped around his neck, and she drew him in for a deeper kiss. Her response caught him off guard, so when her hands moved back to his chest and shoved, he was unprepared. He tumbled backward but managed to catch her by the wrist and pull her into the water with him.

They came up sputtering, spitting river water. Together they struggled back to the riverbank and collapsed, dripping muddy water.

"I'm sorry," Emmett said, once he caught his breath.

"For kissing me?"

Caught off guard again, he stilled. "No. I'm sorry for drenching you." He reached for her hand, streaked with mud, and raised it to his lips. "I'm not at all sorry for kissing you, Lorelei." Her name rolled off his tongue like sweet, golden honey, making him want to say it all over again.

"Oh." She brushed water off her face with her hand. "Oh," she repeated. Then she shoved up to her feet. "We should get back."

Emmett rose as well, feet unsteady in the soft ground. "I didn't mean to make you uncomfortable."

She met his gaze. "You didn't make me uncomfortable, but I think we should get back." Her color was high, and he was somewhat gratified to realize she was as affected by their kiss as he had been. "You wouldn't want to start something you can't finish," she said, and before he could come up with a retort, she whirled, snatched up her pole, and strode away through the willows.

— ⋅◗●◖⋅ —

Lorelei fixed her attention on the road ahead as Emmett—he was now Emmett in her mind, not Mr. Dewey—drove her home. If she looked at him, all she could think about was kissing him. And finding a way to kiss him again.

It's good that he's leaving soon, she told herself. *Lest I wind up heartbroken and pathetic.*

Emmett parked in the drive. As he helped her out of the car, Mrs. Boyd burst onto the porch. "Oh Lorelei, we've got trouble."

"What's the matter?"

"The boys your father hired to help have the mumps. Their uncle came by to let us know."

Da hobbled onto the porch. "It's fine, Maggie darling. I can manage without them."

Momma's gaze shifted from Lorelei to Emmett. "Why are you both all wet?"

"We fell in the river," Lorelei said. "Da, we'll hire a few more workers. We can put an advertisement in the *Rifle Reveille*."

Emmett cleared his throat. "I'd be happy to help out."

Two pairs of dove-gray eyes turned toward him, reflecting relief and suspicion.

"I can't do much at my place." He shrugged. That wasn't entirely true. He could fix the listing gate, and mend the fences, and clean up the pathways and outbuildings. But he knew when God was nudging him, and helping the Boyds in a time of need felt right.

Da extended a hand. "That would be much appreciated, Mr. Dewey. And I'd be glad to return the favor."

Emmett shook the man's beefy hand. "Thank you, sir."

Chapter 8

Rosy light caressed the eastern horizon when Emmett parked the Paige at the Boyds' house again. Fatigue dogged him. He'd spent much of the night questioning God's leading. He never got involved. He came in, improved property value, and left town with the profits in his pocket. Yet here he was, inserting himself into the life of this family, kissing their daughter. . . . It was as if he was planning on sticking around. And that wasn't the case. Was it?

Mr. Boyd sat on the porch, a steaming mug of coffee in one hand and his gouty foot propped on the railing.

"Good morning, sir."

"I didn't expect to see you until midmorning at best." Mr. Boyd chuckled and then scanned Emmett from head to toe. "But before we get started, Lorelei will find you some suitable clothes."

"What was that, Da?" Lorelei asked, drying her hands on an embroidered kitchen towel as she approached the screen door.

Emmett cleared his throat. "I work in these every day, sir. I'm sure it will be fine."

Mr. Boyd dismissed him with a wave of his hand. "Find this fellow some overalls, would you, Lorelei?"

Emmett flinched under Lorelei's inspection. She held the door open and waved him inside. "This way." He followed her into the house, past the parlor and kitchen, and toward the back rooms. He caught a glimpse of Lorelei's room, with a colorful quilt on the bed and dried flowers pinned to the walls. She led him into her parents' room—a utilitarian affair that smelled faintly of liniment—and opened an armoire. From its recesses she dragged a pair of faded canvas overalls and a checkered flannel shirt that had seen better days.

He took the clothes, conscious of the fragrance of the soap flakes the Boyds used for their laundry. He'd smelled the same scent when he'd caught Lorelei in the orchard.

"Boots?" She interrupted his reverie.

"They're in my car."

"I'll go grab them for you while you change."

"Thanks."

She marched out of the bedroom and closed the door. The overalls and shirt were too big, but Emmett rolled up the sleeves and the pant legs. Catching a glimpse of himself in the cheval mirror, he smiled wryly. The last time he'd worn overalls, he'd been a gangly, awkward twelve-year-old convinced he could make a career out of his proficiency with a slingshot.

He folded his regular work clothes into a neat bundle and padded back to the kitchen in his socks, nearly colliding with Lorelei when he rounded the corner.

They both stepped back. She held out his boots. "I was expecting shiny new ones."

He took the scuffed work boots from her hand. "I've had these a long time. They come in handy." He didn't know why he was explaining himself. Most women were more impressed by his usual attire—fancy suits and shiny shoes—than by his old boots.

"Have you ever abandoned a project?"

Was she hoping he would quit work at Otto's and leave? He pulled out one of the cane-backed kitchen chairs and sat down.

"No," he replied, lacing one boot. "Although, I once purchased a building in Florida near the Everglades. When I arrived to start work, I found a six-foot alligator asleep in the sun, blocking the entrance."

She gasped. "An alligator?"

He nodded, picked up his other boot. "I hired local fellas to come in and do the necessary work at twice their normal rate. It was worth it."

"I would say so!" She busied herself with something at the apron-fronted sink, her back to him. "How many properties have you...owned?"

He tucked his laces into the top of the boots, counting in his head. "A dozen, I think. Give or take a few." He looked up. She was staring out the kitchen window, slender fingers drumming rhythmically against the edge of the sink. "What are you thinking?"

"What is it like to buy and sell land the way a grocer buys and sells eggs?" She faced him. Fine lines of tension on her forehead and around her lovely mouth revealed more than she said aloud.

"It's not quite that simple."

"Oh, I'm sure it's not. I just wondered. . . ." Her voice trailed off.

Were the Boyds in financial trouble? Or was Lorelei simply daydreaming? The farmhouse around him was clean and well maintained but small. He could understand a young woman imagining what it would be like to have more. He had spent much of his youth dreaming about *more*. Was that what was driving her to win the pie contest?

Before he could construct a gentlemanly way to ask, she dazzled him with an unexpected smile.

"I'd like to return the favor you're doing for my da."

He blinked. "That's not necessary."

"I know, but it's fair. I was thinking I could go clean Otto's cabin before you start on the renovations."

Emmett looked at her in surprise. It was going to be an unpleasant task. The old man's cabin was one big mouse nest. "Why would you want to do that?"

"Otto was my friend. I know what was important to him. I know the cabin was a disaster while he was alive, and whatever happened after his death. . ." She swallowed. "Let me clean Otto's cabin. Please."

How could he refuse? It would be a help to him, and it meant something to her.

"All right. If you insist."

She smiled again. "I'll head over there now and get started." He followed her glance toward a wooden toolbox filled with cleaning supplies. She'd expected him to agree to her plan.

"I could drive you."

She shook her head. "No, thank you. I'm used to the walk. It gives me time to think." She crossed the room and leaned toward him, so close he could smell the soap scent again, and a fresh, green fragrance that reminded him of sunshine and mountaintops. Her gray eyes glistened with unshed tears.

Her hand clenched his wrist. "My da's gout is the worst it's ever been," she whispered. "He can barely hobble around, and he's too proud to use a walking stick. I'm glad you offered to help." She brushed a soft kiss against his cheek. "Thank you."

She straightened, scooped up the toolbox, and headed toward the front door.

Emmett remained in the kitchen. The spot where her lips had brushed his cheek felt like an echo, calling him, compelling him. His heart pounded as if he'd run a mile at full speed. He was falling in love with Lorelei Boyd, and that put him at a crossroads. Was he willing to change his course to success and settle down? Or would he ask Lorelei to leave her family and travel from place to place with him? No woman wanted that kind of life.

He shook his head to clear it. He would stay through the contest, see if Jimmy wanted to buy her recipe, and then he would move along, for her sake. Maybe he'd sell her the orchard for a song. That idea made him smile.

———— • • • ————

Lorelei kissed her father's cheek as she passed him. "I'll be back for lunch and to make today's pie," she called as she jogged down the steps, cleaning equipment rattling in the old wooden toolbox.

She waved in response to her father's admonition to be safe and set off toward Otto's place. Her skin hummed as though an entire hive of bees had taken up residence under the surface of her flesh. She shook her head to clear the buzzing sound that being around Emmett Dewey triggered.

Good heavens, was she having some sort of episode? Like Mrs. McCauley in town, who'd had a spell last year and, when she recovered, told the whole church congregation that for weeks beforehand she'd heard a buzzing noise in her ears but her doctor had ignored her complaints.

"Oh stop it, Lorelei. Mrs. McCauley is eighty-three if she's a day," she muttered, picking up her pace. She wasn't accustomed to being in the presence of a handsome man near her own age, and it was having an unnerving effect on her senses. Plus, he'd kissed her. She should be offended by the liberties he'd taken. Instead, her skin prickled traitorously at the memory of that kiss. She'd kissed him back, too. And then she'd walked away. She couldn't have a man like Emmett. He was world-wise, an opportunist, a man on a mission for success, and she was a farm girl who needed to stay close to home to help her parents.

"Doesn't matter anyway," she said as she walked—marched—down the lane. "He's leaving once he sells the orchard."

Thoughts of Otto's property being sold reminded her of the letters from the bank. An imaginary claw grasped her chest and made it hard to breathe. She walked faster and turned her attention to her pie recipes. Her personal favorites were numbers eight, fifteen, and twenty-four. And maybe twenty-three. She pictured each individual recipe in her head and contemplated ways to combine the best of her favorites into one pie.

When she reached the corner of the orchard, she slipped through the old break in the wire fence—an as-yet-unrepaired detail she should probably mention—and zigzagged through the trees until she reached the cabin.

But today the cabin wasn't as silent as it should have been. A thin stream of smoke curled from the crumbled chimney, and she was sure she heard voices coming from inside. Other than Emmett, Otto's cabin had been empty since his death. His family hadn't even come to collect his things, which was part of the reason she had insisted on tackling the unpleasant chore herself.

She knew Emmett was expecting deliveries. That was the probable answer. But deliverymen wouldn't have gone inside. Lorelei slowed and ducked behind the trunk of an apple tree. She strained to hear the murmured sounds coming from inside the cabin. Not one voice; at least two, and maybe three. The front door banged open with a squeal, and someone flung a pan of dirty water outside. It spattered the dusty ground with a greasy splash. Raucous laughter followed from within the cabin, and the door slammed shut.

Lorelei's heart pounded. Not deliverymen. She shoved her hand against her mouth and doubled over, praying the men in the cabin wouldn't hear her.

It wasn't uncommon for hobos to hop off the train in search of farmwork at this time of year. Tramps, on the other hand, worked only when they were forced to and sometimes squatted in abandoned homesteads. Most were harmless enough, but there was no guarantee.

A virulent stream of curse words potent enough to straighten her curly hair erupted from the vicinity of the cabin. Lorelei wished she could climb into the anonymity of the leafy branches until the men left. But they might not leave for hours. Or days. And if she didn't come back for lunch, her da would come looking for her, and the results would be ugly and put her father in danger.

She crouched to set the toolbox down in the grass. She could backtrack through the orchard faster without the heavy box. She'd run home, tell Emmett and her da, and they'd call the marshal. She took a deep breath, stood, swiveled to run, and ran smack into the waiting arms of a stranger.

Wiry arms wrapped around her like chains, pinning her arms to her body. She kicked at the man's shins, choking on the stench of old onions and smoke and sweat that emanated from him. She tried to knee him in the groin, but he sidestepped and she lost her balance, giving him the advantage. He pinned her to the ground, her face pressed into the dirt by one firm hand cruelly pinching the back of her neck. He held her wrists together and pressed a knee into the center of her spine.

She struggled, despite the lack of oxygen. She kicked and thrashed and tried to scream. She heard the cabin door bang open and the sound of footsteps.

"Caught me a wild one, Drub," said the man holding her. His voice was raspy, and he was breathing hard. If he hadn't had the benefit of sneaking up on her, she might have escaped, she thought.

"Well, whaddya know? Flip 'er over."

"I ain't lettin' her loose a bit. She's wild. Get some rope or somethin' to tie her up."

"Let me go!" Lorelei shrieked, panic warring with logic. She needed to stay calm, needed to be aware of opportunities to escape.

"Shut her up. If there's anyone in hearin' distance, they'll be coming to see what the fuss is about."

Harsh fingers squeezed the sides of her jaw until her mouth opened, and a filthy rag was shoved inside. She tried to spit it out, gagging as she did so, but another cloth was wrapped around her mouth and tied behind her head. The world started to go black, with shooting stars behind her eyes, and she forced herself to still, to breathe through her nose.

More rough hands bound her wrists and tied her legs together at the ankles. Then someone flipped her over. Tears filled her eyes, and she bit back a cry. She looked up at four dirty, leering faces. The men were young, her age or younger, but they looked desperate. And stupid. She wasn't sure which was worse.

"That's quite a catch." The apparent leader spat a brown stream of tobacco juice into the dirt mere inches from Lorelei's face. He smacked the men beside him with the back of a beefy hand. "Take her inside." Addressing the man who'd caught her, he asked, "Did you find anything, Tweedy?"

The scrawny but strong man shook his head. "Naw, Drub, nothin' but junk. Looks like the place has been abandoned for a while."

"Keep looking. There has to be something worth pawning around here."

Drub—what kind of name was Drub?—strode toward the cabin. He was older than the other three, and his speech sounded like he'd had more education. The two men assigned to carry her scooped her up like she was a rolled-up rug and followed him, with Lorelei swinging between them.

The inside of the cabin was more of a disaster than Lorelei remembered. The men had emptied every box, shelf, and cabinet. They'd even cut open the crumpled mattress on Otto's narrow bed frame and strewn the contents—dirty, broken straw—all over the room.

The two men dumped her on the remnants of the mattress. She wriggled into a sitting position and pushed her back against the wall, watching her captors.

The cabin stank even more now than it had when Otto lived in it, and she hadn't thought that possible. Rotten food, body odor, and the nostril-searing smell of spilled liquor permeated the stale air. Prohibition's laws ruling alcohol illegal had done little to stop its use, sale, or production.

The one called Drub swiveled the cabin's sole four-legged chair around backward and sat down, crossing his thick arms on the back of the chair.

"So, little lady, what shall we do with you?" He smiled, a leering grin that exposed several black gaps where teeth were missing.

She jutted her chin at him, turned her head from side to side, indicating, she hoped, the gag that silenced her.

"You got something to say? How do I know you ain't gonna start a-screamin' again?"

Lorelei shook her head, pleading with her eyes. He stared at her for a long moment and then moved to crouch beside her, far enough away that she wouldn't be able to kick him with her bound legs.

"If you scream, there's no one to hear you, understand?"

She nodded, holding her breath. She held very still as he untied the bandanna and pulled the offending wad from her mouth. She gagged and spat, eyes watering with relief.

"Thank you," she muttered. "Could I have some water?"

"No water in here. Got some moonshine though. That'll clear your palate." He guffawed at his own joke, slapping his meaty thigh with one hand.

"You can let me go. I won't tell anyone you're here."

He frowned, and the corners of his dark mustache drooped to his chin. "Now, little lady, don't lie to me."

Lorelei cursed her inability to hide what she was thinking.

"Then what do you plan to do with me?"

"Well, now. . ." He twisted the ends of his mustache between his fingers. "I don't rightly know. You weren't part of the plan."

"We could take her with us, Drub, use her as bait," said one of the pair who'd hauled her in.

Drub shook his greasy head. "Bait for what?"

"I dunno. Mebbe we could hold her for ransom."

"Look at her, you dolt. She's not rich. No one is going to pay a ransom for her."

"Well, I ain't up for killin' no womenfolk," said the other tramp, shuffling his feet.

"Who said anything 'bout killin' anyone?" Drub said, swatting at the tramp with the back of his hand.

Lorelei shuddered again, this time with relief. Tweedy—surely these weren't their real names—came back inside. He tripped over the threshold and almost crashed head-long into the room. When he'd righted himself, he frowned and addressed the leader.

"Nothing useful out there at all, Drub. Couldn't even round up any chow 'cept for apples. He turned out his jacket pockets on Otto's wobbly table. Apples tumbled out, rolled off the table, and bounced across the floor. One came to a stop beside Lorelei's foot.

Drub groaned. "You're useless, Tweedy."

Lorelei blinked at the apple. She looked through the single grimy window to gauge the sun's height. In a few hours, her father and Emmett would come to search for her, and then there would be a fight. No, she had to escape her captors on her own. She needed a diversion. A Trojan horse. She looked at the apple beside her foot again, inspiration dawning.

"I could bake an apple pie." Four pairs of hungry, suspicious eyes turned toward her. She sat up straight, ignoring the pain in her wrists. "It's my specialty. All the ingredients I need are here in the cabin." All the ingredients, including Otto's morphine.

She made eye contact with Drub. He was the one whose trust she needed to gain. When he didn't disregard her, Lorelei's confidence grew. "I'm entering the Apple Pie Days contest next week, and I would appreciate having some early judges. Let me bake a pie." She looked at Tweedy. "Or two. When was the last time you had homemade apple pie?" She focused attention on the other two and then turned back to Drub. Four pairs of eyes went round and dreamy at the mention of homemade apple pie.

She had them.

"You'll have to untie me," she said. "And I'll need twice as many apples." To her relief, her captors responded as if she'd cast a spell over them. Tweedy grabbed one of the empty sacks by the door and headed back to the orchard. The other two scrambled to begin righting the mess they'd made of Otto's kitchen supplies.

Drub cut the rope binding her wrists. She rubbed the red, raw flesh, willing circulation to return to her fingers.

When he moved to her ankles, he tied a long rope to one leg before cutting the ties that held her legs together. He jerked the long leash tight and tied it to his own waist, putting a six-foot distance between them. "I can't let you wander, you know," Drub said.

"Of course." She pushed herself to her feet. He wasn't much taller than her, but he was as thick as a cottonwood in the middle. Even if he'd been alone, she would have had trouble taking him down.

She surveyed Otto's cooking space. She let her mind drift to her recipes, picked up an overturned bowl, and set it on the table. She started to move toward the wall to grab the flour, but a jerk on the rope nearly sent her sprawling. She faced Drub with a glare.

"Tell the boys what you need. They'll bring it to you."

She looked at the two then blinked. Looking at them she could see they were twins. "What are your names?" she asked.

Drub yanked on the rope again. "You can call 'em Lefty and Righty. That's all you need to know."

She sighed. "Fine. Would you bring me the sack of flour there behind the stove? And the salt and the lard?" They moved in eerie symmetry, complying with her demands. She picked up the apples still scattered over the tabletop, and the ones within reach of her leash off the floor, and piled them together then turned to Drub.

She pointed to the heap of apples. "Those have to be peeled, cored, and sliced." She turned again, found an empty pot within arm's reach, and banged it onto the table.

From the corner of her eye, she saw Drub pull out his knife, pick up an apple, and begin peeling it with the greatest of care. She peeked at each of them in turn as she prepared the piecrusts.

Drub was the only one with any spare flesh on his bones. But he bore the rosy, puffy complexion and labored breathing of a heavy drinker. Tweedy reminded her of one of the blue herons that came through in the fall, all legs and beaky nose. Lefty and Righty—they never switched places, and she wondered if that's how Drub told them apart—were younger than the other two, more nervous.

"Could one of you hand me that box of spices, please?" she asked.

Lorelei sprinkled brown sugar mixed with cinnamon, allspice, nutmeg, cardamom, and ginger over the pot full of peeled, cored apple slices. She bent and sniffed then added a dash of salt and a pinch more ginger to heighten the sweetness and the citrus. . .and to disguise the morphine. She'd chastised Otto for keeping his medications—used when the pain from his arthritis was too much to bear—in his box of spices. Now she was thankful. When she straightened, all four of her captors were staring at her.

"What?"

Drub shook his head. "Last time I saw someone pay that much attention to something was a fella in Kentucky working a still."

"I happen to take apple pie very seriously," she said. "If I win this contest—provided you don't kill me or carry me off as 'bait' for your next heist, or whatnot"—she shook her head—"I can sell the recipe and save my family's farm. At least, I hope I can." She wiped her hands on her overalls. Why had she told them? She hadn't even told her parents what she was planning to do.

She waited for them to laugh, to ridicule.

"What kinda farm, miss?" Righty asked. Or was that Lefty? Did it matter?

"Sugar beets," she replied. She upended the pot's contents into the pie tins. When no one said anything, she continued talking. "My da started getting letters from the bank a few months ago. They wanted to raise the monthly payments on our mortgage. We can't afford more, and my da ignored them. Now they're threatening to foreclose on us." She exhaled. It was relief to share her burden, even if it was with these men.

"Aw, that ain't fair," Tweedy chirped.

She draped the top crust over the apples, rolled the handle of the wooden spoon around the edge to trim the excess, and then used the end of the spoon handle to flute the crust around the edge.

"That's what happened to my uncle in Kansas," Drub grumbled. "He raised me after my folks died. And then the bank took his farm and gave it to the railroad. They tossed him and my nanty out. That's when I took off on my own. They didn't need no extra mouths to feed."

Lorelei's heart constricted. "I'm sorry, Drub. How old were you?"

He peered at her through his beady little eyes. "I was eleven when I left."

"Eleven?" she gasped. "You were barely grown!"

"We was nine when we took to the rails," Righty murmured. Compassion rolled through her. She kept her voice steady as she pinched holes in the top crust for the steam to escape. "What happened to your family, Righty?"

"Our pa went a little crazy after our ma died. He started drinkin' too much. . . ."

Lefty pulled back the collar of his shirt to expose an angry red scar. Lorelei shuddered. "Tweedy? What about you? How did you end up out here?"

The skinny man shuffled his feet. "I never knowed nothin' but the rails and the road, ma'am. My momma died birthin' me, and my pa handed me off to the nearest lady who took pity on me. When I was nine or ten, she sent me away."

That was more than Lorelei could take. "You've never had a home?"

Tweedy hung his head. "No, ma'am."

Tears stung the backs of her eyelids.

"Have you tried to work? Tried to better yourselves?" she asked. Surely there was a reason they'd ended up where they were.

"Every day, little lady. But no one wants to hire us for more than an odd job. We get a meal here and there, and sometimes we find a place to squat, like this." Drub waved a hand to indicate their surroundings. "We do what we have to."

"I'm sorry," Lorelei murmured. She finished preparing the pies for the oven and turned to Drub. "I can't reach the stove with this." She waggled her roped ankle.

"Tweedy, put the pies in the oven," Drub commanded.

Lorelei watched the gangly young man insert the pies into the oven and latch the door.

"Does anyone have a watch?"

All four shook their heads. If they were truly leading lives of crime, beyond taking her hostage, they weren't very successful at it.

"All right. We'll have to keep checking on them."

She lowered herself to a wobbly three-legged stool close to the table and dropped her head into her hands.

Lord, please don't let any of them die. I just want them to fall asleep long enough for me to get away.

She didn't even want to call the marshal on them now. She felt sorry for them. Even Drub. They needed work and hope. Mostly hope. She knew what it was to feel hopeless; she'd been experiencing it since the day she opened the letter from the bank.

The spicy, sweet scent of apple pie began to permeate the room. If her plan failed. . . She raised her head and looked at her captors. Three of them had their eyes closed, sniffing the air with rapturous expressions. Drub stared out the window, a haunted expression on his bloated face. When it came right down to it, the only thing separating her and her parents from these desperate men was a flimsy piece of paper from the bank.

Chapter 9

Sparks flew from the pedal-operated grinder as Emmett held the edge of the hoe against the stone and worked the treadle with his feet, sharpening the tool's edge. To his right lay multiple shovels, spades, shears, and other tools of the beet grower's trade, now sharp and shiny and ready for use. On his other side, propped against the wall of the barn, was a seemingly endless line of implements still in need of care.

When the hoe was done, he placed it in the finished pile. The wheel slowed and stilled, its whirring noise silenced. Emmett took off his driving goggles—he'd gotten them from the roadster after the first bit of rusty metal flew off a spade and smacked him in the face—and wiped beads of sweat off his forehead with his shirtsleeve. Mr. Boyd was perched on a nearby bench, his swollen foot propped on a bale of hay, rubbing saddle soap into a leather harness.

Emmett understood why Mr. Boyd had wanted someone else to work the treadle. It put significant pressure on the feet, something a gout-sufferer would want to avoid.

"How are you doing over there?" Mr. Boyd asked.

"Slow and steady," Emmett answered, reaching for a wide-tined fork used to lift the beets from the ground before the pickers pulled them out, the loppers sliced off the frothy greens, and they were stacked for transport. Mr. Boyd had explained all of this to him the day before. Touching the tools make the task come to life for Emmett.

"We'll knock off in another hour or so. Lorelei should be back by then and ready for lunch."

Emmett picked up the pace on the treadle and began holding the edges of the tines to the grinder, one at a time.

An hour later Emmett used a borrowed bandanna to wipe the sweat from his forehead. It was turning into a scorcher outside, and the temperature in the barn had risen accordingly. He straightened the stack of sharpened tools lined up against the wall. There was something satisfying about doing work that would last longer than a month or two. He wanted, he realized, to see this year's beet harvest, to be here to use these tools.

"You've done more in one morning than I could have finished in three days. I'm mighty grateful."

"I'm happy to help, sir."

"Why don't we head in and see about lunch?"

Emmett's stomach rumbled in response. "Shouldn't Lorelei. . .er. . .Miss Boyd be back by now?"

Mr. Boyd's heavy black brows drew together. He reached into one of his multiple pockets, withdrew a battered pocket watch, and held it at arm's length to read it. "She's a bit late."

Unease spiraled up Emmett's spine and settled, constrictor-like, in a tight band around his skull. Leaving his completed chore behind, he followed Mr. Boyd out of the barn.

Mrs. Boyd met them at the door. "Is Lorelei with you?"

Mr. Boyd hobbled to a standstill. "No."

Mrs. Boyd twisted the corner of her apron between her fingers. "She should have been back by now."

Emmett's discomfort intensified.

Mr. Boyd kissed his wife's forehead. "I'm sure she got caught up cleaning. You know how she is. Once she gets started she doesn't like to stop."

Mrs. Boyd leaned into her husband. "You're probably right. But I can't shake the feeling something is wrong."

The vise around Emmett's head moved to his chest. "I'll drive down to the cabin and pick her up." Emmett did an about-face and jogged down the porch steps toward the Paige.

Chapter 10

Ain't them pies cooked?" Drub groused.

Lorelei shoved her trembling hands into her pockets. The pies were done. She knew the smell of a finished pie. But she hesitated. She couldn't remove the morphine she'd added, and she regretted her actions. Surely now that she knew their sad stories—and they hers—she could talk them into letting her go.

Tweedy rubbed his concave abdomen. "I'm starvin', miss. How much longer?"

Oh, heavens.

She fingered the empty morphine bottle in her pocket. How much had Otto taken when his old joints were aching? How much had she dumped in the pies?

"Come on, missy. Get them pies out," Drub demanded. She reached for a ragged towel marred by multiple scorch marks—Otto's idea of an oven mitt—and opened the oven door. Apple-and-spice-infused steam wafted out, triggering audible groans.

Oh, Lord, please, don't let me kill them.

She transferred the pies from the oven to the scarred table.

"Find plates and forks," she said, reaching for the spatula. The four men scrambled into the mess they'd made.

Tweedy popped up at her elbow first, holding a battered tin plate in one hand, a fork in the other, and a ridiculous smile on his too-lean face. Lorelei suppressed a groan. She should confess what she'd done. She served a slice of drugged pie with a shaky hand as an engine rumbled to a stop outside.

Drub jerked to attention. He gestured to Righty and Lefty to move to either side of the door.

No! Not Emmett, not yet.

Drub reached into his pocket.

A gun? He had a gun?

Lorelei banged the spatula onto the table. "Emmett? Is that you? I'll be right out," she called. Her voice sounded funny: high-pitched and shaky.

Drub grunted, waving his tiny pistol to keep her away from the door.

"Let me go," she whispered. "He came to pick me up. If I go now, he'll never know you're here. I won't tell, I promise."

Drub glowered and shook his head.

"Lorelei? Are you all right? Your mother is worried." Emmett's voice was muffled by the closed door.

"I'm fine. It's taking longer than I thought. I'll be right out. Wait for me in the car." She turned a pleading glance on Drub. "Please! Let me go!"

"No!" Spittle flew from Drub's mouth.

The doorknob rattled. "Who are you talking to? Why do I smell pie?" Righty and Lefty raised their weapons of choice, a skillet and a fireplace poker, over their heads.

Lorelei lunged forward, but Tweedy caught her and yanked her back as the door burst open, striking Righty in the face and knocking him backward. Emmett's eyes widened as he took in the scene, and then Lefty brought the skillet down on Emmett's skull. Lorelei gasped in horror as he crumpled to the cabin floor.

She wrenched herself free and flew to Emmett's side, touching his face, his back, making sure he was still breathing. Then fury flooded through her. She glared up at her—their—captors.

"What did you do that for? You could have killed him!"

Righty bumbled upright, blood gushing from his nose. "He done broke my nose!"

Lorelei turned her wrath on him. "You were standing on the wrong side of the door! What did you expect?"

Drub grunted. A sound that might have been an assent, but she wasn't sure.

"Lefty, take care of your brother. Tweedy, drag him in here and shut the door. I've gotta decide what we're gonna do now." Drub sank into a chair, the gun dangling from his fingers pointed at the floor.

"You're going to let us go, that's what. And here to think I was ready to try and help the four of you find work." Lorelei scrambled out of the way as Tweedy hauled Emmett's prone form far enough into the cabin to shut the door.

"Nnuu nrrr?" Righty mumbled through his swelling proboscis, eyes hopeful. Lorelei glared at him.

"I was. I felt sorry for you." She bent over Emmett again. "You should be ashamed of yourselves, abducting a woman and assaulting an innocent man." *What if he doesn't wake up?* "You may not have had an easy start in life, but if you keep making terrible choices, it's never going to get any better."

The cabin's occupants fell silent. When Tweedy made a suspicious sniffling sound, Drub rose to his feet, shoving the gun back into his pocket.

"That's enough, woman. You be quiet." He paced. Which in the cabin's tiny, cluttered confines meant taking three steps, turning around, taking three steps, and repeating the process.

"Drub, I ain't all right with murder."

Drub glowered at Tweedy. "I have no intention of murdering anybody, you dolt." He turned to Lefty, who had one arm around his twin's shoulders. "You two, get those pies, take 'em out to that fancy car. By the time he wakes up, we'll be long gone."

The Paige! Lorelei's throat tightened. She hated for Emmett to lose his beautiful car. And it was all her fault. She sat up straight.

"You should eat first. Everybody knows apple pie tastes best warm."

Drub eyed her with suspicion.

"Tie us up if you're afraid. Go ahead." She held out her wrists.

Drub spat. "I ain't afraid of either of you." He glanced at the pies, still steaming. "But you make a good point, missy. Tweedy, serve us up some pie."

Emmett groaned and shifted. Lorelei placed her hand on his shoulder and squeezed, hoping he would remain still. If he awoke, they'd be left tied up in the cabin until someone else came searching for them. For a tense quarter hour, with her heart hammering in her chest, she watched the four men devour both pies, chasing the dessert with illegal moonshine.

Emmett twitched under her hand. When his eyes flickered open, she met his gaze. She was thankful his face was turned away from the men. She pursed her lips and gave the slightest shake of her head then pressed his shoulder again. To her relief, he remained still, but the energy in his muscled frame hummed beneath her palm. It cost him something to lie there, passive, in the face of danger.

"You sure there's nothin' here worth takin' with us?" Drub asked. He plopped onto a stool. Was he slurring his speech more than usual?

"Nfn, Dbb," Righty mumbled. His nose was most definitely broken.

"Tweedy, you get our stuff out to that car," Drub ordered.

Tweedy nodded in response then sat down very suddenly on the floor. "I don't feel so good."

Lorelei thought her heart might climb right up her throat and choke her. Was the morphine working? Lefty collapsed against the wall with a thump and slithered to the floor. His brother followed suit.

"Wha' the—?" Drub asked, and then he, too, slumped sideways, toppling off the stool in a snoring heap.

Lorelei held her breath for a beat. Emmett stirred like a rousing volcano under her hand, surging upright. Then he grabbed both sides of his head and groaned.

"Try not to move," she admonished.

"Now you tell me," he growled, head between his drawn-up knees. "What did you do to them?"

She withdrew the empty morphine bottle from her pocket and held it in front of his face. He looked at the bottle then looked up at her with a smile that made his dimples appear. She couldn't help but smile back.

Lorelei helped him to his feet. Together they checked on the four incapacitated vagrants. All four were breathing.

"Thank the Lord. I was afraid I might kill them."

"Not enough in that tiny bottle for all four of them, but I suspect the combination of morphine and spirits did the trick."

She nodded. "Now what? Shall we tie them up?"

"Did you mean what you said? That you felt sorry for them and were thinking of helping them?"

"You heard all that?"

"I did."

Lorelei blushed. "I was trying to stall them—that's why I made the pies—and then they started telling me their stories." She glanced at Righty and Lefty, propped against each other like two rag dolls in the corner. "They're so young, and they've never had a real chance."

"And as you said, they've all made terrible choices."

"Yes, they have, but I don't think any of them ever thought they had any real choices. It's as though they've had to choose the lesser of two evils all their lives." Her fingers curled around his forearm. "Oh, Emmett, that could easily be me or you lying there."

————•◦•◦•————•

Emmett's chest swelled at her use of his given name. It sounded better, somehow, on her lips. He covered her fingers with his hand and squeezed.

"I don't think you would ever fall to such levels, regardless of your situation."

To his shock—and horror—tears filled her gray eyes, reminding him of a summer storm.

"I'm a piece of paper away from being homeless and helpless, just like these men," she said. Her voice was so despondent that he couldn't keep himself from pulling her into his embrace. He patted her back.

"That's not so, Lorelei."

"You don't know." She pushed away, swiping at angry tears. "The bank has been threatening to foreclose for months. Da doesn't have the money to increase his payments, so he stopped opening the envelopes. Without a miracle, we're going to lose the farm."

Her words sank through his pain-addled head before she spun away from him. She stumbled over Drub's legs and caught herself on the stool before she toppled.

"I can help—"

A firm hand wrapped around his ankle and jerked. Emmett kicked out with his free foot, connecting with soft flesh and hard bone. Tweedy grunted and released his grip. Emmett grabbed hold of Lorelei, pulling them both well out of reach.

"Oh dear," she murmured. "Are they coming 'round?"

"They might be. We should go," Emmett said. He bent over Drub's inert form. He withdrew the pistol from the man's pocket. "No need to leave them with this."

Lorelei shuddered. "I suppose we should go call the marshal."

Emmett checked the weapon. "It's not even loaded, and the trigger is so rusty I doubt it would function."

Lorelei frowned. "You see? They're the most pitiful excuses for criminals I've ever met."

"And you've met how many criminals?" Emmett quirked a brow.

She shrugged. "I can't help but feel sorry for them."

A look of despair crossed her features and reminded him of her earlier confession. But this wasn't the time to continue that conversation.

"Come on, we need to get out of here before they wake up," he said, tugging her toward the door.

Outside, Emmett leaned against the door. His head throbbed mercilessly. "Can you find a hammer and a board and some nails?"

Lorelei looked at him in shock. "You plan to trap them in there?"

"Yes. Otherwise by the time the marshal gets here they'll be gone, kidnapping some other young woman. Is that what you want?"

She shot him a look. "Of course not." She marched toward the ramshackle toolshed, returning a few minutes later with a length of board, a handful of long nails, and a hammer.

When the cabin door was nailed shut, Emmett sagged against it. "Can you drive?"

Her eyes widened. "Yes. I mean, I think so. I've driven the farm truck, at least."

He pressed a hand to his head. "I don't think I can focus on the road. I'll talk you through it."

——◆◆◆——

Lorelei helped Emmett into the roadster. He was pasty as an unbaked piecrust and shaking like an old man with the palsy.

"Are you all right?"

"No. But I will be."

She climbed behind the steering wheel, heart pounding. She'd driven the farm truck around an empty field a few times, but that was nothing like the Paige.

Emmett slumped against the car door, sweat beaded on his forehead. Lorelei drove as fast as she dared, wincing every time she bounced through a pothole. The Paige wasn't designed for the rough country roads.

When she braked outside the farmhouse, her parents appeared on the front porch before she was out of the car.

"Momma, help Mr. Dewey. He's been hit in the head. Da, I have to call the marshal. There are four vagrants locked in Otto's cabin." She bounded past them into the house. In the parlor she picked up the telephone receiver. When she'd delivered her breathless message to the operator, who passed it to the marshal's office, she hung up and turned to see her parents assisting a weak and groggy Emmett into the parlor. They settled him on the sofa and propped pillows behind his head and shoulders.

"Young lady, explain yourself," Da said, crossing his arms over his barrel chest.

Lorelei poured out the whole story, from being captured by Tweedy, to baking morphine-tainted pies, to Emmett's arrival and their subsequent escape. By the time she was finished, her mother was in tears and her father was patting her on the back.

She reached up and gripped his hand. "I'm fine, Da. I'm worried for Mr. Dewey."

"Emmett." His voice startled them all, and they turned. He was awake, though still pale. "Back at the cabin you called me Emmett. I think we've been through enough today to use our Christian names, don't you?"

"I suppose we have." Lorelei pulled an ottoman to the sofa and sat down, grateful he was alive.

"I'm going to watch for the marshal," Da said. "Come with me, Maggie." He took his wife by the elbow and steered her out of the parlor.

"Don't you have half-a-dozen pies to make for the contest tomorrow?" Emmett asked.

She touched his hand. "It's hard to care about the contest after everything that happened today."

He interlaced their fingers. "You may not care about the contest, Lorelei, but I do."

"What are you talking about?"

He smoothed the creases in her forehead with his free hand. "There's a man coming on the train tomorrow afternoon. He should be there in time for the contest. His name is Jimmy, and he needs to taste your apple pie. Recipe number twenty-three."

His eyes fluttered shut and his hand fell to his chest. She squeezed his fingers.

"Emmett? Wake up. Who is Jimmy, and what does he have to do with my apple pie? And why twenty-three? That's not my favorite."

She waited. Squeezed his hand again. And then she leaned forward and touched her lips to his. His mouth moved beneath hers, and she pulled back.

"Trust me," he whispered, and then he kissed her with a sweetness that rivaled any apple pie she'd ever made.

Chapter 11

Lorelei was pulling the first batch of pies—recipe number twenty-three, as per Emmett's instructions—out of the oven when the marshal knocked on the door. She nearly dropped the pie tins.

Would she be arrested for poisoning the men? Had they fallen seriously ill before the marshal's arrival?

She hurried into the foyer. Her father and the marshal were headed toward the parlor.

"Wait, Da, Emmett is resting." She laid a hand on her father's arm and addressed the marshal, whose steel-gray handlebar mustache extended almost across his entire face. "Marshal Day, the men who attacked me, are they all right?"

The marshal looked down his nose at her. "They've been transferred to the jail, sicker than dogs, Miss Boyd. Would you like to explain that?"

She hung her head, heart pounding. "I put Otto's morphine in the pies they ate. I thought it would knock them out so I could escape, and then Emmett—Mr. Dewey—arrived and they hit him over the head."

"Quite ingenious of you," the marshal's mustache twitched. "You realize they could press charges against you?"

"That's absurd," Da boomed. "They took her hostage."

"I agree, Mr. Boyd, but it could be argued that she attempted to murder them."

"I'll go speak to them in the morning," Lorelei said.

"You'll do no such thing," Momma insisted, coming up behind Da.

"Momma, I must. I regretted putting the morphine in the pies before I even got them out of the oven. And you don't understand. They all had such sorrowful stories. They need work, and they can't find it."

Da and the marshal harrumphed. "I can't find a way out of work," Da grumbled under his breath.

"Da, you know how things are. They've all been riding the rails since they were children. No one has ever given them a chance to make anything of themselves."

The other side of the marshal's mustache flickered, reminiscent of a cat's tail. "And to soothe your guilty conscience you've determined to take on that role yourself?"

"Lorelei. . ." Momma reproved. "These are dangerous men."

Lorelei gripped her mother's hand. "They are what society and circumstance has made them. Isn't it our Christian duty to show mercy to those who are less fortunate? And besides, we've a harvest coming and no one to bring it in. We could offer them gainful, if temporary, employment."

"But they attacked you!" Da interjected.

"And I poisoned them. . .on purpose. I think that makes us even. I could have killed them. Please, Da, you can come with me. Talk to them yourself. If you feel it won't work, if we simply can't give them a chance, I'll accept your decision."

Momma's eyes filled with tears. "I am so proud of you, my dear."

Da cleared his throat. "Marshal, if you could arrange a meeting tomorrow before the Apple Pie Days festivities begin, we'll be there to speak with these men."

Lorelei smiled. "Thank you, Da."

"I'll see to it," the marshal said. He sniffed the air appreciatively. "And, Miss Boyd, I look forward to sampling one of your pies again this year. Without any additional ingredients, I hope."

"We'll save you a slice, Marshal Day," Lorelei said.

"Do you need to speak with Mr. Dewey?" Momma asked.

"No, ma'am, I don't believe so. If he wants to press charges against the men, he can do so when he's feeling better."

"I'm going to check on him," Lorelei said, excusing herself.

<hr />

Emmett probed the egg-sized lump on the crown of his head with a tentative touch. The swelling was beginning to subside after several applications of ice. His head still throbbed, but he could see straight now and didn't feel like he was going to lose his breakfast. In fact, he was beginning to feel hungry, which he counted as a good sign.

"You must have a hard head," Lorelei said from the doorway.

He smiled a crooked smile. "And that's a good thing. If I didn't, I might not be here."

She frowned and crossed the room. "I'm sorry. I feel like it's my fault you got hurt." She sank onto the ottoman, and he wished she would kiss him again.

"Nonsense. It's no one's fault but that tramp who conked me over the head."

"I need to talk to you about that."

Emmett heard the discomfort in her voice and reached for her hand. She didn't pull away, and he was glad. "What about them? I thought I heard the marshal arrive. Are they in jail?"

"Yes. And I'll be going in to visit them tomorrow."

Emmett raised his brows. "Why?"

"Because I want to hire them, at least during the beet harvest, if Da approves. They need a chance. They need mercy."

He looked at her. "All right. It's not as though you need my approval."

She pulled her hand away. "I wanted to let you know. If you want to press charges against them, that will change my plan."

"Lorelei, if you can forgive them, I can, too." He squeezed her fingers, and she offered him a smile.

"I need to get back to baking if I'm to have all those pies done in time for the contest tomorrow."

"And for Jimmy. Don't forget to save a slice for Jimmy."

"I won't. Do you think you'll be well enough to attend?"

"I wouldn't miss it."

"All right, then," she said, rising to leave. She paused at the door. "Why pie number twenty-three? Why did you pick that one?"

He offered her an easy smile. "I'll tell you tomorrow, after the contest."

She left the room, and he sank back into the pillows. In the morning he would wire his mother and tell her he'd finally found the woman he wanted to marry. He'd build her a house on Otto's land and let her grow every variety of apple tree she could find.

Chapter 12

Lorelei dressed with extra care the next morning. Her fingers fumbled over the tiny buttons on her blouse, and her hair was uncooperative, but she eventually declared the result satisfactory. It was her pies that were to be judged, not her attire.

Emmett waited for her on the porch, hat in hand. He'd put on his fancy clothes again, and she was struck anew by how attractive he was. Her gaze rested on his mouth, reminding her of the kisses they'd shared. That thought sent a rosy flush to her cheeks. She wished he wasn't planning to leave.

"Good morning, Lorelei," he said. "Would you care for a ride into town?"

"Are you all right to drive?" She patted her head, knocking her hat askew. She fussed with the pins to right it.

"I've still got a headache, but otherwise I seem to be fine."

"What about my folks?"

"They already left."

"Oh. I need to get the pies."

"Your mother already boxed them up and put them in the trunk of the Paige." He offered her his arm. "Are you ready to win the contest?"

Her heart fluttered as she slipped her hand into the crook of his elbow and allowed him to lead her to the car and open her door. "I hope so, but the contest still seems trivial after yesterday's excitement."

When they arrived at the festival grounds, she delivered her pies to the contest first. She ignored the stares from the other girls at the sight of Emmett, deftly pulling pies out of the trunk of the bright yellow roadster. Then Emmett drove her to the jail. Her father was inside with Marshal Day. Drub, Tweedy, Lefty, and Righty, who looked very much the worse for wear, were in a communal cell. Drub glowered, and the other three looked at her with wide eyes.

"Whaddya want with us, missy?" Drub demanded.

"Keep a civil tongue, sir," Marshal Day admonished.

Lorelei took a deep breath. "I came to apologize for poisoning the pies I baked for you."

"Is that what happened? I thought we'd had too much moonshine." Tweedy poked Lefty in the ribs with a bony elbow.

" 'Splains the hangover."

"You came to apologize?" Drub asked. He weighed more than the other three and didn't seem quite as miserable as the others. "It's not like we didn't deserve it."

Lorelei acknowledged his admission with a nod. "I know. But when I heard your stories, I felt sorry for you, and I wanted to take it back. But it was too late." She sighed.

"And then Mr. Dewey came in and you hit him, and. . ." Her voice trailed off.

"I'm sorry, too, miss." Lefty said. "We ain't never done nothin' like that before, I swear."

Tweedy rubbed his stomach and groaned. "And we never will again, I can promise you that."

"My daughter"—Da's deep voice echoed off the bare brick walls—"would like me to offer you temporary jobs bringing in our sugar beet harvest. Room and board, plus modest wages."

All four men blinked at him then at Lorelei, in turn.

"If there's so much as an impolite word spoken, the marshal will haul you right out of town without pay. After I'm through with you." Da cracked his meaty knuckles.

Righty swallowed, his Adam's apple bobbing.

"Are you willing to work?" Da asked.

Tweedy, Lefty, and Righty nodded and sat up straighter. "Yes, sir."

Drub was slower to respond, and when he leaned forward, he fixed his gaze on Lorelei. "This your plan?"

She nodded.

"How you expect to pay us when your family's about to lose the farm?"

Her throat constricted as her father, Emmett, and the marshal turned eyes on her.

"You know?" Da asked.

"Yes. I read one of the letters from the bank."

"Did you win that pie contest yet?" Drub asked.

"Be quiet," Emmett said to Drub. He reached for Lorelei's hand. "What does the pie contest have to do with the farm?"

Tears filled her eyes. She hadn't wanted it all to come out like this, especially not in front of Emmett. "If I win the contest, I believe I can sell the recipe. I'll use the money to pay the bank," she said. "That's why I've been so focused on winning. I'm trying to save my family's home."

A broad smile spread across his face.

"What are you smiling about?"

"Trust me," Emmett replied, and to her shock, he leaned in and dropped a quick kiss on her forehead.

Da cleared his throat. "Lorelei, your mother and I never wanted you to be worried about the farm. We'll find a way, with God's help, as we have always done before." Da pulled her into his embrace. "I'm sorry you were afraid."

"Thank you, Da. I'm sorry I didn't say something."

Da spoke to the four prisoners. "If you'll come to work, you'll get paid when the harvest is in. You have my word. If that's not good enough, then you can stay here."

"We'll work for you, Mr. Boyd," Drub said.

"I'll come around and pick you up on our way out of town this afternoon." Da shook the marshal's hand and left the building. Lorelei and Emmett followed him.

Outside, Da squeezed his daughter's shoulders in a one-armed hug. "Sometimes I don't understand what God is doing, but then He gives me a glimpse, and it's always more than I could have imagined." Releasing her, he looked pointedly at Emmett. "I'm going to go find my wife. You two young people go enjoy the festival. We'll see you at the judging this afternoon." He clapped Emmett on the back and strode down the street.

━━━━●●●━━━━

Emmett let Mr. Boyd's not-so-subtle hint soak in. Then he grasped Lorelei's hand and led her down the street, away from the jail.

"What about your car?" she asked.

"It's probably safer in front of the jail than it would be anywhere else," he replied. "Tell me about this plan of yours."

She groaned. "I'm so embarrassed. I should have told my parents. I probably should have told you these past few days. Instead, I told those four tramps while I baked poisoned pies for them to eat."

"Your plan?" he prodded.

"I read an article a few months ago in *Ladies' Home Journal* about a woman who sold her cookie recipe to a fancy restaurant. They paid her twice what my parents need to take care of the bank's demands." She dug in her heels and they stopped. "Is that completely insane?"

Emmett shook his head. "Not at all. You saw an opportunity."

"Did you know I came in second last year and the year before that in the pie contest?"

"No, I didn't know that."

"I thought all I needed was something to set my pies apart from the rest. That's when Otto and I formed our partnership. Well, after he insisted on paying me for bringing him dinner. He wasn't eating well on his own."

Emmett tucked that bit of information away. This woman he'd fallen in love with had a habit of seeing needs and finding ways to meet them.

"And if you don't win today?" he asked.

She shrugged. "I don't know. Like Da said, God has always provided. Who knows? Maybe Drub will dig up a gold brick in the beet field." She didn't sound convinced.

Should he tell her about Jimmy? He opened his mouth to speak.

"Lorelei Boyd! Lorelei!" A beautiful young woman with shining dark hair that rippled down her back trotted up the street toward them. Lorelei let out a little moan.

"Audrey," she grumbled.

"Who's your friend?"

"This is Emmett Dewey. He bought Otto Starkey's place."

"Oh, the orchard," Audrey said. "How convenient. I wanted to wish you the best of luck today."

"Thank you," Lorelei said. "And to you, as well."

"Oh, I won't need it. My uncle and my cousin are judging again," the girl replied then giggled. "I'll save you a slice of my pie, Mr. Dewey, so you can compare." And with a wave and a toss of her fat, dark curls, Audrey headed back the way she'd come.

"Audrey was last year's queen," Lorelei said, by way of explanation.

Emmett grunted. "That would be enough to make me desperate to win the contest myself."

"You didn't find her charming? Everyone else does."

She sounded so despondent Emmett put two fingers under her chin and lifted her face to meet his gaze.

"If you haven't figured it out by now, Lorelei Boyd, you are the only young woman I find charming."

She blushed but turned away. "You flatter me, but you're leaving once you sell Otto's place."

He picked up her hand again and pulled her forward, toward the colored banners and cheerful sounds of the festival. "And what if that were subject to change?"

"What did you say?" she asked, jogging to keep up with him in her heeled shoes. He slowed and interlaced their fingers, enjoying the contact.

"Nothing. Let's enjoy the day. I haven't been to a festival in years."

Lorelei's heart rate sped up to a gallop.

Oh dear. She was in love with him.

The realization stunned and horrified at the same time. She hadn't planned to fall in love with Emmett Dewey, the opportunist. But she was hard pressed to find time to fret about it as Emmett, with childlike excitement, dragged her from one distraction to another.

They watched a parade. Emmett bought a paper cone of fairy floss for them to share, won a stuffed dog in a target shooting game he gave to a small girl in a frayed dress, and then he pulled Lorelei into the middle of an impromptu street dance. When the bell rang to announce the contest, she was flushed, rumpled, and happy.

"I need to go collect Jimmy from the train depot," Emmett said, spinning her around.

Lorelei halted. She didn't want him to go. Didn't want the day to come to an end.

"Trust me," he said again. Before she could ask him about it, he was towing her through the crowd.

By the time they made their way to the contest site, the judges were already in place, contestants lined up behind them. Emmett boosted her onto the dais, and Lorelei slipped into place at the end of the queue. Audrey was in the center, last year's tiara perched on her head.

When Lorelei turned, Emmett was gone. She tried to slow her breathing. If she didn't win. . . No, she couldn't think about that. She had to trust.

I want to trust, Lord. But I'm afraid.

"And the second runner-up in this year's Apple Pie Days contest is Ellie Armbruster," announced the festival's emcee. The crowd applauded. Lorelei's stomach danced.

"First runner-up is. . ."

Lorelei held her breath.

"Lorelei Boyd, for the third straight year."

Lorelei's hopes and dreams dissolved like fairy floss in a cloudburst. That was it. The end. She had failed. They would lose the farm. Emmett would leave.

"And first place, and the title of Apple Pie Days Queen, goes to"—the emcee made a show of opening the final envelope, dragging out Lorelei's misery by painful seconds—"Flora Harding, our new schoolteacher. Congratulations, Miss Harding." The crowd began to applaud.

Lorelei glanced down the line of young women. Audrey yanked the crown from her head, passed it to the emcee, and stormed from the dais. Where was Flora?

A black-haired woman no larger than a half-grown child stepped forward, hand pressed to her heart. *Ah*, Lorelei thought, *that must be Flora.* She'd heard about the new teacher with the childlike features and ability to commandeer a classroom of unruly boys and girls. Apparently, she could also bake a winning apple pie.

Audrey's cousin rose, his acne-scarred cheeks reddening, and kissed Flora Harding's hand. Lorelei smiled in spite of her own trauma.

When she stepped off the dais, her parents were waiting. Lorelei burst into tears when she saw her mother. "I'm sorry, Momma. I tried."

"Oh my girl, you amaze me." Momma hugged her. "Don't be afraid. We've started over before, and we can do it again if need be."

"Lorelei!" Emmett's voice rose over the rumble of the crowd. Lorelei swiped at her tears and turned around. A broad grin highlighted his dimples, and his hair was mussed.

She offered a weak smile and noticed he was pulling someone behind him. The slight, ginger-haired man in a well-tailored, cream-colored suit offered an apologetic smile when Emmett pushed him in front of her.

"Lorelei, this is Jimmy Clarke, one of my best friends."

She mustered a halfhearted smile. "It's nice to meet you, Mr. Clarke."

He bobbed his head. "And you, Miss Boyd."

"Where's your pie?" Emmett asked.

"My pie? I lost. I came in second again," she said, forlorn. He lifted her chin and looked into her eyes.

"I don't care who won. Is any of your pie left?"

Momma stepped forward. "I set aside two pieces, one for the marshal and one for you, Mr. Dewey. Let me fetch them." She disappeared, and Lorelei frowned at Emmett and Jimmy.

"I appreciate your enthusiasm," she said, "but wouldn't you rather taste the winning pie?"

Emmett shook his head. "I've had the winning pie. I sent Jimmy a telegram the morning after I met you."

Momma reappeared, holding a plate with a piece of pie and a fork. She handed the plate to Jimmy.

Lorelei turned on Emmett. "You sent him a telegram about my pie? Why?"

Jimmy sliced a bite of pie with the fork and raised it to his lips.

"Because Jimmy buys recipes for a national chain of lunch counters."

Lorelei clapped her hands to her mouth, eyes wide. "You're joking."

"I'm not. There's no guarantee he'll buy the recipe, but I thought it was worth a try."

Jimmy made a rapturous sound beside them and cleared his throat.

"Is the recipe still for sale?" Jimmy asked, wiping his chin.

"Yes," Lorelei said. "Yes, it is."

"I'll buy it. How much do you want?"

"We'll have to negotiate a fair deal, Jimmy," Emmett said. "And while we're at it, you might ask Mrs. Boyd about her egg salad recipe."

It was Momma's turn to blush.

Lorelei turned to Emmett. "You said you would tell me why you chose recipe twenty-three."

"Because the moment I tasted that first bite I fell in love with the baker." Emmett dropped to one knee. "Lorelei Boyd, will you marry me?"

Lorelei's heart swelled. "Are there terms and conditions? You are an opportunist, after all."

"And this is the one opportunity I cannot pass up. Lorelei, I promise to love you and cherish you every day for the rest of our lives. And I'll build you a house on Otto's property and help you grow all the apples you want."

Lorelei's heart swelled. "I couldn't ask for more." She reached out and pressed the pad of her thumb against the cleft in his chin. "Yes, Emmett, I'll marry you. And I'll love you back, every day."

Author's Notes

The Apple Pie Days Festival in Rifle, Colorado, began in 1908 as a celebration of the completion of a bridge crossing the Colorado River. As the years passed, more contests and activities were added to the event, and Apple Pie Days eventually morphed into what is now the Garfield County Fair.

The Colorado Orange really is the name of an unusual heirloom variety of apples that were grown in Colorado for a short period of time.

Basic Apple Pie

This recipe is from the bottom of a ceramic pie dish I inherited from my grandmother. It's a good place to start when you want to bake apple pie from scratch. Then, like Lorelei, you can begin to experiment with spices and flavorings in the crust and in the filling. Though you won't find the Colorado Orange in your local grocery store, you can choose from different apple varieties to create the perfect blend. Jonathans are a perennial pie favorite. Pie experts say the best apple filling is made from a combination of sweet, soft apples; sweet, crunchy apples; and tart, crunchy apples.

Ingredients:
Pastry for two-crust pie (see page 351)
⅔ cup sugar
⅛ teaspoon salt
¾ teaspoon cinnamon
¼ teaspoon nutmeg
4 to 6 medium apples, peeled, cored, and thinly sliced
1 tablespoon butter

Instructions:
Use half of pastry for bottom crust. Roll ⅛-inch thick. Fit into 9-inch pie pan and trim edges. For top crust, roll remaining pastry ⅛-inch thick and cut several 2-inch slits or design near center.

Combine sugar, salt, and spices (depending on comfort level, play with adding ginger, cardamom, maple syrup, etc.). Sprinkle half the mixture into pie shell. Add apples and remaining sugar mixture. Dot with butter. (If apples are all of the sweet variety, add 2 tablespoons lemon juice and ¼ teaspoon grated lemon rind.)

Moisten edge of bottom crust. Fold top crust in half or roll loosely on rolling pin to lift and center over filling. Spread open to cover pan. Open slits to let steam escape during baking. Trim top crust ½-inch larger than pan. Fold this edge under bottom crust and press together with fork or fingers. Bake in hot oven (preheated to 425°) for 50 minutes, or until apples are tender.

Serve pie warm.

Pastry for Two-Crust Pie

(This recipe is from *Mother Earth News* and uses lard, just like Lorelei's.)

Ingredients:
3 cups flour
1 teaspoon salt
1¼ cups lard, cold and coarsely chopped
1 egg
5½ tablespoons water
1 teaspoon vinegar

Instructions:
In large bowl, combine flour and salt. Using pastry blender or fork, cut in lard until the mixture is very fine. Set aside. In separate bowl, beat together egg, water, and vinegar.

Make small well in flour mixture and add liquid. Mix just until dough comes together in a ball. Divide dough into 4 equal pieces and flatten into disks. Wrap individually in plastic wrap and refrigerate for at least 30 minutes before rolling.

To make double-crust pie with a solid top crust, roll out 2 disks of dough about 1-inch larger than pie plate. Fit one crust into bottom of pie plate. Fill pie with desired filling. Slightly moisten edge of bottom crust. Take second crust, fold it in half, gently place it over pie filling and unfold, centering it on pie plate. Press the edges into bottom crust to seal (you may need to moisten bottom edge with a bit of water). Trim excess dough to leave an overhang of about ¾ inch. Crimp or flute edges (handle of wooden spoon is great tool for this). To allow steam to escape, gently prick top crust with fork several times or slash vents into crust with sharp knife.

For fancy look, use a cookie cutter to cut out two or three small shapes from the crust top before you place it on the pie. Leaves, hearts, stars, etc., are good. You can place the cutout pieces on the crust for a 3-D effect.

Makes 4 single or 2 9-inch double crusts (enough for two double-crust pies or four single-crust pies).

Niki Turner is a novelist, journalist, and blogger. Her first completed manuscript earned second place in the Touched By Love 2009 contemporary category romance contest. She writes for local newspapers and won second place for best agriculture story at the 2013 Colorado Press Association annual convention. She is a coblogger at www.inkwellinspirations.com. Niki is the president of the Western Slope chapter of the American Christian Fiction Writers. Connect with Niki on Facebook or Twitter and visit her website for information on her other books: www.nikiturner.net.

Front Paige Love

by Amber Stockton

Dedication

To Angie Price Booher and Eddie Booher, for always talking and sharing about state and county fairs in such a favorable way, I just had to go and attend one, only to discover just how much fun they can be! I'm giving you both a nod with this story.

Acknowledgments

A great deal of gratitude goes to my husband, Stuart, for helping with our two energetic, creative, and inquisitive children and assisting with household tasks while I write on deadlines. It's not easy keeping the kids away from my desk so I can focus on work.

Thank you to Chere Poole with Clear as Day Copyediting, for offering to review my story before it was submitted to make sure all my T's were crossed and my I's dotted in the right places. And thank you to Ellen Tarver, my amazing editor from Barbour, for all of her help with story ideas, plot development, and strengthening characters. This story wouldn't be what it is without those two.

I'm extremely grateful to Gina Welborn and Cindy Hickey who assembled this project and invited me to be a part of it. It's been a lot of fun working with them and the other six co-authors. What a great bunch of ladies!

Chapter 1

P lease, tell me you're fooling."

Paige Callahan's best friend clutched two corners of the red-and-white-checkered tablecloth as they readied it to cover one of the hand-hewn wooden tables inside the newly built Agriculture Hall on the outskirts of the fairgrounds.

"I wish I could say I was, but that would be a lie." Paige grabbed the other two corners and smiled across the expanse of fabric at Millie as they laid it evenly across the table. "At least Charlie asked to speak to me privately first instead of assuming or announcing it to Mama and Papa."

"Did he ask your father yet?"

"No." And thank goodness for that. Mama and Papa would pressure her to accept and be relentless in providing all the reasons it would be a good match. "He said he wanted to be certain I was in agreement before he arranged to speak with Papa."

"He just dropped it on you though? Like an idea for a business merger? No romantic words? No flowers? Nothing?"

"It was a very matter-of-fact conversation." Paige smoothed her hands across the tablecloth to eliminate any wrinkles. Faint strains of a string quartet playing Gershwin's "Lullaby" floated on the breeze from the orchestra stage across the way. "I must admit, I was a little surprised he managed to gather up enough courage to even broach the subject in the first place." Charles wasn't exactly known for his bold nature, or for taking any kind of risk, for that matter. Proposing marriage? That was a giant step.

"That is a good point," Millie replied. "He sure has earned his 'Conventional Charlie' nickname. Always living life exactly as planned and never straying." She stepped to the next table and reached for the folded tablecloth on top of it. "But are you really surprised? I mean, you two have been pushed together almost since you were born."

Paige poked out her lower lip and released a puff of air, stirring the flyaway strands of her bangs across her forehead. She joined Millie again at the opposite end of the table and caught her end of the tablecloth as it came sailing toward her. "That certainly hasn't been anything I've encouraged, but what other options have I had?"

They made quick work of covering that table and moved on to the next. "At present, there aren't a lot." Millie tugged on her end to even out the sides. "When we were finishing our studies in school, though, the selection was a lot more diverse."

"And then so many of the good ones were sent off to serve in the Great War." Paige's eyes met Millie's. "You lost Christopher, and I lost Grandpa Milton and Uncle Robert.

Papa hasn't been the same since."

Millie pressed her lips into a thin line and inhaled then exhaled slowly. "Between the Great War and then the influenza, I don't think any town was left untouched."

Now, how had their conversation shifted to such dismal topics? Setting up for the annual state fair was always such an exciting time. "That's true, but I think we did an admirable job of recovering and even going on to achieve greater things." Paige swung her arm wide to encompass the Ag Hall where they stood. "Take this building, for example. When the fair was first brought here to Douglas, there was that little grandstand, and people camped in tents out there in the field. Now, we have a brand-new Ag Hall and shiny steel grandstands instead of that old, dilapidated wooden one."

"No more splinters," Millie chimed in with a big grin. She raised her forefinger. "But even with the simple things, we had the best racetrack in the state!"

"Ah, right." Paige winked. "For all those roundup wagon races and horses running around in circles for what felt like an eternity."

Giggles erupted from Millie, and she covered her mouth with her hand. Her eyes shone bright above her fingers. "Correct me if I'm wrong, but I do believe I remember a certain young girl in those early years who was so fascinated by the excitement of the races, she sneaked away from her mama and daddy and hid under the grandstand to watch."

"Can you blame me?" Paige protested. "The state fair and those races are the most exciting thing that happens here in Douglas." She planted her fists on her hips and sent a mock glare toward her friend. As if Millie was completely innocent of any misbehavior or disobedience herself. "And I wasn't exactly alone in my covert observation." Paige wagged a finger. "You were right there with me."

Millie placed her hand on her chest and sighed. "Guilty as charged."

"No wonder we got along so well then. . .and still do."

With her thumb holding her pinkie finger down, Millie pressed the other three fingers together and mimicked the Girl Scout hand signal. "Through thick and thin, best friends to the end," she vowed.

Paige couldn't help but smile at her friend's antics. The Girl Scouts weren't available for them when they were younger, but they knew of a lot of girls enrolled now. At least those girls could go on adventures and add a little excitement to their lives.

"All right, best friend," Paige began as she moved from the now-covered tables to all the items left for them to set up and arrange. "You know Mrs. Waverly is going to be here any minute to check on our progress. We'd better get moving."

Millie scrunched up her nose. "You mean *Sergeant* Waverly?" An appropriate name for the woman who demanded everything be in tip-top shape and wasn't beyond using harsh tones and clipped words to see that happen.

"Exactly," Paige replied. "She won't be happy if this isn't all done. Judging starts tomorrow with the opening of the fair. We don't have any time to waste." She perused everything left to be organized. "Could you make sure the canning table display is complete?" she called over her shoulder. "Showcase our regulars front and center, then fill in any empty spaces with the newcomers and work your magic."

"I can do that!" Millie turned away and headed for that table.

Paige watched her friend's chestnut hair sway with each step. She hadn't been looking for a friend when Millie virtually blew into her life all those years ago. They began as classmates assigned to the same row in the schoolroom. It didn't take long for Millie's unique eye and appreciation for the arrangement of things to earn her a place as the teacher's favorite helper, right alongside Paige, and that had cemented their friendship. Millie's infectious zest for life had wormed its way into Paige's life and heart. Now, she couldn't imagine life without her.

She gave the hall an experienced appraisal. Checkered tablecloths covered every wooden table, aligned to allow ease of access for the fair attendees and for those who had entered their prized items to be front and center during judging. Signs were hung from the rafters, designating each of those areas. Fresh pinecones and well-placed potpourri provided just the right amount of freshness to mask the potential mustiness of a place that remained sealed tight most of the year.

"Oh, I almost forgot to tell you!" Millie's excited voice called to her from among the glass jars of both sweet and dill pickles she now arranged. "Sarah Cooper's engaged!"

"Did Jonathan Brandt finally get around to asking her father for permission?" Paige smiled. Jonathan was one of those mischievous boys growing up who always seemed to be causing trouble and pulling harmless pranks on others. But when Sarah moved into town, all of that changed.

"Aww, don't give him a hard time when you see him." Millie looked up. "It's not his fault Sarah's father was an officer in the Great War and earned several medals. That would intimidate any man, let alone one trying to court his daughter."

"You're right. Jonathan changed a lot after he met Sarah. He deserves happiness as much as any of us, and I'm glad to see he's getting it with Sarah." At least he had found a sweet girl like Sarah and set the course of his life accordingly.

"Then why do I get the feeling you're not as happy as you say you are?"

Paige glanced up and found Millie standing on the other side of the table. Her friendly smile and tender expression warmed Paige's heart.

"Never mind, I bet I can guess," Millie continued before Paige could answer. She folded her arms. "You're thinking about Charlie and what he said to you just before you came here, and you're wondering if his matter-of-fact suggestion is all you're going to get." She wagged a finger in Paige's direction. "And you're back to wishing something different or better would happen. You're dwelling on what you don't have instead of thanking God for what you do."

Her friend was right, but it didn't stop the pain of Paige's predictable life. The man who had never really officially courted her had reached the age of twenty-five and decided it was time to put a check mark in front of the next item on his list for life. And that's when he told her he thought they should talk about when they would marry. No fanfare. No sentiment. Just the facts. It all made sense, but was it what she wanted? Or was it just what everyone expected?

"Charlie is a very nice man." Paige raised her hand. "He's intelligent, hardworking, devoted," she said, tapping out each adjective on a fingertip. "Trustworthy, dependable."

"Always happy to greet you," Millie chimed in. "Content to stay right by your side."

Paige nodded. "Yes. That's Charlie all right."

"I hate to say this, Paige, but you might as well describe your favorite dog instead of a man who has for the most part offered marriage to you."

Paige grimaced. Had it really sounded that bad? "I'm sorry, Millie. I didn't intend to drag you into my melancholy state." She gestured toward the tables around them. "I think a big reason I agree to supervise this part of the fair each year is it gives me something to look forward to. The judging is full of excitement, and it brings me to a place where people come from all over the state of Wyoming to gather in droves for this one week. They're all eager to go home with one of those prized blue ribbons, or maybe even win the one hundred dollars offered by the *Wyoming State Tribune* to the winner of the spelling bee. But each time I walk the fair and see a smiling couple, I'm reminded yet again that I'm alone."

Sympathy filled Millie's eyes. She stepped forward and clasped Paige's hands in her own. "You're not alone. You've got me." Paige raised one eyebrow and Millie conceded. "All right, seriously. You'll find that special someone. You just have to trust God and believe He knows what's best."

Paige offered a quick prayer of thanks for bringing Millie into her life and providing such a dear friend. "My head knows that, but it's not easy convincing my heart, especially when evening comes at the fair and I see all those happy pairs holding hands, oblivious to everyone around them." She released a sigh, blowing a loose tendril of hair from her eyes in the process. "It's enough to send me into a fit of doldrums!"

Millie gave Paige's hands a squeeze. "Be patient. It'll happen for you when it's time."

Paige pulled away and turned toward the back wall. "You know, I can't tell you how old that sage piece of advice is. 'Be patient.' 'God knows best.' 'It's not time yet.'" She repeated the myriad of pat lines she'd heard over the years, each one meant to offer comfort but instead only offering more frustration. "I know God's trying to teach me patience, but I sure wish He'd hurry up and do it!"

A laugh burst from Millie, and Paige couldn't keep a small grin from her lips. Half expecting the words that were sure to come next, she whipped around and pointed a finger in Millie's direction. "And don't you say it!"

Millie held her hands up in front of her and waved them. "I wouldn't dare. I'd be too afraid of your wrath if I did!"

Paige narrowed her eyes and cocked her head as she watched Millie. The woman barely contained her mirth, and a snicker escaped her lips. With a huff, Paige headed for the quilting area.

"Good things come to those who wait," Millie's voice sounded from behind.

"Argh!" Paige looked up at the roof. "Millie, you promised."

Millie skittered back to where she'd been working with a mischievous grin lighting her face. "I know, but I couldn't resist." She winked then bent her head to focus on her task.

"You know, if you were a better friend, you'd be more supportive," Paige called, raising her voice to be heard.

"If I were a better friend, I'd knock you upside the head and shake some sense into you."

"I have plenty of sense."

"Prove it," came her friend's challenge.

"All right, that's enough." Paige stomped in the direction of Millie's voice but didn't find her there. She placed her hands on her hips. "Where are you?"

"Right here."

Millie rose up to be seen over the top of a table full of knickknacks and hand-made items in various assortments. With a mock glare, Paige pursed her lips and exhaled through her nose. Times like these made her wonder how she and Millie ever put up with each other. They needled each other more than anything, but that's probably why they got along so well. They each gave as well as they took.

"Look, just because I get upset over certain things and share my frustrations with you, it doesn't mean I don't have any sense."

"No, I agree. Dwelling on it doesn't help any, though."

But talking helped Paige get her feelings out in the open so she could deal with them. If she brushed them aside, it only made her feel worse.

"What would you do if you were in my shoes?"

Millie turned a random knickknack around and around in her hand and shrugged as she placed it back on the table. "I am in those same shoes, remember?"

Oh. Yes. Millie didn't have a romantic suitor, either, though her friend had never suffered from the lack of them over the years.

"So why does this not bother you the way it does me?"

"Look at how often you talk about it. You spend so much time wishing for what you think you don't have, when you should be counting the blessings in your life. . . like a family who loves you, work you enjoy, and a God who has a plan for your happiness."

"I know, but all the women in my family married young. For as far back as I can remember, they were wives and mothers before they reached eighteen." Paige headed closer to the front of the hall. "Here I am at twenty-two, and the best I can get is a man who seems to have checked 'tell Paige it's time to set a date' off his to-do list."

"Well, I hope you don't miss it when the kind of love you're seeking does manage to find you."

"Oh, believe me. When I find it, I'll know."

Millie placed the final two crafted items on the table and turned to face Paige. She smiled then her gaze shifted to just over Paige's shoulder and her smile disappeared as her eyes widened. With a catch in her throat, Paige froze.

Someone was standing behind her.

A chill ran up her back, but she fought off the shiver. Should she turn around and greet the person, or should she immerse herself in some menial task and leave Millie to handle it?

Before Paige could make a decision, Millie rushed forward. "Can we help you?"

With forced nonchalance, Paige turned then quickly concealed the soft gasp that almost escaped. A well-dressed gentleman stood just inside the main door to the hall. The stranger's dark brown hair, strong jawline, and broad shoulders only complemented his neatly pressed double-breasted tan suit and felt hat set just slightly askew on his head. Even worse. He had to be attractive, too.

"Yes," the gentleman spoke. "My name's Andrew Lawrence. I'm wondering if either of you fine ladies might point me in the direction of the Administration building or the director's office."

Paige fidgeted with the pleats in her skirt and fingered the strand of beads hanging from her neck with her other hand. She swallowed once. Twice. Then, she opened her mouth, but no words came out.

The stranger grinned, one corner of his mouth quirking up slightly higher than the other. "Has the cat got your tongue, miss?"

She tried again to speak. No such luck. Millie came to her rescue.

"If you follow the causeway to the end and turn right, the building you seek will be just around the corner."

"Many thanks," the man replied, reaching up to tip his hat to both of them. "Perhaps once I get my affairs settled, I'll have the opportunity to return and engage both of you charming ladies in more extensive conversation."

With a slight bow and a final glance in Paige's direction, the gentleman disappeared. Was that a wink he'd just given her? No. Surely she'd only imagined it. Why on earth would he wink? They'd barely met, and thanks to her addlepated brain, they hadn't even exchanged any words.

Millie stepped close and gave her a nudge. "Well, that was a first. You, unable to talk."

Paige swallowed and wet her lips. "I honestly don't know what happened. I tried to answer him, but the words wouldn't come out."

"If you ask me, I think you're smitten," Millie teased then glanced toward the door. "He was quite handsome."

"Yes, but. . ."

"Who allowed that reporter in here?" a sharp voice demanded from the side door of the hall. "He's not supposed to be here until tomorrow to cover the preliminary results of the first round of judging." A plump form moved slowly toward the girls.

"Mrs. Waverly!" both girls chorused.

"I told him to make his way to the Administration building and gave him explicit instructions on how to find it."

That gentleman was a reporter? And he already knew how to find the building he needed? So, why did he stop into the Ag Hall, when it was clearly marked on the outside and obviously not where he was supposed to be headed? Paige's chest tightened as she recalled his amused gaze. There was no doubt in her mind that he had heard some of her conversation with Millie. But just how much?

"Did he see anything or take any notes? Was he here long?" Mrs. Waverly's frantic yet irritated voice cut into Paige's musings.

"No, ma'am," Paige replied.

"He asked us for directions, and then he left," Millie added.

"Strange." The dowager woman pursed her lips. "I'm certain I already provided that to him." She waved a hand of dismissal in the air. "Never you mind about that. Let's see what kind of progress you girls have made."

Paige led Mrs. Waverly around the hall, showcasing each area and the neatly arranged tables. She and Millie answered the older woman's questions, but Paige's mind was still back on that reporter. Why *had* he come into the Ag Hall? Was it mere curiosity about all the blue ribbon contender items, or could he have possibly heard them talking from outside and decided to investigate? Whatever his reason, Paige knew she'd see him again the next day. Maybe she'd be able to actually talk to him this time and ask.

Chapter 2

Opening day had finally arrived! Paige waited all year for this week to come. She stood with her hands wrapped around the broom she held and looked north. The location of the Ag Hall afforded her a clear view of the main gate. Fair attendees staggered through the entrance, their clothing as diverse as the prizes in the vendor booths along the midway. The farmers and cowboys came in blue jeans and boots, while the gentlemen came in simple suits with or without outer jackets. The ladies' outfits, however, varied quite a bit more.

Skirt hems settled anywhere from the ankles to just above the knees. Hairstyles varied from the more modern bob or fashionable upsweep to the traditional long braid hanging down the back and everything in between. Paige reached up and touched her own pinned hair that fell to about the middle of her back. Should she follow the fashion and cut hers as well? As she swept, she continued to watch the entrance. She never saw such an array of dress styles and fashions in her everyday visits to town throughout the year.

The well-dressed attendees came mostly from Cheyenne, or even Denver. Folks in Casper and Sheridan or other towns around the state had no reason for those fancier clothes. The state fair and especially the rodeo brought such variety from all over Wyoming and even neighboring states as well.

It was quite a sight to behold.

"Miss Callahan?" The stern voice of Mrs. Waverly commanded Paige's attention.

Paige turned from sweeping the entryway. Clearing the dust might be a futile exercise, thanks to the seemingly constant winds along the eastern plains, but she did it anyway. "Yes, ma'am?"

"I need you to walk over to the Peabody Pavilion and Greenhouse and take a message to one of the judges there." She held out an envelope.

After leaning the broom against the wall, a few brisk steps brought Paige to her supervisor. She reached for the envelope, but Mrs. Waverly retracted it slightly, one eyebrow raised and her head tilted. Paige recognized that look. Despite her hard work and dedication every year for the past six years, Mrs. Waverly still treated her like a child who couldn't be trusted.

"The judges aren't due here to the Ag Hall until after the noon hour, but this message must be delivered with great haste as it pertains to the order and schedule we'll be following this afternoon. Will you be able to handle that?"

The very same schedule the two of them had discussed just two days prior when they were first receiving the entered items for judging? Paige wanted to remind Mrs. Waverly that she was no longer a young girl, but she doubted the woman would even hear her. "Yes, ma'am," she said instead. "I'll go straightaway."

"Very well." Mrs. Waverly passed the envelope to Paige. "Please don't dawdle."

Paige spread her lips into a smile as she exited the Ag Hall. Mrs. Waverly meant well, but she could do with a little improvement in the execution of her requests. She *had* been overseeing the blue ribbon awards since the first state fair twenty years ago, and she'd even kept it running when her husband and two sons were called off to the Great War but never returned. Paige had been assigned as her assistant the following year, and knowledge of Mrs. Waverly's dedication in the midst of her grieving spread throughout all the fair workers. Despite her brusque nature, she'd taken Paige under her wing and trained her in every aspect pertaining to events and procedures inside or around the Ag Hall.

Crossing the narrow patch of grass before reaching the main thoroughfare leading south from the front gate, Paige waited for several clusters of people to pass before she headed for the path between the midway and the arenas. It might not be the most direct, but it was likely the least traveled. "Please don't dawdle," Mrs. Waverly had said. She wouldn't. There'd be time enough throughout the week to enjoy all the fair had to offer.

As she walked toward the greenhouse at the far west side of the fairgrounds, the pounding of horses' hooves sounded from the arena to her left as a cacophony of carnival barkers' voices sang out to her right.

"Ladies and gentlemen! Boys and girls! Step right up and get your tickets to some of the best games and challenges this side of the Mississippi."

"Come and toss the rings. Fifty cents gets you five rings. Everyone's a winner."

"Here's your chance to practice your pitching, boys. Hit the target and send our young man swimming. Three baseballs for twenty-five cents."

Paige smiled. Her older brother, Matthew, had volunteered one year for that booth. He'd vowed to never do it again after the town's baseball team showed up for pitching practice. He'd spent more time in the water than out of it.

As she neared the carnival area, her gaze caught sight of the new steel grandstands, their backs to the carousel and three-story slide. They were about half-full now with a handful of demonstrations and competitions taking place between the three arenas. The midmorning sun glinted off the shiny metal surfaces, and Paige shielded her eyes. A few steps more and she reached the shadow of the grandstands, now on the edge of the carnival area.

"Tickets! Tickets!" another barker shouted to her left. "Get your tickets. Ferris wheel, carousel, pony rides, Over the Jumps, scooter cars, and trolley rides. Get your tickets here!"

Oh, she'd definitely have to make a point to at least visit the scooter cars. Construction of the pavilion that housed that amusement had taken several months. More comfortable on a bicycle than a scooter, Paige didn't know if she'd actually purchase a ticket or simply be a spectator. Sidestepping another cluster of people coming from the direction of the midway and heading toward the Ferris wheel, she turned to the right and made her way to the Peabody Pavilion.

Five minutes later, she stepped outside again and looked south toward the camping sites. A short bit of track for the trolley car ride stretched parallel to the walking path on the outside of the grounds just past the Ferris wheel. The fair committee had certainly outdone themselves this year in presentation and attractions. Paige could hardly wait for the judging in her area to conclude so she could have a little fun.

She turned to the west and faced the river, which bordered the fairgrounds to the west. Papa loved having the North Platte so close to livestock pavilions. Made it easy to get water for the horses he ran in the roundup wagon races as well as what he called his prize-winning bull. He'd been trying for years to see his bull selected for the rodeo. Paige prayed this would be his year.

Raised and heated voices just ahead of her drew her attention as she walked to the rear of the greenhouse. Stopping in her tracks, she took note of five men facing off near one of the livestock paddocks. Three of them stood face-to-face against the other two, and by the looks on their faces, the words they spoke were anything but friendly.

An inner voice told her to keep moving, but the prospect of a possible fight drew her like a child reaching out to touch a hot stove. It couldn't possibly hurt to watch, could it? She'd heard of brawls from Matthew, but she'd never witnessed one firsthand. And the thrill of danger was too tempting to ignore.

"I said I'd teach you a lesson with my fists if I caught you around my animals."

This came from the shortest of the five men, but what he lacked in height, he made up for in bravado.

"And I told you we didn't touch your animals. Your boy here"—the one on the defense pointed at a scrawny lad beside the first one who spoke—"he told you we was. But he should get his eyes checked."

The lad referenced swore loudly and took a step forward, but the shorter one held him back. Paige gasped at the profanity.

"It's my word against yours," the first man countered. "And I say you *was* messin' with my property. No doubt tryin' to rig the livestock show in your favor."

"I say we settle this right here and now."

More expletives came from both sides. Paige had only heard of these kinds of words. Papa was right. They were not for a young lady's ears. No wonder Mama kept her sheltered.

Paige held her breath. She looked around to see only a handful of kids and a few spectators who had gathered. Everyone else went about enjoying the fair. Why didn't someone stop this? Didn't they care? But instead of stepping away, she edged closer, drawn into the small crowd.

No sooner had she found a place than the shortest man threw the first punch with a sickening thud. Paige gasped and covered her mouth. It was three on two, unfair odds in her mind, but the two seemed to handle themselves fairly well. The crack of fist on flesh and bone made her cringe and close her eyes. She peered through one eye and then the other, almost not wanting to know how the fight progressed.

As one man tackled another and rammed them both into the ground, Paige jumped back. The violence had begun in a small area not far from the river, and it now expanded as the men swung at and dodged one another. Well-placed blows knocked them down and widened the circle of their dispute.

All right. She had seen enough. Why any man would engage in this type of atrocious, animalistic behavior was beyond her. Paige stepped back and turned away from the dreadful sight. She had almost made it to the safety of the greenhouse when the thump of one body hitting another caused her to look over her shoulder—just in time to see an airborne man headed her way.

Chapter 3

Andy Lawrence tucked his notepad into the left breast pocket of his suit jacket and let the door to the greenhouse slam shut behind him. He reached into his pocket and retrieved his handkerchief to mop his forehead and neck. Phew! That was one very warm interview. But he'd gotten a great story from one of the farmers' wives on what led her to grow her now prize-winning evening primrose and orange day lilies. His editor would love it. Now, on to the culinary skills and creative craftsmanship at the Ag Hall. . .and maybe even another meeting with the tongue-tied beauty he'd met yesterday. But first, he had to find a telephone.

He turned the corner only to have the wind knocked out of him as his forward motion suddenly changed direction. His kerchief flew from his grasp and his hat followed suit. Sailing through the air for what felt like an eternity, Andy hit the ground—hard.

It took him a few moments to catch his breath and clear his head. Alternating dark spots and flashes of light passed across his vision. Vague awareness filtered through his mind as the shock wore off. Movement on top of him made him open his eyes. He propped himself on his elbows. Pain shot through his shoulder. As he tried to inch backward, he saw the mass of dark tresses splayed out on his chest, some pinned in a haphazard fashion on top of the woman's head while others tumbled free from their confinement.

"Mmmm."

The mumble came from somewhere within the tangle of hair, and the female form on top of him shifted. His senses took over, and he placed his hands around her as he attempted to move into a sitting position. Unable to do so with the weight of the other person, Andy instead slid out from under her and knelt beside her.

The young woman's head rolled to the left and right, but she didn't open her eyes. At least she looked all right. Then again, Andy had absorbed the majority of the impact. He glanced around to see what had caused her fall and saw the unruly bunch of men fighting not ten yards from where he and the young woman now rested. No one seemed to pay him or the woman any attention at all. They were too consumed by the outcome of the scuffle.

At another time in his life, Andy might have been tempted to get involved but not anymore. He turned his attention again to the young woman and smoothed back the hair from her face.

"Miss? Are you—"

He stopped as soon as he recognized her. The young lady he'd met at the Ag Hall. The one unable to talk. Andy hesitantly touched her cheek.

She stirred beneath his touch. Her eyelids fluttered then opened. She blinked several times, as if trying to gauge her surroundings. As soon as she focused on him, she sat up with a start and placed one hand on her chest.

"Oh! I am terribly sorry. Are you the one who broke my fall?"

Well, she obviously had no trouble talking now. Andy opened his mouth to reply, but the lyrical, polished sound of her voice left him speechless. It matched the warm depths of her brown eyes, like coffee with just a little bit of cream mixed in. The young woman didn't seem to notice, though, as she continued speaking.

"It happened so suddenly." She swept one arm outward in an arc around her body. "One moment I was minding my own business and heading back to the carnival area. The next I stopped to watch an awful display of immature behavior." Her gaze stretched toward the ongoing fight. "Before I knew it, one of the men came flying toward me. I tried to escape, but it was too late." She looked back at him, her dark eyes soft and apologetic. "If it hadn't been for your opportune appearance, I might have been hurt a lot more."

Opportune? Perhaps. He *had* just been wishing he'd get a chance to see her again. He didn't expect it to be like this, though. Her head tilted to one side as she regarded him. A dimple appeared just to the right of her mouth, and she scrunched her eyebrows together in a most appealing manner. With a glance downward, Andy realized she still sat in a heap on the ground. *Oh, good grief.* He silently scolded himself as he stood and extended both hands to her.

"Forgive me for my poor manners. May I help you up?"

One corner of her mouth tugged upward, and amusement danced in her eyes. She offered her hand to him and accepted his assistance. When they were both on their feet facing each other, her head fell quite a few inches below his. He stood just over six feet and guessed her to be about a foot shorter. Andy took a step back to see her more clearly. No reason to make her crick her neck to look at him.

As much as he would have liked to stay and talk a bit longer, duty called.

"I'm sorry to rush off, but I was on my way to make a telephone call to my editor when we ran into each other."

"Oh, you don't need to apologize. It isn't anyone's fault I ended up using you as my cushion instead of the ground. . .well, except for maybe those hooligans over there." She glanced again to the group of men who were the real cause of the delay and grimaced. "If it hadn't been for my curiosity, neither of us would be in this mess."

He wouldn't exactly call it a mess. Under other circumstances, Andy might have been more upset. But he didn't mind such a charming young woman delaying him a little.

He regarded her with a curious eye. "Well, as long as you're all right."

She brushed off her skirts, tugged down the edge of her dress, situated her beaded necklace, and reached up a hand to touch her hair. A wince crossed her delicate features followed by a resigned shrug as she no doubt realized the tangled mess was a lost cause.

"I'm fine, I assure you. Now, go make that call to your editor." She pointed toward the Medical Aid Pavilion and Security building. "You'll find a telephone in there."

Andy bent to retrieve his hat from the street and slapped it on his head. "I'm headed to the Ag Hall after this to cover the judging there. Will you be present as well?"

She nodded. "Yes," she replied.

"Perhaps I'll see you there."

"Perhaps," she echoed.

As he started to dash off, he turned his head and called over his shoulder. "I hope the rest of your day ends up better than it started."

The echo of her giggle reached his ears and made him smile. This day just got better and better. First, a solid piece on a local farmer's wife, and then a chance encounter with a rather charming brunette. Now, he'd give his editor a little taste of what was to come with his story, and then he'd make his way back to. . .

Oh no! Andy halted and did a quick about-face. He searched the crowds for any sign of the young lady. He'd been so distracted by their encounter and his desire to keep to his mental schedule, he'd forgotten to ask her for her name. That was twice now. Yesterday, when they'd met, he'd introduced himself, but neither one of the ladies had done the same. Here he'd seen her yet again, and he still didn't know her name. Well, the next time he saw her, he'd remedy that immediately. There was no sign of her now.

As he resumed his path toward the nearest telephone, Andy made a mental jump ahead to that promotion his boss mentioned right before sending him north to this fair. He'd been working at the *Denver Post* for a little over fifteen years, once his days of peddling the paper on the streets of Denver led to his first real job. Paying attention and doing as he was told earned him a steady string of advancements from errand boy to typesetter to copyeditor and then to journalist. And he'd loved every bit of it.

"Can I help you, son?" A weathered security officer addressed him as soon as he stepped inside.

Andy removed his hat and stepped toward the front desk. "Yes, sir. I wonder if I might use your telephone. A friend told me I'd find one here. Got an important call to make to my editor."

"Editor, huh?" the older gentleman remarked. "Does that make you one of those journalists coming from all over to write about our little fair here?"

Little fair? Was the man jesting or serious? "Not meaning any disrespect, sir, but your 'little fair' boasts one of the largest rodeos from here to Kansas City." Andy chuckled. "I'd hardly call several thousand in attendance with over a hundred performers *little*."

The officer shrugged. "It's no Dallas or Coney Island, but we hold our own." Then the man grinned, and Andy caught the twinkle in his eye.

He smiled. "Yes, you do, and I aim to showcase the best of the best in my coverage for the *Denver Post*."

The officer gave him quick perusal from head to toe and seemed to be assessing him with that one glance. "See that you do, my boy," he replied, not appearing to find reason to doubt him. He jerked a thumb toward a room on the left. "You'll find the telephone in there. Close the door if you'd like to make your call in private."

"Thank you." Andy nodded and stepped into the room. After dropping his hat on the only table in the little room, he reached for the upright candlestick and lifted the receiver from the switch hook. He dialed through to the switchboard operator and gave his destination number then waited for the connection to complete.

"Lawrence, is that you?" came the voice of Harry Tammen over the line.

"Yeah, boss," Andy replied. "I'm calling to let you know I got a great story from covering the flower and plant showcase here this morning. Real special interest piece."

"Glad to hear it." Throat clearing crackled along the wires. "I knew I made the right decision sending you up there. Seen any of those rodeo champions yet?"

Andy pressed the receiver tighter to his ear and leaned closer to the transmitter. "Not yet, but most of those performances aren't until later in the week."

"Don't forget about that promotion," Tammen reminded him. "Keep your mind on your job and stay focused."

Andy leaned his hip against the table. It was as if the man could read his thoughts or somehow had his eyes on the fair to see the potential distraction that a dark-haired young lady could be. No, she'd be a pleasant diversion while he was there, but he wouldn't allow it to drive him off course. That lead journalist position was too good to let it slip through his fingers.

"I'm counting on you to turn in some of your best work yet."

As if he'd do anything less. "Won't let you down, boss," Andy promised.

"Very good." Mumbling followed. "Uh, Lawrence, I have an appointment in five minutes, and he's already here in the office. Going to say good-bye for now."

Andy straightened and stared down at the candlestick then raised it off the desk and brought it close to his mouth. "Not a problem, Mr. Tammen. I have another judging showcase to attend."

"Looking forward to what you come up with. Call again at the end of the week."

"I will." He set the telephone back on the table, returning the receiver to the switch hook.

Andy stared at the upright. His thoughts had definitely started drifting away from his assignment since yesterday. It wasn't as if hers was the first pretty face he'd seen during his travels on assignment for the *Post*, and she certainly wouldn't be his last. Good thing he'd made that call to his boss. It helped put things back in perspective and reminded him of his goal. Now, there were a few blue ribbon contenders waiting for their chance at a little black-and-white recognition. He'd better get on it.

Chapter 4

S o, did you set out my jars like I asked?" Mama stood close, stretching her neck to see through the swarm of farmers' wives gathered in the hall.

"Yes, Mama," Paige replied. "Right in front of where the judges will stand when they come to those tables." Some might frown upon giving the previous year's prize-winners special placement, but she'd been put in charge of the culinary division, and the presentation of the entries was entirely her prerogative.

Mama wrung her hands in the folds of her cotton dress. Though she'd accompanied Paige to Cheyenne earlier in the year to purchase some newer dresses in a more modern style, Mama hadn't bought anything for herself.

"Those pretty things might be worthwhile for visits to town or even wearing to church on Sundays," she'd said. "But on the farm? My cotton and calico are much more durable." Then, she'd leaned in and whispered to her daughter, "Besides, I can't imagine tying an apron over one of those fancy dresses. And what would Papa think about me uncovering so much of my legs?"

"I don't know, Mama. Papa might just appreciate it."

And for that, Paige had received a playful swat on her arm as Mama blushed and turned away. Not before Paige had caught the twinkle in her eyes, though. Paige's older two sisters might have married and left the farm, but Paige remained for now, and in the past four years, her relationship with her mother had grown tenfold. Sharing things like this judging experience at the fair had drawn them closer than ever.

"Oh, I don't know if I can take it any longer, Paige," Mama whispered. "When are they going to move on from the pickles and preserves to the jellies, cobblers, and pies?" She clenched the skirts of her dress so tightly, her knuckles were turning white.

Paige slipped her arm around Mama's waist. "Don't fret." She pointed to where the judges made their final notations on their notepads. "There. See? I believe they're finished with the first two tables." She placed a comforting hand on Mama's arm. "Now, I'm going to have to see to my duties and collect the results." Paige caught sight of Millie, who wasn't too far away, and nodded. "Millie's going to come and stand with you, so you won't have to be nervous alone."

Mama barely acknowledged her, eyes trained solely on the tables at the front and the individual items the judges tasted. Millie appeared, and Paige smiled her thanks to her friend then moved to the front of the crowd to stand a few feet to the side of the judges. Mrs. Waverly moved behind them and approached Paige, silently handing her the notations from the first two rounds. Paige accepted the papers and lowered them to her side as Mrs. Waverly resumed her position near the trays of water used to cleanse the judges' mouths between each bite.

As smoothly as the first two tables received their ultimate judgments, the remaining three displayed their wares for the discerning judges while the owners of the tasty samplings awaited the results. With just a small spoon and one tiny morsel, each of the three judges made their pass across the assorted variety and jotted down their thoughts within seconds.

Paige recalled that very first year she oversaw this division. She'd foolishly spoken out about how quickly the judges came to a decision, when they only seemed to test such a small bit. After a soft reprimand from Mrs. Waverly and quiet observance of the proceedings, she came to realize experienced judges such as these didn't need to eat much to know which offerings pleased the palate the most.

"You know, it's a good thing they don't deliberate too long over their conclusions," a low voice spoke from just behind Paige's right shoulder. "These farmers' wives and self-proclaimed culinary experts might revolt."

Paige turned her head and found the reporter she'd all but knocked out just a short while ago. What was his name? Aaron? Adam? Andrew? Andrew! That was it. Andrew Lawrence. "Shh," she whispered. "You're going to distract the judges. And Mrs. Waverly will not stand for that."

Mr. Lawrence peered around her, as if searching for the woman she'd mentioned, then rocked back on his heels and chuckled. "Appreciate the warning," he whispered in return. "I certainly wouldn't want to be on the receiving end of one of her glares."

Paige pressed her lips into a thin line to avoid the giggle that threatened to escape. He'd just given words to the very thoughts in her head on numerous occasions while working with Mrs. Waverly over the years. Yet, stern though she might be, she got the job done, and that was all that mattered.

The reporter shifted his stance, and his arm brushed against hers. He stood close enough for his warm breath to stir some of those loose tendrils of hair that had escaped their pins during her fall earlier. One or two strands lightly tickled her cheek. A tiny shiver traveled up her back, and she raised her arm to hide it. With a few tucks, she managed to confine the few rebellious wisps.

"So." Mr. Lawrence's baritone came low and soft near her other ear. "Are there any creations present that originated from your kitchen?"

Paige glanced over her shoulder to find the reporter bent at the waist with both hands on his knees. He appeared to be using her as a shield and had to duck low to match her height. He'd moved closer to the back wall, possibly to avoid being overheard, or maybe even to better hide from Mrs. Waverly. His nearness was quite unsettling.

His gaze met hers, and he raised both eyebrows. "Well?"

Well, what? She furrowed her brow. Had he asked her something? Oh, yes. Did she have anything entered? Should she tell him? What if she didn't win any prize at all? Oh, pish posh. This was no time for pride.

"Yes. Mama and I have a cherry cobbler entered, and she entered her strawberry jelly for the first time this year, along with her prized raspberry pie."

"Ahh, a combined effort on the cobbler. Excellent." Mr. Lawrence set his notepad on one knee and made some notes resembling a series of squiggly lines and curves.

"What is that?"

"Shorthand," the reporter replied without looking up. He finished writing then tilted his chin toward her. "Can't divulge any of the details of my story, now, can I?" he said with a grin.

"Did you write something about Mama and me?"

"That would be quite difficult, since I don't even know your name."

He said it in such a matter-of-fact way, Paige couldn't tell if he was teasing or not. Come to think of it, though, she hadn't ever given him her name. He hadn't asked for it, either. . .until now.

"Paige Callahan," she said.

Mr. Lawrence made a quick notation on his pad and nodded. "Perfect. And in answer to your question, perhaps. You'll have to wait for the article to appear in the paper to find out."

But she didn't even know the newspaper for which he wrote. How in the world would she know where to look for the article, or even when for that matter?

"Mr. Lawrence, I—"

She didn't get a chance to finish as Mrs. Waverly interrupted their conversation with a quiet but stern clearing of her throat. Paige glanced toward the judges to see they had concluded their proceedings, and all eyes from everyone in the room were now on her and Mrs. Waverly.

"It's time to award the ribbons, Miss Callahan," the woman stated, barely moving her lips. "Would you please retrieve them and bring them to the front?"

"Yes, ma'am," Paige replied and immediately did her bidding. When she reached the front, Mrs. Waverly handed her the final list of names from the judges, save one piece of paper.

"I'll be announcing the cobblers this year," Mrs. Waverly answered. Her tone brooked no argument.

"Very well." Paige accepted the other lists of winners and stepped to the center of those assembled.

Mrs. Waverly set out the ribbons on one of the tables and reached for the first one. Paige read the first two names, and the ladies came forward to accept their prizes. She looked at the top name on the list and smiled.

"And the blue ribbon for the best dill pickles goes to. . .Mrs. Caroline Harris."

Applause followed as demure Mrs. Harris approached, her sweet smile a nice complement to the honor. She'd been runner-up for the past four years. This year, she'd managed to deliver the crunchiest and tastiest dill pickles at the fair. . .according to the judges. And for the first time, she'd be taking home the coveted blue ribbon. Paige made a mental note to talk to Mrs. Harris after the ribbons were all awarded. She wanted to find out what she'd done differently.

Next, it was on to the sweet pickles, then the preserves and jams and jellies. Paige caught Mama's eye. All year long, at various festivals and events, jams had been a tug-of-war between Mama's best friend and Mrs. Greene for as long as she could remember. Every year at the state fair, Mrs. Greene's jams remained the winning entry. This year, though, Mama and Miss Dorothy had worked together, hoping between the two of them, they'd upset the predictable outcome.

With sweet pickles and preserves done, Paige shifted the papers in her hand for the jams category and glanced down. Yes! Both Miss Dorothy *and* Mama were on the list! And so was Mrs. Greene. With great delight, she called Mama's name first.

"It's all right, Paige," Mama said with a smile as she accepted the ribbon for third place. "At least I *have* a ribbon. Not disappointing at all for my first attempt at making a jam worthy of the fair."

Mama was right. They might secretly wish Mrs. Greene would taste the bitterness of defeat just once, but they needed to focus more on what they'd accomplished instead of what they hadn't yet achieved. Paige called Miss Dorothy's name next.

The woman gave Paige's arm a gentle squeeze and smiled. "It just means we'll have to try that much harder next year," the woman who'd been like a second mother to her remarked. Her thoughts almost paralleled Mama's.

Forcing brightness into her voice, Paige made the winning announcement in jams. "And the blue ribbon goes to. . .Mrs. Virginia Greene."

The way Mrs. Greene came forward, as if she had expected to win, made Paige wish all the more that Mama or Miss Dorothy could have bested her this year. If only the woman didn't look so confident and smug at the same time, her winning the top ribbon might be easier to take. With her back erect and her nose raised toward the roof of the Ag Hall, Mrs. Greene only garnered polite applause for her accomplishment. Her jams did possess a certain level of sugary sweetness combined with the slight tartness of the berries she used, but the way she boasted about them left a sour taste in Paige's mouth the last time she'd had some. It would be a long time before she'd purchase any jams from Mrs. Greene again. And now that Miss Dorothy and Mama had teamed up to perfect their own recipes, she had all the jam she'd ever need.

Movement to her right caused Paige to glance in that direction. Mr. Lawrence frantically scribbled on his notepad and flipped the page to continue scrawling. She'd almost forgotten about him in all the excitement. A lock of his dark brown hair fell across his forehead and bounced as he wrote. As if her thoughts had become words spoken directly to him, he looked up and caught her watching him. A slow smile spread across his lips, and Paige quickly looked away, feeling the warmth of a blush creep up her neck.

She looked out again at the ladies assembled, silently praying no one noticed. They all looked back in anticipation, seemingly oblivious. Everyone that is, except for Millie. That observant girl regarded Paige with one eyebrow quirked, her eyes going back and forth between Paige and the reporter. She'd hear about this later. No doubt about it.

All right, time to move on to the last two categories she was announcing, jellies and pies. She read through the names for jellies and moved on to pies. Her mouth fell open a little when she looked at the list in front of her and Mama's name wasn't there. Really? Mama always received a ribbon for one of the top three spots. Friends and neighbors always asked for more raspberry pie whenever Mama made it. Guess this year, things decided to mix themselves up a little.

The third- and second-place spots went to a mother and daughter who had recently moved to Douglas from Casper, about thirty miles to the west of them.

"And the blue ribbon for the best pie this year goes to. . .Mrs. Beatrice Weatherby, for her rhubarb pie."

Well, if Mama had to lose her regular place, it didn't hurt so much seeing that spot given to the woman who would soon become Matthew's mother-in-law. Paige smiled as Mrs. Weatherby made her way to the front. The Weatherbys had moved to Douglas a few years ago from Cheyenne because Mr. Weatherby wanted to spread out a little and have a larger farm. The moment Matthew met Constance, he'd been smitten. Amazing how it had turned her older brother into a mature and responsible man, ready to prove he could effectively manage a farm and provide for a wife.

Mr. Weatherby had taken a shine to Matthew, too, and readily agreed to allow his daughter and Matthew to court. By the time the proposal of marriage came, the Weatherbys approved unanimously. Paige couldn't remember her brother being so happy, and Constance would make a great sister-in-law. Now why couldn't she find the same kind of happiness? Charlie could provide nice conversation every once in a while, but he always spent so much time analyzing everything and planning, she didn't know if he even knew how to just relax and enjoy himself.

"Thank you, my dear," Mrs. Weatherby said, accepting the blue ribbon and bringing Paige's attention back to the present. "You are doing a wonderful job with all of this, Paige. I'm certain your mother and father must be quite proud."

"It's not a difficult task when I love it so much," Paige replied. "Congratulations on your pie."

Mrs. Weatherby winked. "It appears your mother and I need to compare recipes, now that we each have prize-winning pies."

"Oh, Mama would love that, I know." And Mama would, too. Perhaps next year, they would both win a ribbon.

Well, she'd come to the end of her list of winners. Paige angled toward Mrs. Waverly and waited to see how she'd proceed. With no hesitation at all, the woman transitioned smoothly, like they had planned this all along.

"And for our final category, we have the ever-popular cobblers everyone loves to sample this time of year." She allowed a small smile to form on her lips. "It might be a sign that summer is coming to an end, but we're not about to let it disappear without a great deal of enjoyment, now, are we?"

Murmurs of agreement resonated throughout the ladies—and some gentlemen—present. Something was different. The woman almost seemed congenial and likable. Not that others didn't like her. It just took quite a bit of time to truly understand who she was and what motivated her. Most people had trouble getting beyond the brusque exterior.

Paige stepped back and allowed her mentor and supervisor to be front and center, careful not to stand too close to the reporter. He remedied that for her by taking two steps in her direction. Oh well. He didn't leave her much choice. She couldn't exactly step away from him now. It would be too obvious. Let others think what they may. She'd just remain extremely professional. She was, after all, one of the organizers and supervisors at the Ag Hall. It made perfect sense for a reporter to be talking to her.

"Well, now," Mr. Lawrence intoned. "Seems that first-time entry from your mother appealed to the judges' palates enough to earn her third place."

"Yes, she and the lady who won second prize actually made their jams together."

"Trying to come up with a way to best Mrs. Greene?"

How could he possibly have known that? Paige jerked her head to look up at him only to find what was fast becoming a familiar grin on his lips and a gleam in his eyes.

Mr. Lawrence shrugged. "I wouldn't be a reporter worth my salt if I didn't at least do a little poking around beforehand to get a feel for those I'd be interviewing, now, would I?"

He had a point. "No, I guess not." Paige watched the two ladies walk to the front to accept the third- and second-place ribbons for their cobblers. Here it was. The final ribbon for her department.

"And the blue ribbon goes to. . ." Mrs. Waverly paused again for effect, just as Paige had done on all previous categories. Then, her voice caught as she smiled big. "Mrs. Lorena Callahan and her daughter Paige, for their, as the judges noted, 'absolutely divine' cherry cobbler!"

Chapter 5

Paige gasped and immediately sought out Mama, who looked as surprised as she felt. Millie hopped up and down in her exuberance as she clapped loudly next to Mama. They'd won? They'd actually won? Neither one of them moved for several moments.

"I believe they'd like you to come forward to accept your ribbon, Miss Callahan," the reporter teased, his breath again fanning across her ear.

That set her feet in motion. As soon as she took her first step, Mama began making her way to the front. They came together and stood before the panel of judges and Mrs. Waverly, who handed Mama the blue ribbon.

"Congratulations, Mrs. Callahan. The cobbler you made with your daughter was the only entry among dozens to garner such adulation. What did you put in it?"

Mama looked at Paige, and Paige shrugged, so Mama turned back to Mrs. Waverly. "I believe that is one secret Paige and I shall keep." She raised her head with pride and smiled out at their friends and neighbors gathered around them. "We'll leave it to the discerning tastes of those who taste it to try to figure it out."

"Well, I believe you have a definite enthusiast in Mr. Buford, our head judge." Mrs. Waverly gestured toward the stout little man, who beamed from ear to ear at them both. He even gave Mama a little wiggle of his fingers. "Now, can we have all the finalists and winners gather here at the front?" Mrs. Waverly nodded toward the reporter. "I'm sure Mr. Lawrence would like to have a photograph to accompany his article covering the culinary division of the Ag Hall judging."

As everyone else filed out through the three doors on the west, north, and south sides of the building, the ribbon recipients came together.

"If it's not too much trouble," Mr. Lawrence addressed the group as he prepared his camera, "could I have each of you hold up your ribbons and stand behind your entry on the table in front of you?" He flashed what Paige would call an award-winning smile at all of them. "I'd like to feature those prize-worthy entries in the photograph as well."

Several ladies beamed in response as they did his bidding. Paige had a feeling they'd go for a swim in the North Platte if he asked it of them. What a charmer. It no doubt served him well in his profession.

"Is everyone ready?" Mr. Lawrence asked. He raised his camera in front of him and held the handles on each side. "Let's see those ribbons, now," he instructed, and they all lifted their ribbons in response. With a loud *pop*, the image was preserved, and everyone relaxed.

"Congratulations again, ladies," Mrs. Waverly spoke. "Now, go out and enjoy yourself at the fair. There's plenty to see and do." She snapped her fingers. "Don't forget to come back on Wednesday for the judging of the craftsmanship in all of our unique knickknacks and handmade decorative items. If you'd like to see the textiles and larger items, you'll need to go two buildings over to the south and visit our Art Hall. It's been newly remodeled and enlarged to house all of our abundant treasures."

Most of the ladies exited out one of the doors leading to the rest of the fairgrounds. A handful remained and spoke in low tones, sharing their excitement at their prizes. Millie approached from the side where she'd waited while Mr. Lawrence took the photograph.

"Congratulations, Mrs. Callahan! And you, too, Paige." Millie clasped both of their hands in hers and bounced a little. "Can you believe it? Not one, but two ribbons! And one of them is blue!" Her eyes shone bright. "I would love to win a ribbon of any kind, let alone a blue one."

Paige smiled at her friend. "Millie, you have to enter something in order to win a ribbon."

Millie giggled. "I know that, you silly goose." She swatted at Paige and barely brushed her shoulder. "But that also means I'd have to actually bake something, and nothing I make would be awarded a prize."

Mama reached out and squeezed Millie's hands, giving them a gentle pat. "Millie dear, I believe it might be time for you to come for a visit and join Paige and me in the kitchen instead of going over to the barn and paddocks as you always do."

"But I love watching the horses and talking to the sheep and cattle," Millie replied.

"And a certain foreman as well, I'm sure," Paige teased.

Millie blushed and ducked her head. It was no secret she and Carter were sweet on each other. They just hadn't done anything about it yet. Then again, Millie had also caught the eye of a certain bank teller in town. She claimed it was too difficult to choose between them, so for now, she kept things familiar but nonchalant. Paige sighed. Much like how Charlie treated her and their relationship, wherever that stood.

"Excuse me, ladies," Mr. Lawrence interrupted, approaching from where he'd just ended a conversation with Mrs. Waverly. "Mrs. Callahan, Miss Callahan," he greeted formally. "Congratulations again on your notable accomplishments today. I wonder if I might ask the two of you a few questions to add a personal touch to my story." He pressed the tip of his pencil to his notepad and regarded them both. "I promise it will only take a few minutes, and then you can be on your way enjoying the fair."

Millie touched Paige on the arm. "I'm going to walk down to the arenas. Maybe catch one of the calf-roping demonstrations." She raised her eyebrows. "See you there?"

"Yes," Paige replied to her friend then turned to the reporter as Millie bounded out of the building. "I still have a great deal of cleaning and a few things to take down before I can leave, so I won't be taking in the entertainment of the fair just yet." She gave Mr. Lawrence a polite smile. "Mama and I would be happy to oblige you for an interview first, though."

"Marvelous." He placed a hand on his chest. "The chief is going to be quite pleased. I appreciate your time."

Together, they recounted how Mama came to enter a jam for the first time, how long Paige had been working there at the fair, what sorts of things they did throughout the rest of the year, and even shared one of the added ingredients in their cherry cobbler but not both.

"The cinnamon you can print," Mama stated with authority. "But the other shall remain a mystery."

Mr. Lawrence nodded. "I promise not to press you any further, ma'am." He winked. "But perhaps I can persuade you to share a piece with me before you take it with you? I might just be able to figure out the secret myself."

"If you do," Mama replied, "you be sure and come find me or Paige to tell us." She smiled. "There are no guarantees we'll confirm or deny your deduction, but you are more than welcome to speculate."

"I applaud your confidence, ma'am." He gave Paige an approving glance. "I can see where your charming daughter gets her poise and assurance."

Paige avoided his direct gaze and instead fiddled with the strand of blue beads hanging from her neck. Mama looked quickly back and forth between them with slightly narrowed eyes.

Mr. Lawrence cleared his throat, effectively silencing anything Mama might have been about to say.

"I believe I have everything I need. Thank you again, ladies." He bowed. "Should you wish to receive a copy of the paper in which this article will appear, you can reach me here." He withdrew a small card from his breast pocket and handed it to Mama. "It has the address for the *Denver Post* as well as the direct line to my editor. He'll know how to get in touch with me."

The reporter stepped away and retrieved his hat from the table at the rear where he and Paige had stood for most of the judging. After setting it atop his head and tucking his notepad and pencil into his pocket, he again bowed to them both.

"Good day, ladies."

Paige and Mama both nodded. "Good day," they said together.

As soon as Mr. Lawrence disappeared from sight, Paige started clearing the tables and cleaning up the few entries no one had bothered to claim. Mama came alongside her and placed her hand on top of Paige's.

"Why don't you go ahead and join Millie, dear? Mrs. Waverly and I can finish up here." She nodded toward the other woman, who now busied herself on the far side of the hall, then smiled. "Besides, it's been quite some time since she and I have been able to visit." She reached up and touched Paige's cheek. "Go enjoy yourself. You've worked very hard and have earned a rest."

Paige turned to fully face Mama and pulled her into a quick hug. "Thank you, Mama."

Her mother pulled back and waved her hand in an air of dismissal. "Think nothing of it, my dear. Just go and have some fun."

Glancing at the western door where Mr. Lawrence had exited, Paige turned and headed for the one to the south. She wasn't sure if he'd made note of where Millie had said she'd meet her, and for all she knew, he might be somewhere else covering another part of the fair. But no sense in giving Mama any more fuel for her suppositions, if she even had any about Mr. Lawrence and her. Besides, he was a reporter. If he wanted to find her, he would.

Chapter 6

What a morning! Andy had spent most of it walking up and down the midway, observing the fairgoers and taking notes on the various vendors hawking the merits of their booths. He'd been cajoled into trying a few of the challenges himself, though without a prize at the end of his bumbling attempts.

Now, he had some time to himself, and he intended to use it to find Miss Callahan. He'd waited for her after the interview yesterday, but somehow she'd managed to slip past him. After that, he'd been unable to find her, no matter how hard he looked.

He strolled past the grassy areas separating the buildings and dormitories from the rest of the fair and headed for the camping sites. Why he thought Miss Callahan might be there, he had no idea. Then again, he didn't know if she went home each evening or if she *did* have somewhere there on the fairgrounds to sleep. For all he knew, she rose bright and early and had tasks to complete before the fair even opened to the public each morning. He knew she worked in the Ag Hall, but did she have any other jobs? As soon as he found her, he'd find out.

Several ladies he passed resembled Miss Callahan, and Andy almost called out to one or two of them. At least he was getting a good feel for the layout of the fair.

Winding his way around the horse barns and cutting through just behind the grandstands, Andy made a sharp right and walked up to the fence surrounding the main arena. With his forearms resting on the top rail, he propped his right foot on the lowest rail and looked out at the trick pony riders showcasing their skills. Boots, jeans, and fringed jackets were still the wardrobe of choice for these ladies. Oh, and of course the ever-present Stetson adorning their heads.

The audience erupted in applause when the two ladies in the arena successfully managed to swap mounts as they passed each other, without missing a stride. From the corner of his eye, Andy saw a familiar face. There she was! Sitting almost underneath his nose on the bottom row of the grandstands. He pushed away from the fence and turned toward her. With a spring in his step, he approached. She still hadn't seen him.

"Excuse me, but is anyone sitting here?" he asked.

Miss Callahan startled then raised a hand to shade her eyes and stared up at him. "No." She lowered her gaze and extended her hand toward the space on the steel bench beside her. "Please, Mr. Lawrence. Sit down."

"Don't mind if I do," he said, snapping his suspenders before placing one hand on his chest. "And it's Andy. No more of this Mr. Lawrence. The only one who uses my last name is my editor, and he drops the Mr."

She pressed her lips together and regarded him a moment then nodded. "Very well."

She paused. "Andy," she added, almost as an afterthought.

His name sounded pretty good coming from her lips. "And may I call you Paige?"

She nodded then returned her attention to the performance in front of them. As soon as he was settled, he swiped off his hat and ran his fingers through his hair. Paige giggled, and he turned his head to find her looking at him. Or looking at his hair, that is.

"What?" He raised his hands to his head and felt the shocks of hair that had sprouted in all directions. He offered a rueful smile. "All right, so I forgot to brush my hair this morning." Truth be told, his unruly hair was only a testament to the harrowing morning he'd had. But she didn't need to know that. Grabbing his hat, he held it out in front of him. "That's why I have this," he said and settled it on his head once more.

Paige covered her mouth and spoke through her fingers. "If you don't mind, I don't mind."

Andy slapped his hands together as if ridding them of dirt or crumbs then plunked them down on his crossed legs. "Good. Now that we have that settled." He leaned forward and watched the trick riders exit the arena. "Who's up next?"

Paige consulted a crinkled piece of paper that looked as if it had seen better days. "It says here it's the barrel races." She pointed to the far end of the ring. "Look there. They're setting up the barrels."

That paper must be some sort of program guide. Now, why hadn't he gotten one of those? It would've helped him a great deal in knowing where he should be and when. He gestured toward it. "May I?"

She handed him the guide. It didn't have much detail, but it did list the major demonstration and performing locations and what would be taking place at which times.

"This could come in handy," he remarked. "Where would I find one of these?"

Paige pointed to the left. "At the event tent. It's just behind the pavilion where you made your telephone call yesterday."

"Ah, yes, and just across the way from where you were in such a hurry, you knocked me over in your haste," he said, trying to keep a straight face.

Her back straightened, and she pivoted toward him as her fists rammed into her hips. Indignation sent her eyebrows up as her eyes widened and her mouth fell open. "You know very well the reason we collided, and it wasn't my being in a rush."

Andy chuckled and splayed his hands in defense. "I was only teasing." He reached out and chucked her chin. "Relax, doll. Running into you was one of the best things that happened to me yesterday."

A charming blush colored her cheeks, and she immediately relaxed her stiff pose. "I'm sorry," she mumbled.

"Think nothing of it." With one hand on the seat between them, Andy shoved off and hopped to the ground. He turned to face her and extended a hand. "Now, what do you say we take a little stroll, and you give me a guided tour of these grand fairgrounds?"

Paige hesitated only a moment before placing her hand in his and accepting his help to the ground to stand beside him. She started walking away from him, and he followed. "All right. We can begin at the midway not far from the main gate to the north then wind our way around to the dormitories to the east and come full circle."

Andy grimaced as he reached for her elbow to halt her steps. "I already had my fill from a few of the vendors out that way. Spent the morning watching so many hand over their hard-earned money in exchange for baseballs, or wooden rings, or even the chance to shoot a rifle." He rubbed his upper arm and flexed the fingers of his right hand. "Tried a few myself, and while their offerings kept me entertained, I believe I'll take a pass on them for now."

She giggled. "Is that how you ended up here at the grandstands? Your throwing arm needed a rest?"

"Partly," he replied. "I had what I needed from the midway. Then, I realized I never saw you yesterday after the judging or even after supper when the fair was illuminated after the sun set." He slipped his hands into his pant pockets and rocked back on his heels. "So, I decided to take a walk and ended up finding you."

She reached up and ran her fingers up and down the beads of her necklace, an action which seemed to be a nervous habit. "Was there something you wanted or needed?"

Something he wanted? "What?"

"You said you realized you never saw me yesterday before or after supper. I asked if there was a reason you were looking for me."

She'd stated it so matter-of-factly, Andy couldn't tell if she was asking an innocent question or if she was being coy. He regarded her for a moment. She didn't appear to be playing games with him. It had to be the former.

He shrugged. "Nothing in particular. I just figured with all of your experience working here at the fair, you'd be an excellent source of information." He grinned. "And infinitely more charming as an escort than a lot of the other options I have around here."

She ducked her head and fingered the beads yet again. His stomach rumbled and reminded him it was past lunchtime already.

"I believe we should pay a visit to one of the food vendors first," Paige said with a grin. "And then we can make our way in the opposite direction from the midway for our tour."

Andy patted his stomach. "I believe that's a great idea!"

Since he'd already met his quota for the day in terms of story content, he had no reason not to spend the rest of the time with Paige. Or at least as long as she would allow. He intended to stretch that out as much as he could.

After a delicious meal of barbecued beef and baked beans, of which Paige ate very little, she assumed the role of tour guide and led the way toward the Ford Pavilion, stopping just at the corner of the greenhouse where he'd gotten his first story of the week.

"This exhibit pavilion, as you might guess from the smell, is for horses, cattle, sheep, and goats."

Her nose wrinkled in such a captivating manner. He wanted to reach out and tap it, but he held his impulse in check.

"My brother and Papa are thrilled to have this here," she continued. "It's equipped to care for the wants and needs of the exhibitors in a much better manner than in previous years."

"What was here before?" he asked, trying hard to focus on the information and not on the pretty individual sharing it.

"Some rather crude stables and pens and not a lot of privacy," she replied. "Exhibitors had to walk their animals down to the river to drink as there weren't even troughs available for filling."

Andy whistled long and low. "Sounds like folks here have learned quite a bit from past mistakes."

"Yes, and it will only get better." Paige raised her head just a little, and she squared her shoulders. "It's been twenty years since the first fair here in Douglas, and I've loved taking part, watching it all take shape."

She clearly held a great deal of pride for this fair, and her family had a lot invested in it from the sounds of it.

"So," he said by way of continuing the conversation. "Where to next?"

She spun on her heel and faced south. Andy followed suit. "Let's walk toward the carnival area," she suggested. "Maybe you can visit with one or two of the ride operators and ask them what brought them to this particular fair."

Andy nodded. "Excellent idea."

As they passed the area where the midway led off to their left, Paige paused and looked toward the center stage where throngs of people gathered. The resonant sound of bass strings being plucked joined with the saxophone as the closing notes of a woman crooning a bit of jazz mixed with blues reached their ears. After thunderous applause, the upbeat cadence of some vaudeville show tunes followed. Andy watched hope mixed with regret play across Paige's features as her expression brightened upon first hearing the music then dulled as the style changed.

"Everything okay?" he asked.

She sighed. "Yes. It's always been a dream of mine to sing from a stage like that."

She spoke so low, Andy had to lean in to be sure he heard her correctly. "You want to perform onstage?" Now that was something he never expected to hear. . .especially from a farm girl from Wyoming.

Paige stared off into the distance. "Yes, but where would I ever go to receive the training I need in order for anyone to even consider giving me a few minutes to prove I can do it?"

Where indeed? In Denver, there was no shortage of opportunities for anyone wanting to engage in theatrical or performing arts. Here in Douglas, though? "I see your point." Andy reached out and tapped a finger under her chin. "Hey, now," he said softly, and she turned to face him. "Don't give up on that dream." He smiled. "I wouldn't be where I am today if I'd given up as an errand boy at the *Denver Post*." His hand grabbed hers, and he gave it a little squeeze. "Dreams are what keep us going each day. One of these years, I'll get to try my hand at riding a bull. . .and write about it, too." He nodded toward the stage. "If you're meant to be up there, you will be. I have no doubts."

The glistening of unshed tears made her eyes sparkle, and her slow smile brightened her face. "Thank you."

Andy released her hand and tipped his hat just slightly. "My pleasure. Now, let's keep going on that tour."

Paige led him right through the heart of the carnival area, pointing out the unique facets of the carousel and sharing about the hand-carved animals adorning the circular platform. She also mentioned the new scooter cars attraction this year, as well as the trolley rides.

Once past the Ferris wheel, they both looked west toward the river where several Arapaho braves walked around their camp.

"I believe that's Chief Yellow Calf," Paige exclaimed. "At least that's what my brother told me last week when he returned from helping build the ramp for Doc Carver's horse show."

Andy watched the braves interact with one another and the squaws move about the camp. "I'm certainly no expert, but I heard the chief would be present this year on my way into town."

"The Fourth Cavalry used to camp on the grounds here," Paige added. "And both Arapaho and Shoshone have participated in events. Since horse races and relay races are still quite popular, the braves are excellent candidates."

He nodded toward their functional and efficient campsite. "It appears they have made themselves quite at home there on the banks of the Platte. Excellent vantage point, too!"

With a hand barely touching the small of Paige's back, Andy guided her around toward the other established campsite areas. Far different than the way the Arapaho set up their camp. They passed several families, and some of them waved at Paige, who returned their greeting.

Andy remembered that question he'd wanted to ask her when he first went searching for her. "Do you and your family stay on the grounds each year?"

She shook her head. "No. Our farm is only a few miles to the east of the fairgrounds here, so we drive home each night and return again in the morning." She chuckled. "I much prefer my soft bed to the unforgiving ground."

"I won't argue with you there," Andy agreed.

"Still, even these sites are better than the early days, when tents were set up military style with a bugle call to rise and sleep with the raising and lowering of the flag."

Andy grimaced. "Sounds rigid and uniform."

Paige shrugged. "It got the job done."

One final turn brought them almost full circle—at least back to where the Ag and Art Halls stood just to the right. Paige pointed behind them to a cluster of smaller buildings and an assortment of youth, both boys and girls, gathered in groups.

"The dormitories are provided for those from the Boys and Girls Club Works who come to both learn and participate. Since they are with the club, they often don't attend with their families, so the dormitories make it possible for them to camp on the grounds."

Turning away from him, Paige looked left and right, craning her neck a bit and fretting with her bead necklace again. Was she nervous or perhaps just late for something?

"Are you looking for someone?" he asked.

"I wanted to keep an eye out for Millie. She was supposed to meet me here this afternoon." She stopped, and alarm flashed across her face, almost as if she'd just remembered he still stood with her. "If she sees you here with me, she'll pester you with a never-ending stream of questions."

"Are you saying you'd like me to leave?"

"No!" she answered a little too quickly. "That is. . .I. . .uh. . .I don't want you to be forced to endure her interrogation."

"It certainly wouldn't be the first time I've answered for my actions or presence." He chuckled. "The last was when a wealthy socialite I helped showed her gratitude with an enthusiastic embrace that was not seen as such by her powerful and influential husband." He slipped his hands into his pockets and grinned. "Let's just say I had to think quickly in order to appease the man."

A tinge of pink stained Paige's cheeks, and he rushed to continue.

"That wouldn't be us, of course."

Paige met his gaze again. "No, but Millie might assume it regardless." The corners of her mouth turned downward, and her eyes softened. "I am truly sorry to be so abrupt. It has been a delightful afternoon."

Despite her erratic and somewhat befuddling behavior, Andy couldn't be upset. He'd intruded when he'd approached her at the grandstands, and she'd already spent more than two hours with him this afternoon. A very pleasant two hours at that. But if she had plans to meet with her friend, he didn't have the right to command much more of her time. Even though he wanted nothing more than to stay by her side, this was not the time or the place.

"Say no more, m'lady." He stretched his arms high above his head then extended his hand out toward her, waiting until she placed her delicate fingers against his. He bowed and raised her fingers to his lips, placing a brief kiss on her knuckles.

"Until next time."

The smile she bestowed upon him made leaving that much harder. But he must. With two fingers touching his hat, he gave her a final farewell and headed back toward the arenas. At least there he could find something to help take his mind off his beguiling companion from the afternoon. She'd already gotten under his skin more than any other dame he'd met along his travels. There was no room in his life right now for a girl, but if he wasn't careful, Paige might just manage to change his mind. At least while he was here, he could make the most of their time together. He'd deal with the repercussions later.

Chapter 7

Paige stood and arched her back after hunching over the knickknack tables all morning. It took a lot of hard work to develop a layout and methodical plan that would make sense to someone other than her, and she welcomed a little break.

She reached into the low pocket of her dress and withdrew an envelope. After removing the folded paper within, she stared again at the note she'd found waiting for her this morning. Mrs. Waverly had directed her to it not long after Paige had arrived. But what did it mean? She read it for what must have been the sixth or seventh time…as if rereading it might change the words or reveal more about the message.

> *Paige—*
>   *Meet me tonight in front of the Ferris wheel. 7:00. There is someone you must meet. Please come.*
>
> *—Andy*

That was it. No other details. No mention of why they couldn't meet earlier or what he'd be doing around the fairgrounds during the day that day. Nothing.

"Paige?"

Paige looked up. "Yes, Mrs. Waverly?" Her fingers tapped a rhythm on the note as she waited for the woman's next words.

"I know you've already been hard at work finalizing things here, but would you mind assisting me with the preparations for tomorrow's judging on the textiles and fabrics in the Art Hall?" Mrs. Waverly shook her head and released a resigned sigh. "Mrs. Dulaney came down ill this morning and won't be coming as planned."

Paige gasped softly. "Oh my! Is everything all right?"

"Yes," Mrs. Waverly replied. A smile curled her lips upward. "I believe the pending new addition to the family decided to tell Mrs. Dulaney she needed to rest." She arched her eyebrows. "So, will you be able to help?"

An opportunity to see the hours disappear faster? Definitely! Paige had wondered how she'd ever manage to pass the time and prayed evening would come quickly. Now, God had answered.

Paige smiled. "I'd be happy to."

Mrs. Waverly's expression relaxed. "Excellent. You're such a dear." She consulted the pocket watch fastened to her waistband then snapped it shut and returned it to its place. "It's near noon. Take a little time to eat and regain your strength, then meet me at the Art Hall at one. We have a long afternoon ahead of us."

Long afternoon? Paige grinned as she slipped the note back into its envelope and then her pocket. Spending the time working paled in comparison to the seemingly endless minutes ticking by if she'd had to occupy herself. No, this wouldn't be a long afternoon after all.

⬤

After patting her hair and checking the time on the large clock at the Security building for the fifth time in as many minutes, Paige looked again to her left and her right. Was she early? Had she misunderstood the location? The day? No. Andy had left no room for any misunderstanding or even the possibility of misconstrued interpretation. He'd been quite clear in his note. In front of the Ferris wheel at seven o'clock sharp that evening. And that's where she now stood.

Perhaps he'd been detained. As a journalist, being late likely didn't happen often. In fact, he probably made it a point to be early whenever possible. That's why it surprised her not to find him here already, waiting for her.

"Paige! There you are." Andy approached from her right. He looked a little relieved, as if he thought she might not come. "I was waiting over there by the diving show." He frowned, an expression slightly resembling a pout. "Thought maybe you hadn't gotten my note or, worse, simply dismissed it."

"Oh, I would never do that. . .at least not without coming to explain first."

He gave a sharp nod, his self-assured confidence once again returning. "I thought as much."

She furrowed her brow. "Did you just say the diving show? Do you mean the tall ramp near the river? But you asked me to meet you here at the Ferris wheel."

Andy shook his head. "What? No, I'm certain I said the wooden ramp."

Paige reached into her pocket, glad she had kept his note with her all day and hadn't left it behind. "Here," she said, withdrawing the note and unfolding it for him to see. "I'll show you." She pointed to the words he'd scribbled. "This is what you wrote."

He stepped closer and bent his head. The scent of light musk and leather mixed with talc wafted over her. The same combination she'd noticed every other time he'd been near. It distinguished him just a bit with an invigorating freshness. Must be the aftershave he used. Paige peered up at his smooth chin and jawline. The slight hint of a shadow had started to appear, but it didn't hide the evidence of his neatly groomed appearance.

"Well, I'll be," Andy exclaimed. "I thought for sure I said the ramp." He tilted his head, which brought his face within inches of hers as their gazes collided. "Must've. . . had. . .wheels. . .uh. . .wide circles. . .on my mind," he finished, his baritone sounding a bit gruff.

Paige didn't move. Couldn't move, in fact. The intent way in which he regarded her was mesmerizing. His eyes darted down to her mouth, and Paige's heartbeat pounded in her chest. She hoped it wasn't loud enough for him to hear.

All of a sudden, Andy straightened and cleared his throat. As quickly as the moment arrived, it was gone, and Paige released the breath she hadn't realized she'd been holding.

"Come on." He spoke a little too loudly. "There's someone else waiting for us."

Without asking permission, he grabbed her hand and pulled her toward where Doc Carver's Diving Horse Show was located. So much for pursuing those odd feelings further. Unable to do anything but follow, Paige shifted her focus to not stumbling as she quickened her pace to keep up with Andy, who weaved in a zigzag pattern through the crowds.

In less than a minute, they arrived, and Paige paused to catch her breath.

"Andy, my boy," a booming voice greeted them a moment later. "I see you've found our little lady." The man with a thick mustache that came down in a V-shape and hid his mouth offered Paige a half smile. He reached up and tipped the front of his large and showy cowboy hat, the fringes on the sleeves of his thick buckskin coat swishing with the movement. "Doc Carver, miss," he said then jerked a thumb in Andy's direction. "This fella was as nervous as a long-tailed cat in a room full of rocking chairs." He winked and his eyes twinkled. "Glad he found ya."

Paige looked at Andy, who conveniently avoided making eye contact at that moment. Nervous? About her? But why? If this was who he'd wanted her to meet, she couldn't understand what all the fuss was about. Doc Carver might have traveled the world as a renowned marksman and show master, but he seemed very kind and friendly. No reason to fret.

Paige bobbed in a curtsy. "Paige Callahan, Doc. It's a pleasure to meet you."

"Pleasure's all mine. So, Lawrence," Doc Carver said without preamble, "you mentioned this little gal dreams of singing on that big stage over yonder?"

Paige tried to catch Andy's gaze, but he focused straight ahead. He'd told Doc about her? Why?

"Yes," Andy replied. "Were you able to talk with her?"

Talk with whom? Paige glanced back and forth between the two men. Why were they being so cryptic?

"As a matter of fact, I did." Doc nodded then beckoned to someone in the shadows.

Paige turned, and her eyes widened. Bessie Smith was walking right toward them! *The* Bessie Smith, the Empress of the Blues. In all her resplendent finery, complete with the fur-edged robe she wore over her gown. Paige licked her lips. Her breath came in shallow bursts. This time, when she looked at Andy, he was watching her. His grin resembled that of the Cheshire cat from Lewis Carroll's oft-read children's tale. Now *this* explained why he'd been nervous.

"Miss Bessie," Doc began, "I'd like you to meet Miss Paige Callahan."

Miss Smith extended a plump arm, her dark skin appearing from under the confines of the fur-accented sleeve, and Paige accepted the gentle handshake. "Very pleased to meet you, Miss Callahan."

Paige fingered the strand of beads. She swallowed once. Twice. Then, she opened her mouth, but no words came out. Oh no. Not again! She cleared her throat. "Pleased to meet you as well, Miss Smith," she finally managed, surprisingly clear and strong.

"I can't stay long, dear," Miss Smith intoned in her throaty voice. "They'll be calling my name soon to sing some more for those fine folks. But you come on over to the main stage tomorrow, and we'll see what we can do about making that dream of yours come true." She covered Paige's hand with her free one. "Don't make me come and find you, now, you hear?"

"I won't," Paige vowed. Little quivers danced around inside of her, like fireflies searching for a place to light. "Thank you," she whispered, the moisture in her throat disappearing again.

"Doc, it's always a pleasure. Thank Sonora fo the peaches." Miss Smith gave the man a wink and turned to Andy. "And Mr. Lawrence," she said with a stern, motherly glance, "I expect you front and center tomorrow when your gal here takes her first steps onto that stage."

Paige tried to interrupt. "Oh, but I'm not—"

"Yes, ma'am," Andy said before Paige could correct her misguided assumption.

"And I also expect a nice-sized article on me in that paper of yours, too," she said in a playful tone with a smile as she waved to all three of them. "Bye now."

Paige watched the woman leave, head held high and carrying herself as if she floated on a cloud. Such grace and charm. Paige would be lucky if she managed to walk across the stage without tripping, let alone sing to anyone who might be within hearing. Maybe she could show up early before the larger crowds appeared. She could hardly believe Andy had done all of this for her! He chose that moment to slip his hands into his pockets, and Paige shifted her attention away from Miss Smith back to Andy. So many questions flitted across her mind.

"How did you make this happen? When did you have the time to arrange all of this? Why didn't you correct Miss Smith about our relationship? How am I ever going to thank you?" Paige let the questions tumble out.

Doc cleared his throat. "I think I best be getting back to checking the diving ramp and the water levels in that watering hole in the ground they dug for us. Can't have my horse jumping into shallow water, and I don't want Sonora getting hurt as she dives with the horse, either." He regarded them both. "I hope I'll see you at one of the shows before the fair comes to an end."

"Count on it," Andy replied, exchanging a quick handshake with Doc.

"Good night," Doc called as he turned and walked away.

Paige smiled. Doc was everything she'd heard and more. He loved his horses, took great care of his riders, and loved to put on a good show for his spectators. She looked forward to seeing the dive in person and maybe even getting to meet Sonora Webster. Paige had read every article she could find on the diving girl since she first heard the show was coming to the fair this year. But first, a certain reporter owed her an explanation.

As if reading her thoughts, Andy took two steps to the side and leaned back against a post next to one of the ticket booths, hooking one ankle over the other and folding his arms, a knowing smirk forming on his lips.

"Now, to answer your questions, I was interviewing Miss Webster, and the subject of persistence in going after what you want came up." He shrugged. "I mentioned you, Miss Webster suggested I speak with Doc, and the rest you can guess. As for why I didn't correct Miss Smith about us, I didn't see it important enough to interrupt her. And as for thanking me?" He paused as his mouth slid into a slow grin. "Join me for the rest of the evening taking in the carnival rides and entertainment, and I'll consider the matter paid in full."

Amazing. He'd responded to each one of her questions in accurate order, not missing a beat. More of that journalism experience coming to his aid, no doubt. It all seemed so matter-of-fact, the way he'd just described it happening, but Paige knew better. Andy had heard her confession, listened intently, and gone out of his way to utilize his connections. All for her. No one had ever done anything like that for her before. She could at least oblige him in his invitation to a fun evening.

"Very well," she said with a slow nod. "Where would you like to begin?"

Andy pushed away from the post, that spark of mischief back in his eyes. "How about Over the Jumps?" he suggested. "Or the Caterpillar, as they call it in Denver."

Paige took in a sharp breath and grinned. "That's my favorite ride!"

He reached into the inner pocket of his suit and withdrew a long string of tickets. He'd already purchased some for them? Had he been so certain she'd agree to join him?

"Caterpillar it is," he exclaimed, before she had a chance to think on it any further.

With his hand at the small of her back, Andy guided her around the bend toward the ride. As he relinquished two tickets, she couldn't imagine a better close to the day. Just two more days until the fair ended. Then what?

Andy led her to the first empty car and helped her to the inside seat. Once he settled in beside her, he turned to her with a smile. She smiled, too. No. She wouldn't think about two days from now. They had tonight. . .and she'd make it a memorable one.

Chapter 8

Now, you stand right there, Miss Paige," Miss Bessie said, "and you give it all you got as soon as you hear the music start playing."

Paige looked like a deer that stared into the eyes of its predator, ready to bolt at any moment. The first strains of a familiar melody began, but when it came time for Paige to join in with the words, nothing happened.

Oh no! Not again!

Andy had seen how she acted when she was nervous. This time, though, she didn't even lick her lips or open her mouth. She just stood there, frozen. After all he'd done to arrange this, and now it might not happen? What if she couldn't sing? Maybe he shouldn't have gone out on a limb like this for her. Or maybe he should have chosen a smaller venue. Now he'd have to apologize to Miss Bessie, and to Doc. As if thinking of her made her appear, Miss Bessie took a seat next to him and gave his shoulder a nudge. "Son, I'm thinking you better get up there and give that gal of yours a little pluck in her feathers."

Andy shook his head. "I'm sorry. What?" Something about plucking feathers?

Miss Bessie leaned in close and winked. "I believe Miss Callahan needs some prompting and reassurance from you."

He looked from Miss Bessie to Paige and back again. "Oh!" He jumped up and made his way to the stairs.

Paige hadn't moved. The orchestra fell silent, but Andy signaled them to continue playing. He strode across the stage, stopping right next to Paige. He reached for her hand, and she startled. She tried to pull free, but he held tight, and she turned her head to look at him.

"It's okay," he said in a low voice. "Everyone gets stage fright at some time or another."

She swallowed and licked her lips. "I don't know if I can do this," she croaked.

"Sure you can," he said with as much confidence as he could muster. Truth be told, he wasn't sure she could do it, either, but he wasn't about to tell her that. "Don't think about this being a stage or that you're performing." He winked. "Just pretend you're singing to the chickens and cows on your farm."

That at least earned him a small smile. He started to step away, but this time, she wouldn't let go.

"What if I forget the words or I'm not loud enough?"

Andy patted her hand and gave it a squeeze. "I'm sitting right there in the front row. Look straight at me, if you have to, and let everything else disappear."

As if to prove his point, Andy stared, his gaze intent. Her eyes widened, and a soft gasp sounded as she inhaled. A moment later, resolute strength shone forth, and she squared her shoulders. He drew her hand to his lips and kissed her knuckles.

"That's my girl," he said. "Now, just relax and enjoy yourself up here."

He moved offstage and waited once again for Paige to begin. She signaled the conductor below her then looked over at Andy. He nodded. She could do this. She had to. He didn't want to think about the alternative. This was her dream. She needed to see it through. If she didn't now, she might never do it again.

As if coming to that same realization herself, Paige turned again to face forward and waited for the right moment to join in with the words. Her voice started soft and scratchy, but she kept singing. With each word and note, she got a little stronger. Andy smiled. She was going to make it.

Andy resumed his seat and leaned forward with his forearms on his thighs, mesmerized by the rich and tonal quality of the melodic sounds flowing from Paige's lips. Her voice still wobbled a bit as she sang. Whose wouldn't? A glance around the available seating showed minimal spectators, but that didn't matter. Paige's dream had come true. He returned his full attention to the beautiful songbird standing onstage in front of him.

With the shaky fingers of both hands lightly touching the microphone stand and the round top with its center receiver surrounded by coils partially blocking a full view of her face, Paige could've been any one of the performers scheduled to appear that week. Despite her initial protests, her voice resonated loud and clear. Her eyes never left his, as if she drew strength from him in some way. A soft smile slowly drew the corners of her mouth upward as she and the orchestra together eased into the closing of Gershwin's "Someone to Watch Over Me."

The words of the ballad washed over him. From that first day when Andy had overheard the bits and pieces of Paige bearing her soul to her friend, she'd snagged a small portion of him. Now, the plaintive confession offered straight from her heart conveyed an honest truth.

"Quite impressive, that little gal is," Miss Bessie said from beside him.

Andy straightened. He'd actually forgotten the blues singer sat next to him. "Yes," he replied. "Yes, she is." And he'd had no idea just how much. Imagine that. Of all the ladies he'd met and all the ones who'd been temporary dalliances, a petite farm girl from Wyoming had turned his head.

Miss Bessie shifted and nudged Andy with her shoulder. "She's saying something to you, son." Miss Bessie indicated Paige with a nod. "Don't you let that one get away."

Andy mustered some semblance of a reassuring smile in a quick glance at Miss Bessie. What else could he do? He wasn't ready to answer her just yet. She seemed to understand. With a quick pat of his hand, the singer hoisted herself from her seat and made her way back behind the stage. When he looked again at Paige, she was already making her way down the side steps and heading his way. The pure delight on her face made her eyes shine bright and her smile as big as the moon.

"Oh! That was wonderful!" Paige made a fist with one hand and covered it with the other as she pressed her clasped hands to her chest and raised her gaze to the heavens. "Absolutely marvelous," she breathed, her entire upper body trembling.

Andy reached out, hoping to help her relax, when all of a sudden she leaped toward him and threw her arms around his neck. Reflexes kicked in as he caught her about the waist and held tight. Did she have any idea what she was doing to him?

"Thank you!" she said from over his shoulder as she hugged him.

A moment later, she loosened her hold, allowing her feet to touch the ground again. Such joy shined forth from her soul, showcasing itself in her hypnotic gaze. When she attempted to let go, he didn't, and her hands came to rest on his shoulders. Paige furrowed her brows just slightly, and her mouth parted. He could feel the intensity in his stare increase. As he shifted his focus to her lips, he pulled her closer. His head told him this was neither the time nor the place, but his body refused to listen.

"Paigie!" Someone hollered from somewhere behind them. "Paigie, we did it!"

With intentionality, Paige forced him to release her, and they both turned to face the sound of the one who'd interrupted them.

A young man who resembled Paige put one hand on the gate that sectioned off the stage and swung his legs over the top. "We did it!" he yelled again. His shout traveled the distance between them and arrived a few seconds before its owner.

Paige took two significant steps away from Andy and greeted the young man with a broad smile. "Matthew, what did we do?"

Instead of answering, the man grabbed Paige and swung her around in two large circles. Andy backed away to avoid being kicked. Laughter erupted from Paige as Matthew returned her to the ground.

"Old Gordon," he said, his excitement and the exertion of swinging Paige making him breathe a little heavy. "He won! Gordon won the contest. He's going to be a real rodeo bull now!"

"What?" Paige's mouth fell open and her eyes widened. "Are you sure?"

Matthew nodded. "As sure as I am that Pa's about to pop the buttons on his shirt, he's so proud."

Ahh. Pa. This must be the older brother she'd mentioned.

Paige raised a hand to her mouth and covered her soft and delicate giggle. "Is Mama there, too, making sure he doesn't?"

"Yeah." Matthew jerked a thumb over his shoulder in the direction of the cattle pavilion. "I tried to find you before the judging took place, but I guess you were busy." As if he'd just remembered his sister wasn't alone, he nodded toward Andy. "Going to introduce me to your friend?"

"Oh!" Clearly Paige had forgotten about him, too. "Yes," she replied, stepping back to make room for Andy to approach. "Matthew, this is Andrew Lawrence, a reporter from the *Denver Post*. He's here covering the noteworthy news of the fair." She then turned to face him but avoided eye contact. "Andy, this is my older brother, Matthew."

Andy stuck out his hand and initiated the firm handshake. In one glance, Matthew sized him up and sent him a silent warning as well. He might have appeared to be oblivious to the little tête-à-tête he'd interrupted, but his look said otherwise.

"Nice to meet you," Matthew said.

"Likewise," Andy replied.

"Well, look. I'd love to stay and chat," Matthew stated, "but I have to get back over to the pavilion and help transport Old Gordon to the arena." He zeroed in on Paige. "You going to come to and see our bull's first ride?"

Paige smiled. "Of course, I'll be there."

"Great." Matthew backed away, moving up the center aisle toward the gate. "They're cutting him loose at one. Going to do some trial runs before then to see how he does."

"We'll see you there," she promised and waved as her brother again cleared the gate.

We? Was she going to invite him to join her? Knowing full well her parents and brother would be right there watching? That would be rather bold, all things considered, wouldn't it?

"Do you know what this means?" Paige suddenly said and spun to face him.

"Do I know what what means?"

"Old Gordon," she said simply.

Andy spread out his arms, elbows bent and shoulders raised. He shook his head. "What about him?"

Paige sighed and gave him an impatient look. "He's going to be a rodeo bull." She craned her neck slightly forward, eyes wide and head bobbing with each word, as if speaking to a child about something he should already know.

What was he missing? What difference did it make if some old bull was going to join the dozens of other bulls in the rodeo?

She continued in her attempts to get him to understand. "He's never ridden in a rodeo before. It'll be his first time." Again, with the leaning forward and head bobs.

Andy shook his head. "Clearly, I am not understanding." No, his head was still stuck back on that embrace they'd shared a few moments ago. How in the world could she seem so unaffected so quickly and have already moved on to another subject? "I'm afraid you're going to have to spell it out for me." Maybe by then his brain would catch up to the conversation.

Paige grinned. "Don't you remember what you told me on Tuesday about one of your dreams?"

He thought back for a moment. Tuesday. What had they been doing that day? Oh right. She'd given him a tour of the fairgrounds. She'd shared about wanting to sing onstage, and then he'd told her about his various promotions at work and how he'd always dreamed of—

Andy snapped his fingers as realization dawned. "The bull! I remember now."

Laughter escaped her lips, and she shook her head. "Yes. You've always wanted to ride a bull." She made a grand sweep of her arm in the general direction of the pavilion. "And now you have a chance."

He looked over his shoulder then back at Paige and again toward the pavilion. "Wait. You mean your father's bull?" She had to be joking. "You want me to ride Old Gordon?"

Paige clasped her hands in front of her. "Of course. It's the perfect solution. Neither one of you has ever ridden in a rodeo event, so neither one of you will know what to expect."

Andy grimaced. "That's what concerns me. This bull of yours might be volatile and untrustworthy."

She dismissed his concerns with a wave of her hand. "Nonsense. Old Gordon would never behave in that manner."

"But you just said he's never done this before, so how do you know?"

One side of her mouth quirked, and a teasing gleam appeared in her eyes. "There's only one way to find out." The gleam turned into a challenge. "You helped me achieve one of my dreams. Now it's my turn to help you. Will you do it?"

How could he refuse now? When she put it like that?

Andy shrugged. "Let's go meet this bull of yours."

Oh, how he hoped he wouldn't regret this.

A few hours later, Andy jumped up from where Old Gordon had just bucked him off and ran straight for the break in the wall where some of the cowboys had swung open the gate. They beckoned to him with urgency and didn't have to ask him twice. He had no desire to spend any more time with that bull in the ring than absolutely necessary. As soon as he was on the other side of the wall, he cast his gaze around, searching for Paige. She'd moved from her place at the edge of the arena just to the rear of the grandstands as he'd asked.

He rushed toward her, his heart pounding and adrenaline coursing through him. This must have been how she'd felt when she came off the stage earlier that morning. Wow. No wonder she'd been so exuberant in her gratitude.

"Wasn't that the best experience you've ever had?" she asked when he stood just ten feet from her.

Instead of answering, he snatched her around the waist, bent his knees, and swung her around. Not once. Not twice. But three times, before setting her down.

"Yes," he answered her with a big grin. Although, he wasn't quite ready to let the experience end. He wanted to add to it.

Just like before, her hands were on his shoulders, her gaze, her mouth inches from his. Only this time, there would be no older brother and no one else to intrude on their moment. They were quite secluded.

Paige licked her lips as she looked up at Andy. An inner battle waged in those stormy depths. If he waited any longer, he'd overthink it. Before he or she could do or say something to talk him out of it, he lowered his head and pressed his lips to hers. At first, she startled, but when he applied pressure to her back and drew her closer, she relaxed. A minute later, he pulled back and gazed down into her upturned face. That had been all he'd imagined and more.

When she opened her eyes, he smiled. "I've wanted to do that since our little encounter Tuesday morning." Hard to believe it had only been three days.

It took her a moment, but as soon as she realized what he meant, she pulled her lower lip in between her teeth and ducked her head. Andy withdrew one hand from around her waist and gently touched her chin, encouraging her to raise her gaze once more.

"You know, I came up here from Denver with a big promotion on my mind, expecting to find a few nuggets of good stories to give my editor. I intended to show him I have what it takes to be the senior journalist he needs." He chuckled. "I had a plan. But that plan didn't include meeting someone like you."

Paige breathed in and out several times as she regarded him, taking her time, seeming to weigh her words before speaking. "Aren't you still going to go back to your editor with these stories you've collected? I'm sure he'll be impressed."

"Definitely." Andy looked around. "But I'm not sure where that leaves us." There had to be somewhere better suited to this conversation. An idea came to mind. "Walk with me," he said, keeping one arm around her waist as he turned to lead them under the grandstands and back toward one of the main paths.

"You see," he continued, "as you can well imagine, the life I lead isn't a predictable one. I'm sent out, sometimes all over the country, chasing a story and the next best headline."

"Oh, but that's what's exciting about it," Paige interjected.

Andy glanced down as they walked. He'd expected her to agree to the difficulty of his work, not be enthusiastic about it. "You mean, that doesn't concern you?"

She followed him as he guided her through the clusters of carnival seekers and various attendees milling about the fairgrounds. "Not at all. Before we met, I had resigned myself to a predictable life, very much the opposite of what you describe for yours." She sighed. "But secretly, I was hoping something would happen to change that."

He gave her waist an affectionate squeeze. "So, you learned I was a reporter and decided I was as far from predictable as you could get." He grinned. "And that's why you arranged that encounter by the greenhouse."

Paige halted, but he kept on going, his arm slipping from her waist as he rounded the corner of the event tent. When she didn't join him again, he paused and turned. There she stood, hands on hips and righteous indignation oozing from every part of her.

"That is not the way it happened, and you know it," she said, each word spoken with distinct enunciation.

She looked so adorable, Andy almost laughed. Instead, he took two strides to close the gap between them and reached up to tap her pert little nose. "Gotcha!" he said with a wink.

A giggle escaped her lips as she instantly relaxed. Andy extended his arm again and placed a hand at the small of her back, steering them once again toward his plan. When they came to the white picket fence surrounding the center stage, he looked down to see Paige smiling.

"I figured we could sit and listen to the music for a little while." He pulled away slightly. "That is, if you don't mind."

"Of course not."

Andy reached over the fence and undid the latch to the side gate. Swinging it wide, he gestured for Paige to precede him. Once inside, they walked down to the front and settled in seats beside the orchestra pit. Movement to his right made him glance up to the curtains onstage. Miss Bessie peeked out and sought his gaze. Andy nodded and she smiled, clasping her hands together just beneath her chin.

When she let the curtain fall again, Andy slid his arm across the back of Paige's chair and rested his hand on her shoulder. She leaned into him a little and placed her hands in her lap.

"So, what's next for us?"

"I don't know," she said softly. "But I do know when the fair comes to an end, I'll be returning to the farm to tell Charlie I'm not the girl for him."

Andy took a deep breath and grinned. "If that's the same man you and Millie were discussing the day we met, I have a feeling he'll find another gal to fill that line item on his to-do list."

Paige giggled, her shoulders shaking. He tightened his hold and gave her a little squeeze.

"I think I have an idea."

Paige regarded him out of the corner of her eye, her eyebrows raised, waiting for what he'd say next.

"Since I don't know how well you'll take to the big city, why don't we plan a few visits for now between Denver and Douglas and take it from there?" Andy caressed her shoulder and grinned when she shivered. "It'll give us time to get to know each other better and figure out what we're going to do next."

"I'd like that."

"Good."

As the orchestra started to play the opening notes of Gershwin's ballad, Andy stood and extended a hand to Paige. "Dance with me?"

A slow smile spread across her face as she rose and joined him next to the stage. Miss Bessie blended with the wind and string accompaniment and eased into the first words of the song. Andy pulled Paige close and led them in a simple waltz. She leaned forward and rested her head on his shoulder as the harmonic undertones and lyrical melody dictated their rhythm. They might not have a plan for where they were headed, but he'd make certain they would enjoy the journey on the way there.

Tiffany Amber Stockton has been crafting and embellishing stories since childhood, when she was accused of having a very active imagination and cited with talking entirely too much. Today, she has honed those childhood skills to become an award-winning author and speaker who works in the anti-aging and personal development industries, helping others become their best from the inside out. She lives with her husband and fellow author, Stuart Vaughn Stockton, in Colorado. They have one girl and one boy, and a Retriever mix named Roxie. Her writing career began as a columnist for her high school and college newspapers. She has sold twenty (21) books so far, is an active member of ACFW, and is represented by Tamela Murray of the Steve Laube Agency. Three of her novels have won annual reader's choice awards, and in 2009, she was voted #1 favorite new author for the Heartsong Presents book club. Visit her web site for more information: www.amberstockton.com.

Competing Hearts

by Cynthia Hickey

"Can any one of you by worrying add a single hour to your life?"
MATTHEW 6:27 NIV

Chapter 1

Arkansas, 1930

"Turn the lights off!" Pa bellowed from his rolltop desk in the living room. "Our electric bill was a dollar and thirty-seven cents this month. We're in a depression, you know."

Annie Mae Thompkins exchanged an amused glance with her mother. "We'll manage, Papa. I'm entering my quilt in the county fair. I'm sure to win first place, and it's a twenty-five dollar prize. Plus, Mama's canned peaches always win."

"Pipe dreams. What we need is cash in hand today." He entered the kitchen where Annie Mae and her mother prepared soup for lunch. "I'm heading to town to try and get some mill work. I'll be back in an hour or so. Keep lunch hot for me." He kissed Mama's cheek and gave Annie Mae a hug. "Where's the young'uns?"

"Mama told them to tend the garden." Her younger brother and sister were most likely playing in the mud, but at least they were out of her hair. It usually fell on Annie Mae to watch them since Mama took in sewing and did other odd jobs to help make ends meet.

His eyes softened. "If we don't make some money, we'll have to sell the pig."

"No, Pa, not Daisy." Tears stung Annie Mae's eyes. She'd gotten the animal as a piglet and had hand-fed her ever since. She was Annie Mae's most trusted confidant. They'd spent many hours together while Annie Mae talked of her dreams and fears, her secrets, and whatever cute boy she might have a crush on.

He cupped her cheek. "I'll do my best, but hard times. . ." He sighed and grabbed his hat on the way out the door.

"Don't worry." Mama gave her a soft smile. "I'm making the widow Olsen a dress. It'll take care of the electric bill this month and then some."

"I need twenty-five cents to register my quilt." Papa was right. Annie Mae's winning was nothing more than a pipe dream. Her parents were worried about money and here she stood with her hand out. They all worked hard to make enough funds to keep food on the table. Annie Mae would have to work harder. Her parents shouldn't have to shoulder all the burden.

"Take it out of the jar. You can pay me back when you win."

"Surely?" Annie Mae's heart leaped. With her mother's support, how could she lose? She retrieved the coins and practically skipped out the door. "What if I don't win?"

"We'll figure it out. God hasn't let us down yet."

Annie Mae bounded outside, the screen door slamming behind her. Squeals from the garden drew her attention. Robby and Lulu had made a mudhole and covered themselves with the rich clay so thoroughly, it was hard to tell who was who. "You two better get cleaned up before Mama calls you for lunch."

With Mama miscarrying a few babies after Annie Mae's birth, there were ten years between her eighteen years and Robby's eight. Then another two before little Lulu came along. The doctor told Mama no more babies. God knew best. More mouths were harder to feed when the country was in such dire straits. Marcus, her older brother, had been killed the year before in a tragic hunting accident, and life around the Thompkins farm just wasn't the same. Instead of the laughter from Marcus's constant pranks and jokes, a cloud of melancholy as thick as the morning fog hung over their heads.

Life goes on, Pa said. But it was tough when sadness and worry were Annie Mae's constant companions.

Her scuffed black shoes kicked up the red dirt on her way to the general store where she could sign up to participate in the county fair. With each step she took, her excitement grew. Many folks around Rabbit Hollow had commented on her quilt. How the colors complemented one another, how tiny her stitches were. Each square represented a memory. A baby's gown, one of Pa's old shirts. Her steps began to falter as she second-guessed whether or not to enter it. What if someone wanted to purchase the quilt after it won? The money was sorely needed, but could she bear to part with her memories?

"Good afternoon, Annie Mae."

She rolled her eyes and squared her shoulders as Jonathan Mercer, her longtime tease from elementary school, jogged to her side. He'd returned to their neck of the woods a few weeks ago. "Good afternoon."

"Where are you headed?"

"Mason's." She grinned despite her determination not to engage him. "I'm going to enter a quilt in the fair."

"I'm going there, too. Going to enter my Belle."

His pig. Well, if he wanted real competition, she ought to enter Daisy. "That's nice."

She peeked up from under lowered lashes. It was a cruel joke of God's to make such an annoying man so devastatingly handsome. Blue eyes the color of a babbling brook twinkled from under dark lashes. Hair the color of mahogany caught the sun's rays with strands of gold. It just wasn't fair. Not with the way her heart had started fluttering each time she saw him. It was all she could do to concentrate on a Sunday morning sermon with him sitting one pew over!

"It's a nice day."

"Yes, it is." She stopped and glanced up at him. "You don't have to walk with me and make small talk. I'm in no hurry, and with your hog farm and all, I'm sure you're busy."

"There's no place I'd rather be right now than walking down this road with you." A dimple winked in his right cheek.

So not fair. "Very well. Suit yourself." She resumed walking.

The store was a thirty-minute walk from the Thompkins farm. In the colder months, Annie Mae rode their one horse, an old plodding thing that would take a nip out of your leg if you got too close. With the way her senses went haywire every time Jonathan's arm bumped hers, she wished she'd chosen to ride the nag today.

He cut her a sideways glance. "I don't remember you being this quiet."

"You've been gone awhile. I'm no longer the chatty little girl I used to be. Responsibilities weigh on my shoulders now. You were away on a work relief program, right?"

"Yep." Jonathan kicked a rock, sending it bouncing down the road. "I spent some time in Minnesota fighting fires, then when winter got so bad I thought my toes would fall off, I headed to the East Coast to build roads. Now, with Pa hurting his back, it was time to come home and see whether I can't get the farm to produce."

"I'm sorry to hear he's feeling poorly." Folks around those parts hadn't understood why Jonathan had taken off the way he had. A hog farm that size, they had needed more than one able-bodied man to run things. Then again, people needed money to run a farm, and that was in short supply in Rabbit Hollow, Arkansas.

<hr />

Jonathan opened the door to Mason's, smiling at the familiar jingle of the bell signaling the arrival of a customer. He'd missed Rabbit Hollow and its people. Especially the lovely girl next to him who still held a grudge because of the teasing he'd given her once upon a time.

"Annie Mae! Jonathan! What a pleasure to see you two." Mr. Mason, short, trim, with a clean-shaven face, wiped his hands down the front of his spotless white apron. "How may I help you?"

"I'd like to enter the fair, please." Annie Mae plunked twenty-five cents on the counter. "A quilt."

"I'm entering my finest sow." Jonathan added his money to Annie Mae's.

"Wonderful." Mr. Mason pulled a notebook from under the counter. "It's going to be quite the competition this year. This quilt makes number five so far, and as for the sow, well, the livestock is always a people pleaser. I'm glad they decided to have the fair despite the depression."

"Was there concern?" Annie Mae was especially glad they'd continued this year. The fair meant so much to the community. A time to let loose and enjoy the fruits of their harvests.

"When I win," Jonathan said, leaning on the counter, "I'm going to expand the hog herd. Now that I'm home, I'm going to make Mercer Farms something to talk about."

"I've no doubt." Mr. Mason jotted down their entries and gave them each a receipt. "If you'd both sign on the dotted line, we'll be all done here."

"I'd also like two grape sodas." Jonathan paid for the sodas then pulled two from the cooler and handed one to Annie Mae.

"Thank you. My favorite."

"I remember." He remembered a lot about her. She liked to spend her free time reading, her favorite flower was a daisy, and her favorite color blue. When she was bored, she doodled on paper or in the dirt if paper wasn't available. Oh, yeah, he remembered a whole lot about Annie Mae Thompkins. More than she remembered about him, he'd wager.

They headed toward her house, the soda bottle causing condensation in his hand. He lifted it to his mouth and drank deep of the sweet carbonated drink. "Ahh. I could drink one of these every day."

"An expensive indulgence, but mighty sweet." Annie Mae smiled. "You don't need to walk me home."

"I'm headed that way. We live on the same road, silly girl." He tugged one of her curls. "You aren't still mad at me for teasing you all those years ago, are you?"

"No." Her tone said otherwise as she tilted her head. "I didn't think you noticed a child two years younger."

"Don't lie." He placed an arm around her shoulder. "I've always noticed Marcus's little sister." He grew solemn at remembering his friend. He should have been in the woods with him that day. If he had been, maybe another hunter wouldn't have mistaken Marcus for a deer and ended his life.

Annie Mae slipped free of his arm and turned onto her lawn. "Thanks for the soda. I hope you don't mind if I share the last half with my brother and sister."

The pain in her hazel eyes made him want to punch himself. He shouldn't have brought up Marcus. It was still too painful. "Of course not. See you at church."

He trudged home, tempted to throw his bottle into the bushes to hear it strike a rock and shatter. But knowing his family could use the few cents he'd earn by turning the bottle back in to the store, he took a deep breath and headed to his favorite spot.

A large oak tree still held the tree house he and Marcus had built when they were ten. Was it really a decade ago? They'd spent many a peaceful night in this tree with nothing overhead but a thin blanket of stars. It was in this very spot that he'd made a promise to Marcus. A promise he intended to keep. He'd promised to watch over Annie Mae and make sure she was always taken care of if something should happen to Marcus. It was as if his friend had known his life would end prematurely.

Jonathan grabbed a low branch and swung himself onto the platform. He lay on his back, arms folded under his head, and watched the clouds float past through the tree branches. It had taken him a year to come home after his friend's death, but he was here now, ready to care for his family and Marcus's. How, he didn't know yet. He only knew that God would provide a way if he would listen.

"Jonathan!" His mom's yell reached through his thoughts, bringing him back to the present.

"Coming!" He swung down and hurried across the yard. "I'm here."

"I thought I saw you coming up the road. I need you to fetch a sack of flour from the barn. Your pa's back is still spasming."

He handed her his empty soda bottle and rushed to do her bidding. He'd managed to send home quite a bit of his income from the work relief and was glad to see his family well fed. He tousled the hair of his youngest sibling, Eric, who played with a litter of two-week-old puppies. "Did you get your chores done?"

"Suzanne is supposed to feed the chickens today."

"Then that means you're supposed to muck out the stalls." He patted his brother on the shoulder. "Don't make Ma have to yell at you."

"I don't know why Matthew can't do it."

"He's tending the hogs. Now git." He swatted Eric on the rump then hoisted the flour sack onto his shoulder. Whistling a jaunty tune, he carried it into the house and set it on the table.

His thoughts turned to Belle. By Jove, he'd win that competition and not only help his family, he'd buy Annie Mae some store-bought candy. Something a girl in Rabbit

Hollow rarely, if ever, received.

He'd make sure Annie Mae had a lot of things she rarely, if ever, enjoyed. It was the least he could do for his friend's sister. Her family struggled after Marcus's death. If he could make things a bit easier for them, he would.

Chapter 2

Annie Mae hung her quilt on the display rack at the fair. In five days she'd know whether she won and whether or not her family's burdens would be eased. She perused the other quilts, a total of seven, none as vibrant as hers. Her Ohio Star was sure to be a judge pleaser. She waved at Mama, who had entered her peach jam, then, with a little time on her hands before Pa was ready to leave, she headed for the livestock tent.

Jonathan paced the aisle between the hogs and the goats, running his hands through his hair. In front of an empty stall stood the fair coordinator, Mr. Wilson, a man as round as he was tall. His normally jovial face was drawn.

"I'm sorry, Mr. Mercer, I have no idea how that goat got out."

Jonathan whirled. "Got out and let my Belle go! I'm counting on that hog, sir."

"It's a very smart goat." Mr. Wilson's face darkened. "I'll help you search. She can't have gotten far."

"I'll help." Annie Mae placed a hand on Jonathan's arm. "Let's check the next tent. She might have bedded down with the cows."

"I'm frantic," he said, his blue eyes shadowed. "I'll appreciate any help you can give me."

She understood how he felt. If something were to happen to her entry, she'd cry. "Come on."

Belle wasn't in the large animal tent or the corral with animals for children to pet. The fair started early in the morning. It was imperative they find her. The last place to check other than the vacant field was the tent holding the sewing and craft entries. If Belle got in there, she could wreak havoc for sure.

A woman screamed from inside the craft tent. Seconds later, Belle charged out, knocking Annie Mae off her feet.

Jonathan tackled the sow, wrestling the massive animal until he got his arms around her neck. He glanced at Annie Mae. "Are you all right?"

She nodded and got to her feet. "Got the breath knocked out of me, but I'm okay. I'll see who screamed while you lock her back up." The animal was a menace. Daisy would never behave like that. Straightening her dress, Annie Mae stepped into the tent. Tables were turned on their sides. Jars busted. Thankfully, Mama's peach jam was on a higher shelf and thus safe from the destruction. Not so for Annie Mae's entry.

The once beautiful quilt lay in the dirt. Muddy hoofprints marred the fabric, along with a tear in one corner. Annie Mae fell to her knees and gathered the blanket of memories to her chest. Tears rolled down her cheeks, spotting the material. What would her family do? Her hopes lay as crushed as the fabric gathered in her arms.

"Oh." Mama put a hand on her shoulder. "Let me see." She took the quilt from Annie Mae's arms. "Oh, sweetie. It'll never win a ribbon now."

Annie Mae lifted her head. "What will I do?"

"Before we despair, let's think." Mama folded the quilt. "I can wash this for you to keep. It's not a total waste."

"No, about the fair." She got to her feet. "I've nothing else to enter."

Mama grinned. "You know, I won Miss Pulaski County once upon a time."

"Yes, I know."

"They're having the pageant here, as part of the fair."

Why was Mama talking about a beauty pageant? Didn't she know Annie Mae's dreams were dirtied and folded in her arms?

"I'm saying there are other options, dear. You are quite lovely and have a wonderful singing voice. You could enter yourself in the pageant and Daisy in the livestock competition. You'd have two chances of winning a blue ribbon." Mama linked her free arm with Annie Mae's. "Let's find the sign-up sheets. Pa won't mind bringing Daisy out here this evening. Tonight is the deadline for entries."

"Do you really think I could win the pageant?"

"I think you have a very good chance."

Dare she hope? She caught a glimpse of Jonathan exiting the tent where he'd taken Belle. Her spine stiffened. Once again he'd ruined her plans. First, he'd left and wasn't there when Marcus needed him most; now he'd ruined her chances of helping her family through a rough time. "I'll meet you at the truck, Mama."

Annie Mae marched over to Jonathan and poked her finger into his chest. "Your sow ruined my quilt. What are you going to do about it?"

"Excuse me?"

"Are you deaf? It's ruined to the point that not even cleaning it will make it good enough to enter into the competition." Tears pricked her eyes again as she thought of her dashed hopes.

"I'm sorry, Annie Mae. It wasn't my fault. That goat—"

"You should have made sure the gate on Belle's pen couldn't be jimmied open by an animal!" She whirled and stormed away.

He caught up with her, grabbing her arm and spinning her around. "I'm sorry. What do you want? Money? I don't have much, but I can—"

"Oh, you're hopeless." She covered her face and cried. She didn't know what she wanted. The day had ended horribly. "Now I have to enter the beauty pageant. I hate those things. And I have to enter Daisy and then sell her to the highest bidder when she wins."

"I'm a bit confused. What does Belle getting out have to do with all that?"

"You don't understand anything!" She stomped her foot.

"Please, don't cry." He gripped her shoulders. "I'll make it up to you. I promise."

"I don't ever want to speak to you again." Annie Mae pulled free, knowing she was being unreasonable but unable to stop herself.

"Come, daughter." Pa took her hand. "See you later, Jonathan."

"Oh, Pa." Annie Mae buried her face in his chest.

"See what happens when we put all our hope and trust in earthly things?" He set her at arm's length. "Trust in God, child. It will all turn out."

———— •◆• ————

Jonathan had no idea how to make things better for Annie Mae. He knew how much she had relied on winning first place with her quilt. He had the same high hopes for Belle. But he hadn't had anything to do with her quilt getting ruined. If she wanted to be mad at someone, she should be mad at the fair administrator or the goat's owner.

He kicked at a rock in the road. First, he hadn't been there for Marcus; now, inadvertently or not, he'd ruined things for the Thompkins family again. No wonder Annie Mae never seemed happy to see him.

Casting a glance heavenward, he exhaled sharply and continued toward home. His hope of a relationship with Annie Mae was in God's hands.

Wildflowers bloomed at the side of the road, and he stopped to pick a handful. The next house was Annie Mae's. Perhaps the pretty blooms would brighten her day. At the very least he could apologize. Again.

Mr. Thompkins answered Jonathan's knock. "I'm afraid she isn't up to seeing anyone, young man. She's distraught."

"Would you give her these, with my apologies?" He held out the flowers. "I truly am sorry."

Mr. Thompkins took the flowers and set them inside the door. "Come sit a spell, son." He motioned to a pair of rocking chairs on the porch. "There's something I want to say to you."

Jonathan sat, his folded hands hanging between his knees. "If this is about Marcus, sir, I'm sorry I wasn't there. Maybe I could have—"

"That was not your fault. You went away to help your family. There was nothing you could have done to save my son." Mr. Thompkins rubbed his hands down his face. "But his death did change my Annie Mae. She worries now and works harder than she should to help the family out. It seems both of you are harboring guilt that has no place in either of your hearts." He speared Jonathan a glance. "Give her time to get over the quilt. I'll work on her. It was a material possession she put too much stock in. She might win with that hog of hers and things will be bright again." He grinned. "It looks as if the two of you will be in competition."

Jonathan jerked in his seat. He'd been so concerned over the quilt he hadn't thought of her entering Daisy. Now he recalled her saying something about that and also something about the beauty pageant. The day kept getting worse and worse. He was a judge in the Miss Pulaski County pageant.

"Thank you for seeing me, sir." He stood and offered his hand to Mr. Thompkins. "May the best hog win." Lord have mercy, Jonathan was in a deep hole.

If Belle beat Daisy, which she would, he had no doubt, and if Annie Mae didn't win first place in the pageant that he was a judge in. . .well, he didn't want to contemplate the explosion that would ensue. Somehow, he would have to make sure she won first place in the pageant—if he could do it without cheating, that is. She was bound to come in second with Daisy, which paid ten dollars instead of twenty-five. The pageant would give her the twenty-five she sought.

So engrossed was he in his thoughts, he passed his farm and had to double back. Ma stood on the porch, one hand shading her eyes.

"Son, I need you to head back to town. Your Pa is feeling downright poorly. We need the doctor."

"I'll take the truck."

"It's almost out of gas."

"I'll fill it." He had a few dollars left in his pocket from his work relief. He'd chosen to walk to the fairgrounds, but Pa's health was more important than a couple gallons of fuel or coins jingling in his pocket.

Five minutes later, he was racing at ten miles per hour into town. He tossed a wave to Mr. Thompkins, hoeing in his garden, but didn't slow his speed. If Ma was concerned enough to send for the doctor, there wasn't time to answer the questioning look on the other man's face. Most people had sense enough not to speed down the poorly graded road.

Jonathan took the time on the drive to pray for a miracle. They needed not only himself but Pa to make the farm a success. A month was a long time for a man to be down with a bad back. If things didn't improve, the fair winnings might have to be for a specialist rather than for enlarging the farm. That might also mean the entire family being moved to where the work was. Losing the land that had been in his family for generations would break Pa's heart. Jonathan might have disappointed a number of people in his young life, but this was one area he would not fail in.

He stopped in a cloud of dust in front of the doctor's residence. Doctor Morrilton stepped onto the porch, bag in hand. "If anyone comes roaring in here like that, there's a need."

"Yes, sir. Pa is doing worse. We need you to come."

"Was he working the fields again?"

Jonathan shrugged. "I was gone all day, but I told him I'd do it when I returned."

Thirty minutes later, the doctor relieved their fears. Pa had tweaked his back again shoveling manure. With a stern reprimand from the doctor and a prescription for something for the pain, he promised not to do such a thing again.

Jonathan walked the doctor out. He needed to figure out how to keep his pa from working until he was healed, especially with the fair beginning.

Chapter 3

Doing her best not to muss her dress or hair, Annie Mae leaned on the livestock pen holding Daisy. "I know it's a long shot, but I have to win first place in this pageant. You have to win in your division without Pa selling you." She sighed. "A person can't win for losing, can they? We need you to win, but the thought of you being sold rips my heart out. With Marcus. . .gone, this is my way of helping. I can't work the fields or slaughter livestock like he could."

She straightened and pasted on a smile as Pa entered the tent. "Is it time?" Her heart thudded like the engine on a locomotive.

"Yes." He drew her into a hug. "Don't worry. You're the prettiest girl in the county and can sing like an angel. The judges will love you. Besides, all you have to do today is smile. You're only being introduced and telling a bit about yourself."

"I'm still as dry mouthed as a man in the desert."

"Then it's a good thing you don't have to sing." He laughed and led her to the tent where the pageant would take place.

Ignored by the other contestants, Annie Mae made her way to the front of the makeshift stage. She peered through the curtains. At least fifty people sat on hay bales. Behind the judge's table sat the head of the school board, Mr. Washington; the banker, Mr. James; and. . .Jonathan? Why Jonathan? The others were prominent members of the community, not hog farmers. She grinned. She might have a chance of winning after all.

Nine other girls, all dressed in their best, lined up behind the curtain, sneaking peeks at one another. Annie Mae forced herself to stare straight ahead. She wouldn't allow herself to get drawn into any pageant drama.

She pasted on a smile as the curtains opened with a soft rustling and stared into the serious face of Jonathan. He lowered his head and wrote something on the sheet in front of him.

Mama had said they would be judged on poise, beauty, talent, and their vision for the future. Annie Mae had no vision for the future other than helping her parents. With the depression in full swing, a few of their neighbors had sent their children away because they couldn't afford to feed them. She could not let that happen to little Robby and Lulu.

For days she'd thought on what she would say when asked that all-important question and still had no more idea of what to say than she had then. She closed her eyes and prayed. When her name was called, she stepped forward, prepared now for whatever the judges would ask, and wiped her sweaty hands subtly on the skirt of her dress.

Mr. Washington smiled. "State your name and age, please."

"Annie Mae Thompkins, eighteen."

"Your talent?"

"I'll be singing."

"Answer this question to the best of your ability, please, Miss Thompkins. In today's troubled times, those with plenty need to step up and help the less fortunate. How do you intend to help your community?"

Annie Mae was prepared for this one. "Matthew 25:40 says, 'And the King shall answer and say unto them, Verily I say unto you, Inasmuch as ye have done it unto one of the least of these my brethren, ye have done it unto me.'" Tears clogged her throat, but she forced herself to go on. "Neighbors are losing their homes, land that has been in their families for generations, sending their babies to live with relatives who are better off, or sending them to orphanages. Our young men are leaving and seeking work elsewhere." She avoided Jonathan's gaze. "My goal is to help prevent this from happening to the community of Rabbit Hollow."

"This is quite the undertaking. How do you anticipate helping?" Mr. James cocked his head.

"Hard work and perseverance, sir. Food drives through the church, fund-raisers, to name a few."

"I have a question," Mr. James said, raising his hand. "What is your personal goal for your future? Do you hope to marry someday?"

"No, sir. I plan to stay where I am and help my family in the absence of my brother."

"Thank you, Miss Thompkins, you may step back."

On trembling legs, yet feeling proud of herself, Annie Mae returned to her place in line. Prayer had helped, just as Pa had told her many times. Now if only she could remember his words the next time she was insecure and worrying herself sick.

Once the girls had all answered their questions, each question different, they filed off, still smiling, to the backstage area. Once there, they were collected by their family members.

Pa crooked his arm for Annie Mae to slip her hand in and led her to the truck. "You did well, daughter. Very well."

"Thank you. They'll post by tomorrow night each girl's standing in the pageant."

"You'll be in first place. I guarantee it." He tucked her hand close. "Our family is in fine standing with all of the judges. Now, if Horace Smithson was a judge. . .well, you know how we've not gotten along since we both competed for your mama's hand. Not that the judges aren't fair, they are, but with your face and voice. . .well, you're bound to win."

"I was expecting him, actually. I wasn't expecting Jonathan."

"The committee wanted a common man, and the Mercer farm is one of the largest in the county. Since Frank is injured, they asked Jonathan to fill in."

"I was surprised to see him there."

Pa opened the truck door. "It betters your chances, doesn't it? The young man cares for you very much."

"I want to win, Pa, but I want to win fairly." She raised her gaze to his. "I know the pageant is a popularity contest, but if I found out Jonathan fixed it so I would win—"

"I'm talking out of my ears. I'm that nervous for you. Of course you'll win on your own merits."

She hoped so, she really did. With the pageant and Daisy, she was sure to make her pa proud.

<hr>

Annie Mae didn't want to get married? Jonathan shook his head as he gathered his score sheets. That was practically unheard of in Rabbit Hollow. He'd heard the murmurings of the other judges and had hoped Annie Mae would glance his way so he could give her a warning look. Her first question had impressed the judges; the second most likely lost her points.

But he couldn't worry about that now. He had a farm to run.

After heading to the livestock tent and checking on Belle, he drove home to begin work that would take him well past dark. He'd accomplished a lot that morning, but judging the pageant cut into his day.

"I've kept your supper warm," Ma called as he pulled in front of the house.

"I'll eat later. I still need to feed the hogs."

"Your brother did that. Come eat and tell me how the first leg of the pageant went. I've been waiting all evening."

Jonathan planted a quick kiss on her cheek. "How's Pa?"

"I'm fine, boy. Stop treating me like an invalid." Pa scooted to a sitting position on the bed Jonathan had moved to the living room after returning home a few weeks ago.

Jonathan met his mother's exasperated gaze. "See how my days go?" she said. "It's like having another child. Sit." She hurried to the oven and pulled out a plate, setting it in front of Jonathan.

"The girls were lovely," he said, crumbling a slice of corn bread into his milk. "Annie Mae Thompkins told the judges she didn't want to get married."

"Why would she say such a thing?" Pa's brow furrowed. "I thought you wanted to court her?"

"I never said that." Jonathan dipped his spoon into the beef stew on his plate.

"I don't see anything wrong with her comment. Things are changing. More and more women are choosing a career over marriage. It's time Rabbit Hollow caught up with the times. I heard Annie Mae sent a poem to a big city magazine. Maybe she'll be a writer. Nothing wrong with that." Mom sat in a chair across from Jonathan.

"But it probably lost her points, and I was hoping she would win the pageant to replace the money she thinks she would have won with her quilt. Now she's entered her hog and hopes to win first place. The community expects our young girls to be wives and mothers."

"That's not something you can help with, son." Pa shook his head. "There's no way she will win over Belle."

He knew that, and Pa knew that, but Annie Mae definitely didn't. If Belle beat Daisy, there would be one more wedge between them.

"Your face shows what's going on in your head," Pa said. "Don't you dare lose unless it's fair and square. Until I get back on my feet, we need that prize money."

"I've no intention of not winning, Pa." He'd find another way to keep his promise to Marcus and care for Annie Mae. "Don't get yourself riled. The doctor said your blood pressure is too high."

"That's only because of the pain in my back."

"Okay, Pa." Jonathan finished his supper and headed to the barn.

While he mucked stalls, he went over and over in his mind how to help the Thompkins family. Charity wouldn't do—not that the Mercers had much to give, not with Pa's mounting medical bills. Before her answer to Mr. James's question, he'd thought maybe proposing marriage to Annie Mae and combining the two farms was the best answer. Now, he had nothing. The first-prize money would only last so long. They needed a more permanent fix to their problems. Something to keep them all afloat until the depression was over.

If Pa wasn't feeling poorly, Jonathan would see about getting a job at Smithson's lumberyard. But that would take him away from the farm. Sometimes, he felt as if he were running in mud, going nowhere, and sinking with each step.

Pastor Forrest preached that God would provide. To trust in Him. Jonathan believed in God's Word, but when he saw more and more people giving up and heading to the big city in hopes of finding a job, his faith faltered. He'd left home once. He didn't want to do it again, nor did he want to sell the farm and pack up the family.

Suzanne stood in the doorway of the barn wearing her best dress. She twirled, the dress sailing around her knees. "Would I win the pageant if I entered?"

"If you were sixteen." Jonathan leaned on the shovel. "You're too young, sweetie."

She pouted. "They didn't have the fair last year, and I heard they almost didn't have one this year. What if they never have one again? I'll be destined to be nothing more than a wife with ten babies on my hip."

"There are worse things than being a wife and mother." Were all the women in Rabbit Hollow soured on their roles? "You can be anything you want to be, Suzanne. If you want to live the life of a beauty queen, there will always be pageants somewhere."

She tilted her head. "I heard you tell Mom what Annie Mae said. I agree with her. I think I want to go to Hollywood."

"If you still want to do that in a couple of years, I'll do my best to help it happen." Maybe Jonathan was fighting the inevitable. Maybe everyone left home in search of a better future. If so, why struggle to keep something afloat that might be extinct by the time he was an old man?

Chapter 4

"Do re mi fa so la ti do." Annie Mae paced her room while waiting for her pa to call her down. Tonight was the talent portion of the pageant. She needed to make sure her vocal chords were in good condition.

"Hot tea with honey." Mama thrust a mug into her hands. "Sip it slowly. Don't burn your throat."

Mama's nervous fluttering around the house all day kept Annie Mae on edge. "Thank you." She sat on the edge of her bed. "I'm scared. What if my voice cracks?"

"You're in first place, dear. There's nothing to be worried about. Sing as if you're singing in church and the prize is yours."

Annie Mae wished she had her mother's confidence. In her experience, something always went wrong when she wanted something as badly as she wanted a first-place ribbon.

A horn honked outside, signaling that it was time to go. Annie Mae took a couple more sips of her drink then followed Mama outside.

Pa held the car door open. "Daughter, you're riding inside tonight. Ma will ride in the back. We can't have you getting mussed." He grinned.

Annie Mae's eyes widened. It didn't seem right for Mama to sit in the back with the young'uns.

"Time's wastin'. Let's go." Pa slapped the door.

Annie Mae slid onto the worn seat. She wanted to say thank you, she loved them, any number of things, but Mama had made her promise not to speak another word until it was time to sing. That was going to be a near impossible feat. She'd really wanted to talk to Daisy before stepping onto that stage. Which was ridiculous. She needed to speak with people, not animals. Better yet, God. She closed her eyes and said a prayer. When she opened them again, they were at the fairgrounds.

Pa helped her from the truck as if she were royalty. While the rest of the family headed to the front of the tent, he led Annie Mae through the back entrance. "Good luck, sweetheart." He gave her a tender kiss on the cheek then left to join the rest of the family.

Only five girls would showcase their talents, the rest having not made the cut. One was dressed in a flowing gown and would dance the foxtrot with her brother. Another was going to tap dance, another yodel, and yet another was doing a poetry reading. It might not be a pageant by New York or Hollywood standards, but Pulaski County did their best.

Annie Mae ran her hands down the flowing skirt of the peacock-blue dress her mother had sewn for her and took one last glance in the mirror provided for the girls. She was to be the last to perform.

The first girl's name was called, and Annie Mae peeked through a slit in the curtains to watch. The girl's yodels filled the tent. Cows answered from the livestock corrals. Annie Mae smiled and glanced to where Jonathan sat. How could the man sit with such an impassive expression on his face? He almost looked bored.

If he hadn't wanted to judge, he shouldn't have accepted in his father's place. There were other men who would have been very happy to sit in his seat.

As she watched, Sheriff Barton approached the judge's table and whispered something to Jonathan. He paled and bolted to his feet then dashed out of the tent. Mr. Smithson took Jonathan's seat, folded his hands on the table in front of him, and listened as the first contestant finished her talent.

Annie Mae let the curtain fall into place. She didn't have a chance of winning first place now. Not with Pa's nemesis as one of the judges. What could have taken Jonathan away in such a hurry?

Before she knew it, her turn had come. With palms sweating, she stepped into the spotlight, nodded at the piano player, and sang, focusing her gaze on the loving faces of her family. Her voice didn't crack or warble. Instead, had there been rafters in that tent, they would have rung with her praise. Through it all, Mr. Smithson sat stonily, looking everywhere but at Annie Mae.

When she was finished, she thanked the judges and gave a curtsy. She'd done her best.

Fifteen minutes later, after the judges' deliberation, the girls were called back onstage. Mr. Washington, microphone in hand, turned and smiled. "Without further ado, we will announce our winners. In third place, we have Ila Ruth Mason. In second place, Annie Mae Thompkins. Miss Pulaski County 1930 goes to. . ."

Annie Mae didn't hear the rest. She'd lost. Tears burned her eyes. Sure, she'd receive ten dollars, but that wasn't enough. Not nearly enough. All her hopes now lay on Daisy. She plastered a smile on her face as the first-place winner accepted her bouquet of roses and her crown.

As soon as it was polite to do so, Annie Mae bounded down the steps of the stage and into her pa's open arms. "I failed you," she sobbed.

"That could never happen. It was just a bit of bad luck."

"Better luck next time, Thompkins." Mr. Smithson gave a nod on his way past.

"It's cold for that man to take out his grievance with me on my innocent daughter." Pa held Annie Mae close.

"We don't know that's what happened." She forced the words past a throat clogged with tears.

"Of course that's what happened. I know how that man thinks and acts. Come. Let's see how Daisy did."

Lulu slipped her tiny hand in Annie Mae's as they walked to the livestock pens. "You sang real pretty."

"Thank you, sweetie." Annie Mae gave her sister's hand a squeeze. She had sung her best. Unfortunately, circumstances were out of her control.

"Oh." Next to the hog pens, Mama clapped a hand over her mouth and turned to Annie Mae.

"Second place?" Annie Mae glared at the blue ribbon on Belle's pen. Second place for the second time that night, and all because of Jonathan Mercer. On top of the red ribbon instead of blue, two people left messages that they wanted to purchase Daisy.

"Mr. Thompkins, Mrs. Thompkins?" Sheriff Barton stepped into the tent. "I'm wondering whether I could ask for a charitable favor."

"Sure, Sheriff." Pa reached out and shook the man's hand.

"Frank Mercer passed into eternity less than an hour ago. I'm wondering whether your missus could go sit with Harriet. See what the family needs?"

Annie Mae swallowed past the mountain in her throat. She'd had bad thoughts about Jonathan, but no matter how bad she thought her night was, his was a thousand times worse. "I'll go, just as soon as I change out of this dress."

<hr />

Jonathan stared at his pa's lifeless body, his arm around Ma. She sniffed into a lace-trimmed handkerchief. Next to them stood his siblings, features still, but tears filled their eyes.

When he'd arrived home, Ma had told him that Pa had insisted on feeding the hogs. Eric helped the best he could, trying to do most of the heavy lifting, but at the age of ten, there wasn't a lot he could do. Pa had collapsed on his way back to the house.

Jonathan should have been there. Just as with Marcus, he hadn't been around when he was needed the most. Nor had he been there for Annie Mae. Word didn't take long to spread through Rabbit Hollow as to who won first place and where the other contestants placed.

"What are we going to do now, son?" Ma leaned her head on his shoulder.

"I'll take care of it. We'll be fine." He'd done the majority of the work since returning home from the work relief. It wouldn't be difficult to continue doing so. "The children will have to step up and do a bit more work. If we all pull together, we'll be fine."

"What about asking Annie Mae Thompkins to marry you?" Ma peered up at him. "Then we could combine farms and workload. You've always taken a liking to her."

That was an idea. One he wasn't adverse to, but now was not the time to make such a decision.

A knock sounded on the door. Suzanne rushed to get it then called out, "That girl you want to marry is here with a casserole."

Jonathan turned and met Annie Mae's startled gaze. "I'm sorry about that. You know how children are. Come in, please."

"Let me take that. Thank you so much." Ma took the dish and set it on the stove. "I hope you'll stay and have a bite with us. I do believe I smell your mother's potato and ham specialty."

"Yes, ma'am." Annie Mae fussed with her dress. "I've come to express my condolences and to help wherever I'm needed."

"We need someone to slop the hogs," Eric said.

"We could use you to feed the chickens," Suzanne added.

Jonathan wanted to box their ears. "They're trying to palm their chores off on you. Have a seat, we're just saying good-bye to Pa. The coroner will be by soon."

"Oh." Her eyes widened. "I hadn't expected him to still be here."

"Neither did I." The coroner must be walking to retrieve Pa's body. The sooner things settled down, the sooner Jonathan could escape to his tree house and let go the tears blocking his throat. He turned his head so Annie Mae couldn't see.

"Mrs. Mercer?" Annie Mae approached Ma at the stove. "I'll serve the food. Please, go say good-bye to your husband. There's no need to treat me like a guest."

"Thank you, honey." Ma sat on the sofa next to where Pa lay.

Jonathan went to close the front door and saw the coroner and Pastor Forrest driving up. It was about time. Didn't they understand the pain of having your father lying dead in the living room?

"I'm sorry I'm late." The coroner hurried to Pa's side. "I had a flat. If the pastor hadn't come along when he did, I'd still be sitting out there."

"Let me pray for you while he works." The pastor gathered the family in the kitchen and prayed a prayer for strength to get through the tough times ahead.

As he prayed, the tears Jonathan was holding in fell. He was now the man of the house. The burden weighed heavy on his shoulders. Gone was the Mercer figurehead, the man of wisdom who seemed to have all the answers. His head jerked up when the pastor prayed they find joy in their sorrow. Was that even possible?

The children's sobs rose above the pastor's prayer. Ma cried silently, her shoulders moving with her grief. Jonathan came to a decision. If there was joy to be found, he would figure out a way to bring it to his family. Maybe not tomorrow or next week, but he'd see they were all happy again. He glanced to where Annie Mae watched them, her face creased with concern. Maybe joy would start with her.

By the time the pastor and coroner left with Pa's body, Jonathan collapsed at the kitchen table. He couldn't remember ever being as tired as he was at that moment.

"I'm so sorry." Annie Mae handed him a plate then sat next to him. "Tell me what you need."

"Now is not the time for that." He set the plate on a nearby chair. "Sorry, but I'm not hungry."

"You should eat." She twisted a dish towel in her hands. "Belle won first place. Congratulations."

"I'd give you the ribbon if I could. It doesn't mean much to me anymore."

"No, now, with your Pa gone. . .you need the prize money to help support your family. I admit, I was sore at first. And then I came in second in the pageant, too. I blamed you for leaving, not having a clue about why you left in such a hurry. Pa's rival took your place, so there went my chance. I'd lost the moment that man sat down. He isn't fair, like you, and allows his own prejudices to decide for him."

She took a deep breath. He took her hand in his and traced the lines on her palm. "Isn't that why you wanted the money?"

She nodded. "We've two good offers to purchase Daisy. We'll be all right."

"There has to be another way. You love that hog." He thought for a moment, setting her hand back in her lap. "How about I lend you one of my boars? It's not an immediate fix, but you could sell the piglets."

"What would you want in return?"

"For you to be open-minded enough to let me court you after I've finished mourning."

Chapter 5

Goodness. First she walks in to Jonathan's sister saying he wanted to marry her, then he asks her for permission to court her. What was going on in that handsome head of his?

She studied his solemn face. "I don't think it's the right time for this discussion."

"Perhaps not." He shook his head. "But, with my family's future so uncertain, I'd like to finalize any plans that I can." He glanced up, his eyes bloodshot. "We've known each other since we were children. We've grown up half a mile apart. I know everything there is to know about you, Annie Mae."

She doubted he knew how selfish she could be, how insecure she was, or how desperately she wanted to make a difference and save her family from worry. Could Jonathan's proposal be an answer to prayer? She shook her head. She wanted to marry for love.

"Does that mean no?" He took her hand in his. "Won't you even consider me?"

"We can talk about that later. Right now, I'm here to help you through this hard time." She got to her feet and headed for the kitchen where dishes waited. She filled the sink with water and soap. The repetition of washing and the clean smell of the soap helped diminish some of the disappointments of the fair and worry of the Mercer family.

In the background, Jonathan murmured to his family, doing his best to console them, most likely. The man truly did have a kind heart. She exhaled sharply. It wasn't his fault she came in second place in both competitions. Two red ribbons brought in almost as much money as one blue one. And. . .there were always the offers to purchase Daisy.

With the dishes complete, she set bread to rise before stepping out the back door and sitting on the top step. Stars glittered like diamonds on a velvet background. Such a beautiful evening for such a tragedy to have occurred. She couldn't imagine being in Jonathan's shoes. Her pa was her world.

"Walk with me?" Jonathan came around the corner of the house and held out his hand.

"Sure, if it will make you feel better."

"It will."

She slipped her hand into his work-roughened one. Their arms swung as he led her down a path and into the thick stand of trees behind their property. "Where are we going?"

"I want to show you my special place. The place I shared with Marcus."

Her heart hitched. "Why?"

"My pa told me the other day he thought he would die soon. Said his heart had been fluttering in a strange way, and made me promise not to tell Ma because he didn't want to live his last days as an invalid." He stopped and stared down at her. "His death was no surprise. Marcus's was a surprise to us both. I want to share with you something that meant a lot to him. . .to me."

They stopped in front of a giant oak tree. With the help of the moonlight, she could make out a platform nestled where several thick branches met. "This is your thinking place."

"Marcus and I made many a dream here." He pulled her close, slipping his arm around her shoulders. "We were young when I promised him to always look after you. It was as if he knew God would take him home early."

She pulled free of his embrace. "No one could know that. His death was an accident. He shouldn't have gone hunting that morning. The fog was too thick. I begged him not to go." She glared. *He* should have been there. Marcus would have listened to him.

As if he could read her mind, he flinched. "My being there might not have made a difference. Still, you can't blame me more than I blame myself."

Guilt over her childish and unfair behavior filled her. "I'm sorry." She swallowed past a painful throat. "You don't need this right now. Let's talk of happy times."

"Will you be back tomorrow?"

She nodded. "Every day for a few hours for as long as I'm needed."

"Then tomorrow we'll climb up there and think of happy times, just as you wish." He held out his hand again.

She gave him a trembling smile and accepted his hand as a truce. If they could become close friends, despite the sorrow between them, she'd be satisfied until the end of her days. As time progressed and her responsibilities at home became heavier, she could use a friend like Jonathan.

When they returned to the house, she made sure the bread was ready for Mrs. Mercer to bake, glanced around for any last-minute items to take care of, then headed out the door with promises to return midmorning.

"Let me take you home."

"It's a short distance, Jonathan. I'll be fine."

"It's dark. I can't let you walk alone." He fell in step beside her. "Besides, the walk back will give me time with my thoughts."

"Who am I to deny you that?" Despite her feelings that he should have done something to keep Marcus from dying, as ridiculous as that sounded, even to her, she found herself enjoying the time they spent together.

━━━ ◄●► ━━━

After a restless night, Jonathan climbed out of bed and woke his younger brother. "Chores await, my young man. Up and at 'em."

Eric groaned. "Let me sleep. My head hurts."

"That's from mourning. Pa wouldn't want us to lie in bed all day. Not when there is work to be done."

"Pa isn't here." The sadness in his brother's voice ripped at Jonathan's heart.

"That's no reason to shirk our duties." Jonathan yanked the blankets off the bed. "Five minutes. That's all you get."

He banged on his sister's door on his way to the kitchen and was pleased to see her already helping Ma with breakfast. "Make a list of what needs done today. Between us five and Annie Mae, we'll get it done."

"I need to go into town and make arrangements for the funeral," Ma said, her shoulders slumping. "We can do that first thing and be back before Annie Mae arrives."

"I'll drive you as soon as I've fed the livestock. Suzanne, the cow needs milked."

"Done." She placed plates on the table. "And I've collected the eggs. You don't need to look over my shoulder, Jonathan. I know what to do."

He kissed her cheek. "Bless you."

By the time the chores and the unpleasant task of making final arrangements were done, Jonathan and his mother arrived home to see Annie Mae almost finished making sandwiches out of the fresh bread.

"It isn't much," she said. "Egg and tomato, but it will fill your bellies."

"It's enough. Thank you." He hung his hat on a rack by the door, looking forward to alone time spent with Annie Mae in the tree house. Persistence would win over her reluctant heart. She'd followed him around once like a love-struck puppy; he could get her to feel that way again. He grinned. The puppies. "I have a surprise for you."

Her face lit up. "Really? Flowers?"

"No. Better."

"You've piqued my curiosity. Let's eat so you can show me." She set a pitcher of milk on the table, called out the back door for Eric, and waited until the Mercer family was seated before taking a seat herself.

Jonathan led them in a short prayer of thanksgiving, missing his pa more than ever, then picked up his sandwich. "The funeral will be tomorrow. The pastor is going to get the word out to the community."

"Tomorrow night is when they hand out the prizes and officially close the fair." Annie Mae sipped her milk. "Will you be up to it?"

He winked at her. "Trying to steal my blue ribbon?"

"Seriously? You know me better than that. I'm through pouting over my loss, thank you very much."

"Stop teasing, son. Annie Mae is kind enough to help us for a few days. You'll run her off." Ma patted his hand. "Eat, so you can go. Suzanne and I will clean up."

He met Annie Mae's shy gaze across the table. "Pa would have liked getting to know you better."

High spots of rose colored her cheeks. "I feel the same." She gave him a sad smile. "I'm ready to go if you are." She dabbed at the corners of her lips with her napkin.

He stood and pulled out her chair. Having her around helped him feel better. How was he going to cope when she no longer came each day?

"Are we going to the tree house?" Annie Mae asked when they stepped outside. "I wore trousers under my dress and want to hear all your secrets." Her lips twitched.

"We will, but first. . ." He took her hand and pulled her along to the barn.

She laughed behind him as they entered the doorway, the sound like water trickling over rocks in a mountain stream. When he was with her, he could almost forget the trials of the last few weeks.

"Oh, Jonathan. Puppies." She fell to her knees in the straw next to the litter. "They're adorable." She picked up a black-and-white female, rubbing her cheek along its soft fur.

"It's yours. A thank-you for all you've done for us."

"I haven't done anything more than any good neighbor would." She returned the pup to its littermates. "It's another mouth to feed. I can't accept it."

"Think of your brother and sister." He was willing to play dirty if he had to. He knew she couldn't resist making Robby and Lulu happy. "Dogs earn their keep. I won't take no for an answer."

She stared silently at the puppy then nodded, getting to her feet. "Thank you. My brother and sister will be grateful."

Taking her hand again, he led her back to where they'd stood the night before. "Can you climb up?"

"Of course." She grabbed for a board at her eye level and started climbing until she peered down at him from the platform. "You should have built walls." She pulled back so he could join her.

"Remember, we were young. Walls were above our skill level." He lay back, folding his hands behind his head. "Marcus and I dreamed many a dream right here."

She lay on her side, arm bent, head nestled in her hand. "What were his dreams?"

"To take over your family farm, mostly. That, and to make sure the family was taken care of." He cut her a sideways glance. "Why do you work so hard, Annie Mae? Is your pa ill?"

"No, why?"

"If he's an able-bodied man, you shouldn't feel such a burden to take your brother's place."

"I'm the oldest now." She sat up, focusing on her floral dress rather than him. "It's my duty to help my parents. Did you know the Robertsons sent their young'uns to Georgia to live with relatives?"

"Your family would never let that happen." *He* would never let that happen.

She shrugged. "Things happen. You should know that with your pa's passing."

"I suppose, but that's one reason why I want to court you with the intention of us getting married." He sat up and stared into her eyes. "We could combine the farms. It would help both of us."

Her eyes flashed. "I'm not getting married. Ever. And if I were, I wouldn't marry just so you could have our farm."

Have their farm? How did she get the idea he was after their farm? All he wanted to do was help her. He let out a frustrated growl. Why did she have to be so stubborn?

Chapter 6

He almost had her agreeing to a courtship. How could she have been so naïve? Jonathan Mercer was still the tease he'd always been. To use her family's financial troubles that way was downright cruel.

Annie Mae sat on her porch steps and stared up at the very same stars she'd gazed upon with Jonathan. A small breeze announced the coolness of autumn approaching. She closed her eyes and breathed deeply of the crisp air.

She and Jonathan had almost shared a special moment until he opened his mouth and foolishness spewed out. She sighed. It was a good plan, though, to merge the two farms.

"Time for bed." Pa stepped onto the porch. "You look troubled. Are the Mercers fine, considering?"

"Yes. Jonathan said his father's death wasn't a surprise. He'd had a bad heart for a while, and since hurting his back. . .well, they're coping." She stared across the yard.

He sat next to her. "Then what's ailing you?"

"Jonathan wants to court me with the prospect of marriage and merging the two farms." She turned her head to look at him. "That would be a big help to you and to them."

"Who said I needed help?" Pa folded his hands and let them dangle between his knees. "Stop worrying about me, daughter. I'm not fifty yet, and I'm in good health. Although his idea does hold merit. What did you tell him?"

"I wasn't very nice. I don't want to marry, Pa. Now that I'm the oldest—"

"Stop right there, Annie Mae. If I thought for one second that you were seriously contemplating putting your future on hold because of some misguided loyalty, I'd ship you off right here and now so you'd be forced to follow your dreams and not waste your life away here."

She gasped. "But if Marcus were here—"

"He isn't here. God took him home for reasons only He knows. Sure, life might be easier on me if he were alive, but there's no guarantee that Marcus would have stayed on the farm. He might have sought a career elsewhere. Sweetheart"—he took her hands in his—"you need to search your heart and put your trust in God. Stop worrying where there's no need. Do you love Jonathan?"

She took her bottom lip between her teeth as she pondered his question. Did she? "I care for him, yes, but love. . .I don't know."

Maybe if she kept her distance from Jonathan for a while, she'd have time to decide. "I think I'll go to bed."

"Think on his question. Don't marry anyone for less than love, but most importantly, search God's will for your life."

She nodded and went to her room.

The next morning, Annie Mae pleaded a headache and allowed her mother to take her place at the Mercers'. She set to work with a vengeance preparing breakfast then cleaning house to take the burden off her mother when she returned. If she wanted time to think on Jonathan's offer, then she needed to keep her distance. She'd see him that evening at the fair awards. That was enough.

"Get the bandages!" She heard Robby yelling before he raced into the kitchen. "Pa cut himself on a saw."

"Is it bad?" Annie Mae's heart plummeted. This was why she needed to be home and not off caring for a house of her own. You never knew what tragedy would be next on the farm. Someone had to be home in case of emergencies.

Robby shrugged. "He's bleeding."

"It's not that bad." Pa, his shirttail wrapped around his hand, shuffled into the kitchen and sat on one of the straight-backed chairs. "Saw slipped and cut off my pinkie finger." She stared at him in horror as he handed the severed finger to her. "Put that on ice and get me to the doc."

Her stomach heaved, but there was no time to be sick. She grabbed the ice pick, chopped off a chunk of ice from the icebox, then wrapped the finger and the ice in a towel. "Pa, take off that bloody shirt and wrap your hand in this." She handed him a clean piece of flannel. "Robby, run to the Mercers' and tell Mama. Take Lulu with you. Stay together." She narrowed her eyes. "I mean it. You need to be a big boy and listen to me."

"I will." He dashed away.

Thankful that Pa had taught her to drive a couple of years ago, Annie Mae helped him to the truck then slid into the driver's seat. Already, the clean cloth around his hand was soaked red. His skin was pale enough to worry her.

She drove as fast as she dared, which wasn't very fast to some standards. They pulled into the doc's yard, and she laid on the horn until he ran out. She explained the situation.

"Let's get him inside. I'll call for an ambulance. Hopefully, we can get the finger attached, but he'll need blood. I can't do that here." The doctor propped his shoulder under Pa's good arm and helped him into the clinic.

As soon as responsibility for her father was in the doctor's hands, the world grew black, and Annie Mae collapsed to the floor.

When she opened her eyes, she found herself lying on a hospital bed with Ma and Jonathan peering down at her. "What happened?"

"You fainted." Ma's lips twitched. "You don't like blood, remember? But you did a good job getting your pa here. He's in the ambulance. I'm going to ride with him to the hospital, and Jonathan will take you home."

She shook her head. "I'll drive myself."

"No, you won't. You're still woozy. You can retrieve the truck after the awards ceremony tonight."

She'd have to spend all day with him? There went her decision to keep her distance.

After picking up Annie Mae's younger siblings, Jonathan took the Thompkins family to his place where she kept so busy he had no time to talk to her about her remarks from the night before. If he didn't know better, he'd think she was working hard to avoid him.

Now, they stood side by side on the stage at the fair waiting to be awarded their ribbons and prize money. She kept her gaze fixed straight ahead to where his family and her brother and sister sat.

"It's too bad your parents couldn't be here," he said, cutting her a sideways glance.

"Uh-huh."

"I guess the hospital will keep him for a few days?"

"Yes."

He sighed and gave up trying to have a conversation with her. She was as cold toward him as snow.

"First place in the hog competition is Jonathan Mercer!" The announcer handed him a check and a blue ribbon.

"Annie Mae Thompkins took second place in two separate competitions. Her hog Daisy came in second to Mercer's Belle, and she took second place in Miss Pulaski 1930." The announcer handed her a check and two red ribbons. "And her lovely mother, Rachel Thompkins, received a blue ribbon for her delicious peach jam! Give these folks a big hand."

Annie Mae's cheeks turned the same color as the ribbons in her hand. Still, she smiled and nodded to the spectators as if she'd won first place. When the presentation was over, Jonathan escorted Annie Mae to the livestock tent to retrieve Belle and Daisy. The rich odors of hay, animal, and manure filled the air. The smell was sweeter to him than flowers.

He spotted two offers to purchase Daisy and realized he had yet to follow through on his offer of lending the Thompkins a boar.

"Have you accepted one of these offers?" He pointed at the names tacked to Daisy's pen.

"No, I can't bear to, although, now, with Pa's medical expenses. . ."

"I might have a solution. Not an immediate one, but it will help later and you can use your prize money for the medical bills." He propped an elbow on the fence. "Like I told you, I could lend you a boar, and you give me pick of the litter. You can sell the rest."

For the first time that day she looked at him. "I'd prefer that. I'd have to talk it over with Pa, but I don't see him saying no."

"Neither do I. I'll take Belle home and pick up the boar and bring it and Daisy over tonight. Will you be all right driving the truck back in the dark?"

Her eyes narrowed. "I'm not incompetent."

"I never said you were." He ran his hands through his hair. "What have I done to make you dislike me so? How many times do I have to apologize for not being there for Marcus?" He gripped her shoulders and turned her to face him. "I'm here now, for you. What more do you want from me?"

"Time to sort out my thoughts." She stepped back. "That's all. Just time."

"How much time?"

"I don't know." Her words were barely more than a whisper, almost lost among the animals' grunts and snorts.

"Fine. When you figure it out and stop being afraid, let me know." He unlatched Daisy's gate and grabbed one end of the rope tied around the sow's neck. "Let's get these animals to the truck."

"I'm not afraid, Jonathan."

"Yes, you are." He stomped to Belle's pen and retrieved her. Without another glance at Annie Mae, he led the way to the truck where two men waited to help load the heavy sows into the back.

Annie Mae waited in the passenger seat until Jonathan joined her. The ride to the doctor's office was made in silence.

Jonathan turned, resting his arm along the back of the seat. "I'll bring Daisy when I bring the boar. One of these days, Miss Thompkins, you and I are going to have a long talk."

She cast him a glance as she slid from the seat. "Thank you for your help."

With a mental groan, he backed onto the road. He wasn't about to let her drive home without him following. Thankfully, a kind neighbor had agreed to take Robby and Lulu home from the fair. One less thing for him to worry about.

From a safe distance, he followed Annie Mae. She drove hardly fast enough to stir up the dust. At this rate, the children would beat him home.

After an eternity, Annie Mae pulled into her drive with a honk and a wave. Jonathan headed home to drop off Belle and retrieve Goliath. By the time he returned to the Thompkins farm, Annie Mae's siblings waited with her on the front porch. He'd passed Pastor Forrest heading home with Ma, Eric, Matthew, and Suzanne.

He backed the truck as close to Daisy's pen as possible and opened the gate. He could only pray the animals took to each other and provided some income for the Thompkins.

"Thank you again." Annie Mae stopped at his side. "This will be her first litter."

"Hopefully, not her last." He glanced past her to where Robby and Lulu sprinted toward them then climbed on the pen. "Will the three of you be all right alone here tonight?"

"Yes, Jonathan. No need to worry about us." Annie Mae's eyes glittered in the moonlight.

"That's the pot calling the kettle black, don't you think?"

A ghost of a smile teased at her lips.

His heart turned a flip. If the young'uns weren't right there, he'd risk a slap to steal a kiss.

"I guess it is," she said. "I'm working on my worrying nature."

"And who of you by being worried can add a single hour to his life?"

"I get your point, although your interpretation may be a little skewed." She leaned on the fence, her gaze locked on the two animals nosing around each other. "I think they like each other."

"More than you like me."

She whirled around to look at him.

"I've two tickets in my pocket, Annie Mae. I'm picking you up tomorrow and driving into town to take you to the picture show. I'll not waste the tickets by you saying no." He gave her a nod and strolled, whistling, to his truck.

Chapter 7

Annie Mae fluffed her hair one more time. A waste of time, actually. She couldn't go to the moving pictures with Jonathan. Who would watch Robby and Lulu? Pa wasn't coming home until at least tomorrow.

She plopped on the bed. What was she thinking? She'd vowed to never get married. So why contemplate a date with Jonathan? Ugh. Because she was rethinking her decision, that's why. Pa was right. It was time to let the worry go and let God handle things. He was way more capable than she. Perhaps marriage and a family of her own weren't such far-fetched ideas after all.

She giggled, clasped her hands against her chest, and fell back onto the mattress. Oh, she loved moving pictures. She'd find a way to have her brother and sister cared for while she indulged in a rare treat. Still, it wouldn't do to fawn over Jonathan too much. Not until she knew for certain that living on her parents' farm wasn't what God intended her to do with her life. It wouldn't be fair to spawn hope in Jonathan's heart until she was sure.

The breeze ruffling her bedroom curtains cooled, signaling that late afternoon had arrived. Which meant Jonathan would be there soon, and she had yet to put supper on the stove. She shoved off the bed and thundered to the kitchen. Leftover soup and fresh bread, baked that morning, would fill their bellies.

"Supper!" she yelled out the back door.

"Am I invited?" Jonathan entered through the front door, his sister on his heels. "I brought Suzanne to watch the young'uns while we go on our date."

The man thought of everything. "There's plenty of soup. Have a seat." Thank goodness she'd baked bread that morning. The soup was intended to stretch into tomorrow, but she'd figure something else out. Mama said to never turn away a friend from your table.

"Do you like musicals?" Jonathan asked, taking a seat at the table. "The tickets are for *Chasing Rainbows*."

"Oh, I've wanted to see that."

"Ma sent this." Suzanne handed her a bowl of noodles and cheese.

"Thank you." The Lord made sure they had enough food for company. She set the dish on the table as her siblings entered the house, sounding like two bulls charging through a glass house. "Wash up and sit down, quietly. The movie is a telling of life backstage for a vaudeville performer, right?"

Jonathan nodded, dishing soup into bowls. "I've heard good things about the show."

She froze as a picture of the two of them, in a kitchen of their own, surrounded by children, appeared in her mind. The scene was very much like the one in front of her, only the children looked like her and Jonathan. She gulped and busied herself in the icebox, using the cool air to soothe her flaming cheeks.

By the time supper was finished and the two girls were doing the dishes, Annie Mae had worked herself into an internal frenzy. Jonathan laughed and joked with the children, sending her an occasional wink and heart-stopping grin until she didn't know whether to plead a headache or enjoy the attention.

Attention and movie won out, despite her reservations.

Jonathan opened the passenger door to his truck, revealing a rectangular box of chocolates. "Sweets for a sweet gal."

Lordy, things were moving fast. She put her hands to her cheeks. "I…oh, Jonathan." Tears stung her eyes. "I haven't made up my mind about…us."

"I'm in no hurry." He waited until she was inside, then closed the door. Once he was inside, he spoke again. "God knows your heart, Annie Mae, and mine. You've cared for me since you were a little girl. I've seen it in your eyes."

"I've been so cruel to you." She focused on the unopened box on the dashboard. "I've blamed you for everything that's happened to me that was out of my control. Marcus. My quilt. Daisy, the pageant."

"I know." He started the ignition.

She cut him a sideways glance. "Yet, you persist when most men would have given up."

He gave a crooked grin. "You'll come to your senses eventually."

She studied his profile as he drove. What made this handsome man heap attentions on a girl reluctant to accept them? She'd had few suitors in her life, choosing instead to stay home and help her parents. Had she really been so misguided in thinking they needed her as much as she thought they did? What would it be like to be more concerned with new fashions and eligible men, like the other single girls in Rabbit Hollow? Maybe it was time she found out.

<hr/>

Jonathan felt Annie Mae's softening in the lines of her shoulders and the relaxation of her hand. Ma had told him to give her time, and he intended to, but not until after the show. He'd won the tickets at the fair, a surprise prize, and didn't intend to let them go to waste.

He parked in the theater parking lot then hurried to open Annie Mae's door. He intended to treat her like a princess that evening, kiss her good night whether she wanted him to or not, then leave her alone until she came to him. For however long that took, he would wait.

The pink dress she wore fluttered around her knees as he escorted her inside, drawing the attention of several men lounging in the foyer. He glared at them, putting his hand protectively on the small of her back, catching a whiff of rose-scented toilet water. He prayed it didn't take her long to make up her mind. For the first time, the idea of her choosing someone else threatened his peace of mind. If she decided that staying on the farm wasn't something she wanted after all, she might accept courtship from others. If she did, what could a hog farmer have to offer that the others couldn't? He eyed the men's suits then his brown woolen pants, and rushed Annie Mae to their seats.

"Would you like some popcorn? Candy? A soda?" He mentally counted the coins in his pocket.

"I'm fine, thank you."

He sat next to her, wanting to put his arm around and pull her close. Instead, he kept his hands in his lap.

"I haven't been to the movies in a long time," she said, smiling. "Thank you. This is a real treat."

"There's no one else I wanted to bring." He stretched his legs under the seat in front of him then drew them back up. He needed something to do with his hands. "I think I will get some popcorn." He bolted to his feet and up the aisle.

What was wrong with him? He'd known Annie Mae for most of his life. Why was he acting like a nervous schoolboy?

"Who's the looker you came in with?" One of the men from the foyer, a college student from the looks of him, leaned against the refreshment stand. "I haven't seen her around here before."

"She isn't from around here."

"Where's she from?"

"I'd rather not say." Jonathan placed his order, paid the cashier, and turned to leave.

The man smirked. "Is she your girl?"

"Not yet, but she's going to be."

"So, she's fair game for now."

Jonathan gritted his teeth. "I suppose." He marched back to his seat, offering the popcorn to Annie Mae.

She took a few pieces and popped them in her mouth as the lights dimmed and the curtain rose. Seconds later, her soft laughter warmed his heart as she enjoyed the short cartoon preceding the show. The fact that he could take her away from her worries, even if only for a few hours, filled him with immense joy. He wanted to ease her cares for the rest of his life.

Raucous laughter exploded behind them, followed by rude comments. Annie Mae started to turn until Jonathan put a hand on her arm, stopping her. "Ignore them."

She scowled. "They're making it difficult."

"They want your attention."

"For heaven's sake, why?"

"One of them likes you."

"They're acting like children." She stiffened and focused her attention on the screen as the main attraction started.

"Pretty lady, come sit with me." The man behind them leaned over the seat.

"No, thank you."

"You heard her. She's not interested." Jonathan put his arm around Annie Mae. Maybe not the way he'd wanted to get closer to her, but if he could get the man to leave her alone, he'd find another way to make a tender gesture that had nothing to do with an arrogant jerk.

"Please stop kicking my seat." Annie Mae turned to glare.

The man leered at her. "I will if you sit next to me."

"You've been drinking! Jonathan, can you smell the whiskey? Let me have your soda, please."

He handed it over.

Annie Mae stood and promptly upended the drink on the fool's head. "Oops. My apologies. I guess you'll need to leave now."

The man said a few choice words and stormed from the theater.

Annie Mae laughed and resumed her seat, handing Jonathan the empty cup. "That felt wonderful. Let's watch the show."

That was the most amazing thing he'd ever seen her do. For the first time in a long time, he'd caught a glimpse of the Annie Mae not weighed down by the responsibility she heaped on herself. This time, he put his arm around her and pulled her close out of admiration and affection.

After the rest of the movie passed without incident, Jonathan stood and offered his hand to help Annie Mae from her seat. Keeping her hand in his, and a wary eye out for a lurking man covered with soda, he led her to the truck.

On the drive home, Annie Mae opened the box of chocolates and offered him one. "The movie was wonderful."

He opened his mouth and she popped the candy in.

"I enjoyed it. Thank you for coming with me. You were amazing, by the way."

"You mean the jerk behind us? Marcus taught me how to take care of myself. He said if a man didn't treat me like a lady, then I shouldn't treat him like a gentleman. Sorry about your soda."

"From the grin on your face, I don't think you're very sorry at all."

"It was the best thing I could think of." She sighed. "Do you think this is how the city folks live? Going to the theater on a regular basis? I could go every night."

"Then it wouldn't be as special."

When they arrived at her house, he was relieved that none of the children were waiting on the porch. He helped Annie Mae from the truck then put his hands on her shoulders. "I'm going to kiss you now."

Her eyes widened.

"I hope you won't slap me, but I'm betting it would be worth it."

"I won't slap you," she whispered.

He lowered his head, kissing her with all the tenderness in his heart, before pulling back. "Now, I'm going to respect your wishes and give you time. Good night, Annie Mae." He climbed into the truck and drove away, praying he hadn't just made the biggest mistake of his life.

Chapter 8

Two weeks had passed since the night of the movies. Pa was home, minus his finger, and back to work. It took all of Annie Mae's willpower not to step in and try to take some of his load. Why did he keep refusing her offer to help him? After being told that a man wasn't less of a man because he'd lost his pinkie finger, she steered clear of the fields and hog pens. Except for Daisy. To her, she spilled all of the pain she felt because Jonathan hadn't come by once. In church, he avoided her gaze and didn't linger after the service as he used to. He'd even managed to pick up his boar while she was at the store.

"I fear I may have ruined everything this time, Daisy." She folded her arms on the top rail of the pen. "I've pushed him away too many times. Maybe it was my aggressive behavior at the movies, but he said he was impressed that I stood up to that bully." She sighed. "I'm confused and don't have a clue what to do now."

She shouldn't have competed in the hog show at the fair after knowing Jonathan had entered. She'd never had a chance to win against his Belle. All that had accomplished was sore feelings and her acting like a child. She turned and braced her back against the pen, one foot propped on a rail. Glancing heavenward, she thought of all the wasted time spent worrying about one silly thing or another.

Mama and Pa both had told her the family was doing just fine. After receiving her prize money, Annie Mae had added it to the money jar, surprised to see Mama had stashed away at least a month's worth of funds. With Annie Mae's winnings, they were even further ahead. God provided. He didn't need a worrisome girl to keep reminding Him of what needed doing.

While she missed her brother desperately, she now realized there was nothing she, or anyone, could have done to prevent the accident, short of Marcus staying home. For whatever reason, God had chosen to take him.

"Whatcha doin'?" Lulu climbed onto the fence.

"Thinking about life."

"What about it?" Her sister's eyes widened.

"How fleeting it is and how hard."

"It isn't hard to me. I do my chores, go to school and church, and play. What more is there?" She shrugged. "I always find time to have fun."

From the mouth of babes. Annie Mae tugged on her sister's ponytail. "What else, indeed. Someday, when you're older, you can add men to that list. That's when things get confusing."

"I'm going to marry Pa." Lulu scampered down and dashed to the rope swing hanging from a tree.

Annie Mae laughed. Maybe she needed to be more like Lulu and find the fun in life. "Mama, I'm going for a walk."

Her mother turned from where she was hanging the laundry. "Good. Oh, wait. There's a loaf of bread on the counter for the Mercers and a slab of fresh butter. Would you mind dropping those off on your walk? Don't be long. It looks like rain. If it does, stay at the Mercers' until it stops."

"All right, Mama." Maybe she could get Jonathan to notice her and stop pretending she was transparent. She knew what he was doing, letting her miss him and change her mind about marriage and love, but he was going about it all wrong! She wanted him to court her, to shower her with words of affection, to kiss her again.

She collected the bread and butter, placed them in a basket, and set off down the road. She continued thinking of her feelings for Jonathan. Her steps faltered then stopped, and she sat on a fallen tree as the realization hit her that she loved him. From the first time he'd come to visit her brother, she'd loved him. The startling blue eyes that sparkled with zeal, the dark hair that caught the sun's rays, the dimples in his cheeks when he smiled. Those were his physical qualities. His inner ones were more beautiful than she'd imagined. She'd witnessed his kindness and strength time and time again. How could she have been such a blinded fool?

Well, no more. She got to her feet. She intended to declare her love the second she laid eyes on him.

An automobile roared behind her. With a shriek, she dove into the ditch on the side of the road, twisting her ankle and spilling the basket. Tears of pain and outrage sprang to her eyes as the vehicle continued past, not stopping to see whether she was injured.

Standing on her good foot, she peered over the edge of the road, now at chin level. If she didn't find a way out, she might never be found. Gray clouds scurrying overhead announced rain at any moment.

What a predicament. She grabbed at a small bush and tried to pull herself out of the ditch. Instead, she did nothing more than dislodge the bush and shower dirt upon her head. A crash of thunder, and the heavens opened wide.

The other side of the ditch was no better. Annie Mae was stuck, in a ditch, on the side of the road, in the pouring rain. No one would look for her for hours. She groaned and settled the best she could on a boulder, wrapped her arms around herself, and prepared to wait.

By the time the rain stopped, she was shivering. She had no idea how long it had been since her fall, but from the amount of water running off the road, she wouldn't be getting out easily. Leaving the basket behind, she plastered her body against the muddy wall of the ditch, grasped the edge with her fingertips, and fought for a foothold. Inch by tiring inch, she clawed her way out then lay panting on the side of the road. By that time, she didn't care if she got run over by a truck.

———◆◆◆———

Jonathan drove slowly, taking care not to let the truck slide on the muddy surface. He turned a corner and slammed on his brakes. What in the world? He peered through his windshield at what looked like a woman lying there. When the form moved, he shoved open his door and rushed to her side.

"Annie Mae?" He helped her to her feet, wrapping his arms around her as she sagged against him.

"The one and only." She glanced over her shoulder. "Your bread and butter is down there." She collapsed in a fit of giggles.

While he'd waited a long time to hear her laugh with such abandon, the circumstances did anything but fill him with joy. Instead, he worried about her mental state. "Are you injured?"

"I appear to have twisted my ankle, and I'm covered with mud." Her laughter continued.

"Stop it." He gave her a shake. "You're scaring me."

"I'm. . .so–rry. Do you mind carrying me to your truck?"

He wanted nothing more. He scooped her into his arms, unmindful of the mud now smearing his shirt, and deposited her on the passenger seat. Once her giggles had stopped and he no longer feared she was losing her mind, he raced to the driver's seat and climbed in. "What happened?"

She took a deep, shuddering breath. "I went for a walk with the intention of delivering bread and butter Mama had for your family. I jumped out of the way of a speeding automobile and landed in the ditch. I couldn't get out, and it started to rain. It took me a long time to get out. Then, you almost ran me over." She swept her hair out of her face. "I want to go home, please."

"Right away." He turned the truck around.

Mr. and Mrs. Thompkins sat on the front porch. When Jonathan again took Annie Mae into his arms, they bolted from their rocking chairs. "What happened?" Mrs. Thompkins rushed toward them, her husband on her heels.

"I found her lying in the road, laughing hysterically," he said.

"Correction." Annie Mae lifted a finger. "I didn't laugh until I saw the shock on your face after you almost ran over me."

"Mercy." Mrs. Thompkins put a hand to her chest. "Let's get her inside."

"I never made it to his house, Mama. I'm afraid I've lost the basket and its contents." Annie Mae rested her head on Jonathan's chest.

Nothing felt more right to him and he could have stayed like that forever, but she needed to get dry before she caught a chill. He carried her to the kitchen and sat her in a chair across from her wide-eyed siblings.

"Stay for coffee, Jonathan," Mr. Thompkins said. "Annie Mae will need some once her mother is finished getting her cleaned up." It was his turn to carry the muddy girl, and they headed up the stairs.

"I'll heat some water." Jonathan grabbed the teapot and set it on the stove. "Robby, could you carry the tub to. . .wherever they took your sister?"

"Yep." He thundered outside, returning moments later with a large metal tub. He tugged it behind him. "I don't think I can carry it up there, though."

"Watch the water." Jonathan hefted the tub and followed the sound of worried voices. "I'm coming up!"

"Set the tub outside the door," Mrs. Thompkins called. "She isn't decent."

Heat rose up Jonathan's neck and into his face at the implication of her words. "I'll, uh, set the hot water out here once it's ready."

"We'll need cold water, too."

"All right." He hurried back to the kitchen.

After a frenzied hour, Annie Mae was cleaned up and sitting across from Jonathan at the kitchen table. He slid a mug of coffee toward her.

"I don't care for coffee." She wrinkled her nose.

"Drink it," Mrs. Thompkins ordered. "It'll warm you from the inside out."

Jonathan grinned at the disgusted look on Annie Mae's face as she took a sip of her drink. "You scared me."

"I'm sorry I lost control. I was cold and hurting. Then, the look on your face was my undoing." Her lips twitched.

"And how did I look, exactly?"

"Like you saw a creature from the swamp." She giggled again, cutting it off when he narrowed his eyes.

"I'm beginning to think I did see some type of creature. One with yellow hair." He winked.

She shrugged and took another sip of the coffee, grimacing. "Mama sent Pa for the doctor to look at my ankle. I told her it's only sprained, but. . .well, she worries about me."

"So, that's where you get it."

"Get what?"

"Worrying."

"I've decided not to anymore." She squared her shoulders. "Lulu has convinced me that life should be more about fun. That it isn't at all hard."

Jonathan scratched his head. "Are you sure you're all right? You're not acting like yourself."

"I'm acting like the new me." She grinned. "Do you like her?"

"I'm not sure." He studied the woman in front of him. The wet hair, normally the color of corn silk but darkened now to ripe wheat, and the hazel eyes that turned from green to blue depending on her mood. The flush of pink in her cheeks at his scrutiny. "I don't think you could do anything, or change in any way, that would affect how I feel about you."

"Wonderful, because I have something I want to tell you. Something I planned to say when I got to your house." Her gaze settled on his with such intensity his heart beat erratically.

"What's that?" He lifted his cup for another sip.

"I've made up my mind. I love you and want to marry you."

He spewed coffee across the table and across the bodice of her clean dress.

Chapter 9

Time for bed, children." Mama ushered Robby and Lulu out of the room as if they were under siege.

Annie Mae kept her gaze glued to Jonathan's as she dabbed at her dress with a napkin. "Well? Don't you have anything to say?"

"Did you hit your head when you fell in the ditch?"

Was he serious? Her smile faded. For weeks, he'd been after her to decide whether to stay with her parents or pursue a different future for herself. Now that she'd made her choice, he ridiculed her. "Did you change your mind?" She willed the tears away.

"No, but this is going about it all wrong." He ran his hands through his hair.

"Wasn't this your plan? To keep your distance and make me miss you so much that *I* would come calling on *you*?" Had she misjudged him? "I've spent time in prayer searching my heart, and I've come to a place of healing. I know what I want now, Jonathan. Am I too late?"

He shook his head and came to her side of the table. He knelt and took her hands in his. "It's never too late. But I haven't proposed or asked for your father's blessing. None of the things a man does."

"I understand." Not only had he not been able to do those things, he hadn't said he loved her. He'd had the opportunity after her foolish declaration. She pulled her hands free. "I need to clean up the coffee."

He tugged her back when she tried to stand. "I'm going about this wrong, darling. I want to marry you."

"To combine the farms. That's all right. You may come to love me in time."

"I do love you, silly girl." He pulled her to her knees beside him then cupped her face in his hands. "I have a ring passed down from my grandmother. Will you marry me and wear that ring? No more competing in anything, fairs or matters of the heart. I want us to be a team, dear girl."

She let the tears fall. "Go ask Pa. Right this instant."

He planted a quick kiss on her forehead and helped her back into her chair. "Wait here?"

She nodded. "I'm not going anywhere." Even the pain in her ankle couldn't diminish the joy of the moment.

While he went to ask her father's blessing, Annie Mae reached for a wet rag from the sink and set to work wiping the table, her spirits lighter than they'd been in two years. How much easier life would have been if she'd only listened to Pa and searched God's will before sulking like a child because her plans hadn't gone the way she'd wanted them to.

Now she'd received her proposal of marriage in a coffee-stained dress in the kitchen of an old farmhouse. It couldn't be more perfect, except. . .she thought of the small shack on the edge of the farm's property. Built of stone and rich Arkansas clay, it had been her grandparents' home while they'd built the house her family now lived in. With a little work, it would be perfect. She tossed the rag into the sink and waited for Jonathan to return.

He rushed into the kitchen. "We have his blessing. When do you want to get married?"

"I want to show you something first." She stood slowly, grabbed an oil lamp from a hook on the wall, and took his hand. "It's not too far. I can make it if you let me lean on you. Will you come?"

"I'll follow you anywhere." But rather than let her limp, he swooped her into his arms.

She directed him past the hog pens to a small cabin among the trees. "I want to live here. How long will it take to fix it up?"

He cast her a surprised look then set her on her feet and lifted the latch on the weathered door, pushing it open. "It's hard to see, but I guess it has living quarters and a separate bedroom?"

"Yes." She lit a rusty lantern and hung it on a hook. Dust coated the few pieces of handmade furniture left behind and the shelves for holding food. "I'd like some cabinets. I can live with the pump for running water if a pipe could be brought to the house. I thought this would be perfect for us until you could build something better. There's no electricity, so another couple of windows would be nice."

He put his arm around her shoulders. "It's perfect. I can have this ready for us in a month, with electricity."

She turned to face him. "Then I will marry you in thirty one days."

His brow furrowed as he thought. "That's a Wednesday, I think."

"Then the following Saturday." That would give her time to sew a few things to cozy up the place. Excitement coursed through her so strongly she doubted she'd sleep a wink the entire time. "I know we could live with one of our families, but—"

"I understand. Having our own place is better, and this little house is between the two. It won't be a hardship living here with you. I'll count it as paradise."

She snuggled into him. "We'd best get back. One more thing, if you don't mind."

"Anything."

"Could I have another kiss, please? I rather liked the last one."

He laughed and obliged.

———— •◆• ————

Annie Mae sat in the middle of her family's living room and looked around the group of women from church. They were here to bestow gifts and offer congratulations. Once word got out about her upcoming nuptials, the community had been more generous than she could have imagined.

The people of Rabbit Hollow might not have a lot in the way of money, but love and generosity abounded. Annie Mae gazed at the stack of embroidered dish towels, a wedding quilt, and pots and pans, some slightly used or dented, but she cherished every one.

While she planned on using the quilt Belle had muddied on what seemed a day very long ago, the wedding quilt the pastor's wife gave her would make a beautiful decorative item hanging over the faded sofa Pa had found.

Jonathan had asked her to stay away from their future home while he readied it for them, and she'd been dying of curiosity. Pa said things were coming along famously and that her groom-to-be was skilled with a hammer. Ma promised she would get a few of the ladies from church to take over the gifts and other items a woman needed to set up house. Things were moving at such a fast pace, Annie Mae felt she was living in a dream.

"How's the wedding dress coming?" Mrs. Morrillton asked. "Your mother said she was updating her own gown for you."

"It's beautiful. I wouldn't want to wear anything else." She thought of the dress hanging in her bureau. The simple lines of the satin gown made her feel like the most elegant Hollywood starlet. "I'm as ready for Saturday as I can be."

"You've caught our most eligible bachelor," another woman, Mrs. Pruitt, whose family owned a nearby chicken farm, said, tying off the pumpkin-and-gold afghan she'd crocheted. "My Betsy is plumb green with envy. Now she's set her sights on Duane Wilson, the banker's son from Pineville. He isn't as fine to look at as Jonathan, but his pockets are a bit fuller."

"Money isn't everything," Annie Mae said.

"Spoken like a true girl blinded by love. During these times, a few dollars are a blessing."

It pained Annie Mae to think of how she so recently worried about money herself. With Jonathan's quick mind and strong back, they'd want for very little. "I am very blessed." She stood and moved to the table where cookies and punch were laid out.

She needed a moment to compose herself since the woman's words dredged up the feelings she'd fought so hard to suppress. Worry was a part of Annie Mae. A part she would have to work daily to leave in God's hands. She took a deep breath and turned back to her guests. "Please, enjoy the refreshments. I am beyond grateful for your generosity, as I'm sure Jonathan will be."

"I've heard tell your man is so busy on your new house you rarely see each other." Mrs. Pruitt took three cookies. "You'll be virtual strangers on your wedding night."

"We've known each other our whole lives, Mrs. Pruitt." Would the woman ever stop? Annie Mae glanced around the room. When her gaze met her mother's, she silently implored for help.

"Let me help you." Mama filled a glass with punch and led the outspoken woman to her seat. "We appreciate your concern for Annie Mae and Jonathan, but my husband and I believe in letting newlyweds figure some things out on their own. Wouldn't you agree?"

"A wise course of action." The woman plopped into her seat.

Annie Mae exhaled slowly. Mama always knew the right words to say. Annie Mae was nervous enough about starting a new life with Jonathan without some busybody putting negative thoughts into her head.

⚊⚊◆●◆⚊⚊

Jonathan set the last of the new windows in place. He'd managed to purchase a large one from a house being torn down and put that in the front, using the smaller windows in the kitchen and one in the bedroom. He'd no sooner finished than a group of trucks and a backhoe pulled next to the cottage.

"We might as well dig you a new hole for the outhouse," Mr. Thompkins said. "The old one's been filled in for quite a while."

"I hadn't thought of that. Thank you. It's a 'necessity' for sure." Jonathan grinned.

"Horace over there will finish the electricity, and you'll have a day or two to relax before marrying my girl. Her mother is chomping at the bit to pretty the place up."

"I'll be out of their hair tomorrow." Jonathan stepped back and surveyed his work. He'd filled holes with fresh clay, repaired boards inside and given them a fresh coat of white paint, built cabinets and a counter, installed water and a pump. . .the list went on. What with working here and at home, he was bone tired and couldn't be happier. After all, the work was for him and Annie Mae. He hoped she'd be pleased with his efforts.

"You've done well." Mr. Thompkins clapped him on the shoulder. "A lot of work and money went into making this place ready for my daughter."

"It's worth it, sir." He had a hog or two he could sell to make ends meet. They'd be fine. Not to mention the piglets from Daisy. "We'll get together next week and see what chores I can help you with around your place."

"About that. Take a walk with me." Mr. Thompkins led Jonathan past the barn and the hog pens. "There's no reason for us to keep these animals separate any longer. I say we combine the two farms for real. Build new pens between the two properties and split any profit, except from personal animals like chickens and milk cows. That will make us the largest hog farm in the state."

Jonathan grinned. "I like that idea. What will we call ourselves?"

"Something simple like M & T Farms. If you're marrying into the family, we might as well take it all the way." He held out his hand.

Jonathan nodded and sealed the deal with a handshake. "I hope you can give me until next week before I start work on those new pens. I'd like to enjoy my new bride a bit."

"Don't talk to me like I'm the boss, son. We're equal partners. Your father would be proud."

Emotion burned in Jonathan's throat. "Thank you."

"Let's go supervise that crowd and finish the work today."

Together, they headed back to the small cabin, Jonathan's head full of thoughts on ways to improve the farm once it became one. Never in his wildest dreams could he have imagined the wonder of God giving him all the desires of his heart. Not only the prettiest girl in Rabbit Hollow but now the state's largest hog farm.

Annie Mae would never have to worry about anything ever again. He'd make sure of that.

Chapter 10

Annie Mae turned this way and that in front of the mirror, trying to get a good angle of herself in her mother's wedding dress. The veil skimmed past her shoulders and trailed three feet on the floor behind her. The satin dress hugged her bodice then fell past her hips in a pearl-colored sheen. She glanced at the clock. Jonathan was late. Almost an hour late.

"Don't worry. He'll be here." Mama gave a shaky smile and cut a look toward the door. "Your pa will come through that door any minute with the news."

"What if he changed his mind?" Annie Mae perched carefully on a wooden chair. "I took a long time to give him an answer. Maybe this is his way of paying me back?"

"Don't be silly. Do you think he would have spent all that time and money on that little cabin if he wasn't going to marry you? The man is smitten, for sure." Her voice was confident, but she bit her bottom lip.

"Even you're worried." Annie Mae folded her arms. "What if he's been in an accident?" His truck could be mangled against a tree or turned over in a ditch. Mama was right. Jonathan loved her. Only a catastrophe of epic proportions would keep him from their wedding. She bolted from the room. "Pa, take me to look for him."

"In your wedding gown?" His brow furrowed.

"It's only a dress. Please." She clutched his arm. "Something is wrong."

"Very well. Let me tell Pastor Forrest." He left the church's atrium and returned moments later. "The pastor and a few others will search with us."

Annie Mae prayed she wasn't making a big fuss where one didn't need to be made, but her heart told her that Jonathan needed her. She draped her veil over her arm, hitched her dress to her knees, and rushed to the truck.

"Let me help." Mama hurried toward her. "This old truck will smear dirt all over you. If you insist on going without changing, then at least let me help keep you clean." She opened the door and held Annie Mae's dress out of the way while she climbed in. Mama slid in beside her, taking Annie Mae's hand in her lap. "We'll find him. He'll be fine."

Annie Mae closed her eyes and prayed. Surely God wouldn't have brought her this far only to take away the man she loved. Just when she'd begun to put her constant worrying in His hands, she was thrust back into the abyss.

Halfway between the church and the Mercer farm, Pa pulled to the side of the road. "There he is. Looks like a flat tire." He shoved open his door and jumped to the ground.

Annie Mae leaned past her mother. "He isn't standing to greet us. Something is wrong."

"Let me get the dress." Mama held her veil and train out of the way.

Once Annie Mae's feet were on the ground, she pulled free and ran to Jonathan's side, unmindful of her veil trailing in the dirt. She knelt beside him. "What's wrong?"

He gave her a sheepish grin. "You look beautiful."

"Jonathan." She exhaled sharply.

"The tire rim fell on my shoe. I'm stuck."

"Can't you pull your foot out?" Pa asked, squatting next to them.

"I've tied the laces too tight. The rim isn't on my toes, just the tip of the shoe." His gaze never left Annie Mae's face. "I'm sorry, love. I would have gotten there eventually."

"Not without help." She smiled back. "Pa will get the truck lifted."

"The jack broke. That's why the truck fell."

Her heart sank. "What about the wedding?"

He glanced over her shoulder. "I see the pastor."

"You want to get married here?"

"Why not? I've waited years for this moment." He grasped her hand. "I know it's ridiculous, but I can't wait another moment. It'll be the wedding everyone will talk about all year."

"I think it's romantic." She giggled. "All right. I'll marry you here and now."

"Then I'm glad I came along," Mama said, her eyes shimmering. "I wouldn't have wanted to miss a roadside wedding for anything in the world."

Pa laughed. "I still walked the bride down the aisle, in a way. Pastor?"

"Let's get this wedding started." Pastor Forrest motioned for one of the guests who had come along to find a jack to lift the truck. Upon hearing that the man would have to head home then return, the pastor transferred his attention back to the wedding couple. "Dearly beloved..."

When prompted, Annie Mae bent her head and kissed her husband. "This wedding will go down in the history of Rabbit Hollow," she whispered against his lips.

"It's a story to tell our future children for sure." He leaned back on his hands. "I'm sorry. I know this isn't how you planned the day to be."

"It's perfect." She sat on a blanket Mama provided. "As long as I became your wife, I don't care how it happened. Once you're free, we'll head back to the church and join in what's left of the festivities." Surprisingly, the day couldn't be more perfect.

The important thing was that they were married. The sun was shining. Her parents were there to witness the nuptials. God was in His heaven. What more could a girl ask for?

By the time the truck was off Jonathan's permanently indented shoe, the sun had begun its descent over the mountains. Pa got the tire changed, and they all drove back to the church where, thankfully, someone had informed the guests of what had happened.

The women of the church had kept the food warm and the punch cool, and they all lined up to welcome the bride and groom. The events of the day might have happened a bit backward than what was normal, but Annie Mae slipped her arm through her husband's and sailed across the church lawn into the building while rice rained upon their heads.

•───◆◆◆───•

"Does it upset you that we aren't going on a honeymoon?" Jonathan searched Annie Mae's face in the light of the moon. After the ceremony and following party were concluded, and wedding gifts packed into the bed of the truck, he'd invited Annie Mae for a stroll around the farms. After all the subtle joking about the wedding night, he wanted to tell her of his and her father's plans in order to settle her nerves a bit.

"The cabin is our honeymoon." She pressed against his arm. "Someday, maybe, we can take a trip, but it isn't necessary."

"I love you, Mrs. Mercer."

"That's a very good thing, Mr. Mercer, because I love you. Now, tell me of your plans for our future."

"So you won't worry?"

"I doubt I'll worry much with you by my side."

Her trust filled Jonathan with the urge to be the best man and farmer he could be. With Annie Mae as his wife, Mr. Thompkins as his partner, and God over it all, he had no doubt their future would be bright. The depression wouldn't last forever, and America would once again be the prosperous country they loved.

He told her of the plans to combine the two farms into one large farm rather than keeping them separate. He told her how they wanted to expand, beginning with Daisy's litter of piglets. Already, Belle was expecting a litter of her own by a boar with good bloodlines. "The future is bright, my love, as bright as the North Star."

They sat on a rock wall and gazed at the night sky. Annie Mae leaned against him, resting her head on his shoulder. Her hair smelled of the rose-scented shampoo she used. He still couldn't believe she was his wife.

"I'm ready to go home now," she said. "I want to wake up beside you and fix your breakfast. I still haven't seen the cottage with our things inside, nor the changes you've made. Mama said all the lights would be on for us."

"I'm ready." More than ready, if truth be told.

"Rocking chairs," Annie Mae said as the cabin came into view. She clasped her hands in front of her chest. "We can sit on the porch on nice evenings."

"Those were a gift from someone. I've never seen them before." The house was lit up like a grand hotel he saw once. All the curtains were open to let the light spill into the yard, showcasing barrels of flowers.

"It's like a fairy tale." She stepped onto the porch and reached for the door handle.

"Hold on now." He scooped her into his arms. "A groom carries his bride over the threshold."

She giggled and wrapped her arms around his neck. "I guess you'd better do so, then, because I'm growing impatient."

He carried her inside and set her on her feet. Everywhere he looked there was a touch of homeyness. A bright quilt was draped across the back of the sofa. A colorful afghan lay folded on a chair. Lace curtains covered the windows, and blue and white dishes were set on the table.

Tears rolled down Annie Mae's cheeks. "We are so blessed."

He drew her close. "We are." They had all they needed to start their life together. Love, a home, community. He was almost near tears himself.

He grinned to see a slightly used coffeepot on the stove. Someone was superstitious, holding to the old belief that it was bad luck to set up housekeeping with a new pot. He doubted Annie Mae minded using it for a month or so until a new one could be purchased. With all the evidence of love in the many gifts in front of them, he had no doubt their marriage would be very blessed indeed.

With a shy look his way then one toward the bedroom door, Annie Mae took his hand. "Come."

He gulped, then, grin spreading wide, allowed her to lead him to the room they would share. Instead of the blushing bride, he found himself more nervous than she was. Perhaps their walk in the moonlight had been more for his benefit.

They sat on the edge of the bed, hands entwined. "Let's pray," he said. "I want this marriage to start solid."

"I couldn't agree more." She bowed her head.

"Dear heavenly Father. . ."

Dear Reader,

The Arkansas State Fair was sporadic during the time of the Great Depression, and for the sake of my story, I had one held in 1930. At this time, the fair actually closed at Fair Park (which is now War Memorial Park). Officials found several abandoned animals left when the fair closed and built pens to house them. During the 1930s, the Works Progress Administration erected rock buildings, which still stand and are part of today's zoo.

Because of the financial hardship during the Great Depression, thousands of young men left home and entered the Works Progress Administration, where they were employed in the construction of public buildings and roads. At its peak in 1938, it provided paid jobs for three million unemployed men and women as well as youth in a separate youth administration.

I hope you enjoyed *Competing Hearts* and this bit of insight into America's history.

God bless.
Cynthia Hickey

Cynthia Hickey grew up in a family of storytellers and moved around the country a lot as an army brat. Her desire is to write about real but flawed characters in a wholesome way that her seven children and five grandchildren can all be proud of. She and her husband live in Arizona where Cynthia is a full-time writer.

If You Liked This Book, You'll Also Like...

The Rails to Love Romance Collection
Nine historical stories celebrate a spirit of adventure along the Transcontinental Railroad where nine unlikely couples meet. From sightseeing excursions to transports toward new lives, from orphan trains to circus trains, can romances develop into blazing love in a world of cold, hard steel?
Paperback / 978-1-63409-864-9 / $14.99

The California Gold Rush Romance Collection
Nine couples meet in the hills of California where gold fever rules hearts and minds from the lonely miner to the distinguished banker, from the lowly immigrant to the well-intentioned preacher. But can faith and romance lead these couples to treasures more valuable than gold?
Paperback / 978-1-63409-821-2 / $14.99

The Valiant Hearts Romance Collection
In nine historical romances from beloved Christian authors, brave men and women endure some of life's hardest mysteries, challenges, and injustices spanning from war in the 1860s to Prohibition in the 1920s. Will the bonds they form and the loves they develop lead to lasting legacies for nine couples?
Paperback / 978-1-63409-672-0 / $14.99

JOIN US ONLINE!

Christian Fiction for Women

Christian Fiction for Women is your online home for the latest in Christian fiction.

Check us out online for:

- Giveaways
- Recipes
- Info about Upcoming Releases
- Book Trailers
- News and More!

Find Christian Fiction for Women at Your Favorite Social Media Site:

 Search "Christian Fiction for Women"

 @fictionforwomen